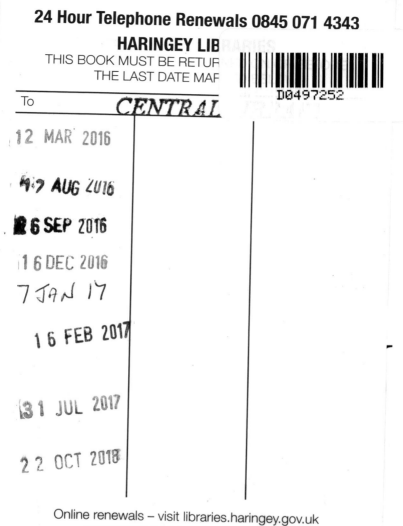

24 Hour Telephone Renewals 0845 071 4343

HARINGEY LIB

THIS BOOK MUST BE RETUR
THE LAST DATE MAF

D0497252

To **CENTRAL**

12 MAR 2016

4 7 AUG 2016

6 SEP 2016

16 DEC 2016

7 JAN 17

16 FEB 2017

31 JUL 2017

2 2 OCT 2018

Online renewals – visit libraries.haringey.gov.uk

published by Haringey Council's Communications Unit 973.16 • 08/12

THE SECOND FOOTMAN

JASPER BARRY

Matador
9 Priory Business Park,
Wistow Road, Kibworth Beauchamp,
Leicestershire. LE8 0RX
Tel: (+44) 116 279 2299
Fax: (+44) 116 279 2277
Email: books@troubador.co.uk
Web: www.troubador.co.uk/matador

ISBN 978 1780883 656

British Library Cataloguing in Publication Data.
A catalogue record for this book is available from the British Library.

Typeset by Troubador Publishing Ltd, Leicester, UK

Matador is an imprint of Troubador Publishing Ltd

Printed and bound in the UK by TJ International, Padstow, Cornwall

My thanks to Patricia Coulson and Martin Village for their help and support.

CHAPTER ONE

Just as a pretty parlour maid may be considered a perquisite by the master of the house, so some of our ladies are not immune to the charms of a handsome footman. Catherine, duchesse de Claireville, being widowed, immensely rich and in addition a Choiseul by birth, employed six. Between serving courses, they flanked the dining-room walls of the Hôtel de Claireville, motionless and haughty, making an excellent display in their wigs, knee breeches and azure swallowtail coats. But, although each had his points and new hirings, it was rumoured, were always put to the test, for the past eighteen months madame's preference had fixed obstinately on Michel: the son of a Belleville horse butcher, a strapping, florid twenty-four-year-old, he was also, by virtue of standing one hundred and ninety-two centimetres in his stockings, numbered first of their rank.

Unsurprisingly, his five subordinates and, indeed, all the lower servants, hated Michel. Oh, there was envy, of course, if not for Michel's additional duties, then for the supposed influence they conferred and the bank deposit that was believed to flourish in his name. But also, it must be said, Michel was not magnanimous in triumph. As first footman, he had been inclined to throw his weight around, delegating his own work and the blame for his mistakes. As madame's established favourite, he was intolerable. So, when Jean, the second footman, decided to return to his family's small-holding in Perpignan, much hope was invested in his replacement.

The new 'Jean' (such was the custom of the house, lest madame be needlessly troubled with remembering servants' names) looked promising from the start. He was tall, tall enough at any rate to cheat the third footman, Fabrice, of promotion, although wanting the one and a half centimetres that would have relegated Michel. He was straight-backed and well-made and, apart from an obtrusive red scar on his left temple running into the hairline, which was anyway concealed by the wig, undeniably good-looking—or so the maids averred. And he had what Michel so abundantly lacked, a refinement of manner that must be his strongest suit. Although his papers proclaimed him to be from the black volcanic mountains of the

1

Auvergne, there was no trace of the country boy in his speech or comportment. Without being foppish like Fabrice, he carried himself with graceful assurance.

True, none of this instantly recommended him to the male servants: they were inclined to take the hint of reserve tempering his elegant manners for standoffishness, for a most unwarranted superiority, considering he came from a far less illustrious house than this (his last situation had been with Reinhardt, the banker). But the distaff side of the household was enchanted. And, on acquaintance, the new Jean proved a pleasant enough fellow, willing to join in a joke or help someone out of a scrape; at such times he seemed to shed his reserve, to become unexpectedly, exuberantly boyish, despite the twenty-three years his papers gave him. Altogether, with his looks and his charm, he appeared the perfect candidate to unseat Michel in madame's favour; spice was added to the contest by the fact that Michel, naturally, loathed him on sight. It was diverting to watch the two rivals, Michel sneering and setting little traps that would bring down the wrath of M Vincent, the *maître d'hôtel*, upon the new Jean's head, the newcomer himself deflecting these assaults, first with incredulity, then irritation, then calculated disdain. Everyone waited for madame to issue the summons. Guillaume, the fifth footman, opened a book on the outcome.

Six weeks after Jean's arrival, the call came. All seemed to go well. For a week the second footman braved madame's bed by night and Michel's jealousy by day. The week grew to eight days. But, on the ninth day, Jean received, via madame's lady's maid, the cravat pin set with a single small diamond that signified his reign was over.

After so much speculation, there was a great deflation of spirits in the servants' hall, particularly since Michel was promptly reinstated. The latter, needless to say, had a simple explanation for his rival's failure. But, to those who had staked their money on Jean and had watched him minutely for signs of draining stamina, this seemed less than convincing. Perhaps it was true, as Pauline, the head parlour maid, opined, that madame, being a lady, found no novelty in Jean's refinement, while Michel, with his coarse features, brutish guffaw and meaty hands, appeared irresistibly exotic to someone who had married a Claireville and been born a Choiseul. The second footman himself offered no enlightenment. The code of the household required minions singled out for such gentlemanly service to display a gentleman's honour in its acquittal: any scurrilous disclosures reaching the ears of M Vincent or Mme Pinot, the housekeeper, would result in the culprit receiving his cards forthwith. But, in any case, the new Jean showed no inclination to drop so much as a hint on the matter. Apparently deaf to the gossip and Michel's jibes, he buckled down to his work. And only a discerning observer would have noticed that, in its rare unguarded moments, his face was clouded by the brooding look of someone who, cheated of an objective, is now unsure where to turn.

However, there was one for whom Jean's failure was easily explained. The third footman, Fabrice, had received an unexpected insight into his character (a revelation, as Fabrice thought of it) on the night of his arrival.

The second and third footmen shared a dormitory—Michel had the luxury of a box room to himself— and privacy was impossible in this airless cranny between the eaves, with its two narrow iron bedsteads separated only by a chair. Shivering in winter, in summer stewing in his own sweat, breathing the stench of feet and farts and rancid linen, the rankness, not just of the two of them, but of generations of footmen, alert to every twitch and snort from the opposite bed, the hiss of urine streaming into the chamber pot, the furtive hand working beneath the blanket, hearing and knowing he too was overheard, Fabrice had learnt far more than he wished about the previous Jean. Now perforce he must learn the new Jean's idiosyncrasies. If only for this, he was bound to take a jaundiced view of the new arrival. And then, of course, the missed promotion rankled. But there was another cause.

Fabrice, with his golden curls, thick lashes and willowy grace, was Michel's favourite victim. Michel would poison the new Jean against him, just as he had the old Jean, and the Jean before that; Michel would see to it that the stranger, although barely able to turn in their confined quarters without jostling his shoulder, would abhor all contact with him as though he had the plague. And sure enough, when the hour came to retire, the usual jokes were trotted out. Fabrice lacked a clear view of the new Jean's face as Michel clapped him on the shoulder and warned him to sleep with his arse to the wall. Certainly Jean did not echo the first footman's uproarious laughter, but his silence as he followed Fabrice up the back stairs clearly manifested distaste.

Fabrice had learned that frigid dignity served him best in these circumstances. Civilly, since the stranger had yet to unpack his box, he conceded him the floor space, retreating to his bed, where he discarded his wig and coat—he would remove his breeches in the dark so that there should be no misunderstandings. Thus trapped, with his legs drawn up and his shoulders wedged into the room's furthest corner, his whole body, as he hoped, signifying distance and indifference, he was nevertheless forced to watch the stranger's proceedings. Understandably after Michel had done his work, the new Jean did not seem disposed to talk, except to enquire politely enough whether a shelf or a coat peg were free for his use, and Fabrice answered in cold monosyllables. Yet he could not suppress a natural interest in the stranger's unpacking.

The new Jean had few clothes: one shabby frockcoat for his Sundays off now hung on a peg beside Fabrice's finery. His only extravagance appeared to be his linen, which, though heavily laundered, was of evident quality. The rest of his box was filled with books, not two-sou adventure stories but grave-looking tomes with battered bindings. When Fabrice considered his own convenience, he could only be comforted by the stranger's sparse wardrobe. And he was pleased to observe, as he watched him stow the books carefully under his bed, that, unlike the previous Jean, this one at least was tidy. But he noted this with half an eye. For there was something else about the newcomer—a dawning familiarity—it was the scar, when he had flung off his wig—Fabrice had seen that scar, that face, somewhere before.

Cautiously he edged his shoulders out of their retreat . "You know, we've met, I think."

The stranger glanced at him over an armful of books. "I don't believe so."

"What's your name?"

"Albert Fabien. And you?"

"Hippolyte Dufour."

Although this exchange struck no chord, that signified little. Fabrice persisted. "Then perhaps you know…?" He reeled off a list of names and places. The stranger emerged from under the bed, clapping the dust from his hands. He shook his head. Yet he was on his guard, Fabrice thought. Turning his back and kneeling beside the tin box, he was making something of a procedure of fastening its latches.

Emboldened, Fabrice swung his legs off the bed. He seized the nearest handle of the box and together they carried it out to the corridor for Martin, the hall boy, to store in the morning. He was not wrong, he was certain of it: as they had lifted the trunk their eyes had met for a moment. He could not be wrong.

"You'll forgive me, " he said, once the door was safely closed. "But I have a conviction I've seen you, either at the Green Monkey or Madame Tonton's."

The stranger was removing his buckled pumps and did not glance up.

"Look, dear heart, I don't gossip. As you'll have noted, it wouldn't exactly be to my advantage."

There was a pause. Then the new Jean lifted his head. He smiled. "Not Madame Tonton's—the fare's a bit rich. But yes, possibly the Monkey."

Suddenly the air seemed to lighten in the poky little room. Fabrice flung himself onto his bed, laughing. "Well, that's one in the eye for Milady!"

Jean raised his eyebrows.

"Oh, not madame. I mean Betty. The Countess of Ka-Ka. That long streak of shit that masquerades as our first footman."

"The rapier wit?"

"But for once, angel, the joke is on her."

It was not strictly true that Fabrice did not gossip. But about life in their shared quarters he respected their freemasonry and kept his oath of silence. He was silent even on the subject of Jean's great nocturnal vice, although he grumbled about it often enough. For it transpired that the library under the bed, a ragamuffin collection culled from Left Bank stalls—histories, works by Voltaire and Rousseau, but mostly texts in Latin or Greek—was not there to gather dust. Although they rose at six, and even if they had been up past one clearing dinner, the new Jean read for two hours every night, filching candle ends for the purpose, since Mme Pinot was known to measure the level of oil in the lamps.

"You'll go blind. If not for the reason the rest of us will."

"Fabrice, you know how it is. If there were any other time…" This was hard to argue with. Their all-too-short leisure hour, after they had served luncheon and eaten their own dinner, was no more than a chance to unleash pent-up energy, to smash a shuttlecock back and forth in the kitchen courtyard or josh the maids, to become briefly, noisily human before they returned to the evening's ritual and M Vincent's chastening glance.

"Anyway, where does it get you? *Amo, amas, amat.* You see? I'm not an ignoramus, I've had an education. But I've still ended up cleaning silver, just like you. That's life, my sweet."

"Not necessarily."

"I'm sacrificing my beauty sleep, am I, so Her Highness can dream? Up her sweet arse I am!"

Yet, despite his resentment of Jean's obstinate hope and the memory it stirred of his own dreams—would he not, if fate had been kinder, be making his mark as a master draughtsman?—Fabrice was bound to be grateful for the improvement Jean's arrival had made to his situation. They looked out for each other; Jean, heedless of the risk to his own reputation, had twice spoken up for him against Michel; in the endless fortnights between Sunday freedom they occasionally afforded each other physical relief. It was friendship of a sort, Fabrice supposed—if such a thing were possible when you fought each other for the wash stand every morning, when, as summer drew in and there was no escape from the suffocating heat, every fly buzzing against the skylight wrought you to screaming pitch. Accustomed to view himself as a pariah, Fabrice was wary of trust, yet he felt there was an instinctive understanding between them. Although he passed for less, the third footman was twenty-six, and inclined to view the younger man, not simply as another of his own kind, but as the very mirror of his own bitter experience. Jean's longing to better himself, his superior breeding for a servant, the fact, as others sometimes remarked, that he never spoke of his people or received letters from home—Fabrice knew too well what it was to grow up a changeling in a so-called decent family, to affront a devoutly Catholic father.

So, when it came to the ordeal of Mme de Claireville, it went without saying how the affair would conclude. At first, Fabrice had been solicitude itself. Bursting into their attic to find Jean there before him, stripped and washing, he had hunted amongst his shirts for the little phial containing the remains of the Spanish Fly and, when this was declined, had at least persuaded the youth to anoint his freshly-shaved cheeks with a splash of his best and very expensive eau de cologne. It was in this sympathetic mood that he had lain awake into the small hours until his bedfellow's return—to prepare consoling words of course—but yes, he had also expected confidences, for what were the house rules between friends? So his solicitude had been severely tested by Jean's silence on this and every successive night. And now that the business was over and he could not help noticing that his erstwhile comrade, instead of regarding this as a merciful release, was morose and depressed, Fabrice grew thoroughly incensed. It seemed to him treachery.

"For God's sake, it's hardly a tragedy, is it? All right, if Betty's to be believed the Empress Catherine tips generously. And I suppose, if Milady of Ka-Ka had flounced off in a huff, they'd have made you first footman. But there's no use complaining if you're just not cut out for it."

The night was heavy with imminent thunder and, though Fabrice had discarded his blanket, his skin itched beneath his night-shirt and he could find no position on the lumpy flock mattress that was likely to encourage sleep. Jean had thrown off even his shirt. By the light of the candle, Fabrice could see the sweat trickling from his forehead and down his left cheek as he sat, naked and cross-legged, grimly focused upon his studies.

Fabrice levered himself onto one elbow, the better to pursue his attack. "Or is it the shame that's eating Her Highness? Is she worried her poor cock-a-doodle-do isn't a match for Betty's mighty member."

A fly had landed on Jean's cheek. He swatted it viciously, but without raising his eyes.

"You've seen Betty make pee-pee, you shouldn't be troubled on that score. And, anyway, eight nights! You fell honourably in the thick of battle. Most of them only fire one salvo—Victor's never even been called to the front. And I told you what happened to me."

"Several times."

"Fainted clean away. The Spanish Fly was no use whatsoever. The Empress had to revive me with her smelling salts. And even then, some things were *quite* beyond—"

"So you said."

"I thought, that's it. Poor Fabrice, sent packing without a reference. But I got my pin, just like the others. So you won't lose your place, if that's what's bothering you."

The fly returned. Jean flicked it away again with a low curse. It buzzed towards Fabrice, who volleyed it back savagely.

"Or perhaps the poor girl's missing madame. Perhaps the Empress reminds her of her darling Maman at home in the Auvergne—" Fabrice was conscious of the cruelty but, after all, it was Jean who had betrayed their fellow-feeling "—or her dearest grandmama, more likely."

This at last brought a response, although not the wounded fury Fabrice had hoped for. Jean raised his eyes from his book and surveyed him over the candle flame with exasperation. "Fabrice, go to hell. Or to sleep. I don't care which."

"That's not kind. Considering everything I put up with. Not kind at all."

The fly, which had been whining in circles around their heads, chose this instant to land on Jean's page. Instinctively he snapped the volume shut. Reopening it slowly, he surveyed the carnage, scraped at it fruitlessly with his index finger, then, wiping his hand on the mattress, cast the book aside in disgust.

Fabrice, sensing his opportunity, leant forward on his elbow: "Oh, I know your love of secrets, dear heart—it's hard enough to get out of you what you did on your day off, short of using an enema. But ever since madame you've been like some old quean with the curling tongs stuck up her arse. So why don't you make a clean breast of it, eh? To your Tante Fabrice."

Jean favoured him with a considering look. "Very well." He paused. "What if I told you it was I who ended it?"

Fabrice stared.

"She was dying for it, but I told her I couldn't go on."

Fabrice continued to stare. "Because you weren't that sort of girl?"

"Because I couldn't spare the time from my books."

"Never!"

Jean's grave face collapsed into laughter. "No, never. You're right there."

Outraged at having been practised upon, if only for a split second, Fabrice was for once lost for words.

"What I'm saying is, don't assume."

"What else am I supposed to do, when nobody tells me anything?"

"There's nothing to tell. She wanted me, then she didn't. That's women for you."

"So your poor little heart is bleeding? You've developed a taste for antique quim?"

"It was a chance, that's all."

"A chance for what?"

Spitting on his finger and thumb, Jean leant over and snuffed out the candle.

Fabrice's voice came, persistent, out of the darkness. "A chance for what?"

"Nothing. Cut it, there's a good boy."

"The chance to be first footman?"

Jean lay still and did not reply.

"So now we have it! Forget *amo, amas, amat*. The girl may dream, but come cold daylight she's a silver polisher like the rest of us."

Usually, once the candle was extinguished, Jean would fall effortlessly asleep. But tonight, even after Fabrice's derision had run its course, he lay, eyes wide open, staring into the shadows. The twitchings and sighs from the opposite bed told him he was not alone in his wakefulness. Jean did not dislike Fabrice, despite their bickering, and he struggled with the longing to explain. For he had not the slightest interest in becoming first footman: what he had wanted from the duchesse de Claireville was of quite another order. But the almost irresistible compulsion that tormented him on occasion to tell someone, just one person, of his grand design, was, he recognised, a stupidity—not merely indiscreet, but inviting danger.

CHAPTER TWO

In his short lifetime our protagonist has already gone by such a succession of names that it is a puzzle for the narrator to know what to call him. Of his two latest—the identity bestowed by the papers he has acquired through Josette's enterprise, or his footman's *nom de guerre*—well, he has no great liking for either. So we shall fix upon the name he gives out to his intimates (rashly, it is to be admitted, but perhaps with a conscious view to laying a trail that will prove his credentials to certain parties). Josette, Mitya Zhukovsky, the painter Van der Meer, and even the renowned Academician Lebas for a brief period, have all called him Max.

Well before he had entered her household, Max had known of the singular duties required of Mme de Claireville's footmen. Old Jouvert had warned him when he had tipped him off about the vacancy, and it had been his main reason for seeking the place. The old boy was always a mine of information. In fact, it was thanks to him that Max had gone into service.

Old Jouvert had been *maître d'hôtel* of a very grand household until possession of the key to its wine cellars had undone him; although he now made his living doing no one quite knew what—the rumour in the Green Monkey favoured money-lending or even blackmail, for despite his greasy frockcoat he was always flush—he still kept abreast of servants' hall gossip, drawn irresistibly to the lost world of his glory days. Which noblemen unknowingly shared a certain actress, which chefs had profitable accommodations with the tradesmen, which lady's maids sold their mistresses' dresses on the sly: locked in Old Jouvert's head, beneath the thin strip of hair pomaded to his mottled cranium, lay the secrets of most of the great houses. Not that he accumulated or disbursed them in the Green Monkey: he plied his mysterious trade elsewhere, only patronising the Monkey to further other interests. Although dignified in drink, as punctilious as if he still superintended a ducal table, he was not one of that establishment's most popular patrons: his grog-blossoms, poisonous breath and tendency to dilate endlessly on days gone by saw to it that, however uproarious the evening crowd, he could usually be found swaying gently over his wine glass, a solitary but still-hopeful wallflower.

He had been alone that night—what was it, just over three years ago now?—when Max had hobbled into the Monkey. Keeping his eyes averted to avoid any of his acquaintance, Max had found his gaze resting on Old Jouvert's corner. His pride recoiled. This would be the second time (he did not count M Lebas' too-generous payments for his sittings for the Apollo, for, although he had come to depend on the bonus, he had never asked for it). The second time. When he thought of the first, the horror of it, the loathsome misery of the last week seemed a judgement he had brought down upon himself. Everything he had done before, everything, at least, since he had come to Paris, had been done freely and for pleasure. But now—well, he must swallow his self-disgust. Lying about his age to the Conscription Board might solve his future problems, but what was he to do about tonight and tomorrow? Rob someone in the street?

Old Jouvert, after all, was ideal: he had money, his needs were known to be simple and—essential, given Max's recent experience— he offered no physical threat. The boy limped over to his table, smiled weakly and sat down. Although the two had never exchanged a word, the old man welcomed him as a dear friend, summoning the waiter to bring a second glass forthwith. But after his first flush of happy anticipation had faded, and when he noticed that Max did not touch his wine, his rheumy eyes grew quizzical.

"If - you - will - forgive my - mentioning - it—" Old Jouvert always spoke infinitely slowly, with a drunkard's heavy precision "—if you will forgive my mentioning it, young man, you do not look yourself."

Max murmured that he had been ill and waited for the old soak to lose interest, to drift, as he surely would, into one of his monologues. But Old Jouvert was not to be diverted

"You look, if I may say so, as if someone has beaten the stuffing out of you."

This was so wretchedly near the truth that the boy could only stare down into his glass.

"Indeed, given the state of your linen and the fact that you have deserted your usual charming coterie, I should go as far as to surmise that I owe this honour to your being in grave need of a square meal."

It was horrifying to the boy that his degradation was so transparent, even to this ancient toper. Shame crushed his resolve, he pushed back his chair. But a liver-blotched yet surprisingly strong hand restrained him. "How old are you, young man?"

"Forgive me, I must—"

"Seventeen? Sixteen?"

The bony fingers dug into his forearm, the watery eyes surveyed him shrewdly behind their lattice of broken veins. If he were to escape, it appeared he must humour the old cove. "For what it's worth, twenty. Now, monsieur, I fear—"

But Old Jouvert , it seemed, was not to be deceived. "Too young to go to the bad just yet. Besides, you've always struck me as being a cut above the rest of your crowd. Oh, come, come, young sir—" Here the old man seized the boy by the elbow, for, despite his attempts to draw himself up, hunger, the effects of his injury and the icy walk from his lodgings had combined to overwhelm him. "Oblige me by sitting down before you fall down."

Since his legs truly did seem unwilling to support him, Max could only submit. Dimly he was aware of the menu being brought and of Old Jouvert urging him to ragout or beefsteak and, when an omelette was eventually fixed upon as being all the boy's depleted system could stomach, adding a medicinal measure of brandy to the order. The old man watched his captive eat, baring his few stained teeth indulgently. And—whether it were the effect of the food or the brandy, which, though he sipped it, confirmed Max's distrust of alcohol by going straight to his head, or simply of Old Jouvert's unexpected kindness— he found himself forgetting where all this must lead, surrendering to the warmth, the companionship, the momentary relief from misery. Oh, he did not tell Old Jouvert about the man at Lebas' party, or about Josette and how she had taken the money won at such cost when she had left him the next morning; nor did he rehearse the foul names she had flung at him (as if she were one to be so particular), although they still rang in his ears. He unburdened himself merely about the outstanding bills and rent, and his conclusion, given the inevitability of his being thrown out onto the street, that he had little alternative but the army.

The old man listened and nodded from time to time. He revolved wine on his tongue thoughtfully. "You're tall. You are, as I'm sure you won't mind my observing, a handsome lad. Have you never thought of going into service?"

And, when Max had shaken his head, Old Jouvert had launched upon his favourite theme. It is fair to say that much of the old fellow's sermon washed over his listener—the dignity of service, the virtues of obedience, the satisfactions of belonging to a household where each could take pride, not only in his own efficient execution of his duties, but in his contribution to an ordered whole, to a mechanism that, hour by hour, day by day, discreetly and smoothly fulfilled its purpose, serving its noble master as dependably as a Breguet clock. Some of this was in any case surprisingly familiar to Max, if in a rather different context— although not the descriptions of table settings glittering with plate and crystal, or the minutiae of etiquette and precedence or the lists of fine wines from venerable vintages lovingly decanted. But what did pierce the brandy mist was this: footmen had regular meals and their livery and a roof over their heads, all found. By the time Old Jouvert had paid the bill and they were leaving for the triangle of waste ground on the corner to conclude their business, Max was inclined to regard him as a saviour.

Mitya Zhukovsky, when Max recounted the plan, was less enthusiastic. Indeed, his friend's broad and usually good-natured face assumed the expression it had worn when Max had confessed to feeling under obligation to Josette, even though her coming child was not his.

"Mitya, this isn't Mother Russia. Servants haven't been slaves here since the revolution. They get days off and wages—not huge sums, granted, but at least something."

"But you're educated."

"I've never taken the *bachot*."

"Even so—"

"I couldn't stick being a clerk again, I'd rather go back to digging drains."

"What about the life classes?"

"It's not regular work. And anyway, I—" Max was conscious of flushing. "I'm done with getting cramp and my balls frozen off. It's either flunkeydom or the military. And you'll agree, I must do something."

Together they surveyed the forlorn room. Most of its moveable contents had already found their way to the pawnshop, even before Josette had stripped it for her flight back to her mother in Arles. Apart from the bed and the broken-backed sofa, little else remained. The second chair had followed its fellow into the grate, where its puny struts sputtered half-heartedly, giving out little enough heat to take the chill from the spring morning, let alone dry the shirt which dripped from a makeshift line strung across the mantel.

"They were her things to take," he said, reading Mitya Zhukovsky's expression. "It was her room. Oh, I know what you think, but there's no denying I owe her a good deal. And as for the last few weeks, well, she wanted the baby in the end, you can't blame her..."

He tailed off cautiously. Zhukovsky and he had been friends from the day the family had moved into the room next door, or at least from the second evening, when Max had been sent to complain about Zhukovsky's violin and, much to Josette's fury, had stayed to listen, entranced. Zhukovsky knew Max's life was not straightforward, owing to a foolhardy moment of effusion—treacherous alcohol again—the night Zhukovsky, with the greater wisdom of his twenty-one years, had absolved him of any duty to enter into a marriage he would instantly regret. With great charity, his friend had apparently forgiven the incident. But now Max dreaded what he—what the whole family—might have heard through the thin plaster.

Yet perhaps Josette's command of idiom had defeated Zhukovsky, despite his excellent French. Or perhaps he did not distinguish this tirade from those preceding it. The family had certainly been the soul of kindness over the past few days, tapping gently on Max's closed door every morning to ask if he needed anything, but leaving him to nurse his shame in private; only Beethoven and Bach had penetrated his solitude, pouring their balm through the wall.

For all that she had not cared eventually whether he lived or died, Max mourned Josette. He did not truly begrudge her the money: let it be compensation for her final disillusionment, for the brutal truth, brought home to her at last by the nature of his injury, that he would never make a respectable bourgeois husband. He did not forget her generosity and sweetness at the start of their affair: what traces of her remained—the hairpins, the tiny scraps of silk, remnants from the flowers she had made to bring in an income during the last stages of her pregnancy—left him disconsolate. But sentimentality was pointless. He had a purpose, a direction, and she had blown him off course. Her departure was painful. But it was also a tremendous relief.

Zhukovsky turned his glance from the ailing fire and dripping shirt. "Look, my friend, if there's any way I can…Of course, I can't run to much…"

"Mitya, you're a good fellow. And thank you, from the bottom of my heart. But really, you know—"

This offer was, of course, absurd. Mitya, his fifteen-year-old sister Vera and their mother lived no more luxuriously than Max himself, crammed into their one small room, which they had partitioned with blankets to save the women's modesty; Zhukovsky, despite his gifts, played at café concerts and weddings to keep the family clothed and fed.

"It's beyond rescue. There's that doctor I fetched to Josette when things started to look bad. And the baby's funeral. And the rent. We owe ten weeks, according to old Mother Richoux, curse her—eleven come Monday. When my future's settled there's nothing for it but a moonlight flit. But in the meantime there's a fellow I know—" he lowered his eyes, for in his friend's presence it embarrassed him to think of his dealings with Old Jouvert "—an acquaintance who'll tide me over."

"All the same…" Zhukovsky's brow remained furrowed. "Service?" He could not prevent himself from spitting out the word. "Forgive me, Maxim, but from what I know of you—"

"I'm no nihilist, Mitya. And, anyway, it has its advantages."

"Bowing and scraping to your so-called betters?"

"There are things I need to learn."

"Waiting at tables and emptying slops? Is aristocratic shit sweeter?"

Max sighed. "As you point out, the Benedictines gave me an education. I have Latin and some Greek, I can discourse learnedly on Augustine and Aquinas. They also, as it happens, taught me to wait at tables and empty slops. But I know nothing about the world."

Zhukovsky's hand swept the squalid room eloquently. "What's this, my dear fellow?"

"Yes, and a wonderful mess I've made of it so far. But that's not what I mean. The cloister isn't exactly the place to learn social niceties. In upbringing I'm a peasant."

"Oh, for pity's sake!"

"No, seriously. I haven't any idea of fancy manners or how to make small talk. I don't know how to leave a visiting card or address a duke…"

But he was obliged to stop, for his friend was staring at him as if he were stark mad.

Mitya Zhukovsky was one of only two people Max had ever been disposed to trust. But instinct told him that, while he had no difficulty justifying his grand scheme to himself, his friend, who had lived a different life and could not in any case be apprised of all the circumstances, might not listen with unqualified approval. Thus it was impossible to explain why going into service, now Max had thought it over, suited his purposes so well.

It was ten months since he and the Other had fled the cloister at St

Pons, eight since he had arrived in Paris. He had not expected the city to be kind, yet he had been confident he could play it at its own game. He was young, clever, resilient, physically toughened from labouring in the fields as they had worked their way from Normandy; and he was free, free at last of God. God was done with him too, for that matter, since he had broken his vows by running away. It would not be taken into account that he had only submitted to the novitiate under duress (curse the Father Superior and his talk of God's will, which was no more than blackmail): he was destined for hellfire now. But apostasy, excommunication—that was all so much shit, myths to keep the faithful fearful.

He had taken enough beatings, had licked enough penitential crosses on the chapel floor for his own sins and the sin he aroused in others, he had heard enough sermons about poverty, chastity and obedience: he had known, had understood since he was eleven that there was no God protecting the orphans in the postulates' *dormitorium*, no all-seeing, all-knowing deity, just or otherwise; and if there were no God, there was no sin. *Mea culpa?* The only amends due were to himself; likewise the only duty he owed. He could take from life, without scruple, the pleasures and advantages the myth had denied him. Only a fool or a coward would hold back.

So he was bewildered by how the city had defeated him, reduced him to this pathetic condition after only eight months. He had been naive, a simpleton, had failed all the proud expectations he had of himself. Certainly he could not pursue his prime purpose while the scar on his forehead still looked fresh, but that hardly excused his staggering helplessly from one indignity to the next. It was as if, in spite of himself, he was determined to justify the Reverend Father's verdict, that a person of his 'disposition', without the protection of the cloister, would be bound to end up in squalor and degradation.

But here Max reminded himself that the Reverend Father had possessed his own reasons for uttering this threat. And perhaps he should not regard his time as utterly wasted; he had learnt something from his failures. Take this vexing matter of money. St Pons had not equipped him to understand it—notes, coins had been foreign to his touch—and even now he cared little about it for its own sake. But he understood a great deal about the lack of it. Poverty was one affair if you had sworn a vow that guaranteed you shelter and food, quite another when it was not of your choosing. Poverty consumed your time, sapped your energy, mocked your hopes. Poverty could shipwreck his grand design before he had even launched it.

During the month before he had met Josette, he had slept in doorways when there was no labouring work to be found or walked the night streets, staring up in wonder at the lofty windows of so many palaces, the flambeaux-lit courtyards, the escutcheoned carriages offering pale glimpses of portentously whiskered gentlemen and ladies in plumes and jewels. Somewhere, behind one of those windows that blazed out into the damp night, was the person who could help him when the time came, the unknown luminary who could tell him where to find the people he sought. But the carriage wheels drenched him heedlessly as they rumbled past, the plumed ladies spared him not a glance as the great gates closed upon them with a boom like a warning cannon.

The poor were faceless and voiceless. They were also expendable—Lebas had taught him that. But Max, who had originally cherished such hopes for the connection, had learnt something else from him too. He had understood it waiting in Lebas' marble lobby to be summoned to the Blue Room, while late-arriving guests in their well-cut tails and spotless shirt-fronts had handed their topcoats to the footman and drifted past him, either with a butcher's look of appraisal or the faintest fastidious sneer. He saw for an instant what they saw: not just his grimy collar or scarred boots or the coat Josette had acquired for him from the crone in the Rue Thouin who dealt in second-hand clothes; but something he gave off, a set of tiny yet unmistakable signals he could not recognise and of which he had hitherto been unconscious, yet which advertised his condition as if he had lettered it on a sandwich board around his neck. He had raised his chin and tried to stare down these wealthy bourgeois who dared despise him. He was as intelligent as they, probably more so; his blood, from what he remembered of his earliest childhood, was by no means inferior. His pride rebelled bitterly. Yet his reason painfully absorbed their judgement.

To the problem of seeking out the elusive notables who would decide his fate was, then, added a second difficulty; he would not gain an audience, let alone convince them, if he came trailing the mire of the street. They would undoubtedly hold that breeding tells, that the pearl will shine even in the midden. They would expect someone who possessed the bearing of a gentleman. At last the frustrating delay imposed on him by the scar seemed decreed for a purpose.

But what was he to do? Where once he might have trusted to his education, he was now, as he had told Zhukovsky, under no illusion on that score. The lowliest tutoring post was beyond his reach as long as he lacked polish, testimonials or even a decent set of clothes. Which left only the odious alternative of office work—and how could he hope to learn the ways of society closeted over ledgers for nine hours a day? If Max still devoured books, it was no longer ambition that drove him (Fabrice was to be quite wrong there, as in most of his suppositions): he read because it was as essential to him as breathing and had often saved him from despair. Moreover at St Pons so many works had been forbidden; here was a limitless feast—Juvenal, Vergil, Ovid, Rabelais, Molière, the *philosophes*, the lives of the great generals and statesmen, Alexander, Wallenstein, Frederick the Great, Napoleon…He had driven Josette mad, lying absorbed on the sofa, not listening to her, squandering his wages on the giddy temptations of bookstalls: it had been a heavy blow when, dog-eared though the volumes were, they had gone to the Mont de Piété with the rest. Yet they were an indulgence. His learning would prove no hindrance later; but no one would be persuaded of his case by his ability to recite Vergil.

He had hoped, when he reached the age for conscription, that his irregular papers would enable him to evade it. All the same, his thoughts now turned naturally to the army, for where else could a man without money or connections improve his lot? He pictured himself rising through the ranks, earning his commission, acquiring medals and useful acquaintance amongst his brother officers. Yet there were disadvantages, the greatest being the absence of a war in which he could prove his mettle: he might spend years as a trooper, or end up languishing in some North African outpost, which would hardly suit his plans. And then Old Jouvert had proffered his alternative, like a gift.

Service held no promise of adventure or distinction (although Max supposed the lives of a soldier and a footman, spent in fancy uniform following mindless orders, might not differ so greatly when you came down to it). It did, however, guarantee him his objective. Even Napoleon, he was compelled to recall, had not risen to eminence entirely through valour; he had been born into the minor aristocracy and had attended an exclusive military college. But in any case, Max had no requirement to become a gentleman by right, he merely needed the appearance. And what better school could he have than the houses of the Faubourg Saint-Germain?

Of course, it would mean surrendering his most precious possession, his freedom—he recalled grimly Old Jouvert's talk of masters and devotion and finely oiled machines. Yet, in truth, there was a part of him that contemplated the loss of this treasure with relief. Perhaps the Reverend Father had not merely spoken out of malice. There was something in Max that longed for the discipline and safety of the cloister just as powerfully as his braver self had longed to leave it. He did not care to examine this contradiction or even acknowledge it, for if he once saw it in clear light he could only despise it. But then he gave no deep thought, either, to those other deviations from his stated philosophy: the guilt he had felt over Josette, or his admiration of Zhukovsky's solid principles; or that, while he saw no theoretical objection to the poor robbing the rich, in practice, even when his situation was desperate, he found himself incapable of relieving some fat bourgeois of his wallet. Later the contradictions in his position would cause him anguish. For now, he merely concluded it was proving harder than anticipated to shed habits of thought drummed in over six years.

As for his bondage, it would only be temporary. He could not but accept that he needed to retire and regroup his forces. For, if he carried on as at present—damn the Reverend Father!—he would soon end up with a dose. Or dead.

Meeting Old Jouvert two days later, as arranged, he took possession of two glowing references testifying to Albert Fabien's abilities as a footman, and a list of three addresses where he would do well to apply. His benefactor also advanced him a small sum at a moderate rate, so that he could present himself in clean linen and with his best clothes sponged free of bloodstains and pressed.

His first situation was in the household of a newly rich department store owner—not ideal for his purposes, but he soon saw why Old Jouvert had suggested it. The mistress of the house, through her capriciousness and harsh tongue, was incapable of keeping servants: his astonishing incompetence for the first few weeks was attributed to the natural stupidity of the serving class, while the harassed butler, resigned to expecting no better, was grateful that Max was at least willing and did not ask for his cards. He stuck at this place for six months, by which time he was proficient enough to aspire to better. Again, the situation with baron Reinhardt was not precisely what he had hoped for, but it was a large, well-run household that entertained lavishly, the baronne was from the minor nobility and the baron's influence in political and financial circles ensured their guest lists were usually gilded with aristocratic names.

It should not be said that he always found it easy. Oh, the work was not difficult, even if its long hours and endless demands at first sent him to bed each night utterly exhausted. No, the work you could do in your sleep, once you had learnt the routine of the household. Nor was the way of life below stairs absolutely foreign to him: the cruel tolling of the rising bell, the silent meals taken beneath the steely gaze of the senior servants, the penitential beds and cheerless dormitories, the reek of unwashed men who barely tolerated each other sentenced to live pressed in together; it was, as Old Jouvert had conveyed, not much different from the cloister. Yet, as at St Pons, his endurance came at a cost. The lost jewel of his freedom had recovered its brilliance. And—Mitya Zhukov understood him too well—he was often obliged to do fierce battle with his pride. Several times in the first year he was on the point of surrender.

Yet he had but to look about him: where else, under one roof, would he find every class of society, from the hall boy who slept on a cot outside the pantry to, on one occasion at baron Reinhardt's table, a prince? Where else could he observe every degree of behaviour— bourgeois decorum, the extravagant vulgarity of the new rich, the negligent assumption of superiority that came with high birth? He had quickly learned the code universal amongst servants that decrees which of their betters merits respect: who tips too much or too little, who is arrogant, who over-familiar, who has money but no breeding or, almost as bad, the reverse. This was a sensible and utilitarian form of snobbery, a small recompense for the many times you were put upon. But he must go further, apply himself to caste's finer nuances. Like a botanist, he must study this rich flowering, this fascinating array of species and sub-species, in order to judge which of these delicate shades and subtle differentiations would best lure his bee.

There were obvious pitfalls. Even the aristocracy could not be counted upon to be consistent: the prince, for instance, tucked his napkin into his shirt front, chewed with his mouth open and belched unrestrainedly, so that, to the uninitiated, little marked him out from the hall boy's father shovelling down pigs' trotters in the Faubourg Saint-Antoine. Then, Max was not the only servant seeking to ape the manners of his betters, which enabled him to note that a lazy eye for detail could yield disastrous, not to say comic, results. Josette's teasing had prompted him to expunge all trace of Normandy from his voice; now he strove to reproduce faultlessly the refinements of Île-de-France. Yet he eschewed the modish verbal affectations favoured, in their private moments, by many of his fellows: the acute ear could not fail to catch when this sort of thing was even a semi-tone off pitch.

He resolved against affectation and flamboyance of any kind. While he was unashamed of the tastes that drew him to the Green Monkey, it was dangerous in the normal way to advertise them and, so far as his own ambitions were concerned, might prove catastrophic. An elegant restraint which, while it spurned bourgeois correctness, avoided any excess was, besides, what suited him best: it appealed to the ascetic in him, to his sense of discipline and purpose; it endowed him with a protective detachment, so that, even as he obediently drew curtains, stoked fires, set tables and ladled sauces without splashing illustrious shirt fronts, he could live by his own rules in his head.

None of this came pat. Mistakes had constantly to be watched for and ruthlessly analysed. Although he had always been quick to learn, his intelligence was of the mercurial rather than the plodding kind, as Magister Jérôme, listening impatiently to his declensions and conjugations, had been pained to point out: Max laughed to think how the old pedant would have been astonished by his dogged approach to this improbable field of learning. Yet, even after three years, he was still liable to forget himself.

Mitya Zhukovsky, having at last found work at the Paris Opéra, had moved his family to a small apartment in Montparnasse, where other musicians, as well as a number of his compatriots in exile, tended to gather of a Sunday evening. These occasions, after Mme Zhukovskaya and Vera had retired, frequently swelled into drunken debates on politics and art or wild extempore performances, as the mood struck, of grand opera one night, folk songs another: one of the Russian contingent might decide to dance à la Cossack and soon they would all be stamping and clapping, balancing on their haunches and flicking up their heels until, one by one, like skittles, they noisily came to grief. The servants' hall would not have recognised Max, sprawling unmannerly elbows upon the table, bellowing to force some point through the din of argument or throwing back his head in full-throated and decidedly non-patrician laughter. When the time came to meet his curfew, he would walk back loudly singing some snatch of the night's music, giddy with ideas, overflowing with the sense that the world was limitless and all things were possible. But as he approached the servants' entrance he would straighten his demeanour along with his hat: nothing was possible without discipline.

Old Jouvert, at any rate, was pleased with him. Max found it sinister that, whenever he dropped into the Monkey on his way to the Zhukovskys', the ex-butler was always well informed of his progress. He could not help feeling a chill in the company of one or two of his fellow servants—one in particular. But it was better not to speculate. He was scarcely in a position to quarrel with the old scoundrel's methods.

He listened to Old Jouvert's account of the duchesse de Claireville's establishment with a leaping heart. It was perfect. And not merely because it was a noble household. Here, at last, was the means to advance his cause.

He had not forgotten staring up at those blazing windows when he was sleeping on the streets. Sometimes he had wondered whether baron Reinhardt were the one who could help, for undeniably the banker had influence; two government ministers regularly ate at his table. But Max had only to glance at the baron, a tight-lipped man, impermeable as a dried walnut, to disabuse himself of that hope: he could not imagine achieving an interview with him, let alone persuading him to listen to his story unless he could quantify its value in stock prices. Mme de Claireville, on the other hand, not only seemed to know everyone worth knowing—according to Old Jouvert at her Thursdays philosophers and poets mingled with diplomats, society beauties and scions of the best families—but she sounded, from her tastes, commendably broad-minded. Besides, being a woman, she could not fail to be influenced by the romantic aspects of his tale. And as for gaining an audience with her—from what Old Jouvert was hinting, Max would be hard-put to avoid it. His one concern was the scar, whether it had faded sufficiently. But he would have to leave that to chance. The duchesse de Claireville was his fate, no doubt of it. She was the face at the glowing window, the unknown patron looking down at him as he had stood and shivered in the rain-swept street.

Thus, once again, he found himself indebted to Old Jouvert. He had paid the money he owed long ago, but over the past three years he had worried periodically that the rest of his debt would be called in, that he would find himself required to carry out some enterprise of espionage or blackmail that he would find hard to refuse, for he had grown fond of the old fellow. But Old Jouvert still asked for nothing. He no longer even required the attentions Max would gladly have afforded him gratis. Certainly, he always seemed delighted to see his protégé, and readier than ever to indulge in reminiscence, particularly since Max was now of the fraternity: he would question him about baron Reinhardt's table and the guests and what wines were served, not, Max felt, for any benefit he gained from the answers, for they contained no sensational detail (the baron was an oyster about his byzantine dealings) but for the sheer pleasure of hearing a colleague talk about his work and for the pictures of fine liveries, immaculate white gloves and spotless napery this talk conjured up.

One evening, as both of them were leaving the Monkey to go their separate ways, Max caught their image in the glass on the opposite wall: himself young, tall and strong, Old Jouvert stooped, emaciated, crimson-faced. As he looked, the old man followed his glance and suddenly drew himself up, not in shame but faintly smiling, as if the sight gave him inordinate satisfaction. With a shiver, Max saw what he saw; that the old fellow had once stood just as tall and straight, with that very same tilt to his chin, that same conscious air of refinement. He, Max, had been chosen as Old Jouvert's heir, encouraged, groomed, sent into the world of service as the old man's expiation, the perfect footman, one day to be the perfect butler. His horror was short-lived, for he was amused and touched by the old boy's faith in him. He was only sorry he was going to disappoint it.

CHAPTER THREE

The bottle of champagne had been left out for him, packed in ice, in M Vincent's pantry. He fetched a tray, then went to the glass cupboard. Two glasses, those were his instructions. He placed the flutes beside the bottle, automatically separating them and covering them with a napkin so that the tray would make no clatter. He was not nervous. He could have done without Fabrice's attentions, which, however well-meant, might have been expressly designed to fluster him. But he was not nervous, why should he be? He was no innocent where women were concerned: he had satisfied Josette, who was nothing if not experienced.

True, madame could be considered intimidating. Since his arrival in her household, he had seized every chance to take stock of her, standing impassive as a waxwork in the salon or the dining room yet studiously noting her conversations, her merest smile and gesture. Although of rather less than medium height and unfashionably thin, with decisive, even mannish features, she appeared to scorn the unfairness of nature; faultlessly costumed *à la mode*, at dinner conspicuously armoured in jewels, she possessed a lacquered brilliance that expected no less than great beauty expects, the right to command and silence a room. That to the petty cruelties of heredity were now added those of age seemed to trouble her little: she powdered and rouged uncompromisingly. Once or twice, when handing round after-dinner coffee, Max had chanced to hear whispers, stealthy and spiteful as pins, concerning the propriety of madame's décolletage or her vigorous resort to henna. The duchesse, of course, could have crushed these junior sisters with one shaft of her hard bright glance. Yet perhaps she would only have shrugged, for it seemed she shared the philosophy of baron Reinhardt's prince: whatever she did was *comme il faut*, because it was she who did it. Another of her characteristics, which ensured the whisperers rarely ventured out from behind their fans, was her forthright tongue; although capable of subtlety when she chose, she usually preferred not to withhold the telling comment or embarrassing question. Max had never witnessed her rage, but it was not pleasant to imagine.

Yet it could also be observed that amongst her innermost circle, by both sexes, she was regarded warmly, not to say adored. Even in the servants' hall her standing was high in spite of her singular tastes: M Vincent and Mme Pinot spoke of her with hushed respect, while the lower servants, although not forgiving her Michel, accorded her a certain jocular affection. She was fair—sharp when she needed to be, but at other times courteous; she remembered names, she even thanked you on occasion; yet she never lowered herself, never overstepped the ordained barrier that stood between servant and served.

Except, of course, in this one notable respect. She was not short of admirers amongst her own kind, could have taken her pick from several elderly nobles. She chose this, Max supposed, simply because she could. Being high-born, rich and disdainful of convention, she saw no reason to distinguish herself from any man of her rank with a preference for youth.

Still, he must not forget himself. He was not Michel or Fabrice, he had a purpose, madame and he would be making a fair exchange. His hand was steady as he carried the tray up the back stairs, his breathing even. On the third floor, M Vincent had left the electricity burning to guide his mission. He stepped confidently onto the landing, avoiding the carpet and walking the parquetry at its border as befitted his station. His footsteps sounded softly but with resolution.

He was glad she was a small woman, he would not have welcomed mountainous flesh. And as for her age, Fabrice was unjust—yes, so far as Max could judge, she could easily be his mother, but she was by no means in her dotage—she still had most of her teeth. Besides, when it came down to it, wasn't she a woman like any other? He had only to recall what Josette had taught him, that the female sex was not straightforward like the male, that women liked to be coy about their lust, tricking it out with diversions and games, as the pillars of a baroque church are concealed by putti and swags of fruit and flowers. He would flatter madame, be tender with her, indulge her in any frippery she wished.

He remembered his first night with Josette. It had all come about by mischance, his being in the doorway and seeing her struggle with the fat man he afterwards knew as M Pintard, and his naturally assuming…How enraged she had been at his efforts to rescue her. She would have thwacked him with her parasol too, would have handed him over to the policeman alerted by the growing crowd, had not M Pintard, hoping to protect his reputation as a respectable married man, made a fatal miscalculation. "I have never seen this woman before." This woman? Who was carrying his child? Instantly switching allegiance, Josette had claimed Max for her younger brother, valiant defender of her honour. And since Max was the only combatant bleeding, the wound at his temple having reopened in the fracas, the gendarme was inclined to give her credence. M Pintard was lucky to escape into the night with a caution, while Josette, having lost her protector but enjoyed a measure of revenge, had made the best of things by taking Max back to her lodgings.

When he recalled that fourth-floor room in Mère Richoux's house he pictured it as ugly and squalid. But this was not how it had appeared to him on that first night. It had seemed a kind of wonderland—the quilt tumbled over the bed, the paper screen with the satin peignoir drooping from it in soft folds, the froth of *broderie anglaise* on a discarded chemise, a tiny slipper, a gauzy stocking. After the life he had lived in unadorned rooms with cold scrubbed surfaces, everything seemed marvellously exotic to his eye, from the fairground bric-a-brac on the mantel to the milliner's block with its partly-dressed hat floating in mists of veiling. Exotic, yes, elaborate, delicate, sensuous; but also disquieting. Here was the manifestation of an alien presence. It hung thickly in the air too, very different from the acid male smells he was used to, a hot sweet scent overlaid with attar of roses and, as you grew accustomed to it, a faint tang of mackerel. It did not move him to desire. Not then. He was too bewildered by its mysteries. She bathed his wound with salt and bandaged it with a strip torn from an old petticoat, and he settled to sleep on the sofa. It was only later, hearing her voice from the bed, hearing her ask if he wasn't cold and lonely lying there all by himself, that it struck him. Here was his chance to commit the sin of sins, the great wickedness thrust on man by the Fall, the transgression beside which yielding to Dom Sébastien and the Père Abbé was venial: the ultimate depravity of fornication.

He had been clumsy, of course, altogether too precipitate, as he realised later. But at the time, lying in Josette's arms with his lips against her breast, he had felt triumphant, the conqueror of a territory he had supposed far beyond his reach. The sin of sins. He smiled to think how pleased his sixteen-year-old self had been with this achievement. He was still smiling as he reached the door to madame's apartments.

Although Michel usually tended to madame's practical requirements, these duties fell to Max on the first footman's Sundays off, so that, as he drew the curtains or banked up the fire, he had been able to note every detail of her bedroom: the gilded pier glasses between the windows above twin inlaid commodes; the silk-hung walls and Sèvres porcelain; the dressing table, with its silver-topped bottles and lapis lazuli-backed brushes laid out in order, as far from Josette's feminine chaos as was possible to imagine; and of course the carved and gilded bed, lying like a ship at anchor on its dais beneath a richly draped canopy surmounted with a coronet. Three years as a footman had left him impervious to such grandeur; he took for granted towering doors, high ceilings and expanses of carpet, no longer wondered at the new-fangled miracle of the electric lamps, although this convenience, like the gas it replaced, had never penetrated as far as the servants' dormitories. These lavish appointments were the matter-of-fact backdrop to his working life, he was at home amongst them, as if, by proxy, he owned them.

Yet tonight this room was different. He had not thought of it as he moved through her boudoir and knocked gently on the inner door, did not think of it until she called to him to enter, but madame had always been absent during his previous visits. Now, even before he saw her, he felt that everything was made unfamiliar by her presence. Suddenly he did not know where to look, although some demon kept drawing his eye to the bed, indecently shorn of coverlet and bolster and with its top sheet ominously turned down. Despite the blazing electric bulbs and the hot May night (under the eaves Fabrice would already be cursing), down here, with the shutters and sashes open and the curtains parted, the air was cool: yet all at once he was sweating. A flood of random sensations and thoughts attacked him; he saw Michel sniggering from that white, naked pillow; he heard Old Jouvert expatiating on the joys of service.

"Jean."

He was forced to look in her direction. "Madame?"

She sat before her mirror, idly dragging one of the lapis lazuli brushes through her hair. She wore white, pure white organza over white silk, and, with the fiery tresses hanging unbound to her waist, you might have mistaken her for a maiden; until she turned and you saw her worn, masculine face, still with its mask of rouge and powder. She seemed a witch, a Medusa, a thousand years old.

"Set down the tray and close the curtains."

There was a mercy in routine tasks, walking slowly from window to window, pulling cords, straightening folds of velvet, working methodically at the champagne cork until it came free with a soft pop and a puff of vapour like gun smoke, but without a drop wasted. He concentrated on pouring the wine, carefully, in stages, letting the bubbles settle, and was relieved that his hand did not waver. He did not stumble as he carried the glass to her. And, if his eye avoided hers as he placed it on the dressing table, that was no more than the etiquette of service required.

"And for yourself, Jean. Fill the other for yourself."

The comfort of rules vanished. He had not ignored the implications of the second glass, but now they struck him in a glaring new light. Servants were strictly forbidden to indulge in tobacco or alcohol on the premises (or carnal relations come to that): no matter that the rule was often broken, it was a rule nonetheless. But now this, along with every other edict that governed his presence here, was to be cast aside. He was to be left floundering where one uncertain step could plunge him into quicksand. This was the reality all his over-confident imaginings had evaded.

"Well? Take off your wig and gloves and pour yourself some wine."

"I—" He stood, absurdly helpless, twisting the wig in his hands. "Where would madame prefer…?"

"Heavens! Set them down wherever you please."

He deposited the wig on the commode beside the tray. He took some moments turning the gloves right side out and folding them meticulously. He began to fill the second flute. This time the bubbles gushed up, foaming rebelliously over the rim. He must take hold of himself, remember what he had come for. As he mopped the glass, it occurred to him: what if he simply told her now? Her view of him would be utterly changed, so that her other expectations would be forgotten. Yes, that was it—tell her now. He lifted the glass and turned, endeavouring to summon the speech he had delivered a hundred times in his imagination.

I come before Madame la duchesse in her livery, as a humble footman. But my position in the world was once very different. I must reveal to madame, in the utmost secrecy, that my true identity is…

But no, that would sound wrong, too rushed, faintly comic.

I stand before madame as a lowly footman. But, owing to an unfortunate sequence of circumstances, for which I crave madame's understanding and compassion…

No, that wouldn't do either, it had a pathetic ring like a begging letter.

Madame, you see before you a member of the servant class. But I must tell you, my blood…

"Your health, Jean."

The long-rehearsed words, now hopelessly jumbled, froze on his tongue. "Madame's health."

The very smell of the champagne disgusted him. No doubt the wine was intended to relax him (and probably to freshen his breath), but now, least of all, was he willing to risk that slackening of control. Nevertheless her eyes were upon him: he took a brief sip. So be it, it was too soon for his speech, too sudden, he would need to win her confidence before he could convince her. But what must he do instead? Was he supposed to act like a lover, set aside his glass and offer to caress her? Or no—that was surely too brutal—should he not be indulging in the sort of teasing, elegant repartee any of her circle would effortlessly summon? But how? He may have acquired the manner, but the content, he realised, was utterly beyond him. Oh, he could talk to her about Voltaire—he had heard her cross swords on the subject with the duc de la Marne and M de Cressy—but he doubted either of those two noblemen would bring the great philosopher to the bedchamber. He found himself wondering what Michel did. But this train of thought, and the images it conjured, brought no comfort at all.

He was aware that she was smiling at him over the rim of her glass. "Now, if you would be so good as to take off your coat. And your waistcoat. And those ridiculous shoes and stockings."

His heart lurched, suddenly behind his eyes hot blood was pounding. Yet what could he do but obey? Standing before her in his shirt and breeches, he felt humiliated, reduced: the sight of his bare feet on the Turkey carpet seemed particularly shocking. But when he looked up she was still smiling. She rose and came towards him.

"And now your shirt, there's a good boy."

Naked to the waist, exposed like some lower creature belly up, he was conscious that, to crown his indignity, his skin had begun to prickle, that every hair on his forearms stood separate and proud from his flesh. She could scarcely fail to notice, for she was no more than a pace away, although mercifully she made no move to touch him.

"Dear me, but I've distracted you. Please drink your champagne."

"I prefer not to, madame."

His tone arrested her. She scrutinised him, head cocked like an enquiring bird. Then she laughed. "A young man of spirit."

She continued to study him, while he, looking over her head into the middle distance, held his breath and fought to control the tremor that was infecting his muscles. It was not his modesty that she affronted—he was unashamed of his body and, besides, he had repudiated modesty along with the other virtues. It was the impropriety of it, this reversal of nature where, even in her bedroom, she continued the master while he remained—no, not the servant, the slave. She did not flirt with him, she did not seek to flatter him as Josette had, he had no notion whether, as she conducted this unendurable examination, she approved of what she saw. She was sizing him up, as some Roman plutocrat might have assessed the trader's shackled cargo. His biceps, his pectorals—at any moment she would stroll round to inspect his dorsal muscles, or peer up into his nostrils, or require to view his teeth.

Fury possessed him. He no longer gave a thought to his cherished enterprise, his reputation in the servants' hall, or even his place.

"Jean?"

She was staring up at him, so that, for the first time, he must look at her directly. His eye moved in reluctant stages before it could bring itself to meet hers, taking in the bony chest above the lace trimming of her night-gown, the lines encircling her neck, the flesh that swagged her jawbone. Damn her to hell! He had little enough inclination to go where Michel had gone, the bastard was welcome to the old witch.

"You are offended." Her glance was penetrating but without rancour. " I won't keep you here against your will. You may leave if you wish."

He continued to stare at her furiously. His rage was increased by her coolness, the shocking indifference with which she was ready to dismiss him. He remembered his ambition and his honour once again. He was damned if he would let her defeat him. He would demonstrate to her that he was not a slave, he would force the recognition upon her with every muscle of his body.

"No. No—I don't wish it."

Her hard, bright eyes expressed neither surprise nor gratification, but merely the flicker of a smile. "Good. Give me your hand."

He submitted to her taking his right hand in hers. This too she examined, turning it in her palm.

"You have fine hands. But then—" here the lines around her eyes puckered mischievously "—well, I shan't trouble to tell you you're a fine-looking young man since you so clearly know it."

"Madame is—"

"Nonsense, all you footmen are impossibly vain, you can't serve dinner without preening yourselves in the silver. Don't think I don't notice. And you, my boy, are one of the worst."

"Madame mistakes me—"

"Shush!" Before he could snatch away his hand, she had drawn it down to his fly. "There. See what anger can do?"

Her chuckle was infectious. Yet his laughter mainly sprang from relief: Fabrice's fate would not, after all, be his.

Her other hand brushed his cheek. "Now drink your champagne."

Thus he discovered there were rules governing this service, as any other: the first being that he should do as madame directed. Surprisingly, this was not the shaming ordeal he had imagined. Madame was not like Josette, she set no store by baroque trifling but stated bluntly and unambiguously what she wanted. While Josette had sought to please, madame's first concern was her own pleasure. Yet, if he could swallow his dignity and submit to her tutelage, his pleasure, too, was increased. That first night he had acquitted himself passably, well enough at least to receive a second command, but as the week progressed he understood how raw he had been. Josette, it seemed, had merely taught him the tune, not the chords and harmonies that gave it meaning. He could not help a rush of pride at his new mastery of this foreign instrument, nor a certain growing confidence that, of the countless others who had plucked these particular strings, including Michel, he was by no means the least proficient. From the way madame pinched his cheek and teased him about the dangers of getting above himself, it would certainly appear she was not displeased.

As for Madame's age—fifty, sixty?—past childbearing at any rate, for she seemed to have no fear of conception—it rapidly ceased to bother him. True, her figure was not rounded and firm-skinned like Josette's. Indeed, its topography was ultimately mysterious since she never removed her night-gown, so that while he grew well acquainted with isolated areas—her sinewy thighs, the dark fuzz of her pudendum, her breasts, fierce-nippled and flat without the artifice of corsetry— the rest remained a hinterland. Nevertheless, when his hands were permitted to explore beneath the silk, what they encountered was angular and lean, a notable relief after Josette's last months of pregnancy. Madame could have been any age; sometimes she seemed infinitely ancient and forbidding, at others, with her salacious and thoroughly unladylike chuckle, a preternaturally knowing child.

He came to hold the days in suspension, to exist for the nights. Madame's scent, a heavy musk with oriental notes, lingered like a ghost in any room she had just quitted, indeed so permeated the lower floors of the house that it formed an essential ingredient of the household atmosphere, of the subtle, individual aroma that distinguishes every building, as unnoticeable to its inmates as the scent of polish. But now, with his senses freshly attuned, he was arrested by it a dozen times a day. In its drift swirled the promise not only of sexual release but a rich assortment of pleasures—soft carpets beneath his naked feet, the smell of starched linen sheets, the joy of clean air and space, an escape for a few hours from his attic squalor. The recollection that all this was usually the prerogative of cloddish Michel could only sicken him. Yet, as the week wore on, his loathing for his rival was tempered by the high disdain that comes from the increasing certainty of triumph.

Beset by such distractions, he might have been forgiven for losing sight of his objective. However it was not forgotten, far from it: every night, as he climbed the back stairs on his way to madame, he resolved that this would be the occasion he broached the subject. But all the same he was no further forward. There was indeed a strict etiquette to his new service; after the first rule came a great many others, every one of which balked him.

He might enter madame, he might witness her abandoned to the extremes of passion, but he was never once allowed to mistake his place. Oh, she was kind, even affectionate. Yet her manner made it clear: the line, sharp as a sword blade, that had divided them when he was merely the minion who closed her curtains still separated them now, and banishment would be the penalty if he presumed to cross it. He was permitted some concessions; he could meet her eyes, he could address her in the second person plural instead of the singular third. But, although he might kiss her in ways that would outrage bourgeois virtue, he must not kiss her on the lips and, once given his cue for departure, he must not hesitate to take it. She might tease him unmercifully but he must beware even the mildest response in kind. It went without saying that she would not welcome any critique of the running of her household, nor be enthralled by servants' hall gossip. And, above all, it was tacitly understood that, however intimate he was with her body, he was not to question her intimately, about her past life with the deceased duke or her present cares and concerns; nor (this was a grave blow to his plans) should he expect personal questions.

Some conversation, of course, was necessary in the intervals between love-making, despite these constraints. Suitable topics were always selected by madame. He need not have worried that he lacked elegant phrases: the woman who discussed Voltaire with M de la Marne and M de Cressy confined herself with Max to a relentless flow of chatter about fashion or the most trivial daily affairs; and while occasionally, out of mischief, she might permit herself some satirical comment on her acquaintance—had Max noticed that M de Cressy's false teeth chattered like castanets, or that Mme de Beaumont-Gramont was the very image of Bismarck?—it was evident that his only appropriate response was laughter, and not some witty elaboration of his own.

He understood, he thought. This—the distance, the rules, the carefully tailored conversation—was how she managed Michel, how she contrived not to be repelled by his boorishness. Max could imagine his rival vainly struggling to extol the flattering properties of crêpe-de-chine. It amused him mightily that the great lover who swaggered in the servants hall was, in the bedroom, a cowed schoolboy. But the shackles designed to keep Michel in his place hardly helped Max's cause. The experience of that first night had taught him that he could not simply blurt out his story. He needed madame's time and attention. And even then…

There was the risk, of course, of being discovered in a lie, for she was shrewd and he would need all his fluency to convince her. But a likelier hazard was that she would not give him a proper hearing, that, with her sharp tongue and caustic chuckle, she would twist his story with so many mocking interruptions that it would shrink to a mere satirical tit-bit, another delicious excuse to tease him. Quite apart from the blow to his pride and his prospects, he must consider the danger this would bring, for if she chanced to amuse her circle with his confession—"Is there no limit, my dears, to the peculiar vanity of servants?"—there was no knowing whose ears it might reach.

His strongest chance, he still believed, lay in the romantic aspects of his tale. Yes, she was masculine in her demands and her candour but for all that, with her love of frivolity and fashion, she was at heart as resolutely feminine as any girl. She read novels: he had seen one of Pierre Loti's exotic romances, lying open spine upwards on the dressing table, tossed aside at his knock. She was not immune to the small tokens of tenderness—gentle hands in her hair, soft kisses to her throat—with which he had learnt to pacify Josette. If he could emphasise the melodramatic aspects of his case, appeal to her sense of justice, invoke her womanly protective instincts...

But finding a way to manage this was not easy. Such openings as she gave him were less than propitious. For instance, on the third night of his service, she suddenly and alarmingly demanded: "Tell me something amusing."

He was tempted to fling caution aside. To hell with it, why not say to her: "Madame, perhaps it will entertain you to know that I—that my lineage, far from being inferior to yours..." Common sense quickly conquered, but his mind, purged of its main preoccupation, was left blank. Michel, he supposed, would have regaled her with the latest filthy joke circulating the male dormitories—and she would probably have adored it. But Max could not bring himself to imitate his rival and besides he had forgotten every joke he knew. Instead all that came to him, inconsequentially, was a story he had heard at the Zhukovskys' the previous Sunday.

It concerned the maestro Richard Wagner and his festival at Bayreuth. For the festival's first performance of Siegfried four years ago a magnificent dragon, complete with serpentine neck and swishing tail, had been ordered from a maker of theatrical machinery in England, who had shipped it over in sections. But, when the Bayreuth curtain rose, the beast was more duck than dragon. Owing to some mix-up, the neck had been sent to Beirut.

A silence fell after Max had finished his tale. He was aware that madame was staring at him. Then she let out a great peal of laughter. "What a strange boy you are," she said, gently tweaking his ear.

While he could hardly deceive himself that the story alone had prompted her mirth, still, he could count it an unexpected success. The following night, when she repeated her peremptory demand, he was ready.

He recounted an anecdote from a memoir he had chanced upon during his furtive perusals of baron Reinhardt's unread library. Madame would perhaps recall the history of the Chevalier d'Éon, who, as well as being Louis XV's spy and a champion fencer, preferred to dress as a woman. Max described the public fencing bout arranged by the English Prince of Wales, where the redoubtable Chevalier challenged the unbeaten champion of the day, the twenty-six-year-old mulatto, the Chevalier Saint-George. Although he was sixty, did not reach Saint-George's shoulder and was considerably impeded by his voluminous petticoats, d'Éon trounced his rival by scoring seven hits.

Again madame considered Max for an instant before emitting a hoot of laughter; again she pronounced him a very strange young man, this time tousling his hair. But he did not care that she mocked him, for he had the beginnings of an idea.

His next offering was the story of Heliogabalus, who had danced for the delectation of the Roman soldiery in the temple of the Sun God until an accident of heredity (and some judicious bribes) elevated him to emperor. The new emperor was by no means prepared to abandon his god: indeed he was determined Rome should be converted. He set up a holy sanctuary next to the imperial palace and, robed in flowing Phoenician purple, honoured the deity with daily sacrifice. His reign was an orgy of religious ceremonial, of outlandish dancing and music, of wine and exotic perfumes, of singing in strange tongues, of festivals and banquets and unbridled licence. The high point of each year was the procession of the Sun God to the emperor's summer residence, during which statues of Rome's traditional gods paid homage. The stone representing the Sun travelled in a chariot encrusted with jewels and, since the god must have precedence, the emperor, holding the horses' reins and with eyes fixed unwaveringly upon his deity, ran backwards before the bejewelled car—a feat he achieved with the aid of teams of courtiers and a path marked out with a carpet of gold dust. The delirious crowd ran along behind him, waving torches, throwing flowers, until, once the requisite bulls and sheep had been sacrificed, Heliogabalus ascended a tower and threw down amongst the mob jars of gold and silver, gemstones and live animals: tearing at each other as they fought for these trophies, many were crushed to death or impaled on the spears of the imperial guard. The blood that flowed was deemed to add to the magnificence of the occasion.

This time Max had taken the risk of spinning out his tale. Yet he must have held her, for she remained with her dark, almost black eyes focused intently on his face, not venturing to interject until he paused, when she enquired: "And were the Romans converted?"

"They had Heliogabalus assassinated and installed his brother in his place."

"Ridiculous child." In a moment of absent-mindedness ignoring her own strictures, she kissed him lightly on the lips.

He could not but feel encouraged. At this rate, he calculated, it would take only two or three more nights of playing Scheherazade to lull the Caliph into a suitable mood to receive his own story. He would introduce it casually, impersonally, like the others. And then, when he had finished and she had ceased laughing, he would reveal the truth and throw himself on her mercy.

The next night, the sixth of his service, he came armed with the curious history of the Bohemian emperor Rudolph II, whom the great warlord Wallenstein had served and whose household had included a lion on a leash, two astrologers imprisoned in a tower and a dodo, whose portrait was painted by a Dutch master. But Scheherazade had reckoned without the Caliph's perversity. Not only did madame fail to give her storyteller his cue: she seemed all of a sudden to have lost her taste for chatter, to favour thoughtful silences over talk of any sort.

Maybe Heliogabalus had proved a little too bloodthirsty. Or maybe she was growing weary of their love-making—although Max doubted it for, if anything, she seemed more passionate. Perhaps he could flatter himself she had at last realised he was not Michel. But most likely, he concluded with some bitterness, she was preoccupied with cares from the real world, the friendships and quarrels within her circle, all the vital concerns of life conducted out of earshot of the servants. She was doubtless exhausted by the demands of society, a ball last night, a *conversazione* this evening... There could be countless reasons why, as they waited for desire to renew itself, she now preferred to cradle him wordlessly on her breast.

Although they played havoc with his original plan, these unexpected silences of hers might still have worked to his advantage. Yet there was a deep and meditative quality to them that challenged interruption, that warned him one ill-judged move could cancel any progress he had made. This renewed need for caution made him almost regret the easy vacancy of small talk. And he missed it, besides, for another reason. If madame were exhausted she breakfasted in bed, but he must rise with the bell at six; although he was practised at foregoing sleep, the exacting nature of his service was beginning to tell.

On the eighth night, he must have succumbed. He awoke to hear madame's voice, faintly, as though from a long way off: "Such a pity... how did it happen?"

"P-pardon me, madame?"

"You're asleep, miserable boy."

"N-no. Positively not."

He lifted his head, blinking to rouse himself. Here was a breach of etiquette gross enough to warrant dismissal. But her lids were heavy, her chuckle soft, as if she too were on the edge of sleep. In contrition, he worked his arms around her. She submitted happily to being turned to face him, sighing and easing her thigh between his, light and bony as a bird as his hands sought her waist beneath the night-gown — strange, he thought drowsily, that someone so small, not much bigger than a child, should have such power over his destiny.

"You were saying, madame?"

"Wretch. Your eyes are closing again."

"I was awake, I swear. It's just that I didn't quite catch…"

"Oh, it was nothing." She ruffled his hair, brushing it back from his temple. "I merely asked how you came by this. It quite spoils your beauty."

As she touched the scar his torpor left him. Here was his chance. Here was the opportunity he had imagined, schemed for, despaired of for seven nights. And now it had transpired so naturally, so easily, that he had almost missed it. His mouth grew dry. Yet he had only to tell this story as he had told the others.

He resisted the impulse to clear his throat. "It happened when I was a child," he said. "My pony threw me."

"Your pony, eh?" To his dismay, the teasing spark flared. "You had a pony?"

"Madame, I…" What was he to tell her? That there had not only been a pony, but a stable of Lipizzaners, not to mention the chargers of Arab and Spanish blood and the mounts belonging to the officers of the guard that had drilled in the courtyard every morning…He began to perceive the flaw in his strategy. Like all good lies, his was immured in truthful detail, yet truth—as his previous stories reminded him—had a way of sounding preposterous. A lie could not be turned into a flippant entertainment, for it would be sunk by the very truths that should keep it afloat. A lie called for gravity, passion, sincerity, the heartfelt delivery of a personal confession, for, unlike the truth, a lie stood or fell upon belief. Besides, he could tell it no other way. This lie, these truths, were his. They were fraught with his hopes, his pain, his entitlement.

"Well, wicked boy? Are you dozing off again?"

Hesitation would undo him. To keep her quiescent, he tightened his arms around her waist. It was encouraging that she did not draw back or rebuke him, more heartening still to see the mocking spark extinguished as her lids grew heavy again.

After eight nights, he must surely have earned the right to gravity, to be treated as more than a plaything. After all, she forgot the rules when it suited her: might not he too be permitted this small indulgence? If he could still her mockery for ten minutes— five…

He pulled her closer, as though to leave the impress of his earnestness upon her body. She smiled and gave a little sigh. He steeled himself.

"Madame, there is something I must tell you."

"Another of your divinely silly stories?"

"No. Not exactly."

"How disappointing. I so adore them."

"This is something—something about myself—"

"Lord! Oh, but I remember now. That pony of yours."

"Yes—that is, no—"

"Well, you may spare me, if—as I surmise from your horribly solemn expression—you intend dwelling on your rustic upbringing in some muddy farmyard or other." She had drawn away from him, her dreamy look had entirely vanished. "That, as you know, has no place here. I should never have let you chatter on about the wretched pony."

"Madame, you are most unjust . All I ask is—" But he was silenced by anger and frustration. It was hopeless. He had bungled things and now he had lost her and could not think how to bring her back. Caress her, make love to her? But then the moment would be gone. Besides, he had little taste for it. He turned his face into the pillow.

Perversely, now she had crossed him at every turn and sapped his will to persist, she seemed disposed to relent. "Absurd child," she said, kissing his shoulder. " What can be so important?…Still, if it matters so much, whatever it is… "

Grudgingly, he turned back to her. After all there was no telling how many nights would pass before his chance came again.

"If you promise, no ponies, no barnyards. Well then, I can't endure sulks—you'd better out with it."

"Madame, I…."

"Don't tease, wretched boy. Out with it."

For certain he would fail again unless he found some means of quelling her. He debated bursting dramatically into sobs but, having schooled himself against tears from childhood, he doubted his performance would convince. Then it struck him—he could not think why it had not occurred to him before—that there was one sure way to soften her, to stir all her sympathetic feminine instincts. There were words guaranteed to make most women amenable, words that had certainly worked their magic on Josette (although, if he had troubled to review their consequences in Josette's case he might have exercised more caution). While he clearly did not expect madame to reciprocate, yet she could not be displeased by the tribute. Besides, since she pressed him, he must say something.

"Madame...I think I love you."

For a moment this appeared to have the desired effect. For a moment her gaze, which remained fixed upon his, grew deep and still. But then from its depths, like a sword rising out of a lake, sprang a cold, sharp light that pierced him, that seemed to penetrate his skull and lay bare the workings of his mind, scornfully displaying them like so many disarticulated bones. She unwound herself from his embrace. She began laughing, not her mischievous chuckle, but a loud, harsh laugh that unbearably went on and on.

She sat up and reached for her peignoir, which was the signal for his dismissal.

"Young man, you are clearly intelligent. Heaven help us if you ever become clever."

CHAPTER FOUR

Very well. It had been a grave infraction of the rules, perhaps the gravest: he could see that now. Befuddled by exhaustion, he had lost his head. But was he to be cast out for an instant's miscalculation? Madame had seemed to like him well enough, he would surely be forgiven. It was true she had not accorded him the chance when, struggling with surprise and outrage, he had sought for the words that would recover the situation. Yet by morning she must see her error. To be called into Mme Pinot's parlour and given the cravat pin in its velvet box by madame's lady's maid, Mlle Lapointe, with her smug little smile, as if she lowered herself to have dealings with him—it was all he could do not to hurl the box at the wall.

His fury was increased by the impossibility of disputing madame's verdict: he had, indeed, been profoundly stupid. For three years he had worked single-mindedly to reach this point and, in one fatal irretrievable instant, he had fumbled it, like a junior housemaid dropping a Sèvres vase.

All the same, he did not reserve his anger entirely for himself. Madame was an old hag who did not know when she was well off, may she enjoy Michel, they deserved each other. Max wore his haughtiest look whenever he was in her presence, although it was doubtful if she noticed: her manner to him in public had not varied when they were lovers and it did not vary now; she made no difference between him, who had brought her to cries of rapture, and any other servant.

Yet Fabrice was right for once, however Max denied it. He missed madame, not just the cleanliness and comfort of her apartments but madame herself, the way she had petted and indulged him, all those tender fripperies he professed to despise: perhaps, just as with Josette, he had truly meant his unfortunate words in the moment he had uttered them.

Of course he disowned this longing for warmth. The vicissitudes of his childhood had left him in no doubt that it was a weakness. It predisposed you to trust what ought not to be trusted. He did not care to dwell on certain episodes, for in that direction lay self-pity, and besides, if you let it, misery could haunt you: he had no wish to recall the place of ashes he had inhabited after Dom Sébastien's kisses had turned to reproaches and threats. You hardened yourself, you took nothing for granted, you became alert to your own treacherous propensity to repeat your mistakes. Now he was an adult, of course, such dangers were behind him. But—curse madame!—if he had meant what he said, even for an instant, what right had she to despise it? Once his grand design came to fruition, she would realise his feelings were not worthless.

He resolved to ask Old Jouvert if he could recommend another situation. Yet he was forced to heed common sense: the old trickster would have his spy in madame's establishment, no doubt of it. And even if he were able to offer a convincing excuse, Max had little to gain from leaving a household that conferred considerable prestige, where he was not overworked or badly treated and which in most respects suited him well enough. If madame were not to be his patron, then he must look for another.

He considered the list of madame's regular visitors, although without much optimism. Granted, the fiasco had yielded one small piece of encouragement: madame had not questioned that the too-prominent scar was a childhood injury; he need delay no further on that score. But otherwise his ambitions faced a considerable set-back. He should not deceive himself: three years' knowledge of the world had reinforced his understanding that one benign word from some pillar of society would lend more weight to his cause than any eloquence of his own. But the obstacles to finding and cultivating this eminence filled him alternately with weariness and impatience.

While it was true that any one of the diplomats and nobles who attended madame's Thursdays might know someone who was ideally placed to help him, there was the usual difficulty of approaching them. Even the bluff ones who tipped well and called you by name could not be counted on to interest themselves in the affairs of someone else's servant and any overture must be finely judged if he were not to risk losing his place. Besides, his difficulties with madame had taught him the impossibility of declaring himself in a quick, glib speech. He would need to choose his target carefully and work upon him, establish himself in this person's view with special attentions and favours, so that when the time came it would seem natural, almost, for him to request a favour in return. He could, he supposed, take a lesson from Victor and Jacques, who both assiduously cultivated the generous tippers, falling over each other to brush the duc de la Marne's hat or run little errands for Colonel Chausson-Laurier, sprinting to open their carriage doors regardless of whose duty it was that day. Max recoiled in disgust from this sycophancy. And anyway he could spend six months brushing hats and opening doors only to find his efforts had gone unnoticed. Curse madame! Curse her for being a capricious, ungrateful old bitch.

Meanwhile the routine of the household proceeded with leaden tread. With escape indefinitely postponed, Max could barely endure the boredom and indignity of his lot. Yet endure it he must, and with apparent good grace. For he had more to concern him now than Michel's sniping and which of his fellows served Old Jouvert.

He had lost face—intolerable in itself, but also fraught with perils for his standing in the household. Certainly the general mood of the servants' hall appeared sympathetic, at least amongst the women: Pauline deliberately sought him out in the break, while Francine, the scullery maid, sneaked him slivers of *foie gras* from the kitchen, blushing scarlet and scurrying away before he could thank her. But, while he received these kindnesses gracefully, he was under no illusions. The advantage of being an unknown quantity was no longer his. He had been defined and reduced by his so-called failure. From now on he would need to guard his back, and not only against Michel. However comradely on the surface, Victor, Jacques and perhaps even Fabrice would seize any chance to exploit his weakness and make trouble for him with M Vincent to their own benefit. Max did not particularly blame them: it was in the nature of the job; caged rats consumed each other when propinquity became unbearable.

He concentrated grimly on performing his allocated tasks with unimpeachable efficiency, on showing willingness to lend an extra hand in the scullery or go on errands, on putting himself in every possible way beyond attack. He even managed to grin at the servants' hall gossip—the progress of Jacques' unrequited passion for the head housemaid, Suzanne, or the joke Victor and Guillaume planned to play on Chef Quintivali when lobsters next featured on the menu— although he steered well clear of the grumbles about Michel and the petty squabbles that could flare up over anything from the rota for answering bells to a pair of misplaced servers. He hoped he appeared impervious. He hoped no one guessed how he struggled with the impulse to ram Michel's over-sized yellow incisors far into the back of his throat. In stony misery, he lived only for his next day off.

It was Fabrice who brought him out of it, so that Max felt

remorseful for his suspicions. Having vented his spleen over the business with madame, Fabrice had succumbed to a new obsession: he was resolved to save Max from the sartorial shame of his Sunday suiting.

Here we should correct an injustice on our hero's behalf. Madame's teasing was not quite fair. It could not be denied he was vain in many respects, but as to his appearance he had remarkably little vanity. Yes, others had taught him he could use his looks to advantage, but—he had only to recall the man in Lebas' Blue Room—they had brought him wretchedness in equal measure. Even in service they had not been an unqualified blessing; there had been other Paulines and Francines, not to mention baron Reinhardt's valet, who had needed to be kept gently but assiduously at a distance. Of course he was proud that his body was well-made and healthy, without Guillaume's bandy legs or Victor's concave chest, but as for his face—he could see nothing particularly agreeable, in fact rather disliked what he observed in the glass.

He had, perhaps, never recovered from the moment in his twelfth year when, troubled by Dom Sébastien's avowal of his 'God-given beauty', proud to have won praise from his idol but at the same time embarrassed and distrustful of its truth, he had crept furtively into the monastery *lavatorium* to see for himself. Until then, since he and the Other had for so long been treated as brothers and regularly mistaken for each other, he had come to assume they possessed roughly the same cast of feature, so that what confronted him when he climbed onto the rim of the washing trough to peer into the monks' cracked shaving glass filled him with disquiet. For the first time in his life, he understood himself as separate, a distinct being, not umbilically bound to the Other by shared dangers and claims of duty, but triumphantly freed, cut loose to follow his own volition; yet the alien features, in which even then he found something indefinable that was not to his liking, also filled him with horror; for if he were not bound, not claimed, he was—apart from Dom Sébastien, that is—alone. He stole back several times to re-examine this revelatory image, always experiencing the same mixed emotions. The last occasion followed Dom Sébastien's tearful pronouncement that his beauty had been bestowed, not by the Almighty, but Satan. This time he understood what made him shiver: he was looking at the face of sin.

He was naturally beyond such superstition now. Yet he never deliberately confronted his reflection except when scraping the razor across his cheeks; nor had it been any hardship to scar himself. He was most comfortable with Mitya Zhukovsky and his crowd, who would not have cared had he been Quasimodo's twin, requiring merely that he could fire a retort to a joke, counter an argument, or sing the entirety of Leporello's '*Non piu servir*' only a little out of tune.

So it followed that he had never concerned himself greatly with the question of dress. His attitude was coloured by the uniforms he had worn for the greater part of his life and exemplified his unacknowledged ambivalence towards his bondage: he loathed the fine worsteds and silks of livery almost as much as he had hated the coarse wool breeches of the postulants' *dormitorium*, or the black habit he had been forced to don at fifteen; yet uniform had its blessings, removing the need for trivial but onerous decisions and sparing the pocket. Inevitably, much of Max's weekly pittance went on books. His one sartorial indulgence was his linen, and here he would claim he answered, not to fashion, but necessity. The routine discomforts of his existence—the sweat-stiffened armpits of his tail coat, its pervasive stench of gravy, the greasy powder from his wig that, however he scrubbed, seemed irrevocably ingrained in the nape of his neck — together with the memory of his former deprivations, of coarse cotton fetid from three days' wear: all demanded the consolation of freshly laundered cambric next to the skin. In many houses exquisite linen was one of the perquisites, the male servants by custom receiving seignorial cast-offs, but Max had usually proved unlucky, being broader in the shoulder and longer limbed than his masters. And, of course, in Mme la duchesse's household there was no such bounty to be had. When his fortunes turned, Max resolved, he would wear nothing but the finest Egyptian lawn, woven from the purest, most delicate threads, as light and supple as silk. But that was the limit of his ambition: he could not see the sense in acquiring debts, as Fabrice did, for the sake of fancy foulards and kid gloves.

Indeed, he could not see any real objection to his despised Sunday suit. Granted it had not been in the vanguard of fashion when Josette, fired by the discovery that he could read and write, had determined he should fill the vacancy in M Cotin's counting house; nor was it truly a suit, but a frockcoat, waistcoat and trousers, all of serge but of different weights worn to varying degrees, so that sunlight revealed a hint of rust in the trousers, while the coat shone faintly green. Once Max's moment came, it would scarcely serve. However, it was perfectly adapted to his present circumstances, being the badge of his other, free life, and not conspicuously worse than anything worn by Mitya Zhukovsky's crowd.

"Well, angel, if you want my opinion—"

"Which I don't."

"You do yourself no good. Not even at the Monkey."

"I do well enough."

"Looking like some *absintheur* in the Place Pigalle? Particularly when you add that frightful hat."

"Who cares about my hat?"

"It's a cruel world. A girl needs to make the best of herself."

The occasion for this conversation was a scene of commendable domesticity. With the oil lamp placed on the chair between them, Fabrice sat cross-legged on his bed applying benzene to a patch of béchamel sauce on the breast of his waistcoat, while Max, having discovered a hole in the toe of his last clean pair of stockings, was inexpertly plying needle and thread. The only flaw in this virtuous picture, had M Vincent or Mme Pinot chosen to view it, was the wine bottle next to the lamp, primed by Fabrice with the dregs of this evening's brandy and smuggled upstairs in the pocket of his left coat-tail.

Fabrice paused from his labours to take a swig. "Certain I can't tempt you?"

The fumes of brandy and benzene mingled unpleasantly, overwhelming the room's usual smells. Max shook his head.

"After all, it's not as if—" Fabrice wiped the sweat from his eyes and took a second libation. "Well, for someone like you—with *ambitions*—I am merely pointing out that looks are not enough—"

"Shit!" Max's fingers were damp and the needle rebellious.

"Quick, suck it, you'll get gore everywhere. Stupid girl! Oh, give it to Auntie!"

Max was ready enough to take over the waistcoat and benzene bottle. Fabrice, having unpicked Max's handiwork with much tut-tutting, threaded the needle and knotted the cotton in one continuous deft movement, then set about the repair with a tailor's agility.

"It's a language, dress. Like your precious Latin—except not dead, thank God. Don't tell me, angel, you haven't grasped that."

"For women, of course."

"For men, too. For men even more so. Mistake the phraseology at your peril— tactless buttons or gauche lapels can mark a girl out for life." Snipping the thread with his teeth, Fabrice held up the neatly-darned stocking for inspection before tossing it back to its owner. Rewarding himself with a generous draught of brandy, he developed his theme. "Consider Monsieur de Bellac for instance."

"Must I?" Aristide de Bellac was a successful popular novelist, whose fame extended as far as England and even to Russia. Though lionised at salons and quite a favourite of madame's, he was not much loved in the servants' hall on account of his rudeness, niggardly tips and general meanness: Max and Fabrice, separately and on more than one occasion, had apprehended him filling his cigarette case from madame's boxes.

"There you are, you see! As with the man, so the tailoring. Did you happen to observe the coat he was wearing last Thursday? That heliotrope lining! And the cut, my dear! Not to mention those spats. Yellow—I ask you—*yellow*? You can tell he came by his precious 'de' where he finds his plots." (Fabrice was as much as stickler for these particulars as any society matron with marriageable daughters—his favourite and only reading was the *Almanach de Gotha*.)

Max laughed. "Yet you won't hear a word against Monsieur de la Marne. Even though his coats look older than mine and the knees of his trousers bag like coal-sacks."

"He's an altogether different case."

"Proving my point, I think. He prefers to rely upon his natural air of distinction."

Fabrice sighed despairingly. "Monsieur de la Marne, my pet, is a duke."

Until now Max had assumed that, if some visitors presented a better figure than others, this was mainly a question of outlay: when his day came, he would simply consign himself to the best tailor he could afford. However, under Fabrice's tuition he learnt this would not suffice; judgements must be made that would prove as vital to his transformation as avoiding solecisms or learning to smile without showing his teeth. Even the apparent uniform of dinner dress was a gauntlet, where one slip as you ran through an infinite permutation of possibilities—quality of cloth, width of trousers, subtlety of braiding, cut of coat, facing of lapels, style of waistcoat, stiffness of shirt front, discretion of shirt studs, knotting of bow tie, height of collar—could leave you bloodied.

Fabrice claimed fashion ran in his veins, since his father was a Lyon silk draper; and besides, with the master draughtsmanship consigned to the realm of might-have-been, he had concluded his best hope was to become a valet. He certainly evinced an impressive command of detail, like an entomologist noting the scarcely visible markings that distinguish identical-seeming beetles. Max still had no intention of discarding the black suit until the occasion arose and he was secretly of the opinion that Fabrice, for all his sensitivity to the placing of pockets and stitching of lapels, was less clear-eyed when it came to his own attire: there was a flamboyance to his Sunday outfits, an exaggeration of cut, an extravagance in his waistcoats, a prominence to his cuffs, that might be said to advertise what he was, just as blatantly as the egregious spats marked out M de Bellac. While conceding Fabrice's scientific observations might prove useful on his own account, Max was sceptical about their wider application—would he recognise a likely patron by the lacing of his boots? But at least it was a game that lightened the tedium. "He must make his valet weep!" Fabrice would declare of certain visitors; soon, coinciding in the kitchen or the pantry passage, they would sum up any new guest with 'tears' or 'joy'.

Such distractions were welcome as the weather grew steadily hotter. The kitchen became a twice-daily inferno, sorbets melted on the way to the table and, despite much mopping with scented handkerchiefs, patrician brows poured sweat, while rivulets trickled between the bared shoulder blades of the ladies and their palms, where their gloves were turned back, left damp patches on the cloth. Out of doors, it was no better. Carriage wheels threw up a gritty dust that pricked your eyes and filled your nostrils and a sulphurous miasma drifted over the city, daring to foul the Faubourg's rarefied air with the stench of rotten eggs. In the first week of July, madame removed to the country.

Only six members of the household accompanied their mistress to Bordeaux: M Vincent, who went by an earlier train to check that M and Mme Roussel, the château's retainers, held everything in readiness; Mlle Lapointe, M Quintivali; and the first three footmen—Michel to wait upon the ladies in their compartment and Jean and Fabrice to see to the luggage. The remaining staff (including Guillaume, Jacques and Victor, who, although they had always known their fate, missed no chance to bemoan it loudly) would endure the stifling city as, under Mme Pinot's command, they swathed furniture in dust sheets and set to work to ensure that, from the highest ceiling boss to the dimmest corner of the most obscure cupboard, the Hôtel de Claireville would offer madame's return an impeccable welcome.

Despite the envy of their fellows, Max and Fabrice viewed their translation to the country as a mixed blessing. For one thing, the work was harder: a house full of guests meant endlessly ringing bells, while they were both likely to acquire extra duties, attending upon gentlemen who travelled without their valets. Then there were the hardships occasioned by the number of senior servants who did accompany their masters and required accommodation. Michel retained his box room, but Max and Fabrice were obliged to share a cramped dormitory with the three local youths recruited to make up the footmen's ranks. It might be expected that the Parisian contingent would inspire a certain awe, given their superior skills and sophistication. But the Bordelais Guillaume, Jacques and Victor, who undertook these roles each summer and were in any case cousins, presented a truculent solidarity that refused to be cowed. They had not forgotten Michel's habit of referring to them as 'The Peasants'; they saw no reason to revise their suspicion of Fabrice's airs and graces; and as for the newcomer and his nocturnal studies—Max was obliged to transfer his candle to a broom cupboard under the eaves and to pray that no one reported him or that M Vincent did not take it into his head to carry out a late-night patrol.

On the other hand, there were likely to be rewards. House guests could be expected to stump up heavy tips. Fabrice entertained the hope that one of the gentlemen he valeted might be so taken with his skills as to offer him a position. And, he hinted, an irregular household such as this could sometimes furnish other perquisites: perhaps with madame's encouragement, certain guests, ladies but also some gentlemen, were not above taking particular notice of her handsome footmen.

Max's project, too, could benefit. Constant proximity would give him an unparalleled chance to decide which guests had the potential to do him service. Some were of course already familiar to him, the standing stones of madame's circle. M de Cressy, for instance, a distant relation of madame's and in his youth, it was said, a great roué, who, having run through two fortunes, had turned this worldly experience to good account by establishing himself as a sage; the marquis de la Rochefontaine, who had briefly led the Republic's embassy to Austria-Hungary and now sat on the boards of three companies with interests in Panama; and Colonel Chausson-Laurier, the renowned explorer and archaeologist. Adding youth's leaven to this distinguished company were two gentlemen still in their twenties: the vicomte de Selincourt-Saint-Antoine and a former school friend of his, M Bécart, who had resigned his commission in favour of a bright future in some ministry or other (Fabrice was not sure which). Then, of course, the ladies should not be neglected. There were the wives, Mme de Cressy and Mme de la Rochefontaine; there was widowed Mme de Beaumont-Gramont with her unmarried daughter (a strapping girl the image of her mother, thought to be the reason for the vicomte's invitation); and lastly, apart from madame herself, the Princess Zelenska (née Trier de Tours), left a grass widow by her Polish husband's missions to foreign courts on behalf of his dispossessed nation: still in her mid-twenties and a noted beauty, she was a recent addition to the Claireville circle and apparently something of a protégée of madame's.

Yet for the first few days Max was unable to give these luminaries his slightest attention. He barely noticed the discomforts of the footmen's sleeping quarters, or the hostility of the Bordelais cousins, or the difficulties of working in this extempore household where you must guess at your colleagues' skills and deficiencies, where the maids, too, and the kitchen staff, were strangers, recruited from nearby villages. He woke with a sense of impending horror, each time a bell rang his heart shuddered, at meal times his hands shook and as he advanced towards a certain chair nausea welled in his throat and he fought for breath; at night, seeking the calm that reading usually brought him, he was blinded by violent thoughts.

CHAPTER FIVE

The cause of Max's predicament—no, that is far too feeble a word for the tides of hate, repulsion and fear that threatened to drown him—was the one guest we have yet to mention, the twelfth member of the house party. And, indeed, Max had never known his name. But he knew him, nonetheless, knew those lubricious eyes, that full pale face, those lips, emerging scarlet and moist like labia from between the flourishing moustache and the silky black imperial. Max had only seen this man once, three years ago, but he was unlikely to forget him: not the smell of him, the compound of goatish sweat, expensive cologne and semen that Max seemed to inhale now, each time he stood beside the man's chair and bent in from the left to offer him a serving dish; nor those large, plump hands, heavy with rings—the right hand, clean, pink-nailed, briefly at rest between graceful gestures, reposing there upon the cloth in dimpled innocence.

The man in Lebas' Blue Room, it transpired, was Achille de Tarascon, essayist, poet, aesthete and a catch for any house party. His slim volume of aphorisms, bound in mauve kid tooled with lilies in silver leaf, was much prized by the ladies, particularly when inscribed by the author as a personal gift, and he had only a fortnight ago returned in triumph from a sojourn in America, delighting the cities of that vast country with his wit. His imposing stature, his thick raven hair, curling artistically just below his collar like some medieval knight's, and his exquisite, if extravagant, manner rendered M le comte de Tarascon a romantic figure to society matrons, who wondered how he had so long escaped marriage. At dinner, naturally, with his repartee and flow of anecdotes, he took centre stage; although his wit, like a cormorant, speared its prey in the belly, he could stir languid Princess Zelenska to peals of laughter, while even stern Mme de Beaumont-Gramont and sour old M de Cressy took pleasure in his malice. He was not, it must be said, unfailingly popular with the gentlemen, M de Cressy apart; M de la Rochefontaine and Colonel Chausson-Laurier remained distant and, after four days of what looked like a blossoming friendship, the vicomte, who, though short and ginger-haired, was not altogether ill-looking, appeared studiously to avoid being in a room with him alone. But M de Tarascon was not in any case one for after-dinner billiards or smoking-room conversations; he much preferred, greatly to their delight, to remain gossiping with the ladies.

Fabrice, predictably, was much taken with M de Tarascon, whom till now he had observed only at a distance on the occasions the great man had graced madame's Thursdays. M de Tarascon, from the drape of his trousers to the braiding of his waistcoats, was of course 'joy' and Fabrice could only lament that he had brought his own manservant.

"You note that dress lounge, angel? I've heard of them, of course, but actually to see one—and in velvet, too…"

Already, in the first week, the two Parisian footmen, tired of communicating in code, had taken to slinking off in the afternoon break, and this occasion found them skulking in the walled vegetable garden, sharing one of Fabrice's cigarettes.

"Naturally he'll have had it made for him during his tour, they're all the rage in America. And, unless this girl is very much mistaken, they'll be everywhere in Paris by Christmas. The tail coat as an item of dress wear will become extinct—"

"Fabrice, don't."

Fabrice stared. Although he had been in the act of passing Max the cigarette, he snatched it back. "Bitch! I saw him first."

"Don't go near him."

This was said with such passion, was in such contrast to his companion's usual reserve, that Fabrice's anger was arrested. "You know him? Or rather—" the third footman tittered nervously "—he's known you?"

Max took the cigarette and drew on it deeply. He remembered, after Josette had thrown him out, crawling upstairs to Van der Meer's empty attic (the painter had been carted away with the horrors to the Salpêtrière). He remembered thrusting his shirt between his thighs to staunch the bleeding, dark blood now as well as scarlet, in a thin but ominous trickle. He recalled hearing over and over, as the fever set in, the talk about the Spanish boy who had suddenly stopped appearing in the Green Monkey. The silent injury, the fatal tear where there was no sensitive tissue, no warning pain. He remembered staring up at the towering canvass on the opposite wall, Van der Meer's daubed and indecipherable painting of him—the start of everything—and thinking, that's it, that is all that will be left.

He inhaled another deep draught of tobacco. "He's a vicious bastard. He doesn't care what he does."

Fabrice raised his eyebrows. "One of those?" He retrieved the cigarette. "Well, you may as well know, angel, we've already had a preliminary skirmish. And thus far she's a sugar plum. Not afraid to put her hand in her pocket, either."

Max laughed bitterly. Demanding his money, oh yes he recalled that too, refusing to take the cab Lebas had summoned in his haste to get him off the premises, refusing to leave the Blue Room until he was paid what he'd been promised.

Fabrice blew a smoke ring. "You're just jealous."

Max considered him for a moment. He sighed. "Then don't meet him too far from the house, there's a good boy."

After all, it must be assumed that M de Tarascon would exercise moderation here, as a guest of madame's, would restrain his behaviour at least, if not his predatory impulse. Suggestive remarks to the vicomte, a frisky pinch, likely as not, administered to at least one Bordelais buttock— Fabrice was naive in believing himself specially singled out. As a matter of fact, Max had already had his own skirmish with M le comte.

He had known it was coming. He had not missed M de Tarascon's leers, even though he had returned them with blank incomprehension. Not that the comte recognised him. Why should he recall a renter, one of many, particularly after three years? He was, Max observed, someone who relished chasing unlikely quarry: he probably believed there was not a man alive who did not secretly, in his hidden heart, share his proclivities. But that by no means meant his instincts were impaired. He would not fail to detect the signals emitted by one of his own kind, no matter how muted.

So Max was surprised only by the suddenness of the assault, and its foolhardiness, coming at the dressing hour and in the open corridor. One moment he was rounding the corner on his way to the Maiden's Tower to lay out M de Cressy's tails, the next he found himself propelled into the alcove that led to the bathroom and water closet, pinned by M de Tarascon's bulk against the wall, with M de Tarascon's hand between his legs.

To his relief—perhaps the violence of the ambush had knocked the breath out of him—he felt astonishingly calm. For this was, after all, what he had feared most, that the man would touch him, whereupon he would immediately beat him to pulp. Repeatedly he had cautioned himself: revenge, justice—call it what you would, anything of the sort was out of the question. If he left a mark on M de Tarascon, he would find himself in prison. Even if he chose some other means of attack— spat in the man's face, for instance—he would be the loser: men like M le comte wreaked easy revenge on flunkeys; Max would find an accusation of theft lodged against him that he would be unable to disprove. He had, as he had reminded himself again and again, but one recourse; politely to disengage himself and take his leave.

Yet—he was not so calm now, feeling the man's breath on his cheeks, seeing those moist lips widening into a smirk, realising the cause, that the thrust to his groin had stirred a humiliating reflex. No, he was not calm now, staring into those pale slightly protuberant eyes that did not know him from Adam. His blood roared as he smelt the man and remembered how he would not stop, how he was powerless himself to stop him without worsening his injuries, how it was only Lebas, panicking that his screams would reach the other guests, who had finally put an end to it. His blood roared, he no longer cared about prison. The urge was overwhelming to batter that flabby, calculating, stupidly smirking face until it yielded up, at least, some glimmer of recognition.

But, as M de Tarascon continued to meet Max's eye, his smirk vanished. He could recognise a threat to his person, apparently, if nothing else. Rapidly withdrawing his hand, he stepped back and, in his face, before it froze into a mask of heavy contempt, something unlooked-for flickered. Max hoped it was fear.

After the count had stalked off, Max was seized by uncontrollable shaking and the urgent need to vomit. Subsequently, however, he grew calmer, if not impervious to M de Tarascon's presence in the house, at least better able to bear it. He had the memory of that flash of fear to console him. And when Fabrice returned from his afternoon tryst bruised and chastened, but with a sum towards the silver-topped cane he coveted, Max was forced to admit that he would not have wanted M de Tarascon on his conscience.

Besides, through some freak of fate and despite the talk in the Monkey, he had survived. When he had woken on Van der Meer's infested mattress a day and half later, the bleeding had stopped. He had remained feverish and in acute pain from his other injuries, but he had recovered. Max was not, as we know, disposed to countenance miracles. Nevertheless, like Wallenstein, who had also cheated death in his youth, he was inclined to view his survival as a portent, confirming that he was destined to travel a singular path.

His concentration revived and he began at last to review madame's guests. Most he could eliminate immediately. Although he was acting as M de Cressy's valet, he could expect nothing from this quarter: even if M de Tarascon had not exploded Fabrice's theories, Max needed no analysis of M de Cressy's wardrobe, the unsparing black of the old-fashioned dandy, to tell him that. The aged buck compensated for his lost wealth and the irritating necessity of living off his relations by dogged assertion of his impeccable lineage: heaven help the minion who failed to address him in a whisper, and then only when addressed. Younger men, Max noticed, were also inclined to stand on ceremony with footmen, as though the merest informality might encourage these coevals in age to forget their place. Besides, both the vicomte and M Bécart, for different reasons, were unsuited to his purpose. The vicomte, though amiable enough and resourceful with a tennis racquet, was less confident when expending mental energy: Max's story would leave him bemused and craving the more congenial topics of hunting and bloodstock. His bourgeois friend, by contrast, seemed never to cease thinking—but largely as to how a conversation or a connection could be worked to his advantage: it was he who paid court to Mlle de Beaumont-Gramont, whose dowry, rumour had it, purged her charms of all defect.

That brought Max to the ladies. By looks and inclination, they divided themselves into two groups; it was as natural that shrivelled, brow-beaten Mme de Cressy should gravitate towards the Beaumont-Gramonts, with their virtuous pursuits of needlework and sketching in watercolour, as it was that worldly Mme de la Rochefontaine and lazy Princess Zelenska should seek the orbit of madame. But even the second group could be discounted; blonde, brittle Mme de la Rochefontaine, years younger than her husband, cared only for gowns and parties, while the princess seemed unable to exert herself to care for anything, unless it was admiration: M de la Rochefontaine could be observed to pay her attentions perhaps in excess of those due to his wife's bosom friend, while M Bécart, too, found himself unaccountably distracted from the solid virtues of Mlle de B-G.

This left the ex-ambassador and the archaeologist. Of the two, Max would have preferred Colonel Chausson-Laurier. Despite his fierce whiskers and clipped manner, there was a reassuring calm about the colonel, as though a shrewd mind coupled with unruffled competence permitted him a latitude, a generosity of judgement denied to lesser men. Of all the gentlemen, he was as ready to listen as to talk, although he by no means lacked eloquence when called upon to describe his forthcoming expedition to Egypt. He made no difference between men, was unfailingly courteous to servants and his refusal to be impressed by M de Tarascon was a further point in his favour. But he was only staying a few days and, by the time Max had reached his verdict, his departure was imminent. Besides—it was a mere niggle, but a doubt nonetheless—Max could not help fearing that shrewdness of his, could not help wondering if his story would withstand it.

Thus there remained only M de la Rochefontaine and, study him as he might, Max continued to find him an unknown quantity. He was charming, urbane; his substantial yet elegant form suggested the sleek contentment of a man who, having won his laurels, now leaves it to others to be ravaged by ambition. Yet there was also something wily about M de la Rochefontaine, a sly cupidity in the urbane smile. Max could not but suspect his real reason for disliking M de Tarascon was not the natural revulsion of finely tuned instincts, but pique that he dominated the supper table. And could it not be said (here Max resorted, after all, to Fabrice's techniques) that the cut of his lightweight alpaca, while exquisitely sensitive to his girth, was rather too youthful, indicating a willingness to deceive himself that might well extend to others? Mindful of his experience with madame, Max hung back from putting M de la Rochefontaine's ostentatious geniality to the test.

And then came a curious occurrence that overturned his thinking. He was pouring mid-morning coffee for Mme de la Rochefontaine and Princess Zelenska as they reclined in wicker chairs on the terrace, when the princess glanced up at him—he would not have said suddenly for she did nothing sudden—but unexpectedly, nevertheless. It was, for all its languor, a startlingly direct glance, a steady look of appraisal that made no attempt at concealment but deliberately sought and held his eye. And although, with the merest whisper of a smile, she let her gaze drift away, was soon chatting in her desultory fashion to the ex-ambassador's wife, he knew he had not been mistaken. This was not a look any lady would usually give a servant.

He recalled Fabrice's remark about madame's generosity with her leavings. Momentarily, his bitterness towards her was unbounded. Yet he could not fail to see that here was his answer. The princess showed no regret for her absent husband and was clearly not above indulging herself elsewhere, provided it did not involve too much effort: perhaps her stay with madame had been planned expressly for this purpose. And, while M de la Rochefontaine and M Bécart were handicapped by entanglements, an affair with a servant involved no such energy-sapping considerations.

It was ideal, now he thought it over. The princess promised all the advantages he had hoped to find in madame. It was true she was frivolous and indolent and it was often hard to tell whether she heard the conversation at supper or had merely perfected the posture of listening. Yet he still believed there were benefits in unburdening himself to a woman, even one as lackadaisical as the princess—she would certainly not put herself to the trouble of asking awkward questions. Besides, little would be required of her: she had merely to effect an audience for him with the prince, who, it was not be forgotten, had diplomatic contacts all over Europe.

There remained only the problem of how to proceed, given the limitations of Max's position. He could wait to see if she threw him another encouraging look. But after two days he concluded that if he waited upon her inertia the venture would be lost. The Zelenski children, two boys of seven and five and a three-year-old girl, were brought out to the lawn to play under their mother's gaze every afternoon. Max set about cultivating their nurse, a plain but jolly girl from Amiens who was always in search of someone to fetch and carry to the nursery. And soon, as the princess reclined beneath her parasol in the shade of the yew hedge, she was able to observe an obliging young footman organising hoop races or giving the baby a ride on his shoulders.

Michel and Fabrice, despite their enmity, could agree on one subject. Both city-born, they despised the country. While the guests enjoyed due respite from suffocating Paris, lolling in shady spots, sipping iced drinks and bestirring themselves only for picnics and excursions, one airless back staircase, one maze of stuffy corridors, one sweltering kitchen with M Quintivali cursing and reducing the skivvies to tears, was very much like another. And, the worst of it was, there was nothing to do on your day off. Michel soon tired of chasing the patron's daughter in the village *tabac*. Fabrice despaired that the nearest town, Angoulême, was an unobtainable carriage-ride distant, and he had a litany of other complaints: the mud and dust conspired to ruin his beautiful clothes, the sun threatened him with freckles; insects bit him—he kept the dormitory awake with his nightly scratching, particularly Max, who slept in the next bed.

Max was more philosophical. In Paris, he was often nostalgic for the tender green of Normandy, the scent of the sun-baked earth, the limitless sky, the infinite silence that was not silence at all but a symphony of tiny echoing sounds, the fiddling of grasshoppers, the beat of a rook's wing, the complacent chuckle of hens, the scrape of milk churns borne faintly from fields away. Here the climate was harsher: the tracts of ripe corn undulated like sand dunes in the shimmering heat. Nevertheless, he rejoiced in the wide horizons, pierced here by a bell tower, there by a column of smoke from already burning stubble; and, since his day off was shared by Guillaume and Victor, who went home to their families, he was able to bask in the rare pleasure of solitude.

Yet it cannot be denied that his yearning for the country was as contradictory as his other desires: within days he was longing for Paris. He missed his evenings at the Zhukovskys' and the company at the Monkey, craved adventure, chafed at his enforced chastity: he might hope in vain on his solitary walks to find some young labourer on the qui vive for a kindred spirit.

Nor had his investment of the princess progressed: indeed it appeared the siege would be prolonged. Where she had devoured him with her glance, now it seemed, however he played the clown for her children, or smiled obligingly, or carefully positioned her chair just as she liked it, she no longer saw him. Setting his irritation aside, he could not help perceiving something disagreeable in her lassitude. Even the children received short shrift: their shouts of triumph could rouse her to only the vaguest of smiles and when the little one grazed her knee it was the nursemaid, Marie, who administered comfort.

Neither did Max find her style of beauty particularly appealing. Like the painting in madame's Paris apartments of odalisques after the bath, she was all sugared-almond curves, from her perfectly rounded face with its sloe eyes and small pink mouth, to her sloping shoulders, dimpled elbows and plump little fingers. At supper the globes of her breasts, pushed upwards as far as her stays could contrive, nestled white as ostrich eggs above the flattering draperies that just concealed her nipples, and from their cleft a strong sweet smell arose, sultry as lilies on a heavy summer night. This was her fascination, Max presumed, the hint that tumultuous passion would reward the lover who woke her from her torpor. But the effect could prove cloying: even her voice, indolent as the rest of her, grated like a knife drawn very slowly across glass.

Altogether, it was uphill work and discouraging, until you remembered the useful husband. (Fabrice scarcely helped, wrinkling his nose, first with disapproval at the foray against the nursemaid, then in disbelief as he divined its true target.) However, Max was comforted to observe that neither M de la Rochefontaine nor M Bécart was making better headway: indeed, M Bécart, being quick to see where his true interests lay, appeared to have abandoned pursuit. The idea occurred to Max, although he endeavoured to push it aside, that his rivals had also received that frankly insinuating look, that it was characteristic of Princess Zelenska's laziness that she did not trouble to conceal her fleeting assessment of any man she encountered, and that therefore, in itself, the look meant nothing.

But then, alas, a further explanation had presented itself. The princess was reserving herself for another suitor.

Perusal of the *Almanach* promised much of the visitor who came in place of Colonel Chausson-Laurier. Unlike the marquis de la Rochefontaine, whose grandfather had been ennobled by Napoleon, M le marquis de Miremont could trace his title back to the reign of Henri II; and that was to say nothing of his vast landholdings and immense wealth. Yet, in the flesh, this august personage disappointed. Max could vaguely remember his once or twice calling at the Hôtel de Claireville (though never on madame's Thursdays), but he would have been hard put to describe him. A man of middle height and middle years, not positively ill-looking but scarcely handsome either, he could be best summed up by what he was not—not witty like M de Tarascon nor charming like M de la Rochefontaine nor eloquent in his opinions like M de Cressy.

Fabrice claimed M de Miremont vindicated his theories: one look at his pocket flaps would tell you he had nothing to say for himself. Though whether the noble gentleman's valet shed tears over this sartorial mediocrity was another matter. It was true that, physically at least, this giant of a man with only one eye and the bearing of an old soldier was more imposing than his master. Yet it was hard to conceive of those huge, clumsy hands, more fitted to prime cannon, meticulously folding trousers or straightening a dress shirt's delicate pleats. And as for social graces—M Thomas made his tongue-tied master appear loquacious. It was amusing, of course, to watch the unease of M Vincent and the upper servants' table as M Thomas, accorded by virtue of his master's rank the place of honour, sat wolfing his food in lowering silence. But, setting aside such satirical pleasures, and granting there was something that instantly quelled ridicule in that one-eyed glare of his, the fellow would not do. Fabrice, who was in awe of M de Tarascon's volatile M Rossini and adulated M de la Rochefontaine's dapper M Gaudier, could not but view M de Miremont's choice of personal servant as a further mark against him.

Max, already preoccupied with the princess, had his own grounds for dismissing the new arrival. He had soon learned, walking a step behind Mme de Cressy and Mme de B-G as he carried their easels and stools to the pavilion, that M de Miremont seldom went into society, preferring to lead the life of a recluse—"Such a trial for his poor family," murmured Mme de Cressy. Besides, Max took a different view from Fabrice: he suspected the marquis's failings—his silences, his vague and distant manner, and even his dislike of society—could be attributed to a snobbery more ingrained than M de Cressy's. Certainly when addressing servants—well, he was invariably polite, that must be conceded—yet he would look through you or around you, as though your physical existence affronted his sensibilities.

Nevertheless he seemed a great favourite with madame, who was continually fussing over him. Furthermore, it gradually became apparent, to Max's astonishment and dismay, that she was determined to effect an understanding between the marquis and Princess Zelenska. Worse still, the princess, mindful no doubt of the noble gentleman's wealth, seemed by no means averse to the idea, indeed became in M de Miremont's presence almost animated.

CHAPTER SIX

Armand de Miremont daily regretted accepting Catherine de Claireville's invitation. He was ashamed of himself, since it was generously meant and he held Catherine in great affection. She had been the closest friend of his beloved sister Léonore and he would not easily forget her kindness during Léonore's last illness. When he saw her on her own, he took pleasure in her sharp mind and independent spirit. But he had allowed himself to forget—Heaven knew how—that Catherine's world was not his. He should have travelled straight from Paris to Beauvallon, or found the courage to go to Greece. He should have paid no attention to Dr Gérard. For was it not what all doctors prescribed when they had no idea how to cure you? "Try a complete change. See what fresh company and unfamiliar scenery may do."

Yet that was unfair to Gérard, who was a good fellow and did not indulge in the usual sophistries of society doctors. Besides, how could he be expected to cure a malady that had no physical origins—or at least none that could be fathomed by powders or pills? In any case, Miremont could not deny the desperation that had led him to follow Gérard's advice. Safe in the company of others, with no space for thought, he could hope his unfortunate symptoms would abate. This had been a delusion, of course. And now, committed to a stay of at least a fortnight, he was wondering how he might decently effect his escape.

Although his life had not been without misfortune, Armand de Miremont generally counted himself extraordinarily blessed. Born to unfashionably enamoured parents, their youngest child, his mother's favourite, he had been brought up secure in affection, in surroundings of dignity and beauty. Due to this accident of birth and thanks to his grandfather's endeavours on returning from exile in England after the Revolution, he would never find himself in want, never know the dire need his mother sought to relieve through her charitable committees. Nor was responsibility to be his burden in return for such privilege. He was the second son. To his handsome, capable brother Edmond would eventually fall the task of running the family estates and administering the fortune in railway stock and other investments accumulated by his late grandfather during the Restoration and now ably stewarded by his father. As the second son, Armand Varon, comte de Brès, would inherit Beauvallon, the small château built by his great-grandfather near Dijon, a graceful neo-classical building, set in an English garden with a lake and follies, where he had spent many of his happiest childhood hours. One day, he imagined, he would lead the peaceful life of a country squire.

Meanwhile he was gloriously free to pursue whatever interests he wished. He became an accomplished horseman and a crack shot (at targets, for family tradition forswore the shooting of game). No one was disconcerted that he was also frequently to be found immersed in a book: in fact, his mother, an admirer of Mme de Staël and Mary Wollstonecraft, was delighted that one of her children followed her intellectual bent and ensured he was rigorously tutored in the classics and philosophy. At seventeen, he made his first journey to Italy, returning with a school of Mantegna *Triumph of Caesar* that cost his entire year's allowance and inspired his interest in collecting. He widened his travels, to Greece, to the Swiss Alps, to Heidelberg, where he spent six months studying philology, to England, where, through his maternal grandmother, the Varons had family connections. He fell in love with the operas of Mozart, wondered dreamily about becoming a poet.

Then, in the space of four months, his adored father was snatched away by typhus and his brother, his admired, level-headed brother, not yet twenty-seven and engaged to marry to a girl he worshipped, was crushed by a tree in a freak storm while out riding at Miremont-St-Fleur, the family's principal estate. Armand had just turned twenty-one.

His mother and his sister, practical in their grief, decided he must be married as soon as possible. Once the period of mourning was over, a match was arranged for him with Aline de Sestrès, eighteen years old, of excellent family and the acclaimed beauty of that season. The new marquis could not dispute the wisdom of the arrangement. He needed the support of a wife and, given how brutally fate had shown it could dash the most certain of expectations, he would be failing in his duty if he delayed producing heirs. Besides, Aline was generally judged enchanting, with her wide blue eyes and innocently flirtatious manner. It was considered, he was later to recall, the wedding of the year.

The story of the marriage, though peculiarly painful to Miremont, is sadly lacking in novelty. It was soon evident that the couple could not agree and, while a daughter, Clotilde, was born after twelve months, there were no further children until the arrival of a second daughter three years later. The baby, Juliette, was barely six months old when Aline ran away to Florence with her lover—she had not troubled to cuckold Miremont with someone of their own rank, but had succumbed to an operatic tenor much fêted by society at that time. Since Miremont still had no male heir and risked imposition, he was persuaded by his advisers to take separation proceedings. But the child Aline was carrying turned out to be another girl, which soon died, while even before the birth the tenor had taken flight. Miremont felt profoundly sorry for her. She was still his wife and, besides, the dishonour to his name must be weighed against his daughters' need for their mother. And, of course, he still needed a son.

Aline could not forgive him for taking her back: it was proof of his insufferable moral rectitude and pitiful weakness. It was soon clear that no further children would be conceived and that the couple could find no way of living together. Since there were also signs that she might repeat her previous escapade, a second separation agreement was drawn up. Miremont gave back her marriage portion, adding to it a substantial capital sum in trust and a generous yearly allowance. In return, she was to retire permanently to Miremont-St-Fleur, taking their two daughters, for he could not countenance their being parted from their mother again. Aline had accepted her exile with less protest than might have been expected: the then object of her affections also possessed an estate in the Loire and would be one of her near neighbours. That indiscretion had doubtless been followed by others but, as she seemed finally to resign herself to country life, society was no longer troubled by the details.

In the first years of his marriage, Miremont had repeatedly blamed himself for its difficulties. He should never have married Aline without loving her—why had he assumed that love would grow naturally from propinquity like mistletoe from an oak? He should not have allowed himself to remain pure until their wedding night. He should have tried to curb his selfishness—for he could not but assume that the unchecked happiness of his first twenty-one years must have made him selfish, since it had implanted in him tastes and inclinations so different from hers. Even so, he conceded to her everything he could, the jewellery, the dresses, the carriages, the endless entertaining and going about in society; the monthly bill from the florists, alone, was apt to leave him startled, but he was happy to give her anything that would make her happy. But there were some things he could not concede: here was another of his failures, that he could not seem to explain this to her.

The Miremont fortune was not his to spend at will, he had a duty of stewardship on behalf of coming generations. He could not, therefore, abandon the trustworthy advisers he had inherited from his father so that her brother Robert could exercise his fancied gift for the stock market. He might withdraw capital to establish a charitable foundation in memory of his mother, but he could not lavish an equivalent sum on transforming the interior of the Hôtel de Miremont according to the latest caprice of fashion. Nor could he, would he, allow servants whose families had attended his family for generations to be dismissed on a whim: a particular sticking point was his own manservant, Thomas.

At first, when those wide blue eyes of hers had hardened into stones and her pretty childish pout had contorted to emit a howl of fury, he had been utterly bewildered. His parents had settled their rare disagreements with amiable compromise. He saw it once again as a defect in him: if he had been gentler, had only found the right words, she would not have been reduced to this hysteria; now, all through his fault, she would make herself ill. But his attempts at tenderness only fuelled her rage. Soon he grew accustomed to seeing her change in an instant from sweet, flirtatious girl to strident harpy. He grew accustomed, but never inured; for although he tried to take these tirades calmly, the relentlessness of her frenzy, the sense that it was unstoppable and without limits, left him mortified, as if he too had given way to madness. Nor was there much consolation in the stormy silences, often lasting weeks, that followed these outbursts: she would merely be storing up fresh accusations to hurl at him—how he showed her no compassion, no human feeling, how he was a self-righteous prig who had never been a proper husband to her. In the end, he gave in to her wherever he could. Where he could not, he locked himself in his study, leaving her to shriek her abuse through the door.

However, during the miserable year following her return from Italy, Miremont's guilt abated, to be replaced in turn by anger, weariness and then resignation. He understood at last that there was nothing he could have done to make the marriage tolerable. Even if he had loved her, she could not have loved him: he was not the sort of man to inspire her love. That required someone of fierce passions and extreme desires, whereas his predispositions were all temperate—he would never, he realised now, have made a poet. Aline was doubtless justified in calling him a dull stick: it was his nature and he had no wish to be otherwise. Yet it must be as painful to Aline as her excesses were to him. He tried to console Léonore, who had never ceased to reproach herself (he was grateful that his mother, whom he had shielded from the truth as best he could, had died before the Florentine adventure): nobody was to blame, for who could have known? The match had appeared as suitable to Aline and himself as to everyone else.

His brother-in-law Constant de Sauvigny, having, like others, advised Miremont against taking Aline back, expressed regret that the law did not permit divorce; as for this second separation, were not its terms undeservedly generous? Why not send Aline into permanent exile abroad? But Miremont would not be persuaded. Certain houses had already closed their doors to her (it was her constant reproach that his forgiveness had not worked miracles): now she was to be banished entirely from the world she considered her natural element; he did not wish to put her at further disadvantage, which might also harm his daughters.

Left at last to his own devices, Miremont was not disposed to brood. (Later, when Léonore died, he reflected that the wretchedness of his marriage was as nothing to the sufferings of poor Constant, who, through a caprice of fate, had lost a wife he respected and adored.) As for his lack of a male heir, Léonore and Constant had two fine sons: the marquisate was assured, if not through his line. His one regret was his daughters, whom he saw only on formal visits to Miremont-St-Fleur, usually at New Year, when the delights of reunion were not unmixed with strain. But otherwise, he could only rejoice in his freedom—he was, after all, not yet thirty. He resumed what he had learnt to call his selfish pleasures. He was to think of the next eleven years as a return to Eden.

He took to picture-buying again, slowly augmenting the collection of Italian masters his ancestors had acquired with works by Watteau and Fragonard, a Goya, two Claudes, and, as he grew more adventurous, canvasses by Géricault, Daumier and Delacroix—he even began to flirt with Corot. He travelled once more. A series of trips to England that included two visits to his second cousins' Norfolk estate fired an interest in advanced agricultural methods, and he started to experiment with some of these innovations on the home farm at Beauvallon. He resumed his study of the classics, idly at first, but soon becoming absorbed.

Even the terrifying events that followed the fall of Louis Napoleon brought him an unexpected gift that was to enrich his life immeasurably. Unlike most of his acquaintance, he took the decision to remain in Paris as the Prussian armies approached. It was not courage that prevented him fleeing to Beauvallon, so much as a feeling that, while his estates were in no danger and could look after themselves, he had a duty to stand by the Hôtel de Miremont and its household. He was concerned, for instance, about his two footmen, who had been drafted into the National Guard: he did not wish them to suffer what poor Thomas had suffered. And then, Léonore and Constant were staying. Léonore joined various ladies' committees and had no difficulty persuading her brother that Aline's empty apartments in the hôtel's east wing should be converted into an ambulance for the wounded.

Although Miremont, in committing himself to the city, expected to share its hardships, he could not say he experienced physical deprivation during the long months of the siege: there was always food to be had if you enquired in the right places and, owing to the obstinate determination of his housekeeper, Mme Mercier, such rarities as chicken and fresh eggs continued to appear on his table in defiance of his protests. Nor was he required to perform any heroic act of defence during the violent rule of the Commune after the Prussians had withdrawn: hidden away behind high walls and iron gates, and guarded by a household that remained obdurately loyal, the Hôtel de Miremont was left unscathed even by the *petroliers*, the women whose final stealthy acts of arson gutted several houses in the Faubourg as the Commune fell.

Nevertheless Miremont found it impossible to harden himself to the boom of the Prussian guns, the rifle fire, the corpses in the streets that became an everyday sight, or to the notion that, cut off from the rest of the world, Parisians were destined to continue slaughtering one another in pursuit of one barbarous political ideal after the next. For long hours he shut out this sickening and nonsensical universe by steeping himself in the formal beauties of Latin verse. He had developed a particular fondness for the poetry of Ovid and, by the time the authority of the republic had been restored and the last barricades torn down, he had completed a monograph on Ovid's *Ars Amatoria*.

Some months later, when the world was back to normal as though the nightmare had never happened, he went to visit the professor who had taught him at Heidelberg and found himself talking about his work. The professor requested a fair copy and an encouraging correspondence ensued which resulted in Miremont, with some trepidation, approaching a publisher. It was pure vanity, this wish to weigh in his hand a bound volume embossed with his name, to open the covers and observe his fallible words marching to the margin with the brash certainty of type: there was embarrassment as well as pride in it, for this was a rich man's indulgence, denied to more talented writers who lacked the publisher's fee. And what was he to do with the results of his caprice? He parcelled up several volumes to send with a letter of thanks to Heidelberg. Then he recalled that one of his former tutors now held a chair at the Sorbonne. Professor Ricard recommended him to the eminent classicist Dr Léon Rosenthal, an authority on the Augustan poets.

The world that was thus opened to him, a world of intricate, absorbing discourse and intellectual discovery, seemed as naturally his element as balls and receptions had been Aline's. His calm and rational temperament was suited to disciplined argument and painstaking analysis. Yet he was not, after all, without passion: he could be fired by the pursuit of an elusive reference, intoxicated by debate, dizzied by the resonance of unsuspected connections; nor did he grow immune to the beauty that was the numinous thread from which he span his own earth-bound work. He collaborated with Rosenthal on a commentary on Ovid's *Poems of Exile* and afterwards wrote a paper on the subject that was published in learned journals in France and Germany. Now, when he travelled, he was as likely to visit correspondents in university cities as to haunt art galleries or walk ancient battlefields. He was not inclined to dispute the verdict of some, that he was merely an aristocratic dilettante; but to himself he acknowledged that this rigorous intellectual endeavour, which required daily dedication, had become the central focus of his existence. He could not be a poet, yet he might become the amanuensis of poets, divining and serving their true intentions. He began upon a compendious study of Ovid's works that he hoped would be his own magnum opus.

His days were purposive and fulfilled. Every morning when he was in Paris he rode in the Champs Elysées, after which, with his secretary M Lesage, who had served his father before him, he went through his correspondence and dealt with family business. The afternoon was reserved for Ovid: frequently he would work on in the tranquillity of the library, reading, scribbling notes, reflecting, until the dressing gong. His routine supplied the hours of solitude that were essential to his being: yet, although he had dropped most of his acquaintance from the period of his marriage and no longer entertained formally, his life was not solitary, for he now enjoyed the amiable and cultivated company of a small circle of close friends. For family, he had Constant and Léonore and his two nephews: he possessed a standing invitation to their house in the Rue de Condé, five minutes' walk away. And then, of course, there was his own house, the setting for this satisfying existence.

As a child he had quite disliked the ancient cavernous palace, lying in the shadow of St Sulpice like a buried giant: the echoing rooms and forbidding corridors had made him long for the light and air of Beauvallon. In Aline's time, too, when it had been thronged with people he neither knew nor cared to know and when its appointments, or lack of them, had been a constant source of contention, he had often felt that of all the burdens thrust on him by the marquisate this was the greatest. But—perhaps the change had come as, seeing it stand undaunted before the threat of invasion and chaos, he had reminded himself that it had withstood the Revolution, two restored monarchies, two empires and two previous republics—he now loved the Hôtel de Miremont as deeply as his Côte d'Or château, loved it and respected it. Like some venerable tribal elder, although unbowed, the building was prey to infirmities—his butler Boussec was forever reporting missing roof tiles, crumbling stucco or sinister cracks—but Miremont begrudged it no care. Its weathered blocks of stone embodied a fortitude that humbled him; yet they inspired in him, too, an almost mystical sense of his own connection with the ten generations that had preceded him.

As he wandered through the ceremonial rooms, he never ceased to be relieved that he had managed to stop Aline wrecking them. Here was the jewelled goblet given to Roland, the first marquis, by Catherine de Médici, here were the family portraits, including the painting by François de Troy of the fifth marquis, Edmond, for whom the hôtel was built (it was a commanding face but Miremont could nevertheless discern faint similarity with his own indifferent features). Much of the furniture in the salons had been made for his great-great-grandfather or, even before that, brought back by the sixth marquis from journeys to Italy and the Far East: the set of carved and gilded chairs and settees in the state apartments had been commissioned in honour of a visit by the Empress Elizabeth of Russia (it had never taken place); in the ballroom the hangings dated from his great-grandfather's time and had been saved by the servants from looters after the fire that had wrecked the east wing during the Terror. Even in his own more modest apartments, Miremont found family history wherever he looked: he wrote letters standing at his grandfather's desk using his grandfather's blotter and ink wells, while his grandmother had given birth to his father on the battered leather sofa he loved to recline upon in his study.

He could still, on occasion, be pulled up short by the weight of this treasure and his duty to it. But more often, when his eye caught some detail and saw it afresh— a painting of nymphs above a door case, the perfection of a gilt lion's head ornamenting a porphyry vase—he would feel intense gratitude that he, the twelfth of his line, for all his inadequacies, had been chosen for this service. His intellectual work had given him individual purpose: his sense of commonalty, of the current of his being merging with the great stream of family tradition and memory, was the other sustaining force of his life.

He could not have said precisely when the serpent entered his paradise. Perhaps it was on his fortieth birthday when, staring at himself in the glass, as he had not for a long time, he saw how lined his face had become and how springy dark hairs had begun to sprout from his nostrils. But more likely his fall began shortly after, with the death of Léonore, painfully of peritonitis after a brief illness.

His father, his brother, his mother—none of these losses had so completely overwhelmed him. Léonore, not yet forty-five and apparently in perfect health until three weeks previously, had been the closest to him of all his family. Mingled with his grief was dull fear, a selfish consciousness of his own mortality. He was the only one left who could remember the happy years of his childhood, the last alive of his own generation. Suddenly the Hôtel de Miremont seemed to mock him, his precious communion with the past appeared a delusion. He sat in the house of the dead and soon he, too, like the dust on the mantelpiece, would summarily be brushed away. He tried to rid himself of these morbid thoughts by burying himself in his work. But here also his joy had vanished: he struggled to concentrate, each afternoon became a bitter battle. However he tried to cage his thoughts, they fluttered restlessly and flew away from him: often they seemed to home with yearning upon some object just beyond his view.

But the worst symptom of his malaise did not manifest itself until eight or nine months later. A young American, son of one of the embassy wives Léonore had befriended while caring for the war-wounded, was staying briefly with the Sauvignys and, since the visitor spoke little French and Miremont possessed serviceable English, he was invited to act as interpreter. Harold Kiddle, although tall and fresh-faced, seemed an entirely unremarkable young man, yet Miremont could not take his eyes off him. In spite of himself, he observed with fascination the boy's habit of running his fingers through his forelock of hempen hair and the way, when listening, he pursed his slightly parted lips: after dinner, as they smoked cigars in Constant's study, the spectacle of the youth's long limbs sprawled in a wing chair so distracted his interpreter he several times fumbled for words. The next day Miremont could do no work and when he was shown into the Sauvignys' salon that evening he was trembling and did not know where to fix his glance. From these and other symptoms, although a stranger to the sensation, he could not avoid identifying this turmoil as desire. He recoiled in horror. And his horror deepened when that night he dreamed about the boy and woke to find his night-shirt sticky. It was unthinkable, appalling. The young man was not charming or even very likeable: in fact, with his brash New-World manners and studied indifference to European civilisation, he could be considered rather obnoxious. Miremont resolved that he would cease to visit Constant and his nephews until Harold Kiddle had left. Yet he went again the next day, he went trembling and aching to luncheon, to dinner, to the opera, to the theatre, and when the boy at last departed for Rome he was bereft.

He sought to analyse the causes of this aberration. He did not, as we know, consider himself a passionate man. All his love had been for his family. In his youth he had never been particularly stirred by any girl and—he must admit it—he had not felt for Aline a fraction of the desire he had felt for Harold Kiddle. Yet his deficiencies as a husband had not been entirely his fault: Aline had shown equal distaste for their marriage bed. And besides, while he had not succumbed to youthful obsessions with women, he had felt no longing for his own sex either. Although…But, no, that was altogether different.

He could not deny his love for the boy at Beauvallon, the lad who had been appointed his groom when he was eight, who had, during five golden summers, watched out for him, supervising his graduation from a pony to horseback, teaching him to fish, to shoot, to skim stones across the lake. He had worshipped this boy, already strong and broad-shouldered, instinctively knowledgeable about horses, wise to the rhythms of nature, where the best mushrooms would grow this year, when the pointer bitch would whelp, how to find a hawk at roost. Then the lad turned twenty, grew restless and enlisted. On finding him gone, Miremont had fled to the hollow oak in the park and sobbed until his throat was raw. But that was natural: he had been of an age when most boys devote themselves to some hero. This pure, idealistic love was profaned by any comparison with his hunger for the American boy. No, he must assume that the Harold Kiddle episode was in some scarcely conceivable way the production of a mind still disorganised by grief. He could reassure himself that something so foreign to his character was unlikely to occur again.

By dint of strenuous effort and self-discipline, he reapplied himself to his work and at last recovered his concentration. After some months he believed his mind was purged of unsuitable thoughts. But his confidence was premature. This time he was betrayed by Ovid.

It had not, of course, escaped Miremont that his poet's major theme was love. But here was the phenomenon as he felt he could understand it—earthy, yes, but safely contained by convention. Indeed, he had penned his little piece on the *Ars Amatoria* precisely because Ovid's witty and cynical manual for lovers was the antidote to chaos. But Miremont was like a man so entranced by some finely crafted piece of marquetry that he forgets he is looking at a table. He had begun a detailed reading of the *Metamorphoses* with his mind attuned to the energy of Ovid's verse, the poet's ingenious layering of myth upon myth, discursive structure, limpid imagery. But he was barely into the second book before these preoccupations were overwhelmed; there was a terrible familiarity to Jupiter's rapacious pursuit of Europa and Io, and on and on it went—Apollo, Pluto, Echo, Biblias, even the Cyclops—blood coursed, hearts flamed and reason gave way to consuming lust, while at every turn there were descriptions of male pulchritude. Miremont's dreams began again, usually with the same ignominious consequences. He grew afraid of sleep and was grateful that it now often eluded him. His appetite fell off. He became prey to alternating extremes of lethargy and agitation.

His friends remarked on the change in him. Catherine de Claireville spoke to him gently of Léonore—she could be the soul of tact when she wished. All the same, when the conversation had found other channels, she could not refrain from giving him a mischievous look.

"Tell me, how long have you and Aline been separated? Twelve years?"

"Almost thirteen."

"Then it's clear, darling Armand, why you're out of sorts. It's high time you took a mistress."

Although Miremont's entire being recoiled from the idea, it was a measure of his desperation that for two or three days he considered it. Instead, he decided to consult a doctor. He remembered the man Constant had called in to give a second opinion in Léonore's case. Dr Gérard had struck him as sensible and dedicated, less renowned than Dr Chevalier, the family's usual physician, and certainly less grand, but probably more competent. His honesty and unwillingness to flatter had appealed to Miremont, but he had also shown a diffident gentleness which suggested, in marked contrast to Chevalier's polished manner, that every patient was particular, that here was a rare being, a doctor with imagination. This did not incline Miremont to disclose the full extent of his troubles, for how could he speak of that to anyone. But these abhorrent psychological symptoms must have some physical cause, which a perceptive doctor would easily detect.

Dr Gérard, having given Miremont a thorough examination, found nothing amiss with his heart, lungs or reflexes. Apart from suffering mild eye strain and being a little underweight, the marquis was in good physical condition for a man of forty-one.

In person, Gérard was large and shapeless, with a moon face the colour and texture of putty. His entirely unexceptionable morning coat did not flatter him, but merely accentuated his ungainliness. From the gingerly way he perched his bulk on the chair in Miremont's sitting room, to his speech, which was slowed by a slight lisp, his whole demeanour suggested—no, not clumsiness, but rather a concern not to be clumsy, a delicate wish that, despite his shambling form and bumbling gestures, he should overbalance neither chair nor patient. At least, Miremont observed thankfully, he had discerned that his verdict might not bring reassurance.

"I could, of course, prescribe a sleeping draught for the insomnia and a tonic for the feeling of debility you describe. But these would merely be palliatives. I sense, monsieur, that you would consider them worse than useless."

Miremont nodded.

"I remember the comtesse de Sauvigny, of course. I first became slightly acquainted with her years ago, during the war. She was a kind and courageous woman. They say grief passes, but where the person is so close to you, a sister or a mother, that is not strictly true. The feeling of loss diminishes but never disappears."

"And may take—unusual forms?"

The doctor looked at Miremont, but did not immediately reply. He studied his hands, which were large and furred with indifferent-coloured hair: he folded them carefully, with circumspection. "You are not married, monsieur?"

Miremont stirred irritably. "The marquise and I are separated."

"It may be—" The doctor paused. "Sometimes, when men reach our age, they realise that there are certain things—things they have denied themselves, satisfactions they now regret are missing from their lives…"

Miremont could barely contain his disappointment. He had not called in Gérard to hear a repetition of Catherine de Claireville's advice. "I have no wish to find myself a mistress."

"No. Of course not, monsieur. That will only serve for a certain type of man."

"And for others?"

The doctor spread his palms, then retracted them quickly, as if he feared knocking over some invisible vase. "Acceptance perhaps? That some things cannot be. That there are other satisfactions."

Miremont stared at the doctor. Clearly his faith in him had been utterly misplaced. If Miremont had required platitudes he could have consulted Chevalier, who would have delivered them more eloquently. Acceptance? Had this sanctimonious idiot any notion what he was asking him to accept?

But no, of course, as Miremont recalled, Gérard had not, since his patient would sooner die than confess. Nor, to do the doctor justice, had he sounded complacent. Rather, he had spoken tentatively and, far from concluding with a smug smile like Chevalier, had remained serious, even lugubrious. Miremont considered afresh the grey, melancholy face, then the awkward hands with their ringless fingers. Forgiveness came to him.

"You are married yourself, monsieur?"

"Ah no. Sadly not. When the time was right, I was busy building up my practice. And now—" Gérard smiled hastily, as though to absolve Miremont from compassion "— my sister keeps house for me since our mother died. She takes excellent care of me. It is not an arrangement I should care to unsettle."

Miremont suddenly discovered a liking for the doctor, although his visit had been well-nigh useless. Having detained him in conversation for a while, he found himself clapping him amiably on the shoulder as he took his departure and inviting him to play chess one evening.

And perhaps, after all, there was something in what Gérard had said. Perhaps Miremont's affliction was aggravated by his struggle against it, perhaps acceptance was the answer. Yet what, precisely, was he to accept? That his symptoms were, in fact, the disease? That this spore had always lurked within him, waiting for the climate that would nurture its vile fruit? If he were to accept that, he must accept that he was someone he no longer knew and must despise. It did not matter that his depravities were of thought, not deed. Merely to desire what he desired was to dishonour his name, to break the sacred trust his heritage conferred. He would, in all his relations with the world, with his friends, his academic acquaintance, even his servants, be a fraud. And that was as nothing to the wrong he would do his daughters.

The previous summer, while he had been struggling with his work, his elder daughter, just turned eighteen, had married Raymond Thierry-Le Puy, the son of the Burgundian neighbour who had caused her mother's second downfall. The marriage had required no involvement on Miremont's part, except to pay the bills and make a stiff visit to Miremont St-Fleur to give away the bride. Yet here were his girls, whom he had scarcely seen for twelve years: little Julie, almost fifteen now, fair and beautiful, the image of her mother's youth, completing her education at a convent school in Bruges; and Clotilde, grown up, a married woman. What kind of father would he be to Julie's innocence? How could he face Clotilde, who now lived in Paris, in the house in the Square de Luynes Miremont had bought the couple as a wedding present, and who paid him calls out of daughterly duty, heavier each week with her coming child?

Accept? He had never been devout—indeed his parents' infrequent attendances at mass had been to satisfy social obligations—but, one afternoon of despair, he stole into St Sulpice and made confession. No comfort came to him from the other side of the grille. It was as he had concluded: even thought was sin.

And yet, all the while, another voice was struggling to be heard above his cries of self-accusation. Had he forgotten that he could call the ancient world in his defence? The Greeks would have found his desires perfectly natural, not inimical to the social order, nor inferior to the love of women and certainly no sign of moral or physical weakness: Xenophon maintained the bravest regiments were made up of pairs of lovers, Achilles' love for Patroclus was as celebrated as the champion's legendary martial prowess. Homer, Plutarch, Pindar, Plato, and the Romans, too, Vergil, Horace, Catullus, Juvenal, even Ovid, for all his pursuit of the female sex—the corpus of classical literature endorsed Miremont's inclinations: even the gods were not immune to the charms of boys, witness Apollo and Ganymede. Miremont's reason told him that, if what was once considered a normal channel for desire was now an abomination, it was not human nature that had changed, but society. His heart hardened against the pious voice behind the grille, ordering penitence, sullying with its venal prohibitions what the greatest civilisation in the world had found natural and glorious. He began to permit himself his forbidden thoughts, even allowing himself to take pleasure in them. And it is possible he might have found some measure of peace, had he not been visited by Achille de Tarascon.

CHAPTER SEVEN

Tarascon was Aline's friend, not his. Indeed, Miremont had conceived a particular aversion for him from the days when the house had been haunted by every social butterfly in Paris. Although not usually given to violent dislikes, Miremont recoiled from the man's exhibitionism; he loathed the ill-will that was the fount of Tarascon's supposed wit; and there was something else too, something in his posturing, in his suggestive moues and whinnying laughter, that seemed to stop just short of indecency. For years Miremont had been unable precisely to define what that something was. But, at Clotilde's wedding, from his new position of enlightenment, he was appalled to discover he knew too well. Furthermore, although in his agitation he might have been mistaken, he received the impression that Tarascon knew he knew, that every meaningful leer, every innuendo, was produced for his benefit.

He should have declared himself not at home when Tarascon called at the Hôtel de Miremont unannounced. Perhaps horrified fascination prevented him. The man's excuse was flimsy enough: the information on classical mythology he required for some lyric verse he was composing could be found in any schoolboy crib. His conversation, though avoiding outright declaration, was nevertheless remarkably frank and not inhibited by his host's distant manner. In fact, Miremont was left in no doubt that Tarascon found him utterly transparent, read his vilest thoughts, his basest urges, so that for weeks afterwards he would check his deportment in the glass, wondering which look, which unconsciously effeminate gesture had so egregiously betrayed him. Worst of all was the complicity, the unspoken assumption of fellowship and Tarascon's evident glee, the joy of a priest making a convert. After the man had gone, Miremont sat at his desk with his head in his hands. Greek love? The manly ideal of lovers dying side by side in battle was myth, Achille de Tarascon the reality. Miremont would not, could not sink so low.

But soon afterwards his affliction entered a new and more alarming phase. He could not go for a short walk without finding his gaze hungrily distracted. A red-cheeked butcher's boy out on a delivery, a waiter bending over a café table, a smocked workman, muscles straining as he wielded his pick—this fuel for Miremont's helpless lust would keep it stoked until the night hours when, as he had been obliged to for some time, he would joylessly resort to what his nursemaid had termed 'evil habits'. He experienced a constant and intolerable sense of physical strain, as if his fevered body were on the point of dissolution, as if the hairs that sprouted from his ears and nostrils were not merely signs of middle age but the start of an inexorable, irreversible transformation from man to beast, like the punishments meted out by the gods in the *Metamorphoses*.

He would not give in. No matter that his mental resources seemed to have deserted him. He would find some way to force his flesh into submission. That summer at Beauvallon he rode, swam, walked; he acquired dumbbells and for an hour each day performed exhausting gymnastic exercises. On his return to Paris, he hired a fencing master and, three mornings a week panting and sweating in the ballroom, set about retrieving his youthful skills with the foil. But what had brought some measure of relief in the country was useless in the city where temptation once again surrounded him.

With insistence, there returned to him Achille de Tarascon's sly references to adventures in the Champs Elysées and the Bois de Boulogne. In the Bois there was less chance of Miremont's stumbling into someone he knew—Tarascon had mentioned the area near the Porte Maillot, well away from the lakes—but there were other terrors beyond contemplation: what if he were seized in a police raid? All the same he made his way there by cab one icy night. The resulting transaction beneath the leafless trees brought him release at last, but its effects were ephemeral. And, although he went again, steeled himself on two further occasions, he was conscious each time it was over of a feeling akin to grief. This was not what he wanted.

Nevertheless he must accept that he had crossed the line, must now call himself a Uranian, an invert, a Greek of Achille de Tarascon's tribe. His fall was complete, all his notions of himself were shattered. Aline was right: he was a contemptible hypocrite.

As his sense of himself slid away, so did other certainties. His religious belief, always vestigial, vanished entirely. His interest in pictures died and could not be rekindled even when the dealer Korsakov tempted him with another Claude. What was the point? He had never been a royalist, had never espoused any political position, had fancied he stood above such things; but now he saw, in the pictures, the portraits of his forebears, the accumulation of artefacts, in the very fabric of the Hôtel de Miremont, a homage to ancient privilege that celebrated, not tradition and continuity, but decadence: perhaps the

Communards had been right, perhaps it was the people's turn at last, perhaps this monument to the *ancien régime* that mocked the events of the last hundred years deserved to be swept away. Clotilde had been delivered of a boy, the long-awaited heir to the marquisate, yet Miremont struggled to rejoice, for when he looked into the guileless unformed face of his grandson he thought only: I cannot be to this child as my grandfather was to me.

As for his work, he was forced to acknowledge he had achieved nothing of significance over the last year and must accede to his critics: he was an aimless dabbler. He was ashamed in the presence of Ricard and Rosenthal and, where their company had brought him stimulation and delight, he now made excuses to avoid them. One afternoon he assembled the preparatory notes he had made for his work on Ovid, the sketched ideas, the painstaking textual references, the outline structure and draft chapters on the *Amores* and *Ars Amatoria*, and, having evaluated them with a cold and, it seemed to him, newly realistic eye, fed them, every last scribble and jotting, to his study fire.

He was now, like Ovid, in exile from everything he knew and loved. And, as with Ovid, there seemed no hope of clemency. For the Furies, the serpent, Nemesis—whatever this evil genius was—continued to pursue him. The longing for what he could not see and could not reach, that indefinable something just beyond his vision, was not appeased by his degrading pilgrimages to the Bois; on the contrary, it seemed every day to grow more consuming. As for his furtive excursions, he swore to put an end to them. But he already knew this resolve would be broken.

One morning he woke to find himself weeping uncontrollably. That evening Gérard was expected for chess. Miremont, who had always set so much store by self-restraint, was appalled to hear himself blurt out that he feared he was losing his reason.

He had been aware of the doctor scrutinising him with a professional frown over the past few months: Gérard, in his roundabout way, had even enquired if he would care for another examination. But of course Miremont had declined, for it was more impossible than ever to explain the true cause of his trouble. Now, as he stammered out a confused account of his failure to work, he wished he had never uttered his despairing admission. However, this time Gérard was not to be put off: indeed, his tone was unexpectedly firm as he proposed returning with his medical bag the next morning.

The results of this new examination were far from encouraging.

Gérard found the patient's pulse dangerously accelerated and his heartbeat irregular. Taking this, a slight temperature and certain other symptoms into account, as well as the patient's own description of his agitated condition, the doctor concluded that Miremont's attempts to force himself to work had brought him close to collapse and in imminent danger of brain fever. The only remedy was a drastic and immediate alteration of routine. He must rest. He must altogether abandon his punitive physical regimen. He must not think of opening a book. He must not be too much alone and it was imperative he seek out a complete change of scene as soon as possible.

Having delivered his verdict, the doctor glanced at his feet as if expecting to find the floor strewn with broken china. "You won't care for it, my dear sir, I know that. I shouldn't care for it." He gave Miremont a sad, wry smile. "But I should take it as a favour if you'd consider it. Nobody likes to see a good player squandering his bishops as, forgive me, you have been apt to lately."

Touched by Gérard's friendship, Miremont submitted. He even accepted the doctor's renewed offer of a sleeping draught. After all, he himself had no answer to his predicament and, while Gérard was undoubtedly alarmist to speak of brain fever, he had certainly been brought close to total exhaustion. As for the empty life of an invalid, would it be any emptier than his existence now?

The question of a change posed a greater problem. That it would remove him from the temptations of the Bois was much in its favour. But, if Beauvallon were ruled out, as it must be—his life there was solitary, it could not be strictly accounted a change and besides, in his current frame of mind, like the Hôtel de Miremont it would only make him wretched—where might he go? He had often spent some part of the year travelling, but always alone, and he recognised the sense in Gérard's advice, more sense than the good doctor knew. For already the incubus that had lodged in his brain was up to its duplicitous tricks, discounting England, where any unsuitable adventure might land him in jail, but recalling that Tarascon had hinted at the delights of North Africa. Tunis, Tangiers, Algiers…Or there was Greece, not of course the country of ancient legend with its armies of lovers, but modern Greece, where nevertheless…

No, he could not under any circumstances contemplate travelling alone. Perhaps he could persuade Léon and Ruth Rosenthal to accompany him. Or Gérard, if his practice permitted. But yet—he understood with horror that even then he could not trust himself, far away in a foreign country and freed from the usual constraints: he would be looking to his friends as guards, not companions.

No solution had yet occurred to him when he was visited by Catherine de Claireville and foolishly mentioned Gérard's advice.

"Oh but, darling Armand, it is quite simple. You must come to La Boissière. I shall be going down in a fortnight for the whole summer and you can stay as long as you wish. No, don't say it—I know how hopeless you are about invitations—but this time you shan't escape me."

So there he was, a house party guest, obediently making small talk and allowing himself to be organised into games and excursions. He could not fault Catherine's hospitality: she went out of her way to ensure his comfort and find the means to amuse him. But here, vividly recreated, in the conversations, the preoccupations, the personae, was his life with Aline. He struggled to conceal his misery. He had seldom felt so out of place.

It did not help that he had lost the art of social chitchat or, rather, had an ingrained resistance to re-acquiring it. He should have liked to talk to Hugo Chausson-Laurier, whom he had met once or twice at the La Marnes: he would have been happy to listen for hours while the colonel expatiated on Egyptian burial practices and the difficulties of travelling in the desert; but sadly Chausson-Laurier had already departed to supervise the preparations for his expedition. The remaining guests presented Miremont with no such ready topics. What was he to say, for instance, to poor, foolish Jean-Marie de la Rochefontaine, who had floundered in Vienna and was bound, according to Constant, who knew about such things, to take a tumble over his Panamanian ventures? How was he to respond to Gilbert de Cressy, a dedicated supporter of Orléans' lost cause, who assumed that Miremont must inevitably share his views? In his present state of self-distrust, he tended to avoid the young men, who might have proved more congenial. As for the women, they also confounded him, chattering about parties he had not attended or gossip he had not heard. Perhaps he should be grateful that the dinner-table was largely monopolised by Achille de Tarascon.

Tarascon. One of the precautions Miremont should have taken before accepting Catherine's invitation was to enquire about the guest list. He should also have recalled the irregularities in her life that exerted their influence on the society she kept and on the very atmosphere of her house, which could be described as—well, the word that came to mind was 'louche'. He had fled from Ovid's lustful nymphs and gods only to find the same perilous currents here. Intrigue seemed to seethe all around him.

He could forgive Catherine Iphigénie Zelenska. It was typical of Catherine, having decided he needed a mistress, to provide one for him. The woman was pretty —beautiful if you admired the work of Ingres—and, though conversationally more baffling than all the others put together, apparently embarrassingly willing. However, while he accepted that the gesture was well meant, he wished that Catherine had reflected a little. Even if he had been capable of seducing the princess, he should have avoided it: as a betrayed husband he would shrink from cuckolding another, no matter how complaisant; nor did he find her ready infidelity an attractive characteristic. All the same, Catherine had apparently raised the lady's expectations and now he was put to the task of shaking her off as kindly and discreetly as he could manage. Perhaps she would settle for La Rochefontaine, whose small, round, over-optimistic eyes constantly strayed to her breasts at dinner.

But Princess Zelenska, of course, was not Miremont's worst difficulty. He had been distantly aware of the rumours about Catherine's footmen. But, as he had not dined at the Hôtel de Claireville in years, he had no distinct memory of these young men, other than as fleeting, handsome figures who attended to his coat or saw him to his carriage. At La Boissière, however, it was impossible to escape the spectacle of these six good-looking boys, processing into the dining room or standing haughtily to attention behind the guests' chairs, nor was it easy to forget their special terms of service. And, if Miremont struggled to do so, Tarascon would not let him.

On his first afternoon, Miremont had been standing on the terrace observing a rather charming tableau being performed on the lawn leading to the Italian garden. Iphigénie Zelenska's elder son, Stanislaw, was learning to ride a bicycle. His mother and one of the other ladies watched from the shade of their parasols, while a nursemaid superintended the two younger children and a footman held the boy in the saddle. The laughter hanging in the windless air, the pure white of the ladies' dresses and the children's sailor suits, the preternaturally clear tones of grass and sky, like colours in a nursery painting— Miremont, his senses lulled by the heat and the unaccustomed fatigue of having nothing to do, looked on indulgently at the distant figures, finding the scene one of refreshing innocence. There had been several false starts and one near catastrophe, but now Stanislaw was pedalling confidently with the footman running behind and still gripping the saddle. Miremont's gaze caught the liveried figure at the instant the lad let go, held the graceful arc of the vigorous young body as it straightened up, arms still outstretched, carelessly abandoned to the joy of the moment, held the image with fascination: so that it was not until he saw the young man suddenly sprint forward that his attention was wrenched back to the by-now wobbling bicycle.

At that point, when, in the split second before disaster, the runner had intercepted the machine and was steadying the child and both were laughing, a voice said in Miremont's ear: "I see you are admiring Catherine's horticultural triumph."

Miremont started.

"Her delightful flower garden. The Hyacinths and Narcissi whose blooms she generously permits her friends to pluck."

Only then, as understanding sank in, did Miremont become aware of the impropriety of his gaze. He was appalled that it had been obvious and shocked, too, that Tarascon addressed him so crudely, without disguise, as though brotherhood were now agreed between them. The fellow did not even trouble to moderate his voice. Miremont glanced around anxiously, but his persecutor was not to be discouraged.

"Ah yes. The lilies and roses of youth, only waiting to be—" But here, shielding his eyes to acquire a clearer view of the liveried figure, he appeared to recoil. "Though some of them are best left on the bush, my dear. If you wish to spare yourself thorns. Or the worm in the bud."

Tarascon's long sight was evidently more accurate than Miremont's, but in any case Miremont was grimly determined not to look. "My dear Tarascon, as I'm sure my wife has told you, I am a very dull man. I fear your recondite observations are wasted on me. Now, monsieur, if you will excuse me... "

It was pompous, priggish, not the glittering stiletto his tormentor would have administered. And, besides, Miremont might ponder the wisdom of snubbing a man who perceived his own guilty secret. For, while Tarascon spared him further private indiscretions, in public he appeared readier than ever to advertise their fellowship, as though he took vindictive pleasure in dangling Miremont's reputation in his jewelled fingers. Miremont found it extraordinary, wonderful given the man's excesses, that none of the company, not even worldly-wise

Catherine, saw Tarascon for what he was, until he remembered his own former innocence. Yet all the same Tarascon seemed to enjoy flirting with them, daring them to discovery. Watch me, he seemed to be saying to Miremont with every artful glance, every veiled allusion, see how close to the sun I fly, and be sure if my wings melt you too will plummet.

And this was not the limit of his malice. It became an ordeal for Miremont to take his place at table, or even to request a newspaper or a pot of coffee, for he had but to glimpse an azure tail coat to recall Tarascon's insinuations. He had fled to the peace of the country, only to find it a place of greater temptation than the Bois. But he would not succumb. He was not Achille de Tarascon, he accepted no association with him however it was thrust upon him. He would not permit himself the indignity of allowing his gaze to stray again.

He feared he was a sad disappointment to Catherine's kindness, although he struggled to be a rewarding guest. Constantly on his guard and concerned also to evade Princess Zelenska, yet obliged to appear at ease, happily occupied while idle, able to conjure talk out of thin air, he grew increasingly exhausted. True, he had some successes. He could not forever continue avoiding Charles de Selincourt-Saint-Antoine or Maurice Bécart and was relieved to discover they stirred nothing untoward, that he might feel as relaxed in their presence as he did with his nephews. Of the two, he preferred Selincourt, who seemed a sensible and unaffected young man. They had several undemanding exchanges about fencing and horses, and Miremont was fascinated to learn that the vicomte was planning to join Chausson-Laurier's expedition. He had made some headway with the watercolorists too, genuinely admiring Mlle de Beaumont-Gramont's technique and uncovering in Mme de Cressy a surprising enthusiasm for Delacroix. But he was aware that on the whole he merely endorsed his reputation as a dry stick.

When Achille de Tarascon took his departure at the end of the week, Miremont was immeasurably relieved. But even this could not make him easy. Selincourt was also amongst the departing guests, along with Bécart, and in their place came others who were unknown to Miremont or merely passing acquaintances—the novelist Aristide de Bellac and two young nephews of Gilbert de Cressy—so that he had the sense of beginning his endeavours all over again.

He envied Bellac, who took Tarascon's place as the supper-table raconteur, regaling the company with endless stories of his visits abroad—the notables who had honoured him, the ladies who had written him scented letters—and who was always delighted at the slightest prompting to discuss the sources of his inspiration or rehearse his creative struggles. Miremont could not imagine the luxury of unburdening himself about his own work in this fashion. While it was considered elegant and accomplished to publish a novel or a slim volume of aphorisms, his own scholarly toil was viewed at best, by Catherine and his society friends, as harmless eccentricity and at worst, by his immediate family—or so he gathered from remarks let slip by Clotilde—as a social affront, a bourgeois activity that demeaned his rank. Yet suddenly he longed to talk about poetry, ideas—real things, things at least that seemed real to him. He bitterly regretted the destruction of his writings, which appeared to him now a senseless act akin to self-mutilation. He longed to revive his discussions with Ricard and Rosenthal. He missed the doctor, too, and their leisurely exchanges over the chess board. And above all he craved—he did not care if they were forbidden him—he could no longer survive without books.

It was true that Catherine had lent him one of Bellac's works in preparation for the great novelist's arrival: its confection of winsome and deserving orphans, wealthy tyrants and noble young idealists, salted with social realism and liberally spiced with romance, was apparently characteristic and could not be judged too taxing even for an invalid. But, alas, the first volume of *The Quarryman's Daughter* proved more effective than Gérard's sleeping draught. Miremont recalled his conversation with Selincourt. If he were not permitted the gods of Rome and Greece, he might surely divert himself with Ancient Egypt, with Isis, Osiris, Horus and Amun Re.

That afternoon, while everyone else was in the garden, he made his way furtively to the library. Such was his guilt, not so much at disobeying Gérard's advice as at letting the side down, at putting his personal pleasure before his duties as a guest, that he was taken aback to find someone else in the room. But it was only one of the footmen, tidying away some books. Adopting his usual precautions, he nodded to the young man but directed his glance firmly towards the shelves and soon, hearing the door quietly close, understood he was at last blessedly alone.

La Boissière's library was not well-used nor generously stocked, but its tranquillity, its reminiscent smell of dust and fading leather, was balm to Miremont. Having found little to his purpose, not even a general history of the Pharaohs, he wavered reprehensibly before the shelves of Latin and Greek before crushing the intemperate urge for poetry and compromising with Tacitus. He consoled himself with the familiar pages of the *Annales* until it was time to dress for dinner. He felt alive again.

Yet at dinner he was once more overwhelmed by exhaustion. He would stifle without solitude. The next day, a Sunday, an excursion was planned to a church some kilometres away, to inspect the petrified stalactites in its crypt. Miremont, pleading mild indisposition, was shamed by the tender concern of Catherine and the other ladies. But as he watched the carriages roll down the drive after luncheon he could feel his weariness lift.

This time he would not bury himself in the library, but seek light and air, break another of Gérard's prohibitions, the edict against exercise. He thought of borrowing a horse from the stables, but decided to walk. Striking out through the gardens and across the park, he was soon beyond the château's domain and in open fields.

Although it was the height of a blazing day, he did not care that sweat gathered in the inner band of his hat and ran down into his eyes or that his shirt stuck to his back. There was something pleasing, virtuous even, in these effects from his exertions, a soothing purpose in his swinging arms and the brisk crunch of his boots upon the cart track. All around him, waist high, was ripe corn, barely rustling in the still air. In the field of wheat to his left, the harvest had overruled the imperatives of Sunday worship: he watched the double file of bent figures moving slowly but systematically forward, the men reaping, the women catching and binding the fallen stalks, two lines a measured distance apart but working as one perfectly attuned organism, the flash of the blades, the bobbing of the women's kerchiefs all governed as though by some primordial rhythm. The margins of the fields were starred with flax and white butterflies danced across his path.

He felt that his sweat purged him, that reason and common sense flowed back to him with every step. He could not begin to understand why he had come to La Boissière. He had somehow allowed his troubles to grow out of all proportion. He was not, as he had feared, in the grip of mania: while it was true that on occasion he entertained improper feelings, he was perfectly capable of controlling them—had he not proved this over the past week? Certainly, this sin, fault, transgression against nature—if that were what it was—shamed and diminished him, but how had it come to overwhelm everything else in his life? Why had he punished himself by destroying his work, cutting off his friendships, abandoning his interests, exiling himself from all that might be redemptive?

Every morning of his stay here he had woken wretchedly homesick for the Hôtel de Miremont and Beauvallon. If he were an unworthy guardian, he was nevertheless the only one they possessed. Looking out across the fields, he felt his yearning for Beauvallon swell. There, too, they would be bringing in the harvest and, supposing the promises of his steward Calvert could be trusted, work would at last be starting on his model cottages. If he made his excuses to Catherine this evening, he could arrive tomorrow or the day after: Thomas, who had nicked him twice with the razor this morning (always a bad sign), would be only too delighted to consult the railway timetable. And then his secretary must be sent for. With Lesage's assistance, he could begin upon the labour of reconstructing his manuscript. He would write to Rosenthal, apologising and asking his advice. He would instruct Lesage to contact Korsakov expressing interest in the Claude if it were still available. He would spend the rest of the summer at Beauvallon. And on his return to Paris? Was it so grievous to admire a young man's beauty, if that admiration were unexpressed, constrained to the realm of the Platonic ideal, as one might yield to art or music? To look but not to touch. It would be painful, yet there was a poignancy in it that more nearly met his longing than any perfunctory physical act.

The cornfields had given way to vineyards and then to pasture, to his left sloping steeply upwards, to his right running to the horizon in a flat plane broken only by occasional small outcrops of rock and, far ahead, a copse. The cart track had dwindled to a narrow path and there was no longer any sign of habitation, not a cottage, not a cowshed, just the patchwork of fields, spread indolently beneath the scorching sun. He had not the slightest notion where he was, but it would be a simple matter to retrace his steps. He strode on, elated.

It amused him to think that he had found the cure for his ills by breaking every edict of the doctor's prescription. Poor Gérard. But really—brain fever? Miremont saw now, quite clearly, that his gloomy phantasms had been spawned by his shutting himself away in miserable introspection for the last year. Here, of course, thrust relentlessly into the company of others, deprived of his greatest pleasures, cut off from everything he valued, it was easy to realise the error of—But there he paused. Then let out a hoot of laughter. Poor Gérard, indeed? Miremont had a clear vision of the doctor, his large, pallid face opaque save for his slightly raised left eyebrow: it was just the expression he wore when Miremont had left his king exposed.

In front of him, now, loomed the copse. He could follow the path, which veered to the right towards a distant gate and, beyond it, the penitent gold of a field of sunflowers. But, for all his bravado, he was beginning to feel the effects of the heat. The shade appeared inviting and he was arrested by an unexpected sound that increased its allure, the chatter of running water. And indeed, as he grew nearer, he caught a gleam of silver between the thickly growing trees. Pushing his way past overhanging branches, blinking at the sudden diminution of light, he found himself all at once in a clearing dominated by a jagged spur of rock. The woodland pressed in on the crag from three sides and crooked saplings thrust their roots into its clefts, while from its summit gushed a spring, bubbling in crevices, cascading over promontories, leaping from the heavy boulders at the rock's base to create a wide and shallow pool that almost filled the clearing, lapping the furthest roots of the trees where Miremont stood.

He was entranced. The green, subterranean shade, the sunlight slanting between the trees to dapple the surface of the pool, the glittering, dancing beads of the waterfall—here was a scene so remote from the parched fields and punishing heat that it appeared unaccountable, mysterious, brought to his mind Ovid's solitary nymph-haunted pools, Hermaphroditus diving into the embrace of Salmacis, Narcissus, spied on by Echo. Settling himself on a cushion of leaf mould beneath the nearest tree, he took off his hat and mopped his brow.

It was as he lowered his handkerchief and glanced up—perhaps some sudden movement had alerted him—that he realised he was not alone. To the right of the waterfall, where the rock was hollowed out into a shallow cave and the water was darkest and presumably deepest, a sleek wet head, dark as the water itself, crested the surface. The bather remained in the shadows of the cave, submerged and perfectly still, watching him. And only now did Miremont notice the pile of clothes, lodged tidily between the roots of a neighbouring tree.

CHAPTER EIGHT

For a moment the two continued to stare at each other, Miremont frozen with surprise and embarrassment, the bather also assessing their situation. Of course, Miremont knew perfectly well what he must do. No matter that, having stumbled upon such a place of enchantment, he was reluctant to leave: the poor fellow in the water had found it first and had counted on privacy. And he was on the point of going, had reached for the nearest tree root to lever himself to his feet, when the bather too reached a decision. He rose from the water.

He was tall, so that even at its deepest the pool made no concession to his modesty, but he had apparently resolved to brazen it out. He stood, pushing back his wet hair, water streaming from his raised forearms and from his shoulders and flanks, cascading down over the flat plate of his stomach to where the rippling surface barely lapped his groin. Then he waded out from the shadow of the rock and into the sunlight, a young man—even from this distance Miremont could see that he was not much more than a boy—unabashedly, magnificently naked, the sun glinting on the wet curves of his pectoral and shoulder muscles and bleaching his skin to the whiteness of marble. Miremont, reminded of the statues of antiquity, thought he had never seen anything so beautiful. Except that this, of course, was dangerous living flesh. And he must go.

Yet he was transfixed. The boy, treading shingle, advanced like a tightrope walker with both arms outstretched, so that, although the water was by now only up to his calves, he was still unable to protect his decency, while Miremont still could not tear away his guilty, starving glance. Only the thought of how this must strike the poor young man recalled him to his senses.

The boy, however, appeared to have noticed nothing untoward. Nor did he seem unduly concerned by his predicament. As he drew within earshot he called out a respectful "Good day, monsieur," compelling Miremont, who had been earnestly studying the waterfall, to respond in kind.

"The water…looks pleasant."

"Wonderful in this heat. I recommend it."

And, with that, stirring muddy clouds in the shallows as he cleared the last of the pebbles, he lengthened his step and strode confidently up the bank. As he passed, Miremont glimpsed the pale flash of buttocks and long, well-muscled thighs. Then the boy was gone, making for the tree where his clothes were piled, disappearing safely from view on the far side of it.

Again Miremont cautioned himself. But their exchange had complicated matters. To leave now would seem unmannerly, almost a calculated snub. All the same, however determinedly he stared out across the water, he could hear the crackle of fallen twigs as the boy energetically towelled himself with his shirt. He felt the young man's presence with every nerve in his body.

No question of it, he must go. A courteous goodbye would hardly give offence, and the boy would be grateful to have his solitude restored. He would wait at least until the poor young fellow was dressed, then he would…

Glancing, in spite of himself, towards the forbidden tree, his eye lit upon the coat the youth had left behind when he had gathered up the rest of his clothes. Something had slipped from the pocket and lay amongst the dead leaves, equidistant from the two tree trunks and, if Miremont stretched out his arm to the utmost, just within his grasp. Merciful refuge. A book.

He was struggling to extract his pince-nez from his waistcoat pocket when the boy reappeared, barefoot and in his shirt sleeves. As he observed Miremont with the book in his hands, a disconcerted look flashed across his face: perhaps this was occasioned by the start Miremont had given on seeing him, but more probably he was offended by such impertinent curiosity on the part of a stranger.

"Forgive me, monsieur. I…"

But the young man was smiling. "It is you, monsieur, who must forgive me." He indicated his dishabille. "It is unfortunately necessary if I'm to dry my shirt."

In other circumstances Miremont would have been much amused by the irony of this solemn apology for the lack of a waistcoat and jacket. But, as things were, he could only stammer: "N-not at all."

"Ah, what heaven! To feel clean again…It's too shallow, of course, to swim properly. And you need to beware the mud in some parts. But to feel cool water on your skin—as I say, monsieur, I cannot but recommend it."

The boy had flung himself down on the leaf mould beside Miremont's tree and was pulling on his stockings and boots. Close to, with his collar flapping inelegantly from one stud, he no longer seemed a creature of the gods: his features wanted the perfect proportions beloved of Praxiteles and, where he had combed back his wet hair with his fingers, a scar, curved like a billhook, marred his left temple. Yet these marks of humanity only served to increase his dangerous beauty. Miremont could not help noticing how, as he bent to attend to his boots, the milky fabric of his shirt clung to his body, moulding itself to the muscles of his back and revealing his skin in glowing splashes like sun through mist. Even his feet were beautiful; long, slim, straight-toed, gracefully arched. Seared by desire and shame in equal measure and by a horror of the repugnance this innocent youth must feel could he read his thoughts, Miremont was no longer able to look.

He opened the book at random. Even through his pince-nez the print danced, so that for a moment he struggled to make out the text. He found to his surprise that he was reading Latin. Latin verse; the voice singular, instantly recognisable.

He could not help turning to the boy. But the young man had also decided to break the silence.

"Monsieur, I—"

"Tell me, monsieur—?"

As they both faltered, Miremont found himself accidentally meeting the boy's eyes. They were blue-grey, he noticed, the colour of slate, and deep-set, which had the effect of intensifying their gaze. He looked away hurriedly. "Forgive me. I interrupted you."

"No, monsieur. Please. It was nothing of consequence."

"If you're certain…? I was merely intending to ask…you are studying Latin?"

"When I can, monsieur."

"Then you are evidently…these verses…"

"Catullus."

"Yes. Not the easiest of texts. What do you make of him?" Too late Miremont realised the foolishness of his question, that he was about to stoke fire with fire.

The reply confirmed his danger. "He is incomparable. Rome's greatest poet. Certainly Rome's greatest love poet."

For all his confusion, Miremont could not bring himself to disavow Ovid. "But surely—?"

"In my opinion, that is, monsieur."

"Yet the language is raw. And the syntax—I'll grant you, it's spare, but it can seem inelegant."

"I admit, monsieur, that I came to Catullus only recently. So you will forgive me if…Oh, but—" here the boy's enthusiasm mastered his respectful constraint "—but you cannot deny it is the rawness and compression that give his voice such power. Such astonishing ability to convey passion. The Attis poem is extraordinary."

It seemed to Miremont that the covers of the book began to burn his fingers. He would prefer not to discuss Catullus's Attis, he-she, castrated by his own hand in frenzied worship of the goddess Cybele, then torn by equal frenzy at the loss of his manhood. There were also a great many other poems that must be avoided, poems with unsuitable references or expressions of desire. Even a conventional exercise like the hymn to Hymen alluded to the love of boys, despite being a celebration of marriage. Heaven knew, in his present state he would find it awkward enough to deal with the poet's tormenting passion for his mistress Lesbia. Yet he had begun this, had unstoppered this intoxicating yet poisonous bottle. He must set clear limits, steer the discussion into the safer waters of meter and imagery, concentrate on those few poems he could recall as harmless—the verses on Peleus and Thetis's wedding quilt, the translation from Callimachus.

"I agree," he began. "The Attis poem is fine, very fine indeed. Remarkable, even for Catullus. And I concede, there is a freshness, an energy in the way he treats myth. Consider, for instance, Ariadne and Theseus and the killing of the Minotaur…"

The words rolled from him, hurriedly and, it seemed to him, at random, on and on, so that he, who was not much given to pontificating, could have set up in competition with Bellac or Tarascon. The boy managed to interpose a comment once or twice, but then grew silent. Yet it seemed to Miremont, who spoke without looking at him, that he was still listening, no doubt with the silent contempt of the young for the prolixity of their elders, so that in Miremont's mind this profusion of words became the manifestation, like a great murky tide, of his shameful incontinence: for all the while as he spoke, hardly hearing himself, he was thinking entirely of what he must avoid, thinking of it, being goaded by it, whipped by it into a frenzy of desire that was worse, far worse, than any of the agonies he had endured for the last three years, until the pain rose up and constricted his throat and the words, crushed by the great burden of what they could not say, slowed. Then ceased to come.

There was a long and profoundly discomfiting pause. It was the boy, eventually, who broke it.

"You make no mention of the poems to Juventius."

The quiet way in which the young man said this compelled Miremont to look up. Instantly he regretted it, for he knew his shame was written in every contour of his face. But the boy looked back steadily. Then he smiled. It was a smile, Miremont was bewildered to realise, of complete understanding.

The young man rose to his feet and set off round the edge of the pool furthest from the waterfall, where the bank of mud and leaves appeared to open a pathway to the dense foliage behind the rock. After a moment's dazed hesitation, Miremont followed.

His disgrace and mortification were now complete. He could not bring himself to look at the boy, for he knew the picture he presented, standing there with his fly barely undone, fumbling for his handkerchief. An old man with an old man's lack of self-control. This was worse, even, than the Bois. He could not bear—it sickened him to recall the weary contempt of those pinched young faces, obliged to requite the lusts of repulsive lechers like himself, their sole emotion a burning impatience to extract payment and escape. But the boy, he discovered, was surveying him with an expression of sympathetic concern, as though he ascribed Miremont's over-eagerness to his own lack of finesse. He redirected Miremont's hands. It was apparent, astonishingly, that he thought, indeed expected, that Miremont would be capable of giving him pleasure.

Afterwards he said with a grin: "You can't refuse now."

Miremont stared at him.

"To bathe, monsieur. You really cannot refuse to bathe."

For all his reluctance to uncover his middle-aged body before this glorious specimen of youth, Miremont was a strong swimmer who usually rejoiced in the liberating shock of the water. Besides it was impossible for two bathers, even two strangers, splashing in the small expanse of the pool deep enough to keep them afloat, to continue constrained with each other. Their second encounter behind the rock was of an altogether different order. They swam again. Then both sat under the trees letting the warm air dry their linen.

All around them, apart from the chatter of the waterfall and the cawing of rooks, was silence. During their retreats to the fastness of the rock, during the time they had spent in the water, no single soul had disturbed them, no other walker on the path beyond the trees, no peasant driving his cattle: yet Miremont was dazed to find the bank as they had left it, the young man's coat tossed aside carelessly, the book still lying where it had dropped from his hands.

A sweet warmth flowed over him. He stretched and his muscles responded luxuriantly. Sitting with his throat uncovered and his hair falling damply over his forehead, inhaling the peaty, brackish smell of the water drying on his shirt, he felt, for the first time he was able to remember, unashamedly, expansively comfortable in his own skin. It was as if he had been unstrung and remade. He was filled with gratitude to the boy, who could scarcely be aware of the miracle he had worked.

Indeed, they were once more talking of books, no longer awkwardly it was true, but with the politeness required by chance acquaintance. But at least Miremont now dared study his companion. Yet, when he pondered the stroke of fate that had brought this miraculous young man here, at just this moment to just this seemingly enchanted spot, he found the boy something of a puzzle.

Of one thing, there remained no doubt: Miremont was struck anew by how extraordinarily handsome he was, of face as well as body. His hair, now it had dried, proved not to be dark, but a fine soft brown a shade or two lighter than the leaf mould, yet still in pleasing contrast to his clear pale skin. His jaw was definite, his cheekbones high, his nose straight and well-shaped. But the main force of his beauty resided in the interplay between his over-wide mouth with its full and sensuous upper lip (Miremont shivered to think he had been permitted to kiss it) and his penetratingly blue eyes. He had a way of smiling that seemed mysteriously protracted, so that, like the instant before a candle flame flares, there was a delay before the light reached his eyes, bestowing the smile at last like a beneficence—it took Miremont a while to realise that this resulted from the boy's odd habit of smiling without parting his lips.

Yet, despite this curious but charming quirk, he appeared pleasingly unconscious of his beauty. There was nothing girlish about him, none of the simpering prettiness Miremont would have found disagreeable, nothing to offer any intimation of his singular accomplishments. Taken as a whole, his was already a strong face, whose looks would be refined rather than destroyed by maturity, a distinctive face, not easily forgotten: in fact, fleetingly it seemed to Miremont that he did recall it, or at least that it reminded him of someone; but he could not have said who, and in any case the feeling, which was probably the product of such concentrated scrutiny, vanished as suddenly as it had come to him.

However, there were other puzzles. The boy's age, for instance? His complexion retained the flawless clarity of extreme youth, so that he might have been—Miremont, as his own years mounted, found it increasingly hard to judge—no more than eighteen: yet his assurance argued he must be older. Then, he seemed oddly hard to place in regard to his station and class. He was certainly no son of the soil; his well-kept hands and freedom from sunburn would have discounted that, had his education not so conclusively dismissed it: moreover his inflection strongly suggested the capital. Yet neither was he the son of local landed people for, while his manner was refined, it was a little too correct to be entirely gentlemanly. Furthermore, it was impossible not to notice that his shirt cuffs were frayed and his trousers were of cheap material that had seen better days. Then Miremont remembered their first conversation. So far as he could reconstruct that strained and painful exchange, he recalled the boy had talked about his studies. A university student. Of course. The promising son of some modest family hereabouts, forced by the scholar's traditional choice between eating or paying the rent to return home for a spell.

Miremont dared not enquire. He was grateful enough that the young man, from natural delicacy or perhaps following established etiquette in such situations, asked no questions about his own circumstances. Indeed, if they had not had books to talk about, conversation might soon have faltered. But, as it was, they continued absorbed, concluding the contest between Ovid and Catullus in amiable laughter—Miremont could not remember when he had last laughed unrestrainedly—then moving on through a veritable shelf of other authors. The boy was impressively well-read considering his youth, and not merely in the classics: he proved ardent about Baudelaire, praised modern poets—Verlaine, Mallarmé—who were unknown to Miremont, and had just finished Shakespeare's *Macbeth*, albeit in translation. He argued his points fluently, though sometimes with a young man's rashness, and if his studied correctness slipped occasionally, his fervour getting the better of the deference due to Miremont's years, Miremont merely liked him the more for it. He would have been delighted by the conversation in any ordinary setting. Here, by the waterfall, as the shade deepened, it seemed a further unlooked-for joy in an afternoon overwhelmed with pleasure. He gazed at the boy and longed once more to kiss that scornful, voluptuous mouth. But there was always the dread that someone might finally come along the path, and he felt a certain diffidence too, a fear of violating the arcane code that ruled their proceedings.

Besides, it had grown cooler and the light had left the water. The boy, glancing up at the position of the sun, went to find the rest of his clothes, while Miremont inspected his watch and recalled with consternation that he had a long walk ahead of him. He was already far too late to greet his returning fellow guests as a virtuously rested invalid, and in another half hour or so Thomas would begin wondering at his absence. The weight of duty descended on him again. True, supper on Sunday, when half the servants were off, was a less formal affair with dishes placed on the table in the old-fashioned manner, but he would still be expected to appear punctually and properly dressed.

They walked together as far as the start of the cart track, where the boy indicated he would take the fork to the village. Again Miremont was seized by the longing to kiss him but that, of course, was an impossibility now they were back in the world. Nor was it possible for Miremont to say what was in his heart for, had he dared, the words eluded him.

"Monsieur, I have much enjoyed—that is, I…"

The young man favoured him with his candle-flame smile. "I too, monsieur." Yet he was already turning, in a hurry to exchange adieus. To watch him disappear, to part without touching, without hope, was all at once insupportable.

"Shall you go there tomorrow?" Miremont called after him.

He paused, glanced back. "Not for a while." But, as though repenting the finality of this, he returned a few paces, seeming to hesitate, so that for an instant Miremont hoped once more. However, all he said eventually was: "We shall meet again, I'm sure of it." Then he was on his way, his coat swinging from his shoulder, his heels stirring a wake of white dust.

It was as it should be. A chance encounter, not to be repeated—for how was that possible when they had not even exchanged names? The act of repetition, the attempt to reproduce this perfect afternoon, would be like trying to recreate one's first taste of strawberries or one's first breath of sea air. Miremont was happy as he strode back towards the château and, if his happiness were commingled with regret, that merely intensified its sweetness. He would never again inhale the scent of leaf mould without recollecting the young man. He would never smell leaf mould without recalling this healing certainty, now, of what was natural to him.

As for his resolution to take flight for Beauvallon, well, he had not abandoned it. In fact, in his new frame of mind, he fervently longed to end his self-imposed exile, to repossess all that was loved and familiar and begin constructive work once more. But he had arrived back far too late to speak to Catherine before dinner and at table he was shamed by her forgiveness of his truancy.

"My darling Armand, I am only delighted our air is at last proving beneficial. You look positively transformed."

What could he do but smile benignly? He would broach the subject tomorrow.

Max, too, was in excellent spirits as he struck out for the village, where he would while away the remaining hours of his freedom at a corner table in the *tabac*, smoking and reading. He walked with a light step, playfully kicking the stones that fell into his path, sometimes singing, occasionally laughing out loud.

What a turn-up, what a complete stunner! He had craved an adventure and, while this had not been exactly what he had envisaged, it had certainly set his thoughts racing. What joy to see Fabrice's face when he discovered how they had both misread the old chap. Except, of course, that Max would not tell him (even supposing he could get a hearing, for, since the indignity of having to valet for M de Bellac, Fabrice had only one topic of conversation). But all the same, it was hard, this need to keep his jubilation to himself. His hopes, his future prospects restored—here was a prize to bring back from a Sunday off!

Max had not, of course, been so delighted when he had first observed an intruder in what he had come to regard as his own private retreat. And when, with the keener sight of youth, he had immediately recognised the figure in the straw hat and crumpled linen jacket, his annoyance had not diminished. What was the old fool doing here, when he was supposed to be admiring the geological marvels of St Mathilde? It seemed the old boy existed for the express purpose of plaguing him. Max did not forgive him the difficulties he had occasioned with Princess Zelenska. And now he, Max, would be required to quit the water, leaving pool, shade and solitude to the uninterrupted enjoyment of the noble gentleman forthwith.

Yet here was a thing. He had felt the heat of M de Miremont's glance even as he was obediently wading shoreward. The sly old bastard. So much for the princess! But yet, damn it!—Max should have guessed, if not merely from his rival's comical flight from her advances. There was bound to be some spark smouldering in such a resolutely damped grate. At any rate, here was the starchy old marquis quite obviously in the grip of a conflagration. Even before he had properly assessed the possibilities, Max had no doubt of it—this was a windfall.

Then had come his second surprise. From M le marquis' response when he wished him good-day he gathered the old boy did not know him. Yet Max was not altogether astounded. Certainly it was difficult for house guests to persist in ignoring their hostess's servants; usually, if they did not go so far as to remember names, or even clearly distinguish between individuals, they vaguely recalled faces. But M de Miremont, as Max had observed, seemed to exercise an extreme patrician fastidiousness in respect of the lower orders, preferring to deny their existence altogether. It was clearly to Max's advantage to continue unrecognised. All the same, it could prove tricky.

What if some enlightening shaft penetrated the carapace of the old fool's snobbery? Max was alarmed to find him in possession of the book. It seemed impossible that he should leaf through it and not come across madame's plate inside the front cover. Drawing the marquis' attention to his identity would at least divert him from this more damaging discovery, as well as saving embarrassment later. Max had been on the very point of confessing when the old boy had begun talking about Catullus. After that, confession had become increasingly impossible.

Max grinned to himself. They had certainly been comic, the marquis' stutterings and stammerings. Yet who would have thought he had anything in his head but lists of precedence and armorial bearings? As the afternoon progressed, the old boy had turned out to be made of surprises. Take his astonishing innocence, for example—where had he been all his long life? It was tempting to mock. But dangerous too: there had been that awkward moment that had threatened Max's entire enterprise, before he had grasped the true state of affairs. However, to M de Miremont's credit, he had not taken flight, nor tried to save his dignity with angry bluster. On the contrary, like Old Jouvert that wintry night amongst the rubble and the brambles, he had proved pathetically grateful, indeed had continued grateful for the smallest attentions, as though a couple of clumsy kisses were an unimaginable privilege.

In spite of himself, Max had found this unexpected humility rather touching. Nor could he help warming to the old boy's courtesy.

Whatever his draconian line with minions, with someone he rated worthy of his notice the noble gentleman showed no side at all, was generous with his cigarette case, seemed modest, unassuming and, unusual for madame's circle, somewhat unworldly.

He was not, when you came down to it, even so old. His hair was still thick, without traces of grey and, once he had overcome his prudery and stripped off his clothes, he had turned out to be in good shape for a man of his years, flat-bellied, muscular, unexpectedly athletic. Even his lined face, a little rumpled like his jacket, had been transformed by their literary debate: his eyes alight and his damp hair falling recklessly over his brow, he had appeared, if not youthful precisely, then certainly unrecognisable as the waxwork who graced madame's table.

Indeed, it was no longer such a puzzle to divine what she saw in him. In defiance of society's strict measure (not to mention Fabrice's theories), M de Miremont turned out definitely to have his points. He might be an innocent old fool in some respects, but in others—well, his erudition could crush Messieurs de Tarascon and Bellac, if ever he felt their need to perform intellectual gymnastics for the company's admiration.

Max was still exhilarated by their discussion. Deprived of his Sundays at the Zhukovskys', subjected nightly to Fabrice's jeremiads and to the hostile lowing of the Bordelais contingent (whom Fabrice, no kinder than Michel, had christened the Oxen), starved, in short, of anything to exalt the spirit, he had found this unexpected chance to engage his mind as invigorating as the water. He felt he had acquitted himself well enough: the marquis had acknowledged his views respectfully and without the slightest trace of condescension.

M le marquis de Miremont was altogether so much better a proposition than Princess Zelenska. Polite conversation would not be a problem, which was more than could be said for the princess. Nor would Max need to play the ludicrous and incomprehensible games that seemed indispensable to women: he knew what M de Miremont required better than the old boy himself. And surely, for all the gossip, a man of his rank would hardly lack illustrious connections (Max had gathered from the dinner table that he counted the duc de la Marne among his intimates as well as madame, so he could not be a total recluse). More pertinent still, Princess Zelenska was yet to be conquered (and if Max were truthful, she was probably a precipice he lacked the stamina to scale). Whereas M de Miremont was already his —Max had only to recall the old chap's face at their parting.

But this was not his only reason for filling his lungs and hurling joyful snatches of Beethoven like firecrackers across the empty fields. He was under no real illusions as to the limits of M de Miremont's civility. If the marquis had treated him as an equal it was because he had thought him—well, not a true equal obviously, but someone whose station in life was not so greatly beneath his own. Max had passed. He had passed, even to the most discerning eye, as a gentleman. The scar would stand scrutiny and now so, too, would he. After three years of relentless work, observing, analysing, crushing his natural inclinations, he had achieved his transformation.

There remained, of course, one obvious difficulty. The truth would come as a shock to the old boy and it might have been kinder to prepare him, although in the end it had proved unthinkable—the joys of equality had been too sweet. However, Max was confident the marquis could be brought to see the folly of his prejudice. He placed great faith in that parting look.

CHAPTER NINE

Armand de Miremont slept without recourse to Gérard's sedative draught and awoke refreshed, if earlier than was his habit. Ringing for Thomas to shave and dress him and noting the dew was still on the grass, he decided upon a stroll in the gardens before breakfast. His recollection of the previous afternoon was vivid yet still delightfully without shame: he was warmed once more by unaccustomed happiness. But, for all that, he was clear-headed. Today a luncheon was planned, alfresco, at some vantage point an hour's drive away. Thus Catherine was bound to appear downstairs by mid-morning. He had only to take her aside before the carriages set out and, without inconvenience to her or her household, he could catch the earliest train tomorrow. He could tell her with sincerity that he would cherish his memories of La Boissière.

However, not for the first time, Miremont was experiencing that remarkable phenomenon of the human mind, its capacity to entertain simultaneously two coherent but entirely contradictory strains of thought. While his reason was preoccupied with railway timetables and packing and the need to write to Lesage, a rebel voice, which he recognised as the incubus, was cursing the picnic because it deprived him of the chance to visit the waterfall again (true, the boy had said he would not be there, but he might change his plans). He fretted that he knew neither where the young man lived, nor even his name: yet was his ignorance an insuperable obstacle? Such a notably handsome and intelligent youth would not go unknown in the village. Miremont's enquiries must be discreet, of course, he must think of some pretext— that he had offered to lend the boy a book. But, if he breakfasted hastily, he could walk to the village and be back before the carriages set out at noon.

Thus Miremont, as he returned to the house, was at the same time on a train to Beauvallon and walking up some muddy cart track towards a cottage door, where a respectable, aproned matron, dusting flour from her hands, was smiling and calling into the shadowed interior that her son must come at once, he had a visitor…Except— damn Gérard—Miremont could hardly pillage Catherine's library and otherwise the only book he could lay his hands on was *The Quarryman's*

Daughter. Never mind, over breakfast he would think of something.

Miremont usually took his coffee and brioches in the privacy of his bedroom, but this morning, since he was up and dressed, he had instructed Thomas that he would be breakfasting downstairs. On entering the breakfast room he immediately regretted this decision. It was true the atmosphere was one of hushed calm: although the windows to the terrace had been thrown open the blinds were partly drawn, so that despite the brilliance of the early morning sun the room was plunged into a soft, aquatic gloom, in which the footmen, shadowy in their morning livery of corbeau tails and trousers, glided noiseless as underwater swimmers from sideboard to table. Nor was the company large: all the ladies, following Catherine's example, appeared to prefer lingering in bed and there was thankfully no sign of Aristide de Bellac; Cressy and his elder nephew, Amadé, were deep in newspapers, while the younger nephew, Ignate, was silently brooding over his coffee and La Rochefontaine was preoccupied with his post. All the same, everyone looked up when Miremont entered and he was obliged to exchange pleasantries. His two strands of thought were instantly sundered by his dread of enforced conversation.

But there was worse to come. He was no sooner seated and had been presented with his own letters and newspaper, than he was struck by the most extraordinary sensation, at first pleasurable but increasingly shocking. He had no need—he did not dare—to look round: he knew, even before a well-remembered voice enquired if he would care for coffee, who was standing beside his chair. He watched the liquid pouring into his cup, he stared at the gloved hand tilting the pot, the outstretched arm in its dark worsted, so close to his shoulder it seemed to scorch him. He continued to stare as the arm retreated, as the presence moved away and was all at once in clear view. There was no mistaking that straight back, that set of the head, no mistaking the profile as its owner bent to dispense coffee to Gilbert de Cressy. Mesmerised, Miremont watched the boy go the rounds of the table, to La Rochefontaine next, then Ignate de Cressy. Oh there was no question: without the wig, it was even possible to make out that distinctive scar on his temple, not quite hidden by the way he brushed his hair. He wore the look all good servants wore, oblique, impassive, but with the touch of hauteur footmen liked to affect. Yet, as he straightened up from attending to Amadé de Cressy, he seemed, quite deliberately, to meet Miremont's eye and on those provocative lips— Miremont was not mistaken about this—the ghost of a smile flickered.

Then he was gone, disappearing in the direction of the sideboard. Miremont could feel his presence somewhere behind him, like heat.

He was aware that his forehead was damp and his face must be scarlet. Much to his relief, the table seemed oblivious: Amadé de Cressy was reading a newspaper article to his uncle, while Ignate, who had pretensions to being a poet and did not espouse his family's Rightist views, was affecting sardonic detachment; La Rochefontaine remained engaged with his letters. Nevertheless, Miremont dared not mop his brow or reach for his coffee cup. Yet he must do something to hide his turmoil: shakily he retrieved his pince-nez, which had slid from his nose, and tore open the first envelope from the pile beside his plate.

Of the emotions that buffeted him— shock, embarrassment, shame and even, for one unthinking second, a flash of wild joy—what predominated was horror. The boy had lied to him. If he had been aware for one instant, if he had understood this apparent stranger had any connection with Catherine's household, if he had realised the youth had known exactly who he was, he would never, good God, never have put himself in this position. But the boy, who had seemed such a charming companion, had lied to him.

Yet who was to blame? The boy, most certainly, for deceiving him. But he could no longer pretend the young man had been a total stranger. With the shock of discovery had come the terrible certainty that this was the footman who tidied the library shelves, the footman who was teaching the Zelenski child to ride a bicycle. Miremont should have exercised more caution. But, old fool that he was, blinded by lust, he had allowed himself to be entrapped. For what had Achille de Tarascon implied about this particular footman—that he was a bad lot?

Miremont, recalling the boy's covert smile, found sinister meaning suddenly in that faint twist of the lips. Was that it—blackmail? The unread letter quivered in his hands. He must leave at once, forget the customary civilities, write Catherine a note pleading some emergency. He could no longer sit here, feeling the boy's glance and sensing that the very set of his shoulders betrayed him, knowing how well-satisfied the young man must be by his consternation. He must summon Thomas and instruct him to pack. Seizing his post and mumbling his excuses to the table, he rose and made blindly for the door. Mercifully it was another footman who opened it for him, but he was acutely aware of his persecutor, standing respectfully to attention by the sideboard; and he felt certain, though he did not dare divert his glance, that the boy again shot him a meaningful look.

Upstairs in his room, which he had quitted in such a different mood not an hour previously, Miremont struggled with his misfortune. He could not even seek sanctuary at Beauvallon, he realised, for blackmailers were persistent, the contagion would follow him there, or to Paris: with a shudder he imagined Lesage, in the performance of his daily duties, innocently opening the inevitable letter. Miremont's only recourse was the one most distasteful to him. He must confront the youth here and now, discover his price and pay him off. After that, he would probably be well-advised to go abroad for a spell.

But arranging such a confrontation was fraught with difficulty. He could not ask to have a particular footman sent to him without drawing attention to the relationship he was at such pains to conceal. Nor could he guarantee finding the young man on his own, in circumstances where an interview of this nature would be possible. In his despair, Miremont wondered what Tarascon would do. But of course, it was obvious, even to someone as innocent of the workings of the criminal underworld as Miremont: the blackmailer would come to him. Miremont shivered. He had only to wait upon the young man's whim.

The grounds of a derelict convent provided the picturesque setting for the picnic, at the summit of a hill whose escarpment dropped precipitously into a valley terraced with vines, in which, far below, the huddled buildings of an ancient hamlet were strung like ivory beads on a river's silver thread. To delight the visitors, as well as the views of the wooded hills beyond and the panorama afforded to the west across open countryside, there were the convent buildings themselves, most particularly the chapel, decorated by the nuns with primitive frescos of the life of Our Lady. The chapel had been deconsecrated, the frescos were faded and worn away completely in many places, consumed by a mange of damp and decay. But all the same most of the visitors were keen to view this curiosity while the servants were setting up the table for luncheon, particularly as its dim and echoing interior offered some respite from the enervating heat. Few stayed long before seeking the more congenial shade of the convent's overgrown garden: the corroded masonry gave off an uncanny chill and the stench of damp was overpowering, while several of the ladies wrinkled their noses at the guano encrusting the sanctuary flagstones where the altar had once stood. Miremont soon found himself alone.

This ruin, with its vaulted columns soaring vainly towards a rotten and gaping roof, its melancholy odour of fervent yet blighted yearnings, exactly suited his mood. His panic had not subsided: when he had eventually been obliged to leave the safety of his room he had flinched at the mere glimpse of a livery, so that, finding himself seated opposite Catherine in her open landau with the two footmen perched on the tailboard in direct view—one, inevitably, his nemesis— he had suffered acutely. But other emotions now contended with his fear. In spite of Tarascon, it was hard to believe the boy was irredeemably bad. Miremont was not one of those, like Aline's brother Robert, who proudly maintained they were an unerring judge of character: yet all the same—it was not simply the young man's physical beauty that swayed him—Miremont found it difficult to accept that the sympathy he had felt between them had been pure illusion. Undeniably, the boy had lied and must have done so for a purpose. But how could Miremont, who had never suffered deprivation himself, know what someone could be driven to by debt or family troubles? He could not bring himself to hate the boy. As he watched a pair of martins chase the glancing sunlight in through the shattered timbers, swooping to their nest above the chancel window, his strongest emotion was grief.

The creaking of the door brought him up with a start.

"Monsieur will forgive me…"

The boy stood framed in the white light of the doorway, so that he appeared faceless, a mere dark shape in a tricorne and tail coat, a sinister silhouette. Miremont's panic repossessed him. So this was it. The words burst from him: "What do you want ?"

"Madame requests me to inform M le marquis that luncheon is served."

Miremont stared at the boy. Now that he had moved from the door, halting a few respectful paces away, and his expression was plainly visible, it was possible to discern only the blank, impervious mask of the well-trained servant. No smile, no insinuating look, not even a hint that he was ruffled by Miremont's tone; his glance, as was proper, avoided all contact.

An inner voice told Miremont that he was a preposterous idiot, that his fears had been entirely fanciful, the product of his own shame. The young man had clearly understood from his demeanour at breakfast that there could be no further connection between them. Miremont was free to go to Beauvallon whenever he pleased and forget the entire incident. However, a second voice—the voice of reason?—warned that this was cowardice.

"I asked you what you want of me."

"Luncheon, monsieur, is—"

"Don't prevaricate. You lied to me. You told me you were a student."

The servant's mask slipped as though the boy were genuinely taken aback. "Forgive me, monsieur, but I know I did not."

"You told me you were studying the classics."

"When I was able, monsieur. "

Miremont was dimly aware that this might well be true: however he could not allow himself to weaken. "All the same, you did not alert me to the fact—you did not tell me the truth about your situation."

"I assumed you knew me."

This was said with such conviction and contained, for Miremont, such a justifiable reproach that for an instant he was inclined utterly to believe it—until he recalled yesterday's parting. "You were well aware that I did not. You deceived me. I require an explanation."

"Monsieur—" the boy glanced towards the door "—forgive me, but luncheon is waiting—"

"You refuse to explain?"

"I should be glad to. But, as I'm sure monsieur realises, for discretion's sake, this is not the moment."

"Then tell me when?"

"Tonight? After the company retires?"

Miremont hesitated. "Very well. Where?"

"The Italian garden? The pavilion?"

Miremont blanched. He could not imagine anything more compromising than being discovered with a servant late at night in the gardens. "No. Impossible."

"Then where, monsieur?"

There seemed only one place where privacy could be guaranteed. "My room. You know how to find it?"

The boy nodded. "As monsieur wishes."

As Miremont walked out into the sunlight with the boy two or three paces behind, he was chilled by his own folly—here was a meeting-place more unsuitable, even, than the pavilion. In obeying the dictates of reason, he had somehow managed to compromise himself further. If it had been reason speaking, that is.

*

Miremont sat in the window embrasure of his tower room listening to the sounds of the sleeping house. He still wore his tails—he had dismissed Thomas early—and he hoped he presented the picture of composure. Nevertheless, every creaking board, every distantly closing door, made him start.

Since luncheon, reflection had wrought a considerable change in his mood. He no longer believed the boy intended blackmail and was ashamed to have imagined it. Indeed, he was altogether rather ashamed of himself. Miremont would have been shocked by Max's harsh assumptions, for he hoped he extended to servants the courtesy he showed his equals. In this instance, however, he must admit he had been remiss and deserved the boy's reproach. For here was the footman, he now discovered, who stood in waiting behind him every mealtime, who pulled out his chair and unfurled his napkin. He should certainly have known him.

There were excuses he might offer. It could be difficult to place someone outside his usual sphere and in different dress. For years, until the old man had retired, Miremont had been on friendly terms with Gervais de la Marne's first footman, Etienne, chatting to him about his sister and his numerous nephews and nieces. Yet one day last winter he had been mystified when an elderly stranger in a well-worn covert coat had tipped his bowler to him: Miremont had tipped in return, of course, but it was not until hours later, back in his study, that he had identified his mystery acquaintance.

A stronger excuse was that he had been misled by the boy's erudition. On reflection, it had been absurd to take him for a student: his manner and stringently barbered hair clearly marked him for what he was. Yet how many footmen chose Catullus for their Sunday-afternoon reading? Was it not natural to assume that any young man with such gifts, however poor his circumstances, would want to put them to better use?

But Miremont was uncomfortably aware that none of this would wash. His own capacity to deceive himself had assisted the boy's deception. All the same, he could hardly explain the ridiculous and, as it turned out, futile precautions he had taken to avoid being tempted. Nor could he describe the curiously bifurcated, contrary instrument his mind had become since his affliction, how it could resolve upon one thing and promptly choose another, how it could know something and not know it, receive the indelible impress of that lithe and joyful figure setting free Stanislaw Zelenski's bicycle and yet deny all recognition of it, absolutely.

It saddened him, of course, that the boy had not told him the truth, but perhaps in the circumstances that was understandable. In his new mood of penitence, Miremont deeply regretted his unpleasant suspicions, which had tainted the precious memory of yesterday. He did not forget the debt of gratitude he owed. This interview, rash as it was, at least gave him the chance to make it up to the boy, to offer some token—a sum for books, perhaps—by way of affectionate farewell before his departure.

The contemplation of this gesture and the pleasure it would bring should have soothed Miremont, but his heart was racing: when at last the soft knock came upon the door, he trembled.

Fearing to call out lest he be heard on the landing, Miremont rose and admitted his visitor. The boy, who still wore his livery, though not his wig, entered silently and without smiling. When Miremont, discomfited by the bed's looming presence, directed him to the armchair near the window, he shook his head.

"If monsieur will excuse me, I prefer to stand."

This was not at all what Miremont had been expecting. It appeared the boy, too, had been turning over events, to rather different effect. Miremont was torn between his obligation to rebuke this cold hostility and a surge of dismay. At the same time, the scornful tilt of the boy's chin left him helplessly noting, all over again, how beautiful he was.

"My dear young man—Jean—it is Jean, is it not?"

"Monsieur, if you will give me leave—you asked me here to account for myself."

"By all means. But should you not be easier seated?"

"I shall try to be brief and not waste monsieur's time." The boy's eye suddenly fixed Miremont's. "What if I told you it was I who failed to know you?"

This was calculated insolence but, since Miremont already conceded the point, he chose to overlook it. "You are quite right, of course. I can make no excuse, I should have recognised you. I owe you an unreserved apology."

The boy seemed taken aback: to Miremont's relief, his expression softened. However, while Miremont was unwilling to stand upon his dignity where he felt himself to be in the wrong, he could not, even to propitiate the young man, concede what should not properly be conceded. He paused, choosing his words carefully.

"I was guilty of great incivility. But all the same, you know—I fear we were both at fault. Once you realised my lapse, you had a duty to make yourself known to me."

He seemed to have struck the right note, for the boy smiled faintly. "It was not the occasion for an exchange of visiting cards."

"I appreciate…naturally…" Miremont was ashamed to feel himself blush. "Nevertheless, in this case, given the circumstances, complete honesty would have been best."

"So I lied to you?"

This sudden change of tone startled Miremont. "I am merely suggesting you should have been more open."

"First I am accused of pretending to be a student—"

"We are agreed, I was mistaken. "

"Now I am charged with lying in general."

"No, of course not—"

"I lied to you, with some underhand purpose."

"Young man, you are twisting my words—"

"Were you not unhappy, yesterday, in my company?"

"Unhappy? I hope you know what pleasure it gave me."

"You were pleased to sit talking with a liar and a crook?"

"Oh, my dear young man—"

"Yesterday it was 'monsieur'. Today I am 'young man'. Yesterday it was 'Tell me your view of the *Ars Amatoria*'. Today it is 'Give me an explanation,' and 'What do you want of me?' Well, monsieur, I want nothing of you. I want nothing today, I wanted nothing yesterday. Except what, unless I am deceived, you were not averse to yourself."

To emphasise his words, since he must perforce keep his voice down, the boy had abandoned his haughty stance and had begun furiously pacing the carpet. Miremont flinched from that last sally. He wondered in bewilderment how they had arrived here. It came to him that, all along, whatever he had expected from this interview, his greatest hope had been to embrace the boy and cover him with kisses. But the young man seemed implacable. It was as though he took a perverse delight in his anger. Indeed, if he had paused, it was apparently to muster strength for a further outburst.

"I came here to explain my conduct, monsieur, as requested, and if I had been allowed to offer my explanation—though I suppose I should not expect it to be believed—"

"Young man—Jean—this is preposterous!"

"If I had been allowed, I could have assured you that I did try to tell you who I was. Twice. When first we began to talk, and then again when we came to say our goodbyes."

Miremont recalled the boy's hesitation as they had stood at the cross-roads, and his own thirst for hope. He spoke more gently: "But you said nothing."

"The first time—well, as you will remember, monsieur, events overtook us." Here, surprisingly, the boy smiled, as if he, too, found the memory not altogether disagreeable. "And when we were parting— it was stupid I know, it certainly seems the utmost folly in retrospect, for I had nothing to gain from keeping silent and you were bound to find out anyway—but I could not bring myself to do it. I did not think you would thank me."

"Why ever not?"

"For spoiling your afternoon."

Miremont's conscience was caught. "Oh, but that is absurd. My dear boy, you do me—you do us both an injustice."

"Do I, monsieur?"

"I should never have...This morning, you must understand, I received a severe shock—but yesterday...Well, I should have been surprised, of course."

"Surprised?"

"Well, yes. Naturally. You have such excellent Latin."

The compliment, Miremont was puzzled to see, far from pleasing the boy, caused him to stiffen. Miremont felt battered by these mercurial changes of mood. It struck him that he was being played with. Worn out by the strain of standing (for, since the boy had refused to sit, he had scrupled to make a pointed assertion of rank by doing so himself) and frayed by the ever-present fear that, despite the tower's thick walls, they would wake Ignate de Cressy in the room beyond his dressing room, he found himself suddenly, absurdly, close to tears. The boy stood no more than six paces away. The incubus urged him to have done with pride, to cross the strip of rug that divided them, fling himself upon the young man's neck, beg him to make love to him. He retreated so that the barrier of the armchair stood between them. Leaning on its back, he lowered his head and took a deep breath.

"We have—there have been misunderstandings on both sides. But let us not part at odds."

At least the boy seemed to assent to this.

"Nothing can alter the fact that it was a delightful afternoon."

"Yes, monsieur. It was."

"I shall remember it warmly. And I should like to show my appreciation." Miremont moved to the writing desk for his notecase. "I should like, at least, to—"

"No!"

Miremont was halted with the notecase in his hands.

"Monsieur is gracious. But no. Thank you."

"My dear boy. Out of friendship. To assist with your studies."

The young man was staring at him. His face was white, his eyes blazing. "You did not offer to tip me yesterday."

"This is not a tip, merely a gesture of—"

"You felt no need to make gestures yesterday. When we sat and talked like two human beings."

"Oh, my dear fellow—"

"But clearly the man you talked to yesterday no longer exists." No question this time the boy's anger was real: his voice, as he continued, was icy. "That being the case, monsieur, you have no more cause for worry. Yesterday you met a man who does not exist and did certain things with him that cannot have happened, during an afternoon that never was. Your reputation and honour are safe!"

CHAPTER TEN

Max had never intended to go so far. He had meant only to shake the old boy up a little, to teach him the error of his ways before relenting. But the destruction of his illusions and the affront to his pride had proved more than he could bear.

He was in the right, of course. Yet, as he crawled out of bed the next morning and belatedly joined the dormitory scrimmage for hot water and the shaving glass, he had seldom been more depressed. Usually set-backs to his grand plan spurred him to anger or impatience, but now, for the first time, he found himself questioning his own capacities.

It was not simply that three years' hard work had apparently gone for nothing. A student! Perhaps Fabrice, curse him, was right and Max should have consulted a tailor. But in any case, if M de Miremont had been for an instant deceived, which seemed unlikely, his prejudices were now fixed like thumb prints in mortar. Given that this was so, had it not been a grave miscalculation to humiliate the old boy? Wallenstein and Napoleon had furthered their careers, not merely by courage and skill, but through acute political instinct. Yet here was he, Max, still making elementary misjudgements, ignoring reason, as much a prey to his passions as when he had fought the restraints of the cloister. First madame, now this. Did he imagine his opportunities would be limitless? Was he happy to spend the rest of his life catching Fabrice's elbow in his ribs, tripping over Guillaume's boots, one more piece of lumpen and already sweating humanity jostling to pull on the trappings of his servitude?

It would be politic to apologise to the old boy. Yet it was by no means certain how M de Miremont would receive an apology. After rising late the marquis spent most of the day closeted in the library, giving Max little chance to judge his mood. At luncheon, it was true, one remarkable alteration could be noted in the old fellow's behaviour: he addressed all the footmen punctiliously by name and made a point of looking at them directly. But, as he gravely thanked Max for pulling out his chair, there was no hint of familiarity, nothing conciliatory or suppliant in his manner, merely a melancholy dignity that was as impenetrable, in its way, as his previous blindness. Max, studying the

nape of the old boy's neck, would have given much to swap places
with Fabrice standing opposite. All the same, there were certain
indications, particularly at dinner—a dejected droop to the old fellow's
shoulders, a marked reluctance to take food —that suggested his pride
might crack. Max pondered the wisdom of risking a second nocturnal
visit uninvited. It was hard to judge: he might merely be giving the old
boy another opportunity to put him in his place.

Besides, there was a further obstacle to apology, a difficulty which,
despite the promptings of reason, Max could not bring himself to
overcome. If he climbed down over the money he would be lowering
himself irretrievably in M de Miremont's eyes. He would become to
the old boy as he was to M de Tarascon. For him, too, it would be as
though the conversation by the waterfall had never happened.

The certainty that he could not, would not back down did nothing
to console him. That night as, without the heart to read, he lay
listening to the snoring of the Oxen and Fabrice's scratching, he could
not help remembering M de Miremont's own courteous apology, nor
prevent himself from thinking that the old boy's offer, however insulting,
might have been generously meant. Yes, right was on his side. But he
could not escape the feeling that he had treated the old fellow badly.

Max's spirits would hardly have been lifted had he known of the
marquis' plans for flight. Armand de Miremont had resolved to rise at
dawn and give Thomas his orders without further shilly-shallying.
That he had sunk so low, that he had been obliged to hold himself
back from pleading with the boy—this was a disease far beyond
Gérard's prescriptions. However in the morning he had felt too
wretched to stir from his bed.

To rouse himself, he sought to nurture his offended feelings into a
flourishing conviction of his own righteousness. But he was merely
reminded miserably of Aline. Whatever efforts he had made to be fair
and generous, she too had always twisted his words against him. Yet he
allowed—must allow, particularly given his new and guilty self
knowledge—that he was as much at fault. And was it not, after all, to
the young man's credit that he had rejected the money? As for the lad's
anger—when Miremont recalled his own unworthy suspicions he could
see too well how his benevolence might be misunderstood. Besides,
supposing their positions had been reversed? By what right did he
assume that the boy, because he was a servant, must be grateful for
condescension? Miremont, whose good fortune it had been never to

be troubled by such considerations, was ashamed to realise the blow he must have dealt the young man's amour-propre.

If he had hurt the boy, it was incumbent on him to make amends. And here the incubus chimed in to offer sudden hope: the previous night's interview had not, after all, been without its encouraging moments. As ever, of course, opportunity was a problem. But perhaps fate would be kind to him. Having summoned Thomas, he dressed and went down to the library, where he rang the bell for coffee. But fate sent him the young man with the heavy thighs and the prominent mole on his upper lip, one of the local lads, rather surly—Guillaume, Miremont thought his name was. And when the tray was retrieved, the boy who came was Victor, a slimmer version of Guillaume, perhaps his brother, red-cheeked and more obliging, though that was little comfort.

But it was not until luncheon that Miremont's hopes were utterly dashed. He had persuaded himself that the boy, too, was wretched. Perhaps he had even expected some small gesture of reconciliation, a fleeting look, a return of the covert smile. But the youth who pulled out his chair and nodded to him respectfully might have been a stranger: his face was such a model of blank indifference that Miremont had to turn away hastily to hide his anguish. Nor was his pain diminished when later, having retired once more to the library, his sightless contemplation of Horace's *Odes* was interrupted by the crackle of gravel and shrieks of laughter. He looked up in time to see Stanislaw Zelenski fly past the window on his bicycle with Jean, at full pelt, in pursuit. They appeared to be engaged in some sort of race, at any rate their antics seemed to amuse them both mightily: as they shot out of sight in the direction of the stable wing, their laughter drifted back, the child's high giggle and the boy's staccato gasps, winded, punctuated by shouts of mock protest, but entirely unfeigned.

Dinner was torture. Miremont had never given thought to it before, but the business of waiting, of being waited upon, the attentive yet impersonal presence at his left elbow, considerately offering dishes, removing plates, concerned to gratify his slightest whim, seemed a ghastly parody of intimacy. As they bent towards each other, hands all but brushing in the joint endeavour of transferring artichoke hearts or turbot fillets to his plate, as he heard the boy's soft impartial words of encouragement—"A little more, monsieur?"—and felt his breath on his cheek, Miremont lost the power to hold the servers steady.

Yes, his situation was ridiculous. He recalled acquaintances from Aline's time, grown men reduced to idiocy by some actress or other.

He had never understood it, yet here was he showing all the symptoms of similar folly. He thought of Tarascon again. Would Tarascon allow himself to be crushed by a chance encounter? Would Tarascon have worried about the boy's feelings or even cared whether he were a liar? It seemed to Miremont that he was hopelessly ill-equipped for the curious new world he had entered.

Already Catherine was fussing over his long face and lack of appetite, enquiring whether his indisposition of Sunday had returned. He should have made clear his intentions then, of course, but once again it would have seemed a churlish response to her kindness and, besides, it would hardly have been civil to announce his departure before the company at large. However, go he must. He could not allow himself to be delayed by sentimental notions. The boy's indifference proclaimed that any parting interview was pointless. Besides, he no longer trusted himself to speak.

Yet, after another wretched night in which sleep eluded him until dawn, he woke, as before, numb with misery. Sending back his breakfast tray untouched, he had resolve only to struggle as far as the library, where he once again sat blindly staring at Horace.

In Paris, the middle of the morning offered certain gifts to footmen. With madame breakfasting in her room, no visitors expected until the afternoon and M Vincent safely closeted with Mme Pinot discussing household matters, chances arose to truant, to pretend some errand and stroll the boulevards. But in the country, as well as the laying, serving and clearing of breakfast and the laying-up of luncheon, there were bells ringing incessantly. Only Michel continued to exercise the footman's unwritten prerogative: if taken to task by M Vincent, he justified his disappearances by claiming some urgent command from madame. As for his work, he would bully or blackmail someone—usually Fabrice—into doing it for him.

Despite his acid tongue, Fabrice was curiously incapable of shrugging off Michel's insults. Whether the years of persecution had worn him down, or whether the first footman's jibes, crude though they were, evoked some other distant but more telling voice, his protests usually crumbled and he could even be brought close to tears. Neither had his lot been improved by the arrival of Aristide de Bellac. Certainly his complaints were long and loud, but they were not without warrant. For it was not merely the famous novelist's wardrobe that offended his sensibilities. M de Bellac having been too mean to bring his own man (or perhaps his valet had deserted—that was not unlikely), Fabrice was deputed, as Max was with M de Cressy, to help the literary gentleman dress for dinner. However M de Bellac wilfully ignored this limitation, harrying Fabrice as though he had been gifted to him as his personal servant. The mornings, when M de Bellac lay in bed reading his post and writing to his many devoted readers, saw Fabrice up and down stairs as though on elastic.

"'Plump my pillows, file my nails, shave me, fetch me more violet ink!' She lolls there with her great hairy belly straining her night-shirt like a—like a pregnant sea lion. Yesterday—can you imagine, dear heart?—she demanded I scratch her back!"

Fabrice had complained to M Vincent, but to no effect. Michel, too, was unmoved by his sufferings; they merely sharpened his appetite for sport. That morning, coming in from the garden, Max could hear Fabrice's voice from the other end of the passage, plaintive, teetering towards hysteria.

"You *know* I can't. You *know* I'm already at my wit's end!"

"Oh dear, oh dear, fetch the smelling salts. Frightened, are we, of getting our dainty feet wet?"

After days of sun, the household had woken to a deluge: sheets of rain veiled the gardens, rain hammered on windowpanes and rattled from gutters; the sky trembled with thunder and indoors lamps and fires had been hastily lit. Max, whose duty it was supposed to be this morning to attend guests on the terrace, had been forced to rush out at the rising bell to check that nothing had been left astray on the lawns, and, now that breakfast was cleared, suddenly recalling Stanislaw Zelenski's bicycle, he had once more plunged into the downpour to ensure it was under cover. His cape left a watery trail as he came down the passage and into the thick of the altercation.

From what he could gather, madame had left Michel a note for the head gardener about the day's flowers, but Michel was not disposed to make the sodden trek to the hothouses when he could find more comfortable employment (such as pursuing the under-parlour maid who had recently seized his fancy).

"You'll manage, Nancy."

"Don't call me that!"

"It'll only take a minute."

"I haven't *got* a minute. As it is, M de Bellac wants his boots polished—he doesn't care for the way Alphonse does them. *And* I'm on bells this morning. I'm utterly at his mercy!"

"Oooh dear! Oooh my! So we'd rather be at the mercy of Cardinal Vincent, would we? When he finds out where that bottle of cognac disappeared to last night."

"Oh, for Christ's sake, Michel. Leave him be!"

Max always fought the urge to intervene on Fabrice's behalf, indeed rather resented its demands. It reminded him forcibly of the Other, of that bond not of his choosing that had brought him countless beatings, that had taught him well-intentioned actions can have dire consequences, that there is a tenacious power in weakness for which strength is no match. Besides, since his so-called failure with madame, he was on dangerous ground. True, he sensed that Michel, despite his sneers, remained wary of him. But there were obvious risks in taking Fabrice's part: even if Max did not damn himself by association, he was courting trouble. Nevertheless, although he had concentrated with determination on hanging up his cape, natural impulse and his present grim mood had proved too much for him. And all thought of caution died when Michel pointedly ignored the interruption.

"Yes, Nancy. The Cardinal would love the answer to that little mystery. Though if he puts a match to your breath—"

"I said, leave him be."

"Did somebody speak?"

As Michel turned to square up to him, Max once more felt the urge to divest madame's favourite of his over-sized front teeth.

"Well, bless me if it isn't Milord Merde. Poking his toffee nose in where it's got no business. What are you, Nancy's big brother? I've told you before—"

"And I've told you."

"You don't tell me anything, shitface. In case you've forgotten, I'm first footman."

"Do the job and I'll remember."

"Yes, do your own work for a change!" chimed in Fabrice, not altogether helpfully.

Michel turned briefly to spit. "Jesus, you're a pair!" His lip curled at Max. "You're almost as bad as he is. We all know what's in your trousers isn't much to write home about."

"At least," said Max levelly, "I don't keep my brains there. And, since we're talking of mysterious disappearances, perhaps the Cardinal would care to hear about that candelabrum that went missing just before we left Paris. Or those cases of champagne that got lost on the way from the wine merchants—"

"Why, you fucking—"

"Gentlemen! Gentle-*men*."

All three froze. M Vincent was not physically imposing, being a slight, sleek, olive-skinned man, neatly but delicately made, and being given, into the bargain, to certain vanities that might have been risible in another of his age; his oiled black hair, where it caught the light, displayed a pigeon-breast sheen that betrayed the dye bottle, while his hairless and unnaturally pale hands were always redolent of lavender water and the frequent application of emollient lotions. Yet no one mocked M Vincent. He compensated for his lack of avoirdupois with a steely impassivity: his lizard eye, the imperturbable calm of his curiously unlined cheeks, his very capacity for stillness had evoked for Fabrice the menace of the Inquisition, from whence had come his nickname. His voice was velvet—the softer it grew, the more it conjured visions of endless scullery duties or docked wages. Such a man must have found it galling to accept the compromises foisted on him by Michel's position in the household. However, he never behaved as though his power were less than absolute, so that even Michel dared not cheek him. Indeed, from the first footman's present sickly look, it was evident he was in some terror of what M Vincent, approaching with his panther's tread, might have chanced to overhear. But Max's wits were, in any case, faster.

"Fabrice and I were sympathising with Michel, monsieur. He has an errand from madame to M Goujon in this terrible weather."

"How comradely. Although your concern, gentlemen, seems more vociferous than the case would warrant." The *maître d'hôtel* favoured the first footman with his chilling smile. "I am sure such a great strapping lad is not afraid of a little thunder and lightning, eh, Michel? And look—there's a cape on that peg over there."

Under the Cardinal's eye, Michel was obliged to don the dripping cape. As he set off sulkily down the passage he contrived to shoot Max a vengeful stare.

"Fabrice, according to the rota you are answering bells with Jacques—please do not let us detain you. And now, Jean, this *brouhaha* has reminded me that the storm has robbed you of your duties. I am somewhat concerned as to how the roof is faring, particularly the section adjoining the Knight's Tower. I should be obliged if you would go up into the attics and take what measures are necessary. Use the fire buckets—you know where to find them. Well, gentlemen, be so good as to get to it."

Once M Vincent had gone, Max and Fabrice reconvened at the door to the servants' hall.

"So Betty's scared of thunder! How delicious!"

On his way in from the garden Max had been contemplating the problem of M de Miremont: the realisation that the weather had left him with time on his hands had sown the germ of an idea; now he did not intend to let it wither, despite M Vincent's unfortunate interference. "I think, my friend, you owe me."

Fabrice looked fleetingly shame-faced. "Only it's hardly a deliverance, is it, angel? I'll still get veins running after the Lion of Literature all morning."

"Then let me do you another favour."

Fabrice studied him narrowly. "Oh yes?"

"Change with me."

"Putting buckets under leaks?"

"Out of sight and out of mind."

"She's so horribly insistent. It'll be like yesterday, when I was trying to lay up luncheon. She'll have me fetched."

"Not from the attics."

"Anyway, His Eminence will notice."

"He'll be sampling the Roussels' anisette for the rest of the morning."

Fabrice continued to eye Max suspiciously. "And what prompts this noble act of self-sacrifice, if I may enquire, dear heart?"

"I'm scared of spiders."

Fabrice laughed and, since he could not begin to adduce what advantage Max stood to gain, permitted himself to surrender. "Well then, angel, put me truly in your debt. If Madame de Bellyache asks you to shave her, be so good as to cut her throat."

According to Jacques, M de Bellac had rung down twice about his boots, already highly displeased by Fabrice's absence. Of the Oxen, Jacques, the youngest, was the most malleable, particularly when not in the company of the others. Sturdy and apple-cheeked like his cousins, he evinced, unlike them, a lazy softness of flesh, a mild and indifferent eye and a blank grin that often appeared without discernible cause— possibly he was a little simple-minded. At any rate he readily accepted Max's explanation that Fabrice had been called away by the Cardinal on special duties. M de Miremont, on previous form, would appear in the library at about eleven, Max would not have long to wait.

However, it was just his luck that, at a quarter to, Marie came down from the nursery in quest of hot milk to soothe Izabela Zelenska's colic. Strictly speaking he had no further need to cultivate the princess's nursemaid. All the same, he liked her stoic cheerfulness and, while their flirtation was a harmless game no girl of her sound practical sense would take to heart, it would be needlessly unkind to start treating her coldly. Nor could he suddenly drop the Zelenski children. It was almost eleven by the time the tray with the boiled milk and a dish of macaroons (Colette, the head kitchen maid, had a soft spot for the little ones) was ready for him to take upstairs. And of course there could be no question of his simply handing over his burden at the nursery threshold. Stanislaw and Antoni, deprived of outdoor recreation, were drawing pictures with pastels: Max must admire these and make preposterous faces to cheer little Izabela and exchange further pleasantries with Marie. When he returned to the pantry, the clock showed twenty past eleven.

Jacques was absent but reappeared almost immediately. "Took your time," he observed, although placidly and without reproach—to do him credit, his was not the sort of laziness that abhorred its reflection in others.

Max shrugged. "Busy?"

"Writing paper to Monsieur de Cressy in the Yellow Salon. Coffee to Monsieur de Miremont in the library."

Shit!

"Took Monsieur de Bellac his boots. Didn't like how I done them. Wants Fabrice to shave and dress him. Keeps ringing. Blow me if that's not him again now!"

However, to the relief of both, it was madame's bell—Mlle Lapointe, no doubt, wanting madame's breakfast tray cleared.

"Now here's a suggestion," said Max amiably. "You've had your fair share of Monsieur de Bellac. You take Mademoiselle Lapointe, and I'll deal with the gentleman when he rings again."

Jacques was not inclined to reject such an offer. He was barely out of the door when the novelist's bell began to jerk frenziedly upon its coiled leather strap. Max had no wish to cause Fabrice further trouble. On the other hand, M Vincent was unlikely to be any more enamoured of M de Bellac than the rest of the servants' hall: if the Lion of Literature complained to madame, Fabrice would doubtless escape with a mild caution. Ignoring the clamour, Max set off for the library.

M de Miremont did not appear to heed his knock, although the doors stood open. Indeed the old boy was barely visible, hidden, but for one arm and the faint suggestion of a profile, in the depths of the wing chair he had drawn to the fire. Facing north and shadowed by two ancient cedars, the library, despite its painted and gilded shelves, was always gloomy: today the murky light cast by the rain-smeared windows and two or three half-hearted lamps hardly encouraged reading, yet the old fellow seemed engrossed.

Nevertheless, Max did not hesitate, for he could not afford to give his actions too much thought. Quietly he closed the doors and approached the mantelpiece with assurance.

"Monsieur rang."

M de Miremont had been so startled by the intrusion that he had knocked a teaspoon from the tray at his elbow. The book in his lap was closed, Max noticed, and the coffee Jacques had poured for him remained untouched. Max bent to recover the spoon. When he rose he found the old boy staring up at him with a look of great agitation.

"Monsieur is doubtless bothered by the storm."

"I—no—I—"

"If he will permit me, I shall close the shutters."

This time he met M de Miremont's eye and held it until it seemed a thin shaft of enlightenment began to pierce the old boy's confusion. At any rate, the marquis offered no protest, indeed appeared bereft of speech, as Max went from window to window, unfolding and latching the shutters (a needless precaution, perhaps, since who would brave the rain to peer in). All the same, as the third pair fell heavily into place and the library was plunged into flickering half-light, Max prayed the old fellow, in his nervous innocence, had properly understood his intention, would interpret the motion of his hands as he paused, back still turned, before the window, and would not balk at the risk.

But it seemed his anxiety was groundless. As he swung round and walked into the firelight, the marquis emitted a curious muffled sound, part sigh, part sob, before sliding from the chair onto his knees.

The shutters could not remain closed indefinitely without attracting suspicion. While the boy, once more the well-trained servant, was throwing open the room to the shuddering sky and to the spectacle of hail stones as big as pearls bouncing from the gravel, Miremont reclined thoughtfully in his chair. No one would have disputed his transformation from the hunched figure Max had found staring into the gloom. Yet a stray furrow still marred his brow.

"My dear Jean—"

" Max. Jean is just what they call me here."

"My dear Max. Please—leave the tray for a moment."

"It is my alibi for the pantry, monsieur."

"Only for a moment."

The boy lowered his burden. The china clattered a little, as though, despite his outward composure, he took a certain apprehension from Miremont's gravity.

"There is something I...something that must be said..." A crack of thunder allowed Miremont to collect his words. "We are both, I think, proud. Perhaps excessively so."

The boy raised his eyebrows. "Monsieur, I—"

"My dear fellow, if I have stood too much on my pride of late, I ask you to forgive me."

The boy's defensive air vanished, he seemed momentarily dumbfounded. "Monsieur, there is no need—I...You meant to be generous, monsieur, the fault is mine."

It was Miremont's turn to be touched, for he could not avoid noticing the effort this cost. "My dear fellow...Let us not fall out again over who is the most to blame!"   Reaching out, he caught the young man's hand: as its fingers briefly returned his grasp, he was seized with the impulse to press it to his heart. Yet he feared such an effusive gesture would alarm the boy. God knows, as it was, he must have seemed contemptibly over-eager.

"Now—I must let you go." Nevertheless, watching Max carry the tray to the door, he could not bear his departure, yearned for some token that all was settled between them. "Only—one last thing."

"Monsieur?"

"I cannot seem to find Madame de Claireville's Catullus."

"Indeed, monsieur?"

"She possesses a copy, there is a gap in the shelf. I was wondering if, by chance..."

"I might happen upon it?" The boy grinned. "And if I should? Say, tonight. May I assume it is monsieur's pleasure—?"

"It is my dearest wish."

CHAPTER ELEVEN

It was generally remarked how much better Armand de Miremont was looking. Mme de Claireville was naturally gratified that, with the benefits of her country air, stimulating company and excellent cuisine, he had at last thrown off the ailment that had lowered his spirits. Not that he had suddenly turned loquacious—indeed there were times when he seemed more abstracted than ever, in a veritable daze—yet he was given to smiling beatifically, as though the least doings of his fellow guests gave him infinite pleasure.

Strolling with him in the Italian garden, Mme de Claireville was reminded of the man she had known when Léonore was alive. Certainly her friend's brother could not have been judged handsome, with his thatch of dark but lustreless curls that defied the barber's art and his sallow, crumpled countenace—a face like a widow's handkerchief, according to some wit, probably Achille de Tarascon. Yet penetrate his shyness and there was something not unappealing about that odd prematurely lined face, the expressive eyes, the vivacity of his conversation once you got him on his own, the unaffected joy he took in his various recondite enthusiasms. Catherine de Claireville had always found intelligence an attractive quality, at least in men of her own rank. It was a pleasure to her to hear him laugh again, to listen to him praising the beauties of the local countryside with all his former animation, to observe him at meal-times, no longer staring at his plate or toying with his napkin, but alert to his surroundings, seeming to anticipate with delight the serving of each new course, and often with that dazed, tender smile drifting over his lips.

But perhaps it was not merely the curative properties of country air that accounted for the smile. Mme de Claireville did not fail to note that, in the afternoons, when Iphigénie Zelenska watched her children at play, Armand, instead of skulking in the library, now joined the little court attending her. Oh, he might pretend to arrive by chance and shyly fix his gaze on Jean's antics with the children, but his hostess was not deceived. Just deserts for Aline, who had been too obtuse to value him! Altogether his stay promised to be a considerable success.

*

Miremont was befuddled with pleasure. He felt much as he imagined a sixteen-year-old virgin must feel in the power of an accomplished seducer. He experienced no qualm at surrendering the privileges of age and rank as he gave himself up to the boy's tuition. The boy, instinctively it seemed, knew what would please him: parts of his body he had always assumed mute became organs of exquisite sensation; intimacies, smells, tastes that would once have shocked him now brought him to rapture. But his greatest discovery, his deepest joy—something he had glimpsed at their first meeting, yet had scarcely believed—was that, despite his clumsiness, he too could give pleasure. Lying late in bed, still feeling the imprint of the boy's flesh upon his, still smelling the scent of his scalp upon the pillow, Miremont would contemplate the miracle of his awakening and of these strange stolen nights. He was bound to recall his only other experience of physical intimacy and to gain a measure at last of all that had been missing from his marriage.

As he sat at table, endeavouring to exchange conversation with Catherine on his left or Amélie de la Rochefontaine on his right, while all the time giddy from the boy's presence behind his chair, he would exult tipsily in this new double life, in how this tedious social ritual was a mere shadow of the rich existence he was promised in—oh God, still another three hours—and how the Miremont they observed, nodding, smiling, attempting to feign interest in Bellac's eternal anecdotes, was a shadow too, how, if only they knew, the real man was ardent, aching with desire. But often he feared they might come to know it. He fancied that there were already whisperings, sideways glances.

Not that he could fault his lover's discretion. Catherine, of course, had posed an immediate problem: might Miremont not be poaching on her preserves? But Max had merely laughed, assuring him there was no difficulty there: madame (incredibly to Miremont) preferred the heavy, florid youth who was her first footman. As for the practicalities of their liaison, once again Miremont could rely on the boy's precocious worldly wisdom: he was mindful of details that would have utterly escaped Miremont, taking precautions to avoid the chambermaids gossiping, ensuring he left no trace of his presence to alert Thomas in the morning.

Ah, but Thomas…If Miremont dreaded discovery, then, he must admit it, he did not so much fear his fellow guests as this silent, morose man who had served him for over a quarter of a century. It could not be said that master and servant enjoyed a perfect understanding, for

Thomas, even after all these years, still refused to speak except in absolute necessity, still appeared to live, resolutely armoured, in his own world: nevertheless, if the servant's thoughts often remained opaque, the master was uncomfortably aware that his own perhaps did not. He remembered when he had decided to be rid of his moustache. Although the growth was an ungainly specimen, Thomas had tended it like some hothouse fern, so that perhaps his disapproval was natural. Yet this was during the Alfred Kiddle episode, and Miremont could not help detecting in Thomas's rebellion, in the unpressed trousers, the shirts lost in the wash, the little nicks to his chin where his valet's deft cut-throat was suddenly wont to slip, the uncanny perception that Miremont's wish to look younger was not solely born of vanity. It had horrified him. It still horrified him to think that Thomas, of all people, might see him for the sham he was, a disgrace not just to his rank but to the simple principles of manly decency. It was as if he had broken the silent pledge he had made twenty-six years ago when he had taken Thomas into his service.

Yet guilt inflamed the imagination: Thomas could be cussed about any number of things—new-fangled boot trees, some minor innovation below stairs. In the first days of their sojourn here Miremont's chin had been in constant danger, although he forgave Thomas, realising his own misery was as nothing to his valet's—a man who did not speak and treasured the protection of familiar routines, thrust headlong into the enforced sociability of an alien servants' hall. When Miremont had plunged into despair, Thomas, by contrast had grown almost lively, as though he had read his master's thoughts of timetables and packing. But now he had relapsed into baleful gloom and Miremont sported a blob of bloody lint just above his collar.

Miremont studied him anxiously for other signs. Yet could not the poor fellow's silent rumblings be easily accounted for? Miremont had capriciously cheated him of escape. It was absurd, this superstitious watchfulness, like some faithless husband tiptoeing around his wife. Thomas did not, after all, read his thoughts. Where he might be alerted, where he might rise up, teeth bared like a vengeful Cossack, was at any incursion upon his command—a bottle out of order in Miremont's dressing case, missing shirt studs, confusion in the strict ranks of the collar drawer (or a moustache shaved on a whim, perhaps?). If they remained careful, as, thank Heaven, the boy was, Thomas, sealed in that angry shell of his, would continue unaware.

*

Max could not but be amused by M de Miremont's anxieties and the curious blindness of the nobs. Complete discretion, however desirable, was wishful-thinking in a house such as this. For instance, the old fellow must have some inkling of how his own footmen were quartered; or perhaps he preferred to ignore such lowly details. At any rate, it was merciful he was not privy to the conversation Max found himself having with Fabrice during their break, two or three days after he and M de Miremont had effected their reconciliation.

"You ought to mind yourself, angel."

This meeting in the walled garden was a token that Fabrice had at last forgiven Max for the savage dressing-down he had received from M de Bellac. The afternoon was sultry and they sat on the rim of the well, breathing cool air from its depths. Max yawned.

"I mean it, dear heart. The Oxen are banging about in their stall. The leader of the team, in particular."

"The beastly Guillaume." Max yawned again, more deeply.

"She complains you're ruining her beauty sleep crashing in at three in the morning."

"Stupid bastard. Remind me not to cover for him when next he sets luncheon without any forks."

"It's serious, angel. He's threatening to report you."

"Then tell him I'm reading. In the broom cupboard. As was his bovine wish."

"No good, dear heart. Yesterday night he saw you shaving in the sluice room."

"Well, then tell him…" Max scraped up a stone from the path with the toe of his pump, kicked it, caught it. "Tell him you can't tell him anything. Gallantry forbids."

Fabrice stopped fanning himself with his handkerchief and wrinkled his nose. "Not the nursemaid?"

"Oh, for pity's sake."

"You mean, her mistress?"

"I naturally cannot be expected to betray a lady. However, you may hint that it is with madame's knowledge and consent."

"Surely not the princess?"

Max tipped the stone lightly from palm to palm. "Let us just say, a certain lady."

Fabrice raised one eyebrow. "Curious, but our mousey little marquis seems to have blossomed of late."

"A certain lady, tell the Chief Ox. With madame's blessing. And if he—or anybody—breathes a word..." Max consigned the stone to the well and, after some seconds, was rewarded by an echoing and eloquent splash.

Max certainly did not share M de Miremont's optimism about M Thomas. Fabrice might be fond of repeating Mme Corneul's dictum, 'No man is a hero to his valet', but Max required no epigrams to convince him that M le marquis stood naked before his: he soon experienced a disagreeable encounter with the old Cyclops.

In the general way of things, of course, their paths did not cross: M Thomas ate with the upper servants and otherwise kept himself aloof. But it so happened, when Max was coming out of the laundry with newly pressed trousers for M de Cressy and M Thomas was making his way in on some similar errand, they all but collided in the narrow passage. They stood for a moment chest to chest and Max, seeking to move aside, discovered his way barred. The apology he was obliged to render his senior died on his lips. He grew acutely aware of the menacing size of the man, the heavy arms, the barrel chest, the dominating shoulders, his sheer height, so that Max, his glance drawn unwillingly to the old monster's face, had the unusual experience of being forced to look up. And what a face, with its grim jaw and vacant eye socket. The single eye, an icy blue and slightly bloodshot, froze Max with its glare; the narrow lips drew back in a silent snarl; Max felt rather than saw the massive fists slowly clench.

It was over in an instant. The giant lifted his grizzled head and strode forward, forcing Max against the dado, out of his path. Afterwards, of course, one could laugh it off: the brute was clearly touched. Still, it must be admitted, there had been a chilling lack of ambiguity in that Cyclops stare. Michel, Guillaume, and now this— Fabrice was right, Max must guard his back. But at least—here he grinned to himself—you could guarantee the Monoculus would not gossip. And besides, these were trivial worries when generally circumstances were working so entirely to his advantage.

It was a marvel to Miremont, who had learnt to view any lapse in his guard as infinitely dangerous, how comfortable he was with the boy. To talk, to laugh, to lie, bodies entwined, in spent and sweat-soaked silence—now that their differences had been resolved, Miremont felt that an extraordinary current of sympathy flowed between him and this boy, Max, Catherine's footman, his lover.

Perhaps it was that Max already knew his darkest secret; or that, knowing it, he appeared to think nothing of it, as though Miremont's guilt were the aberration, the departure from the natural order of things; or perhaps that, as their love-making conceded space for conversation, there never seemed time enough in these clandestine hours to extinguish a tenth of the subjects that took fire between them. They talked not only of books; Miremont found himself frankly confessing the crisis of confidence that had afflicted his work; he was even drawn to revive memories shared with no-one since Léonore's death, recollections of his childhood, or of Paris in the horrifying aftermath of the siege. Yet what most excited his interest was the subject of Max himself. For, despite their instinctive fellow-feeling, the boy was in many ways still a riddle to him: the contrast in their circumstances decreed that.

It was part of Miremont's pleasure, this voyage of discovery through an exotic and unknown landscape. The terrain, although always intriguing, was often ploughed with contradictions. The boy was by turns disconcertingly assured and unexpectedly gauche; for all his sophistication in carnal matters, when it came to how the world worked he sometimes betrayed a naivety that Miremont found both startling and endearing. He was capable of sensitivity, generosity, even gentleness on occasion, and his intellectual judgements could be surprisingly mature: yet he could be crude and facile too, as though from a perverse desire to shock. And then, of course, there were his servant's affectations, which waged constant battle with his natural vitality: the Max Miremont liked best was the boy who showed his teeth when he smiled, who laughed with abandon, who burned with a reckless feral energy that Miremont found quite indecently exciting.

What had gone into the making of him, this strange young creature, who, with all his intelligence and pride, seemed content with a life in service? It was folly to guess, as Miremont had discovered on their very first night.

It had been painful for him to part with the boy and, as they had lain for a last few moments in each other's arms, he had been rocked by a furious onrush of feeling, a longing to express he knew not what, such a confusion of happiness, gratitude and embarrassing sentiment that he was hard put to contain it. "Oh, my dear…"

Max grinned. "*Futuimus bene.*"

"*Futuimus optime*—disgraceful fellow." Miremont kissed him, glad to be rescued from his folly. "Although, strictly speaking, shouldn't we say *paedicavimus*? By the way, my dear boy, you have never mentioned where you came by your Latin."

"In the cloister." As he watched the effect upon Miremont, Max's studied nonchalance dissolved into laughter.

Miremont too had laughed, at first with incredulity, then, as the boy had doubtless intended, titillated despite himself by the unsuitable images this astounding confession invoked. But he had soon ceased laughing as he had listened to Max's brief account of the postulants' dormitory, his enforced vows and his flight to Paris. It was a story that rang with the shocking echo of a bygone age, particularly when Miremont recalled his own indulgent childhood. Yet, as he lay dwelling on it in the darkness after the boy had finally left him, he did not disbelieve it. The scepticism that had hardened in him over the past two years told him it was not beyond the Church to persist in such practices despite a century of attempted reform. And, even if he had been disposed to doubt, there had been, for all the boy's attempts to disguise it, an edge to the narrative, a bitterness that compelled belief.

Miremont ached with tenderness for him. It was bad enough that the poor lad had not known parental affection; Miremont grieved that all the other riches of childhood had been stolen from him as well. But perhaps Max had caught a hint of that 'poor lad', for the next night when Miremont sought to reopen the subject he was at his most insouciant.

"Oh, it wasn't all praying and fasting. Quite often when they wanted to punish me they banned me from the library and sent me to work with Brother Bernard. One of the lay brothers. He kept the pigs. They despised him because he stank and could barely sign his name. But he let me work the cider press and steal the apples and help him when the sow farrowed. He taught me to snare rabbits. I remember—" Max laughed suddenly, a laugh so warm and affectionate that Miremont felt an instant's fierce jealousy of Brother Bernard "—they kept an ancient piebald nag to draw the dog cart and when his back was turned I used to mount her bareback and gallop her around the meadow like a charger. Doubtless you were brought up in Paris, monsieur. Or did you ever hunt rabbits and climb trees…?"

Thus the topic of the cloister drifted away and was never properly recovered. Miremont's curiosity about his lover's past did not diminish, nor did he cease to long for an equal freedom in their nightly exchanges.

But for the sake of the boy's pride he was cautious, working with delicacy, always holding back at the first signs of resistance, as though unfurling gold leaf.

If madame were all rules and regulations, M de Miremont seemed to set no rules at all. Indeed the old boy positively urged Max to talk. Of course it was frustrating—although perhaps unavoidable—that they had got so early onto the subject of St Pons: for, while M de M seemed fascinated by it and would not let it drop, it was not really part of the story; or rather, for all its tedium and misery, not an important part. However, Max perceived that his reticence only stimulated the old boy's curiosity; and that was certainly no bad thing.

The fiasco with madame had taught him he could not simply blurt out his story. If he had occasionally longed to unburden himself to Mitya Zhukovsky, and latterly to Fabrice, it had not been a longing, he now understood, to tell the story itself, but to show off the full glorious architecture of his grand design—its ambition of scale, its ingeniously deceiving perspectives, the daring of it, but also the justice of its symmetries, the indisputable foundation of entitlement on which the whole soaring, glittering edifice rested. He had wanted, in a foolish moment, to witness their astonishment and to hear his own voice quivering with elation. But the story itself was another matter. As he had discovered with madame, it required a careful approach and a cool head. Besides he was not made for glib disclosures; Fabrice was right, secrecy was ingrained in him, the past twelve years had seen to that. So it suited him to treat M de Miremont's questions with reserve. Let the old boy worm his confession out of him; that way it would seem all the more convincing.

Meanwhile he could take proper measure of monsieur. For perhaps it was not entirely correct that the old fellow imposed no rules. Consider his exacting definition of truth. Max must remember that fastidiously truthful people, with their unfair tendency to ignore all notion of degree, could trip you up on the smallest detail, something that had no relevance to the greater scheme of things: for instance, there was the matter of Max's false papers, which he would be obliged to confess: supposing M de M allowed himself to be distracted by this minor irregularity at the expense of all else?

It also paid you to watch your tone with the old boy. He seemed less fond of the truth when it came unvarnished. Despite his intelligence and his learning, despite—or perhaps because of—the lofty peak of rank and wealth from which he impartially surveyed the world, the old chap was unsettled by disrespect for authority. He might happily admit he held no particular brief for religion, but he had blanched when Max had declared that there was no God and no sin. Then there had been the moment when Max, attempting to explain why the Reverend Father had pressed him into the novitiate in spite of his lack of faith, had said, with thoughtless bravado: "Perhaps he was afraid of what I could tell the Provincial." It was evident that the old boy had not liked this, and it was in any case a miscalculation, for Max had no intention of mentioning Dom Sébastien or the Reverend Father's singular regime of chastisement (any more than he was likely to speak of Josette or his career as a life model), so that he was obliged to laugh as if he had essayed a dubious joke.

Yes, you could be lured by the old boy's flattering interest into carelessness. It was not that the marquis was a prig exactly, but rather that his ignorance of the real world caused his sensibilities to recoil from its harsher manifestations. Small wonder he had struggled to deny his inclinations all these years. However, he was shaping up very well in that regard: Max viewed monsieur's transformation with a certain pride, a satisfaction in his own achievement that made him feel quite protective towards the old fellow.

Even if M de Miremont had not been essential to his plans, Max would have enjoyed these nightly visits to the room in the tower. They transported him once again to the luxuries of clean, unconfined space, of feather mattresses, of crisply folded towels, of soap that lathered the instant you touched it and did not scrape your skin. Their intrigue, like a rush of ether, swept away the dead air of La Boissière's routine. And then there was the affair itself, of which Max, who generally preferred the freedoms of fleeting encounters, had in truth not expected much beyond a release from frustration. Yet he was surprised to discover that familiarity, far from inducing ennui, could intensify pleasure. Of course it helped that M de M was evidently besotted with him. No need for rash declarations to spur the old boy's interest; indeed, after madame, the whole business was blessedly straightforward.

However, Max's greatest delight, after the day's bowing and scraping, was to be treated at last as a sentient being. He was bound to admit M le marquis had learned his lesson from their brief estrangement. He was by no means a bad sort, monsieur, despite his foibles. Oh, it would have been easy to take his willingness to apologise, his gratitude, his sentimental tenderness as marks of weakness. Except that there was always something about M de M—Max could not precisely define what—that prevented you. Dignity, perhaps? The old boy's tale of destroying his life's work, which might have seemed pathetic, had actually been rendered quite affecting by his utter lack of self-pity. Or perhaps it was that peculiar modesty of his, which seemed to set so little store by his learning or his rank.

Modesty was a quality that puzzled Max. He was reminded of Mitya Zhukovsky, who could apply horsehair to gutta percha and summon up the soul's darkest yearnings, yet shrugged off this accomplishment as though it required no more skill than sawing wood. The first time M de Miremont had spoken of his country estates, Max had been ready for resentment—his own father, his real father, had acquired an estate, which Max had visited only once when he was six but which he would have inherited had fate permitted. But M de Miremont did not boast of hectares owned, servants employed and horses stabled: his childhood reminiscences, like Max's own, were of simple, down-to-earth pleasures.

Indeed, the old boy seemed to eschew any kind of show, whether it were verbal fireworks at the dinner table or the studied reminders of influence, like the laying down of spoors ('When I was last in audience at the Hofburg…' or 'The comte de Paris has positively confirmed to me…') favoured by such as Messieurs de la Rochefontaine and de Cressy. Even monsieur's personal effects resolutely shunned ostentation. Max was well-placed to observe that, while M de Cressy's dressing case, despite that gentleman's impecunious state, was a very grand affair, its every brush and stopper belligerently armorial, M de Miremont's, from the article's battered leather and antiquated design, had seen service with his father and perhaps his grandfather before. Even the old boy's watch, a very plain if unusually slender hunter on an unadorned chain, was silver, a trifle beside M de la Rochefontaine's resplendent gold half hunter or the Literary Lion's timepiece set with diamonds.

This lack of show could not be accounted for by parsimony. The coats Fabrice despised, although not in the latest fashion, suggested by their material and cut that monsieur's tailor's bill might rival the ex-ambassador's. Yet somehow, although he could not be accused of affecting the duc de La Marne's nonchalant shabbiness, he never rose to elegance. It was as though, despite his titles and châteaux, he was intent on persuading the world that he was really an ordinary sort of fellow.

But no, of course that was not it, any more than Mitya disavowed his passion for the violin. Rather, the titles and châteaux were so central to monsieur's being that he could afford to wear them negligently. It might shake him to discover he preferred footmen to chambermaids, but in every other respect, Max realised with envy, he possessed an unfaltering certainty of who he was, a certainty that was bred into his bones, beyond thought.

Max was no longer surprised that the old boy had seen through his gentleman's manner. Indeed, it seemed to him that he had been almost as simple-minded as Fabrice. He too had concentrated on externals—voice, bearing, the acquisition of a certain air. Yet it should have been obvious that such things, to convince, must appear to flow from this state of majestic certainty. Admittedly fate had not gifted him with M de Miremont's advantages—not yet. But surely states of mind were not impossible to learn; here was the old boy before him nightly as a primer.

It was gradually born in upon him that M le marquis did, in fact, have a great many rules: Max began dimly to discern an entire complex code touching upon questions of honour, form and taste, a code so instilled into the old boy's very marrow that where fashionable conventions contradicted it he simply disregarded them. Not that he was eccentric—he would no doubt consider the deliberate cultivation of eccentricity, in his own person at any rate, to be in very poor taste. Nevertheless, in his own quiet way, he was as indifferent to opinion as madame.

Max was bound to admire this sublime disregard, just as he was drawn to the restraint that masked it. In a way, the old boy was not unlike that watch of his, which, on closer inspection, proved, with its chaste curves and austere surfaces, to be an object of some grace and distinction, and not silver either but, from the sheen of the metal, white gold.

Altogether, Max could not have chosen better than M de Miremont. Not only could he learn from the old fellow; without doubt he could rely on his help—once monsieur had given his promise, the code would see to that. Max's glorious future suddenly took on a sharper definition. He was impatient for it, impatient to see the old boy's face when he told him, impatient for his look of startled reappraisal, of new respect. And yet...If it all went wrong, as it had with madame, if he ended up back where he started...These few nights, the snatched escape from squalor, the delights of being flattered and adored, could hardly compare with the vista once his future was certain. And yet...There was no immediate hurry, monsieur seemed to have no thought of departure. Max had already brushed aside the inevitable question about the scar with the vague explanation of 'a childhood accident', indeed had turned aside several possible openings. Better to be certain of the old fellow...

It was a paradox, amusing to Max, that while M de Miremont was obsessed with discretion, he was the least equipped of anyone to manage an affair discreetly. His code was one obstacle. When Max attempted respectfully to hint that it would be useful cover if monsieur, instead of fleeing Princess Zelenska, pretended to requite her interest, the old fellow was horrified.

"My dear boy, I couldn't possibly."

"Monsieur, I don't suggest you throw yourself at her feet. Just a mild flirtation. A glance here, a smile there."

"Out of the question. Quite apart from the likely appalling consequences—" here monsieur shuddered: it was the closest Max had observed him come to commenting on one of his fellow guests "—quite apart from that, it would be improper."

Max raised his eyebrows: impropriety seemed a curious scruple in relation to the princess.

"Since I have no interest in the lady, it would be entirely wrong, not to say unkind to raise her expectations."

"All the same, it can do no harm if you at least join her when she's with the children. Besides which, your watching us surreptitiously from the terrace could occasion comment..."

Miremont, remembering the incident with Tarascon, was reluctantly won over, at any rate so far as the gatherings on the lawn were concerned. To his relief, no disagreeable consequences ensued. In fact, as Max perhaps might have predicted, the princess, finding the elusive marquis suddenly willing to pick up her handkerchief or hold her parasol, at once fell into a torpor of indifference; what sultry glances she had energy to muster were bestowed on M de la Rochefontaine. Only when the Lion of Literature took it upon himself to join their circle, bathing them as usual in the stream of his eloquence, did the princess consent to pay attention to M de Miremont, whether it were to shoot a stifled yawn in his direction or a shrug of languid despair; but Miremont, though at first somewhat alarmed, was soon comforted to discover that her sloe-black odalisque eyes remained as blank as if he were not there.

The code, however, was not the only difficulty. Like all worshippers of the truth, monsieur was unskilled in the simplest practices of deception. His too-expressive face might have schooled itself to withstand the routine depredations of boredom, distaste or irritation, but it was helpless against assault from a more forceful impulse.

"Monsieur may just as well ask me to take out my cock."

"God, dear boy, would that I could."

"How am I to concentrate on the children? This afternoon when I was swinging the little one onto my shoulders I nearly dropped her."

"Blame those scandalous breeches of yours."

"Monsieur could look elsewhere. Fire a few of his lustful arrows in the princess's direction."

"Heaven forefend."

"Conscience surely can't prevent you now madame has turned cold. Why not take a few lessons from Monsieur de la Rochefontaine?"

"I could learn all I need, my boy, watching you with that young nursemaid."

Max was by no means displeased to find that monsieur was not above jealousy.

Miremont himself perceived another paradox in discretion: the more you feared discovery, the more you were driven to risk it. He was reminded of the phase of his mortification when he had seen temptation on every street, yet the harder he had fought his unbidden urges the wilder and more fantastical they had grown. Now, of course, the daily torture of seeing the boy, of longing for the forbidden, was salved by nights where his desires could be extravagantly satisfied. It should have been enough: but he was like the drunkard for whom a sufficiency is never sufficient, but urges upon him the 'one last little drink' that propels him under a passing carriage. The torture had become an exquisite part of the pleasure. Whereas at first he had trembled even to look at Max in public, now from his waking moments he was weak with excitement, keenly anticipating the day's chances to court danger.

The sly caresses, the snatched embraces in the library, the ever-present memory of the thunderstorm, fostering wanton images that surged with him into the dining room where, fertilised by the suggestive intimacy between the server and the served, they burgeoned into the most indecent fantasies—only add to this the realisation of foolhardiness, how one misplaced glance could bring catastrophe: all contrived to put him in an ecstasy of pain that was scarcely supportable until the saving hour arrived.

Max, it is true, did his best to urge caution. But he was delighted that the old boy should betray this unexpected talent for mischief; nor was he a stranger to the aphrodisiac properties of risk, while, as the nights wore on, he himself grew dizzy and rash from his usual affliction, lack of sleep. Besides, as time strengthened their secret fellowship, it was impossible not to catch the infection. They so instantly read each other's thoughts, so easily found the tiny, teasing gesture that would burden one or both with the need to suffocate treacherous laughter. Standing behind monsieur's chair at dinner, Max would will him to arousal and, observing the altered set of the old fellow's spine, would feel his own answering excitement; when he drew back the chair he would be sure to adopt his haughtiest look, while monsieur, rising somewhat breathlessly, struggled to wrench his eyes from the contradictory and compelling message manifesting itself elsewhere.

It was a game, a delicious game. For Max, too, the dinner table—the jewels, the shirt-fronts portentous with decorations, the talk of politics and literature, the Oxen clumsy in their livery, Michel oiling up to madame, M Vincent's chilly eye—all receded from reality. He laughed to think that these self-important people had no notion of the true purpose of their existence, which was to provide for himself and monsieur, like the grit in the oyster, the frustration requisite for immoderate pleasure.

"Are you quite mad!"

Max and Fabrice were in the Grand Salon, clearing away the card tables and retrieving coffee cups and glasses now that madame and her guests had retired. Fabrice had made a great point of setting aside his tray and peering down the enfilade, but Max, anxious to get the work over and be on his way to monsieur, had paid scant attention. However, the candles, all flickering at once in the draught from the closing doors, made a suitably dramatic setting for Fabrice's explosion.

"Really, if you must fuck your little marquis in public, why not do it here on madame's Shiraz where the entire household can enjoy it?"

Max, busy gathering up playing cards, paused, but only for a moment. "Oh, it was you, was it? Thank god for that. We heard someone, but when he went away I assumed he hadn't seen us."

"You're lucky it wasn't the Cardinal. He wondered why you weren't serving coffee and sent me to find you."

"M de Miremont asked me to help him search for his pince-nez. He thought he might have left it on the terrace."

"Or in your fly."

"Oh for heaven's sake! We were only kissing."

Fabrice slammed down his tray with an agitated clatter. "Angel, are you demented? Has relieving Little Miss Mouse of her bonbon completely gone to your head?"

"Monsieur de Miremont to you, my friend."

Fabrice spluttered. "I fear for you, dear heart, I truly do. As if dinner wasn't bad enough—I've never seen anybody make such a folderol of ladling hollandaise over asparagus tips. And then—couldn't you at least have got Little—*monsieur*—as far as the shrubbery? Behind a planter on the terrace! *Only* kissing! *Only*?"

Max carried the boxes of playing cards to the Boulle cabinet. "I suppose it was a trifle incautious."

"Incautious? What if it hadn't been me? What if it had been the Cardinal? Or Betty?"

Max stowed the boxes tidily away and closed the cabinet doors. "Monsieur le marquis is quite a pet of madame's. I imagine, if she can tolerate the comte de Tarascon, she'd be lenient with Monsieur de Miremont's peccadilloes."

This was too much for Fabrice. He collapsed heavily into a chair. "And of course she'll extend her leniency to you."

Max was brought up, suddenly as much startled as Fabrice by what he had said.

"Tell me, angel," enquired Fabrice, "have you recaptured your lost innocence? Or perhaps you're in love."

"No, of course not!"

"Nothing like love to make blancmange of a girl's brains. I remember, in my first situation—"

"Cut that! He's useful to me. That's all. "

"Very useful if she gets you sent packing without a reference." Fabrice shook his head sadly. "Remember, dear heart, I speak to you as a friend—even though you can't spare me a word these days, despite the trouble I've gone to with the Oxen on your behalf. We'd all be glad of a rich Auntie, a very rich Auntie who no doubt showers her niece with delightful presents. But some of us wouldn't let our head be turned or give ourselves airs. Just wait till you're out on the street, angel. See how generous Auntie Mouse is then."

Max wondered what Fabrice would say if he told him he had not accepted a penny from M de Miremont. But, if you set his jealousy aside, Fabrice was right, damn him. Max had allowed himself to get carried away. M de Miremont's momentary terror at the footsteps on the terrace had somehow blinded him to the fact that he and monsieur did not play their game of chance with equal odds. He could not believe M de Miremont would have left him in the lurch—the old boy's code would surely not permit it. But nevertheless a chill went through him. M de M was such a confounded innocent, it should have been his, Max's, responsibility to ensure the game remained within bounds.

Besides did he not have just as much to lose as the marquis? This was not Paris, with its fleeting anonymities. A public scandal would hardly serve him well when he confronted his destiny. He had lost sight of his objective. He had become so dizzied by the old boy's adoration, so drugged by constant arousal, that it had taken Fabrice to remind him—monsieur was supposed to be useful to him. Furthermore, he had not only lost his focus, he might have lost his opportunity, for monsieur's interest, instead of being heightened by his evasions, had appeared perversely to wane: now Max considered their recent conversations, he could not recall the old boy asking him a single personal question.

He must take the matter in hand. If an opportunity did not present itself over the next couple of nights, then he must create one.

CHAPTER TWELVE

Armand de Miremont had now been Catherine de Claireville's guest for three weeks, a week longer than he had planned, although Catherine could not have been more delighted, urging him to stay for the rest of the summer. Meanwhile the La Rochefontaines had gone—Amélie had seemed to part rather frostily from her bosom friend Génie Zelenska—and Mme and Mlle de Beaumont-Gramont had also taken their departure, leaving Mme de Cressy to ply a lonely brush in the Italian Garden and rendering Ignate, who had sought to supplant M Bécart in the marriageable young lady's affections, even more morosely poetic.

In place of the ex-ambassador and his wife had come the comte and comtesse de Corvignac, a couple unfamiliar to Miremont yet so similar to the La Rochefontaines—he portly, urbane and on the board of several companies, she blonde, burnished and brittle—that Miremont was hard put not to feel he already knew everything worth knowing about them. On the other hand, a novel and startling ingredient was introduced by the arrival of Baroness Donyani, the noted blue stocking. Tall, with a formidable jaw and an embonpoint to match, dressed even for the country in flowing robes of Grecian influence, Beatrice Donyani, to steal the thunder of Ignate de Cressy, was a celebrated poetess, with several volumes of 'advanced' lyrics to her credit and a verse drama reinterpreting the story of Salomé from the point of view of the New Woman. No one knew what had become of her Hungarian husband—according to Achille de Tarascon, he had been eaten at first mating—but she was attended by her niece-companion, Mlle de la Falaise, a pretty, kittenish girl of eighteen or thereabouts, who showed commendable devotion to her aunt, frequently throwing impulsive arms about her neck.

Like the view from a vertiginous cliff, Mme Donyani was not without a certain awesome charm, whether teasing Gilbert de Cressy about the Woman Question or adroitly wheedling from M de Corvignac tit-bits of the latest financial scandal. Her smile was generous and she and Mlle de la Falaise had soon taken poor bereft Mme de Cressy under their wing. Even Miremont, with his hazy vision, could see that the baroness had shaken them up: the glittering fragments of their kaleidoscope, seemingly fixed by weeks of familiarity, had now settled into an entirely different pattern.

Not everyone was delighted. Catherine, of course, was still empress, holding undisputed sway over her courtiers. But within the court, smaller spheres of influence had grown up. Génie Zelenska was less than enchanted to find herself vying every afternoon with the baroness, who, expressing a great fondness for children, would hitch up her skirts and join in their races, egging on her niece to do likewise and creating such a spectacle as to divert attention properly due to the children's mother. Nor was Aristide de Bellac overjoyed by the baroness's arrival. More than Ignate de Cressy he had reason to bear a grudge. Not only was Mme Donyani apt to spoil his anecdotes with amusing interpolations; the poetess had been permitted to declaim her latest work to the company one evening, an opportunity their hostess had not vouchsafed Bellac, despite his international renown.

But the novelist had other troubles besides. Even Miremont could perceive from his woebegone glances that he was smitten with the princess. She, of course, repelled his overtures with bored disdain, escaping them, just as she had sought to escape his verbosity, by soliciting Miremont's protection. Gallantry hardly permitted Miremont to refuse, although he was disconcerted to find that when the company was assembled the princess was usually at his side, smiling at him faintly or engaging him in desultory conversation; and he was still more startled to receive venomous glances from the rejected suitor. Surely the wretched fellow must soon realise his misapprehension. For Miremont could not have said what he and the princess talked about in such a vague, disjointed and yet apparently absorbed manner: his mind was on Max and hers, from her reassuringly vacant gaze, was also far away.

Miremont was approaching his third Sunday at La Boissière, a day he liked to regard as an anniversary and which, according to the rota, once again fell to Max as his day off. Catherine made no demur when Miremont expressed the desire for another of his solitary walks: it seemed she was so pleased with his recovered health that she would deny him nothing, even insisting the kitchen make him up a picnic basket in case his exertions left him peckish.

Miremont set out first—Max could not leave until luncheon had been cleared—and as he strode through the heat, sweating the more profusely from the extra burden of the hamper, his anticipation at spending an entire afternoon with his lover was not unmixed with anxiety. Their meeting at the waterfall had been a moment of such perfection—had he not warned himself at the time that it could never be repeated? He was seized with the superstitious dread that someone else had taken ownership of their secret place, trysting lovers from the village or some peasant come to water his cattle. Certainly the countryside all around him lay deserted, deep in Sunday slumber now the harvest was over, the fields an empty golden plane shadowed only by haystacks or occasional corn stooks not yet gathered in for threshing; the silence, apart from the cawing of rooks swooping over the stubble, was heavy and complete. Yet it was with intense relief, as he reached the copse and forged his way through its tangled branches, that he saw before him the pool, the rock, the waterfall, steeped half in fierce white light, half in verdant shadow, mysterious, untrammelled, just as they had left it. By the time Max arrived—no longer in livery but wearing his battered hat and shabby frock coat, so that, seeing him anew, Miremont was struck anew by his beauty—the hamper was stowed in shade, its bottle of Chablis was chilling in the water, wedged for security into the cleft of a tree root, and Miremont himself, already in his shirt sleeves, was propped against a beech trunk smoking a cigarette, in satisfying and unchallenged possession.

It was as before. They made love behind the rock, they bathed, wrestling in the deepest part of the pool, tasting the musty water in each other's mouths as they kissed. At last, exhausted, they dressed and settled on cushions of leaf mould to let their linen dry. The boy, when shown the hamper's salmon pâté, plovers' eggs and pastries, fell gratefully upon them, but refused the wine, preferring to slake his thirst from the pool. He was bending, scooping water in his hand, when something beneath the surface caught his eye. He stretched out his arm to show Miremont. In his dripping palm lay a stone the size of a thumb joint, blood-red and shot with two slender white veins.

"Agate?"

Miremont shook his head doubtfully. And indeed the glorious jewelled crimson was already drying to a dull rust.

"Just a pebble." The boy shrugged. "No matter. Behold!" Like a child swallowing a bonbon, he slipped the stone between his lips.

Miremont envied the pebble, found himself transfixed by an absurd longing to follow it, to be as it was, swallowed up, utterly contained by the sweet warmth of that mouth, completely possessed. He could hardly bear to look as Max caressed the stone with his tongue before spitting it into his palm.

"You see, monsieur? Alchemy."

"Idiot boy!" Miremont's laughter struggled with an unaccountable impulse towards tears. Lowering his glance to the water's edge, desperately seeking distraction, he too found his eye drawn to a pebble, flat, grey, with no potential for transformation, but excellently formed for purposes of another kind. He weighed it in his hand. Then, drawing back his arm, he sent it skimming towards the rock.

Miremont had always rather prided himself on his skill at ducks and drakes. He could remember long and happy hours in his childhood, endeavouring to defeat the impregnable expertise of Arthur, his companion and groom, his boyhood hero. Even these days, as twilight began to fall over the lake at Beauvallon, he was not above sitting on the bank below the summerhouse and watching with pleasure his proficiently aimed missiles describe a series of perfect shallow arcs over the darkening water. But if he thought to impress the boy, he was to be disappointed. The pebble struck the pool's surface with a moribund splash and sank.

Max, however, was scrutinising the still-widening ripples with a knowledgeable air. "Forgive me, monsieur, but it's too shallow. You need to aim further out. And then, even if the wash from the waterfall doesn't defeat you, there's not enough distance before you reach the rock. You'll never do it. Not even one bounce."

"You challenge me?"

Max was already fishing for suitable pebbles.

For the next half hour they contended with each other, trousers and shirt sleeves rolled up, knees muddy, absorbed and obstinate as schoolboys. They trawled for pebbles of a certain size and shape—was small and light better under these circumstances or was the degree of flatness all, was brown stone more buoyant than grey, was marbled stone luckier? They experimented with different trajectories and elaborate flicks of the wrist. By the time they had collapsed from laughter and frustration, Miremont had achieved three skims, and Max four—although this was disputed, since on its fourth arc his pebble had vanished into the cave.

Thrusting hair from his eyes, Miremont glanced across at the boy. He had been a redoubtable opponent and Miremont, again recalling Arthur, wondered, not without a twinge of jealousy, whom his teacher had been. "My dear, I concede defeat. Is this another trick you learned from the worthy Brother Bernard?"

The question seemed to puzzle Max. "No, from when I was quite small—is it not like whistling, you simply pick up the knack?" He frowned suddenly. "I don't recall …an older boy perhaps…there was a lake, a great sheet of water, with fountains…" He continued to frown, as if something essential eluded him. "It must have been…anyway, that was years ago, before…"

"Before you went to the monastery?"

Max nodded.

"Then you do remember a little? Of your parents, your family?"

The boy turned away, an abrupt movement that freed his shoulders from Miremont's arm. Lowering his head, he seemed preoccupied by the small heap of pebbles at his feet.

"My dear, forgive me, I didn't intend—"

"No. It's no matter." Max toyed with the stones, then, with a sigh, selected one and lobbed it into the water. "No, monsieur. I should like to tell you."

What did Max remember? He and the Other had thought of time as sliced in half by the disaster, like an apple. There was Before, green and sweet and smelling of Eden, and After, black, rotten and poisonous. There had certainly been mothers and fathers in plenty. Those Max recalled most vividly were the pretend parents from After; their Pretend Mother, her ringlets, her pointed chin, her thin nose and the two tiny bones at its tip that grew stark white when she was crossed; and their first Pretend Father with the gap between his front teeth that made him appear always to be smiling, even when he was coming for you breathing firewater and clenching his fist—smiling, smiling.

Of his real mother, Max could recollect little, but then he had been sent away from her before he was of an age to remember. There had been a portrait in his father's apartments depicting a heavy, square-jawed woman with an expression of grim piety, but it had stirred no filial longings in him. Nor can she have greatly mourned his absence, from his memory of their only reunion, when he was six and had been sent to the family estate to recover from an illness; her duty visits to the sickroom had been conducted from the foot of the bed and with an air of resigned disapproval—of what? —his malady or his very presence? She had smelt strongly of camphor, like a piece of ancient linen stored away unregarded.

His real father he could picture more clearly. A short-legged, broad-chested, vigorous man with whiskers like palm fronds and a nose like a button, a man undoubtedly awe-inspiring to certain adults but to a child's eye, as he puffed himself up in his blue and gold uniform, somehow ridiculous. Perhaps it was his father's voice, unnaturally high, almost a falsetto, that had encouraged Max's derision, although these piping tones were remarkably versatile, ranging, to suit their audience, from simpering obeisance to razor-blade savagery. But Max knew his contempt was actually a defence against shame. Somehow he was aware, as though he had absorbed it from the atmosphere, inhaled it with the scent trailed by the ladies in evening gowns who visited the nursery, that his father was not quite as he should be, jumped up, irredeemably unworthy of his gold braid and his estate and his shiny new nobility.

Then there were the parents he must lay claim to. The mother, of course, neither he nor the Other had known. She too was just a portrait, pretty and pink and gold in a frothy white dress. The father…? It irked Max that he could not remember him better, for even during his frequent absences his was the presence that informed everything— the whispers of the scented ladies, his real father's simpering, the shouts of the commander of the guard, the footmen ramrod still in the silent hallways. Yet, beyond a faint dread, all Max could summon was a tall figure; a dark figure in a dark uniform.

Other people were clearer by far. Their nursemaid, the warm bolster of her apron-front smelling of aloes and boiled milk. The old footman who served the nursery and who, when no one was looking, had let them skate along the marble corridor to the orangery, past the rows of dead men's heads on plinths. The doctor, their tutor, the French governess…

They could not forget their governess, no such mercy was allowed them. And so, during the year—Max calculated it must have been a year—that they had been shut away from the sunlight, he and the Other had found it better not to think of people. In the game they had played, the deadly serious game they had conducted in whispers to ward off the damp and the darkness and their terror, the game of memory that was their lifeline, that would ensure, whatever befell them, that the idyll of Before would always be there to give them succour, they had concentrated on sounds, smells, places, objects, the names of horses and dogs.

They would send themselves to sleep by describing the view of the courtyard from the nursery window with the soldiers far below, ranked like marbles in a solitaire board; the distant crunch of boots on gravel, the boom of the chapel bell; the sweet fug of hay and dung that clung to your clothes from the Riding School, or the lingering smell of cabbage in the nursery. They would reconstruct the marvels of the Gold Room from the awed glimpses they had been allowed, its ceilings heavy with gilded leaves and sunbursts, its mirrors weighed down with cherubs and garlands, its dais supporting the two lofty chairs whose backs were formed from the spread wings and sinuous necks of twin gilt swans; nor should the ballroom be forgotten, where the cherubs and flowers were as white as icing, nor those other strange rooms at the Summer Palace, whose pillars, friezes and statues looked to be carved from stone, yet up close were as flat as your hand, a painter's trick…When their breath froze in the air, they would warm themselves with detail—the ciphers on the door locks, the devices denoting rank on military buttons, the exact configuration of the cracks in their bedroom ceiling. When the Other was whimpering and feverish, Max, his own brain fevered too, would shake him and force him to count out the number of marble chequers from the gallery to the orangery. Eighty? One hundred? One hundred and twenty? How many ink spots on the school-room table, how many puppies did Freya have last summer, how often does the guard change? Count, damn you, don't give in or we're both finished, you must, you can remember…

"I can remember a little," Max said, taking the cigarette M de Miremont offered. He could not have asked for a better opportunity, so why, just as with madame, did his heart sink? He lit the cigarette from the old boy's match and inhaled deeply.

"First, monsieur, I know I insult you by asking this, for it goes without saying, but I beg you not to mention to anyone what I shall tell you. Not for the time being at least. It could be dangerous for me."

Shit! While this caution was necessary, he could tell from monsieur's raised eyebrows that it was the wrong beginning, too melodramatic by far. Now he could only soften its effect by compounding his difficulties.

"My papers are—somewhat irregular. They state that I was born in the Auvergne, but that is not strictly correct."

It was true that M de Miremont frowned, but only briefly. "My dear boy, what you tell me in confidence—yes, it does go without saying—I shall not repeat."

Max reached out to squeeze his arm and felt the old boy's hand on his, returning the pressure. He drew again upon the cigarette. "Not only have I never set foot in the Auvergne, I am not French. I was born in Waldavia."

"Waldavia?"

"In Rittenau, the capital."

"You are German?"

Remembering that the old fellow had endured the siege, Max felt compelled to add hastily: "South German. Waldavia may now be part of the Prussian Reich, but it remains an independent kingdom with its own ruler—"

"My dear Max, I hold no personal animosity against the Prussians. And, while I have never travelled further south than Heidelberg, I am aware that, *pace* Bismarck, there is not yet one Germany." Monsieur was smiling. "If I seem startled, it is because you are an endless store of surprises. How old were you when you left Waldavia?"

"Seven, I think. Some things are—it is hard to recall exactly."

"But you do recall your homeland?"

"I still have strong memories of it."

"And you can remember something of your parents?"

"Not my mother, she died when I was born. All I know of her is that she came from Russia. But yes, monsieur, I can remember my father." Here Max hesitated, struggling to make this true, but meeting once more only the mysteriously blurred dark image. "He was tall— considered handsome, I think—rather aloof. But then I suppose he had a great many important affairs to attend to and I recall he was often away."

"He was a person of some consequence?"

"He was—" But no, despite the good beginning, it was too early for that, better to ease the old boy into it gently. "He had—a certain position. I was his only son, his heir, so I can have lacked for nothing. But—it is absurd—what I remember best are the little things, foolish things that stay in your mind as a child. Our dogs, for instance. Old Wotan, my father's mastiff, I can see him now—he looked as fierce as a bull, but you could ride on his back. Whereas Freya, the wolf hound, she'd give you a nip if you tried that trick with her, especially when she was in pup. I'd been promised two of her next litter, I was going to train them myself. And then there were the horses, of course. My pony, Bobik. Actually, I was rather afraid of Bobik, he had a vile temper and hated children. You once asked me about this, monsieur." Max touched his scar. "It's my souvenir of Bobik—he threw me several times. My father was displeased with me, I think. He was a superb horseman. He insisted we were put in the saddle as soon as we could walk—"

"We? Had you sisters?"

"There was another boy. Because I was an only child and held to be of a nervous disposition, I fancy my father thought I should not be too much alone. One of his household had a son of about my age and he lived in the nursery with me."

"A friend for you."

Max swallowed the bitterness that threatened to betray him. "I believe he was devoted to me." For a moment he exhaled smoke slowly. Then he smiled. "The nursery was our little world. A safe world, or so it seemed then. During the winter we were always in Rittenau and it was bitterly cold despite the big tiled stove—the ink used to freeze in the schoolroom and we'd make our teeth chatter like the abacus to annoy our tutor. Sometimes we were allowed downstairs, although we had always to be on our best behaviour and we were forbidden to slide on the marble floors. And we went to the Riding School every day, of course. But in the summer, there was the park to play in—"

"The park with the lake?"

"You would call it a vista, I suppose— a great bale of water rolling out to the fountains far away on the horizon. And then, when it was very hot, we went to the mountains. There was a room there filled with stags' heads, from every wall glassy eyes staring down at you, a forest of antlers. And a ferocious bear rearing up on its hind legs. And everything smelt of pines, like the ointment Frommchen, our nurse, rubbed into our chests in winter..."

The cigarette had burned down to Max's fingers. As he threw it into the water, he shot M de Miremont a covert glance. Truth, plain truth. The detailed, meticulous truth he and the Other had stored up for salvation during that terrible year. Yes, this was the best way. Not to start with the main point, which was how he had failed with madame, but to pour out these truths, the more jumbled the better. They were evidence, after all: M de M would be able to repeat them when, as he well might be, he was questioned as to what Max had told him. So long as the old boy was not becoming sceptical or, almost as bad, bored. But no, he continued to wear a sympathetic, if intrigued, expression.

"Childhood, as you know yourself, monsieur, always seems perfect in recollection. But I do, even now, believe those years were a time in paradise."

"And yet—" he heard M de Miremont's delicate hesitation "—and yet it came to an end..."

"When I was seven, my father died."

"My dear, I am sorry."

"An accident, they said. But we knew, even in the nursery, that he had shot himself."

"Oh, my poor boy!"

"It was the start of everything terrible. It…" He faltered, silenced suddenly by those other memories, devoid of consoling images, screaming not to be shut out, threatening his composure and his judgement.

He felt monsieur's hand on his shoulder. "My dear Max, if it is too painful…"

"No." Shit, he was nearly there, the old fellow was in his palm. "No." Finding he had screwed his eyes shut, he forced them open again. "I said I wished to tell you. Anyway, the rest you mainly know."

"Your guardians brought you to France?"

"To France. And then St Pons. But I have never for a moment forgotten Waldavia."

"Of course not. How could you?"

"In the cloister, or when I was sleeping in doorways, or now, when I'm—when I am as you know me—I have never forgotten my country. Or my birthright." This was it, at last, the perfect moment. Max heaved in breath. "My father—"

But M de Miremont was also speaking, already softly intoning words that drowned his.

"Ich hatte einst ein schönes Vaterland.
Der Eichenbaum
Wuchs dort so hoch, Die Vielchen nickten sanft.
Es war ein Traum.

Das kusste mich auf deutsch und sprach auf deutsch
(Man glaubt es kaum,
Wie gut es klang) das Wort: << ich liebe dich!>>
*Es war ein Traum."**

---

*I once had a fine Fatherland.
The oak trees
Grew so tall there, the violets nodded gently.
It was a dream.

It kissed me in German and spoke in German—
You'd scarcely believe
How good it sounded—the words "I love you."
It was a dream.

'In a Foreign Land' - Heinrich Heine

A sick chill had begun to spread over Max.

"Do you not know it, dear boy? *In der Fremde*. Heinrich Heine. One of your finest poets. He too was an exile here, he is buried in Montmartre."

Although he must offer some response, Max could not look up.

"It seemed apposite—yet, now I consider it, perhaps the last line of the verse is not so appropriate."

"I—"

"And indeed, on reflection, the entire poem is…Forgive me, I can see it has upset you. I did not intend—I hope you don't think I meant to imply…"

"Monsieur, I don't—I cannot—" The chill had broken out on Max's forehead in icy sweat, yet behind his eyes the blood was pounding. "I have not read Heine. I—I have lost my German."

It was true, a truth like all the others. During his time with Josette, when he had been free to explore the bookstalls, he had come upon a tattered copy of Goethe's *Faust*. For an instant his spirit had soared at the sight of gothic print, he had snatched the book up hungrily. But it had been then as it was now—the type had blurred, a cold nausea had gripped him, his heart had begun to thunder as if all the blood in his body would burst from its veins and choke him. Oh, they had been thorough, the baroness and Major von Eisen. During the time he and the Other had been kept in the cellar, every syllable of their native tongue had been beaten out of them.

It was true, on his life, true! Yet M de Miremont's hand had fallen from his shoulder, Max could sense his incredulity, knew that should he bring himself to meet his eyes he would see questions flicker, doubts already flaring into disbelief.

"When we—when they…" But the bile rose in his throat again, he could not do it, could not speak of the time in the cellar. Damn it all to hell! He should have remembered monsieur's professorial acquaintance in Heidelberg, should have predicted the old boy would have fluent German. He folded his arms across his knees and lowered his forehead to rest on them, defeated.

However, as his blood stilled, he heard the leaf mould rustle. The old boy seemed to be shifting uncomfortably.

"My dear Max—" monsieur gave vent to a little anguished cough "—my darling boy, you must believe…It was never my aim…I was reminded of the poem by your longing and stupidly thought it would touch you. It did not once occur to me…" The old fellow's fingers tentatively skimmed the nape of Max's neck, hovered, then settled there diffidently. "I beg of you—you intended to say more, I think— please forget my foolish interruption."

So all was not utterly lost? Raising his head, taking pity on the old boy's consternation, Max essayed a smile. Yet the propitious moment was shattered. Moreover, as long as his lack of German remained unexplained, he could hardly press on without appearing not merely a liar, but deluded. Besides, he had neither the strength for it, nor the appetite. Even the precious memories of Before filled him with sudden distaste.

Time was what he needed. Some day his inquisitors would require him to anatomise After in every grim detail; why shrink from rehearsing the ordeal before M de Miremont? But he would need time to nerve himself, time to regain the old fellow's confidence.

Yet that was not impossible. For several days he had been turning over an idea that was to serve should he not get his chance to speak. But it had, in any case, many advantages. And now…He pondered his muddy feet for a moment, picking the leaves from between his toes.

Raising his eyes, he found the old fellow watching him still with the same agonised concern. He could take assurance from that look. Suddenly he had straightened his shoulders and was smiling.

"Please don't trouble yourself, monsieur. It was nothing. Nothing that will not keep."

All the way to the cross-roads, Miremont was inwardly berating himself. He had never meant to shame the boy. What devil was it that had put into his mind that wretched poem? The same, presumably, that had mocked his superstition, that had persuaded him to believe it was possible to replicate perfection—only to confound him by ending the afternoon so badly.

Yet perhaps his sensitivities exaggerated the disaster. For Max, who might have been expected to stand upon his pride, had shrugged it off. That was the most extraordinary thing. One moment he had been wretched, so painfully humiliated he could not look Miremont in the eye—God, Miremont would have given anything not to have inflicted that pain—yet the next he was smiling, laughing. He had seemed in high spirits as, noticing how the sun had shifted, they had hurriedly washed away the muddy traces of their competition, rescued the wine bottle and pulled on the rest of their clothes. And now, as they walked, they were engaged in an energetic but thoroughly amiable argument about the relative merits of Corneille and Racine. If Max secretly burned with anger and resentment at being found out, Miremont could detect no sign of it.

All the same, he fretted that his clumsiness had shattered their understanding. When they reached the cross-roads, the ambiguity of a formal parting seemed too much to bear. No longer caring what watchers might be hidden in the surrounding fields, he flung his arms around the boy's shoulders and pressed his mouth to his. The kiss, their sustained embrace, the boy's answering grin as, for good measure, Miremont could not forbear asking: "Until tonight?"—all should have reassured him. He had been forgiven, it seemed. Nevertheless, as he picked up the hamper and began his solitary walk to La Boissière, he remained deeply perturbed.

Why, in heaven's name, had the boy told such an outlandish lie? For it was a lie, no doubt of that. Of course it was possible that someone who had left his native country as a child might forget the language of his birth through long disuse. But not Max. Not Max, who chose Catullus, Juvenal and Horace as his everyday reading, who was proficient in Greek, who desired to learn English so that he could read Shakespeare in the original, who apparently even spoke passable Russian.

Why, then, had such an intelligent boy not acquired at least a smattering of German to authenticate his story? Although, more probably, the whole thing had been a spontaneous invention, conjured up to satisfy his, Miremont's, accursed curiosity. In which case, Waldavia was an inspired choice—one of those tiny German states that few people ever visited, whose doings, if they were reported in newspapers at all, rated no more than two lines at the bottom of an obscure page. To lay claim to a life such as the boy had described and then set it in France was to invite awkward questions: what château was this with the vista and the fountains, in which *département*, belonging to which branch of which distinguished family?

Yes, the German setting had certainly lulled Miremont's suspicions. After the boy's revelations about his upbringing in the cloister, it had not even seemed so extraordinary. And perhaps it was also true that Miremont had wanted to believe. He had wanted to think that his tall handsome lover, with his fine features and physical grace, was not the son of some Auvergne peasant, but the scion of a noble if impoverished house, with a bloodline not so far distant from his own. Romantic nonsense of course. Yet could it be…? Could it be Max also longed to believe it?

'*Es war ein Traum*'. Again Miremont cursed the thoughtless facility with which Heine's double-edged poem had risen to his lips. A dream, a fantasy. It seemed scarcely credible that precocious, clever Max should harbour such notions; until Miremont reminded himself of the boy's naive streak. And after all, was it so improbable, so unforgivable, that a boy left an orphan should spin fantasies of noble parentage? Or that a young man of Max's qualities, condemned to life in service, should dream himself the equal of those who, while they might be his superiors in rank, were not always so in nature?

Miremont remembered Max's other lie. That, too, had been absurd—again the boy, despite his intelligence, had seemed not to consider that he was bound to be found out. And that too had touched upon his dignity.

Miremont's heart muscles tightened. The after-taste of the lie, which, for all his shame at his own tactlessness, had lingered like corked wine, was washed away. To discover this unsuspected fragility in the boy redoubled his tenderness for him. He was all the more mortified not to have sensed it, to have blundered in where affection should have forewarned him.

Two mornings later Miremont awoke and knew, even before he distinguished the gentle rhythm of someone else's breathing from the other soft murmurs of first light, that Max still lay beside him.

He opened his eyes. Such was the heavy heat of these nights that as usual they had thrown back the covers, so that the boy's naked, sleeping form was revealed at full length. Miremont was stirred by concern—he had exhausted the poor lad, who might now end up in trouble. But this worry penetrated his still-fuddled brain only briefly, for it was soon obliterated by other emotions, joy at his lover's proximity and a poignant delight in observing him innocently abandoned to sleep.

Miremont studied him with fascination. Yes, he was beautiful— perhaps he truly was some aristocrat's bastard. And young, so young, lying there with his cheek pillowed on his hand; twenty-three was another falsehood, although Miremont forgave it, he must be eighteen, nineteen, no more. To watch him thus, stretched out on his stomach, oblivious, to see his shoulders gently stirred by the rise and fall of his breathing, his upper lip dewed with sweat where a barely perceptible morning shadow crept; to note the unexpected length and thickness of his lashes; to search out the place, beneath the damp tangle of brown hair revealed by his out-flung left arm, where, in contrast to the muscles of his torso and thighs, his skin was soft as a child's: this was at once an affirmation of their intimacy and a revelation. The tranquil profile, unguarded, its contradictions stilled, touched Miremont with its innocent transparency; and yet, with its complex workings shut away, it also seemed, as never before, inaccessible, profoundly mysterious.

Miremont's eyes burned once more with inexplicable tears. Again he ached to reach out and touch that mystery, to clutch it to himself, possess it, be possessed by it, be absorbed, at one with its essence, utterly consumed. The confused words crowded to his lips, danced there feverishly, then resolved themselves into a simple sentence, which he heard himself speak soundlessly, once, and then again.

He did not know why he should be surprised. The instant he said it, he realised it had been true since that first Sunday. He loved the boy, loved him with a ferocity that far exceeded the voraciousness of mere desire, loved him as he had never loved anyone, as he had once hoped to love a wife.

As if Miremont's thoughts had pierced his oblivion, Max sighed. Drawing back his arm, he turned onto his flank, revealing that his dreams were now far from enigmatic. At Miremont's touch, he opened his eyes, closed them again briefly, then began slowly and luxuriantly to smile.

They were already too engrossed to heed the forecourt clock when it started to strike the hour. Only as the echo of the sixth chime died into silence did Max suddenly freeze.

"Shit!"

He seemed to be listening to some other sound, carried on the echo but too distant for Miremont to hear.

"Shit—forgive me, monsieur—but that's the rising bell! How in heaven's name did I—? Oh damnation!"

Groggy with frustrated desire, they stumbled over each other gathering up the scattered items of Max's livery and he struggled into them, tugging on his shirt back to front in his haste and muddling the legs of his breeches.

"Curse these ridiculous stockings! Thank god, here's the other under the bed. Shit, how I loathe this fancy dress!" But at least he was laughing as he finally stood dishevelled but, apart from his pumps, fully clothed.

Miremont had pulled on his dressing gown. "My darling boy, this is my fault, I should have made sure to keep awake—"

"I'm the one who had no business falling asleep."

"But will you be in trouble on my account? And what if…?" Miremont faltered, ashamed of his cowardice.

"There are awkward questions? Don't worry, monsieur. Should it come to it, I'll confess to the vice of reading in the broom cupboard." Max grinned. "My main difficulty is escape. The back stairs will be swarming. And even attempting this corridor is dangerous."

As though to prove his point, there were distant footsteps, knocking, the sound of a door opening.

"One of the maids bringing Monsieur and Madame de Cressy their morning tisane. Madame Donyani also likes to be woken early."

They both paused. The Sangrail Tower, which housed Catherine's apartments, had a spiral staircase of its own with a separate entrance; but the smaller Maiden's Tower and the rooms abutting it, like those next to the Knight's Tower, gave only onto the landing. Max's escape did indeed seem cut off.

"What shall you do?"

"Give up and come back to bed." Miremont's heart lifted wishfully, but the boy was laughing. "No, there is nothing for it but the window."

Miremont stared at him.

"Oh, not in here. Your dressing room. The casement is wider, and there is a drainpipe I fancy I can reach." Max was already pulling off the coat and waistcoat he had donned so hastily. Rolling them into a bundle with his pumps, he thrust them into Miremont's arms. "If you would be good enough, monsieur, to throw these down after me."

"My darling boy——"

But Max seemed fired by the challenge. His eyes gleamed as if he relished nothing better, as if the lunacy of the enterprise made it irresistible, and Miremont could not help being swept along by his mood. They were laughing as they rushed into the dressing room, where Max rapidly unlatched the casement, vaulted onto the windowsill and swung his legs through the opening. As he sat for a moment, back turned, legs dangling, Miremont could glimpse beyond his right shoulder the drainpipe descending from where the tower's turret met the pitched roof of the wing; it was newish-looking and appeared sturdy enough.

Max turned his head and grinned. "Trust me, monsieur. I shall cover my tracks. All will be well." Then his right arm reached out to grasp the pipe, his left arm flew after it and his body launched itself into air.

Miremont's smile died. Craning into the space the boy had vacated, he watched with horror as Max hung wildly by outstretched arms while his legs fought for purchase. The lead looked suddenly frail and insecure and Miremont's stomach lurched as he took in the sheerness of the drop. The struggle seemed interminable. He was numb with his own helplessness. But, just as he felt he could not continue to look, the boy's knees and feet connected with the pipe and he began to slide slowly downwards. Miremont suffered a second shock as, without warning and still some way from the ground, Max deliberately let go. Yet he landed neatly and, although he crouched for an instant leaning on his palms, when he sprang to his feet his upturned face wore a smile of triumph.

Miremont's entire body shook with relief. It was only the boy's urgent signals that prompted him to remember the bundle he was holding. The parcel unravelled as it fell, but Max managed to catch one of his pumps, waving his thanks with it. Scrabbling for the other and pulling on his waistcoat, he sprinted off round the perimeter of the tower, struggling into his coat as he went.

Miremont staggered into the bedroom and sat down heavily. If he had been in the slightest doubt, he could question it no longer—the boy's life was his life. He could not think how he had agreed to these insane heroics. Yet Max had escaped harm. And, after a while, Miremont could not but recall the farcical aspects of their predicament. He smiled in spite of himself. Slowly the light of a dizzy happiness began to suffuse his face.

CHAPTER THIRTEEN

"All will be well." It was merciful monsieur did not know the half of it. Euphoria and racing pulses had propelled Max towards the service wing. But here he had encountered a further danger: the route from the garden to the stairs would take him directly past the open door of the servants' hall and, as he paused to catch breath, he realised it was not only his dress livery that would make him conspicuous; his gloves and shirt-front were blackened, his stockings torn, and one of his calves was bleeding. However, by forcing a storeroom window at the other end of the passage, he had succeeded in making his way up to the footmen's dormitory, causing confusion amongst the maids trying to descend from the floor below, but without being apprehended by the Cardinal. Arriving in the dormitory, breathless and sweating, he had been aware of Fabrice clicking his tongue and sarcastic comments from the Oxen, but there had been no time to respond, no time for anything except to splash cold water on his face and haul on his morning livery. Still, the after-glow from his exertions remained. To hell with the Oxen! He could rely on his alibi, cloaked as it was in the sacred code of gallantry, a secrecy made doubly impregnable by the supposed imprimatur of madame. He felt invincible.

Alas, this mood could not endure. It was gradually born in upon him that his palms, although he had protected them with his gloves, were burning, while the material of his trousers had bonded painfully with the blood congealing on his leg. Then there was bound to be trouble with Mme Roussel when he put out his dirty laundry; his shredded stockings would be hard to explain. Furthermore, it was deeply disagreeable to start the day unwashed, although thankfully, since he had shaved as usual before his visit to monsieur, his jaw would pass muster until the afternoon's change of livery. Altogether, he could have done without Fabrice's knowing comments, which he could not escape since the two of them were answering the morning's bells. Fabrice was in any case tetchy, dreading M de Bellac's jangling summons. Max too waited, for the consolation of eleven o'clock when monsieur would descend to the library. Meanwhile, as his elation drained away, his eyelids grew heavy and he could scarcely stifle his yawns.

Fortunately it was an unexpectedly quiet morning. True, madame sent her tray down much earlier than was her custom. But the Lion of Literature's bell remained silent—according to Fabrice he had taken liberal enjoyment in madame's armagnac after dinner and was presumably sleeping it off. M de Miremont must also have succumbed to sleep, for there was nothing from the library bell either, although it was past eleven. When Fabrice, on an errand for M de Cressy, disappeared for some time and the servants' hall remained blessedly empty, Max seized the chance to sit back on the bench, prop his shoulders against the dado and close his eyes.

"My, my, angel! Who's well and truly in the consommé?"

Max recoiled, blinking, from Fabrice's excitement. "Where the hell have you been?"

"In the kitchen, if you must know, talking to Colette. And you'll never guess what I've just heard."

"I'll never guess."

"Don't take that tone with your Auntie, my petal, you'll need her. Your excuse for breezing in this morning stinking of spunk and looking—"

"I've told you, cut that, I'm sick of it."

"Oh, you'll be sick, no question, when you hear what Colette's just told me."

Max could not but read the ill omens in Fabrice's relish. With a sigh, he straightened his back.

"Colette had it from Lise—you know, that house maid who looks like a Charolais heifer—who had it from Coeline, who had it from Simone, who had it direct from Mademoiselle Baudin—"

"Mademoiselle who?"

"For heaven's *sake*, angel! Mademoiselle Baudin, lady's maid to Madame de Corvignac. Well, anyway, Monsieur and Madame de Corvignac have taken a carriage to Angoulême today—apparently they have a fancy to see the cathedral—so Madame la comtesse asked to be called bright and early—"

"Get to the point, won't you. If there is one."

"There certainly is, dear heart, and this is it. When Mademoiselle Baudin turned into the Knight's Tower landing with her tray, she saw someone further down. Sneaking out of somebody else's bedroom."

Max's instant alarm at these words was quickly hushed by common sense. If Mlle Busybody Baudin had been in the Knight's wing, she could not possibly have seen anything that would compromise him or

M de Miremont. This was some other guest's indiscretion and Fabrice was mischievously using it to stir him up. Relieved, he slumped back in his seat.

"Don't go to sleep. You'll want to know who."

"Don't count on it. "

"Madame de Bellyache no less. Mademoiselle Baudin's quite certain. How could you miss the monstrous lump in that lurid dressing gown of hers? Besides, she made no attempt at evasion—stared La Baudin straight in the eye, then waddled back to her own room calm as muck."

Max yawned. "Look, Fabrice, I share your sentiments about the Literary Lion. But, grotesque as the old goat's nocturnal gallivanting might be, I simply can't see it's any business of mine."

"Not if she came from the tower room?"

Max yawned again.

"Wake up, angel! Who sleeps in the Knight's Tower?"

"Oh, for pity's sake!"

"You should know, dear heart. Of all people."

"Why ever—?" But Max stopped abruptly, all at once wide awake. He drew in breath. "Nonsense. The princess can't stand Monsieur de Bellac."

"She makes believe she can't abide La Bellyache and she flirts with your Little Miss Mouse. When she was hot for the Mouse, she flirted with Monsieur de la Rochefontaine. Women's wiles. Spurn them and drive them wild. However, don't ask me, angel, I'm hardly the expert."

Max groaned.

"Exactly. So, since it's all over the entire household—Mademoiselle Baudin, who makes the Delphic Oracle seem discreet, is bound to have told Mademoiselle Lapointe, so even madame knows by now—you'll have to find another excuse for your own nocturnal frolics."

Max ran his hands through his hair. "Madame de Corvignac?"

"*Really*, angel. Even if you'd managed to escape La Baudin, the Corvignacs, in case you haven't noticed, are novices in the state of wedded bliss and still at the spooning stage."

"Mademoiselle de la Falaise?"

But Fabrice merely uttered an incredulous shriek. "You poor sweet thing!"

"Look, I don't see—"

"You're the girl with the classical erudition. Have you never heard of Sappho?"

"Truly? You mean—with the baroness?"

"Which leaves Grand-mère de Cressy. And I doubt even the Oxen would credit that."

Max sighed. "I suppose I can't claim the nursemaid."

"Now you're losing your head, petal. Improper relations with another servant? That will instantly get you your cards."

In fact shortly afterwards Max was called to the nursery, where he could manage only perfunctory exchanges with Marie and was hard put, even with the children, to counterfeit jollity. On his return, his heart sank still further, for he could immediately tell that Fabrice had fresh news to impart.

"It's a mercy, angel, that the Oxen don't talk to Betty—or rather that she won't give them the time of day."

"Michel? What has he to do with anything?"

"I bumped into her in the passage. She's just been over to the hothouses for madame. Where she hears something utterly fascinating. At about ten past six, one of the gardener's boys saw a figure shinning down the drainpipe beside the Maiden's Tower. Strange enough, you might think. But, although the boy was some distance away, so he can't absolutely swear to it, he's fairly convinced that when the figure ran off he caught sight of a footman's tailcoat."

"E-extraordinary."

"Oh, spare us!"

Max swallowed. "Michel thinks it was me?"

"You were the one late down to the servants' hall. Even a brain the size of Betty's can make that deduction."

"Shit!"

"Who did you think you were, angel? D'Artagnan?"

"If the boy can't absolutely swear—"

"He can swear to the drainpipe. And he can also swear he saw someone throw something out of the window next to the tower. The window, as even Betty can work out, of Little Miss Mouse's dressing room."

Max contemplated his knuckles for a moment. He raised his chin. "Who cares! If Michel plans to report me, he'd better realise it will do him no favours with madame to compromise Monsieur de Miremont. Besides which, he might recall he has one or two dirty little secrets of his own which—"

"Oh, I don't think that's her game."

"Then what?"

"You know Betty. You know her favourite sport."

Max winced.

"She seemed no end entertained when I met her in the passage. Sniggering. Leering. Oh, I can't bring myself to repeat what she said, you know how disgusting she is."

"He can cut all that if he wants to keep his teeth. He can't prove anything. It's the gardener's boy's word against mine."

"Don't fool yourself, angel. Look how she is with me, and she's never caught me *in flagrante*. But then this girl's discreet. Whereas I'm amazed Betty hasn't already spotted you ogling Miss Mouse over the andouillettes. God, it's not as if I didn't warn you. *Why*? Whatever *possessed* you? "

Max shrugged. "It was amusing."

This, for some reason, drove Fabrice into a passion. "You know your trouble, dear heart? You never think of others. It never occurs to you that you might have duties, responsibilities."

"I shall do everything in my power to keep monsieur out of it."

"Sod fucking monsieur! What about your duty to me? Your friend? You know how I suffer already. Thank God, this girl can stand up for herself. But if I'm to stand up for you as well…I haven't the strength, my poor back isn't broad enough—"

But here Fabrice was silenced by the angry chatter of the Famous Novelist's bell, and before Max's astonishment could turn to outrage, he had swept out, trailing curses in his wake.

Max closed his eyes again and leant back against the dado. His gloom deepened. The Oxen on one side, Michel on the other, and who knew what rumours wafting malodorously towards M Vincent's sensitive nose. It would be far too dangerous to visit monsieur tonight. He must try somehow to arrange a meeting—a pity the old fellow had preferred his bed to the library, but there would always be after luncheon. Max would need to be sparing in his explanation, of course, lest monsieur take fright. But once the old boy's disappointment had sunk in, he could salve it by outlining his proposition. This was not how he had planned things but, given the circumstances, monsieur could not but be receptive. Max's despondency lifted. Damn them all—Fabrice, Michel, the Oxen—he would show them.

However, monsieur was not at luncheon. The loving couple was much in evidence, Monsieur de Bellac pretending to be bashful but unable to restrain his swagger, the princess as enervated as ever, yet with a new eloquence in the droop of her neck and her wilting lashes. But M de Miremont's place to the right of madame was taken by M de Cressy; and Max gathered from the conversation that on a whim the old boy had decided to accompany the Corvignacs to Angoulême. It was so startlingly unlike monsieur that Max wondered for a moment—had he heard something? But no, that was impossible: the Cyclops was no Mlle Baudin. All the same, the old boy's absence was a blow. It was not merely that it presented practical difficulties; Max somehow could not accustom himself to it. He glared at the scraggy nape of M de Cressy's neck as if he were an usurper.

Sleep, it seemed, was intent on revenge for Max's nights of neglect. Sneaking off alone in the break, he stretched himself out on one of the vegetable garden's grassy paths, shaded by currant bushes and concealed from view by the feathered curtain of the asparagus bed. He stared up briefly at the cloudless sky. Somehow, in between his afternoon duties and assisting M de Cressy into his evening clothes, he would find the opportunity to slip away and speak to monsieur. With a little ingenuity, they could meet in the garden after supper. Everything would resolve itself. He closed his eyes.

"So this is where you've hidden yourself, angel."

Max moved not a muscle, but the presence hovering over him refused to be discouraged. He heard the scrape of a match, then smelled tobacco.

"A peace offering, dear heart. After our words this morning."

Although he was obliged to respond, Max kept his eyes firmly shut. "Thanks, but no offence was taken. Now, if you don't mind, dear chap—"

"You should have told Auntie, she'd have understood." The closer proximity of the voice and a sudden powerful waft of cigarette smoke suggested that Fabrice was now squatting somewhere near his head. "You should have said you and the Mouse have had a falling out."

Max's lids quivered. "Don't be absurd."

"Then that's not why she's leaving?"

No reserve of will power could have kept his eyes closed against this. Yet opening them was a mistake, for Fabrice, he knew, read his bewilderment and alarm.

"Packing up, bag and baggage. I overheard the One-eyed Monster telling the Cardinal just now."

"T-that's ridiculous. The Cyclops doesn't speak."

"She can when she wants to, angel. It isn't melodious, I'll grant you. But I distinctly heard her asking Monseigneur about trains. Oh, and could Alphonse bring down Little Miss Mouse's boxes in good time tomorrow, in case there's confusion with all the preparations for the ball."

"Tomorrow?"

"The Mouse is staying for the ball, apparently, then leaving next day at first light. But, angel—forgive me—I took it for granted..."

"Of course I knew." Heaving himself into a sitting position, Max took the cigarette from Fabrice's fingers. He prayed, as he drew on it, that Fabrice would not notice how his hands were trembling. "Of course I knew. I simply didn't—I must have misheard him."

"No doubt, angel."

"Monsieur de Miremont has always intended to visit his own estate this summer. I hadn't understood it would be so soon. That's all."

Fabrice fell silent. He even failed to protest when Max took a second and third pull on the cigarette. Eventually he sighed. "Auntie did warn you. It never does for girls in our position to become too attached."

"Oh, for god's sake!" Fabrice's pity was more of a scalpel in Max's wound than all his malice. "How many times must I tell you? I am not, as you put it, 'attached' to Monsieur de Miremont. The old boy and I have a—an understanding —that's true. But it is of a purely practical nature."

Fabrice raised his eyebrows.

"It really makes no odds that he is leaving. So far as I am concerned, it's all one whether he goes the day after tomorrow or in a month's time. We have already come to an arrangement that should prove greatly to my advantage. No need to trouble yourself on my account—you'll see."

CHAPTER FOURTEEN

Once he had collected himself, Miremont had dressed in his night shirt to present a respectable appearance to Thomas when he eventually arrived to wake him; then, since Max had not had time for his usual meticulous housekeeping, he had cast a careful eye around the room, straightening the sheets and kicking a soiled towel beneath the bed. He was still concerned that the boy might be in trouble—but, after all, Max had seemed so confident he could disguise his absence that Miremont was inclined to be reassured. When he climbed between the covers, the desire which had been so brutally cut off burgeoned again; he set about satisfying it in a contented and leisurely way. Afterwards, with his hand still resting gently in his groin, he lay in a kind of dream, a stupor of happiness. He loved the boy. He felt all-powerful, ecstatic, capable of transcending his mortal shell, of attaining unimaginable heights, and at the same time weak with an excess of joy and pleasure.

It occurred to him that, at last, he was capable of understanding Aline. In the well-ordered surroundings of the Hôtel de Miremont, in the dry and passionless atmosphere of his study, he had found completely mystifying her willingness to abandon all—her reputation, her home, even her children—for a rootless Italian she had met at a musical evening. But now he could fathom—now he could feel—the extraordinary force that must have carried her away, the imperative stronger by far than reason and caution, the glorious heedless courage of love. He had been unjust to her, had not even done her the honour of jealousy, because all this had been as foreign to him as the forests of the Amazon. With his cold reason, he had perceived only that Signor Ogetti was an adventurer, not of her rank, a man who liked conquest but would soon tire of her; he had thought her blindness astonishing— could she not see she would make herself ridiculous and get nothing but pain for her folly…?

But here he stopped. His caressing hand fell away. He saw his own situation with terrible clarity.

He was no less foolish than Aline. It did not matter how dearly he loved Max. The boy could not love him. Twenty-three years—perhaps more—stood between them. He was a clumsy middle-aged man; hair grew from his nose and ears, in sleep his mouth fell open like a dead man's, he grunted and snored. To someone of Max's youth and beauty, he must seem unthinkably old and repulsive. All he had to commend him was rank and wealth; but that could not inspire affection, let alone overmastering tenderness or transcendent joy. Every night, going to him, the boy must steel himself; every night he must come away shuddering with relief. How grotesque he must find Miremont's groans of passion, how ludicrous his sentimental effusions; how his beautiful sensual lip must curl at this pantaloon fancying himself as a lover.

Oh, but—in all reason—Max had just risked his neck on his behalf. And could Miremont honestly say that he had ever noticed these signs of reluctance, which, given the remarkable current of sympathy that flowed between them, could surely not have escaped him? Yet what sympathy, what current? Did this mysterious understanding actually exist? Or could it only be found in the glass of Miremont's love, his own reflection beguilingly thrown back at him?

Max might seem to enjoy their friendship and their love-making; he might be respectful, outwardly engaged, even surprisingly gentle on occasion—Miremont remembered how, that first night, the boy had brought soap and water from the dressing room and, with great care, bathed him where he lay: it was tempting, oh yes, irresistibly so, to view all this through the haze of the distorting glass, to take encouragement from it, expectations, portents. But it must be remembered that Max was a servant, tutored to conceal his true feelings. And in any case—

A pain Miremont had long struggled to ignore surged up to intensify his misery. Before Max, he had never—more fool he— believed himself capable of jealousy. Yet, lying half asleep after the boy had left him, he would wonder where his lover had learned his art and, with a stab of anguish, he would think of Achille de Tarascon. Now the pain returned in full force. What did the boy do on his days off in Paris? How had he come to be known to Tarascon? Tarascon and who else, what other tongues, mouths, cocks had feasted on that adored body? A vision of the street arabs in the Bois rose up. The unfocused and inexhaustible potency of youth had no difficulty feigning pleasure where none was possible. And as to why Max should stoop to this deception—as with the youths in the Bois, it was absurd to ask.

Oh, please God, no! Besides Max had never demanded money, he had been insulted to be offered it, he had sworn he wanted nothing. Yet what otherwise was Miremont's attraction? Wealth and rank might not inspire love, but there was no denying their other compelling qualities. Miremont screwed up his eyes in anguish. He could not bear to think of Max in this way, he recalled what he had felt as the boy had hung, flailing, above that neck-breaking drop. Yet, like hail stones, the thoughts assailed him.

What did he actually know about Max? That he was intelligent and well-educated. Very little else. Except, of course, that he had a slender hold upon truth. Perhaps even his tale of the cloister had been invented to manipulate Miremont. It was impossible to tell. It was impossible to know, in spite of their intimacy, what was true and what invented to serve some hidden purpose.

Yet Miremont did know—felt—could not believe...Dear God, could so much pain be possible? He loved. True, he had never loved before. Yet he could not believe he was mad enough to love where nothing was returned but falsehood. And even if that were so, would his love cease? Could he turn it off like gas? Would its flame not continue to burn wishfully, long after only shadows remained? Did it matter that Max could not love him? Did anything matter, except this certainty Miremont felt now, that whatever the boy was, blameless or deceitful, generous or mercenary, to be parted from him would be more than he, Miremont, could support?

Yet, of course, part they must, and some day soon. He could see, with his new cruelly clear vision, that this was inevitable. He thought of Aline and her tenor again. He thought of her with envy. If Ogetti had not tired of her as their money had dwindled and her body had swelled with child, they could have enjoyed a life together—not in society, as she would have preferred, but a life nonetheless. But what could Miremont hope for? What could he hope for even if his love were returned? Could he run away like Aline? He and Max could live openly nowhere. But it was anyway unthinkable that he should renounce his duty to ten generations, abandon the heritage he held in sacred trust, let alone sully it with such an unmentionable disgrace. Unthinkable, too, that he and Max should meet in Paris: how could he risk assignations with a nineteen-year-old boy, a servant, under the eye of his family and friends? Only here, at La Boissière, in this hot-house of Catherine's with its ill-assorted blooms and its air heavy with ambiguous scents, was this furtive love possible.

He had been too much bedazzled to think of endings. But now he had thought, now he understood, that was all he could think of. He would never see Max again once he left La Boissière. The agony of it filled him. It tore him as though something deep within him and fundamental to life had been wrenched from him. He bit his knuckles till they bled, but it did not relent. It would be his from now on, like a familiar. Every day he continued here he would view his existence from its shadow—his love, the boy's disdain, the inevitability of their separation. There would be no shaking it off, only a gradual and hopeless surrender.

Better to end the torture now. Better to find the strength to endure the unendurable and go. It would be a kindness to deliver Max from the futile burden of his love.

Such thoughts brought him close to weeping. But he had made his decision and, if he wanted to save himself and spare the boy, he must act on it. He flung himself out of the bed, in which he could, in any case, find no comfort. By the time Thomas arrived with his breakfast tray, he was already in his shirt sleeves at the escritoire, writing an urgent note to Catherine.

Catherine's response was unexpectedly prompt, given her usual habit of not rising before eleven, although when she received Miremont in her boudoir she was still *en déshabille*. She listened sympathetically but also with a certain abstracted air as he stammered out his gratitude and his regrets: alas, this morning's post had brought a letter from his steward obliging him to leave for Beauvallon immediately; there was some difficulty concerning the building of his English model cottages that could not be resolved without his personal intervention.

"But, darling Armand, your company has been such a pleasure. And I had hoped—at least until now—that we had afforded you pleasure too."

"And so you have, my dear. Truly, I am most grateful. But Calvert, my steward—although, do not mistake me, he's a good fellow—he is fond of a glass of wine. Apart from which, he has little understanding of the project. I believe he thinks it a nasty foreign fad…"

Miremont faltered. In fact, when Thomas had returned almost immediately with Catherine's reply, he had been taken aback. He remained true to his grim decision, it was the only course possible, but nevertheless he was shocked to find himself so instantly born along by its consequences. Besides, his treacherous mind had forked again: the maverick part, regardless, was wondering where Max was, hoping the boy had recovered from his escapade. He focused with difficulty on what Catherine was saying.

"My dear friend, I know you must be disappointed. But please try not to take it too much to heart."

This brought him guiltily to attention. Did Catherine know—was Max right, had he been all along so utterly transparent? But no. She would certainly not be favouring him with that affectionate smile, the sweet and surprisingly tender smile she reserved only for her intimates.

"For myself, I cannot think what has come over her. In fact, I am really rather vexed. He is such an astounding bore. I simply cannot imagine why I invited him."

Miremont had no notion what she was talking about. However, since it did not seem to touch upon his own preoccupations, he could only be relieved.

"And now we are to lose you. Today, this very minute. It really is too bad."

"Catherine, I could not be more sorry—"

"Oh, I know. Those cottages. But surely they won't fall down before our ball?"

"I—"

"The ball tomorrow? In honour of dear Génie's birthday—although I'm not at all sure she deserves it. I was relying on you to protect me from the local notables."

"Forgive me, I—"

"And consider, is it politic for you to rush away so pointedly? It could be taken as bad grace."

While Miremont could not imagine the princess would be in the slightest perturbed by his sudden departure, he was arrested by a more compelling thought: what of its effect on Max? He had acted in haste, without proper consideration, had somehow taken for granted in his misery that the boy would remain unmoved whatever he did. But even if Max were utterly indifferent, they had been lovers for a fortnight; the very least Miremont owed him was due warning and a proper goodbye. To contemplate this parting scene was excruciating. Yet, in the midst of his pain, the other voice whispered soothingly that if he took Catherine's suggestion he could spend two further nights with the boy.

"My dear…I am churlish…I confess I had allowed the ball to slip my mind"—that at least was true "—but, of course, if you are counting on me…"

"I shall think it unpardonable if you desert me."

"Only, if I am to stay…if you are so generous as to wish me to do so…there is something…some business I must attend to."

For, of course, it was not merely a matter of goodbyes, he could not leave without doing something for Max. Money—he pushed aside his contemptible speculations—was clearly out of the question. Linen? He had observed Max examining one of his shirts with a look of envy. But they would scarcely fit the boy and besides cast-off linen was a servant's present. Books were an infinitely better idea. He must find a bookseller.

"I should be most grateful for the use of a carriage today."

"Yes, of course."

"I—I should like to buy the princess some little token for her birthday."

Catherine smiled her sweet smile. "Darling Armand, that is most generous of you. Under the circumstances, more than generous. And now I recall, you are in luck— Charles and Helène de Corvignac are this minute setting out for Angoulême."

To be confined in the jolting prison of a sweltering carriage, exchanging small talk for several hours with relative strangers, would have taxed Miremont at the best of times and, in his present mood, seemed purgatory. It scarcely helped that Mme de Corvignac, who affected a lisp and a child-like manner, when not exclaiming in wonder at every passing sight upon the road—peasants with milk churns, urchins pursued by hissing geese across a meadow—emitted a ceaseless flow of enthusiastic prattle, which her husband was disposed not only to indulge but to encourage. They were amiable enough people and merely discharging the obligations of politeness, so that Miremont could not be proud of his misanthropy; but, desperate to be alone with his thoughts, he was soon reduced to feigning sleep.

A remark of Mme de Corvignac's, delivered with a blush and an exculpating giggle, had explained to him the puzzling elements of his conversation with Catherine. Although inclined to share Catherine's estimate of Aristide de Bellac, he was all the same moved by unlikely fellow-feeling, glad that the man, after his days of suffering, had at last been united with the object of his passion: Miremont would not wish his own misery on anyone.

For, in addition to his other afflictions, he had inevitably begun to feel deeply ashamed of himself. How had he brought himself to think so badly of the boy when he professed to love him? Had he learnt nothing from the blackmail episode? Would he, indeed, have entertained these suspicions, even for a moment, if Max were of his own rank?

Certainly the boy lied upon occasion. But was he, Miremont, in a position to judge him? Without compunction, he had told Catherine at least three untruths this morning and had just now treated the Corvignacs to a fourth, maintaining his business in Angoulême was with a notary (for he feared, if he repeated the story about the present for the princess, Mme de Corvignac's feminine expertise might be volunteered to assist him). He was not so pure. In one way or another, he had been lying to himself and to others from the moment he had entered Constant's salon and set eyes on Arthur Kiddle. Fate had decreed that lying should be a condition of his existence. And so it was, too, for Max.

Images floated up before Miremont: the boy unashamedly devouring pastries, smearing his mouth with cream; how his eyes had blazed as he had defended Racine; how his laughter seemed sometimes to possess his whole body; his careless grin as he had flung himself into the void this morning. He gave generously of himself. Perhaps he truly was indifferent. But in their love-making, in their friendship, he was bountiful nonetheless.

Miremont's heart fluttered with sudden hope. Was age, after all, such an insuperable obstacle? Here, sitting opposite him, was Mme de Corvignac, no more than twenty-two, yet gazing with adoration at her middle-aged spouse. Love, enduring love, was a conjunction of minds as well as bodies. Where such a rare and precious thing existed, surely differences of age and even rank—

But here he stopped himself. To take encouragement from the Corvignacs was preposterous, they lived in a different world. If he had flung himself at the feet of some actress or were the sort of man who chased parlour maids, he would have more hope than he possessed now. Even if the boy were able to entertain some feeling for him—the thought both dizzied him and crushed him with a fresh access of pain—it would alter nothing. Their situation was without remedy. He had understood this and accepted it, there was no going back. Having drunk the hemlock, he must now submit to its effects. This hot and interminable drive was merely the beginning of a long and wretched journey.

To distract himself, he applied his mind to his errand, for at least there was pleasure in thinking what he might give the boy. Yet here too he struggled. Books, yes. But which exactly? Max had told him about the library he kept under his bed, but Miremont had no precise idea of what it contained. Catullus was one obvious omission, but what else? By the time the carriage had rumbled through the outskirts of Angoulême and begun the climb to the cathedral, Miremont had made, amended and rejected several mental lists.

Having excused himself from the Corvignacs, he set out through the maze of cobbled streets that nestled in the shadow of the great black steeple. It was now the hottest part of the day and many of the shops were shuttered. However, he found a bookseller and breathed with relief the reassuring aroma of dust and binding glue that assailed him as he entered. But alas he had stumbled upon a purveyor of religious tomes. There was no Catullus to be had, and precious little else from any of his lists. And, besides, it struck him, as his eye withdrew, disheartened, from popular lives of the saints and treatises on Aquinas, that books would be a mistake. Particularly in any number, they were too bulky for discretion. Better some small, easily concealed object that did not invite explanation.

Oh, but what? He stumbled out into the light again, mopping his brow, and wandered aimlessly, staring into shop windows, gazing sightlessly at faded displays of ribbon or patent medicines. At last he found himself in an alleyway, peering into a small window, partly shuttered and very grimy, so that it was some moments before he took in the legend painted in chipped letters on the glass: 'Watchmaker'.

Max, he knew for certain, did not possess a watch. It would be a practical gift, but also, in a particular way, personal: Miremont could not restrain the fancy that, every time the boy took it out to discover the hour, he might be prompted to think of the giver.

With decision, he pushed open the door. As his eyes adjusted themselves, he gradually made out an immense clutter in a small space; wall clocks up to the ceiling, disembowelled clock cases, disembodied faces, fragments of workings, pieces of silver and plate, lengths of chain. The stuffy air throbbed with the ticking of the clocks, and yet, like the stillness at the centre of a vortex, it was heavy too with silence, the deep quiet of concentration. At a counter beneath the window, where a thin soup of light trickled through the murky glass, two men in shirtsleeves and aprons sat at low stools so that only their bent heads and shoulders were visible, and their hands, deftly working with tiny instruments on the delicate mechanisms pinioned, like the quivering hearts of birds, just beneath their chins. Although one was young and pallid and the other grey-haired and stout, they must, from their shared domed foreheads and negligible chins, be father and son.

The father rose and, discarding his jeweller's eyeglass and apron and snatching his frockcoat from a peg, came out from behind the counter ceremoniously to greet Miremont.

What might he do for monsieur? Did monsieur have anything in particular in mind? Silver, gold, hunter, half hunter, open-face, repeater? When his customer hesitated, the watchmaker obligingly fetched timepieces from cupboards and drawers and, rolling out a length of black velvet over the empty portion of the counter, spread them before Miremont in bewildering profusion.

Miremont felt acutely uncomfortable. He was reminded of the furtive nature of his errand, and the constraints it imposed. He would gladly have given Max the most expensive timepiece in the shop if it had been pleasing enough, but he could not do so. He must reject the handsome gold half hunter the watchmaker was entreating him to weigh in his hand: someone in Max's situation suddenly flourishing a gold watch would prompt questions. It grieved Miremont to stint the boy, he hated the cruel parsimony of fate, which not only denied them any life together, but was even niggardly in the matter of parting gestures.

But he was also troubled by the obliging watchmaker. The man affected good nature, yet all the same Miremont seemed to detect something overbearing and even contemptuous in his manner. It was as if the fellow had somehow divined that there were questionable circumstances attached to this purchase.

Was it for monsieur's own use or intended as a present? For someone he knew well or a distant acquaintance? A gentleman like himself? Or a younger gentleman? Miremont shrank from this interrogation, which seemed ominously intrusive, and at the last enquiry he feared he visibly blenched. Yet civility obliged him to answer. "A young man—a nephew."

"A young gentleman." The watchmaker's glistening face crimsoned with triumph. "Now, at last, monsieur, we are getting closer. In fact, dare I say it, we have the very thing." And, almost snatching away the sober silver hunter Miremont had been toying with, he set in its place an open-face watch.

"Anti-magnetic minute and seconds chronograph and second hand, keyless lever movement, jewelled in ten holes, compensation balance, adjusted for temperature variations, solid silver case. All the rage with discerning young gentlemen."

Miremont stared doubtfully at the complicated face with its inset dials, multiplicity of numerals and bewildering array of hands.

"It is, as I'm sure you'll agree, monsieur, not so much a watch as an instrument of science. These other pieces are fine, very fine indeed some of them, of unmatched quality, though I say it myself. But the young man of fashion wants something—monsieur, forgive me—more up to the minute."

Miremont managed a faint smile. But he was mainly beguiled by the thought of Max, in his shabby frock coat, as a creature of fashion. As for the watch, he continued to stare at it in perplexity. Not only did its scientific pretensions strike him as vulgar; he questioned that it would be in the least bit useful for telling the time.

However, it seemed the watchmaker would not countenance his doubts—yes, there was definitely something of the bully about the fellow. "You won't find anything to equal it, look where you please, monsieur, in the whole of Angoulême. In fact, you're fortunate we can still offer you this piece. We had three, but the other two went in a day. The young gentlemen can't get enough of them, isn't that so, Félicien?"

The sickly youth, who until now had remained mute, lifted his expressionless face with its huge blank forehead, and said, in the tones of an automaton: "That is so, Papa."

"There you have it, monsieur. We're, excuse my saying so, another generation. But take it from Félicien here. Your nephew will be delighted."

The ugly inutility of the watch, the cowed look of the boy, the father's hectoring tone and the slight but sinister emphasis he seemed to lend to the word 'nephew'—all urged Miremont to flee. He was suffocating in this narrow crammed room, where the whirrings and tickings, the flutterings beneath the pale boy's mechanical fingers, resembled the protests of small captive creatures struggling vainly for life and where the curious contradictory stillness he had noticed no longer appeared tranquil but to emanate from dumb resignation. Just at that moment, as if in confirmation, a great cacophony broke out, a churning, grinding and wheezing like the death rattle of the entire menagerie, so that he was obliged to grasp the corner of the counter to steady himself. But it was only the clocks all beginning to strike.

He was overwrought. The chiming of the hour warned him that shortly he would be obliged to rejoin the Corvignacs. Perhaps he was wrong about the watch. Perhaps there was sense in the fellow's odious reminder: Miremont was indeed of another generation and Max might well be amused by the novelty of the chronographs. Perhaps, however many watches he inspected in his present fluster, he would never be able to come to a decision. Yet decide he must, or go back empty handed, for he had still to make good the pretext for his journey.

He chose a simple fob chain to go with the watch. No, he did not require the case to be engraved, he was only passing through Angoulême, leaving within the hour. He avoided the watchmaker's eyes as he said this, for he feared to read in them the understanding that this was a gift which must remain devoid of all inscription, even a single initial that might identify the giver.

But the fellow was busy hunting out a shagreen box for the purchase and, as he wrapped the package neatly in brown paper, Miremont could find no trace of insinuation in his red, sweating face, nor anything, in his gratitude for monsieur's esteemed custom, more sinister than excess. Perhaps the poor man had merely been desperate to make a sale. All the same, Miremont was glad to leave, to close the door on the agitated insistent pulsing of the clocks and the boy automaton in their midst.

From a draper two streets away he hurriedly purchased for the princess a mantilla of Brussels lace, which, since it would be judged for its expense, could be certain of a favourable reception.

CHAPTER FIFTEEN

The party from Angoulême arrived back after the dressing bell, and dinner was held in waiting while they washed away the dust of the road and changed. Thus the first Miremont saw of Max was when the boy pulled out his chair. Although to general appearances Max's face remained appropriately devoid of expression, Miremont, who understood better, saw that he already knew he was leaving and had received the news, not with indifference, but with shock. Miremont endured dinner in anguish. The longing to grasp Max's arm or seize one of his white-gloved hands as they offered him the servers, to press it, to utter his whispered contrition, was almost more than he could master. But all that was possible, once the meal was finally over and he was rising from his chair, was to concentrate into the one brief look he was able to direct at the boy the urgency of his need for a meeting.

Yet he must stay his impatience, for although Max responded with a scarcely perceptible nod and although later, through the open windows of the grand salon, Miremont thought he glimpsed him fleetingly on the terrace, Catherine was determined to claim her old friend for the rest of the evening. Pointedly, as Bellac strewed anecdotes at the languid feet of the princess, their hostess took Miremont aside and talked to him with the greatest show of animation and intimacy about shared friends, about his daughters, about his English cottages (God, how he wished he had never mentioned them): she even insisted on helping him turn the pages of a volume of Piranesi etchings which she had been promising to show him for the past three weeks, but on which, it now seemed, his immediate opinion was vital to her existence. He was quite unable to escape her misplaced kindness until it was time to retire.

He both yearned for and dreaded the boy's stealthy knock. And when it came, the desire to blurt out that everything was a mistake, that he had no intention of going, left him momentarily bereft of words.

"I have offended monsieur? Monsieur is displeased by my blunder this morning?"

Max did not come forward to embrace him but remained stiffly to attention near the door, and Miremont noted with pain his use of the third person.

172

"No, my dear fellow, my very dear…Good heavens, no, I…"
Lying to Max, he realised, would be a very different matter from lying
to Catherine. "There are difficulties at Beauvallon. I ought to have
gone there, you understand, a week ago and now…this wretched
business, which cannot be helped…I meant to tell you myself, only I
was obliged to go to Angoulême—to consult a notary."

"Then you are not angry with me?"

"My darling boy, why should I be? Except with your idiotic bravado
this morning. But then, I ought to have prevented you—"

"You have not—nothing at all has happened to displease you?"

"Of course not. It is just this business at Beauvallon…" Miremont
paused, for he felt in another moment he would launch into the
unnecessary elaborations that had undone him with Catherine. "It
was all decided suddenly when the post arrived this morning. I ought
to have told you immediately…if I had only been able to get word to
you…"

He hated himself for lying to the boy, and he felt the boy should
hate him too, should hurl reproaches at him, fight back against this
grotesque deception with every atom of his pride. But instead Max's
expression had softened, he even appeared relieved, so that it struck
Miremont with consternation that he might truly have imagined he
had offended him in some way.

"Oh, my dear boy! You cannot possibly think…" But here
Miremont struggled with new difficulties as the words rose up that
would contradict the lie, the incontinent effusions that would burden
Max and encourage his own delusive yearnings. He could only continue
lamely: "You must know I meant to tell you…And you? I have not yet
asked you—did you escape mishap this morning, after you had terrified
me out of my wits?"

"Oh, that. There was no trouble, I was not missed." The boy was
smiling suddenly—nonchalantly, almost—no longer stiff and defensive,
but coming forward to embrace Miremont with every appearance of
affection. As Miremont held him, he felt the measure of his impending
loss. But, once he could speak, all he could permit himself was: "Oh,
my dear, we have two more nights."

"Then let us make the most of them."

For all his fears, Miremont had secretly hoped for some expression
of distress or regret. And yet there was nothing indifferent about the
boy's love-making: he seemed driven by a new urgency, an intensity of
passion that had no time for niceties, that brushed aside Miremont's

concern about the gash in his calf, that thrust and battered and consumed as though it would obliterate the very idea of Beauvallon; and Miremont was soon beyond anxiety and guilt, beyond thought.

Afterwards, just as he had on their first night together, Max brought water and a towel from the dressing room and bathed Miremont with great gentleness as if he were a child. Then he lay down again so that Miremont could take him in his arms. For a while they said nothing. Miremont did not speak because he dare not. But Max, it seemed, had been preoccupied, for he suddenly disengaged himself and sat up.

"Monsieur."

Miremont was seized, quite against his resolve, by a ridiculous hope. "My dear boy, what is it?"

"I once said I would never ask you for anything. I would not break my word, except—well, in what I ask there are advantages for both of us."

Hope shrivelled as though blasted by a north wind.

"Take me into your service, monsieur. Employ me as your secretary."

Miremont could only stare at him, appalled.

"You know I have serviceable Latin. My Greek, I admit, does not match it, but I am working to remedy that."

It could not be escaped: with every word the boy condemned himself and confirmed Miremont's worst suspicions. There was no boundary to Miremont's disappointment.

"I realise there would be other duties apart from helping you with your work. Correspondence, business matters—"

"My dear fellow, please—"

"But I am quick to learn, you would not find me—"

"Please, my dear Max. You must not…I cannot…I already have a secretary."

The boy was checked, but only for an instant. "Does he understand your work as I would? Is he as willing as I would be?"

"Monsieur Lesage has been with our family for forty years. He was secretary to my father."

This time Max definitely faltered, yet he was not to be stayed. "Then employ me as your copyist. I am told I write a good clear hand. In the cloister I also learnt calligraphy—I may be a little out of practice, but I have not entirely lost the skill. Look —if you have ink and paper I can show you." And, before Miremont could prevent him, he had swung his legs out of bed and was striding, naked as he was, to the escritoire.

"Please, my dear fellow, you must desist!" It was bitter enough for Miremont to discover his jaundiced speculations had been all too accurate, that Max had indeed been pursuing his own advantage: he reeled from the effrontery of the young man's ambitions—that he should imagine Miremont might contemplate taking him into his household, where he would be encountered by Constant, by his nephews and, worse still, by his daughters.

Yet ought Max to be blamed for his lack of understanding? Miremont was bound to recall that, while he had spoken frankly of his childhood and had referred, though in the briefest and most factual terms, to his separation from Aline, discretion had compelled him to omit all reference to his daughters, as though shying from a profanity. No, the boy, in his naivety, could not be blamed for his unrealistic hopes. Despite the pain of his own disillusionment, Miremont felt pity for him: it was understandable that he should wish to better himself; Miremont heard with anguish the desperation in his eagerness.

Reaching for his dressing gown, he continued more gently: "My dear fellow, I am grateful—I am honoured by your offer. But alas, as you must see, it is impossible for me to accept it. I should have no work for you—"

"Not even copying?"

"As you know, there is not a manuscript at the moment. And if, God willing, there ever is again…well, Monsieur Lesage has always made my fair copies. Not that I doubt the clarity of your hand, or your capabilities. Not that I doubt for a moment that in other circumstances you would make me a first-rate secretary—"

"Other circumstances?"

"Well, as I say, if things were not…as they are, with Monsieur Lesage. So, you must see…I beg you to understand…what you ask is not within my power to grant. It is sadly impossible."

Max said nothing. But, as Miremont rounded the bed, he saw a look on his face he had never seen before, not even when he had tactlessly recited the Heine poem. The boy's disappointment was raw. He averted his head as Miremont approached—it might have been from resentment but, rather, Miremont sensed his shame at not being in command of himself—so that, despite the impulse to take him in his arms, Miremont was obliged to draw back. He watched helplessly as Max reached for his clothes.

"Of course, although I am not able to employ you myself, that is not to say…I do not mean, my dear fellow, that you ought not to entertain such ambitions. On the contrary, it is absurd that your abilities are not put to good use. If I should hear of anyone of my acquaintance who requires a secretary, I shall not hesitate to recommend you. In fact, when I return to Paris, I shall make enquiries of Doctor Ricard and Professor Rosenthal. There is sure to be someone at the university who would leap at the chance to employ a young man with excellent Latin…"

"Monsieur is kind." The boy's face, as he pulled on his coat, was now perfectly controlled, devoid of reproach, devoid of any emotion, utterly opaque, his servant's face.

Miremont was stung by this withdrawal. Yet it was no more than he deserved. He had behaved, was behaving, shabbily. And, at the same time, the maverick voice sang out that the lies, the hypocrisy, the shabbiness—all of it was needless. What better existence could he hope for than the life the boy had offered him? A vision shimmered of nights giddy with love-making matched by purposive days that were also filled with pleasure, mornings where he woke to the prospect, not merely of work and duty, but of laughter, debate, common amusements, natural affinities. Would anyone truly notice that the young man who copied his manuscript also shared his bed? Was it fine moral scruple that held him back, or simple cowardice?

"Oh, my dear Max, " he murmured, "if I could only…"

But the boy, it seemed, was not listening. He had drawn himself up to his tallest and had raised his chin, as though coldly determined to deliver some prepared speech. "It seems I have already troubled monsieur enough. All the same, I have the impertinence to request a second favour. I do not expect to be believed, I was not believed before, but nevertheless, monsieur, I beg you to listen. You are proud of your blood, I too am proud of mine. Although misfortune places me in my present situation, so that any claim I make invites mockery, I must tell you that my father—"

"Darling boy, in God's name, stop!" It broke Miremont's heart that Max, for all his pride, should reduce himself with this childish fantasy. "Don't you think I know your worth? Do you imagine this has anything to do with rank?"

"Monsieur misunderstands me—"

"No, dear Max, you mistake me. Do you think if I were free to choose…if I were able for one minute…My God, if I could even begin to tell you the pain it causes me to—"

However, just in time, he caught himself. One glance at the boy was enough to make clear, if it were not already clear enough, that he had no feelings for him. Besides, his first instinct had been correct. He had only to remind himself of Clotilde visiting with his infant grandson, or Juliette, sweet innocent Julie, returning from convent school, and horror replaced the maverick vision of happiness. He had moved towards Max with his arms outstretched but now he stepped back and sat down heavily on the bed.

Max seemed about to speak, then to reconsider the usefulness of it. With a faint shrug, he turned to the door. "Monsieur, I must go now."

Miremont was at once alert with anxiety. "Until tomorrow?"

"It is difficult, monsieur. It was not easy tonight. And tomorrow there is the ball, we shall be working till all hours."

"But you will…I should like to…" Yet Miremont could scarcely hold out his gift as an inducement, since it would seem infinitesimal beside what he had refused to give. "My dear fellow, we surely cannot part without saying our goodbyes."

His desperation must have been patent, for the boy, if he did not precisely smile, unbent a little. "I shall try my best, monsieur."

For the entire next day, the house was thrown into turmoil. Tradesmen and workmen arrived in carriages and carts and there was a great deal of shouting and hammering— hammering, as Miremont recalled from the time of Aline, was a necessary precursor to balls. Barrow-loads of flowers were transported from the gardens and hothouses, furniture was everywhere in disarray, bells went unanswered; luncheon was served in the old fashioned manner with guests fending for themselves and the Zelenski children forewent their afternoon games.

The ladies greeted the commotion with a resigned air of *noblesse oblige*: they would do their best to assist their hostess with her annual entertainment for her neighbours, however draining the exposure to provincial manners and fashions. Princess Zelenska, the excuse for the occasion, was naturally the most resigned of all, accepting her birthday tributes, from Miremont's lace to a sonnet specially composed for her by Aristide de Bellac, with a faint smile of heroic fatigue. Nevertheless, as the day wore on, there was a hum of suppressed excitement in the corridors, a scurrying of lady's maids with dresses over their arms and pincushions at their wrists. The men on the other hand were inclined to be tetchy: Ignate de Cressy retired to the pavilion with a volume of Baudelaire, while his father and brother, routed from the Yellow Salon, their usual sanctum, invaded Miremont's solitude in the library; only

Aristide de Bellac appeared in excellent sorts, no doubt buoyed both by the delights of love and the prospect of a fresh audience.

At last evening came. The twilight resounded with the screeches and sighs of a string orchestra tuning, Chinese lanterns glimmered on the terrace, the Italian garden blazed with flambeaux, on the lawn various wooden structures had been erected to assist the firework display, as well as a flower-decked stage, on which a troupe of dancers, conveyed specially from Paris, would perform a ballet of Baroness Donyani's devising, loosely based on the Hebrew legend of Lilith. Carriages began to rumble into the forecourt. The local minor nobility and gentry, the mayor of the commune, even the curé; prosperous gentlemen with rotund waistcoats, nervous matrons; families with marriageable daughters blushing in overawed anticipation: all were announced sonorously by M Vincent to Catherine, waiting, gracious in her diamonds, to receive them; and soon a clamour arose to compete with the orchestra as though an aviary of multitudinous birds had been let loose, and the air grew close with the smell of tallow, lilies, pomade, scent and sweat.

Miremont did his duty. Despite the glowers of Aristide de Bellac and Catherine's anxious glances, as though she wished she could spare to him the cruelty of the ordeal, it fell to him, as the highest ranking man present, to lead off the dancing with the honoured guest, the princess, and to take her into supper. However, as soon as he decently could, when it was plain Catherine had no further need of his services, he pleaded his early start on the morrow and retired.

All day, Max had been no more than a retreating back, or a distant figure carrying chairs or nailing up lanterns; tonight, too, Miremont had only caught glimpses of him, replenishing glasses, hurrying away from the supper table with empty platters. A sense of unreality had overtaken Miremont, accentuated by the crush, the explosions of the fireworks, all the tumult and glare and disorder of the ball—things could not fall apart in this nightmarish way, tomorrow Max would bring him his coffee, as normal, in the library, this could not be the end, he could not be leaving. Yet he had but to enter his room to feel a new emptiness, to encounter the cold reminder of his valises in the dressing room, already neatly packed by Thomas, with only his travelling clothes left out for the morning.

He was taking the right course. Honour, duty and decency demanded it. If he still cherished doubts, he had merely to observe Thomas as he went about the business of undressing him, his jaw

rigid, his one eye resolutely declining to encounter his master's:
Miremont could not imagine how far his head must have been in the
clouds to think Thomas deceived, or to believe his recent transition
from cantankerousness to quiescence had been anything other than
the setting in of dumb mutiny. He again recalled his vow on taking the
poor fellow into his service, remembered it was to his father that the
promise had been given. His parents, in their generous and unaffected
virtue, his brother Edmond, gallant and capable, so much better
equipped to carry the burden of the family's honour, his beloved
sister—he had let them all down. But at least he might now make
recompense to the living; if he could not save Thomas' feelings he
must bear that as a penance; but at least he could ensure the contagion
did not spread.

Yet it was remarkable what scant comfort it brought him, this clear
recognition that he was doing his duty. It was extraordinary how, given
proof positive that Max had merely manipulated him for his own gain,
he was still racked by the feeling he was treating the boy badly. Nor
had Max's duplicity in any way diminished his love, but merely
increased the pain of it.

To distract himself he turned his mind to the watch. He was still
uneasy about it and, after Thomas had gone and he was able to free it
from its wrappings, his uneasiness grew. It was not merely that the
object reminded him disagreeably of his encounter with the
watchmaker: what had even then seemed in doubtful taste now
appeared inescapably hideous. Certainly Max was young, yet Miremont
could not but feel he would share this judgement.

Miremont's own watch lay on the escritoire. It was not, as so many
of his possessions were, imbued with memory, patinaed with the touch
of previous generations. In fact he had bought it on impulse one day,
while his grandfather's hunter was being repaired. He had been visiting
the Bibliothèque Française—it was a pleasant afternoon and he had
decided to send his carriage home and walk—and he had been
attracted to a curio shop in a small passage near the Palais-Royal. The
watch was hanging in the window amongst a host of other objects,
coral and amber beads, embroidered reticules, scraps of tapestry, a
faded Kelim, but it had caught his eye at once because of its striking
simplicity. It was clearly no curio, but of modern manufacture, which
the shop's proprietor, a Greek, confirmed: the watch had been made
by his late brother-in-law, a craftsman of great talent and with certain
firm theories about the relationship of design to function that were

perhaps ahead of their time, for they had failed to please popular taste. However, they had greatly pleased Miremont and he had continued to wear the watch even after his grandfather's timepiece had been restored to him; it still gave him pleasure to look at its clean Roman face, to weigh its slender mass in his hand and find it unexpectedly heavy, like a well-balanced knife.

Here at least was something worthy of the boy. Fortuitously, since it had been acquired originally as a temporary measure, and although Miremont had later meant to have his initials set on the inside of the cover, it had never been engraved. Thomas, indeed, was the only drawback—Miremont must provide some account of its disappearance that did not provoke a search or awkward questions; but no, shamingly, he realised, Thomas knew enough by now to make his own deductions.

The watch looked well inside the shagreen box, an immeasurable improvement on the other. Yet new worries assailed Miremont. Would such a present appear ungenerous? Would he seem to be giving the boy a cast-off, the consequence merely of some last-minute thought? Finally, by way of compensation, he took out his notecase and folded the highest-value banknote it contained into a neat square, which he slid out of sight beneath the watch. There would be difficulties when Max discovered it, but he would smooth them over somehow.

He sat in the window embrasure with the box beside him, smoking, waiting. Downstairs, the music ceased and the sounds of revelry dwindled. He had not allowed himself to doubt that Max would appear; yet, as the forecourt clock struck two, his certainty faded. Good sense required that he should extinguish the lamp and go to bed, for he must rise in four hours; but he feared to sleep lest, against all hope, the boy's knock came and he failed to hear it. Nevertheless, he must have dozed where he sat, for suddenly Max stood before him.

"Forgive me for waking you, monsieur, but I can stay only a few minutes."

Nothing was as Miremont had imagined it. As he rose, blinking stupidly, from the window seat, he saw that Max had exchanged his livery for the black frockcoat; he did not miss the declaration in this gesture, or the tension in the boy's face, which, despite the dark circles beneath his eyes, seemed more than the product of fatigue: yet it was not merely the boy's pride that rendered their embrace a stiff, formal affair, devoid even of kisses. Miremont had never been more conscious of the great wall of words that divided them, words on both sides of bad faith and duplicity, multiplying the others that must remain unsaid.

If any current of mutual understanding had ever existed beyond Miremont's delusion, it was dammed up now. They had already parted.

In his sorrow, Miremont almost forgot the box. Max seemed genuinely surprised to receive it and was inclined to protest, but once he had lifted the lid his look of pleasure was gratifying. He revolved the watch delightedly in his palm, clicked open the cover, admired the face.

"Monsieur, it's beautiful. It is exactly like..." But here realisation clouded his face. "No. No, I couldn't possibly accept—"

"My dear boy, I wish you to have it. It has always kept good time for me and I hope it will serve you as faithfully. Just as long as it pleases you—"

"Of course it pleases me—"

"Then it is yours."

"But I cannot—"

"It is yours. And we will have no further argument."

Max hesitated, but then smiled, which Miremont could not but take as a satisfying rebuke to the watchmaker. "Thank you. Thank you, monsieur, I..." Yet the smile faltered, for in returning the watch to the box Max had noticed the square of coloured paper lodged in the bottom. Setting aside the watch, he began to unfold it.

Miremont thought it best to pre-empt him. "And there will be no arguments on that score either. I had hoped to buy you books, but it proved impossible."

But the boy had already stiffened. "Monsieur, is not the watch enough, more than enough? This is not—well, in any case it is an absurd sum."

"If you refuse it I shall be most offended."

"Then one of us must be offended."

"Idiot boy, it is not a tip. I require you to make me a present in return."

Max stared at him. He gave a short, dry laugh. "Now monsieur mocks me."

"My dear fellow, only something small. Even a button—"

"A button?"

"Humour a foolish old man. I too should like some memento of our time together."

Max continued to look at Miremont for a moment. Then he shrugged and began to turn out his pockets. A handkerchief, crumpled and somewhat ragged, a coil of string, a paper twist of tobacco, matches and several centimes fell in a bedraggled pile onto a nearby commode, then, from his trouser pocket, something that dropped with a clatter and skidded across the polished surface of the wood. A rust-red stone, about the size of a thumb joint, shot with two white veins.

"My dear boy, I should be very happy with that, if you are prepared to give it to me."

"This pebble?" Max picked it up, glancing sceptically at Miremont. "If that is what monsieur truly wishes." With due ceremony he handed over the stone and watched Miremont stow it safely in his dressing gown pocket. He laughed. "You give me riches, monsieur, I give you a pebble."

"Oh my dear Max!" All Miremont's resolutions were suddenly forgotten. "Oh, my darling boy, are you truly unaware of all you have given me, have you truly no idea, no conception—?" He recollected himself abruptly, but not before he had seized the boy by the shoulders, so that he found himself staring helplessly into his eyes. They looked at each other in silence for a moment.

"*Futuimus bene,*" Max said softly. Then he took Miremont's right hand and pressed the palm to his lips.

Miremont struggled for breath. Something cold and metallic constricted his throat. It was only the tears that gave him the strength to save himself, withdraw his hand, turn away, stumble towards the window.

"I shall not forget—" although he swallowed hard, his voice came thickly "—I shall of course not forget my promise to you. If I hear of anyone who requires a secretary—we may not write to each other, that goes without saying—but if I am successful, I trust I may send word to the Hôtel de Claireville. And you, my dear fellow—if by any chance you decide to leave Madame la duchesse's employ, perhaps you would be so good as to let me know—just a brief note, giving the address of your new situation. Although, I am sure, once I return to Paris, it will be only a matter of days before—"

But he was interrupted by the sound of the door closing and when he turned the boy was gone.

CHAPTER SIXTEEN

Curse the old hypocrite! So much for his so-called code of honour. May he rot! Fabrice was right—M le marquis de Miremont was no exception to the rule, for all his sentimental speeches: the nobs looked after their own interests, and to hell with anybody else.

Max still reeled from the old boy's treachery. When he sought for explanations, when he tried to comprehend how he could be adored one moment, expendable the next, he could reach but one conclusion. The conversation about Waldavia might have occasioned some awkwardness, but that had been a couple of days ago and the cloud had seemed to pass over. No, it had been oversleeping that had done for Max. The old boy, despite his denials, had been thoroughly panicked. Maybe he had caught wind of the gossip, but most likely not: the thought, the very thought that he had narrowly missed being found with a footman in his room, had been enough to put him to flight.

It was as simple as that: Max kicked himself for his failure to grasp it. Bewildered by such a mercurial change of heart, he had believed the old boy might be turned, like a ship momentarily blown off course. He had been quite unprepared for the look of horror his perfectly sensible proposition had inspired, but even then he had not given up hope, even then he had imagined the old fool merely needed time to reflect. He had returned on that last night, at great risk, still hoping, expecting, still deceived by the old fellow's sighing and heaving. In his stupidity he had continued to credit monsieur with finer feelings. But here was the brutal truth: once risk outweighed pleasure, Max had served his purpose.

And where did that leave him? Every minute he expected to hear that Guillaume had reported him. Undeniably it had been foolhardy to visit monsieur again after the drainpipe incident—he hardly required Fabrice to harp on about that. Despite his flourishing a candle-end and a copy of *The Illiad*, nobody had believed he was reading in the broom cupboard, so that the next night, the night of the ball, he had been reduced to climbing into bed and waiting until the dormitory was asleep; because of the late hour the Oxen were soon snoring, but nevertheless Guillaume had looked at him suspiciously the next morning.

And why not? What was more calculated to confirm everybody's suspicions than monsieur's hasty departure? Add the remarkable coincidence that Max no longer disappeared at night, and you would be a bigger fool even than the Oxen not to draw your own conclusions. Michel was certainly making the most of it and Max already felt the frost of M Vincent's frequent glance. The moment could not be far off when he would be called into Mme Roussel's parlour to be sent packing. There was only one thing that might save him, and this was but a faint hope, for it could equally prove his final undoing.

Of course the old fellow could hardly be blamed for failing to see the extent of Max's predicament, for it had been politic to conceal it from him. Yet even so, if he had thought, if he had troubled to exercise his imagination…But grand gentlemen like monsieur, as Max should remember, had not the slightest notion of the realities of life. Doubtless his conscience was clear—had he not paid Max off handsomely? But here again the old boy's grasp of reality was laughable.

At first Max had been touched by the gift of the watch, and not merely because he had always admired it; yet it was so instantly recognisable as monsieur's that he could never wear it or even allow it to be discovered amongst his possessions—to protest that it had been a present would sound, to say the least, thin. The same was true of the money: a note of that size was of no use unless he could change it, yet he could imagine the glances he would draw presenting it at a bank. Perhaps Old Jouvert would break it down for him when he returned to Paris (if, in the event of his ignominious dismissal, Old Jouvert still gave him the time of day). But until then the note, and the watch too, were an incriminating burden that must be hidden, the watch under a floorboard beneath his bed, the banknote in his frock coat, stitched into the hem.

Useless presents, useless risks. Damn the old boy to hell! Max wondered what it would take to disabuse Fabrice of the ludicrous fancy that he had entertained some affection for the old fossil. Certainly Max's mood was black, but mawkish fantasies were hardly required to account for that. Yes, it was true that, just as with madame, there were things he missed, the flattering attentions, the escape from the squalor and hostility of the dormitory. Yes, he would even go so far as to admit that on occasion he missed the old fellow himself; he still could not get accustomed to another taking the old boy's place at table; he still craved the refined agonies of their game of risk; in the midst of mindless tasks, preoccupied with some idea or other, he would still anticipate the pleasure of debating it later with monsieur and suffer, as he caught himself, a moment's wrenching loneliness. And yes, of course, he was only human, he missed the fucking.

But what did that amount to? Certainly not an 'attachment', as Fabrice so odiously described it. Ironically, that last night, misled by the old fellow's crocodile tears, Max had been tempted to tell him he loved him: it had seemed the gust that might save the floundering vessel. But it was as well he had been forewarned by his experience with madame; as things had turned out, he would have achieved nothing except complete humiliation. In any case, declarations of love, while they might increase your power with women (or at least had done so with Josette), diminished it with men. Max winced as he thought of Dom Sébastien.

What was love anyway? It was like that stone the old boy had made such a performance about, agate one minute, a pebble the next. Damn Fabrice, with his cloying solicitude and maudlin memories of his dalliance with the younger son of his first house. Max's stupidity was of another kind. It was not love that had been betrayed here: Max had let his guard down so far as to trust the old boy. He should have known, of course. There had been only two people he had trusted up to now—Brother Bernard and Mitya Zhukovsky. You did not trust anyone who wanted something. M le marquis, despite his show of affection and for all his apparent devotion to truth and honour, was, when you came down to it, no different from Lebas or even the comte de Tarascon.

Max had been taken for a fool. He shuddered to recall his false hopes, and how he had made an even greater idiot of himself, boasting of them to Fabrice. As the days passed, his heart hardened against all reminders of monsieur. When his next day off came—if he were spared to enjoy it—he would take the watch to the pool and hurl it into the water.

Miraculously, the blow from M Vincent had not fallen by the time that Sunday arrived. Alone in the dormitory, after waiting impatiently for Guillaume and Jacques, whose Sunday it also was, to change and take their departure, he prised the watch from its hiding place and thrust it, without looking at it, into his pocket. He imagined skimming it like a pebble across the lake, he saw it flying with the full force of his rage in a great gleaming arc towards the deepest water, where it bounced once, before sinking, neatly, roundly, with the satisfying finality of a full stop. But when he reached the waterside, he could not do it.

He did not know why. He even got as far as swinging back his arm but could not bring his fingers to let go. With the watch in his palm, he sat staring out towards the cascading water and the straggly trees clinging like goats to the rock and, once again, an inconsolable loneliness seized him. He shoved the watch back into his pocket. Ah well. It was, after all, a beautiful thing, and valuable besides: like madame's diamond pin, it would raise a useful sum at the pawn shop.

Yet—to hell with it all!—he should not permit himself to be distracted from the main point. Which was, of course, that he had lost his patron. He would have to begin his search all over again.

He was obliged to admit his anger on this score was pointless. He had been given the perfect opportunity and had muffed it, had bungled it so badly that, on his second try, he could not even persuade monsieur to listen. That day nearly four years ago it had seemed so simple— seize the moment, take what was his, what, at any rate, was his just entitlement. All it required was one convincing lie. But he was learning that the lie was not his greatest obstacle. What constantly confounded him was the truth.

The long-awaited chance to describe the glories of Before should have been an exalted occasion, so why had he experienced that curious distaste? Perhaps the memories could no longer be kept pure but were irrevocably tainted by what befell later. It was true enough that they had ceased to be a talisman. To recount them out loud, to give them substance, to utter them recklessly to a stranger, was to invoke the curse of After in all its power. Twice since that conversation with the old boy he had suffered the nightmares that had tortured him in his first years at St Pons—the rats scampering over his sleeping face, the engulfing darkness, the stench, in which something beyond the oozing walls and the slops pale and the rotting straw, something sweet and putrid, rose up to take your breath: his screams had not increased his popularity with the Oxen.

Yet there was more. That death's-head smell reminded him. The full horror of their captivity lay not in these physical deprivations, but in a realisation that had come to him early on. It was the Other they wanted. Whatever plan they had concocted, Major von Eisen and Baroness Zetter, it stood or fell on their possession of the Other. He, himself, was superfluous. As to why they had bothered to keep him alive until now was a puzzle, but one thing was certain: if the Other died, so would he.

And so it had begun. Not from altruism, not from liking—the two of them, for differing reasons, had never enjoyed any fellow-feeling—nor from duty as the Other chose to assume; but from his own cold fear. When the Other wet his bedding or forgot to speak French, he would confess to it and take the beating. When the Other complained of hunger, he would sacrifice his own meagre ration. When the Other sucked his thumb and retreated to infancy, he invented the game of Before to bring him back. When the Other cried at night, or whimpered and fretted from any of the small ailments he had always been prey to, he would nurse him with all the care their beloved Frommchen had bestowed. Once, when the Other's cough had turned to fever and his breathing had grown alarming, he had crouched over him all night, desperately forcing his own breath into his lungs; towards morning, lying limp across the Other's body, he had woken from a doze to find himself drenched: he could still recall his joy at realising the sweat was not his own; the fever had broken, his frantic prayers had been answered, the miracle had been granted that restored them both to life.

Nine months, a year—he could never be sure—all this time locked in dark limbo thinking the Other's thoughts, racked with the Other's pains, feeling the Other's hot piss leaking into their palliasse as though he pissed it himself: gradually he had ceased to know where the Other ended and he began. Once his life had been contingent on the Other's: now they were one organism. If they still had little liking for each other, their differences were the opposing forces at war within any human heart; if the Other must be judged the embodiment of worth and virtue while he was the repository of sin, that merely confirmed their indivisibility. In all the alien, frightening places they had ended up afterwards, culminating in their abandonment at St Pons, their union had seemed their only certainty. It burdened him, he resented it, but he did not question it. Until the day he had peered into the *lavatorium's* spattered glass and seen a face that was not the Other's staring back at him.

Yet now they must be one again. He had allowed for this of course—that he must describe Before through the Other's eyes, with the Other's prejudices and weaknesses—yet, until his conversation with M de Miremont, he had not known how violently he would recoil from it. And there was something else he had not reckoned with, something only born in upon him as he had heard himself speak: the golden vision of Before—that too was the Other's. He, Max, was the boy with the truckle bed in the corner, the boy who dutifully held Bobik's reins, who walked a step behind. He might not be the peasant his papers declared; his father, his real father, may have boasted a newly acquired 'von' before his name: but in one way or another—or so it struck him now—he had always lived in servitude.

Not that this, any of it, shook his determination. Rather, every nightmare, every painful memory argued the justice of his cause. But he must own it: he faced a practical problem. If, as was likely, his life in service was over—and shit, he had had his fill of it! —how was he to proceed? His three years in great houses had strengthened his belief that influence was all, yet his hope of that was ended if their gates were to be closed to him. True, there was M de Miremont's vague promise to find him a secretarial position, but he set little store by that, it had been the old boy's way of fobbing him off. He must accept it, he was on his own.

Still, was that such an irretrievable disaster? Perhaps it made no odds. If they had taught him one thing, Mme la duchesse de Claireville and M le marquis de Miremont, it was the impenetrable complacency of their kind; war and revolution might have shaken their ineluctable superiority, but only for the blinking of an eye. Why, when they reaped all the riches of *La France*, when they stood, or so they believed, at the epicentre of the civilised universe, should they stoop to consider the struggles of a small and distant country of which they had barely heard? What had happened to Max must seem so remote, so fanciful that, if he had ever succeeded in making his declaration, they would most likely have taken him for mad.

He needed the help of someone who knew Waldavia. But here once more was the perennial problem: how, without connections, to find this personage, when one injudicious enquiry, one word in the wrong place, could prove—no, not merely dangerous, but fatal.

Or did he exaggerate the dangers? Perhaps the two men Brother Bernard had found lurking near the barn had come to St Pons with no malign intent, perhaps they were merely lost or Brother Bernard had drunk too much cider that afternoon. Their appearance had certainly terrified the Other, scared him enough to wheedle Max into taking him with him in his flight, although the Other had loved monastic life as fervently as Max had loathed it. But Max, though he might scorn to show it, had also been afraid. Fear had been a lesson driven home by the strap from the time before the cloister—avoid glances, shun questions, suspect strangers, dread pursuit. That they might still be pursued after nearly a decade did not seem improbable. And now, four years later—yes, the lesson still stood: do not draw attention to yourself, cover your tracks.

Still, he must take the risk. After all, he was not a fool. He knew better, for instance, than to go anywhere near the embassy. And cafés, too: although there would doubtless be some dingy establishment in a Paris side-street that exiles frequented, it would be like the cafés where Mitya's compatriots met, haunted by anarchists and thus a magnet for spies. Libraries, journals, newspapers, a trail of yellowing paper stretching back twelve years, that was where he must start.

It would be a tedious and lonely business. Yet his heart lifted. If he lost his situation, so much the better; he would be free to devote himself, body and soul, to his quest. Suddenly he saw a purpose for the banknote and the watch and was moved, almost, to gentle feelings for M de Miremont. Yes, it was infinitely better this way, on his own, his own master. As for the danger, after the tedium of life in service, he welcomed it. He would triumph, they would see, he would astound all of them: it would be the old boy bowing and scraping if their paths ever recrossed.

Sometimes his thoughts ran in this vein. At others he plumbed the depths. On black days he found himself thinking once more of the army.

As with nations and religions, so with house parties: identifying a common enemy fosters the general good. In the early days at La Boissière, M de Miremont had risked being cast in this role, except of course that he was protected by his lineage; and besides, for all that he was silent and solitary, his diffident courtesy discouraged ill-will. In any case, there had soon appeared a much better candidate. There had been instant accord amongst the gentlemen that Aristide de Bellac was a bounder, while ladies as unlike as Mme de Corvignac and Baroness Donyani could share the currency of lifted eyebrows, stifled groans and cutting comments exchanged at his expense. Such unity in suffering brought all other feuds to a truce and prompted, amongst the company at large, exaggerated displays of friendly feeling.

But then Bellac had gone too far. Not an eyelid would have flickered at his adulterous liaison if the fellow had only been discreet. Alas, the famous novelist in love was like an untrained puppy, bounding about noisily and, when not gazing at his beloved in moist-eyed adoration, pawing her waist or slobbering over her hand. Outrage at this disgraceful lack of tone was led by their hostess: there came an evening when, on three separate occasions, as Bellac commenced one of his anecdotes, she was moved to remark she had heard the story before. Even Bellac's thick hide could absorb her message—in fact, in matters appertaining to his literary renown his skin was mere gauze. The day after his departure the princess also discovered a pressing need to return to Paris.

Yet harmony was not restored. Lacking the irritant of the literary gentleman, the guests grew irritable with one another. No children's voices refreshed the afternoon air and everyone was sick to death of the heat. It was the dog-end of summer and minds fatigued by rustic pleasures longed for the city and civilisation. Besides, the Corvignacs had gone and the baroness and her affectionate niece were departing for Vienna, where one of the poetess's verse dramas was to be staged. Soon only the Cressys remained. Left with her relations for entertainment, Mme de Claireville kept increasingly to her own quarters.

As in the salon, so in the servants' hall. Michel was the chosen enemy: even here in the country most of the Bordelais were regulars and knew him of old. But, it seemed, the balance was swinging. Against all expectation, Michel and Guillaume had forged an alliance.

Guillaume had not reported Max to the Cardinal. For that Max had Fabrice to thank. Fabrice had spotted that the Oxen, on their Sundays off, were in the habit of taking home souvenirs of their service at the château—oh, these were magpie gleanings, silver teaspoons, a match-holder or two, once even a cake-stand, not peculation on Michel's scale, yet peculation nonetheless. The Oxen fell quiet for a day or so. But it was not to last.

Guillaume's loud objections to Max's nocturnal escapades, had, it turned out, been prompted by resentment: why was there one rule for Max and another for the rest of the dormitory? That there might be more to it, a graver indictment, did not initially sink in. Heaven knew why not. How could Guillaume, country boy though he was, miss the import of Michel's oh-so-amusing falsetto or of him shouting "Backs to the wall, boys!" whenever Max or Fabrice appeared? Yet enlightenment, if it came but slowly, did dawn at last. This was an abomination! Guillaume was a normal healthy man—his brother Victor, their cousin Jacques, they were all three normal decent lads from respectable families. Yet they must share a dormitory with this—

with these…Only the pilfered silver prevented Guillaume from rushing to protest. His next brainwave was that Max and Fabrice should be given a sound thrashing; but here Michel intervened (he surely did not want his own pleasure spoilt) by reminding him that fighting incurred instant dismissal.

However the upshot was that Guillaume forgot Michel had always despised him. He became the first footman's comrade-in-arms, eager to hammer home whatever lesson in morality Michel might devise for the denizens of Sodom. And naturally where their leader went the other Oxen followed—although Jacques still wore his bemused smile and seemed to forget his moral obligations when his cousins were absent.

While Michel was not clever, he had all the cunning of the street. He knew from experience that taunting Max would bring only limited satisfaction. But he could get properly under his skin through Fabrice. Accordingly—and as Fabrice himself had predicted—a renewed campaign of persecution was mounted, now zealously assisted by the Oxen. When Fabrice was deputed to clean the silver, he would turn his back for the briefest moment only to find his handiwork smeared; when he carried a laden tray to the scullery, a foot would shoot out from nowhere to trip him; items of his livery went missing; on one occasion he found fresh turds in his pumps, on another the dormitory's slops were emptied into his bed. His duties for M de Bellac (for the Famous Novelist had not yet been sent packing) were a particular target; the Literary Lion's newly polished boots would vanish, his newspaper would be soaked in dishwater, his breakfast chocolate, if left for an instant unattended, would be spiked with salt: Fabrice must withstand the literary gentleman's outraged eloquence, only to return, trembling, to a chorus of sniggers and jeers.

Max was beside himself. It was effort enough to shrug off the crude insults; had Michel but known it, under Max's chilly disdain his pride was burning. The white hot rage he had first experienced during his encounter with M de Tarascon was now an ever-present threat; his face was stiff, his body shook with the struggle to contain it. Several times he was close to giving in; once, spurred by a vile remark about M de Miremont, he had actually stepped towards Michel with his fists clenched when M Vincent had appeared in the passage. Yet all this was easier to stomach, by far, than the assault on Fabrice.

The worst of it was, Max was powerless to stop it. Where once Michel had been wary of him, now he was another nancy, another *petit jesus*, no longer any threat. Besides Michel's confidence was puffed up by the Oxen; he had an audience to play to, which drove him to further excess.

If Max had ever resented Fabrice's dependence, that resentment vanished. To the humiliation of being forced to stand by while Fabrice suffered the indignities that should have been his was added the sting of guilt. For, after all, Fabrice had warned him, but he had chosen not to listen. Now, having brought disaster down upon them both, he did what he could, kept constant watch, searched for what went missing, helped clear up the mess; when the tray of glasses was smashed, he went to Mme Roussel before Fabrice could prevent him, taking the blame and the cut in wages himself: but it was not, it would never be recompense. Nor could it calm his fury.

Strangely—and this added to Max's pain—Fabrice did not give vent to the expected reproaches. Certainly he had wept at the excrement smearing his stockings and defilement of his bedding, but by and large he was uncharacteristically stoic in his martyrdom. He seemed to find perverse compensation in the fact that Max, too, had been brought low: like Max's supposed adversity in love, it was a strengthening of their kinship, even if he, Fabrice, must suffer unfairly for it. "Well, at least, dear heart, there are two of us," he was wont to murmur resignedly.

This solidarity became their sole comfort. Since most of the Bordelais servants were either related to the Oxen or from neighbouring families, the word that the two Parisian footmen had been declared pariahs was quick to spread. Generally the reason for this was not fully understood, despite Guillaume's dark hints: the edict was quite sufficient by itself. Some independent souls stood out—Colette in the kitchen could see no cause for depriving herself of a gossip with Fabrice—but it was notable that in the break he and Max no longer required subterfuge to meet by themselves.

"I'll kill the bastard."

"What I pray, angel, is that some great brute gets her up a dark alley one night and gives her what she's been asking for all these years."

"I mean it."

"A coal heaver. Or a hulking midshipman from Marseilles."

"I mean it, my friend. I'm reaching the point where I can't be answerable."

They sat propped against the stonework on the shady side of the well. Fabrice, cross-legged and in his shirt sleeves, was inspecting his forearms for insect bites. Max, with his legs drawn up and his chin resting on his knees, stared grimly into space. Their gloom, if it could not be increased, was not eased by their having run out of tobacco.

"I tell you, it's on my mind day and night, I think of ramming those rotting yellow—"

"Oh *please*! It won't get us anywhere, angel, this obsession with Betty's tombstones. Can't you see, that's exactly what she wants you to do?"

"Then let the bastard have what he wants."

"Come on, you're a clever girl. You hit Betty, she calls the Oxen as witnesses. They'll swear blind it was unprovoked. More than likely, they'll also give you that thrashing Guillaumetta is forever creaming her kecks about—"

"Like hell they will!"

"Your cock-a-doodle won't crow for weeks, but naturally they'll claim it was self-defence. And when they explain to Monseigneur Vincent what they were defending themselves from ... "

"Balls to them!"

"You yearn for the gutter?"

"I'd manage." Max reached out to tug savagely at a frond of grass. "Anyway, it would be worth it. To beat the arsehole to pulp."

"And when you've offered yourself up as a ritual sacrifice? Tell me, what's to become of this girl?"

"Once I'm gone, they'll let up."

"Now they've developed an appetite?"

A miserable silence fell, in which Fabrice scratched a horsefly bite and Max chewed vengefully upon the grass stem. Eventually, however, he hurled it aside in disgust.

"I will fight him. I'll find a way. I shan't rest until I have that bastard's guts."

The catalyst was M de Bellac's favourite waistcoat. Fabrice was taking it to the laundry room to have it sponged and pressed when, distracted by M de Corvignac's valet, who was asking for sealing wax, he laid it aside on the servants' hall table. It was, of course, gone when he turned round. Colette reported seeing Guillaume and Victor playing ball with it in the passage but no trace of it could be discovered, until just before luncheon when Max found it in a coal scuttle. It seemed unusually bulky, but that was accounted for by the moderate-sized pike that slithered from its folds.

The reappearance of the missing fish brought down upon Fabrice the full wrath of Chef Quintivali. But this would be mild compared with the Literary Lion's reaction.

"Look at it—just *look*! As if the coal dust wasn't enough without the scales and the slime. And the *smell*! Nothing on earth will get rid of it. What am I going to tell him, angel? What *am* I going to do?" Fabrice was powerless to check the two large tears that rolled slowly down his cheeks.

That break time, Max marched into the yard behind the service wing, where Michel was holding court. The suddenness of his appearance and the deliberation in his stride startled even Michel into silence for a moment. It was just time enough for Max to draw off his left glove and slash it across the first footman's face.

Michel's astonishment gave way to a guffaw. "Honestly, is that the best you can do? See that, lads? Take my advice, Nancy, try a feather duster next time."

Ignoring the sniggers of the Oxen, Max flung the glove at Michel's feet. "Pick it up."

Michel's laughter was arrested. "*What* did you say?"

"Pick it up."

"Now listen, you little cocksucker—"

"Pick it up." Max's note of cool purpose did not waver. "It's a challenge."

"Oooh, a challenge, is it? Hear that, boys? Rents his arse to the aristocracy, thinks he's a sodding aristo himself. What does Madame la marquise propose—pistols at dawn?"

"Fists."

Michel emitted a hoot. "Itching for your cards, are you?"

"We'll fight away from the house and there'll be no visible injuries. Our seconds will agree the rules."

"Seconds, eh?" Michel made a show of wiping the mirth from his eyes. "Your ladyship is a regular caution! But now you've had your joke, bum boy, you'd better run along to your little chum. And take this with you—" here he kicked the glove contemptuously "—before I stuff it up your poxy arse!"

Max made no move to retrieve the glove, nor even looked at it. His eyes remained fixed upon Michel. "That's your answer? Your final answer?"

"You heard. Now sod off!" This was endorsed by jeers and menacing gestures from the Oxen.

Max stood his ground. "You know, I've never doubted you were a coward."

"I said, you've had your joke—"

"It would seem—" Max allowed his glance to drift briefly towards the Oxen "—you're afraid to fight me."

"Your mother! I could take you on with one hand—"

"He'd whip you," chimed in Guillaume. "He'd give you the whipping you deserve."

"He'd make sawdust of you!" added Victor with relish.

"Sawdust!" echoed Jacques, though somewhat feebly.

Max permitted himself a faint smile. "Then why won't he?"

"Now hold hard, lads." It could not be denied that Michel looked uncomfortable with the turn things were taking. "I wouldn't because— because I wouldn't dirty my hands. I only fight men!"

Although he produced this last with a note of triumph, by now the Oxen's blood was up and this was not what they had hoped for from their hero.

"But if he's asking for it—" protested Victor.

"He's flaming begging," snarled Guillaume. "Come on, Michel, we agreed, didn't we? The arsehole needs a beating. He needs thrashing into the middle of next week. You could do it without hardly breaking sweat. Look at him!"

Michel was looking and finding in Max's icy composure a reminder of why he had once been wary of him. "But that's the thing, lads, it's too easy—"

"You don't, I will. He's insulted you! A – a—" Guillaume struggled for the word "—a flaming degenital! He called you a coward!"

This was a corner from which, even Michel must grant, there was no escape. Besides, a gaggle of maids had been lured over by the altercation, including Coeline, the under-parlour maid whose skirts he was hoping to lift. To save his dignity, he worked up a ball of saliva and spat prodigiously. "All right. Somebody give me the sodding glove."

At a nod from Guillaume, Jacques bent for it and thrust it into Michel's hands. The first footman made a display of crushing it in his palm. "Just remember, shit-hole, you asked for it!"

"My second will meet your second," Max said with a small, cold smile, before turning on his heel.

CHAPTER SEVENTEEN

"You do recall, angel, that Betty was born in Belleville? She's been street-fighting since she was out of swaddling clothes. Whereas you, unless I am much mistaken..."

They had tobacco again—Colette's brother had brought supplies from the village—and Max's reply was a nonchalant smoke ring. However, it was true: apart from scraps with his fellow postulants, his only taste of fighting had been the fracas with Josette's M Pintard, from which he had hardly emerged with glory. He must rely on whatever advantages nature had given him: he was fit and strong, there was little to choose between Michel and himself in height and, although Michel was heavier, he was likely to be faster on his feet. In any case, if he lacked brute force, he possessed another, surely more potent asset: his anger.

As Max's second, Fabrice worked diligently. Dealings with Guillaume were not the ordeal he might have predicted. Not only was the campaign of persecution suspended until the outcome of the fight, but Guillaume on his own—and Fabrice had wisely insisted upon this—was a far more tractable beast, still surly and bristling with manly indignation but no match for Fabrice's sharp wits and forced, besides, to recall that it was Fabrice who had spotted the cake-stand, that if tales were to be told nobody would escape unscathed.

The contest would take place during the afternoon break. A fighting ground was selected, a patch of parkland suitably distant from the house, and a set of rules was drawn up. Biting, kicking, kneeing, gouging, butting and blows to the privates were forbidden. Most importantly, blows were to be delivered to the body only; a combatant striking the face, where the resulting injury could not be concealed, was immediately to be disqualified; furthermore, his opponent would be entitled to inflict similar damage to ensure they both met an equal fate. Here Michel, who had been raising niggling objections throughout, suddenly announced he must withdraw.

"She claims it's unfair," Fabrice reported. "You may be able to hide bruises to your body, but what if she's called to madame?"

"Unfair? He's the one with madame's protection! He could appear with a torso like a black pudding, he won't be the one to lose his place.

Tell him, worm though he is, he can't wriggle out now!"

Fabrice retreated slightly from this explosion. "I merely mention her objection, dear heart, because it raises a question that relates to your own interests."

Max raised his eyebrows.

"What if madame asks Betty who she's been fighting? Or why?"

"She won't." Max remembered all too well the humiliation of attempting conversation with madame. "And if he tries to explain, she won't listen. Her ears are closed to the doings of us subterranean creatures. Michel knows that as well as I do. Tell him I have no hesitation in standing by my challenge—the challenge he has accepted. And, while honour, I realise, is a concept utterly foreign to him, unless he wishes the world to know what a snivelling funk he is, he had better hold to his word."

It was, indeed, impossible for Michel to back out, for although the fight was supposed to be a deadly secret, to be kept above all from the senior servants, gossip hummed amongst the lower tables in the servants' hall and bets were already being placed. Max was reminded of their previous duel, over madame: then he had been the general favourite, now he was the outcast, the one marked for defeat. Ah well, he would have to fight the harder, and perhaps this time luck, in its perversity, would bless him.

Now he was taking action, he felt on the whole extraordinarily light-hearted. Fabrice too was in better spirits, and not only because his sufferings had been temporarily relieved. In the matter of the waistcoat he had enjoyed an unexpected escape. The very night of the incident, he had been ordered to pack M de Bellac and the manner of Literary Lion's going had been such as to prevent his recollecting the waistcoat. Yes, many of Fabrice's burdens had been lifted. All the same, he could be observed to look at Max narrowly from time to time with a worried furrow cleaving his brow.

If the contest itself was a poorly kept secret, Fabrice had done his best to ensure the precise date and location remained unknown. All the same, quite a little crowd had gathered at the fighting ground; Alphonse the boot boy, a giggling cluster of housemaids including Coeline, Colette with the girls from the kitchen, as well as contingents from the stables and gardens, all waiting in high excitement for the contenders to arrive. Both fighters were in shirtsleeves and wearing their Sunday trousers to preserve their livery breeches. Michel strutted ahead, attended by the Oxen in a body. Max and Fabrice followed at a disdainful distance. It was another remorselessly hot day and at this hour the sun was still savage; the crowd was already sweating, the women fanning themselves with their handkerchiefs or clustering beneath Coeline's parasol; when Guillaume tested the parched brown grass with the heel of his shoe, it gave the muffled ring of earth baked to rock.

Scarcely propitious conditions for fighting but Max barely noticed. Instead of the emotions he had thought to experience—fear, elation, nervous anticipation—he felt only a numbing detachment. Even his anger, his precious powerful anger, was gone. He looked around him hardly remembering why he was here, let alone the occasion for the quarrel. His fingers encountered the mascot in his trouser pocket, a tiny wooden Our Lady lent to him by Colette and carved by her grandfather, that she swore had always brought her family luck. Yet, touched though he was by her gesture, even luck seemed irrelevant to him now. Nothing seemed worth his attention because everything was beyond his power, already decided. This, he thought, must be how a man feels going to his execution.

Fabrice pressed Max's shoulder and he roused himself sufficiently to return a smile of thanks. Michel was stripping off his shirt. Max followed suit, handing it with Colette's Our Lady to Fabrice for safekeeping. A clamour arose from the crowd, cheers, giggles, whistles, as they compared the fighters' physiques. Agreed, Max was broad-shouldered and well-muscled, but surely his hips were too narrow, his body too graceful for strength. Everything about the first footman, his solid torso matted with blond curls, his meaty arms, his bulky thighs, even the roll of flesh above his waistband, suggested intimidating force. When he raised his arms to acknowledge the approval of the crowd, the muscles of his back rippled ostentatiously.

Shouting for silence, Fabrice proceeded to read out the rules of the competition. To his suggestion that the contestants should shake hands, Michel's only answer was to spit. Max shrugged. Fabrice and Guillaume stepped to the side. And the contest began.

Or rather, the combatants stood, facing each other, on their guard, but not moving. Max seemed unable to shake off his fatal detachment; Michel too, despite his bluster, appeared irresolute, uncertain how to proceed without the usual tools of his craft, a pick handle or broken bottle. When at last they began tentatively to circle each other, neither seemed willingly to make the first sally. It was only when someone—

Fabrice thought it was Victor—yelled "Go on, kill him!" that Michel suddenly plunged forward and hurled his right fist into Max's ribs. Taken by surprise, Max failed also to parry the left-hand thrust that followed. He staggered and fell and, while Guillaume struggled to hold off Michel, Fabrice began counting.

Dimly, Max heard the cheers and boos of the crowd. His chest hurt and he was temporarily winded. But at last the fog had lifted, his mind was sharp. Pausing on one knee to recover his breath, he rose on the count of nine with a look of purpose. Fabrice, whose voice, as he counted, had grown shrill with dismay, allowed himself a sigh of relief, for Max easily dodged the next punch swung at him by the emboldened Michel, was all at once quicksilver, luring his opponent on then dancing out of range, jabbing at him, forcing him to dance too, even penetrating his guard with a creditable thrust on occasion.

However, the intention was not lost on Michel, who, face scarlet, chest heaving, was already feeling the heat. When his opponent next closed in, he ended the indignity of this exhausting gavotte by breaking through his guard and clenching him in a bear hug. As they grappled, he worked his foot between Max's legs and hooked his ankle. Max fell with the full weight of Michel on top of him and in an instant Michel's hands were round his neck. Fabrice, despite his official duties, could not bear to look. But when he opened his eyes, Max had somehow freed himself, and both were scrambling to their feet.

There were other occasions when Fabrice could scarcely forbear to avert his glance. Once Michel was within a whisker of gripping Max in a headlock, which would leave Max powerless as he pummelled his back and ribs. But Max was learning. This time it was he who tripped Michel and they wrestled inconclusively on the ground for some moments before he sprang free. When Michel manoeuvred him so that he must fight with the sun in his eyes, he returned the pressure, jabbing and dodging until their positions were reversed.

By now both combatants were larded in sweat, so that when they grappled their hands slithered over red and glistening flesh. Michel had begun by goading his opponent with salvos of abuse, while Max had remained grimly mute; but now Michel too saved his lungs and they fought in a silence punctuated by groans, howls, and the bellows-roar of their breathing, fought oblivious of the crowd, with increasing savagery. Yet Michel, it could be noticed, was tiring: although he had kept Max on the defensive and had hammered home several punishing blows, Max, younger, nimbler, quicker to recover, had so far cheated him of the decisive thrust. Furthermore, as Michel's swings grew wilder, his foe seemed at last to find his aim.

Fabrice permitted himself a whoop as Max jolted Michel with a volley of hard and accurate punches. Yet this joy was short-lived, for Michel, lumbering forward, clutching Max about the waist as though to grapple, suddenly stamped upon Max's left foot. Max let out an agonised gasp.

"Foul play!" cried Fabrice.

"Not against the rules!" yelled back Guillaume.

But Michel was in any case deaf to restraint. Now his enemy was off-balance he grasped his moment, seizing Max by the forelock to dangle him helpless while he drew back to commence a relentless assault on his belly.

"Separate them!" howled Fabrice.

"Not against the rules!" screamed Guillaume, although his words were drowned by boos and hisses.

Max heard neither the crowd nor the seconds. Although his anger had revived with Michel's first blow, until this instant he had kept it in check. But now rage overwhelmed him. Impervious to pain, not caring that he left a tuft of hair in Michel's grip, with an almighty twist of his neck and shoulders he tore himself free. Then, seizing Michel by the upper arms, he pushed him, hurled him away from him with full force.

Michel staggered backwards, stumbled, fell. Fabrice began counting. Michel lay where he was for the moment, blessing the chance to heave in breath. But, limping, implacable, Max came after him.

"Get up!" Max spat.

Michel, his chest juddering, levered himself effortfully to his feet. The crowd fell silent as they faced each other. They stood, maddened, swaying, half-blinded with sweat.

Michel lunged first. There was no mistaking the intended direction of the blow. Max, with his own arm drawn back to strike, swerved to dodge it, cheating it from landing full in his face but helpless to avoid it glancing off his nose.

The crowd gasped. Fabrice began to scream "Fou - ou - ou - oul!" But, although Max had recoiled from the impact, he had righted himself and his punch was still travelling, instinctively following the sideways motion of his body, driving into the space left unguarded by his enemy's still-raised right arm. The time in the cellar, St Pons, the comte de Tarascon, monsieur's betrayal, the cruelty to Fabrice—the stored fury of years powered his fist as it flew, gathering to itself the momentum of Michel's own flesh as, still moving forward, it came to meet the blow, which hurtled, exactly where Max had aimed it, into the flabby fold of gut below the ribs.

Michel tottered. He clutched himself. His legs folded and he collapsed, writhing.

Fabrice and Guillaume were uncertain whether to count, for, according to the rules, Michel being disqualified, the fight was already over. But the crowd, caring less for technicalities than justice, was counting for them. And sure enough, with the shout of "Ten!" a distant echo, Michel still lay on his side, curled like a foetus, groaning and clutching his stomach.

Max stood where he was, staring at his handiwork. He seemed stunned and, although blood gushed from his nose and crimsoned his chest, he did nothing to staunch it until Fabrice rushed up with a handkerchief. Surrounded, suddenly the universal favourite, blown kisses by Coeline, clapped on the shoulder by Alphonse, hugged by Colette despite his bloodstains, he mopped his nose and tried to smile, but his eye remained fixed on his stricken enemy, who had rolled over to vomit.

"All yours." Looking round, Max found Jacques at his elbow. "All yours, friend."

Fabrice was astonished by Max's perplexity. "He means, dear heart, your dreams have come true. Betty's ivories are at your disposal."

And indeed Guillaume, that stickler for the rules, had Michel by the hair and was offering up his vomit-smeared face to receive the blow.

Max struggled to repress a shudder. His contempt for Michel was absolute, but he had already taken his revenge. Besides, when he recalled the joy, the pure animal joy that had coursed through him when his fist had hit home, he could not view its effects without a measure of self-disgust.

He spat the blood from his mouth. Linking arms with Fabrice, he set off back to the house.

CHAPTER EIGHTEEN

There was, it seemed, no part of Max that did not hurt. He moved gingerly, like an ancient dowager tight-laced. His knuckles were torn and his hands so swollen that he and Fabrice strained to force them into his gloves. Although his nose was not broken and had ceased to bleed, it, too, was puffy. But that, they hoped, could be disguised by a careful application of Fabrice's face powder. Not so Max's left eye, around which a massive bruise was already purpling: Fabrice did his best, but within hours Max would sport a badge of conflict no cosmetics could hide.

"Fuck that bitch Betty! You were so valiant, I was so proud of you, angel. Why didn't you do it? It was in the rules. Why didn't you belt Betty Kaka in her ugly great kisser?"

Max attempted a shrug but discovered that this, too, was acutely painful. Instead, he managed what he hoped was a reassuring grin. "Look, old friend, it's not so bad. At least I'll get back to Paris."

Fabrice's lip twitched.

"You could join me. I happen to—well, I've got a bit saved. And I know someone who can help us. Or at any rate he'll help you. Things aren't so bad, you'll see."

Nevertheless, he was already in trouble, they both were: Fabrice was supposed to be laying dinner, while Max should be with Victor attending to guests on the terrace; Victor, who had grown suddenly obliging, would cover for him, but his absence could not indefinitely escape the Cardinal's notice.

As luck would have it, madame was on the terrace, taking iced sherbets with the baroness and her niece, who were to leave the following morning. Max did his best to linger in the background and keep his head averted. But madame's eyes were sharp.

"Jean?" She scrutinised him, it seemed not with outrage, but with intrigued amusement. All the same, her command was stern: "Be so good as to find M Vincent and ask him to come here immediately."

After that, it was a relief to present himself to the Cardinal and be ordered to stay in the dormitory until he was sent for. As he gratefully lowered his aching body onto his bed, he felt once again a sense of inevitability. They would return to Paris. Old Jouvert would find

Fabrice a situation as a valet. He would take a room, begin his quest. After M de Miremont's money ran out he would enlist. Everything was decided, there was nothing more for him to do. His eyelids dropped and he fell instantly asleep.

"I tripped on the stairs, monsieur."

"The same stairs, I assume, that tripped Michel?"

The Cardinal, sitting behind the table at which Mme Roussel did her accounts, looked more judicial than ecclesiastical, his preternaturally smooth face an impartial mask, his voice at its silkiest. The parlour was crammed with furniture, including an abundance of chairs, and Max would have given anything to sink down upon one of them. But the court required the accused to remain standing. Max fought a fierce urge to yawn.

"I am given to understand—" unblinking behind his half-moon spectacles, M Vincent's obsidian eyes considered the defendant "—I am informed that these fisticuffs were intended as some sort of duel. And that you, Jean, were the instigator."

Max deemed it better to say nothing.

"Of course, had I realised for one moment that such an incident was taking place, or heard the slightest whisper that it was planned, I should have taken immediate steps to ensure that it was stopped."

From which Max inferred that Monseigneur, whose ear was nothing if not acute, had possessed his own particular reasons for declining to act. This was certainly interesting and might have seemed hopeful. Yet there was little to bring hope in the Cardinal's lizard glance, nor indeed in his next question.

"You are aware, my lad, that fighting amongst male servants is a very serious matter? A matter that cannot be countenanced? Well, speak up."

"Yes, monsieur."

The Cardinal reached for a china cup at his elbow. Having taken a delicate sip and replaced the cup fastidiously in its saucer, he emitted what was always considered to signal the greatest menace, his sorrowful sigh. "You came to us, Jean, highly recommended. With extremely high recommendations from a most trustworthy source."

So it was as Max had always suspected: M Vincent was Old Jouvert's spy in madame's household. As he had previously calculated, this might influence his fate either way; now it seemed clear it would tip the balance against him.

"You are a good servant. You are capable and reliable. You have an excellent manner. You don't drink. You don't steal. I should not have disputed that you might eventually prove worthy of higher things. Until we came here, to the château. Since when, your behaviour has been—erratic is too mild a word."

The Cardinal again paused to drink, then turned to the plate of *langue du chat* biscuits beside his cup. He picked one out, snapped it, bit into one half, chewed unhurriedly. Only when the pause was growing intolerable did the movement of his jaws abruptly cease. Snatching off his spectacles, he fixed Max with a piercing stare.

"It is admirable, Jean, for us to emulate our betters. But not in every respect. There are some things—tastes, inclinations—which, though generally offensive to society, when indulged in by our betters may be overlooked. But they will not be overlooked in us. We do not have tastes, we do not have inclinations." M Vincent remorselessly held Max's eye. "And if, my lad, we are foolish enough to forget that, we not only risk the worst kind of disgrace. We do no service to those who know that wisdom stays in the shadows."

Having confirmed Monseigneur's connection with Old Jouvert, Max was not as surprised as he might have been by this. But he was struck by the rebuke. As no moral lecture could, the reminder that he had betrayed the hidden brotherhood left him shamed and subdued.

"So—" the Cardinal was the only person Max had ever encountered who could shout by lowering his voice "—so, you will agree your behaviour deserves exemplary punishment. And that is before we consider this latest charge against you. Brawling with another footman. Can there be any excuse for such conduct ? Well, come on, lad, astonish me—if you have anything to say in your own defence, you had better out with it."

"I offer no excuses, monsieur."

M Vincent considered Max briefly before returning to his cup. His eye lighting upon some biscuit crumbs, he became immediately and agonisingly absorbed in sweeping them to the edge of the table, brushing them into his palm, then tipping them meticulously into his saucer. Finally, dusting his hands together, he deigned to look up. And Max saw with amazement that he was smiling, freely, quite without his usual menace.

"Well, my lad, you are in luck. Madame, it would seem, is under a slight misapprehension as to the reason for your set-to with Michel—a misapprehension which, I fear, I may have compounded. While she cannot condone your behaviour and naturally holds herself above it, she is rather taken by this notion of a duel on her account—ladies find such things romantic and madame is no exception, as I'm sure she'd forgive me saying. So she has asked me to be lenient with you."

Max stared.

"You will hand over your livery to Alphonse, who will wait at table and perform your other duties while you perform his. You will continue backstairs until you are once again in a fit condition to appear before your betters."

This was unheard of. So unexpected was the reprieve, so certain had Max been that his life was about to be fixed upon an entirely different course, that he was for a moment unsure whether to be relieved or disappointed.

"Eh, lad? Nothing to say?"

"T-thank you, monsieur."

"What's up? Are you in need of a doctor?"

Dazed, and exhausted besides by the effort of standing, Max had begun to sway. He dragged his wincing body to attention. "No, monsieur. Thank you, not at all."

"Good lad! Pity the same can't be said of our first footman. He's complaining you've crushed his kidneys and cracked his ribs."

Guillaume had assured Max that Michel had suffered no serious hurt. "Monsieur, I never intended—"

"Oh, he'll live." The Cardinal seemed to find Max's look of horror highly entertaining. In fact, a curious change was overtaking his face. Little fissures were appearing in the impassive mask, cracks around the eyes, rifts across the brow, fractures at the corners of the mouth that spread rapidly to the cheeks, quivered in the neck, migrated to the shoulders, until Monseigneur's entire form was quaking like a reflection in choppy water. He, who never laughed, was consumed by laughter. "By God," he spluttered, "I would have given something to see that punch! Oh yes, indeed. What I'd have given!" Then, as suddenly as the disintegration had begun, it ceased. "But just you mind, my lad. If I ever have to speak to you again, you'll be on the street before you can say knife."

By the time madame returned to Paris, Max's black eye had faded to a faint primrose yellow and he was in livery again. After the deprivations of the country, he and Fabrice found their tiny malodorous room under the eaves almost luxurious. Starved of books for weeks, Max hurled himself into his nocturnal studies. To burn with ideas again, to see opening up, beyond the hurdles of this sheep-pen, plains, mountains, limitless sky, to feel his spirit soar—he could not but think of M de Miremont and ache for the answering call from that wild, unbounded universe. But he was forgetting himself. It irritated him that he continued to dwell upon the whole stupid business. The old boy, when he called upon madame, as etiquette decreed he must sooner or later, would merely be a personage whose topcoat Max took.

Besides, if Max wanted debate, laughter, riotous flights of fancy, music—shit, how he longed to hear music again—he need look no further than the Zhukovskys. They were sure to be on exceptionally good form, as Mitya had written that he was soon to set out on a concert tour of Italy that would launch him as a soloist. Max's day off fell on the first Sunday after his return to Paris. His heart light with anticipation, he climbed the stairs to the Zhukovskys' apartment two at a time.

Yet he had barely to cross the threshold to know that something was amiss. Oh, there was nothing scant in the greeting he received. Mitya embraced him with his customary warmth; Vera came out of the kitchen, where she had been supervising the maid, brushing damp hair from her brow and smiling joyfully; and Mme Zhukovskaya, who had been lying down, appeared within a few moments of Vera's call, more stooped by rheumatics than ever and leaning heavily on a cane, but showering him with affectionate exclamations as he took her tiny stiffened bird-claw in his own hand to kiss. Nor was there anything ill-omened about the apartment: in the salon the usual happy disorder prevailed, Mitya's violin case open on top of the piano, music sheets everywhere, books, newspapers, hanks of brightly coloured wool from Vera's weaving; a candle flickered before Mme Zhukovskaya's treasured icon, the samovar burbled, from the kitchen promising smells wafted. Vera bustled about, offering Max the most accommodating chair, bringing him a glass of tea, slicing lemon. All the same, something comfortless hung in the air. The setting of the dining table in the alcove revealed that for once no other guests were expected. And after the first effusions of their reunion conversation grew uncharacteristically strained.

Mitya, usually so good-natured and full of energy, seemed peculiarly subdued: Max noticed, that contrary to habit, he had gulped down his tumbler of vodka in one draught and was pouring another. Vera, now past her eighteenth birthday, had lost her childish diffidence and blossomed into a capable young woman whose natural seriousness was tempered by a teasing smile and an irrepressible giggle; but at present her fingers played uneasily with the fringe of her shawl and her round blue eyes were solemn. Only Mme Zhukovskaya, from long practice in the salons of St Petersburg before her late husband's arrest and exile, rose gallantly to the occasion.

"Tell us, please, my dear, all about Bordeaux. Did you go about much, did you visit the cathedral at Angoulême? Here we longed for the country—the heat has been stifling."

"Yes, do tell us, Maxim Alexandrovitch." The patronymic was Vera's invention: long ago, preferring her own country's custom to the chill formality of "M Fabien", and being told by Max that his father was unknown, she had said: "Then you shall borrow ours—it will be as if you are our brother." Now, as she pronounced the syllables of this generous gift, he seemed to hear in them a muted sisterly plea.

Of course it was obvious what was missing, what should have been the first topic of conversation. Max balanced the dictates of friendship, the instinct to sympathise with the desire to spare pain. Yet silence would not lift the pall that oppressed them. "I should much rather hear how the plans for Mitya's tour are progressing."

Mme Zhukovskaya sighed. Vera parted her lips, then hastily closed them. Mitya flushed scarlet and looked away.

"My darlings, we are bound to speak of it sooner or later," said Mme Zhukovskaya, sighing again.

Mitya drained his glass and slammed it down, shaking the little table beside his chair. "Maxim, I have been a complete bloody fool!"

"You are not to be blamed, darling Mitya," said his mother, gently.

"We all of us agreed," protested Vera.

"But it was I—I who allowed myself to…" Flinging himself from the chair, Mitya strode to the mantelpiece, where he stood with his back turned, staring fixedly into the fire. "God, twenty-five years of age and I'm still wet behind the ears!"

Once Mitya could be coaxed away from the fire, it all came out, the whole unfortunate story. He had been introduced by a friend to M Stahl, the impresario for his Italian tour, and general enquiry had elicited no reason to doubt the fellow's reputation. They had met often to discuss arrangements; Mitya had seen convincing letters from promoters and concert halls in Rome and Milan. He had thrown himself into learning the repertoire they had agreed and three weeks ago had resigned from the Opéra. A solo career was, as Max knew, his life's ambition: so, when Stahl had come to him, two days after he had left the Opéra, a mere six weeks before the date of his first recital, and confessed to a temporary embarrassment—it was a complicated story involving another tour and a promoter in Salzburg who had let Stahl down badly—Mitya felt he had no choice but to listen. Funds were needed to pay the printers in advance for posters and flyers, without which audiences in Italy could not be assured. Mitya had talked the matter over with his mother and sister and with their agreement— with their encouragement, they both stressed—had handed over the family's savings. But, after that, well, Max could guess—the impresario had become first evasive, then elusive. Finally, two days ago, Mitya had gone to his office only to find the shutters up and other creditors banging on the door. The gentleman himself might be anywhere by now, Berlin, Vienna, Geneva…

"So there you have it, Maxim. Through my stupid ambition, I've thrown away everything. My job. Our savings. The happiness of my mother and sister."

"Hush, Mitya," murmured Mme Zhukovskaya.

"Of course I shall get work. I'm on good terms with Farrant at the Opéra, he'll think of me when they're short of a fiddle. But it won't be regular money—"

"I shall work," said Vera, lifting her chin. "In an office. Or I could give piano lessons."

"Under no circumstances."

"Or perhaps—" here, in a vague sweep, she gestured at the exotically patterned fabrics that decked the mantel, swathed the sofa and glowed like stained glass from the walls "—perhaps I could sell these fripperies of mine. Someone might give me a commission."

"That will not be necessary." Mitya had been known to inveigh at length against the oppression of women but his present injured pride seemed to have reversed his principles. "I shall find work. If need be, I'll play at weddings and cabarets again. But we must tighten our belts. Florente must be let go, which means you'll have more than enough to occupy you, Verotchka. And, oh God, if that were only the worst!" He paused to bury his face in hands. "Damnable idiot that I am! I took a gamble. I was so convinced, you see, that there would money coming in from the recitals. We are already a month behind with the rent, but I was so certain we could make it up. And now…Look at me, Dmitri Alexandrovitch Zhukovsky, the great genius! Landing us up exactly where we started. Back at Mother Richoux's."

His shudder eloquently evoked the squalid room in the Rue Mouffetard partitioned with blankets to preserve his womenfolk's privacy. Once again, he covered his face.

Max, who, apart from the occasional sympathetic interjection, had so far listened in silence, gently touched Vera's arm. "Do you by chance have a pair of scissors?"

"I—I beg your pardon?"

"Scissors, Vera Alexandrovna. If you would be so good."

Mitya glanced up startled as Vera went to her work basket. "I realise, Maxim, that I must appear utterly contemptible—"

"Bear with me, old fellow."

"But I hardly thought you would repay me by playing the fool."

"Shush, Mitya!" said Vera, handing Max the scissors.

"My goodness, Verotchka," said Mme Zhukovskaya, peering from the sofa, "whatever is the dear boy doing?"

In spite of herself, Vera's giggle burst out. "Lifting his coat tail, Mama... snipping a hole in it...and pulling out...a slip of paper. No, good heavens, it's..."

Carefully smoothing out the banknote, Max crossed the room to lay it beside Mitya's vodka glass.

Mitya stared at the note and then at Max, and Max was appalled to see what he had never thought to find in the eyes of his dearest friend, a flash of suspicion.

"Yes, of course, Dmitri Alexandrovitch. I murdered one of Madame de Claireville's guests in his bed and pinched his pocket book."

"Oh, my dear M Fabien!" exclaimed Mme Zhukovskaya. "I'm sure Mitya thinks no such thing."

"Of course he doesn't." Vera, who had been gazing at Max with wonder and admiration, rounded on her brother. "Really, Mitya, how could you?"

Mitya Zhukovsky took in the frozen face of his friend. He hung his head. "Oh, my dear chap, forgive me. This whole wretched business— once you learn distrust, it becomes a habit. Naturally, I did not mean—"

"The money, I can assure you, is mine to give."

"Old friend, I do no doubt it."

"And it would please me greatly to give it to you."

"I told you I was an idiot. A stupid, ungracious idiot. I beg you, forgive me."

Seeing that Mitya actually had tears in his eyes, Max could not but unbend. They embraced.

"But of course you realise, old chap, we cannot possibly accept it."

Max drew back. "Why ever not?"

Mitya's glance strayed to Max's decrepit black suit, the trousers of which, for all the remedial efforts of the laundry maids at La Boissière, had not been improved by the fight. "Maxim, you are more than generous. But this is all you have."

"I am in no need of it. Consider it the repayment of my debt."

"What debt? You owe us nothing."

"When I was on my uppers, you offered to help me."

Mitya laughed. "An empty offer. I had not so much as a spare sou."

"But you would have given it to me, had you possessed it. When I was ill, you played me Bach and Beethoven, your mother and sister left food outside my door—"

"Look, old fellow, this is ridiculous." Mitya sighed and rubbed his forehead. "In my black mood, I may have exaggerated our difficulties— I should not have spoken of Mother Richoux's, it was melodramatic, another of my stupidities. We truly cannot—we could not be more grateful, we cannot thank you enough, but we cannot accept this money."

"And you, Mitya, accuse me of pride?"

"I am sure Mama and Vera agree with me."

Vera's solemn blue eyes were fixed upon Max as though she were torn. But only for an instant. Loyally, she turned to her brother. "We shall manage. As I keep saying, I too can work. Although it will be hard on Mama…"

"Oh, don't concern yourselves with me, children." Mme Zhukovskaya drew herself up as far as her crooked spine would allow. "At my age one can live happily on very little."

Max considered them briefly—Mitya, whom misfortune had made suddenly so touchy and obstinate, and the two women, whose love, with equal obstinacy, would support him, right or wrong. Max was consumed by envy, affection and intense exasperation.

"Very well." He walked calmly to where the banknote lay, untouched, beside the vodka bottle. He picked it up. "I truly have no need of this. In fact, it is something of a burden to me. So it may as well go on the fire."

Vera's eyes were round as moons. "Mama, I think he means it!"

"Maxim, you confounded lunatic!" shouted Mitya .

"Children, children!" Mme Zhukovskaya hammered the floor with her stick. "Have we all gone mad?"

Max straightened up from the fireplace. Only a corner of the note had caught; with his finger and thumb he crushed the tiny spear of flame.

"It seems," said Mme Zhukovskaya, "that, since this dear silly boy is quite determined to make us surrender, we had better do so gracefully."

Max and Mitya faced each other. It was Mitya who broke first, his smile widening like paint dipped in water, washing over his broad cheekbones, spreading light to his eyes and colour to his face, until he looked quite his former self again.

"Of all the pig-headed..."

"My darling brother," carolled Vera, "hear who is talking!"

Her laughter infected them all. Mme Zhukovskaya watched, beaming, as her son and his friend clapped each other on the shoulder.

"My dear chap, we'll pay you back as soon as possible."

Max shrugged. "There is no need."

"Of course we must repay you. With interest."

"Then let it not be until I have attended your first recital. And as for interest—I don't understand these complexities and care for them even less. Might it not be enough that you give me extraordinary pleasure?"

A very agreeable evening followed and Max left the apartment with Bach still resounding in his ears. It was only when he was half way to the Hôtel de Claireville that he recalled his original intention for M de Miremont's banknote. Ah well, so much for that—it must be the army, after all. He did not in the slightest regret what he had done. He could not think of a better use for the money and indeed, he had not been entirely untruthful—he felt the lighter for being rid of it.

CHAPTER NINETEEN

Armand de Miremont remained at Beauvallon until the end of October. It was not that he had been soothed and sustained by his beloved country retreat—on the contrary, he found himself wretchedly immune to its pleasures—but rather that he lacked the will to return to Paris.

At first he would wake to see the sunlight slanting through the faded hangings of his bed and there would be a moment, a deceptive instant, before he remembered his loss. But after a while his eyes opened only upon a bleak vista of grey. His housekeeper at Beauvallon, Rosalie Durand, had always been remarkably sensitive to his moods: now no invalid could have been treated with more concern or delicacy; the housemaids glided through the passages, flitting from his path like ghosts; the kitchen was kept on its mettle offering the consolation of his favourite dishes—quails on a bed of *foie gras*, salsify fresh from the vegetable garden, lemon soufflés light as angels' wings—but, like the venerable burgundies Zacharie Durand brought up from the cellar, they tasted only of the fog.

At the beginning Miremont had been determined to lose himself in work; he had written to Lesage, instructing him to hunt down references that would help him reconstruct his notes. But Ovid provided no solace: his facile cures for lovers merely brought home to Miremont that the poet's notion of love was an elegant, artful crystalline thing, far removed from the messy contradictions of real passion.

He recalled a debate with Max where he had cautioned the boy against ascribing modern motives to the Augustans: Ovid and Catullus were not Baudelaire, they did not speak as individuals but as everyman, their Corrina and Lesbia, with their caged birds, obliging maids and vigilant husbands, were not drawn from some dark torment of the soul, but were a pleasing reiteration of a well-understood convention. And he remembered how Max had argued that this was not true of Catullus, that the poet from Verona had transformed the convention with his own raw pain. Perhaps Miremont should have conceded the point: for, if Ovid's artifice jarred him, he could not, without tears, look at a page of Catullus. Only Ovid's *Poems of Exile*, where the poet's mellifluous verse was soured by his loneliness, his feelings of injustice and his longing for Rome, brought some comfort: at least here the misery and self-pity were heartfelt. But after a while Miremont was forced to admit his attempts to work were futile.

Riding, shooting, the dumbbells—it was the same, whatever he took up to distract him; in the end he had not the energy or the will for it. The footings were not yet laid for his model cottages and altogether Calvert was making an appalling botch of the project, but Miremont lacked the strength to get annoyed. He spent many hours by the lake, not swimming nor testing his skill with the stones, but merely contemplating the trees as they put on their autumn colours or watching the midges dance or charting the ripples on the water.

He had acted for the best, as he kept repeating to himself. Clotilde had written to say she was again with child, he received a rare letter from Julie, more impersonal than he would have wished, it was true, mostly a stilted account of school routine, but, with its large rounded artless hand, vividly recalling to him her unblemished sweetness. The incubus might whisper that he had fled, not for the sake of morality or decency, but from simple fear. But the incubus had no notion of duty.

As witness that his misery was a necessary burden, Miremont had Thomas daily before him. It could not be said that the poor fellow had forgiven him, he might not hope for so much. Yet Thomas' grim mien had noticeably softened, indeed there was about him a certain triumphant—one might almost have said ebullient—air as though, like some trusty mountain dog, he were congratulating himself on having dragged his master back from the chasm. Or perhaps, Miremont reflected, noting how the cut-throat dexterously skimmed his chin, how all at once his every need was anticipated, it was the other way about: he, Miremont, was the hound, to be trained out of his shameful habits by rewards for good behaviour.

As he sat by the lake, Miremont pondered his ties to Arthur Thomas. He had been sixteen when his hero had returned to Beauvallon after his discharge from the army. Poor Thomas, it had been his abominable luck to be stationed in Paris when Louis Napoleon had declared himself emperor. True, the city had only seen three days of violence, there had been nothing to equal the riots that had preceded the July monarchy or its fall in 1848, nothing approaching the subsequent bloodshed of the Commune; but that was because the new emperor had held the army at the ready. Thomas had been injured on the third, last and bloodiest day, when cavalry, whether obeying an order or, as some claimed, simply from panic, had stormed the boulevards, firing into the crowds on the pavements and at innocent bystanders in houses and cafés. Had Thomas caught fever with the rest? Miremont would never know. Apparently he had been felled in the Boulevard Bonne-Nouvelle, where the charge had begun: perhaps he had not even had time to raise his musket before the stone, flung from somewhere in the terrified crowd, had ended his military career.

Returning to Beauvallon for his sixteenth summer, Miremont had been ignorant of all this. When, during his first week, he had seen the filthy ragged figure loitering furtively near the stables, he had registered no shock, for this tramp reeling from drink was as far away as possible from his imaginings of Thomas, tall and erect in his blue uniform on some distant parade ground. However, assuming the fellow must be some indigent peasant seeking his mother's help, Miremont had mentioned the encounter; whereupon, reluctantly, for it seemed she and his father had feared pointlessly to distress him, his mother had told him of poor Thomas' fate.

Doctors could detect no serious damage to Thomas' brain from the missile that had put out his eye, but nonetheless the young man had suffered a drastic change of character. He had apparently been struck dumb at the moment of his injury: although his vocal cords remained healthy and intact and although every effort had been made to draw him out, he could not—or would not—speak. But this was not his only refusal. He seemed altogether to have turned his back on life. Eventually, deemed a hopeless case, he had been committed to the Salpêtrière, where he might have remained in perpetuity, had his family not begged the marquis to intervene. A return to Beauvallon, everyone hoped, would work the cure that had eluded science.

However, although Thomas had been offered employment in the stables, where he could be close to his beloved horses without overtaxing his strength, it appeared he wanted no part of it, could no longer abide horses nor any other outdoor work, as though he had conceived a loathing for the very countryside itself. He refused to take the slightest care of his person or sleep in his bed at his parents' cottage, but preferred to roam the park like a vagrant. All approaches, from moral lectures to gentle exhortations, had failed and it was by no means certain that Thomas even understood them. The poor man, said Miremont's mother with a sigh, was to all appearances an idiot and it might have been kinder to leave him in the asylum.

Miremont did not sleep that night. But when he went in search of

Thomas the next morning he was nowhere to be found, not in the vicinity of the stables, not in the park, not in any of their former most secret haunts. In desperation, Miremont called at the family's cottage, but the embarrassment this occasioned, the fluster to Mme Thomas at finding herself without warning receiving the younger son of the château, together with the simple dignity of her grief, all made him feel a clumsy and pointless intruder. He must accept what she had accepted: the army had taken away the man they had both loved and returned a stranger in his place.

And yes, perhaps, despite his pain, he would have accepted it had not Rosalie Thomas waylaid him a day or so later. She was the parlour maid then, barely twenty (this was years before she married Durand) but tall, like her brother, her figure already promising its later amplitude, her strong-featured handsome face already possessed of that smile that made you think of bread warm from the oven. She knew where to find Arthur—in the ruins of the Old Manoir, not above ground where Miremont had searched, but in what remained of the cellars. She met her brother there every day, brought him food in her break and, if Miremont would only accompany her... "He thought the world of you, Monsieur Armand. As if you were his own flesh and blood. If he ever talks to anybody, he'll talk to you."

Miremont doubted he could possibly succeed where the curé and Thomas' own family had failed. But he could no more resist his longing to work the miracle than he could ignore the quiet despair in Rosalie's plea. After luncheon he set out with her for the ragged piles of stone that had once presided over the estate as the *grand manoir* of the *seigneurs de Beauvallon*, but which had fallen into dereliction years before his great-grandfather had built the present château. She showed him the entrance to the cellar that Thomas had forged, still concealed by tangled bushes and heaps of rock, then thrust the cloth-wrapped package of bread and cheese and two candles into his hand.

Ah, youth and inexperience. Looking back, Miremont could clearly remember the horror of that afternoon, the fusillade of emotions that had bombarded him where his idealism had told him he would feel only love and pity. Yes, of course, he had felt both. But revulsion, impatience, overpowering anger that his hero allowed himself to slide into this degradation—these less creditable feelings were often foremost.

Once he had managed to light a candle he had immediately seen the empty eye socket with its angry scar, but that had disconcerted him surprisingly little, and in any case Thomas had instantly turned his back. No, it was the stench of that animal lair amongst the shattered masonry that overwhelmed him, the feral stink of Thomas' filthy clothes and beard, the thick black dirt under his talons, the repulsive noises he made wolfing the bread and cheese, as if he had sloughed off all trace of humanity. Yet perhaps this disgust was not entirely for Thomas, but in some part a reflection of his disgust at himself. Persuade Thomas to speak? He too was for some while speechless, and when he found his tongue it was only to mouth platitudes or ask questions that Thomas, in full possession of his wits, might reasonably have disdained to answer. After half an hour he could stand it no longer and made his escape.

As cover for his flight, he had promised to return the next day. Loyalty to all Thomas had once been, to all he had taught him, forbade Miremont to break his word, yet he could not but hope the poor fellow would be as anxious as he to avoid a second encounter. However, Thomas was there, crouched in his fetid earth, and, although once again he turned his back almost immediately, Miremont sensed he had been waiting for him. So it was, the next day and the next. Miremont found himself talking to fill the silence, talking wildly and too much, acutely conscious, as he had never been formerly with Thomas, of his own inadequacy and shyness: at first he tried to provoke some response by recalling the old days, but later he spoke of anything that came to mind, of Paris and his studies, of trivial comings and goings at the château; once, in desperation, he retold classical myths, Theseus and the Minotaur, Dido and Aeneas, the wooden horse and the fall of Troy. In return, he received not a syllable, not so much as a grunt, although Thomas turned his back less frequently now and sometimes his single bloodshot eye was focused on his companion with an expression Miremont could not fathom.

In the end, Miremont too fell silent, not merely from exhaustion, but from distaste for the vacuousness of his words. They sat, side by side in the candlelight, amidst rotting scraps of food, ordure and empty wine bottles, often scarcely looking at each other, shifting only to avoid physical discomfort, like two monks engaged in grim meditation. And it was odd but Miremont fancied he began to hear Thomas' thoughts, or at least to feel emanations from him like magnetic waves travelling through the silence.

Miremont had early concluded that the doctors were mistaken, that Thomas' mental faculties remained intact. Nor was he always as far gone in drink as might be supposed. Despite his degraded state, he even displayed a certain obstinate dignity. The flame of humanity still burned within him and Miremont understood that it was stoked by anger—though whether at the general who had ordered Thomas' squadron to shoot into the crowd, or at the insurrectionist who had hurled the stone, or at the emperor himself, Miremont, to this day, could not tell. Yet in spite of this, he felt, Thomas' rejection of speech and civilised manners was not rebellion, but an appalling sort of penance. He had noticed that when he had spoken of their summers together Thomas had seemed for a moment to register sorrow; and later, when he persuaded him to come up into the air and walk in the park, the poor fellow strode on with his one eye fixed straight ahead, not looking at the waving grasses or the blue clusters of scabious nor at the young saplings whose promising growth he would previously have marked, not hearing the skylarks or the distant drilling of a woodpecker, as deaf and blind to all around him as if he were in some drab city street. Yet it was not apathy that occasioned his blindness—or that, at any rate, was how it appeared to Miremont—but rather an agonising effort of renunciation, as though he, who had been so perfectly attuned to nature's rhythms, now felt himself irrevocably divorced from them.

God, how simple the world is to the youthful idealist! It had certainly seemed to the sixteen-year-old Miremont that he had only to coax Thomas into forgiving himself for whatever offence against nature he felt he had committed for all to be well. But whenever he tried to broach the subject, Thomas turned his back. One humid afternoon, when the air in the cellar was more than usually rancid, Miremont found himself crying out in desperation: "What is it, Arthur? What do you want?"

Whereupon Thomas made a curious noise, reminiscent of the grinding of a rusty lock, yet just intelligible as speech. "Nothing." And Miremont suddenly understood the frequent expression in Thomas' orphaned eye: nothing meant nothingness, oblivion, extinction. Overwhelmed by horror and by mortification at his own uselessness, Miremont left soon afterwards.

He did not go back. He perceived his shaming arrogance. Who was he to try to save Thomas? Whatever fixation the stone had lodged in Thomas' brain, it was of such complexity, its roots so deep, that a few glib words would not erase it. What had Miremont hoped for—to transform the poor fellow, as if by some painless spell, back into the man he had once been? Thomas, he of anybody, understood that this could not happen. And if Miremont had truly loved and respected him, he would have understood it too, would have abandoned his senseless exhortations and left the poor man in privacy to come to terms with his loss.

However, four days later, when Miremont was dismounting from his morning ride, he noticed a tall figure, keeping its distance from the stable boys but pointedly waiting; and once again Miremont was astonished to see a Thomas he barely recognised. This Thomas had shaved his beard and cut his hair; even his clothes, while obviously borrowed from some shorter member of his family, were passably clean. He did not smile and was as silent as ever, so that Miremont, having learnt his lesson, forbore to give vent to his joy. But, as they walked without speaking beside the lake, he rejoiced nonetheless. What could this mean, except that Thomas was at last prepared to accept his help? If Miremont could not cure him, he could after all save him. He could find him work, a purpose, a refuge from the horrors that beset him.

Now that Miremont was sixteen, his father had decided it was time he had his own manservant and it had been suggested that the young under-footman at the Hôtel de Miremont might suit the position. It would be no easy matter to convince the marquis that Thomas should be considered instead. Even if he could be trusted to continue in his reformed ways, even if one set aside his lack of speech and other eccentricities, the former groom had no experience of life in a household, let alone the skills required of a valet. Yet Miremont reminded his father of Thomas' military service: he was used to discipline, regulations, the rigours of the barracks; he must have learnt, too, to care for his uniform and equipment. Besides, Miremont's needs were few and easily explained. Thomas himself, although it had taken a period of days and considerable delicacy, had been persuaded to nod his assent. Miremont would take full responsibility for his new valet's conduct; in fact, he promised his father that, as long as Thomas served the family or held any connection with it, he would consider his welfare his personal duty.

There were a few uneasy moments at the start, including a two-day disappearance from which Thomas returned smelling powerfully of absinthe. But on the whole he proved an exemplary valet. Miremont had feared that the move to Paris might revive dreadful memories, but Thomas seemed to be happier in the city, where he was not taunted by everything he had lost. In fact, he built his own world, the world of Miremont's dressing room, a universe of insensate things as far removed from nature as possible, in which rigid order was all. He had not lost the dexterity that had tied delicate fishing flies and gently tweaked mucus from the nostrils of new-born pups; now he expended it on recalcitrant shirt studs and the sewing-on of buttons. As he had settled in, Miremont had renewed his hope that he would begin to speak. But Thomas' meagre store of words was reserved for barking orders at porters or relaying his master's wishes to the servants' hall. Eventually Miremont not only grew resigned to his silence, but came to cherish the peace it conferred.

There had only been one crisis in their relations, and that had been occasioned by Miremont's marriage. Aline and Thomas, from the outset, could not abide each other. Aline's complaints about Thomas were loud and various, but at first mainly directed at his appearance. When Thomas had entered Miremont's service there had been some talk of fitting him with a glass eye but, since his scar was already healed, rendering the success of the operation uncertain, the idea had rapidly been abandoned. Besides, Miremont had never been troubled by his valet's empty eye-socket, indeed had soon ceased to notice it. However, to his wife it was an outrage, a deformity quite unacceptable in the personal servant of a nobleman. Thomas must wear an eye-patch or go. Miremont was not prepared to insist on something he knew affronted his valet's dignity, even had he believed his insistence would have the slightest effect. But it was not merely Thomas' deformity that enraged Aline. His refusal to speak was insolent, his general manner was intolerable, he disobeyed her orders and thwarted her at every turn. This last, Miremont was obliged to admit, was all too true. Since Thomas regarded his master's personal effects and even his master's person as his fiefdom, he snarled at any incursion; worse still, he seemed, like an over-zealous mastiff, to believe it was his duty to protect Miremont from his wife. Perhaps Aline's demands for Thomas' head were not altogether without justification. But it did not matter how much she stormed and raged and even, on one frightful occasion, frothed at the mouth: Miremont, despite surrendering so much else, could not break the promise he had made to his father.

In the end, of course, it was Aline who had gone. After that, master and valet had settled back into their accustomed routine. At sixteen, Miremont had been shocked to find himself the adult and his hero all at once the child. But during the course of twenty-six years he had come to take this for granted: Thomas had his foibles—once or twice a year he would return from his day off hopelessly inebriated and would need to be helped to bed—and he had certainly grown more cantankerous with age; but Miremont was disposed to look upon his lapses benignly, as he might indulge Julie or his grandson. It was not to his credit, perhaps, that after all this time he understood little more of what went on inside Thomas' head than he had during their silent hours in the Old Manoir's cellars; yet it was not indolence that had made him give up the attempt, but Thomas' dogged resistance.

Thus he was deeply perturbed to discover that what he had dreaded during the past two years of torment was not neurasthenic fancy: he himself posed no such riddle, Thomas did indeed divine his thoughts. Nor, it seemed, could he any longer take for granted his adulthood. Now he was the one to be coddled and humoured yet steered firmly away from the erring path.

Miremont submitted to his valet's stern ministrations: he rose when Thomas decreed the shutters should be opened, unprotestingly wore his overcoat when the winds grew colder, changed his boots when they were wet, obeyed the silent injunctions to swallow Dr Gérard's potions. He offered up his obedience as witness to his contrition. Only on one point did he rebel.

Although it was scarcely consistent with his good resolutions, Miremont treasured the pebble Max had given him: when he could be certain of solitude, he would take it out and contemplate it, gripping it in his palm as if its cold surfaces could still transmit the warmth of the boy's mouth, or guiltily pressing it to his lips. He had placed it for safe-keeping in his stud box—foolish, of course, for Thomas, even if he had no notion of its significance, could hardly countenance such an offence against good order: Miremont had twice narrowly prevented him from throwing it away. Thomas had seemed, if reluctantly, to give in to his master's whim. Until one afternoon two weeks later when Miremont went to the box and discovered the stone had vanished.

Miremont had never thought himself capable of rage. Indeed, he could not remember once in twenty-six years having spoken in anger to Thomas. But his hand was quivering as he touched the bell. And when Thomas appeared, he was hardly aware of what he said, only of being born along, powerless, as if by a seething tide, scorching, blinding, intemperate, unstoppable.

When the flow at last ceased, he could see that Thomas, most unusually, had blanched. Miremont felt instantly ashamed. His fury was in any case pointless, since the pebble must long ago have been disposed of by the housemaids. Yet when he came to dress for dinner and Thomas, his face a mask, opened the stud box, there it was, miraculously restored to its place.

The time came when Miremont's departure for Paris could no longer be postponed. Beauvallon, without gaslight, was inconvenient during the winter months, damp from the lake's proximity and whipped by unforgiving draughts; besides, Lesage's daily letters were heavy with business that required Miremont's attention.

It was impossible to banish the thought that he was once again in the same city as the boy, that on drives, on his morning rides in the Champs Elysées or his constitutionals in the Faubourg, he might glimpse through the crowd a familiar tall liveried figure. Yet the excitement that possessed him merely heralded a fresh access of pain for, in the unlikely event of such an encounter, he must turn away his glance and cross the street.

A duty visit from Clotilde, tedious sessions with Lesage, deliberations with Boussec over the dry rot in the east wing—the routine of the Hôtel de Miremont, once such a source of pleasure and comfort, pressed down upon him like the lid of some vast dank sarcophagus. On the first Thursday of Miremont's return, he and Gérard resumed their chess evenings. As he rose in greeting, Miremont observed the doctor's smile falter, change fleetingly to a frown, and then to a look that suggested his friend feared leaving a veritable roomful of broken chairs in his wake. What could Miremont say to the poor fellow? That his nostrum had been all too effective, yet, alas, it had left the patient susceptible to a new infection, a malaise as common as the head cold and equally beyond the art of medicine to cure?

CHAPTER TWENTY

Amongst the many matters Miremont had neglected, as he was uncomfortably aware, was his promise to the boy. Oh, from Beauvallon he had written to Gervais de la Marne, who, he seemed to recall, was at present without a secretary, but his friend had replied that his lack had been remedied. Miremont had been unaccountably relieved to receive this letter and afterwards had done nothing further. But now that he was in Paris and bound in due course to see Ricard and Rosenthal, his conscience was pricked.

He wished, as he and Lesage pored over endless papers, that he did not keep remembering the boy's offer, that he did not keep imagining the boy's shoulder next to his, the boy's breath, and not Lesage's, warming his cheek, the boy's long fingers leafing through these documents and ledgers. But here was the incubus at work again.

Not that he lacked a strong argument for providing Lesage with an assistant, a compelling and compassionate argument—in other circumstances, if Lesage had been another man...But Miremont knew his secretary too well, Lesage had been with him for over twenty years, almost as long as Thomas: it was quite impossible.

Lesage had originally been taken into the household as tutor to Miremont's elder brother and when Edmond had outgrown his services had been promoted to his present post, although at that time, of course, he had served Miremont's father. From his childhood, Miremont remembered the secretary as a somewhat formidable personage, very precise in his speech like someone spitting plum stones, exact in his gestures too, always officiously busy and inclined, with children and his inferiors, to adopt a superior air. In his person, he was also exact and dapper; slim, of middle height with sloping shoulders, possessed of a luxuriant poll of dark hair and features which, although set in a face overly long and thin, seemed precisely, not to say delicately, moulded. He had been, Miremont seemed to recall, not without charms for the fairer sex: indeed, several years after becoming secretary to the marquis, he had contracted a match with a friend of his sister's from his home town of Nogent, the daughter of a local school master or a notary; but although Miremont's father had offered to settle a generous sum on the couple, the engagement had foundered for some reason.

When first Miremont's father and then Edmond had died, Lesage had proved invaluable. In the bewildering aftermath of his loss, Miremont could not have been more grateful for the secretary's exactitude and his encyclopaedic command of the family's affairs; and if Lesage were apt to convey that he considered the new marquis half the man his father had been, Miremont felt he could hardly rebuke him, for this appeared to Miremont himself no more than the truth.

Perhaps if he could have foreseen that twenty-one years later Lesage would still retain this view and indeed from time to time not scruple to express it, he would have been less tolerant. If he were the adult to Thomas' child, to Lesage he would definitely remain the irritating little boy in knickerbockers, the second son who would never amount to much. Yet Miremont choked back his annoyance. Poor Lesage—Miremont could well see why his life with the twelfth marquis had been a long trail of disillusionment.

For, if Lesage hankered for anything, it was not his service with the tenth marquis, but the time of Aline. To see the doors of the Hôtel de Miremont thrown open every night to the cream of society, to converse with duchesses instead of brokers and lawyers, to set aside dreary correspondence for invitation lists and table plans—to Lesage, who loved nothing better than a title, it must have been paradise indeed.

The couple's separation had dealt the poor fellow a bitter blow and Miremont had not the slightest doubt Lesage considered him solely to blame. And, if it were not bad enough that his wife's departure had drawn Miremont back into his dull old ways, there was a new burden to contend with—his academic pursuits. Although Lesage had very adequate Greek and Latin, he had not the least interest in the texts themselves. What to Miremont was adventure was to his secretary dusty drudgery. Furthermore Miremont suspected from Lesage's weary but disdainful resignation that he shared Aline's view—this was no suitable occupation for someone who could trace his title back to Henri II.

Yet the man had his virtues. There was his extraordinary efficiency, of course. He could be entertaining, too: while he was as voluble as Thomas was silent and frequently exasperating with his petty snobberies, he had not entirely lost the wit that had once charmed the ladies. When Miremont was at home, it was his custom to lunch with his secretary and, if he did not take dinner in his own apartments, to dine with him as well; over the last desolate years there had been occasions when he had been all too grateful for the company his amanuensis provided. And, although inclined to waver in matters relating to Aline, Lesage was otherwise the model of loyalty—Miremont might fail his exacting standards, yet Miremont was still a marquis, and Lesage's marquis to boot.

Poor fellow—Miremont could not but feel his secretary had paid a high price for his devotion to the nobility. Although well into his seventh decade, he remained slim and dapper and his poll, if now pure white, was still luxuriant; yet the skin had shrunk over those finely modelled features so that their bony pinions were revealed like veins in a dried leaf. Life in the rarefied air of the Faubourg had desiccated him. While he never visited his sister in Nogent, nor spoke of her, his friends in Paris were few, two or three aristocratic widows in straightened circumstances who welcomed him to make up a card table on his days off and for whom he ran errands and performed other small services. Beyond that, the Hôtel de Miremont was his entire existence and, as Miremont had long since accepted, he would die there.

But for some time now Lesage had been giving Miremont more immediate cause for concern. It was not that his legendary exactitude was failing, for his memory remained as acute as ever: all the same— unheard of previously—he was inclined to mislay things. His immaculate hand was also deteriorating and often, in those fair copies he so hated making, there were words and sometimes entire sentences missing. He had worn spectacles for years, but Miremont could hardly fail to notice that by degrees the lenses had grown thicker and once or twice he had chanced to find him working with a magnifying glass— Lesage had started and quickly stowed the object away, as if apprehended in some misdemeanour.

Cataracts, Gérard opined, which must eventually ripen into blindness. Not that Gérard had been permitted to examine the patient. Lesage was adamant that he was as healthy in body and as keen in all his faculties as any thirty-year-old. Nor was he willing to accept any gesture of help that acknowledged his difficulty: when Miremont offered to hunt for mislaid letters or suggested his writing desk be moved nearer to the light, he responded with extreme irritation. Miremont was not sure what the poor fellow most feared, blindness itself or that he would be summarily cast off if he admitted his incapacity. Naturally Miremont had no such intention and endeavoured constantly to reassure him. But it seemed the subtlety and tact required prevented Lesage from grasping his meaning; perhaps the secretary's forty years in the Faubourg had taught him to assume that those of rank had a perfect right, indeed a duty, to discard minions who had ceased to be of use. Or perhaps, rather, it was Miremont's generosity he dreaded, which would see him comfortably pensioned off, forced to forsake the Hôtel de Miremont for the social extinction of lodgings in an unfashionable quarter or, worse still, retirement to Nogent.

An assistant would be of immeasurable help to the poor fellow. An intelligent young man like Max could be his eyes and sustain him in his post for years to come. But Miremont knew how his secretary would respond to the very hint of such a notion. Eventually something must be done, although Miremont was perplexed to know what. In the meantime they must continue with their daily pretence that Lesage was no more than a trifle short-sighted. Miremont closed his ears to the incubus. An assistant was impossible.

Four days after his return, Miremont went to dine with Constant de Sauvigny and was astonished to find Achille de Tarascon amongst the company. He was little enough pleased by this discovery on his own account, but when he learnt that Tarascon had been invited by his younger nephew Roland, and when he furthermore observed that the boy was hanging on the famed wit's every word, he was horrified. Roland, whose inheritance combined the Sauvigny auburn curls with the Miremont dimpled chin, was an attractive young man not yet twenty. It was surely Miremont's duty to speak to the boy or warn Constant. Yet how? How could he explain his horror of Tarascon without also laying himself open to suspicion?

In the event no occasion presented itself and Miremont resigned himself to calling on Constant the next day. However the guests took their departure in a downpour: Miremont, since he lived only five minutes away, had come on foot, and Tarascon offered him the shelter of his carriage. His first instinct, naturally, was to decline, but when Tarascon proved insistent it struck him that here, after all, was his opportunity—a discreet appeal to the fellow's better nature would be by far his best course.

The brief drive left him no opening, for Tarascon, to whom talk was a drug, was still scattering epigrams like sparks, still aflame with the elation of a successful evening. But, as the carriage paused for Miremont's gates to open, the count inspected his watch.

"My dear, at this hour only disreputable people are tucked up in bed. May I suggest we repair to the bath-house. Or there is an interesting establishment, much frequented by the military, where—"

Once again Miremont was taken aback by the man's obnoxious directness. However, he did not forget his purpose. "I thank you," he said hastily. "But since we are at my door, perhaps you will honour me by accepting my hospitality."

Much to Miremont's surprise, for he could hardly furnish the excitements of the bath-house, Tarascon appeared to welcome his offer, even to greet it with alacrity, and they were soon seated before a newly lit fire in the smoking room, partaking of Miremont's brandy and cigars.

Once the servants had been given permission to retire for the night, Miremont cleared his throat. "My dear Tarascon, there is a matter—my nephew Roland—"

"Roland de Sauvigny."

"My nephew, yes.

"If you knew, Miremont, what rapture it is to speak that name, to hear you speak it. It is pure poetry, is it not?"

"My dear sir—"

"Roland de Sauvigny. He of the hyacinthine hair and the rose-petal lips. With a name like the breath of the gods!"

"Monsieur!" Miremont, who had expected to lead gently into his subject and to encounter at least some token evasion, could not contain his outrage. "My nephew is an innocent!"

"Ah, innocence. A commodity that is of value only to those who have lost it."

"Monsieur, I will not—"

"To the innocent it is like the chicken pox—they itch to be rid of it."

"Monsieur de Tarascon, you go too far. This is intolerable!"

But Tarascon merely shook his head in amusement. "Miremont, Miremont! Trust you to make a necessity out of virtue. I adore your nephew, but alas the divine youth is in no danger from me."

"The boy is impressionable. It was quite evident tonight that you set out to dazzle him."

"My dear, he was amused by me as one is by a performing seal. But, had you not been blinded by moral indignation, you might have observed he was dazzled by Mademoiselle de Sainte-Foy." Sighing, he drew deeply on his cigar. "It is my doom, my dear Miremont. To love what I cannot have and have what I cannot love."

Miremont looked at him dubiously.

"Have you ever been in love?"

The question caught Miremont off guard. He feared that he flushed. "No."

But Tarascon had not missed his hesitation. He inspected Miremont over the lip of his brandy glass with surprise and renewed interest. "Then you will know all too well how it is. Lovers, dear boy, are like over-dressed women—they never learn from their mistakes. Certainly it has ever been so with me."

He paused and Miremont, observing that his glass was empty, felt obliged to refill it. Yet perhaps Achille de Tarascon needed no more brandy. Although his hand was steady and his cheeks, above the raven beard and curled moustache, retained their usual waxen pallor, his eyes were suddenly filmed with a sentimental mist that might presage tears. To Miremont's alarm, he drew his handkerchief from his sleeve and noisily blew his nose.

"But surely, Tarascon—" Miremont sought to lighten the air "—to a cynic like yourself—is not love an illusion?"

"Illusion is the purest form of reality. It is the real that is unreal. And you mistake me, Miremont. A cynic requires the world to sink to his expectations. I, on the other hand, am hope's slave. What else can I be when I bestow my love exclusively on those who find it unthinkable or unspeakable?"

A stir of fellow-feeling compelled Miremont to nod.

"I have been in love a hundred times, yet I am the soul of fidelity for I have loved only once. Let me tell you the story of Raphaël Clément."

Tarascon had momentary recourse to his glass. When he resumed speaking it was in a lower, gentler voice, far removed from the high artificiality of his dinner-table utterances.

"Your nephew, the exquisite Roland, reminds me of him, of course. Raphaël too was an Adonis, a gold and ivory god resplendent in his rose-white boyhood. He was a school-fellow of mine. Not that I was one of his intimates then—he was four years ahead of me and considered brilliant, while I was a pale overweight boy inclined to eczema. I worshipped him only from afar and perhaps in time I should have forgotten him. But, when I was barely eighteen, I encountered him by chance while out walking with my sister in the Luxembourg Gardens. Naturally, it was I who recognised him—at twenty-two he had merely grown more beautiful. But I flatter myself I had improved a little too, for, though I introduced myself with the greatest diffidence, he immediately put himself out to be charming. We discovered there and then that we were twin souls. He had been intended for the bar—his father was a lawyer—but he had thrown it over to become a poet. We spoke of poetry, the theatre, the opera, until my sister, who has always reserved such flights of enthusiasm for the weightier topic of hats, became quite faint with impatience. So what could we do but arrange to meet again the next day?

"We saw each other almost daily that winter, whenever Raphaël could find time from the journalistic endeavours that brought him a meagre income: we would read each other our verses, we commenced working together on a poetic dramatisation of the life of that unfortunate and much-misconstrued emperor, Heliogabalus; often we would repair to the delicious gothic squalor of Raphaël's lodgings to smoke a hookah and soar aloft on an Arabian carpet of jewelled dreams. My people grew so accustomed to Raphaël's presence in our house that they began calling us David and Jonathan.

"When summer came and we removed to the country, naturally Raphaël was invited to join us. My joy was unconfined, for now we could spend every waking moment together. I was certain my passion was returned, for his hand was always upon my shoulder, we walked with our arms about each other's waists, it could not be long before those crimson lips permitted my awed and ardent kisses.

"We had not been in the country a week when he proposed to my sister, who, since he lacked the attributes that sway a tender-hearted girl—rank, fortune and future promise—turned him down without ceremony. He left that afternoon and I never saw him again."

Tarascon paused, hung his head, toyed blindly with the emerald on his third finger. He seemed all at once so unlike himself—smaller, humbler, painfully, fallibly human—that Miremont's sympathy could not but be roused; besides, Tarascon's anguish inevitably recalled his own.

As much to break the silence as anything, Miremont asked: "What became of him?"

"He married a diamond merchant's daughter, went to live in Amsterdam, grew very fat and never wrote a line of verse again. He died three years ago, I discovered from another school fellow, struck down in a duel with five dozen oysters. But, of course, he is immortal. He lives for me in your delightful nephew, as he has lived in all those other young gods I have worshipped incontinently but in vain."

Miremont struggled with himself. Faced with Tarascon in this new flesh-and-blood incarnation, his dislike of the man melted and he was powerfully tempted to lay his own heart open. But, beyond the embarrassment and difficulty of putting his misery into words, he could not avoid seeing where this would lead. He might hope that Max had been safely numbered in Tarascon's impervious pantheon, but supposing it had been otherwise? In the end, all he could bring himself to ask was: "And have you—has your love never been returned?"

"It has been my fate to suffer immoderately. But what wiser credo than immoderation in all things?" With a sudden laugh and an extravagant flourish of his cigar, Tarascon recovered his former self. "Pain is pleasure, pleasure is pain. The exquisite torture of unsatisfied love is not without its rewards: such love is never tested; thus, unlike Madame de la Rochefontaine's diamonds, it will not prove to be paste. And while love is beyond price, lust, mercifully, is a few francs on every corner."

Miremont flinched slightly, only to be admonished by the count's mobile cigar. "There is only one truth, my dear Miremont—to be true to oneself. The man who is true to others is an incorrigible liar."

Afterwards, Miremont was driven to reflect on this curious conversation. He had not revised his opinion that most of Tarascon's talk was pernicious nonsense: how could someone who was not true to others ever be true to himself? But the glimpse Miremont had received of the face behind the domino, of the real Tarascon, as it seemed to him—over-given to sentiment perhaps, but nevertheless unashamed to own weakness and despair—was bound to moderate his judgement. He was reassured, too, about Roland; closer scrutiny confirmed that the comte was right, his nephew's greatest danger was Mlle de Sainte-Foy. But, if Miremont no longer studiously avoided Tarascon's company, it was most of all because of the comfort the conversation had brought him.

He did not regret resisting the urge to confession: nor was he merely held back by jealousy, but by that sense of form that had once prevented him divulging, even to Léonore and Constant, the state of affairs with Aline. Yet to talk frankly for the first time with a member of his own circle—to abandon evasion, to discuss Hellenic love as if it were no more out of the ordinary than Roland's passion for the little Sainte-Foy girl—this was a hitherto unimaginable consolation.

But if he were willing to dine with Tarascon occasionally, he would not go so far as the delights of the baths. Lust for a few francs— at least that craving had evaporated, so that he was now thankfully indifferent to waiters and butcher's boys, while the very thought of the Bois filled him with revulsion. Not, of course, that desire had deserted him: it tortured him nightly. Yet it had but one focus.

He could not forever put off calling upon Catherine. He had written to her on his departure from La Boissière and had corresponded with her regularly, but friendship decreed that, on his return to Paris, he must present himself in person. Indeed, he did arrange to call, only, at the last moment, to plead a head cold. But he could not continue to absent himself without causing justified offence.

The visit might work his cure, he told himself. He would encounter Max and the illusions spun by memory and longing would unravel: here would be an ordinary, insignificant youth, just another footman. All the same, he instructed Thomas to lay out his new coat, delivered only the day before and of an uncharacteristically fashionable cut. And while he waited for the carriage he could not forbear continually glancing at the clock, though it would have been hard to say whether in dread or anticipation.

CHAPTER TWENTY ONE

"No more apologies, my dear Armand. It is I who must apologise to you."

The footman who had opened the carriage door was one of the usual Paris contingent, although Miremont could not recall his name. The footman who had taken Miremont's overcoat was a dark, olive-skinned youth whom Miremont was almost certain he had never seen before. And, although his heart had once again raced as Catherine had touched the bell for English tea, he was due only for further disappointment: the footman who had appeared, well-remembered from La Boissière, was the fair slender boy with the girlish mouth, Fabrice.

"My dear," continued Catherine, "I have been horribly afraid that you were displeased with me. Indeed, I wonder what I could have been thinking of. Génie Zelenska would not have suited you at all, she is quite unworthy of you. In fact, given the tasteless way in which she and that odious windbag have been carrying on since they returned to Paris, for all the world as if they were Anthony and Cleopatra, I can only conclude she is losing her wits. And as for him! Oh for an asp! After boring us all to extinction and thoroughly overstaying his welcome, do you know what he had the effrontery to do? Write me a long, pompous letter about some article of his—a cravat or a waistcoat or some such thing—which he claims one of my servants has stolen. Fancy! Even the servants have more discrimination—"

However at this juncture Fabrice reappeared with the tea tray, temporarily quelling conversation.

Watching the footman unload the silver teapot, the basin of sliced lemon, the cake-stand heavy with tartlets and choux pastries, Miremont seemed to recall that Fabrice and Max were on friendly terms. Yet what could that serve him? Catherine's presence prevented him from so much as catching the young man's eye. Besides, Fabrice, like Max, cultivated that hauteur which had often amused Miremont, that look of ostentatious disdain more aristocratic than the aristocracy: while his hands executed their various tasks with precision, his glance was loftily distant. Only when he was bending to retrieve his tray did he unexpectedly look up and stare directly at Miremont. And even then Miremont could not be sure; it was so quick, a mere instant, he had probably imagined it. All the same, he was startled. For the glance, if he had truly seen it, had been spiked with hostility.

Catherine poured Miremont a measure of watery liquid. He would have much preferred coffee, but what matter since his trembling hand dared not lift the cup.

"Of course," she went on, "Génie will soon discover the insufferable Bellac is all talk and no money. For now the inevitable has happened."

Miremont endeavoured to collect himself.

"Naturally she has taken her usual measures under the circumstances—a hasty visit to the prince in Geneva. Poor man! He must wonder. But perhaps Génie has told him premature births run in her family."

Realising from Catherine's dramatic pause that some response was required, Miremont grasped the only word he had caught distinctly. "Geneva—as I recall—is quite pleasant at this time of year. Cold but quite pleasant."

His friend stared at him, first in astonishment, then in pity. Impulsively she leaned across from the sofa to take his hand. "My darling Armand, what a stoic you are—at any minute I expect you to tell me about your model cottages. But you cannot deceive me. It is generous of you to try, but I know how little I deserve your generosity. All I can hope is that, now I have told you the very worst, you will cast Iphigénie Zelenska utterly from your mind. You must see she does not merit a single thought of yours, not one regret, not one painful memory. There are other women far more worthy of your heart."

Now it was Miremont's turn to look astonished. "My dear Catherine, you cannot seriously imagine—?" In spite of himself, he laughed. "You do not truly suspect me of falling in love with the princess?"

"Why else were you a changed man during your time with us in the country? Why else did you leave the instant she took up with the monstrous Bellac? Yes, you have every right to be angry and refuse to come to see me, for I, fool that I am, put the notion into your head."

Miremont pressed the hand that lay in his. "My dear, if I have not called, it is not because—you must not think...I swear to you, without wishing to be ungallant, the princess—well, she is charming of course, but her charms are not for me. And as for that fellow Bellac, yes, I allow he is a boor, but he seemed so thoroughly smitten with her. If the poor wretched husband must be betrayed, as it seems he must, then I hope the two of them find happiness together."

"So you are not vexed with me?"

"My dear, far from it."

Catherine continued to clasp his hand as she scrutinised him thoughtfully. A teasing smile widened her lips. "Then, if it was not Génie Zelenska…?"

Miremont floundered in the pit he had dug himself. "T-the country air. Your country air, your splendid hospitality and your friendship." And, knowing too well that she could not be counted upon not to press the point, he hastened the conversation on to other topics.

Yet as they talked, he could not but think of Max, busy at some task somewhere under this roof. Would Fabrice alert him to Miremont's presence? That perplexing look of enmity argued against it. Still, Miremont could not prevent his eye drifting towards the doors, could not restrain the hope that a sudden knock would herald Max's appearance on some pretext. By the end of the visit, his nerves could scarcely bear the strain. Surely when Catherine touched the bell it would be Max who came to escort him downstairs. Whenever he had imagined paying this call, on all the occasions he had lain awake thinking of it with longing or trepidation, it had never occurred to him that he would not encounter the boy at all.

However, it was Catherine who took his arm and walked with him to the head of the stairs. And when he looked down, the only livery visible belonged to the dark-haired stranger, who waited respectfully with his coat.

As Miremont struggled to fit his arms into the sleeves, he could not resist one last desperate glance around the hallway. Whereupon another footman did indeed appear, this time the thick-set Michel, whom Max had declared to be Catherine's paramour. Observing Miremont's tussle with the topcoat, Michel gave the dark boy his dismissal.

"You may leave Monsieur le marquis to me. There, that's better now, isn't it, monsieur?" Michel lowered his voice confidingly, although the dark youth was already out of earshot. "I trust you will forgive Jean, he's only been with us a week or two."

Jean? Miremont recalled Max explaining that new servants in Catherine's household took their predecessors' names. He could not prevent himself from staring aghast at Michel. And it seemed to him that this did not escape the footman, that the fellow's smile, as he presented Miremont with his hat, was replete with malice.

The boy was gone. As Miremont climbed into his carriage, his shock struggled with disbelief. Max had undertaken to write if he changed his situation. Miremont must have misheard, Michel had not said

Jean, but some other name. Perhaps his overwrought nerves had imagined everything, from Fabrice's enmity to Michel's knowing leer.

Hidden from curious eyes within the sanctuary of his carriage, Miremont buried his head in his hands. The boy was missing, he had not imagined that. He was gone, and discretion denied Miremont the means to find him. Nor, as was clear from his failure to keep his promise, did he wish to be found.

And yet—supposing he had not left Catherine's of his own accord? Perhaps this had been the true meaning of his fellow footmen's sinister behaviour. Was the poor lad in trouble? Or ill perhaps—was he wasting of a fever in the Hotel-Dieu?

But no, Miremont must face it, the boy was not languishing somewhere desperate for his help. He had shown his contempt by vanishing. All Miremont's agonising, all his homilies to himself about duty and self-denial, all his longing and his pain and his futile attempts to kill his love had been a mockery. The boy had already decided the matter.

Such was Miremont's turmoil that he did not notice his carriage had halted. Only his longing to reach the safety of home and shut himself away with his grief made him finally aware that the brougham was not merely stationary but had been so for some time. Pulling down the window, he leant out to make enquiries of Théo, his coachman: a vintner's cart five vehicles ahead had apparently swerved to avoid an approaching omnibus and toppled several wine casks into the road.

Resignedly, Miremont was about to draw up the window and sink back into his seat, when something stopped him dead. A figure amongst the crowd on the pavement. A tall figure whose blue tricorne overtopped the heads of other passers-by, whose long buff coachman's cape swung unbuttoned to the rhythm of its wearer's stride, revealing a glimpse of azure beneath. He was carrying a parcel, a brown paper package the size of a glove box, and it too swung negligently by its string as he walked. He was almost level with Miremont now, another second would bring him within arm's reach. His eyes moved incuriously to where Miremont's head and shoulders were framed in the carriage window, were arrested, flickered—there was no mistaking it—with startled recognition; then, rapidly withdrawing his glance, the boy walked on.

Miremont did not stop to think. Leaning out to unlatch the carriage door and jumping down into the street, shouting up to Théo that he would walk home, he set off in pursuit. The boy's long stride had already carried him some distance and Miremont was held back by the stream of pedestrians flowing around him in both directions. Desperation battled civility. In the end, out of breath and clutching his hat, he could see nothing for it but to call out "Max!"

The buff cape continued without faltering for several paces. Then, just as Miremont was wondering whether he should outrage public dignity by shouting again, there was a sudden turbulence in the human tide ahead. The boy had turned. As his livery obliged him, yet with no show of urgency, he retraced his steps and tipped his tricorne.

"Good afternoon, monsieur. May I be of service to you?"

Max's footman's mask was firmly in place and his icy formality narrowly skirted disrespect. All the same, Miremont was not to be stayed. He knew he must present a ridiculous figure, his own hat askew, his chest heaving, but he no longer cared. "Max—Jean—are you still in Mme de Claireville's employ?"

With some surprise, the boy's free hand indicated his livery. "As you see, monsieur."

"It is only that I—well, I have just come from there and—"

"I have been on an errand, monsieur."

"An errand?"

"Again, as you see."

Miremont glanced down at the parcel. "Yes—yes, of course."

"Now, if monsieur has no further need of me—"

"My dear boy—Max—Jean—" Beside himself though he was, Miremont could not ignore the passing crowd, still less the row of stationary carriages, some with faces peering from their windows, that, as a consequence of the accident, now lined the kerb. His pride no longer restrained him from pleading with Max, but to be overheard doing so would be perilous for them both. He coughed suddenly and raised his voice: "As I say, I have just come from your mistress and you can indeed do me a service." Then, in a low tone, almost a whisper, he added: "*May we meet?*"

"What service is that, monsieur?"

The boy's expression had not changed, perhaps he had not heard. Miremont tried again. "I believe I have left something of mine at the Hôtel de Claireville. *Is your day off still Sunday?*"

"Something, monsieur?"

"Something important. My – my…" But here Miremont's limited talent for improvisation ran dry. He was wearing his gloves and still clutched his cane; he could not think what other possession he might have mislaid. To cover his confusion he began an elaborate mime, feeling in his pockets and patting his coat. If he had seemed ridiculous before, now he cut a preposterous figure. Two young girls passing with their chaperone put up their gloved hands to stifle their giggles. And Max, it seemed, was also not immune to this comic performance. For all his hauteur, the corners of his mouth began to twitch.

"May I suggest that in these circumstances monsieur usually mislays his pince-nez?"

"My pince-nez, yes, of course!" Suddenly both were laughing. Miremont was emboldened to make a further attempt. "My pince-nez. I believe I left it in the Rose Salon. *Are you free this Sunday?*"

"On one of the consoles perhaps? *I might be.*"

"I could have dropped it anywhere. *At, say, three o'clock?*"

"Most likely it has fallen under a chair. *Possibly.*"

"*Oh, my dear boy*——"

"Or slipped behind some cushions. *Where?*"

Once again Miremont's inspiration deserted him as he sought for a meeting- place that guaranteed anonymity.

"I shall search the Rose Salon. I shall also search the vestibule, the staircase and the landing. Trust me, monsieur, no effort shall be spared. *Le Jardin des Plantes?*"

"Yes, of course. Very commendable. *Whereabouts?*"

"*The Menagerie. The big cats.* Monsieur may be assured I shall leave no cushion unturned. Although——" the boy grinned "——I fear it will be fruitless. The article concerned is hung about monsieur's neck. "

Miremont made a pantomime of thrusting his hand within the lapel of his coat and producing the pince-nez on its ribbon with a flourish. "How foolish! I am most obliged. *The big cats, three o'clock.* How glad I am, my dear Jean, that I can count on you."

But this last was a mistake. The boy, apparently feeling he had made sufficient concessions, immediately withdrew his grin.

"*Count on nothing, monsieur. I said possibly.* Now, if monsieur will excuse me, I am late and shall be missed."

Miremont arrived early at the Jardin des Plantes and, with some false starts, found his way to the big cats' enclosure. It was a bleak afternoon, leaden, with a chill wind that whipped up the last of the fallen leaves; the arms of the trees thrust out dark fingers to bar the sky, bones picked clean like the iron ribs of the cages, the joints of a vast winter skeleton sprawled across the park.

Nevertheless, this was not the solitary meeting-place Miremont had hoped for. On his way past the zebras and the elephants, the paths had been thronged with promenaders in their Sunday finery determined to enjoy the day of rest whatever the weather. Bowler-hatted tradesmen and clerks with ornately milinered ladies on their arms mingled with working men in caps and mufflers; tired young women carried babies swathed in shawls, while small boys in stockings and breeches tugged at their skirts and pointed excitedly to the animals, or chased the bowling leaves as if they were hoops. Even here, a fair crowd craned over the railings that held back the populace from the bars of the big cats' cages, although most of them had retired to the shadowy recesses of their quarters and there was only a solitary leopard in view.

The leopard paced the brief length of its cage, indifferent to the bespectacled young man lecturing his two female companions on the habits and characteristics of the species, blind to the little girl in her Sunday frills held up to see by her doting father, impervious to the three bare-legged boys who tried to goad it by poking a stick through the railings. The beast went back and forth, back and forth, without enthusiasm but methodically, as though each imprint of its great paws on the dirty straw marked out the hours, days, years of its captivity. Yet sometimes, as it turned, it would raise its eyes and in that baleful glare and in the flash of the bars across its splotched pelt, like the play of light on some far-off savannah, there was just for a moment—or so it seemed to Miremont—a quickening, the recollection of something unsurrendered, before it resumed its convict's tramp.

Miremont turned away in disquiet. It was not just the plight of the beast, caged and forced to deny its nature, that made him uncomfortable. Amongst the bowlers and black suits, his top hat and fur-collared overcoat felt disagreeably conspicuous. And besides, he had a superstitious fear that if he diverted his attention for an instant he would miss the boy.

Despite Max's warnings, Miremont did not countenance the notion that the boy would fail to appear, he could not. Over the past few days he had thought of very little but this meeting. At first he had rued the blind impulse that had suggested it, had castigated himself for his lamentable failure of self-control. What good could come of such an encounter? For the boy it would be a disappointment since he could offer him nothing, while it would only exacerbate his own pain. Yet after a while, as he toiled in the swamp of self-recrimination, he saw firmer footings within reach. He checked himself—but no, this was not the whispering of the incubus, it was perfectly possible: there was a way for duty and love to be reconciled, for him to keep the boy near him, yet violate no trust. Everyone—the boy himself, even Lesage—would benefit. Miremont's excitement grew as he elaborated his plan. It gripped him now as, retiring to one of the benches set back from the railings, he anxiously consulted his watch. Max would not fail him, he must not.

Yet when the boy did appear, he almost did not see him. Or rather his eyes, in quest of a shabby frock coat and battered stove-pipe hat, at first passed over the youth in the pearl-grey suit until the stranger came towards the bench and raised his bowler.

Miremont stared at the boy in shock. He had always admired that natural grace which, whether Max wore livery or his tattered black, seemed somehow to set him above his station. But in these curious garments, the jacket cut indecently short, the material slightly shiny and too flimsy for the season, some tailor's concept doubtless of fashionable elegance, designed to render him a 'swell', he looked, alas, only what he was. Or worse. With his pomaded hair and prominent cuffs, he seemed to exude a musk of depravity.

The thought that they might be noticed together dealt Miremont a discreditable stab of shame. But more reprehensible still was the urge that followed, the mad agony of desire that craved for the boy to go with him now, somewhere, anywhere, into the nearest clump of evergreens, to relieve its torment.

This was so counter to Miremont's resolve that it was all he could do to stammer out a greeting. Nor was his shame decreased by the fear that Max had divined his weakness.

"Monsieur will forgive me but I cannot stay long, I am expected elsewhere."

"Yes, of course…my dear fellow…I am grateful…" Miremont struggled to collect himself. "I trust you will pardon me for accosting you in the street, but I feared you had gone?"

"Gone?"

"You have a new footman in your household—"

"Guillaume?"

"Guillaume, is that it?"

"The old Guillaume left while we were in the country." Max gave Miremont a puzzled glance. "But, as to why monsieur would—"

"A misunderstanding, my dear fellow. That first footman of yours, Michel. I must have misheard him, but I could have sworn he said Jean."

"Ah!" A light flashed in the boy's eye, a savage light that reminded Miremont of the leopard. But it vanished in an instant, Max dusted away the subject with a negligent flick of his hand. "Michel is a pea-brain. Is that why you wished to meet me?"

"Good heavens, no. I…" The boy's coldness had sobered Miremont, but he still required time to gather his thoughts before embarking on the impartial, business-like conversation he intended. "Please, my dear fellow, let us be seated."

As Max settled beside him and crossed his legs, it absurdly comforted Miremont to observe that he still wore his old boots, cracked in places at the toes and with scuff marks that defied polish. Even more reassuring was the familiar chain adorning the boy's waistcoat; at least he did not disdain to wear the watch. Miremont cleared his throat and began.

"You will recall that when I—when circumstances unfortunately required me to leave Bordeaux—I made you a promise."

Max raised his eyebrows. "I recall, monsieur, that you paid me off handsomely."

"My dear boy, I did not—"

"I cannot see that you are under any further obligation to me. Or I to you."

This was hardly a propitious start. Nor was it the discreet exchange Miremont had hoped for, so that he glanced around nervously. But everyone seemed intent on the leopard; even those drifting away from the enclosure scarcely spared the bench and its occupants a glance.

Reminding himself that the boy was entitled to every atom of his injured pride, Miremont persevered. "I promised to help you better your situation. I agree, I have been tardy in keeping my promise, and for that I ask your pardon. But I believe I have at last found something that may suit you."

"Monsieur is too good—"

"It is no more than I—"

"But it may be that I have plans of my own."

Miremont stared at the boy. It was all at once born in upon him, as it never had been with such force and finality, that Max was not only lost to him, but had been so, irrevocably, since his cowardice at La Boissière, and no ingeniously hatched schemes, no delusions of beneficence, could win him back. If Miremont wished to preserve the last shreds of his dignity, then his best course was to leave now. After all, the boy too was anxious to leave, he had another engagement, probably with another lover.

But, as Miremont reached for his cane, Max unexpectedly laid a hand on his arm. "Monsieur, I didn't mean..." He bent his head. "Michel is not the only one who keeps his brain in his boots. You are generous and I am ungrateful."

Miremont looked at the hand. He seemed to feel the imprint of its fingers through the weight of his overcoat and all the layers beneath. Slowly, he looked up at the boy. "Impossible, dear fellow, is the word I should have chosen."

All at once—he hardly knew how—both were smiling. The unflattering bowler and the dreadful suit receded from Miremont's vision and he saw only the boy's clear, intelligent gaze and the generous beauty of his mouth, its full upper lip no longer scornful but contrite.

"So has this impossible idiot lost the chance to hear your proposal?"

"But, my dear boy, your plans—"

"They are not yet carved in stone."

It was as much as Miremont could manage not to close his own hand over the fingers still resting lightly on his arm. Yet this would not do. He must recall his firm intention to be businesslike. "Very well then. There is, as I say, a situation available— should you decide it is congenial. "

"You have found an eminent mathematics professor who requires someone to slave all day copying simultaneous equations?"

"This is—something more in accordance with your original wish."

"At the Hôtel de Miremont?"

Miremont nodded.

Although the boy's eyes widened for an instant, it was hard to fathom his expression—was he surprised, pleased or merely wary? Certainly, his brows shot up. "But you have a secretary."

"I am offering you the post of librarian. Your first task would be to catalogue the books."

Now Max did appear genuinely taken aback.

"As I recall, you worked in the library at your monastery."

"Mending bindings, copying manuscripts. Under Dom Aloysius's strict supervision."

"There you are—an excellent start. My requirements are not complicated, I have every confidence you will do a splendid job. Your other duties will include assisting me with my work—looking up references, suggesting suitable quotations. As for the rest, as you will realise, the position—if you are willing to consider it—offers a considerable improvement on your present situation. And not just in terms of remuneration and standing. To one of your abilities, the work will not be arduous. It is my hope that you will find yourself free—say, for a couple of afternoons a week—to pursue your own studies."

Miremont paused. However, although regarding him intently, the boy gave no response.

"Of course, it is not a secretary's post. Perhaps that disappoints you. Perhaps—" here Miremont essayed a light laugh "—you would rather the simultaneous equations…Well, at any rate, I could hardly expect you to decide at once. You must have questions you wish to ask…Or at least you will need to think it over. My dear boy, please, take whatever time you require, there is no urgency, I…"

But the boy's glance had drifted away, he now seemed more interested in the leopard and the crowd at the railings. Clearly he had once again been vanquished by his impossible pride.

Miremont sighed. "Max, if the situation does not suit you—"

"No."

The boy had turned back so suddenly and had spoken with such emphasis that Miremont was startled. "No?"

"I mean, yes. Thank you. Of course it suits me."

"Y- you do not wish for time to think?"

"There is no need, monsieur. I should like nothing better than to accept."

"Well, in that case…" Miremont was quite bewildered by this unlooked-for surrender. "Oh, my dear boy…"

He stared at Max. The boy was smiling that strange slow smile of his, the candle-flame smile that seemed like a beneficence. All the mad, confused, sentimental words, the words that must not be spoken, surged at once to Miremont's lips. The need to be businesslike was remembered only with the greatest difficulty.

"My dear, may I say—how truly delighted—"

"I too, monsieur."

"You will want…I desire it too…we must arrange it as soon as possible. There is just one thing…" Miremont hesitated, yet the matter in question, which had seemed in all his calculations so very awkward, now appeared, in comparison with winning over the boy, a mere wrinkle. "I should be most grateful, first of all, if you could oblige me with a favour."

"Of course."

"It would be politic if you were to present yourself to Monsieur Lesage."

"Your secretary?"

"In your new post you will, of course, be accountable to me. But the practical details of your employment will fall to Monsieur Lesage. It is no more than good sense that you should meet him beforehand."

"So he may approve me?"

"My dear boy, it is mere formality. For politeness' sake. So as not to ruffle his feathers."

"And what if he doesn't? "

"Approve? Of course he will. You will dazzle him with your Latin and leave him no choice."

As the boy considered this, his frown was succeeded by a mischievous grin. "And am I to tell him the nature of my present employment?"

Miremont too smiled. "We may need to be less than frank on that score."

"So is he to suppose I have simply dropped from the heavens?"

"The difficulty has not escaped me, dear boy. Having given it some thought, I have concluded that you were recommended to me by Doctor van Zuylen, a respected authority on Ovid with whom I correspond from time to time. The doctor tutored you in the classics so that you might enter a seminary in Bruges. But alas you have discovered the priesthood is not your vocation. Having returned to France, you are now in search of some other livelihood, and your mentor, who cannot speak highly enough of your industry and ability, has kindly thought to refer you to me."

"Very ingenious, monsieur. But what if your secretary happens to meet the doctor?"

"Monsieur Lesage and Doctor van Zuylen have never met, nor are ever likely to. The doctor lives in Antwerp, besides which, sadly, he is bedridden. Even his correspondence is infrequent—Monsieur Lesage will not think it odd that this is his first reference to his protégé. Altogether, there is no risk of—wretched boy, why are you laughing?"

"Monsieur is coming along a treat."

Miremont attempted to look indignant. Yes, he was conniving with the boy to tell Lesage a pack of lies, but during the hours he had spent concocting the story he had consoled himself with its virtuous purpose, of which Lesage would be the principal beneficiary. All the same, the boy's laughter was infectious. "Impudent, I see, as well as impossible!"

"I am impressed by monsieur's command of detail. You'll tell me which seminary I attended in Bruges?"

"I shall leave the finer points of your seminary life to your own unparalleled powers of invention. But, truly, my dear Max—" it was hard for Miremont, now they seemed on their old terms, not to squeeze the boy's thigh or fling his arms about his neck "—truly, we must be serious. There are other obstacles to be negotiated. Monsieur Lesage will not see you on a Sunday."

"I can sometimes escape in the middle of the morning. Mondays and Tuesdays are best. But for no more than about an hour."

"Very well. I shall tell Lesage to expect you Monday week—say at ten? Is there somewhere he can send to if there is a change of plan?"

Max borrowed Miremont's notebook and pocket pencil to write down the Zhukovskys' address.

"Excellent. Now, my dear boy, there is only one other small detail—well, two perhaps…" Miremont bit his lip. "Your—your present attire is a little—smart—for an indigent seminarian. Do you still possess your frockcoat?"

The boy nodded. To Miremont's considerable relief he did not seem in the least offended; on the contrary he laughed. "And do not worry, monsieur—" his hand went his watch chain "—I shall not wear this."

So there it was, the business was concluded. Everything had eventually fallen out in the most satisfactory manner, leaving Miremont no excuse for prolonging the interview. And in any case the boy had another appointment. Yet it was with the greatest difficulty that Miremont adhered to his good resolutions. His only consolation as he rose from the bench was that Max did not seem impatient to be off: at least they might walk to the gate together.

The crowd at the railings had dwindled, for the leopard had ceased its pacing. Now it lay, neck stretched out, eyes closed, inert as a roll of carpet, with one resigned forepaw hanging limply through the bars.

"Poor beast," Miremont murmured.

Max shrugged. "It was careless. It let itself be caught."

It occurred to Miremont that the creature might never have seen the wild but had been born in this prison. He pushed the thought aside, not wanting to blight his mood, which, even despite his imminent parting from the boy, soared as it had not for months. Besides, Max was asking him about his work. As they walked he described his first tentative steps to reconstruct his manuscript and, although possibly he exaggerated a little, he truly began to feel he had made good progress, that the work at last had an optimistic future. In turn, he enquired what the boy was reading, which transpired to be Suetonius on the Augustan Emperors—Max seemed fascinated by the ruthless political instinct with which the upstart Octavian had recreated himself as the mighty Augustus.

In this way they arrived at the gate giving onto the Rue Geoffroy Saint Hilaire almost without noticing it. The sight of the public highway made Miremont once again aware of their suspect disparity in age and dress, so that he held back from even a formal embrace. Yet he could not resist touching the boy's arm. Nor could he contain his feelings entirely.

"My dear boy, I have missed your company."

"And I yours, monsieur."

Platonic love. Had not Miremont considered this solution, albeit in the abstract, during the wretched weeks before he had gone to Bordeaux? His conversation with Achille de Tarascon had revived the idea: if Tarascon were capable of worshiping his young gods from afar, then so was Miremont, all the more because he had the strongest incentive for the sacrifice. Every obstacle to inviting Max into his house was swept away if improper relations no longer took place between them. He could safeguard his daughters, honour his duty to Thomas and assist Lesage with a clear conscience. And, so far as the boy himself was concerned—well, Max would reap the benefits of a loving friendship uncomplicated by selfish desire. It would be a relief to the boy, of that Miremont was certain. And for Miremont, in addition to the pleasure of having Max near him, there would be the delight of watching him thrive in his new circumstances and of knowing that any help, any advantage that he, Miremont, bestowed was motivated only by pure affection.

Of course, it would not be easy. He had been much disconcerted by the virulence of his hunger in the Jardin des Plantes. The daily presence of the boy would put him severely to the test. Yet he recalled that certain Sufis deliberately set themselves in the way of such temptations to assay their spiritual strength. And was not the celibacy of priests of the same order? Did he truly believe he was unequal to the sacrifice, he who had managed to live entirely without passion for his first forty years? The rewards would outweigh the trials. It was clear from their meeting that the affinity between them was not merely a figment of besotted desire, but arose from some instinctive communication, both of mind and spirit, that was more powerful than the boy's wounded pride or his own physical urges. That would be Miremont's talisman; that bond of affection and understanding would protect him against weakness.

The immediate trial, however, would be of his diplomacy: Lesage must be persuaded to grant the interview.

"Monsieur your father saw no need for a librarian."

Miremont sighed. Lesage sat opposite him at his study table, censure in the very stiffness of his spine against the straight-backed chair, the very angle of his chin above his high starched collar. Guilt sharpened Miremont's irritation; the deception was bad enough, why must the wretched fellow make it so difficult?

On the other hand, he could not avoid noticing a stain—egg, soup?—on the lapel of his secretary's waistcoat that would have mortified the poor man had he known of it and which, even two or three months ago, would never have escaped him. Miremont was instantly softened. It was his great hope that the presence of the boy, junior in years and experience, would bring out Lesage's natural propensity for command; trivial tasks he refused to surrender for fear of admitting weakness he would find himself happy to delegate if this demonstrated his superiority; what he was ashamed to accept he would be delighted to exact. Miremont swallowed his scruples and pressed on.

"There were not so many books in my father's time. We have acquired a considerable number since the library was moved downstairs."

Lesage sniffed. Miremont's only significant alteration to the house—the relocation of the library from a modest room in the east wing of the *piano nobile* to the former state apartments of the marquis on the ground floor—had never met with his approbation. "The books were all replaced in strict order after the removal. If you recall, monsieur, I supervised the task myself."

"But that could not be said of the new books. They have taken their places on the shelves wherever there was room."

"We always know where to find them."

Miremont laughed. "I often wonder how."

Lesage appeared shocked. "We know the library."

"Did we not hunt for Lamartine's *Méditations* for at least six weeks? We have never found our copy of Aesop. And only last month— remember that poem by Stéphane Mallarmé that the booksellers looked out for me and sent over specially? It disappeared almost the instant it arrived, vanished into thin air."

"I trust, monsieur, you do not suggest some shortcoming on my part."

"Oh, good heavens, my dear fellow, of course not. Nothing of the kind." Miremont, while he did indeed suspect his secretary in the matter of the avant-garde verse, was chagrined to think the poor man might take his observations as a comment on his infirmity. "It is merely that we can no longer rely on instinct. We need a system, a proper catalogue of reference."

"And this young person of Doctor van Zuylen's, who knows nothing of this house or our ways, will provide what is required?"

"My dear Lesage, even if the task were a fitting use of your talents, I could not possibly spare you. However, I am sure you will give the young man the benefit of your advice."

As Miremont had hoped, this temporarily silenced Lesage, who would indeed have considered the job beneath his dignity. However, he reverted to a previous tack. "Nevertheless, monsieur, we know precious little about this individual—"

"Albert Fabien. Albert Maxime Fabien."

"I wish I had seen Doctor van Zuylen's letter, I cannot understand how I did not."

"As I explained, I found it tucked inside that copy he kindly sent me of his latest monograph. And—" Miremont felt a fresh pang at his new and dreadful fluency "—well, since you were occupied with more important business, I dashed off an answer myself."

"All the same, is it not somewhat presumptuous of the doctor to assume this Monsieur Fabien will suit us? Can he offer further references? What do we know of his family, his connections?"

"Although apparently from humble beginnings, he has pulled himself up by his own efforts. Doctor van Zuylen regards him as a most deserving young fellow and has always considered it his duty to assist him."

"So now the good doctor passes his charitable obligations on to us. How many more waifs and strays will we be expected to take in?"

But here, impatience triumphing at last, Miremont resorted to the one argument Lesage knew better than to question. "We may take the measure of Monsieur Fabien next Monday. We certainly cannot refuse to see him. I have given my word."

CHAPTER TWENTY TWO

Once Max had seen M de Miremont into a cab, he had retraced his steps and strolled aimlessly about the gardens. It was a bore; while he could not have undone the lie without losing face, he was not due at the Zhukovskys' for hours and it would have been pleasant—very pleasant it seemed to him now—to have whiled away the rest of the afternoon with the old boy.

Undoubtedly this was a weakness. Yes, of course it was a weakness to allow oneself to be flattered and won over by someone who had shown he was not to be trusted. In any dealings with M le marquis de Miremont Max would be well advised to exercise caution.

All the same—caution be damned! This was the chance he had hoped for and believed lost. What sort of fool would he be to refuse it? Since Bordeaux, his dislike of service had grown to loathing. How could he pursue his quest when he had but one niggardly free Sunday a fortnight? In any case, he was heartily sick of the tedium and petty backbiting and Michel's endless attempts at revenge. The chance to live in the Hôtel de Miremont as monsieur's lover—Max inhaled the dizzying scent of freedom.

Not that he entirely liked the sound of his new employment; 'librarian' inevitably conjured Dom Aloysius's rheumy stare and the sting of his ruler across one's knuckles. Besides, books were for reading, not for tending like caged canaries. But the old boy would not expect Max to remain walled up in the library—had he not said as much? And think, only think of the advantages.

Max would have ample scope for his researches, but perhaps they would no longer be needed, for he could return to his previous plan. In due course—who could doubt it?—as monsieur came to trust him, he could resume his confession where he had left off; and this time it would not be disastrous, this time he would conquer the minor obstacles—the troubling memories, his lack of German. Meanwhile every day he spent at the Hôtel de Miremont would serve to prepare him for that moment. Living intimately with monsieur, he would finally acquire that inner certainty of being, that negligent assumption of right that, like a last layer of varnish, would seal to perfection his gentlemanly veneer. Add M de M himself, eager to throw the weight of his rank and fortune behind his claim—how could Max not convince, who would dare disbelieve him?

Yes, here finally was the stroke of fortune that would transform his fate. Was it after all surprising that he felt a certain warmth towards the old fellow? If the old boy had not seen fit to apologise on this occasion, nonetheless repentance was written in his every line and furrow, he was as transparent as ever, in this as in other matters—and here Max could not forbear to chuckle. Altogether, there was no shame in being pleased to see the old chap again, in finding amusement in his halting attempts at intrigue; honour was not dented by a longing for civilized conversation, a craving to rekindle the mind after months of cinders.

Satisfied on this score, Max was left free to contemplate his future. And so agreeable was the prospect as he stood, dreaming, smoking, lounging against the rail of the parakeets' enclosure, that he scarcely noticed the man who settled himself a hand's breadth from his shoulder. Even when the stranger asked for a light, Max was disinclined to respond; with his head full of the Hôtel de Miremont, he could not but feel an obligation to monsieur. Yet it was nearly twilight, the garden would soon close and there was still an age before he was expected at the Zhukovskys'. He glanced round at the man, who was freckled, stocky and about his own age. They exchanged smiles. Disentangling themselves from the railing without a word, they left the crowd and strolled off towards the trees.

Max had rather exaggerated the ease with which he could desert his post. It was true that there was usually a lull on Monday mornings but one could never predict when a crisis would arise. Furthermore, although Michel's attention was fortunately diverted by the rumour that the new Guillaume had received his summons to madame, there was still M Vincent to be reckoned with: since Max's discontent had begun manifesting itself in lackadaisical ways, he had forfeited most of his credit with the Cardinal. He would normally ask Fabrice to cover for him; yet instinct told him that if he explained his errand his friend would sulk and refuse. Better simply to go. After all, there was little risk, this interview was a formality. And besides, once Fabrice found he was missing, comradeship would oblige him to tell the requisite lies.

Accordingly, with his old Sunday black parcelled and concealed under the folds of his cape, Max slid out of the servants' door at a quarter to ten and repaired to the café three streets away, where, by prior arrangement, he could change out of his livery. This was cutting it fine—even walking at speed he would struggle to be punctual. He prayed this Lesage was not given to verbosity: half an hour was as much as Max could spare him.

The carriage gates of the Hôtel de Miremont stood open but the forecourt was deserted, except for a leather-aproned man leaning in the doorway of the cobbler's in the arcade and the distant whinny of a horse from the stable courtyard beyond the arch to Max's right. The great grey facade, imposingly pedimented and adorned with statuary, stared down at him blank-eyed, so that he hesitated for a moment.

"Monsieur? If you please—you will find the tradesman's entrance to your right and round the side."

He had not noticed the concierge peering officiously from his cubby-hole in the gate arch. Curse his Sunday black! He summoned all the hauteur he could muster.

"I have an appointment with Monsieur le marquis' secretary, Monsieur Lesage."

Not sparing the fellow so much as a backward glance, he strode towards the carriage entrance, a pair of high black doors flanked by two more statues and crowned with a spherical triangle bearing the Miremont arms in an elaborate cartouche. He had scarcely set foot on the step when the doors opened: the footman must have been watching him through a spy hole.

They considered each other briefly, the footman taking in the visitor's shabby appearance, while Max assessed him with a professional eye. Unlike madame's footmen, he was middle-aged and balding, sober as a sacristan in his plain morning livery, yet with an affable, even avuncular manner. However, there was something in this cheerful indifference which, more eloquently than scorn, suggested that Max would have done better to heed the concierge.

Notwithstanding, when he gave his name, raising his chin defiantly as he added that he was expected, the old cove nodded. Max was led into the foyer, relieved of his bowler and gloves and instructed to wait.

Although he was sufficiently used to great houses, he could not but look round him with extreme curiosity. To his left soared a staircase far grander than madame's, balustraded in iron and gilt, but otherwise a veritable monument to the stone mason's art, supported on pairs of Corinthian columns and carved on every visible surface with masks, floral swags, birds and allegorical scenes. A little to his right towered a marble sculpture of Apollo, Italian, Max assumed, and of some antiquity, while in niches there were other sculptures and busts in marble and bronze. Ahead of him, a pilastered door case surmounted by a relief portraying some classical theme—he thought it might be Psyche awoken by Eros—gave on to a dim antechamber; at the far end of the foyer, across an expanse of black and ochre marble, beyond a second columned arch supporting the upper landing, another similar doorway allowed him to glimpse more sculptures, ornate *torchères*, massive paintings in gilt-encrusted frames.

Everything seemed of monumental proportions. Yet Max's principle impression was of shadow and silence. Despite the thin winter light trickling in from the stairwell and through the small panes of the tall windows, and despite the gas burning in the great wrought-iron lantern—M de Miremont, it seemed, had not yet discovered the modern convenience of electricity—the outer reaches of the foyer fell away dimly and in the rooms beyond Max sensed drawn blinds and half-closed shutters, while over all lay an eerie stillness; he felt the smallest sound, the click of his own heels, a coin let fall several rooms distant, must reverberate like a dropped missal in a cathedral.

But he had no further time for contemplation, for there were sounds now, the ringing of footsteps, and he saw someone slowly descending the stairs. For an optimistic instant he thought it might be monsieur. But a small man appeared, treading meticulously, a thin elderly man with a wizened face and a crest of white hair that recalled the cockatoos in the Jardin des Plantes. He wore a frock coat, a collar of punitive height and stiffness and a pair of pebble spectacles, through which he peered at Max disapprovingly.

"Monsieur Fabien?" He did not extend his hand. " Follow me, if you please."

Miremont fought the impulse to go down to the library. Stealing out onto the second-floor landing, he had heard Georges admit the boy shortly after ten, but Lesage's dignity would be offended if he seemed to be interfering in the proceedings and, besides, to show too much interest would be unwise. All the same, it was torture to remain shut away in his study, he could not hold his mind to anything, kept picking up and discarding books and letters or going to the window to stare out at the courtyard. When the clocks struck eleven he was tempted to risk the landing once more. But no, Lesage would surely be on his way upstairs to report to him.

By eleven thirty he could stand it no longer. Touching the bell, he instructed Philippe, the younger footman, to summon his secretary.

Lesage appeared some ten minutes later, clutching a sheaf of papers. "Forgive me, monsieur, but this morning's distractions have left me behind with the correspondence. Here is the letter to Maître Ladurie for your signature, and the instructions to Monsieur Korsakov regarding the delivery of the Claude—"

"But what about the boy?"

"Ah yes. The young man. Albert Fabien." Lesage pursed his lips with ominous satisfaction. "I have taken the liberty of drafting a letter for you to Doctor van Zuylen. I am afraid he will not do."

"Good heavens, why not?"

"Regrettably he does not possess the qualities that would suit us."

"But what about his Latin? It is excellent—or so I am assured."

"Alas, Monsieur Fabien is like so many of our young men. He is slapdash and places no value on reflection. "

Miremont's brows rose in astonishment.

"I set him a passage from Ovid's *Fasti* to copy and translate—the twelfth of May, *The Games of Mars the Avenger at the Circus*. He was in such a hurry to be done his nib barely paused before he began the translation, he simply rushed it off without thought. And when we come to the Greek—Cassius Dio on the Parthian wars—perhaps if he had allowed time for due consideration, he might have avoided his more egregious mistakes."

"May I see?"

"Monsieur, you will hardly wish to waste—"

"My dear fellow, much as I respect your judgement, I should like to see for myself."

Lesage's affronted look suggested he would claim to have left the boy's work downstairs or even to have disposed of it. But perhaps he caught something unexpectedly dogged in the set of Miremont's jaw, for, on second thoughts, he began to hunt through his pile of papers, after much leafing and peering grudgingly extracting several sheets from the very bottom.

"As you wish, monsieur. This is the Greek."

"And the Latin?"

The Latin too was pushed across the table with a pained sigh.

Apart from the scrawled address in his notebook, Miremont had never before seen Max's hand. As he held the pages of script and observed how it slanted elegantly to the right, noted the firm regular descenders and the grace with which each curve turned the stroke from acute to oblique, he might have been reading a love letter, so strongly did these details appear like a revelation, so fierce was his longing to press the paper to his lips. It was some moments, and not until he had placed the sheets flat upon the table to conceal his trembling, before he was able to review the contents; and by then they scarcely mattered, for merely to trace the ink with his fingertips was to nerve himself for battle.

Besides, it was as he had suspected: the Ovid was the breach in Lesage's defences, the copy perfect, the translation accurate and fluent despite the speed of its execution. The Cassius Dio, as Miremont was sure Max would allow, was not of the same quality, but the errors were scarcely as manifold as Lesage had implied.

Miremont glanced up at his secretary and smiled. "My dear fellow, are you not a trifle harsh?"

"If you refer to the Ovid, I am merely pointing out that the language is too free, that with less impatience and more judgement——"

"We must not expect perfection. He is, after all, barely into his twenties. Between the two of us, I am sure we can help him improve his Greek. And you have omitted to mention that he writes an excellent hand."

However Lesage, as was his wont, defeated on one flank, was massing his troops on another. "When I ventured that he might not suit us, monsieur, I was not referring exclusively to his scholarship."

"Meaning?"

"As you say, he is a mere youth. I fear he will not prove steady."

"Oh, come, Lesage——"

"He has already changed his mind about the priesthood. He may change his mind again. Besides which, his character strikes me as having in its makeup something rash, not to say headstrong——"

"My dear Lesage, he will be cataloguing the library, not investing in stocks. Nor should we expect him to possess the maturity of judgement you have acquired over decades."

But Lesage, as usual, refused to be conciliated. "And there is something else. Granted he is well-spoken and has presentable manners. But he is not—how may I put this delicately?—in a house such as ours, he may not feel at ease."

"Must we consult the *Almanach de Gotha* before hiring a librarian?"

"Monsieur your father would have known precisely what I mean."

Miremont sighed. "Very well. If it will reassure you, we shall take the young man on three months' probation."

"I really cannot advise—"

"We shall write to him to that effect. Today."

For several days Miremont lived in fear that Max had been put off by his encounter with Lesage. But at last his secretary saw fit to inform him that the boy had replied accepting the post. In view of Miremont's usual duty visit to the Loire to celebrate the New Year with his wife and daughters—this year's festivities would include the baptism of his second grandchild, Clotilde having just been safely delivered of a girl— it was decided the new librarian should take up his situation in the second week of January. This seemed an eternity away and Miremont was tempted to arrange another meeting in the Jardin des Plantes before he left for Burgundy; but that would hardly be in accordance with the rules he had set himself; Lesage, for all his grumbling, was conducting the business now and Miremont had no excuse for further dealings with the boy, none, that is, which would stand scrutiny.

He must be content with the promise of the future and the joys that would reward him after his grim three weeks with Aline. Everything was perfectly well settled. Or rather, there was only one matter that still troubled him.

As Max had so forcefully taught him, there was little chance of his acquaintance recognising his new librarian as one of Catherine de Claireville's footmen. Tarascon might perhaps, but Tarascon could surely be prevailed upon to keep the secret—honour amongst thieves. However, Catherine herself was another thing entirely. Given the particular interest she took in her footmen, Miremont would not put it past her to throw out some comment in front of Lesage. And then there was the tricky question of etiquette. In the normal run it would not signify—while he had never given it thought, since most of his own household had been with him for years, he supposed people quite commonly poached one another's servants—but this was not the normal run. Although Max had assured Miremont that Catherine had no interest in him, could Miremont be certain she would not be piqued? Would it not be mere politeness, particularly to such a close friend, to own to his theft and have done with it? After all, he could not keep the poor boy imprisoned in the library every time she called. Besides, would avoiding the subject not seem in itself suspicious? Whereas, now he had made his resolve, there was nothing suspicious, no cause for shame, nothing whatsoever improper in the boy's presence under his roof: he could explain it without resorting to a single untruth.

Accordingly, when Catherine paid her next call he steeled himself. Having gone to inspect the new Claude, which, after some reordering of the overcrowded walls, was at last hanging in the picture gallery, they had repaired to the little salon in the east wing that had once housed the library. Miremont was particularly fond of this room, the redecoration of which had been supervised by Léonore; without seeming out of place amongst the baroque splendours of the rest of the *piano nobile*, its pale painted panelling, soft Chinese rugs and display of English porcelain—the blue and white Worcester and Spode much prized by his mother—lent it an informality not so far removed from the comfortable simplicity of his own apartments. Since the sky threatened snow, the lamps had been lit early and a generous fire blazed in the grate. Catherine had teased him about the Claude—she had always found his taste in paintings stuffy—and now she was commiserating with the forthcoming rigours of his visit to Miremont-St-Fleur. He should have felt easy, but he was only too grateful when she lit one of her small cheroots, permitting him recourse to his own cigarette case.

"My dear, I—I have a confession to make."

She paused with the cheroot midway to her lips. He would have preferred it if she had not appeared so interested.

"Oh, it is nothing. Well, I hope it is nothing. I am stealing one of your footmen."

To his relief, her interest seemed to abate. "Darling Armand, steal them all. Wretched, vain, idle, empty-headed bunch that they are, you are welcome to them. They are poor Vincent's burden, not mine."

"I am comforted. I felt, out of courtesy you understand..."

She gave a wry smile. "You are very considerate. Though I confess I am astonished. Why should you want one of my louts when you have two perfectly serviceable fellows who aren't forever preening and squabbling like caged monkeys?"

"I shall not be employing the young man as a footman. He is to assist my work—well, only in a manner of speaking, for of course I already have Lesage—"

"Proving, my dear, that your beatification is imminent."

"For now, the young man will look after my library."

"Good heavens! You have suddenly developed a very cavalier attitude towards your beloved books."

"It transpires the boy has excellent Latin and Greek."

"Truly? And which of my rabble, may I ask, is such a paragon?"

"Jean."

"Jean?" Was it Miremont's imagination or did she look startled—no, not startled but stung? It was impossible to be certain, for in the next instant she had veiled her eyes with smoke. "Jean, eh? Well, I suppose I should not be surprised. He is certainly a very curious young man—the vainest of the lot, cocksure in every sense of the word. Are you certain he is not spinning you one of his tall tales?"

He had not been mistaken, she was definitely nettled. While he had accepted that Max, as a condition of his employment, must once have shared her bed, he had never before confronted the notion; but now he was seized by a jealousy as fierce as any he had felt towards Tarascon. Yet Catherine was one of his oldest, closest friends. He should have trusted his first instincts and never begun this conversation: he must certainly conclude it as rapidly as possible.

"Lesage has put him to the test. It seems he has received an education unusually thorough for one of his class and, understandably, wishes to make use of it. Which, my dear Catherine, with my help and your blessing, we shall both enable him to do. And now, since my household arrangements are scarcely a fascinating topic, let us—"

"Oh, but this is. Quite fascinating. Latin and Greek, eh? How ever did you discover the boy had such talents?"

"We—he was aware of my interests and we fell into conversation. Now truly, let us not—"

"Here, in Paris?"

"While I was staying with you in the country. "

"At La Boissière?"

"He used to bring me coffee in the library. We would talk about what I was reading and naturally—well, I was surprised by his knowledge, I…" Miremont's discomfort was acute, yet the topic seemed impossible to escape, to bind them in sticky strings like toffee. "My dear Catherine, I cannot but feel—"

"So that was it! That was why…"

Miremont took in with horror her look of enlightenment and the darker emotions—shock, revulsion, contempt, disillusionment?—that surged up in its wake. Without a word she rose and, with a hiss of silk, strode to the window. For some while she stood, back turned, arms folded, gazing out at the courtyard and puffing furiously on her cheroot. Miremont had also risen but he could only watch her helplessly. She had stripped him naked, there was nothing he could say to redeem himself. At the same time he could not but see how desolate she seemed, standing in frigid isolation by the window, how frail and angular her stiffened shoulder blades appeared, like fledglings' wings, how small she had grown suddenly.

At last, visibly girding herself, she turned. She cast aside the cheroot. She surveyed him fiercely. "Armand, may I presume to advise you? It requires that I speak frankly. As you are well aware, I run a disorderly house. No, no, do not interrupt—we shall get nowhere without candour. I sleep with my servants and, as we all know, that is a reversal of the natural order of things—certainly for a woman, although there are men of our acquaintance who find it quite as natural as farting after dinner—but that is by the by. I was widowed at twenty-nine and ever since, although I was no beauty even then— Armand, I beg you!—there has been no shortage of men anxious to save me from my widowhood. Generally they have been a sorry bunch—or perhaps it has been my misfortune that, where I might have proved susceptible, the men concerned were already married, albeit to featherbrains incapable of showing them the slightest appreciation. At any rate, when I considered these brave suitors of mine, I could find no good reason to deliver myself, or my money, into their care. Nor did I wish to take a regular lover, for the same objections applied, I had no appetite to be governed like some petty apanage, I had come to love my independence. But I am not made of stone. So I settled upon the arrangement you are aware of."

"My dear Catherine—"

"Armand, I insist you let me finish." She continued, as before speaking rapidly and angrily, though whether her anger were for him or for herself, Miremont could not be sure. "It is disorderly. But there is order in my disorder. There are rules—there must be if I am to remain mistress of my own house. I shall not bother you with the strictures that apply to the young men. But I have a particular rule for myself. I favour those who combine a zealous performance of their duties with a complete absence of superfluous distraction—the more uncouth they are, the more lacking in brains or sensibility or any other attribute that might persuade me in a moment of weakness to think fondly of them, the better. And if I ever find myself becoming even remotely attached to one of them, I drop him like a burning coal."

She fixed Miremont with a glance so ferocious that he could only lower his eyes. His shame crushed him. Yet, though he had been guilty, was he still guilty now? If ever he had questioned his new resolve, he was never more glad of it than at this moment.

"Catherine, I am—I fear we misunderstand each other. Lesage, poor fellow, is losing his sight. I am taking Max Fabien—that, by the way, is his real name—into my household partly to benefit the lad himself and partly because in these unfortunate circumstances his assistance will be invaluable."

She raised her eyebrows.

"It is true I have developed a liking for the boy—well, yes, I admit it, I am fond of him. But, as you see, there is nothing untoward about his employment. It is all quite innocent."

"You are innocent, Armand, as a baby. That is not what troubles me. Or rather, perhaps it is."

For all his shame, suddenly Miremont too was angry: by what right, his jealousy demanded, did she presume to judge Max, assume a knowledge of the boy's character more searching than his own? "You are hard, Catherine. The lad may have one or two rough edges. But he is an orphan, his life has been difficult in ways neither of us can imagine. I have no doubt whatsoever that his heart is good."

Her glance flashed, her lips were ready with an acid retort. But all at once she fell silent. After a moment of consideration, she came quickly towards him and seized both his hands.

"My dear, let us not quarrel." He was perturbed to see her eyes were moist. "We have been friends, good friends, for what—twenty years? Let us not fall out over a wretched, silly boy."

CHAPTER TWENTY THREE

So far as Max was concerned, Lesage's letter, with its crabbed erratic hand, could not have come soon enough. The old bird had kept him such an unconscionable time as to exhaust even Fabrice's powers of invention; Max's wages had been docked and he was back on scullery duties.

"The marquis de Miremont?" murmured the Cardinal, glancing sideways at Max as he surveyed the thick velum with its discreet crest. "I note they do not ask for references. Fortunate, is it not, my lad?"

Max found it politic to describe his new situation as assistant secretary, this sounding altogether more exciting and influential. But if he hoped to be congratulated on his sudden rise in the world, he was to be disappointed. True, Pauline wished him well and Francine hid red eyes as she stood scraping potatoes. But amongst his fellow footmen his elevation drew mockery rather than awe. Michel, buoyed by a double triumph—Guillaume had managed only a single night with madame and now his sworn enemy was leaving—was naturally the one to set the tone, but the others were not slow to follow. Jealousy, of course, played some part. But the reaction was instinctive, as Max realised when he cast his mind back to baron Reinhardt's household and the way they had regarded the secretary and the tutor.

"Neither flesh nor fowl," pronounced Old Jouvert, when Max, who had forfeited a day off through his misdemeanours, was at last able to meet him. "Despised alike by the salon and the servants' hall. Service, young sir, as I have impressed upon you often enough—as, God help me, I believed you to comprehend—is a dignified and honourable occupation. Must I remind you that, like the nobility, we have our codes, our traditions, our loyalties? A butler, like a prince or a duke, is a man of the highest rank, deferred to by his inferiors, respected by his peers, in possession of great power which, with judgement and through the imposing dignity of his person, he exercises to maintain the supreme virtues of order and discipline that ensure the common good. But a secretary!" And here the old toper spat wine eloquently into the Monkey's sawdust.

Max was not troubled by this warning, for he would enter M de Miremont's household with special privileges; but he did not forget

Old Jouvert's kindness and was sorry to repay it by shattering his hopes. Fortunately, after several hours and the best part of two bottles, the old chap seemed disposed to a grudging forgiveness.

There appeared, on the other hand, no means to conciliate Fabrice. "How gracious of Little Miss Mouse to have a change of heart," he had said when Max had told him. "I daresay, angel, in your position I should do the same—abandon all my friends the instant some rich old quean clicks her fingers." Then he had stretched out on his bed, turned his face to the wall and refused to favour Max with another word.

Of course this was preposterous. Fabrice would do exactly as Max had done, given the opportunity—had he not even entertained hopes of the comte de Tarascon? All the same, however Max tried to shrug it off, the silence day by day as they jostled elbows in their tiny room cut him like a whip.

Ironically, too, he had never been in more need of Fabrice's advice for, as he prepared for his new life, he was obliged to consider the thorny question of clothing. A footman had his livery all found. But a secretary—and by that token also a librarian—must provide for himself. Max would require a good set of everyday clothes and evening dress as well. Furthermore, he need not recall the way that old buzzard Lesage had looked down his beak at his ancient black to know that certain standards must be met. There was his new suit, of course, bespoken under Fabrice's supervision from Fabrice's own tailor: Max never felt entirely comfortable in it—it seemed to cling everywhere yet to fit nowhere, while its light colour required frequent ministrations with the benzene bottle; however Fabrice had assured him that it was the latest thing and besides it had hardly been worn. But a suit of tails, a dress shirt and waistcoat, studs—and that was not to take into account the new boots he needed, new shirts, collars, a new cravat—quite apart from the sartorial pitfalls he risked, it would all add up to quite a sum.

Money was a vexing, not to say loathsome topic: yet Max was forced to consider it. He was still paying Fabrice's tailor, he had lost a week's wages and furthermore there would be a gap of three weeks between his leaving the Hôtel de Claireville and going to monsieur's, during which he would receive no wages at all; while the Zhukovskys had offered to put him up, he could not reward their friendship by failing to pay his way. Of course, once he reached the Hôtel de Miremont he would be, if not rich precisely, unimaginably better off, so princely were the old boy's promised wages compared with his footman's stipend. It would not be inappropriate, nor indeed unusual in these circumstances, to ask for an advance to cover his expenses and he had hinted as much in his reply to a second letter from Lesage confirming the date of his arrival. But, in monsieur's absence, the mean old buzzard had chosen to ignore his request.

Old Jouvert, it was true, might lend Max the money, but their reconciliation was fragile and besides, he had another more pressing favour to ask his former mentor. That left M de Miremont's watch. It was of no use to Max, since he must not be seen wearing it in the Hôtel de Miremont, and he could doubtless raise a tidy amount from such a valuable object, enough to see to all his wants. It was pure sentimentality that made him flinch every time he imagined it lying on the pawnbroker's greasy counter.

Altogether, the working-out of his notice was a time of endurance, however Max endeavoured to fix his mind on the future. Even madame appeared set against him: he was sure he did not imagine that whenever he encountered her she was wont to spear him with a look of frigid displeasure. Damn her, damn the lot of them! Well, one day they would look back and feel exceedingly foolish.

He was still afflicted by the nightmares invoked by his conversation with monsieur about Before. During the penultimate night before his departure he must have been in the throes of one of these when he awoke to find himself violently shaken and pummelled.

"Cut it! Let a girl sleep, can't you! Let a girl fucking sleep!"

His assailant crouched over his bed, a spectral shirt-tailed figure dimly illuminated by the freezing moonlight.

"If the Mouse only knew! If she knew what I had to put up with!" And without warning Fabrice began to weep, not with the easy copious tears he had shed over the Literary Lion's waistcoat, but with sobs that shook his whole frame and brought him to his knees.

Heaving him up by his armpits, Max dragged him onto the bed, manoeuvring his limbs until he lay sprawled on top of him. It was thus, before their estrangement, that they had often lain chastely during these bitter nights, like two cards in a pack, defying the narrow mattress to seek warmth from each other's bodies. Fabrice's feet were icy now and shivers commingled with his sobs. Max pulled up the blanket. In the darkness, although he could see nothing but the mass of Fabrice's shoulders heaving beneath the coarse wool, he felt his friend's misery flowing into his own flesh like a mesmeric current.

Embarrassed, perplexed, yet stirred by obscure guilt, Max was at a loss; the most comfort he could offer was to stroke Fabrice's spine where the vertebrae told like beads through his shirt. Meanwhile, his friend continued to snort and gasp, his breath damp upon Max's neck and smelling faintly of purloined brandy.

Eventually, when Max was losing sensation in his right arm, Fabrice rose on one elbow and blew his nose on his shirt sleeve.

"Don't flatter yourself, dear heart, that I shall miss you."

"I know. You're overjoyed to be rid of me."

"No more yelling and screaming fit to bring on the Apocalypse."

"No more candles burning all night."

"No more risking my immortal soul telling outrageous lies on your account. No more darning your beastly stockings."

Fabrice shifted, relieving Max of most of his weight by wedging himself in sideways next to the wall, so that for a moment both were preoccupied with ensuring Max did not fall out of bed.

"Of course," continued Fabrice with a sniff, "when the Cardinal finds me a new Jean, she will bear in mind that I am particular in my requirements."

"Shoulders like a bargee."

"Cheeks like pumpkins."

"Cock like a smoke-stack."

"Very likely, angel. Why should I imagine she'll be like all the rest? A mean little shit who'd love to beat me to a fricassée—if she wasn't so scared of catching a nasty disease."

Max squeezed his shoulder. "My friend, there is an answer."

"You think I'm surrendering my virtue to that disgusting old sot in the Monkey?"

Max sighed. But this was not the moment to press the case. They were silent until Fabrice suddenly put out a hand and touched his cheek.

"You're young, angel. A mere infant. Too young to be in love."

"Fabrice, how often have I told you—"

"All I'm saying, dear heart, is don't trust the Mouse. Certainly, she has a taste for chickabiddy. But her appetite will wane once she spots your first pin feathers. Listen to Auntie. Or you'll end up a silver polisher again."

"I think it's fairly certain—"

"That you've polished your last epergne? You can't know. None of us can. Especially where love is concerned. You don't know the first thing about love, angel, not the very first thing."

It was impossible to read Fabrice's expression in the darkness, particularly as he lay in the shadow of the eaves, but Max understood he was crying again, quietly this time, as though to himself. Working his arms around Fabrice's waist, Max drew him away from the wall and set about comforting him in the only way that seemed possible.

Thus, when Max returned to their room on his last night, while his heart leapt at the sight of his box jammed between the two beds, ready to be packed and sent on to the Hôtel de Miremont, his feelings were not unmixed. Besides, that day it had been as if all past feuds were forgotten. When he had handed back his livery to Mme Pinot, she had not scolded him for the dent in his tricorne or the tear in his breeches. The Cardinal, who had been uncharacteristically affable all week as though he were in possession of some joyful secret—he had even been caught humming snatches of Offenbach—had welcomed Max heartily when he had gone to collect his cards, clapping him on the shoulder and murmuring: "By God, lad, I shan't forget it. That punch of yours. If I'd only seen it!" Francine had filched him a pot of caviar and, although Michel had spurned his outstretched hand, most of his fellow footmen had wished him well. By morning, when he had taken a private farewell of Fabrice before sitting down to eat his last breakfast in the servants' hall, he almost felt tearful himself.

But he had only to step out into the street on his way to the Zhukovskys' for the weight of sentiment to slide from his shoulders, cast off with as much regret as his footman's cape. Soon he was jauntily swinging his canvas valise and whistling.

Ah, freedom! To rise and retire when you wanted. To wear clothes that did not stink of food. No wig to scour your scalp like an infestation, no orders, no routine, no intrigues, no permanently looking over your shoulder. Fresh air and the indulgence of stretching your legs whenever you desired. Although he had resolved to make better use of his liberty than he had the last time—there was no reason, for instance, why he should not immediately begin his research—it must be said that he was so taken with enjoying this precious commodity, just for its own sake, that his three weeks at the Zhukovskys' raced by.

But then, there were so many distractions. Music, for one: Mitya practising or improvising cadenzas, Vera playing him Chopin nocturnes, while he lay on the sofa surrendering to sensation, by turns ravished and exalted. Then there were the customary dinners, the fierce debates over what could be done to save Mother Russia, upon the future of painting and whether Rossini were a genius or an organ-grinder. Mme Zhukovskaya was nowadays frequently confined to her bed and Max would keep her company, even venturing to read to her in his stumbling Russian; the soul of Petersburg *politesse*, she showed no irritation when he mangled Pushkin or Gogol with his misplaced stresses and execrable accent, although, at his own request, she did correct his more ludicrous mistakes, always sweetly and with laughter, so that he would close the book feeling guiltily that his own gain had been rather greater than hers.

In short, he was thoroughly spoilt and altogether made much of. By night, even though the sofa was not equal to his length, warmed by the dying embers and cocooned like a Bedouin in Vera's outlandish blankets, he slept soundly, without dreams.

This luxurious indolence, it must be granted, was not utterly without achievement. The new Jean not only realised Fabrice's worst fears, he might be Michel's twin—or so Fabrice proclaimed when Max met him at the Monkey on his Sunday off: thus Fabrice's resistance to being introduced to Old Jouvert was at last overcome. The two, although they had long known each other by sight, had never exchanged a word and to Max's dismay neither warmed to the encounter. However, after much wine and some flattery on Max's part, the old rogue agreed to find Fabrice a situation as a valet.

Max's sartorial difficulties were also resolved. The pawnbroker, miserable skinflint, feigned disbelief that the watch was gold and would lend only a pittance on it, so that Max had no choice but to visit the old crone in the Rue Thouin. Here, however, he found a very serviceable suit of tails: true, Vera, who had accompanied him, worried that the jacket might be tight across the shoulders and the trousers somewhat short in the leg, while he himself acknowledged that the cut would scarcely have satisfied Fabrice; yet the suit, as the old witch pointed out, was of quality material, hardly worn, and she was willing to throw in a nearly new pair of boots for the price. Besides, the air in the shop, which was barely a crack in the wall, was so thick with the sweat and toil of the numerous forgotten souls whose coats and jackets hung there like carcasses that both he and Vera craved the street. Although he afterwards discovered the boots were inclined to pinch, he was not displeased with his bargain. And, on top of this, Old Jouvert had agreed to a small loan, admittedly at rather stiff rates, so that he could order new linen and buy presents for the Zhukovskys.

As the day neared for his move to the Hôtel de Miremont, a part of him was loathe to leave the simple comforts of his friends' apartment: in the midst of music, chatter and laughter, he was daunted by the memory of the hôtel's cathedral-like silence. Then there was that old brute of a valet, with whom he did not relish further encounters, not to mention the martinet Lesage. However, neither of these two personages need concern him. It was M de Miremont who counted.

CHAPTER TWENTY FOUR

No matter that Miremont had mentally rehearsed Max's arrival a hundred times: confusion still struck him when Lesage shepherded the boy into his study. He was aware of his new librarian playing his part admirably, hanging back with respectful diffidence, making a little formal bow as he was presented; he noted that Max's hair was heavily pomaded and that the boy wore his renter's suit, which once again stirred in him a perverse excitement; but his main thought, as he stumbled through his speech of greeting, was that after all these weeks this was no sort of welcome, that on such an occasion, despite his vow, something more might be permitted.

"Monsieur Fabien, you must tell me—how is Doctor van Zuylen these days? I was much concerned to hear from his last letter that he is still troubled by nephritis. Perhaps, if Monsieur Lesage can spare you for a moment…"

At last allowing his eye to meet the boy's, Miremont was rewarded by a flash of complicity. But it seemed they had reckoned without Lesage.

"Monsieur Fabien was just telling me, monsieur, that, as circumstances have obliged him to stay in Paris, he has not seen Doctor van Zuylen for some months."

"All the same, he has written to me," Max cut in quickly. "Not two days ago. It was his particular wish to be commended to you and he enjoined me to—"

"Well, we shall not bother monsieur with all that now. Monsieur's time is precious and so, young man, is ours. Duty calls us to the library." And, with an imperious flourish, before Miremont could recover from this effrontery and formulate a riposte that would neither arouse suspicion nor appear a humiliating rebuke, Lesage had swept Max to the door.

Yet Miremont supposed he should be grateful. At least so he told himself afterwards, as he sat at his study table with his head in his hands. The weight of his disappointment measured the baseness of his intent. God, that he should possess such a capacity for self-deception. While he had known his vow would be burdensome, he had reckoned without the sheer guile of the incubus. Yes, he must be grateful to Lesage for saving him from himself. So, when his secretary appeared some minutes later, this time alone, Miremont made no attempt to reprove him. Indeed, he started somewhat guiltily at Lesage's first words.

"It won't do, monsieur."

"What's that, my dear fellow?"

But Miremont might have predicted the cause of his secretary's pursed lips. Lesage's sight might be fading, but it was still acute where infractions of form were concerned. "The young man's attire. You must have noticed."

The very mention of the suit revived the incubus. All the same, there could be no argument. Miremont sighed. "Send to Mathurin, let him have someone come to measure the boy this afternoon."

"If that were all…"

Miremont sighed again.

"The boots, monsieur, cannot have escaped your attention. And the cravat. And the hair—setting aside the noxious aroma of bay rum, no gentleman would permit his barber—"

"Oh, very well. Arrange whatever must be arranged." However, as Miremont was waving Lesage away, the sudden vision of Max recreated in his secretary's image, from the sombre frockcoat to the constricting collar, made him pause. If he were to buy the boy new clothes—and the novelty of the idea entranced Miremont—then they must make some concession to his youth and beauty. "On second thoughts, my dear fellow, ask Mathurin's man to call upon me when he arrives."

"If you think that necessary, monsieur."

Miremont again feared he had aroused suspicion. But no, Lesage's sniff merely betrayed his usual grievance—that his judgement had been slighted. Miremont essayed a conciliatory smile.

"My dear chap, where should we be without your instinct for detail? Only— well, I'm sure I need not mention—I know when you put the matter to M Fabien you will go gently. When we are young our pride is a tender flower."

Had the boy felt humiliated? When Miremont next saw him, at luncheon, it was impossible to tell, for the continued presence of Lesage meant Max must keep to his role of deferential stranger, nodding and smiling where appropriate but otherwise maintaining his servant's opacity. Nor did it help that Lesage took it upon himself to monopolise the conversation, first with tedious business matters and then with gossip about his noble ladies, so that, while Miremont tried to draw the boy out, he found little opportunity.

Still, dinner was bound to prove more propitious. By that time Lesage, having made the boy familiar with every aspect of the library, would also have shown him over the *piano nobile*, not failing in the process to take him downstairs to the picture gallery.

Accordingly, when they reassembled in the dining room that evening, Miremont turned the conversation to painting. "Well, Monsieur Fabien," he enquired with a smile, "and what is your view of my latest acquisition?"

"The Claude Lorrain?" The boy, who had been staring into his plate, glanced up, yet to Miremont's disappointment hesitated. "It is... very fine...the river, the ruins, the reference to Ovid's Pyramus and Thisbe..." But then suddenly his servant's face vanished, his eyes caught fire, and Miremont saw with joy that he had not forgotten their old ways. "However—forgive me—I cannot help finding it contrived and lifeless. I should give two of it to possess that Delacroix of the Arab horseman fighting the lion."

This was much as Miremont had anticipated. But, as he was about to press for reasons, a severe voice rang out.

"Monsieur Fabien! I think we may spare monsieur your artistic judgements. Particularly since, by your own admission, you have never even visited the Louvre."

Max flushed. And Miremont, although he had noticed Lesage's tendency to fix upon the boy through lowered spectacles every time he opened his mouth, was so considerably startled that he knocked a knife from the table; the sound of its fall seemed to echo in the silence, even after Boussec had noiselessly retrieved it.

Miremont struggled to be gentle. "My dear Lesage, you forget that I invited Monsieur Fabien's opinion."

"But, monsieur, I hardly think—"

"I agree, it may be unprofitable to compare works painted two centuries apart. But we cannot be certain of that if Monsieur Fabien is forbidden to explain himself."

Given this invitation, Max was obliged to rehearse the Delcroix's merits—its spontaneity, its drama, the fierce energy transmitted by its strong colours and vigorous brush work. To which Miremont (who secretly conceded that in his youth he too would have preferred the valorous tribesman) could not but counter with the Claude's enduring fascination, the mystery inherent in the contrast between the two tiny figures menaced by the spy in the shadow of the ruined wall and the lyrical play of light over the idealised Roman countryside; yes, this was painting to a set of fixed conventions, but they were conventions of Claude's own devising, a sign of his great originality.

Yet neither argued with their wonted passion, for it was impossible to ignore Lesage, censoriously dabbing his lips with his napkin. And when Max, contending that the mastery of the painter should transcend the conventions of his period, offered the painting above the dining room mantelpiece, a Titian portrait of a young Venetian nobleman, as proof of his case, Miremont, who loved this masterpiece acquired by his great-great-grandfather—the more so since he had lately noted in its subject's youthful hauteur a certain resemblance—was glad to give his agreement, bringing this travesty of their former debates to a conclusion.

Besides, he was already distracted by other troubling thoughts. It was his custom, when there were no guests, to take his coffee and brandy alone in his apartments. And oh, it would be so easy—Max knew where his rooms were, a smile, a look as he rose to retire would be enough to signify his wishes. As he glanced at the boy, whose eyes were once more downcast, he longed to offer some consolation for Lesage's insult.

But no, he must recall that, duty aside, his vow was also taken for the boy's protection. For it struck him forcibly, as it had not before, that by admitting Max into his employ he had incurred further moral obligations. At La Boissière, Max, whether indifferent or not, had come to him from choice. But now, if commanded, the poor lad would feel constrained to obey. The idea that he would appear to be invoking *droit du seigneur* was so disagreeable to Miremont that it instantly crushed the incubus. Rising to his feet and announcing his departure, he strode towards the doors without looking to right or left.

He passed a wretched night. He knew Max was quartered near Lesage on the floor above, although he was uncertain in which room—over his study perhaps? At any rate, he could not dispel the thought that somewhere close by, separated from him only by timber, lath and plaster, the boy lay sleeping, and inevitably, as he had a hundred times since, Miremont remembered waking beside him at La Boissière. The recollection of that unconscious, unguarded form, the love that had overwhelmed him as he had studied it, and the agony of desire—all acted like yeast upon his present longing. But when he attempted the sole relief now permitted to him, it was an empty, effortful exercise that left him more miserable than ever.

*

The next morning, when Lesage was with him in his study sorting through the post, Miremont took his secretary to task.

"My dear fellow—I know you mean it for the best—but you really must not be so harsh with Monsieur Fabien. The poor lad must be permitted to speak."

"Not if it is nonsense."

"He says what he thinks. Surely that has a certain charm?"

Lesage lowered the letter that he was holding close to his nose, Miremont's presence precluding his open use of the magnifier. "Personally I have never found ignorance charming. If you, monsieur, are disposed to indulge the young man, that is all very well. But what if Monsieur de la Marne had been present, or Madame de Claireville?"

Miremont bit his lip. He could hardly explain that, although Max might never have visited the Louvre, he had spent his daily life in surroundings where works of art were commonplace: Catherine, for instance, aside from her enthusiasm for Ingres, possessed a Bellini Madonna, three Poussins, several Davids, a Velazquez, a very fine Vermeer and a masterly painting of fighting ships painted by Claude's heir, Turner. Nor could he give vent to his privately held view that Lesage, for all that he might expatiate upon art, had never taken much interest in it, even when his vision had been unimpaired; it was, rather, the prestige and distinction which the ownership of works by revered masters conferred that preoccupied him, the size and value of the canvasses, the ornate gravitas of the frames.

"All the same—"

"All the same, monsieur, it is a burden. I shall do my best to teach young Monsieur Fabien our ways, but it is a burden I did not look for, and against which, if you recall, I strongly advised."

"It was never my wish, my dear fellow, to increase your load—"

"Perhaps you think I am unequal to it."

"No. Of course not." Miremont ran his hand through his hair. "But I'm sure now you have set Monsieur Fabien on the correct path, he will be able to find his own way. Who knows, he may even prove useful to you, there may be things—routine tasks you find irksome, but which he—"

"Ah! So you do think me unequal."

"No, no! My dear Lesage—"

"I have given your family—you and your esteemed father before you—four decades of my life. But all of a sudden I am found wanting. I am, I admit, no longer youthful. And nowadays youth is all. Well, monsieur, I am sure Monsieur Fabien's knowledge of business affairs is as much to be relied upon as his appreciation of art and his taste in dress. Perhaps you would care to give him these—" Here Lesage brandished the sheaf of letters like a battle standard. "Then see how your affairs prosper!"

For a moment, Miremont was tempted to take him at his word. However, he had only to remember what prompted Lesage's touchiness to regain his patience. Yet, by the time he had reassured his secretary and generally smoothed things over, his head ached. In search of peace and solitude and to leave the poor fellow free at last to employ his magnifying glass, he quitted his apartments and went downstairs, intending to visit the picture gallery. But he was halfway across the foyer when he heard footsteps in his wake.

"Monsieur!"

Miremont, who had expected Max to be at work in the library, turned with a smile of surprise and delight. "My dear boy…" But then, his initial thought—that here, at last, for the first time since Max's arrival, they were alone together—was succeeded by anxiety that they were in plain view, that Georges might appear from the servants' door at any minute, and also by the realisation that the boy could not have come upon him by chance.

In confusion he began what was almost a repeat of his speech of welcome. "Well, my dear fellow, I hope you are settling in and have everything you need. I trust you find your room comfortable—if there is anything you lack, please do not hesitate to ask Madame Mercier. And I am sure Monsieur Lesage has taken you through your duties…"

The boy, holding Miremont's glance, smiled his curious, delayed smile. "Some of them, monsieur."

For an instant Miremont feared he would choke. But he managed to conquer the combined forces of panic and temptation. "You have no other duties. It is enough that you are here. Now, Monsieur Fabien, if you will excuse me…"

It was difficult to see how the boy had taken it. Or, rather, he showed no sign of being distressed. True, at luncheon, when Miremont sought his first impressions of the work to be done in the library, his answers were brief. But the most likely explanation for his reticence was fear of provoking Lesage. The balance of evidence, no matter how the incubus tried to gainsay it, was that Miremont's words had been accepted, as he had predicted, with indifference or relief. It should have been a relief to Miremont, too, to have all ambiguity resolved at last, it should have been the final affirmation his vow required; he struggled valiantly to see it thus.

But at least Lesage, although he continued to train a minatory glare upon the boy, did not interrupt or correct him. Miremont was comforted to think that this morning's conversation had, after all, had its effect.

He should have known better. That evening, David Ricard and Léon Rosenthal were expected to dinner and Miremont was certain Max would enjoy the impassioned literary discussion the occasion promised. The presence of guests imposed the obligation to dress and Thomas, whose reaction to the boy's arrival had been much as expected, had somehow mislaid his master's favourite dress waistcoat, so that Miremont, descending late to the Elizabeth Salon, found that David and Myriam Ricard had already arrived. Lesage was dutifully playing host in his absence. However, of Max there was no sign.

Miremont was surprised by the boy's tardiness, then irritated. But, when the Rosenthals had long since been announced and Max remained absent, he grew alarmed. Yet it was only as the company was preparing to go in to dinner that the opportunity arose to draw Lesage aside.

"Monsieur Fabien is taking dinner in his room, monsieur."

"Good heavens, man, why?"

"His evening dress is—unsuitable."

A bolt of blinding anger struck Miremont. "This is preposterous. Do you suppose our guests would care?"

The tip of Lesage's nose twitched disdainfully—Miremont had long suspected him of sharing Aline's view that bourgeois professors, who, worse still, were Jews, were not fitting acquaintance for someone of Miremont's rank. "Even they, monsieur, would notice the stench of mildew."

Miremont shook. He was on the point of sending Philippe to ask Max to join them, now, this moment, whatever his state of dress. Yet this, of course, given the embarrassing explanations it would provoke, would merely compound the poor boy's humiliation. Miremont was obliged to hold his anger in check until his guests had departed.

He hoped Lesage was chastened. He had been milder than he had originally intended because he had come to feel that he was partly to blame. If he had only considered, he would have seen that Max would find it difficult to equip himself suitably on a servant's wage. Except that—he recalled the banknote he had given the boy at their parting, then immediately disliked himself for the thought, for if the money were spent, however extravagantly, then it had been a gift for Max to use as he liked. No, if Miremont had considered more deeply, he would have asked Lesage to offer the boy an advance on his wages.

At any rate, the upshot was that the tailor was called in again; and that, when Miremont next saw Max, at luncheon, the boy, as well as saying little, had that tilt to his chin that Miremont well recognised. Again Miremont longed to offer comfort. But he understood now that he was not only held back by his pledge: every mark of favour shown to the boy increased Lesage's hostility.

Thus Lesage took possession of M de Miremont's new librarian. Miremont had guessed rightly that his secretary would delight in lording it over an underling; where he had been wrong, as he now knew, was in his hope that Lesage would be persuaded to delegate some of his load; on the contrary he perceived it as his duty to supervise every aspect of the boy's work as well as carrying out his own. Nor was Miremont allowed to be alone with the boy for an instant; if he drifted down to the library, Lesage, guided by some sixth sense, would appear moments later; if books were to be delivered to Miremont's study—properly, one of Max's functions—it was Lesage who brought them; once, when Miremont, finding his secretary fully occupied with some legal documents, had the temerity to ask the boy to copy his notes, the copy was returned to him by Lesage marred by smudges and blots that Miremont was certain were not of Max's making.

All this extra endeavour, when combined with the daily struggle already imposed by Lesage's affliction, took its toll. Letters went unanswered, documents were mislaid—but here again, if for nothing else than the distraction he created, the boy could be blamed. Miremont lost count of the times Lesage reminded him that young M Fabien was only on probation and must be brought to account after three months. He soon even gave up his customary reassurances, for he observed that, in his secretary's beleaguered mind, they merely reinforced the opposite notion, that the boy was definitely intended as his replacement.

Torn, as usual, between anger and pity, Miremont felt helpless. He was, however, not unconscious of the irony of the situation: Lesage, while remaining oblivious to his struggle, had become the gatekeeper of his virtue. Yet, if Miremont's chastity were assured, the compensations he had hoped for—the boy's conversation and companionship—were resolutely denied him. This was not at all as he had planned.

There were some small pleasures to be had. Mathurin's man, when he was sent for again, took the opportunity to deliver Max's new suit. Whether it was because, owing to some confusion over Lesage's message, suggesting the garments were for M le marquis himself, Mathurin had arrived in person to take the measurements, or whether his assistant, returning for the fitting, had been inspired to extra zeal by the comeliness of his client, the suit and matching waistcoat, although of unpretentious charcoal-grey worsted, contrived to flatter Max's broad shoulders and narrow hips to perfection, to suggest a gentlemanly elegance that belied the modesty of its cloth. Miremont, once again astonished that this novelty was within his gift, could not have been more delighted and even Max seemed not displeased with his new attire. Lesage, of course, opined privately to Miremont that it was far too good and would give the young man ideas above his station. A great fuss ensued over whether the suit would be ruined by the dust from the books. Miremont was applied to for a dispensation allowing the boy to remove his jacket in the library and a footman's apron was borrowed to protect the rest of his clothing.

So it was that Miremont, drifting down to the library, settling in his chair by the fire and taking cover behind a book, could watch Max ascending and descending the library steps, could, even in Lesage's presence, poignantly observe how, as the boy reached for the topmost shelves, his straining linen disclosed his biceps and how, as he manoeuvred himself on the ladder, the worsted now embraced his calves, now his thighs, now his cheeks.

The boy's presence blew through the house, too, like a gust of ozone. It was not that he was clumsy or thundered on the stairs: on the contrary, his time in service, and doubtless in the cloister, had taught him to move noiselessly. Yet his healthy young masculinity, the easy vigour of his movements, stirred the calm spaces of the Hôtel de Miremont with an exhilarating turbulence, seemed to let in light and air like a sapling pushing skyward through dead wood. On his days off, Miremont felt his absence keenly.

Although it was unworthy, he could not help wondering what Max did during those Thursday evenings and Sundays, where he went, whom he saw. For it was notable that, although his manner had grown wary since the disagreeable events of his first two days, and his conversation subdued, he seemed, on the morning after these absences, altogether more carefree, so that Miremont was racked by jealous speculation.

Yet, if it were wounding that Max was happiest when he escaped, it was forgivable. Miremont, as his heart went out to him, felt proud of him too. His manners remained impeccable; despite that occasional rebellious lift of his chin, he did not give way to his pride or his impetuous streak. All the same, the business of the cataloguing was not proceeding without disagreement, as Miremont could overhear during his visits to the library. Even if Lesage had not been driven by his demons, it was, Miremont supposed, inevitable that their approaches would clash: the boy's quick intelligence took a wide sweep, while Lesage had ever been fettered by detail. As their voices reached Miremont's chair, he could hear, more from tone than substance, for his presence constrained them to respectful whispers, that Max was endeavouring, politely but firmly, to refute Lesage's dogmatic pronouncements. Not that he could win, of course, poor boy: carefully reasoned argument was no match for Lesage's devotion to tradition and that mysterious entity by which he set so much store, 'the dignity of the house'.

Thus the scheme for reordering the library, when it was presented to him, confused Miremont extremely. Max was allowed to attend and brought notes, from which, on Lesage's periodic prompting, he read in an obedient but toneless voice, but the exposition of the plan was given verbally by Lesage himself. Miremont could see, despite his secretary's many digressions, that the basic notion had been as simple as could be: to classify the books according to subject matter—Science, History, Literature, Ancient Literature etc—adding subsections where necessary, as for Latin and Greek, and then ordering the books alphabetically according to author, with the wider bottom shelves reserved for quarto and folio volumes. But somehow, like a seedling meeting an obstacle in the way of its growth, this simple conception had become strangely distorted. Why were the third marquis' volumes of Montaigne, for instance, classified under Mineralogy? Why did the alphabetical ordering of French History jump arbitrarily from B to G? Why were genealogy and heraldry categorised as Philosophy, not History or possibly Science?

There were so many of these bewildering quirks that Miremont knew any request for enlightenment would be futile. Even the two or three questions he did ask out of courtesy seemed merely to agitate Lesage. Miremont sighed inwardly. If, as was his hope, his secretary could gradually be brought to see that Max presented no threat, then he would serve the boy ill by rejecting this plan, however bizarre and impracticable. Accordingly, after playing with the ribbon of his pince-nez for a minute or two so as to seem to give the matter due consideration, he looked up, smiled, and offered the two of them his congratulations. Lesage was immediately all triumphant bustle, beaming at Miremont from behind his spectacles and shooting the boy a smug glance as he motioned to him to gather up his papers. But Max, as he rose from the study table, paused to give Miremont a look, which, while indecipherable by his persecutor, was not lost to Miremont's keener sight. Incredulity, anger, contempt—it was a glance like a knife.

A day or so later, the boy having been at the Hôtel de Miremont by now some four and a half weeks, Lesage came down with a cold. Although he was clearly feverish and sneezed persistently, his anxiety resisted any suggestion that he should take to his bed. The result was that in a couple of days Miremont too was infected. Miremont had no scruples about retiring to his apartments: here, shut away from Lesage, the boy, the whole abominable mess, he could be alone with his wretchedness. He was nursed with devotion by Thomas, who, as Miremont had hoped, had come to see that his worst fears were groundless and who was also enjoying Lesage's discomfiture. The secretary and Thomas being natural enemies, Lesage was never permitted further into Miremont's apartments than the study; now, from the distant protests cut off by Thomas' growl and the eloquent slamming of the outer doors, Miremont gathered the poor fellow was banned altogether, an edict he chose not to reverse.

Miremont remained in seclusion for four days. He felt something of a fraud, for his symptoms were not severe, certainly not grave enough to summon Gérard. But he could no longer bear to see Max and know the boy despised him; and besides, from fretting about the treatment Max might receive in his absence, he had come to think that the reverse might be true—without the constant need to prove that he was indispensable, Lesage might deal with the boy more gently. Between spells of agonising, Miremont read and slept and, on the fourth evening, it being a Thursday, Gérard called anyway, for their usual game of chess. They spent, as ever, an agreeable evening, with Gérard's conversation and the cut and thrust of the game proving infinitely more curative than the vile-tasting linctus the good fellow insisted on prescribing. Miremont came downstairs on the Friday feeling almost optimistic.

He was shocked when he encountered Max at luncheon. The boy's eyes and nose were red, his hair was lank, his skin blotchy and he sported a pimple on his chin; shorn of his beauty, he seemed all at once pathetically young, a whipped schoolboy. But when Miremont suggested fetching the doctor—against Lesage's inevitable protestations that young men like M Fabien were as strong as oxen—Max, glancing up as though with supreme effort from his soup plate, merely thanked him and shook his head.

It was then that Miremont understood, from that lacklustre glance in which there was no longer any trace of rebellion or even contempt, that the boy's depleted state was not purely due to his head cold. Miremont was reminded suddenly of the leopard in the Jardin des Plantes.

He had made a terrible mistake. What he had meant as a gesture of love was, he saw with horror, an appalling cruelty. He had indulged himself. He had installed the boy in his house as though he were another Cannova Apollo, another Titian portrait, but with less care or forethought than he would have given to either. Youth, beauty, zest—he had refused to see that the dust and the silence would stifle them, that this house of old men would crush the life out of the boy as surely as it had sucked Lesage dry. But for Max, at least, it was not too late. If Miremont truly wished to show his love, he must set the boy free.

The pain of this realisation was well-nigh intolerable. When he had taken his vow, he had never understood that the sacrifice would be of this magnitude. Once Max left the Hôtel de Miremont it was unlikely he would ever set eyes on him again. And then there was the difficulty of how it could be managed. By enticing Max away from service, Miremont had fastened his cage with double bolts, for the boy would scarcely wish to return to that life, yet where else could he go? Of course Miremont must help him—but how? Give him money—in effect, pay him off? Miremont doubted Max's spirit was yet so crushed he would be immune to the indignity. Find him another position? After all, that had been Miremont's original idea, but it would take time. And again, supposing this new post were not to Max's liking...?

Truly, it was an impossible situation. When Miremont remembered his plans, when the incubus reminded him what might have been, in another world where he had no obligations...Confound Lesage! It was one thing to steel oneself to abnegation, quite another to have someone impose it on your behalf. Compulsion fostered disobedience as honey drew wasps. The incubus urged Miremont to hurl his vow to the floor and watch it shatter into irrecoverable fragments.

But it was unseemly to blame poor half-mad Lesage for an impasse that was of no one's making but his own. After a day or two Max had shaken off the infection and returned to robust health; yet he still spoke only when spoken to, still wore that look of apathy. Miremont must summon him privately to his study. Oh, but it was not so easy— the difficulty of choosing the right words, the pain, the dreadful finality of it—perhaps Miremont was being too precipitate, perhaps, as Lesage's fears lessened and the boy grew more accustomed to his situation, matters might yet resolve themselves…

Several evenings later, Miremont attended the opera, sharing the La Marnes' box and making up one of the company for supper afterwards. Inevitably, the effort of social exchange drained him and into the bargain it was an unusually bitter night; however tightly he wrapped the rug about him on the drive home the cold pinched his nose and drove the blood from his fingers. The habit of years summoned a warming vision of the Hôtel de Miremont. It was only when he was at last within the familiar portals and handing his hat and cloak to Georges that, with a sudden heaviness reminiscent of his marriage, he recalled his present difficulties. Turning towards the stairs, he instructed Georges that, if everyone had retired, he might extinguish the gas and retire himself.

"Monsieur Fabien is still in the library, monsieur."

Miremont could not help it, his heart lurched. "And Monsieur Lesage?"

"Monsieur Lesage has already retired."

Miremont's exhaustion vanished, his spirit soared—only to plummet again as he realised that here was the perfect moment for the promised conversation. Nevertheless, telling Georges he might go to his bed, he made with determination for the library.

The mantels at the nearest end of the room had already been extinguished, so that the chaos occasioned by the cataloguing—the empty shelves, the floor stacked with teetering piles of books—was veiled in shadow. The boy sat at the far end, where order still reigned, in an island of light from the dying fire and the lamp at his elbow. Ensconced in Miremont's favourite chair, he was absorbed in a folio volume propped on the reading stand but, as Miremont's footsteps resounded on the parquet, he leapt to his feet.

"Monsieur Fabien—my dear boy—please don't disturb yourself. Georges told me you were here and I—please, dear chap, do be seated—I was concerned you were still working."

Max smiled—a little guiltily Miremont thought. "Pursuing my own pleasure, I'm afraid, monsieur. The book is too large to take to my room. And anyway—well, when Monsieur Lesage went upstairs, I took the liberty of coming down again to get the benefit of the fire."

Miremont, who was already feeling the chill pressing in upon him from the unheated expanses of the vast room, and who, bending to hold his hands before the embers, could measure the frailty of their glow, glanced up at him with concern. "Does the fire in your room not draw? My dear fellow, we must ask Philippe—" But he was halted by the boy's look of perplexity. "You surely have a fire?"

Max's puzzlement turned to unfeigned surprise.

Miremont cursed Lesage for his petty cruelties. "But this is absurd! It is too late now, even Georges has gone to bed. But tomorrow morning, you must ask Madame Mercier to instruct the maids—no, I shall tell her myself. Really, this is too bad. My dear boy, what must you think of us?"

Max seemed disposed to shrug off the omission. "I cannot say a fire would not be welcome. Thank you, monsieur."

"All the same, I fear we have not...we are not..." But suddenly Miremont found himself stumbling into territory that, despite his earlier determination, he did not wish to visit—at least not now, not at this minute, when, for the first time for days he had the boy to himself. "Well, it shall be remedied tomorrow, you have my word on it."

An awkward silence fell. It pained Miremont, when he remembered their conversation only weeks ago in the Jardin des Plantes, that they now addressed each other as strangers. "Anyway, my boy, I am interrupting your reading. What is it that keeps you up so late?" Moving away from the fire, he edged towards the chair so that he could peer at the reading stand. "Good heavens! Frederick the Great."

Max laughed. "His poetry is dreadful. I doubt I shall manage all six volumes."

"Thirty-three, if you intend soldiering through his complete works. He was certainly industrious. He also composed a over a hundred flute sonatas and several concertos."

"But the interesting thing is that he writes in French. Although he was King of the Prussians, he did not speak German."

Max gave this observation curious emphasis. However, its significance was lost to Miremont. He was beginning to be distracted by their proximity, by the ease with which, as he hovered behind the chair, he could have reached out and squeezed the boy's shoulder.

"But he knew Prussian dialect when he needed to rouse his troops." God, it was overwhelming now, the urge to ruffle the boy's hair, to bend and kiss that delicate place beneath his ear, to devour his neck with kisses. "Oh yes—" and here Miremont tore himself away desperately, retreating for sanctuary to the fire "— he might not speak *Hochdeutsch, Der Alte Fritz*, but he knew his people's tongue when it suited him." Even to himself, his voice sounded thick and, when he made a business of taking warmth once again from the embers, he was ashamed to see how his hands shook.

There was a pause. Then he thought Max spoke, but the blood was pounding so fiercely in his head that he could scarcely hear. With a struggle, he composed himself.

"My boy, forgive me. What was that you said? I believe you asked me something."

"Oh, nothing. It was nothing." To Miremont's discomfort, a faint smile hovered suddenly on the boy's lips. "I was only going to enquire, monsieur, whether you had enjoyed the opera. Mozart, was it not?"

"*Don Giovanni.* Yes—thank you. Patti was in great voice."

"'*Batti, batti, o bel Masseto*'."

"Indeed. You know the opera?"

"I have never had the good fortune to see it performed. That, or any other opera. But I do know the aria. I've heard it sung—" from Max's broadening smile it was evident the recollection delighted him "—or rather rendered, that is a better way of describing it. To a piano accompaniment."

The laughter in his voice invoked instantly for Miremont the mystery of his days off, the questions, the agonising questions—whom did he see, what company was it that so pleased and amused him? The pain, the longing, the torture of their estrangement was all at once more than Miremont could bear. He wanted to throw himself at the boy's feet, beg him to forgive him, abandon all shame and speak his love at last, utter those confused, terrible, ecstatic words so that they rang out in the furthest expanses of this freezing room and could never again be stifled.

In the end, it was not his vow that stopped him. Damn his vow! It was not duty or obligation, nor even the thought of his daughters and grandchildren. He was restrained only by the memory that had haunted him since he had bowed to Lesage over the catalogue: he saw, with fresh horror, Max's look of utter contempt.

Turning away, he muttered something about his exhaustion and the late hour. Then, cautioning the boy not to strain his eyes by reading too long, he fled.

CHAPTER TWENTY FIVE

"You'll burn in purgatorial fire! Your immortal soul will writhe in eternal agony."

"And what about sneaks? What circle of hell do they go to?"

"I didn't sneak!"

"You blabbed to our esteemed Father Superior."

"I did not!"

"Oh, so it wasn't you telling tales about Dom Sébastien?"

"I had to answer the Reverend Father honestly, before God—"

"You're a lily-livered sneak!"

"You couldn't expect me to commit a mortal sin on your account—"

"The times I've taken the strap for you! The times I've stood up for you when the others were ragging you—"

"That was your duty."

"Not any longer."

"It will always be your duty, as ordained by God."

"We're equals now."

"You can never be my equal. You'll always be beneath me! You're a vile filthy sinner and I hope the fire boils your brains and shells your eyeballs like peas. I hate you, I hate you, I hate you, I hate you…"

It rang out, the Other's voice, so clearly in the darkened room that Max reared up from his pillow. This was not one of his usual nightmares, although he was still beset by those, but a kind of waking dream so vivid that he expected to see the Other standing at the foot of the bed. But there was nothing: only the bulky shadows of the wardrobe and the bookcase, looming like galleons adrift in fog, and the clock of St Sulpice lugubriously tolling four as though from across the water.

Perhaps it was the house that had conjured this apparition, for there was something about the Hôtel de Miremont with its chilly expanses of marble and parquet that made Max think of Before. But more likely it was his own guilty conscience. This was a disagreeable reminder that he was no further forward with his task. But then, how could he be? God, but he was the fool to crown all fools! How had he let the old boy pull the wool over his eyes, yet again?

Oh, he made the best of it to the Zhukovskys and Fabrice. He extolled the comforts of his new situation: his room, large enough to encompass fourfold his former attic; the linen sheets, the feather mattress, the water closet down the passage, the baths twice a week, filled with piping cans brought up by the housemaids. He allowed them to admire his new suit—even Fabrice was obliged to show approval, despite its want of certain stylish embellishments his own tailor would not have omitted. Oh yes, the unaccustomed luxuries, the generous increase in means and leisure—Max took pains to appear entranced by the pleasures of sitting at a marquis' table; for he would rather have had his teeth pulled than admit that Fabrice had been right.

If you set aside—and how was it possible to do so?—the pain and humiliation of being spurned; if you convinced yourself that you had misread the signs, that the old boy had not, by his every look and gesture, held out the special privileges accorded to a lover; if you were capable of taking the conversation in the Jardin des Plantes as simply the mundane commerce between employer and employee; well then, you would still be left with the bare and brutal facts of the case: M de Miremont needed no lessons from Max in deceit and false pretences.

Where, in this rag-heap of threadbare promises, should Max start? Perhaps with the old boy's airy assertion that Max's reporting to that stuck-up stuffed parrot of a secretary was a 'mere formality'. If only he had found the decency to come clean, if he had but said outright that he was disposing of Max to the evil old buzzard, body and soul, like a serf!

To begin with Max had not fully understood the extent of his predicament. In the confusion of the first two or three days and even after his rejection—which, though it was a harsh blow at the time, Max could not but believe would soon be retracted—he could see some purpose in the old boy's machinations.

It had not occurred to Max during their initial meeting that, despite the bottle-glass spectacles, Lesage was blind as a mole, for he had attributed his finicky movements and his fastidious regulation of the objects on his desk to his generally starchy disposition. Only on his first day, as they had traipsed round the house so that M Lesage could imbue him with a suitable reverence for its history, had it gradually dawned upon him: when the old buzzard pointed out artefacts of interest—the goblet given to Roland de Miremont by Catherine de Medici, the fifth marquis' collection of Etruscan bronzes or the seventh's of ancient surgical instruments—he often seemed, despite his authoritative disquisition, to be looking at some point to the side of these fascinating articles, as if diverted by a trespassing fly. In the picture gallery, when they reached the wall on which some paintings had clearly been rearranged to accommodate the Claude, he expatiated on the virtues of a Corot while standing before a Fragonard—the Corot, of similar proportions and similarly framed, was hanging several paintings away; and, when they passed through the dim anteroom that led from the picture gallery into the music room, the sudden winter sunlight from the courtyard windows seemed for an instant utterly to disorient him, so that, although he had navigated salons crammed with furniture, he stumbled into a chair and would have fallen had not Max caught his arm.

Nor was the poor fellow's near sight much better. During their morning in the library, as Max now realised, he had been most ingenious; where his remarkable instinctive knowledge of the shelves had failed him, he had used Max as his eyes, commanding him to take down volumes, read out titles, without ever arousing his suspicion.

Max rather admired the old buzzard. Long habitude clearly assisted him, but all the same such a comprehensive memory of his surroundings, such an ability to chart every object in his path, to recall the rank and order of family portraits, the carved detail of an overmantel or the gilding of a looking glass—it was extraordinary. And brave too. When Max considered how he himself would fare if he must blunder through a perpetual fog that obliged him to give forethought to buttoning his boots or tying his cravat, let alone the simple, yet now seemingly miraculous, feat of reading words on a page, his imagination struggled to measure the immensity of the deprivation. He did not even mind that, when he had reached out to save M Lesage in the music room, the old fowl had shrugged off his grasp as if he had committed a gross impertinence. He too would wish to guard his pride, would loathe to be treated as a pitiable cripple.

However none of this could alter the cruel truth, that M de Miremont was in need of a new secretary. M Lesage himself was at pains to point out that his responsibilities weighed upon him. It seemed obvious to Max that his own relegation to the library was temporary, that at the end of his 'probation' M de Miremont would pack the Buzzard off to a well-earned retirement.

So inevitable was this course of events that M de Miremont had felt no need to spell it out. And as for his strange and inconsistent behaviour, well, he was anxious, in these first few crucial days, that nothing untoward should spoil his plan. Of course, it would have helped if he had explained himself—but then, from his wild-eyed look when Max had confronted him, he was in the grip of an attack of nerves like the one that had driven him from La Boissière.

The ever-present Lesage; that older footman, Georges, whose jovial manner did not disguise a hard, sharp eye; not to mention the Cyclops, although he at least would not gossip: yes, Max conceded, there were spies aplenty. And there were other complications too. For here again the old fellow had scarcely been honest. Max had received the impression that, in the years since his separation, the old boy had lived bereft of the comforts of family. Yet now it appeared he had a married daughter and two grandchildren, who lived just off the Rue de Grenelle, only a short drive distant, and visited him every Sunday (there was another daughter, besides, though not in Paris). Then there were the brother-in-law and two nephews who lived four streets away and could also be counted on to call frequently. And the two elderly ladies, great aunts or second cousins twice removed, who inhabited the second floor apartments overlooking the forecourt. And heaven knew however many other relations likely to drop in at any hour without warning.

Max could understand all this would momentarily make the old fellow take fright. Yet he must have weighed up the risks beforehand. The instant his head cleared he would see what was self-evident—that no one would be remotely surprised that he was training a successor to Lesage; within a week Max's presence in the house would go unremarked.

God, how Max had deluded himself in those first two or three days! Why, he asked himself, had he been so eager to find excuses for the devious old bastard? So monsieur had neglected to explain his plan to him? He had also neglected to explain it to the Buzzard. However savagely the Buzzard had shaken off Max's help in the music room, that was as nothing to the ferocity with which he guarded the letters and documents, the weighty testament to his master's confidential business, over which he pored with his furtive magnifying glass—woe betide Max if he so much as rescued a paper that fluttered to the floor!

There was no plan, there never had been. Purblind though he might be, the Buzzard was apparently indispensable to M de Miremont. The old idiot deferred to his secretary's judgement at every turn. And as for Max, the Buzzard might humiliate him however he chose, monsieur could not be troubled—or did not dare—to rise to his defence.

For did the Buzzard return monsieur's respect? During their tour of the house, as they had inspected the family portraits in the Empress Elizabeth Salon, M Lesage had paused reverentially before a heavily whiskered gentleman in a long frock coat.

"The tenth marquis. Monsieur Guy de Miremont."

"Monsieur de Miremont's father?"

"Ah, there was a man who embodied the dignity of this house."

The sententiousness of this irritated Max, so that, despite its being his first day and the Buzzard as yet a relatively unknown quantity, he ventured: "As, surely, is Monsieur de Miremont."

But the secretary's only response was to move on to the next portrait with a sniff.

Such blatant disloyalty, and in the presence of a new and junior member of the household, left Max considerably taken aback, as well as furious on M de Miremont's behalf. Although every day that followed stoked his own disillusionment with monsieur, he retained the memory of this lese-majesty; while it fed his contempt for M de Miremont, it also nourished his growing loathing of the Buzzard, which no pity for the old fowl's infirmity could temper.

Oh yes, Max might swagger before Fabrice, but he had been most comprehensively rooked. Hours for study? The Buzzard made sure his every moment was occupied in the library. As for his notional increase in wages, he had never been poorer: monsieur's turpitude was woven into the weft of that much-admired suit, for, as the Buzzard had made very clear, it must be paid for, along with the evening clothes, boots and other items, in instalments that would fall due long after it was in rags.

The worst of it was—and he disliked to admit this even to himself—he was abominably lonely.

All his life, he had craved a room of his own. There had been his cell during his brief novitiate, but that had been no more than a cubicle with a permanently open door. And, of course, there had been that paper-partitioned room in Mère Richoux's hovel after Josette's flight, but, crushed by debt, he had been in no mood to revel in his solitude. Now here were solid walls, space—so much of it that his treasured library barely filled one shelf of the bookcase—and solitude enough for him to read far into the night by a lamp trimmed daily for his legitimate use. Yet dark thoughts shadowed the page and in sleep he tossed like an unmoored craft on the wide billows of the mattress. He longed for the dormitory he had shared with Fabrice, the narrow eaves, the fetid air, Fabrice's complaints and the companionable sound of his scratching.

He longed for the camaraderie of the servants' hall, too. The back-biting and Michel's enmity were forgotten as he recalled how you could always find someone to share a cigarette or a joke, how they looked out for one another, an élite troupe, the footmen, comrades united in adversity. He could imagine Georges and Philippe, at dinner here in the servants' hall of the Hôtel de Miremont, tilting back their chairs after the upper servants had retired, teasing the parlour maids, exchanging winks, guffawing uproariously at their own innuendo, and the image filled him with all the pain of loss.

For, needless to say, Old Jouvert was right. Max could no more claim fellowship with the servants now than he could feel at ease at M de Miremont's table. If anything, of the two camps the servants were likely to hold him in the greater contempt.

The Buzzard had seen to that. It was not that the servants' hall cherished any particular respect for M Lesage. The secretary's years of devotion to the house of Miremont could not alter the fact that he inhabited the same ambiguous territory as Max and must likewise be viewed as exacting service on false pretences. But the Buzzard, predictably, felt no need to moderate his manner in his dealings with the lower orders; rather, he had made it his duty to supply the peremptory tone his master lacked. Thus, while it was evident that the servants regarded M de Miremont with respect and even affection, it was equally evident, to Max's trained eye, that they hated Lesage. Oh, Max could not but watch Georges and Philippe with admiration. They might dream of seasoning the Buzzard's escalopes with rat poison, and who knew what happened to the old fowl's plate on its way from kitchen to table (Max recalled that the soup tureen at baron Reinhardt's had been regularly fortified with spittle, or worse) but their impassive faces never showed it. They attended to the Buzzard's wants with a most fastidious correctness; they even did their best to assist him, anticipating his difficulty in judging distance by stealthily rescuing his wine glass or moving condiments within his reach; and, when detected and roundly rebuked for their pains, they would, without the flicker of an eyelid, offer solemn apologies before calmly proceeding with their duties. No, you could not fault them. Although, carried the smallest degree further, this imperturbable competence might be taken for ridicule.

But it did not follow that the servants would feel sympathy for Max, as another of the old fowl's victims. To the contrary. If Lesage were despicable, how much more so his whipping boy, whom he did not scruple to humiliate in their presence?

Besides, Max had further reason to be wary. Doubtless the Cyclops would keep his customary silence; but, knowing servants' hall gossip as Max did, he must reckon it inconceivable that some word of his previous employment had not been picked up by now, to be passed on to the generality like scarlet fever. He thought he could see it in the appraising eye of the housekeeper, Mme Mercier, in the heavy, gloomy stare of Boussec, the butler; he sensed it in the very impassivity of Georges and Philippe when, despite his years of study, he became confused by the panoply of cutlery and glasses set before him.

Not only was he the Buzzard's plaything. He was 'jumped up'. To the crime of false pretences he had added the sin of disloyalty.

He was thus at every possible disadvantage in determining his own manner towards the servants. Too haughty and he was a thousand times more worthy of scorn even than Lesage. Too friendly and he would be perceived as making assumptions that no longer befitted him. Of course, he could take for his model M de Miremont's unassuming courtesy. Yet, since Max did not enjoy the special dispensations of rank, in him modesty could too easily be interpreted as timidity and over-politeness as grovelling. What matter that a comfortable existence in any household depended on the good opinion of the servants' hall—he was lost, whatever he did. He no longer even had the doubtful privilege of one of Old Jouvert's spies to protect him.

He must rely on his own natural reserve and on making no demands, except where absolutely necessary. But it was a strain, constantly holding himself in check and praying he did not overstep some unseen but ineluctable boundary. He could scarcely wait for his days off. Yet even then he must watch himself lest any slip should cast doubt upon his supposed good fortune.

True, he could be certain of distraction at the Zhukovskys', as long as he could evade Vera's acute glance. The Sunday night circle had acquired a new member, Sergei Lyudin, a cellist, who was hoping to persuade Mitya to abandon his soloist's ambitions and join him in forming a string quartet. This led to heated discussion, yet nothing was ever resolved and the subject usually drifted away after the second bottle of vodka, whereupon Lyudin, a gangling fellow who put Max in mind of a poorly assembled easel and who, sober, was abominably shy, was prevailed upon to indulge his surprising talent for mimicry, which included a formidable falsetto—his Adeline Patti was a particular favourite at the candle-end of the evening.

Max's meetings with Fabrice usually cheered him too. The new Jean, apparently, was a perfect monster who made Michel look like a sainted virgin. Furthermore, inside a fortnight, he had ousted Max's old enemy in madame's favour—Michel had left in a huff without serving out his notice. It was all one to Fabrice, off himself at the end of the week to his new situation as valet to a millionaire newspaper proprietor in an *à la mode* mansion overlooking the Parc Monceau. But the Cardinal—you'd think he'd be beside himself. Yet here was the curious thing. This monstrous Jean was like a simpering altar boy in the Cardinal's presence. Turned out the crafty old quean had only gone and hired his own nephew. Yes, my uncle, no my uncle. No wonder Monseigneur was whistling these days.

Yet, back in the frigid luxury of his room, no longer warmed by the Zhukovskys' well-tended stove or the press of bodies in the Monkey, Max would feel his loneliness steal up on him again, like the draughts that came down the empty chimney, spreading their chill into every corner and penetrating his very marrow. Perhaps it was this bitter gust of misery that forced open the shutters and let in the Other.

"But there might be papers—"

"Cut it! Dom Ignatius will catch us. And you know full well who he'll pick to get the thrashing."

"He can't see us from here. If there are papers, documents, saying who we are, who I am—"

"We've been through this a thousand times. You truly think she left any evidence when she abandoned us here? Why would the Reverend Father have bothered us with his endless questions?"

"But if there was something he overlooked? And they come searching for us—"

"After all these years? They won't come now. And who are they anyway? We don't even know who 'they' are?"

"Go on, scoff, that's just like you! But it won't only be me who's in danger."

"Oh, for pity's sake!"

"They'll torture you to find out what you know. If they don't kill you too. Most likely they'll kill both of us, to be on the safe side."

"Ghouls! Phantoms! Made up by the two of them, she and the Major, to keep our mouths shut. Now cut it, will you! Dom Ingnatius is looking this way!"

But the Other would not cut it. He kept reverting to it whenever there was the smallest chance for them to talk.

"There may be something—"

"There's nothing, I tell you! What did we find when we searched the Chapterhouse? Oh, I'm sorry—we? You, I seem to remember, were scared by some ghostly rat—"

"It was real, it ran over my foot in the dark—"

"And you ran too. Leaving me to grope around with a candle, risking weeks pulling turnips for Brother Bernard. Thank the Lord Dom Jérôme snores for perdition and didn't notice I was missing. And all for what?"

"There's the Reverend Father's office."

Max knew what was coming next, he had expected it for some time. "No chance. He wears the key on his belt."

"But when he gives you a beating—"

"No!"

"He locks you in there while he's at chapel for None, then comes back to give you a second dose of the strap. You said so!"

"I tell you, no!"

"You could easily search then. Give him some excuse to punish you, which you shouldn't find difficult—"

"No. And there's an end to it."

"Why? What's another strapping to you? Or is it all a lie when you say you don't care? You're just a coward, aren't you? Always making excuses not to do your duty. You're just a liar and a coward!"

"Or perhaps I've been listening to your lectures on my immortal soul."

"What do you mean by that?"

"Doesn't it occur to you that, in asking me to do something that involves a mortal sin, you will be in a state of sin yourself?"

"It's true that, strictly speaking, searching the Reverend Father's desk is sinful. But it's only venial and God will understand it's in a just cause."

"You know that's not what I mean."

"I do not!"

"Oh come, Pierre. Ask yourself why our beloved Father Superior in his wisdom chooses to thrash me and not you. Is it because you're such a saint?"

"Not this again! I won't listen!"

"Why does he single out some of us for the special privilege of baring our flesh to his belt—me, Marc, Xavier—and leave the rest of you to Dom Jérôme?"

"Of all your vile, filthy lies, this is the vilest, the filthiest."

"Why does he lock us in?"

"I tell you, I'm not listening. That you should slander the Reverend Father, the holiest of men—pray that God in his mercy does not strike you down for even thinking such a depraved and disgusting thing."

"Disgusting? Yes, if you care to know, it does disgust me. I'll take what I must take, but I won't volunteer for it. Now we'd better cut along before we're missed."

The Other was silent for a moment, his eyes screwed shut as if he were plunged in effortful thought, or possibly praying. "Our Heavenly Father tells me that if I don't believe your lies it is no sin for me to ask what I'm asking of you. On the other hand, it is a grievous sin for you to refuse to honour your debt to me."

"What debt, exactly, is that?"

"Have you conveniently forgotten that I saved your life?"

"You? Saved *my* life?"

"One word from me and they'd have killed you, the two of them. They only kept you alive because they thought it pleased me."

And so the argument continued, then and in the days that followed. But eventually Max was bound to give in. It was not that he disavowed the games of concentration or the times he had protected his fellow captive's body with his, but that he was obliged to remember that in keeping the Other alive he had hoped to preserve his own expendable existence. Yes, the Other's claim was just, even if its reasoning were faulty—Max did owe him his life.

It was also true that, however much he sneered, he was not immune to the Other's fears: how could he be, when the threat of 'them', the Pursuers, the evil ones who would murder him and the Other if they were discovered, was so seamed into his consciousness that reason was powerless to unstitch it? Documents could indeed be dangerous. He found none, of course—well, none of the dangerous sort anyway: only, in the great oak chest, after he had made use of the lock-picking skills he had learned from Brother Bernard, a yellowing paper promising the Chapter a substantial benefaction in return for the board and education of the two young postulants, Pierre and Paul Lambert, up until their novitiate; needless to say the names and the signature upon this document were false and, as various notes attached to it testified, not a sou had been received, the mysterious lady benefactor having vanished without trace.

This was a gloomy discovery, for it confirmed what Max had always sensed but shrank from acknowledging; he and the Other were prisoners at St Pons, as surely as they had been in the cellar. They would repay the baroness's debt with a lifetime of service: the Other would not object, indeed he longed to take his vows; but he, Max, was already being groomed to replace Dom Aloysius in the library when the palsy finally took the old boy, and nothing—not his lack of vocation nor even his growing lack of faith—would be permitted to prevent it.

Nor was the Other grateful when Max returned empty-handed. If he had found nothing, then perhaps his search not been assiduous enough. And as for the sacrifice he had made—the Other, as usual, stopped his ears.

Thus it was that around this time Max made his first plan to run away. It was hardly a well-organised plan, consisting merely of his stealing out of the dormitory when Dom Jérôme began snoring, and creeping across the muddy yard to Brother Bernard's outhouse in the hope that his friend might be persuaded to hide him in his cart when he drove to market the next morning. That night was principally memorable for being the first—and the last—occasion Max would ever allow himself to get drunk, resisting all Bernard's attempts to wrest the cider jug from him, so that he had no recollection of how he got back to the cloister in time for Matins: he supposed Bernard must have heaved him over his burly shoulder and carried him. For the rest, he could recall the familiar stench of the sow and her piglets, and how the heat of their straw rose up with the cider fumes to clot the air beneath the rafters; he could remember the reassuring homeliness of this fug, and how, sitting across the scarred deal table from Brother Bernard, with the guttering candle between them and his jar clasped in both hands, he had grown flushed with confidence, felt he had attained manhood at last, that destiny was finally his to control: yet this mood cannot have sustained him for long, for his strongest recollection was of the fountain of vomit that had suddenly spurted from his mouth, and, more humiliating still, how, when he had retched and vomited until his belly hurt, he had burst out in childish sobbing.

Whereupon Brother Bernard had hauled him up and towelled his face with a rag and held him to his broad chest; and Max, still snivelling but inhaling, along with a powerful gust of the farmyard and ancient sweat, a solid, consoling warmth, had wondered blearily what the price of this comfort would be. But only for an instant and from force of habit. For, of course, Brother Bernard had wanted nothing.

Of the conversation that had led up to his disgrace Max had virtually no recall, except for one fragment. He had, he fancied, been proclaiming loudly that God and all His trappings, from Heaven and Hell to Our Lady and the Stations of the Cross, were simply poisonous rubbish. But Bernard had merely laughed.

"If you mean their God, over there——" here he jerked his thumb in the direction of the cloister "——I won't quarrel with you, Paul lad. But grass grows, apples ripen——there's a God all right."

"Then why has He created me as the embodiment of sin?"

"Who says He has?"

Max had never spoken to Brother Bernard about Dom Sébastien, not even during the terrible days before the latter was sent away; nor had he hinted at what happened behind the Father Superior's locked door: only the Other knew (or chose not to know) that. It was not merely shame that restrained him; he sensed that, for all Bernard's dealings with the outside world, and despite the flexibility of his conscience when the Bursar's back was turned, he was in many respects an innocent and it would be unkind to trouble him with such knowledge. "Well——why do I get so many thrashings?"

"Hush, lad! They'll thrash you again if you can't keep your voice down."

"Well go on, tell me! Or I'll tell you. They beat me because I'm steeped in sin and I tempt others to sin."

"They beat you, my lad, because they can. And maybe because they see in you a spark of the God that ripens apples——that wouldn't suit their book. But you know what your real problem is? That sour-milk brother of yours."

"How many times do I have to tell you, he's——"

"Not your brother? So you say."

"We were brought up together, but we share no blood."

"Still, everybody sees you as brothers. Pierre and Paul, stands to reason. Added to which, you're as thick as herrings in a barrel. And it strikes me, the thicker you two get, the more you're likely to end up in trouble."

"You're wrong, we loathe each other."

"Well, it defeats me then. You're not brothers, he's not your blood and you loathe him——so why do you, who's got brains, or so they say, always jump when he tells you?"

"I do not! But he's…I can't…Bernard, you wouldn't understand."

"Oh, pardon me, Your Majesty."

"No, I didn't mean...We're bound together, he and I. By fate." Max hesitated, for, though he trusted Bernard and despised his own superstition, he still feared the retribution he might call down by going further. "I can't explain. He owns my life, I own his...Oh, it's hopeless, I can't find the words..."

Bernard snorted. "Paul, my lad, do you want to know the difference between you and your so-called brother?" To Max's astonishment, he pushed back the sleeves of his robe and spread his arms wide with a flourish that took in the pigs and his rickety corner cupboard and the water bucket and even the rafters, for all the world like a priest displaying the host to his congregation. "Tell me, lad, what do you see?"

Max laughed.

"Go on, tell me what you see."

"I see a disgraceful old reprobate in need of a shave and smelling of pigs."

"Mind yourself, lad! But seriously, what do you think your high and holy brother would see?"

"Well...the same."

Bernard shook his massive head triumphantly. "He wouldn't see anything. Not a thing. He'd notice Juno here and her little ones before he'd deign to cast his eyes over yours truly. You may have more than your fair share of mischief in you, but you're not so bad at heart. Just so long as you can get free of your sainted brother."

Free? Max would never be free. Shivering in his chilly bed at the Hôtel de Miremont, he saw once again the ruined farmhouse just outside Versailles, not a day's walk from Paris, where his brother-in-fate had forfeited his name and his existence and become the Other. After it was done, Max had sat for a while over the fire they had made, oblivious to his throbbing temples and the blood still smearing his hands and face. There was no God, there was no sin.

He had been unprepared for the emptiness that had engulfed him once he had finally understood that the Other was gone forever.

CHAPTER TWENTY SIX

The Hôtel de Miremont was something of a puzzle to Max. Baron Reinhardt's mansion in the Avenue Foch, with its expensive new furniture, exotic plants and ceiling frescos imported from some decaying Florentine palace, had been quite clear in its intentions, as the peacock is clear when it spreads its tail. The Hôtel de Claireville, while it had no need for such protestations, did not scorn the latest contrivances of fashionable upholsterers; like an Arab stallion, it was not above flaunting its high-mettled elegance. By contrast, the Hôtel de Miremont seemed to Max like a great whale that had indiscriminately gulped the plankton of history into its maw.

Reminders of Before had been fleeting: those vast rooms, as he remembered them, had so dazzled the eye with their gilding that it was like looking into the sun. The great silent spaces of the Hôtel de Miremont, their blinds drawn against the thin winter light, their sparse lamps dimmed, their colours fading timidly into shadow, were veiled in a greenish-grey gloom as if they had risen up from the bottom of the ocean. Floating out of this watery half-light came a bewildering profusion of objects, chosen over the centuries without any guiding principle of taste: ingenious cabinets from China and every country in Europe; chairs of all shapes and sizes, carved with lyres, lion's heads, serpents, gryphons, whose only common feature appeared to be the frailty of their brocade; malachite coups, tourmaline bowls, porphyry obelisks; Etruscan terracotta, cloisonné tea sets, primitive masks, ecclesiastical embroideries; satyrs, naiads, ancient Egyptians, classical Greeks and imperial Romans, rendered in bronze and every hue of marble...Even Lesage, for all his eagerness to impress his listener with the dignity of the house, was unable to find space in his commentary for more than a fraction of the contents of each room.

Furthermore, the juxtaposition of these objects was entirely haphazard, without regard to their beauty or value, or so it seemed to Max, accustomed as he was to the studied perfection of the Hôtel de Claireville; you might come across a rack of old clay pipes or a withered fan, relics of some obscure Miremont scion, granted a place amongst the lapis lazuli caskets and Meissen vases. Indeed, without denying the grandeur conveyed by its sheer size, the Hôtel de Miremont seemed surprisingly shabby for the principal residence of a man of considerable wealth. The furniture in the Elizabeth Salon was in patent need of regilding, while in the cavernous ballroom—a room seldom heated, in which, as you crossed it during this season of the year, you puffed out clouds of your own breath —the silvering in the mirrors was altogether shot; and as to the draperies, which according to the Buzzard dated from monsieur's great-grandfather's time, before the Revolution—well, even Lesage would have been put to it to say what colour they had been originally. In M de Miremont's apartments, from what little Max had been privileged to glimpse, a far greater simplicity prevailed, yet still without pretence at elegance; there were ink stains on the study table, clearly visible between the piles of books, while the scarred leather divan sagged wearily.

Yet, if the Hôtel de Miremont wore a faded air, it was not from neglect. When Max rose early he was likely to encounter a flock of housemaids, who snatched up their polishing cloths and dusters and took flight giggling the moment he appeared. The master of the house himself could be observed, several days after Max's arrival, standing in the forecourt with the ever-gloomy Boussec and two frock-coated gentleman, all four of them peering up critically at the facade as they considered some renovation or other; another day, playing brief truant from the library, Max encountered the old fellow deep in conversation with a picture restorer, who had his ladder up to one of the paintings above the lobby doors.

But by then Max had remembered the old boy's battered dressing case. Truly there was nothing so puzzling about the house after all, for it was of a piece with its owner, with his dislike of show, his indifference to fashion, his inveterate preference for the sentimental worth of objects.

That so much of the Miremont collection had survived the Revolution was due to the forethought of the present marquis' grandfather, according to Lesage: after the fall of the Bastille, the family treasures had been hastily packed and despatched to the country, some to the two Burgundian châteaux, but most to the family's other estate in the staunchly Royalist Vendée. The hôtel had not escaped the Terror; in 1792 an incendiary attack had destroyed the east and service wings and what valuables still remained in the building had been saved from looting only by the valiant resistance of the servants. Miremont's grandfather, restored to his patrimony and created a peer of the realm by the returning Bourbon monarchy, had rebuilt the two damaged wings, adding the picture gallery to the ground floor of the east wing and creating the arcade that ran along the eastern side of the forecourt.

The result of this latter innovation was that, in contrast to the eerie stillness of the house, the forecourt bustled with the life of the city. The carriage gates remained open until evening to admit the customers of the cobbler, silversmith and purveyor of religious images who inhabited the booths in the arcade. Horses clattered across the cobbles from the stable yard and Max, when he managed to dawdle in the lobby without being smartly sent back to his duties, would catch occasional glimpses of the aged second cousins who lived in the apartment above, hunched bombazine figures swathed in furs, being helped by Georges into their carriage. These ladies, the princesse de Vaux and Mme d'Ancy-Miremont, never came to the main house, although Max gathered M de Miremont visited them twice a month and they were on Lesage's list of noble ladies; but sometimes Max would see Mme d'Ancy, the plumper of the two, being wheeled out in a bath chair by their paid companion, a wraith-like woman in grey; or on Sundays he would glimpse the princess, alone and clutching her missal, off to mass in St Sulpice: so that he would find himself wondering about these separate intricate lives continuing mysteriously upstairs above his head, and about the lives of the others who came and went from the arcade, some hurrying about their business, some braving the cold to stop and gossip, in what, though he was cut off from it only by panes of glass, seemed another world.

But his greatest escape was the picture gallery. He had been piqued by Lesage's taunt about the Louvre. It was true that since he had arrived in Paris, despite living in houses well-stocked with works of art, he had never been moved to visit Napoleon's great collection. Partly, he did not wish to be reminded of his days as a model or of how they had ended. But also the hours he had endured sustaining contrived poses while frozen and fighting cramp had left him with a certain contempt for artists: not just Lebas with his stiff portraits and hackneyed classical tableaux, but the students in the ateliers, so convinced of their own genius and yet, to Max's untutored eye, so conventional and uninspired.

Van der Meer, of course, had been another matter. Yes, he was always so drunk you were amazed he could hold a brush, and on bad days he would see snakes coiled around the washstand. But he had possessed something—fire, madness, a vision from the gods? The strange thing was, he could draw, truly draw, not like the students; he had spent hours making painstaking sketches of every aspect of Max's anatomy: yet, when he had begun to translate his vision onto canvas, it was as if he had thrown all that hard work away. What emerged was not anything resembling his stated intention to portray the naked male body in motion, but a strange, blurred distorted image; yet it came whirling at you, that image, it assaulted you, as if he had somehow captured movement itself. Max, while not understanding what Van der Meer had done or why he had done it, had stood in awe of that painting. The old sot had not been able to sell it, of course, any more than he could persuade any dealer to take his other paintings. Thus it had still been there, propped against the wall, mocking Max with his own living essence during the night he had lain on Van der Meer's mattress praying to cheat death. He wondered how he would react if he ever saw it again—would it now provoke only a shudder of revulsion? Yet the old toper had doubtless died in the Salpêtrière, and the painting was long gone, sold off by Mère Richoux to the rag merchant with the rest of the artist's meagre possessions.

The picture gallery, of course, contained no paintings remotely resembling a Van der Meer—M de Miremont appeared to find Corot and Courbet daring. But his debate with the old fellow had left Max intrigued: he wanted to understand what it was that M de Miremont saw in the Claude and also to explore his own reactions; for, while he could see why he had instinctively responded to the Delacroix tribesman, he could not have explained the precise qualities of the Titian portrait that had moved him, beyond repeating to himself the generalised theory of 'great art' he had offered M de Miremont, which even to him had begun to seem facile.

So, whenever he could be certain of the Buzzard's absence, he stole into the picture gallery. And, although he would never have given his enemy the triumph of admitting it, on his days off, before trying his chances at the Monkey or calling on the Zhukovskys, he visited the Louvre. Here, after wandering dazedly through room after room crammed with spoils from two continents, he let himself be guided by Titian: even though the paintings of the Italian Renaissance by and large filled him with indifference—with their endless pious Madonnas and haloed infants, they recalled the crude reproductions exhorting reverence at St Pons—he forced himself to study them. Attempting to read them as he would a poem, he analysed their composition, their symbolism, emphases and tropes. Then, returning to the picture gallery, he would confront M de Miremont's Italian masterpieces, his

Mantegna, his Raphaël, his Annibale Carraccis, interrogating them in the light of his discoveries, hoping to wring from them the answer to the riddle: why did the old fellow and the world in general judge them to be repositories of some sublime truth?

The gallery's two long windowless walls, stretching the length of the east wing, were amply furnished with rosewood chairs plainly upholstered in olive-green watered silk, so that one could contemplate in comfort whichever picture one pleased. Illuminated by natural light from two skylights and the tall windows at each end, and with its length broken at equal intervals by two arches supported by marble columns, while it boasted its inevitable quota of busts on plinths and candelabra upheld by Nubians or gilded cherubs, it was less stiflingly cluttered than the other ceremonial rooms: even its deep silence seemed to a purpose. But Max did not loiter in the gallery merely to clarify his thoughts. He hoped that sooner or later he would encounter M de Miremont engaged in the same contemplation. Yet, since Max was best able to desert the library when the Buzzard was upstairs with the old fellow going through the morning's business, it was a faint hope and daily fainter.

About the library, Max was naturally in two minds. On the one hand there was the dreadful irony that, having escaped from the clutches of Dom Aloysius, here he was, similarly imprisoned, sniffing up the dust of ages and craving fresh air. But, on the other, there was a perverse comfort in that familiar scent of foxed paper and ancient leather. And besides he was conscious that, in different circumstances, if he were not chained to it for long hours of tedious and often back-breaking labour, he might have found the place rather agreeable.

He was not surprised to learn from Lesage that the library was M de Miremont's one contribution to the evolution of the house. The Buzzard seemed disposed to regard the room as his master's folly but, to Max, it was like the watch: functional, even austere when you compared it with the other grand rooms, yet pleasing in the very simplicity of its appointments, it testified to the old fellow's tastes when he was not shackled by his obligation to history.

This was no rich man's toy with neatly calibrated rows of imposingly bound volumes in matching sets, designed to suggest erudition, not to offer it; this was a true, working library such as Dom Aloysius would have approved. Buffered from any sounds from the entrance hall by the anteroom housing the seventh marquis' cabinet of minerals, it otherwise extended, in parallel to the picture gallery, the full length of the west wing. On three walls, interrupted only by two graceful chimneypieces in pale, veined marble, bookshelves of lightly varnished oak soared to the ceiling, with a brass-railed mezzanine giving access to the upper shelves; its furnishings were serviceable— deep armchairs, upright chairs of polished mahogany with generously upholstered seats, low side tables, a writing desk, three sturdier tables that would support piles of books; apart from the Turkey carpets spread over the parquet, the spines of the books—umber, ochre, crimson, ultramarine, sage, viridian, cadmium red—provided the dominant source of colour: light came from four sets of French windows opening onto the inner courtyard, affording views of a stone fountain (at present dry for winter) set within a formal garden of topiaried box.

Then there were the books themselves. Aside from the volumes you would expect any great house to possess—Montaigne, La Fontaine, Pascal—the shelves reflected the diverse preoccupations of successive marquises, from alchemy (the second marquis) and metaphysics (the fourth) to natural sciences (the seventh) and bloodstock and heraldry (the eighth). M de Miremont's grandfather and father had both contributed copiously to the weight of tomes on history, philosophy and political theory. But the old fellow himself had outdone all his ancestors, expanding the library at a prolific rate; as well as adding considerably to its store of ancient literature, M de Miremont had succumbed to a whole series of passions: Shakespeare and the English novel, poetry, travel, topography, architecture, archaeology—even, unexpectedly, land management and animal husbandry.

The result of the old fellow's addictions was that whatever order had prevailed after the library had been moved had long since broken down. New arrivals had been piled haphazardly on empty shelves or jammed into gaps in full ones; and every week a fresh package still came from the bookseller. For Max, had he possessed his leisure, this chaos would have been treasure trove, an Arabian Nights' cave crammed with unimagined jewels. Even now, as he dutifully carried down books and sorted them into piles, he was tempted by the curiosities he unearthed—a seventeenth-century treatise on debauchery, complete with woodcuts, Deschanel on magnetism and electricity, the memoirs of Lorenzo de Medici; but, of course, if he so much as flicked open a page here or there, the Buzzard would swoop.

It could not be denied that the library needed to be catalogued. But it was equally true, as Max rapidly discovered, that the enterprise was doomed. After all, who had created the original system by which the books had been ordered? The Buzzard, who now relied on his remarkable memory of that system to conceal his infirmity. Max could not but have sympathised, if that had been the only difficulty. But, as he was gradually to find out, there were other problems. M Lesage, though he would have despised baron Reinhardt, appeared at one with the banker on the true purpose of books—that is, they were for decoration, to confer distinction (the dignity of the house again), for anything but reading. Max's simple alphabetical system violated Lesage's firmest tenet: that the oldest, most valuable and most beautifully bound books should be on the lower shelves, where they would immediately be seen by visitors, not relegated by some quirk of the alphabet to the mezzanine, or forced into company with M de Miremont's vulgar newcomers. Indeed, such was the veneration in which the Buzzard held some of these sacred relics that he seemed reluctant to let Max's unhallowed fingers touch them at all; when, early on, in a foolish attempt to find favour, Max had confessed that he knew how to repair aged bindings, the secretary had brushed the information aside with one of his characteristic sniffs—M le marquis used an antiquarian book specialist in the Palais-Royal for such services.

Classification also caused difficulties. Although in general the Buzzard was supremely indifferent to the content of books, he had certain fixed obsessions. Max wished he had not wasted two hours trying to argue him out of the view that the eighth marquis' volumes on heraldry and genealogy should fall under Moral Philosophy, on the grounds that they dealt with the honour and dignity—yet again!—of great families and thus embodied a moral precept. Lesage would also have liked to emulate St Pons in having a locked cabinet of Indexed books: but the Buzzard's heretics included Proudhon, St Simon, Voltaire and Napoleon, as well as the entire German people.

Max placed his faith in M de Miremont. The old fellow might be a fool but his intellect was rigorous. He would be certain to reject the shabby patchwork of compromises that was all Lesage would agree: Max scarcely minded that he would inevitably take the blame, so long as the old boy tore up the plan.

The meeting in M de Miremont's study marked the moment Max gave up hope. There was nothing to be done, the old idiot was utterly in thrall to the Buzzard. And what had he, Max, achieved, during the long month he had spent under monsieur's roof? He was not a lover, he was not a secretary, he was not even a librarian. His freedom was more circumscribed than when he had been a servant and he was now also tied by debt. And, although the Other still haunted him nightly, he was no further forward in engaging the old boy's support for his great endeavour. He had nothing whatsoever to lose by asking for his cards. The Zhukovskys would put him up for a week or two and then—there was no longer any way out—it was the army for him.

Perhaps he would quickly be made an officer, despite his lack of money and connections. That frightful old snob, the Buzzard, might disdain him. But, examining the effect of his new evening dress in his cheval glass, he felt fairly certain he could now pass as a gentleman. The clothes, of course, must be returned—that was a point of pride, since he could not pay what was owing for them. But something of the accursed dignity of the house of Miremont must have rubbed off on him. An officer's uniform would play well with the personages he must impress. And, in the meanwhile, he would not fritter away his time at the Zhukovskys', as he had at Christmas. He would penetrate the Bibliothèque Mazarine, hunt down old newspapers, find names, seek out exiles, identify once and for all whom he must approach to be certain of a hearing. He was not a child any longer to be frightened of 'them'.

On principle, Max would not give notice to the Buzzard: nothing less would serve than an interview with monsieur himself. But here, just as he had determined to wait not a day longer, M de Miremont frustrated him by retiring indisposed. Again curse the Buzzard, snuffling and spitting and cunningly ensuring everybody suffered twice, first from having to endure his playing the martyr, and then from his affliction. Apart from that dimly remembered spell as an invalid on his father's country estate, Max had always enjoyed unblemished health, indeed had taken pride in it—it was the Other who had always been sickly. And this was no serious illness, merely a head cold: it was humiliating how he was laid low by it, weakened by his fever, prevented from thinking by his thick head, starved of sleep by his endless coughing and sneezing, so generally crushed, so filled with disgust for his own sweating, phlegm-choked, disobedient body that his resolve drained away and he fell back into despair.

Was it the unfeigned concern he detected in M de Miremont? Or perhaps the useful information he had gleaned from a little-frequented shelf of the library? Whichever the cause, when his head cleared and his mood lightened, he was no longer in such haste for action. Oh, his determination had not weakened, but good sense suggested that, whatever a military future might offer, when it came to pleading his cause with illustrious personages, M de Miremont remained an ideal champion. Given the effort Max had expended on the old idiot, what was to be lost by one last try?

The night M de Miremont attended the opera Max was still martialling his case in preparation for that final, decisive interview. He had blessed his luck that the Buzzard had decided to retire early, so that, on hearing the old fowl's door close further along the corridor, he could creep out of his own room and hurry back to his research. But he could scarcely believe his good fortune when monsieur himself appeared. Or was it, after all, so fortunate? Taken by surprise, Max allowed his opening gambit to go to waste. Yet perhaps there was another reason why the old boy could not bring himself to concentrate on Frederick the Great. Max was sure he was not mistaken. But before he could exploit this unlooked-for opportunity, the old fellow had rushed off as if pursued by Beelzebub.

Max did not encounter M de Miremont until luncheon the next day, where the marquis was distracted and irritable, barely pretending to listen to Lesage and favouring Max himself with not so much as a glance. Yet this was not necessarily discouraging—Max remembered their brief estrangement at La Boissière. No, the main difficulty was determining how to press home his sudden advantage.

While a formal audience might have served his previous plan, it scarcely suited the present situation: monsieur, thus confronted, would take fright, as Max had cause to know. Nor was the spontaneous approach that had succeeded so admirably in the lenient atmosphere of La Boissière practicable here: M de Miremont's wavering chastity might collapse when ambushed by overwhelming temptation, but it would soon be restored by horror at the danger he had courted. Discretion must be all.

Work in the library had entered a mid-winter phase, where it was hard to imagine spring ever coming. A third of the shelves was now bare and, while in places a few sparse volumes heralded the green shoots of the new order, the main evidence of Max's toil lay in an encroaching snowfall of books that looked set to threaten even M de Miremont's sanctum. Narrow paths through the banked-up volumes allowed passage from one end of the room to the other, to the shelves and to the sole remaining table, where Max kept the tools required for his other various tasks—the glue pot for replacing book plates, the goose quills for recording the classification of each volume.

All afternoon, Max, in his footman's apron, dutifully trudged these paths with stacks of books. But, for once, he was barely conscious of the dust that caught his throat or the sweat that trickled into his eyes despite the coldness of the room: he was back in Bordeaux at the height of his affair with M de Miremont, seeking some clue as to how he should proceed with the old fellow.

Recently these memories had served mainly to remind him of his own gullibility: all the same, it was amusing to recall their awkward first encounter, their ridiculous games, the time the Cardinal (only it had really been Fabrice) had almost caught them *in flagrante*; when Max came to the morning he had hurled himself from the tower, he could not forbear laughing aloud.

Whereupon Lesage, who had chosen this moment to make one of his regular incursions, enquired testily what he found so entertaining.

If the old fowl but knew! Cheeking Lesage was not likely to improve Max's situation, as the latter recognised in his more sober moods. But, for the instant, he was light-hearted, buoyed by these reminders of a time when he was not a mere serf in a footman's apron, so that he could not resist a retaliatory dig.

"I was just wondering, monsieur," he said, assuming an air of innocence, "about that book that miraculously came to light when I was hunting for blotting paper this morning. You recall—*L'après-midi d'un faune*? By Stéphane Mallarmé, a limited edition. Granted, it's a slim volume. But how odd, don't you think, that it could work itself into the gap behind my drawer without sustaining the slightest damage?"

The Buzzard favoured his underling with an unpleasant smile. And he was just embarking upon his by-now-familiar encomium to true poetic values, as exemplified by the romantic flights of Alfred de Vigny, when he was interrupted by Philippe, appearing at the door with a small pile of books that monsieur had sent down from his study.

Max stared at the books as they passed from Philippe's hands to Lesage's and then, accompanied by a curt nod of command, to his own work-table. Shit, it was so obvious! Here it had been, the solution to his problem, right in front of his nose all the time.

Most mornings, after he and Lesage had gone through the post, M de Miremont gave his secretary a list of the books he required for his day's work. The Buzzard would then carry this list, written in monsieur's own hand, down to the library and give it to Max, with instructions to assemble the volumes as quickly as possible. Once Max had done his bidding, the Buzzard would convey the pile upstairs to his master. In the beginning, he had been most punctilious in checking the books against the list, but more lately he had relaxed his zeal. Max knew better than to imagine he had won the old fowl's trust; rather, he suspected, this dereliction was due to the Buzzard's reluctance to make overt use of his magnifier: while he still gave an elaborate performance of scrutinising the paper before handing it over, he undoubtedly had but a hazy notion of its contents. Nor was he likely to recognise any of the books, for they were not the gorgeously gold-tooled treasures that he revered but most often M de Miremont's plainly-bound new acquisitions. As long as the number tallied with the number of titles on the list, he would take the stack upstairs without question.

Here was an open gate for a Trojan horse.

Max must wait, of course, until the Buzzard had performed his usual ritual at the close of the afternoon, fussing and finicking, picking random books from the top of various piles and moving them here and there, shuffling the volumes set aside for the restorer. Dutifully, Max gathered up the returned volumes on his table and replaced them on the shelf he reserved for M de Miremont's books-in-use. Dawdling, he untied his apron, stuffing into its pocket the gloves he wore to keep his hands free of grime and reaching for his jacket from the back of his chair. Finally, to disguise his impatience and as a gesture of defiance, he pasted a bookplate into the Mallarmé. But at last the Buzzard, satisfied that he had made his point, bustled off to receive monsieur's orders for tomorrow morning.

Contrary to appearances, the maze of books had been constructed to a plan and, unless foiled by the Buzzard's infuriating sorties, Max knew which path would lead him to his quarry. As it happened, he had come across the book he required a couple of days ago; he had noted it particularly and even recalled its binding. A slim, earth-green volume with plain end-papers and only the title and author picked out in gold. And, yes—it slid easily into his jacket pocket.

CHAPTER TWENTY SEVEN

Dinner had seemed interminable, the old fellow silent, Lesage more than usually tedious and an air of gloom hanging over the whole proceedings. But at least the fire which Max had been surprised to find blazing in his grate when he had come upstairs to change his linen was still giving out a luxurious warmth—he must grant the old boy had kept his word there. Max drew one of his two armchairs to the fender and, casting off his jacket and cravat and rolling a cigarette, settled himself in unlooked-for comfort to study the Catullus.

He was at first inclined towards poem LXXXV:

odi et amo. quare id faciam, fortasse requiris?
*nescio, sed fieri sentio et excrucior.**

He could not but feel intense admiration for the artistry that could capture the paradoxical agonies of love in two spare lines. But, on second thoughts, as an overture to M de Miremont this was too forceful by far. It might offend the old fellow. And, quite apart from the fact that if Max truly were suffering he would rather swallow hot coals than confess it, did it not greatly overstate the case?

Besides, it conjured painful memories of Dom Sébastien.

After an hour or so flicking backwards and forwards through the pages till their type danced before his eyes, Max settled on XCIX, one of the poems to Juventius. True, if one were to be literal, M de Miremont could not be characterised as a young man. But in all other respects the verse suited Max's purpose perfectly, relating, with a conventional hyperbole that was not unreminiscent of Ovid, the agonies of a lover rejected after one stolen kiss.

---

* I hate and love. Perchance you wonder how I do this?
I know not. But I know the pain and it is torment.

...nam simul id factum est, multis diluta labella
guttis abstersisti omnibus articulis,
ne quicquam nostro contractum ex ore maneret,
tamquam commictae spurca saliva lupae.
praeterea infesto miserum me tradere amori
non cessasti omnique excruciare modo...[*]

Yes, that would serve very well. Finding paper, he tore off a thin strip and marked the page.

The next morning, he smuggled the book onto the shelf that held M de Miremont's regular reading. Then he endeavoured to teach himself patience. The Buzzard would not be summoned upstairs until monsieur returned from his ride. Meanwhile, Max must sharpen a new quill and apply himself to calligraphy.

Before the books in the maze could be returned to the shelves, he must record their details—title, author, place and date of publication, classification—on foolscap sheets which, when the cataloguing was complete, would be cut up and pasted alphabetically into heavy leather ledgers. Although it was a clean job, it required concentration—one mistake and the entry must be begun again—and besides Max was out of practice with a quill. On the whole, despite the dust, he preferred emptying shelves: at least that was a task which did not tempt the Buzzard to peer over his shoulder every second minute, tut-tutting when his overloaded nib inked in letters or left a blot, as if the old fowl had taken lessons from Dom Aloysius. And today Max was more than usually prone to mistakes. It seemed an age before Georges arrived to inform the Buzzard that monsieur awaited him.

In the event, Max would be obliged to contain his impatience for a good while longer. When in due course Lesage reappeared, he brought no list. True, there were rare days when monsieur did not require books and—curse Max's wretched luck!—this must be one of them. But he dared not ask, for fear of alerting the Buzzard's suspicions. Nor was his luck to improve. Monsieur sent word by Georges that he would

---

[*]...As soon as [the kiss] was done, having washed your lips with quantities of water
You wiped them with every one of your fingers,
Lest any contagion from my mouth remain,
As if it were the foul spittle of a tainted whore.
Nor, moreover, have you scrupled to render up my woe
To merciless Love and to torture me in every way...

not join them for luncheon. Again this was not unprecedented, although, recalling the old boy's disappearance at La Boissière, Max was inclined to see it as an ill omen. Yet there was probably some simple and undramatic explanation for M de Miremont lunching alone in his apartments. Max urged himself to be philosophical. The Catullus was there, safe on its shelf, and monsieur was bound to need books sooner or later.

Then, all at once, stoicism was redundant. Max had barely returned to his work table when Lesage was standing over him.

"Monsieur Fabien, if you please."

Shit, why was his heart suddenly racing? He forced himself calmly to blot his work and lodge his quill in the inkstand before taking the scrap of paper the Buzzard thrust at him. Again, shit! He had hoped the old boy would send a screed of requests, so that Lesage would be less likely to notice the intruder; but here were only three titles (although he observed that the first was a commentary on *Metamorphoses* by one Cornelius van Zuylen—that at least must be propitious).

He fetched the Van Zuylen and monsieur's second request, then took down the Catullus. Quickly, without thought, just as when he had launched himself from the tower, he placed the Catullus on the top of the other two books and handed the pile to the Buzzard. To his own eyes, the slim green volume, smaller than its companions and with its tell-tale paper marker, looked horribly conspicuous—how could the Buzzard not be tempted, in defiance of his dim sight, to inspect it on his way upstairs? But, as if to prove Max's luck was turning, Lesage, who had been in a vile mood since luncheon—he too seemed put out by monsieur's truancy—merely set the books aside and rang the bell: this, it seemed, was one of the days when he had decided his elderly legs should not be taxed with such a burden. A few minutes later, Philippe appeared and bore the pile safely away.

That was it, then. Ah well, what should Max care if he had invoked disaster? He had nothing to lose. He picked up the quill and endeavoured to settle to his work.

M de Miremont could hardly be expected to risk Lesage's scrutiny by bursting into the library; Max's ear was trained for Philippe's footfall in the anteroom, which must imminently announce that he was required upstairs. But no such signal came. Nothing. After luncheon, it was the Buzzard's present practice to attend to his master's correspondence at the escritoire in M de Miremont's sanctum (although he would have been far more comfortable retiring to his own study); as

Max strained to penetrate the silence, all he could hear was the angry scratch of the secretary's steel nib and the irritating nasal grunts the old fowl emitted when he was concentrating; beyond that, there was only the ticking of the clock on the mantel behind Max's chair.

The clock, as if to taunt him, proceeded to chime the half. Three thirty. How long, damn it, would it have taken Philippe to reach monsieur's study, how long for the old boy to look through the books? Not an hour, for pity's sake!

It was borne in painfully to Max that, while he had warned himself to expect the worst, he had secretly counted on a positive answer. Perhaps he had merely been seduced by nostalgia for La Boissière, but, like a fool, he had wanted...Yet what the hell did it matter what he wanted? He had better brace himself: the longer it took the old fellow to respond, the more likely the news was to be bad.

Work on the classification was now impossible; he had misspelled words, omitted letters and smeared even his few correct entries when he had blotted them. He slid the spoilt sheets into the wastepaper basket—Lesage would have heard him tearing them up—and turned to his glue pot. *L'après-midi d'un faune*, which he had left out to dry overnight, was still on his table. To read might calm his nerves. But no, even that was denied him; Lesage, although he could not possibly see him, possessed some uncanny power of divination that would be alerted in moments. God, to be up to your elbows in books but forbidden their solace, like the shipwrecked mariners on the raft of the Medusa, lost in great wastes of water, yet dying of thirst.

Just before four, Philippe at last reappeared, but only to close the shutters, turn up the gas burners and stoke the fire; he addressed a few words to the Buzzard but paid Max not the slightest attention.

Despite the footman's efforts, it was abominably cold in Max's unheated section of the room; his fingers were numb and he was shivering, although this last was more likely from agitation. He would be better off moving books. Yet supposing the old boy's summons finally came? He had no wish to present himself in his demeaning apron, sweating and with his face streaked with dust.

These thoughts propelled him unwillingly towards another. Suppose there were to be no summons? It was nearly half-past four, two hours after the books had gone up. Supposing it was not a question of news, good or bad, but of no news at all? Supposing M de Miremont had simply decided to disregard the poem, had judged it better to continue as if he had never seen it? It was not unlike the old fellow to ignore disagreeable truths. Not unlike at all. Did Max forget that his sojourn under monsieur's roof had been a chapter of evasions?

Of all possible outcomes, this was the worst, this nothingness, this limbo, this fog of denial. Truth? The old fool was utterly false to his god. He could not face truth if it were blazing before him in conflagration.

Just after the clock had once again chimed the half, the Buzzard, who, although enjoying the benefit of the fire, had also complained of feeling cold, announced that he would take his work upstairs—his vigilance, Max gathered, had finally succumbed to the yawns which had latterly punctuated his grunting. Naturally the secretary could not leave without issuing a great many instructions. Max nodded dumbly and closed his ears—all this was no longer of the slightest moment. He was only sorry his departure would give the old fowl such satisfaction.

At least, now he was alone, he could move about to calm himself. With difficulty he conquered the urge to sweep the ink and glue pots off his table and aim vicious kicks at the piles of books. Pacing backwards and forwards in front of the fire restored the blood to his fingers but did not bring release; he ran up and down the spiral staircase to the mezzanine until he was breathless.

On his final ascent, as he lent on the rail, shoulders heaving, he found himself staring down at the stacked books. Seen from above, spines hidden, they no longer echoed the jewelled colours of the rugs (which had in any case been taken up); instead, their ordered masses resembled rows of ancient sarcophagi, blotched here and there with orange and yellow lichen, tarnished with the dank blues, kidney browns and purples of decay.

Books! 'Vessels of sacred truth', Dom Aloysius used to say. At St Pons, they had held out the hope of freedom. Later, they had been Max's tutors, his inspiration, his pleasure. All for the joy of reading, he had strained his eyes and starved himself of sleep, he had twisted his limbs into uncongenial spaces and even risked his situation. He had happily given his last sous for books or stolen them when his pockets were empty. Yet now, all at once, he could hardly bear the sight of them. He was sick of the reverence accorded to them, these dead things, whose dust tasted metallic like long-dried blood, whose yellowing pages gave off the musty smell of grave cloths. Above all he was sick of the pretence that these desiccated objects held the truths shaping human existence, when it was clear that in reality it was shapeless, brutal and wretched. He was glad he was destined for the army, for a life of action where he need never pick up a book again.

Unable to bear the library for a second longer, he made his escape to the gallery. This was even colder than the library, with both fires unlit, and gloomier too, for the lights were turned low. But it was not his wish to contemplate the pictures—they contrived their own snares; he was grateful merely for a room without books. For some while he sat in the chilly half-light, nursing his misery.

When he eventually dragged himself back to his post, Lesage had reappeared and was fussing over the volumes set aside for the restorer.

"Ah, Monsieur Fabien, at last you honour us with your presence."

Max could scarcely rouse himself to reply. "I was answering a call of nature, monsieur."

"And what a pity it is that nature always calls you to idleness. It had slipped your mind, I take it, that you were supposed to parcel these up for Monsieur Grimaux's man to collect tomorrow morning?"

But Max was staring at his work table. The three books, one brown, one red and one smaller, slimmer and green, sat neatly stacked, as if untouched, exactly as he handed them to Lesage after luncheon. Max could see that even his paper marker was still in place. He must have been harbouring some last vestige of hope, for he felt this discovery like a punch in the stomach.

"Monsieur sent back the books?"

"Evidently they were not what he wanted."

"But did he say—?" Max halted abruptly, for this was a question he could not possibly ask. "I—I mean—did he say he wanted others?"

"Monsieur appears not to know what he wants." And Max distinctly heard the Buzzard add sotto voce: "As usual."

Yet he was distracted by something curious. As he disconsolately approached the table, he realised the returned books occupied the space in which he had left the Mallarmé. But of that there was no sign. Surely the Buzzard would not go so far as to make away with it a second time?

"But of course," Lesage was saying, with a certain note of triumph, "if you had not had found entertainment elsewhere, you could have asked monsieur yourself. Needless to say, discovering him here alone and unattended, I made what excuses for you I could. Alas, he appeared unimpressed."

So M de Miremont had taken the Mallarmé. The old boy had brought the books down himself. Max's heart was suddenly pounding. As he came within arm's reach of the table, he glanced again at the

Catullus. Now he was close enough, he could see that the marker was not where he had placed it, but nearer the front cover.

All Max's warm affection for books came flooding back. His hand was drawn irresistibly to the small green volume.

"Young man, what do you think you are doing?"

"Putting these away, monsieur."

"We have other business to attend to. Be so good as to fetch me the instructions for Monsieur Grimaux you wrote to my dictation."

However at this moment the Buzzard was distracted by the arrival of Philippe with brown paper and twine. Max was given just long enough to discover the marked poem was XLVIII:

mellitos oculos tuos, Iuuenti,
si quis me sinat usque basiare…[*]

But in any case he required to read no further, for he easily recalled that, were the poet permitted to kiss the young man's eyes, he would bestow upon them three hundred thousand kisses and still hunger for more…

---

[*] If someone gave me leave continuously to kiss
Your honey-sweet eyes, Juventius…

CHAPTER TWENTY EIGHT

Max might have been spared much anguish if he could have seen M de Miremont open the Catullus, but he would also have been puzzled. It was most extraordinary, the way monsieur would stare at the book, then jump up from his chair, then fling himself back down again and bury his head in his hands, before commencing the whole sequence all over again. Indeed, if you took account of his dazed smile and his sudden gasps and the wild little laughs he uttered from time to time, you might conclude the noble gentleman had suffered a paroxysm. However, you would be compelled to grant he no longer resembled the melancholic who could scarcely drag himself from his bed in the mornings.

For two days Miremont had been struggling with his duty. His duel with the incubus in the library had merely affirmed his decision: the boy must be sent away, for his own good. Yet whenever he imagined himself uttering the words his strength failed him.

It had not helped that this morning Lesage had treated him to a lengthy enumeration of Max's supposed faults. Miremont might once have been able to deflect his secretary by reminding him of Max's probationary period, but what could he say to Lesage now, when he too had decreed the boy should not be allowed his three months? What could he say to the boy? However he explained it, Max would believe he agreed with Lesage. How could he add this final blow to the destruction of the boy's expectations? Yet, at the same time, the interview with his secretary served as an unpleasant reminder that he must act.

Thus, for different reasons, he could face neither Lesage nor Max at luncheon. He lay on the divan for a while but sleep, which had visited him only fitfully in the last two days, continued fugitive. At last he forced himself to be resolute: he would speak to the boy the next morning, without fail, first thing after breakfast. Meanwhile, although work seemed impossible, he must find some distraction.

However, when Philippe brought the books, Miremont was still stretched out on the divan and barely gave the footman or his burden a glance. Only later did he bestir himself reluctantly.

Whereupon, having instantly recognised the Catullus and

understood who had sent it, yet hardly daring, as his hand had fumbled for the marker, to give shape to the hope that suddenly stopped his breath, he had subsided into the curious state in which we observe him.

Yet, as he sat with his head in his hands, the marquis was not worrying about the innocence of his daughters, or the curiosity of his brother-in-law, or his duty to Thomas or his obligations to generations of Miremonts, past and future. His mind no longer forked, but was set on one single path, which it travelled over and over, as though scarcely believing it must inevitably reach the same destination: the boy was not, could not be, indifferent to him. Periodically, Miremont rose from his chair, intent on rushing down to the library to take Max in his arms; but now it was merely the ubiquity of Lesage that restrained him: for, like a man who wakes one day to find some chronic pressure on a nerve has ceased, he no longer feared the incubus or gave it a moment's thought; perhaps, as he was later to reflect without regret, he had stopped dreading its incursions because it had entirely subsumed him.

"Oh, my darling boy, I owe you an apology—"

"First, monsieur, do you not still owe me two hundred and ninety-nine thousand nine hundred and ninety-nine kisses?"

Thus had Max laughingly brushed aside the speech Miremont had been endeavouring to compose while he had waited for him to arrive in his apartments. In truth, even if Miremont had known where to begin, he had been in such a ferment of anticipation since their rapid exchange of glances at the conclusion of dinner that the solemn phrases of explanation and contrition had refused to take shape, or were quickly obliterated by other thoughts that flared and darted like so many fireflies. And now what words that came, in the moments that allowed speech, were those long suppressed, all the foolish endearments and declarations, all the joyful, reckless incoherence of his passion. He would happily have told Max he loved him three hundred thousand times, simply to relish over and over the unfamiliar taste of the words, which was indeed as sweet as honey.

Yet, in the end, as they finally lay together exhausted on the rug before the bedroom fire, explanations could not be avoided. It seemed to Miremont a matter of honour that he should bring himself to account, for he was now agonisingly aware that the lofty moral precepts which, mere hours ago, had justified his renunciation, were nothing more than pitiful self-deception.

To begin with, Max listened in silence. Only when Miremont

came to the matter of his vow did the boy's eyes widen. Then he let out a great hoot of laughter.

Miremont could not help being a little offended. "My dear, I wanted to help you without exacting any return."

"Monsieur, I have already lived in the cloister."

"But I could not be certain…If you had felt obliged…It would have been abhorrent to me if, against your inclination…"

Here it was Max's turn to be offended, at least in show. "I had no idea I was such a lacklustre lover."

"No, my darling boy, that is not—"

"If monsieur is not satisfied, I must do my best to remedy the situation."

"No! Please! My dear Max—" From the brief skirmish that followed, Miremont emerged gasping with laughter and begging for mercy. "Enough! Don't taunt me with your youth, you wretch. *Futuimus bene.*"

Max had rolled away onto his stomach, from where, with his chin propped on his forearm, he grinned at Miremont. "Well, that's a relief. At least I shan't have to leave tomorrow."

"L-leave?" Miremont started guiltily, recalling this morning's absurd decision and wondering if, uncannily, the boy had read his mind.

"If Plato had triumphed over Catullus, I was intending to ask for my cards."

This should not, Miremont realised, have come as such a shock. After all, he had seen that the boy was miserable, even if, as it now appeared, he had attributed his dejection to the wrong cause. But somehow, as the keeper of the big cats sees the frustrated pacing of the leopard, yet takes for granted that it is powerless to escape, Miremont, in all his agonising and in spite of knowing the boy's obstinate pride, had neglected the possibility that Max might take command of his own fate. Even now, he burst out with "But, dear boy, where would you have gone?"

The answer made him shiver, for he could not but be reminded of poor Thomas. To ward off the vision of Max lying mutilated or dead in some blood-sodden colonial furrow, he drew the boy back into his arms. "God, I've been such a confounded fool! And yet I believed I was acting from the highest motives."

But Max merely grinned. "You don't give a fig for Plato, monsieur. And never did."

"No, truly, I…" Yet it was pointless to protest. He could not shirk his duty to be rigorously honest. "Oh, my darling boy, when I say I am a fool I flatter myself. The truth is, I've been an abject coward."

He hung his head, fearing Max's satirical glint. But the boy looked at him steadily, without a trace of mockery. Then, as if in absolution, he laid his lips on Miremont's brow, so that Miremont was momentarily threatened by the second disgrace of tears.

"My dear, daft monsieur, there is nothing shameful in self-preservation. Both of us should avoid scandal as we'd avoid smallpox."

"Darling boy, I no longer care. Now that I have you back, I'm resolved to be valiant."

"But you should care. And I too—I have no interest in seeing my future prospects blighted. I shall make you a vow, one that won't carry the curse of eternal chastity. I promise that no word or action of mine will compromise you and I shall make it my unfailing duty to safeguard your honour."

Miremont was touched by the solemnity of this declaration. "Dearest Max, you know I have always trusted your discretion."

"But should you have trusted it? I ought never to have allowed us to tempt fate as we did at La Boissière."

"Ah, but it was all so delightful."

"And dangerous, monsieur. We must never again take such risks."

Miremont smiled wistfully. "No more hunting for my pince-nez?"

"No more cream with your coffee in the library."

"No more heroic leaps from windows?"

"Definitely not."

"Well, that at least is a blessing."

"And, monsieur, there is another pressing necessity. We must somehow make you a better liar."

Miremont was considerably taken aback. "Ah but, darling boy, that is unfair! I thought I had done rather well with dear old Van Zuylen."

"Granted, it was a promising beginning. But what were you thinking of this afternoon?"

"Of you, of course, and how ridiculously happy you had made me."

But Max, though he returned the kiss that accompanied these words, refused to be diverted. "It was madness to go down to the library yourself. And then, what about dinner?"

"Ah, well, yes. I allow that was a slip."

"'I must thank you, Monsieur Fabien, for recovering the Mallarmé.

I had forgotten your remarkable talent for retrieving missing books.'"

"How could I help recalling Mme de Claireville's Catullus?"

"A remarkable talent indeed, when I was in Bruges and had never met you. The gift of clairvoyance."

"I don't believe the poor fellow noticed. He was distracted by your wickedly handing him credit for the Mallarmé."

Here Max's feigned severity, which had in any case been wavering, collapsed into laughter. "God! He didn't know whether to be furious or to lap up your paean to his efficiency."

"Poor Lesage, it was unfair and I must make it up to him. But I craved the pleasure of seeing you smile again—even if it were only to grin into your soup."

"I caught your look, monsieur. And all your other looks. And if old Lesage could see further than his nose—"

"My dear Max, don't." Miremont stroked the boy's cheek. "No more lectures. I adore you and naturally I wish to show it. Oh, I'm not quite fit for Charenton yet, I know that isn't possible, for your sake as much as mine. But all the same...to treat what is between us as a sordid secret...I shall try to become a more proficient liar, but I was brought up to value truth. "

"Ah, truth," Max could not help murmuring with a wry smile.

"I fear it is ingrained in me. 'Truth is the fount of honour'—so my father always said."

"But which truth? Beauty's truth or the one at the bottom of a bottle? The church's or nature's? The truth Aristotle prefers to Plato or the sort Voltaire reserves for the dead? Forgive me, monsieur, but it seems a rather slippery creature."

"The simple truth that flows from one's own conscience. 'To thine own self be true.' That was another favourite of my father's. 'To thine own self be true and it must follow, as the night the day, thou canst not then be false to any man.'"

"To thine own self?"

"Yes, of course, one must always..." But Miremont faltered, for unless he were to gainsay all he had come to understand about himself in the last few hours he could not avoid the paradox.

The boy was grinning. "And there it is, monsieur. If you and I are to be true to ourselves, then, as night follows day, we must be false to the rest of the world."

Not long afterwards, when the clock had warned that the boy must depart and when Miremont sat in his dressing gown in the welcome ease of an armchair—for all his romantic sentiments, he had found the sensuous pleasures of the fireside and Bukhara silk rather unforgiving of middle-aged bones—one of Tarascon's aphorisms came to him suddenly. What was it? 'Be true to yourself, the man who is true to others is an inveterate liar'? Miremont recalled he had considered it specious. But now, watching the boy pull on his clothes and dreading, as he must, the imminent moment of their parting, he was inclined to hear consoling wisdom in Tarascon's words.

Of course Miremont did not altogether give up fretting about his daughters or feeling guilty about Thomas and Lesage or agonising over his duty to his lineage; it was no more in his nature to do so than it is for water to flow uphill. Nor did he cease to ponder the vexed question of integrity: was it possible for a man to live honourably when what was at his life's core must school him in every refinement of deceit? But these concerns no longer crushed him, for they were outweighed by his happiness.

It remained an immeasurable pleasure to tell the boy he loved him. Miremont recalled making this declaration to Aline in the first months of their marriage; he had uttered the words because, with the naivety of youth, he had believed it to be his duty and because he had hoped that, once planted like magic beans, they would take root and grow. But now, in this troubling debate about truth and lies, these three words were at last his to speak with absolute veracity. Not that he did not soon become aware of the perils of repetition; what had begun as a simple statement of fact could easily turn itself into a question, or even a demand.

He longed, he must confess it, to receive the echo of his words from Max's lips. Yet when it did not come, he endeavoured to rein in his disappointment. The boy had sent him the poem, he too had been made wretched by their estrangement, he was as passionate and affectionate as Miremont could have wished. It was the curse of love, as Miremont ought to know too well, this urge to ignore the riches already spread before one and peer obsessively into gutters, chasing after small change—a frown, a sigh, longed-for words not spoken, even the boy's curious concern for his 'future prospects', when where should his future lie except at Miremont's side? Love, if one let it, would always want more and would not rest until it had gambled away its fortune. Though Miremont, in his present elation, could scarcely bring to mind the precise degree of his suffering over the past months, he did recall it had been needless. He must learn to be content with what he had.

If guilt were a hard habit to break, so too, it seemed, was cowardice. For a week or two, Miremont's heart still lurched when callers were announced. But the foundations of the Hôtel de Miremont did not quake. On the contrary, the visitors Miremont feared most—his family—appeared supremely indifferent to the boy's existence.

True, Max was generally hidden away in the library and Sunday, when Clotilde and her family paid their weekly filial visit, was the boy's day off. But when Clotilde did chance to call on an errand from her mother—there was always some complaint about the amenities of Miremont-St-Fleur that the marquis' elder daughter felt it her duty to relate—Miremont, as he accompanied her downstairs, was startled to see Max crossing the hall. His first and craven impulse was to ignore the boy. But no, that in itself would appear questionable. He called Max back.

"My dear, this is Monsieur Fabien, who is cataloguing the library."

But Clotilde merely answered Max's bow of the head with a nod and a murmur, before continuing her account of baby Agathe's remarkable precocity as though the interruption had never taken place.

Much the same occurred with Constant and his sons. Constant was moved to remark (thankfully out of Lesage's hearing, since Miremont felt it wisest not to complicate matters by correcting his brother-in-law's misapprehension) that it was certainly time Miremont got in some young blood and retired that damn-fool secretary of his. But otherwise the boy, having once been formally acknowledged, was of no further interest.

Miremont supposed he should be grateful. He should be glad they considered him such an old fogey that he could not be guilty of the merest peccadillo, let alone this enormity. He should be—he was—thankful to Max for keeping so punctiliously to his vow, for maintaining a correct and modest demeanour only one degree less opaque than his footman's manner. Yet Miremont also nursed a perverse resentment: he did not forget the lesson of their first encounter and every time he saw Clotilde look through the boy with the gracious myopia she reserved for servants he felt ashamed on her behalf. Likewise it chafed him that his nephews, much of an age with Max and usually agreeable generous-hearted lads, would never for one instant consider him their equal. Once again Miremont was stung by the injustice of it—that

Max should be held back by the misfortune of his birth, that he could not, like Edmond and Roland, glory in the freedoms of youth, but must stand always in the shadows.

Yet, as successive dinner guests—the Rosenthals, the Ricards, the La Marnes—raised no eyebrows at the boy's presence at his table, Miremont could not but admit his abiding emotion was profound relief.

Thomas, needless to say, was another matter. By now Miremont understood that, however carefully Max covered his traces, Thomas would not be deceived. But he had not bargained for the preternatural sharpness of his valet's intuition; or perhaps Max was right and, despite his care to conceal his agitation as Thomas had undressed him that first giddy night, he had been pathetically transparent. At any rate the next morning, from the savagery with which Thomas slammed down Miremont's bowl of chocolate and tore aside the curtains, it was plain that he knew. Miremont was unsurprised to be splashed liberally with foam as the brush clattered angrily in the shaving bowl and to sustain a wound to his earlobe that took some minutes to staunch. Nor had things improved when he returned from his morning ride; his clothes were not laid out but heaped, crumpled, on the bed, while Thomas tugged at his riding boots with such ferocity that he was nearly hauled from his chair.

Apart from a few growls on Thomas' part and the occasional grinding of his teeth, this war was waged in silence, for Miremont knew rebuke was futile. He did, however, despite dreading what he might see, several times try to force his valet to meet his glance. But, whether during the shave, or when Thomas was tying his riding stock unpleasantly tight, or later when the simple business of fastening Miremont's collar threatened injury to his Adam's apple, although their faces were so close that Miremont could see every taut sinew in his servant's jaw and smell his breath, which this morning reeked of aniseed, Thomas still contrived to evade him.

Only at the last, as the valet was belabouring his master's shoulders with a brush, did their eyes accidentally meet in the glass; and this time it was Miremont who looked away quickly, whatever mollifying words he had intended—God knew which—dying on his lips. What he had glimpsed in that single grim eye was a look he had not seen for many years, yet vividly remembered, since it had made him shudder then as it did now: a blank, hard annihilating look that prompted him to count himself lucky his shave had endangered no more than his ear. That was unworthy, of course; Thomas would not harm him, however provoked. But all the same Miremont felt a sudden concern for Max.

So it was even something of a relief when Boussec came to see him in the late afternoon: Thomas, Boussec regretted to inform him, had disappeared after luncheon and had not been seen since; if monsieur permitted, Philippe would dress him for dinner. Thomas would do as he always did when he went missing, Miremont supposed—return after several hours still fractious and stinking of drink but with the rebellion drained out of him by the time he awoke the next morning.

Miremont, as we have seen, did not readily feel anger at his valet. But now—perhaps to assuage his guilt—he was consumed with righteous fury. How dare Thomas try to blight his newfound happiness! For twenty-seven years Miremont had put up with his silence and his moods and his grotesque antics. Would any sane man take one week of such behaviour from his manservant? Did twenty-seven years of tolerance not deserve some loyalty? When Miremont had sworn to his father that he would look after Thomas, he had not sworn also to surrender his life to the fellow. Plenty of men, if Tarascon's gossip were only half-believed, indulged in pleasures more exotic than the conventional string of mistresses—did their valets presume to sit in judgement on them? If Thomas's conscience was too fastidious to brook the only love Miremont was capable of enjoying—yes, shameful in the eyes of the world, but no longer shameful to him—then damn the fellow, he could go back to the country.

In truth, Miremont's happiness that first day was too overwhelming to be blighted by Thomas; his anger and indeed Thomas himself were soon forgotten as he contemplated the night ahead: even the following morning, he could greet the news that his manservant continued missing with a mere shrug of irritation. But the second day slipped into the third and Georges, who had been sent out by Boussec to scour the wine shops and cafés, returned alone yet again and with nothing helpful to report. Thomas had never been gone so long before. Miremont, like a man waking from a dream, confronted his own indifference first with astonishment, then with horror.

He recalled the Arthur Thomas, tall and strong and clear-eyed, who had been the hero of his youth. He recalled—and this with the force of revelation—how much he had loved him, how he had wept at his loss. He recalled, too, crouching in Thomas' filthy lair beneath the

Old Manoir; he saw again how Thomas had looked at him when, with all the folly of his sixteen years, he had sought to console him; and it was borne in upon Miremont that this look, even when he had seen it in his cheval glass not three days ago, for all that it invoked dissolution and extinction, threatened no one but Thomas himself.

Miremont summoned Boussec. Georges was reinforced in his search by Philippe, Théo and the grooms. Boussec was deputed to contact the local gendarmerie; after all, it was not impossible Thomas had been arrested. For Miremont the thought of Thomas stubbornly, silently awaiting rescue from a police cell was comforting compared with the other visions that assailed him—Thomas' water-logged body being hauled from the Seine or laid out for public view on blood-stained zinc in the Morgue.

That night, since he had instructed Boussec to come to his apartments if there were any news, whatever the hour, Miremont was obliged to forego his visit from Max. Besides, it seemed profane to abandon himself to pleasure—he was still mortified by his previous indifference. He spent a wretched night, battling with his gruesome imaginings and with other familiar demons that plagued him with the words 'judgement' and 'retribution' in apocalyptic tones.

But in the morning, Boussec, bringing Miremont's chocolate himself, announced, with only a slight tempering of his usual lugubrious air, that Thomas had returned. Far from having made away with himself, Miremont's valet had been found snoring in a confessional at St Sulpice when the priests had arrived to say early mass. One of them had recognised him; although he had never attended services, the Father had on several occasions noticed his distinctive figure in the chapel of the Virgin Mary, bowed in prayer before the votive candles, and had deduced from his dress and bearing that he must be a servant from the great house nearby.

Delivered to the ministrations of Mme Mercier, Thomas was found to be still half-drunk and covered in blood from a gash above his eyebrow; his jaw had come off the worse from some earlier fight, he had lost a tooth, the overcoat Miremont had given him at New Year and every last sou in his pockets, and he was inclined to limp. But otherwise, although no one could discover where he had spent the preceding three nights, he seemed to have suffered no great harm, indeed appeared rather more tractable than he often was after such episodes: Mme Mercier had applied a compress to his forehead and he was at present devouring tartines as if he had not eaten for weeks; it was Boussec's view that all would be well if he were left to sleep it off as usual.

Miremont heaved a long sigh. He sent Boussec round to the church with a contribution to the offertory and Philippe to Gérard, for, while Boussec might be right, no harm could come from calling in the doctor. Miremont's relief left him too exhausted to ride. Yet gradually, as the morning progressed and he sat, enervated, in his study, unable to concentrate, some of his former anger returned: he was grateful that, despite the thundering voices in his head, he had not been tempted to strike some binding deal with fate. Whatever Thomas' dialogue with Our Lady—not that Miremont had ever before heard mention that he was in any way devout—he must accept Max's presence. Miremont would speak to him sternly but fairly. And perhaps, given the gravity of the moment and if only to acknowledge the alarm and confusion he had caused, Thomas might for once be moved to speak out too.

But in the event, when Thomas reappeared the next morning, neither spoke. Miremont found it an impossibility and his valet was his usual mute self. It could not be said, however, that they continued as if nothing had changed, although Miremont could hardly complain about the precision of his shave or the care with which his shirt and riding breeches were laid out. The alteration in Thomas' manner was certainly not due to penitence, nor did it suggest resignation—rather, as the valet went about Miremont's apartments, still limping but quietly performing his customary tasks, it was as if he were there only in effigy; though he was clean-shaven, correctly dressed and this morning exhaled violet cachous, the real Thomas had abstracted himself, had withdrawn once again to the unreachable depths of his lair.

This was not at all as Miremont had hoped (he realised how greatly he had longed for some exchange of words, some few broken syllables of conciliation); however, it was enough to restore a precarious harmony to the household.

CHAPTER TWENTY NINE

Although Miremont's fear of callers had proved generally unfounded, there were two visitors who were bound to cause him anxiety. Or rather, there were three; but the third was unexpected.

Dr Gérard still came for chess every week, but, since this was always on a Thursday, Max's other evening off, the doctor had yet to encounter the boy. However, when he was called in to attend Thomas and went upstairs afterwards to make his report, Max was in Miremont's study—Miremont, after their separation the night before, had found a pretext to extract the boy from the library for a few precious minutes.

Miremont had grown to feel more at ease with Gérard than with almost anyone else he knew: he had always trusted the doctor's lack of affectation and valued the sharp mind beneath his clumsy exterior; but as, little by little in the face of Gérard's inveterate modesty, he had gleaned more knowledge of his friend's life—the doctor, it transpired, worked gratis two afternoons a week at the Hotel-Dieu and had published papers on the spread of infectious fevers amongst the indigent—so Miremont had come greatly to respect a dedication that seemed immune either to selfish considerations or to the prejudices of society, and to think his friend the model of impartial kindness.

Of course, he should have allowed for the acuteness of Gérard's perceptions; and for the fact that on Thursday, not two days ago, the doctor had noted his miraculously restored spirits. Perhaps he was not as much on his guard as he should have been.

All the same, he and the boy must have appeared innocent enough—they stood apart on either side of the mantelpiece and, besides, the doors through to the sitting room were thrown wide open. Miremont was unprepared to be fathomed so instantly, to observe how, as Max was presented to him, Gérard, after his gaze had taken in the boy, glanced quickly at Miremont, then back at the boy, not questioningly but rather, it seemed, for confirmation. Nor was Miremont any less perturbed by the rapid sequence of expressions that crossed the open landscape of the doctor's large grey face. For they included shock, followed by distinct disapproval.

Gérard evidently knew he had given himself away; after Max had taken his departure and he and Miremont were alone, there followed a moment of distressing awkwardness in which he clasped and unclasped his big pale hands and seemed not to know where to put himself, regarding the chair Miremont indicated to him with trepidation, as if expecting to wreak its immediate destruction. When he was finally persuaded to sit, one of his elbows chanced to knock several books from the table, rendering his mortification complete. He hurriedly conveyed his opinion of Thomas' injuries: none was serious, a sprained ankle, various cuts and bruises—even the contusion to the left brow looked worse than it was and should heal quickly. Then, saying he had promised his sister to call in on a charity bazaar run by one of her committees, he made his escape.

All thoughts of Thomas displaced, Miremont sat for a long time with his head in his hands. Naturally he feared he had lost the doctor's friendship. But other more complicated emotions beset him. For what had startled him most about Gérard's reaction was not his shock nor even his disapproval; it was his expression when he had first looked at Max. Miremont could recall that pent-up hunger only too well, the flash of desire sparked indiscriminately by any passing glimpse of male pulchritude.

He was as certain as he could be that his friend did not realise he had caught this flicker: indeed it was impossible to tell whether Gérard himself had been aware of it; perhaps the poor man believed he was now so inured to temptation that he was at last immune. Fellow-feeling, compassion, a deeper understanding of the sympathy between them, even joy—all these emotions commingled with Miremont's distress. He also felt remarkably foolish. For it was clear that all along, despite his litany of misleading symptoms, Gérard had perfectly understood the cause of his affliction.

He recalled their very first conversation, remembered how Gérard had talked of acceptance and renunciation, of seeking satisfaction in work. The doctor had conscientiously taken his own prescription and had expected Miremont, like-minded as they were, to do the same. Not a week ago, Miremont was startled to realise, he would have agreed and redoubled his efforts to remain celibate.

But now, when he thought of all his friend had renounced, he grieved for him. Gérard bore his sacrifice stoically; apart from an occasional faint melancholy he had never struck Miremont as unhappy. But that, as Miremont now understood, was because he could have no true measure of his loss. Miremont mourned on Gérard's behalf the joys, so richly deserved by such a generous-hearted man, that were denied him.

And yet, exalted by love though he was, he admired Gérard's strength of will and even felt ashamed that he lacked it. He was saddened to have embarrassed and disappointed his friend. If any of his confused emotions predominated, it was not pity, but a fresh access of affection for the doctor, so that it wrenched his heart to think their friendship might cool.

However, Gérard, who had so patently regretted betraying his disapproval, seemed resolved to stifle it, if not banish it altogether. Neither the incident nor its cause was ever referred to and, albeit that a certain constraint stiffened the first moments of their next encounter, the chess evenings resumed their comfortable intimacy.

Miremont was thankful; but, although there was no diminution of the friendship, two things grieved him: that he could not speak honestly to the friend who, above all others, should have been able to understand him; and that their friendship must perforce exclude Max, so that Gérard would never come to appreciate the boy's qualities nor see why Miremont was bound to love him.

The other two visitors Miremont anticipated with a certain dread were Achille de Tarascon and Catherine de Claireville.

Tarascon would have little trouble accepting that Miremont required a handsome youth to catalogue his library; on the contrary, he would probably chalk it up as a victory for his proselytising powers. Miremont's difficulty lay in two other directions.

The first was that Tarascon might remember Max from La Boissière or the Hôtel de Claireville. Miremont had reconsidered his original plan of confiding in the comte, for he was unconvinced that Tarascon would honour any promise he might give. All the same, Lesage was a great admirer of the poet and wit—if by some chance Tarascon did remember, he might not scruple to pass on such an interesting piece of information.

The second presented a further compelling reason for not taking Tarascon into his confidence and was still so disturbing to Miremont that he wished not to think of it. He remained haunted by his suspicion that Max and Tarascon had been lovers, that this beautiful boy, every hand's breadth of whose body he adored, had willingly lent himself to Tarascon's grubby pleasures. It made no difference that he was now on better terms with the comte and, as long as it were judiciously rationed, quite enjoyed his company; every so often, if only for a second, he would be assailed by this sickening vision. But let it remain merely that—a vision, a suspicion, vague, flimsy, lacking the repugnant substance of fact. Miremont held a superstitious fear that, should the two of them meet, he would be forced to read the truth in their faces.

Of course, when he was with Max, he knew that this was nonsense, that his absurd jealousy did the boy injustice—at La Boissière, Tarascon, viewing Max in his footman's livery and at some distance, had simply mistaken him for another youth. All the same, Miremont was relieved that circumstances kept them apart. His own encounters with Tarascon were generally at the opera or at Constant's and, on the rare occasion the comte paid him a call, he was duly grateful that Lesage kept Max hidden. Two months after Max's arrival at the Hôtel de Miremont Tarascon had still been granted no sight of the boy. However Miremont was painfully aware this could not continue forever.

One March afternoon when the comte called and the conversation had turned to his favourite theme, whether art could have any moral purpose—Tarascon naturally thought not—he cited as proof of his thesis the vagabond poet François Villon, who was supposed to have written his first testament, *Le lais*, to provide him with an alibi for murder. Whereupon Miremont, who was tiring of the topic, foolishly mentioned that amongst the contents of his library was the fifteenth-century first edition of Villon's works. The comte was keen to see it and Miremont said he would send for Lesage to bring it upstairs; but Tarascon insisted he would be delighted to go down to the library— besides he was interested in how the catalogue was progressing.

In vain did Miremont describe the dust, the confusion, the piles of books still carpeting the floor; Tarascon waved all that aside with a flash of his emerald.

"My dear, I shall not be denied. From what I am told by your faithful amanuensis"—he meant Lesage—"it is a task of such magnitude as to make the Great Library of Alexandria seem a bookstall."

When Miremont and Tarascon entered, Lesage was at the escritoire at the far end of the room and Max, in shirtsleeves and apron, was poised at the summit of the library steps. Lesage, at the sound of Tarascon's voice, came forward with an effusive greeting. Meanwhile, Miremont was thoroughly flustered: he was no longer quite sure what he expected and hardly dared look at Max.

Tarascon having already proclaimed to Lesage the purpose of

their visit, the boy was in any case despatched immediately to the mezzanine, where the medieval manuscripts were kept. While they awaited his return, the comte and Lesage exchanged tittle-tattle: Tarascon was always delighted to confess he had just dined with Princess This or driven in the Bois with the Duchess of That and Lesage, who remembered these personages from Aline's reign, would ask about their health and their near relations as if he were one of their intimates. This interval enabled Miremont to observe that yes, the comte's attention, which was never properly held by any conversation not entirely centred on himself, did drift to follow the movement of the boy's buttocks and thighs as he ascended the spiral staircase—but, as even Miremont must admit, it was only a fleeting interest, certainly no more than to be expected from Tarascon, and appeared to vanish altogether once the Villon was produced.

As for the boy, he was unsmiling and—perhaps this was merely Miremont's fancy—rather pale. Miremont also noted that, when Max brought down the book and removed its protective chemise of linen, he handed it quickly to Lesage, so that it was the secretary who settled beside Tarascon at Max's table, opening the metal clasp that fastened the oak covers and assisting the visitor to turn the fragile pages as he perused their woodcut miniatures. Yet this was no doubt as Lesage had decreed. Altogether, Miremont could not have said there was anything in Max's manner that was not dictated by discretion; and when, as he and Tarascon were leaving, he took advantage of Lesage's profuse farewells to shoot the boy a smile, he was reassured by the grin that answered it.

As he and his guest walked back through the anteroom and across the hall, Miremont felt relieved and not a little foolish. What cataclysm had his preposterous jealousy anticipated? Max was clearly indifferent to Tarascon and Miremont should have cherished the moments of sanity that told him Tarascon did not know the boy.

But, on the first landing, the comte paused. "That youth?"

Miremont's heart stopped. "I beg your pardon?"

"Your amanuensis's cup-bearer. The Adonis in the tantalising apron. I could swear I've seen him before."

There was a possibility—no, a probability, which Miremont clung to—that this was merely a manifestation of the lesser threat, that Tarascon remembered Max from Catherine's. Miremont essayed a shrug, praying his physiognomy was at last responding to Max's tuition. "Most unlikely, my dear fellow. Monsieur Fabien came to me from Bruges."

Tarascon appeared satisfied with this and they continued on to Miremont's apartments. It was only after another half an hour, when the comte announced he really must depart and was extinguishing his cigarette, that he suddenly fixed Miremont with a portentous look.

"My dear Miremont, I should beware."

Miremont's cigarette shed ash on his waistcoat.

"I now recall my encounter with that young man of yours. He's no Adonis, my dear fellow, but a centaur who devours human flesh. Or rather a Siren. Not last week, he sang to me sweetly and lured me onto the rocks of the Champs Elysées, whereupon he stole my purse and attempted to break my head."

"But—that's impossible!"

"Impossible it most certainly was. He left me without money for a cab and I was obliged to walk home. The young have stripped sin of all decency. They set a dreadful example to their elders."

"My dear Tarascon…" The requirement for clear thought struggled with Miremont's outrage. "Last week, you say? What day, exactly?"

"Miremont, Miremont! You really must not sully the purity of truth with facts. It may have been the week before. I cannot tell you the date, I am not a calendar."

"Well, was it after dark? If so, you could easily be mistaken—"

"I should not mistake that scar on his temple." The comte, as he rose to leave, reached out to pat Miremont's shoulder. "My dear fellow, I speak as your friend. The boy is a worse ruffian than Villon. Count your spoons and lock away your knives."

Miremont did not doubt for a moment that Achille de Tarascon's story was a calumny. Even if the comte had answered him by naming a Thursday or a Sunday, Miremont would not have believed him. But that still left the question—why had he troubled to tell such a lie? Miremont could discover no motive that did not foment his own jealousy.

He had resolved to say nothing to Max. Yet that evening he could think of little else and by the time Max arrived in his rooms his agitation was so apparent the boy enquired if he were unwell.

Miremont waved him to an armchair, then sat down himself, rather heavily, on the chaise at the end of the bed. He took a deep breath. "My dear boy, do you know Monsieur le comte de Tarascon?"

"Monsieur de Tarascon?" Was Max's surprise a trifle overdone, or was that once again Miremont's fancy? "Well, naturally I know him, not least because he was here this afternoon."

"I mean, have you—are you in any way acquainted with him?"

"No, how should I be?"

"He seems to know you."

"My dear monsieur, is that the trouble? Just tell him he's mistaken. He can't be positive he saw me at Madame de Claireville's. Monsieur le comte's interest in the lower orders doesn't extend above the waist."

Miremont could not escape the notion that the boy was fencing with him and besides this last remark, although delivered with a smile, had an edge that did nothing to still his fears. He did not wish to press on but felt he was left with no choice.

"Monsieur de Tarascon insists he has met you before. And dear boy, forgive me—when we came into the library this afternoon I could not help observing that you were—how shall I put it?—more than usually on your guard."

"I don't like Monsieur le comte. And neither, I think, do you." Max rose all at once and, coming over to Miremont, put his hands on his shoulders. "The answer is no, monsieur. I would sooner thrust my cock into a running sewer."

"My darling boy, I had no intention…I was certainly not going to…"

"Indeed you were." The boy laughed. The alarming ferocity that had gripped him a moment earlier seemed to vanish as suddenly as it had appeared. He sat down beside Miremont. "Whatever did he say to you?"

Miremont no longer knew what to believe. For all Max's professed skills in the art of deception, he thought he could tell when the boy was truthful. And, although he had been startled by his vehemence, he had seen that Max was startled by it too, that he had not intended to reveal so much of himself, so that it was hard not to conclude his denial was heart-felt. Nor was it unreasonable that Max should instinctively be repelled by Achille de Tarascon; after all, he was right, Miremont had shared—still shared—the same instinct. He wanted to believe the boy and, besides, his mortification at finding his jealousy was so apparent encouraged him to drop the matter. But, all the same, there was the unresolved question of Tarascon's behaviour.

Miremont put his hand on the boy's knee. "My dear, forgive me, I never truly thought…I hope you can believe…I gave no credit to Monsieur de Tarascon's absurd allegation when he made it and I give no credit to it now." Reluctantly he repeated Tarascon's story.

"What the—? The vile old goat!" There could be no doubt this time that Max's astonishment was genuine. "And you believed this, monsieur?"

"No, my darling boy, of course not. As I have said, I thought it a preposterous fiction from the outset. But what disturbs—what puzzles me, is why he should have invented it?"

Max returned Miremont's gaze, returned it, as Miremont was comforted to see, without flinching. "Perhaps Monsieur le comte's amnesia is miraculously cured when he is scorned."

"Then he did…?"

"Of course. In Bordeaux. He tried with all the footmen. And his fairy tale is almost accurate in one particular. He could see I should resculpt his profile if he persisted."

"Oh, my dear boy. "

Max laughed. "But I'm afraid I flatter myself. Monsieur de Tarascon does not know me from Adam. The answer to the puzzle is a good deal more obvious."

Miremont sighed. "Alas, not to me."

The boy gave him a wry smile. "He wanted you to think exactly what you were thinking."

From then on, Miremont was not at home to Tarascon and kept him at a careful distance whenever they chanced to meet.

Catherine had been away for the month of January, staying with Princess Orsini in Tangier, but she was bound to call on her return to Paris. Miremont could not precisely understand why he failed to anticipate her visit with his usual pleasure.

Of course, in her absence his altruistic motives for taking Max into his household had entirely broken down, but that should hardly present a difficulty, since she had never believed them. Moreover, after their first painful conversation, she appeared to have reached a generous acceptance of the situation, even viewing it with what, if he were not talking about Catherine, Miremont might have described as motherly interest. But perhaps that was the problem.

Catherine did not inspire in him the sort of sickening, debilitating jealousy that he felt towards Tarascon; yet he could not quite forget that the boy might once have shared her bed, for there was something irritatingly proprietorial in her concern: it was as though Max were on loan to him like a picture or a vase, whose qualities only she understood and knew how to show to advantage. She was bound to claim a right to inspect the boy to ensure he was suitably installed in his new location.

Miremont was not mistaken. Catherine allowed herself to describe the company at Princess Orsini's—it had included Beatrice Donyani, with whom she had become firm friends; nor did she omit to relate the latest scandal about Aristide de Bellac and Iphigénie Zelenska—Bellac had lost a fortune backing some literary journal, the name of which temporarily escaped her, which had occasioned Génie, although now visibly in an interesting condition, to turn her interest elsewhere. But when, fixing Miremont with her sweetest smile, she remarked that she need never have gone away, for she realised, looking at him, that if she sought rejuvenation she should have stayed at home with Ovid, he could be in no doubt the moment had arrived.

"My dear, he's downstairs, in the library. With Lesage."

"Then send for him. I wish to see him."

"Dearest, we have not chipped or cracked him in your absence."

"Don't be provoking, Armand."

Miremont sighed. "You must understand, it is not so easy—Lesage is bound to wonder why Madame la duchesse de Claireville—"

"Truly, you are impossible! Why not just ask him to bring up a book?"

"Because Lesage will take it upon himself to bring it."

Catherine pushed aside her teacup in exasperation. "Then is it, my dear Armand, beyond the scope of your invention to think of some other excuse? You must have told that old ninny some fable when the boy arrived."

When Miremont related the story he and Max had concocted, Mme de Claireville could not restrain her laughter. "A seminarian, eh? Well then, say…say I wish to consult the boy on a point of theology."

The absurdity of this made Miremont laugh too. He touched the bell to summon Philippe and shortly afterwards Max appeared in the Little Salon. Miremont, whose own proprietorial feelings were stirred, was pleased to note this was not one of his days for moving books—his hair, which was growing out of its brutal servant's cut, was tidily combed and his face bore no smears of dust. Miremont stood back with some pride as Mme de Claireville, with approval he thought, looked the boy up and down.

Thus he was all the more astonished when she turned to him peremptorily. "Thank you, Armand. You may leave us now."

"But, my dear—"

"We wish to talk. You may return in ten minutes."

As Miremont took his departure, Mme de Claireville appeared

preoccupied with peeling off her right-hand glove. Only when she heard the doors close did she rise from her sofa and walk across to where Max was standing. She smiled at him.

"Well, Jean—Max—Fabien—whatever you call yourself—I must congratulate you. You have certainly gone up in the world. That suit must delight your vanity."

Then, drawing herself up on tip-toe, she raised her right hand and struck him with full force across the cheek.

"That is a warning. M de Miremont is one of my oldest, dearest friends. Indeed, I would go further—he is the brother nature denied me. So, if I ever hear so much as a whisper that you are up to your usual tricks, you shall have me to answer to."

A little breathless, she stepped back to inspect her work. While he was very pale, so that the mark of her palm showed crimson beneath his left cheekbone, she was obliged to admit he had taken it rather well, rocking a little from the impact but otherwise remaining stock still. Nevertheless, he could not quite master his injured pride; it blazed in his eyes as she scrutinised him.

"Excellent," she said. "I'm delighted that is clear." With a swirl of her train, she returned to the sofa to retrieve her glove.

But he did not take his dismissal. Instead, as if to remind her that he was no longer in her service, he moved from his respectful retirement near the china cabinet and, although he did not go so far as to seat himself without permission, stood with his hand resting lightly on the back of a chair.

"Madame is most—emphatic. But not, forgive me, clear. What are these tricks that madame refers to?"

Mme de Claireville paused from easing her fingers into their second skin of kid. "Insolence, for one. Not to mention your tall stories."

He raised his eyebrows.

"I trust you will not lie to Monsieur de Miremont as you lied to me."

"I have never lied to madame."

"By swearing your undying love?"

"That was not entirely a lie."

If madame's expression were inclined to soften, she quickly rearranged it. "It was not entirely the truth either. And then there is the brawling."

"Brawling?"

"Which you managed to convince my poor Vincent was an affair of honour. So that I, hardly less gullible than he, took pity on you, when I should have turned you out on your ear. Poor Michel was never quite the same again."

"Some might count that a blessing."

"Wretched boy! Mind you, I cannot but admit his bruises were impressive."

Max touched his cheekbone. "He was fortunate not to find himself on the wrong side of madame."

Here Mme de Claireville, for all her effort at unbending severity, gave way to laughter. "Appalling child, you have not improved since you left me. You are still heartless, ambitious and as tricky as a brace of jackdaws. Indeed, you are worse—more cocky than ever and, regrettably, more handsome."

"But not yet clever?"

It took her a second to retrieve the reference. Then she let out another robust laugh. "That stung, eh?"

"What stings, madame, is your wishing to deny M de Miremont what you have no use for yourself."

She abruptly stopped laughing and shot him a hard glance devoid of any play-acting. "That is casuistry, my little seminarian. I have explained what my concerns are."

"So eloquently that if I were to promise M de Miremont had nothing to fear, I should be wasting my breath. Yet after all it is monsieur's affair whether he trusts me not."

But Mme de Claireville, as she considered Max, seemed to be pursuing some reflection that chastened her. "You are a strange child. Perhaps I am unduly harsh. Here—stop looking disdainful, it suits you far too well, and come and sit by me. We shall have our theological discussion."

Now it was Max's turn to laugh.

"No, truly." She patted the space beside her on the sofa. "We shall pray you never become clever. And debate our belief in miracles."

When Miremont reappeared from his impatient turn around the *piano nobile* and found them sitting together laughing, he did not know whether to be troubled or reassured.

Of course, there was one person whom M de Miremont should have feared above all, one person uniquely placed to form suspicions. Lesage saw monsieur and the new librarian in each other's company daily, both at meals and on those occasions, increasingly frequent, when Miremont could not resist visiting the library. It was possible that Lesage's infirmity prevented him from noticing the small betrayals of glance and gesture that, for all their caution, the two of them unwittingly fell into as their affair progressed; but he could not remain unaware, since monsieur much against his advice encouraged the youth to talk at table, of the curious habit they were acquiring of commencing a topic in the middle of the debate and of snatching up each other's unspoken thoughts, so that the conversation, which usually involved some recondite subject that anyway bored Lesage, resembled one of those irritating puzzles that required you to join together seemingly random dots.

Despite his cataracts, Lesage was certainly not blind to all this. Nor was he lacking in suspicion: to the contrary. But, as he noted the favour M de Miremont bestowed upon the interloper and the way monsieur, as he had never permitted himself with his loyal secretary, sometimes absently addressed the youth as *tu*, his mounting sense of persecution blinded him utterly to any possible cause but one.

A cleverer man than Lesage, suspecting there was a rival for his position, might have befriended the boy, putting him under such a sense of obligation by the generosity of his advice and the thoughtful kindness of his many small attentions that the young upstart would scruple to pay him back with deceit. A cleverer man, observing that monsieur displayed a partiality for his rival, might have echoed this good opinion, or at least guarded his tongue and kept his execrations to himself. But Lesage's cleverness, while it equipped him to flatter a duke and grasp the finer points of the *Code Napoléon*, did not extend to Machiavellian strategy. And in any case, for our cleverer man to practise such subtleties, he must be capable of overcoming not only the injury to his amour-propre, but also his fear.

Lesage, though racked by both, believed his continued opposition sprang from a more noble cause. If he spoke frankly about the boy's defects, he could not be blamed, for he was merely asserting a truth which M de Miremont, had he been more discerning, would have grasped without trouble. If he sought every opportunity to remind monsieur of his own superior skills, length of service and arcane knowledge of the family's affairs, he was endeavouring to prevent the marquis from falling into a great wrong that monsieur's father would never have countenanced. If he demanded due recognition and the banishment of his rival, he did so not from selfish motives but to save the house of Miremont from the stain of injustice, not to mention the other disasters that must inevitably befall it once its affairs were in the wrong hands.

It did not matter what assurances Miremont offered: Lesage was armoured for his crusade and the words glanced off him.

CHAPTER THIRTY

Unsurprisingly, Max was also pondering the problem of Lesage.

Certainly his renewed intimacy with M de Miremont had improved his situation. Leaving the old fellow's bedroom in the small hours, exhausted, yet with his mind still fired by their conversation, Max forgave him the deprivations of the last month. But he was wary, too. This time he would not be caught out. M de Miremont's professions of love were by no means disagreeable to him, but he was inclined not to lend them too much weight. Oh, he did not doubt the old fellow's sincerity. But he did not forget Dom Sébastien. Give monsieur a month and his abhorrence might be equally heartfelt.

Max feared this moment had come, even earlier than expected, when the Cyclops went missing. Although he could scarcely comprehend the to-do over the old monster, he thought it only proper to volunteer for the search. But the momentary look of shock that M de Miremont could not hide and the sadness with which the old boy shook his head combined to impress upon Max that his offer was misplaced; and when he understood he was also to be banished for the night he was in no doubt: if the Cyclops met with misfortune, while M de Miremont would take the blame upon himself, he, Max, would not escape its consequences.

But old Monoculus was recovered safely. And Max began to realise that, in making his declaration, M de M had done what he found most difficult—he had come to a decision; furthermore, having reached it, he would daily be strengthened in it, so that it would be as hard to reverse as it had been to make. By now Max had seen enough of the Hôtel de Miremont not to underestimate the risk of this obstinate bravery—while he had meant every word of his vow, he could hardly protect monsieur from the vagaries of fate—and he was tempted to find it convincing proof of the old fellow's affection. Although he would still be wise to take nothing for granted, it seemed that the compact they had made in the Jardin des Plantes was at last being fulfilled. Now he could set about improving other aspects of his life that were less congenial.

Of course, there were some situations no influence could remedy: nothing could alter the distaste with which he was now viewed by the servants. Even if the significance of Monoculus's delinquency had not been grasped, there would have been whispers, gossip amongst the maids—if M de Miremont's relations lacked the faculty of observation the servant's hall did not. Max felt the change almost immediately: from being someone who scarcely deserved notice, he became the focus of an unexpressed but palpable hostility, as though wherever he went he let in an icy draught.

The shock of their master's fall from grace, though it must have been deeply felt, was never made obvious in the servants' treatment of monsieur himself. There may have been a few chilly days, yet perhaps this was merely Max's perception: M de Miremont, who, in spite of the Cyclops, still cherished the illusion that the household in general would remain oblivious, did not appear to notice. Besides, in monsieur's case, the frost was brief. Disaffection would not last in a household whose members and their forebears had served the family for so many years. Max remembered how, even in the friable atmosphere of the Hôtel de Claireville, loyalty to madame had pardoned her eccentricities. True, M de Miremont's transgression was of a different order, but M Boussec, Mme Mercier and the cook, Mme Dussardier, would soon remind themselves how hard it would be to find another situation in which they were treated so considerately; and where the upper servants led, the rest would follow. Affection for M de Miremont would be restored by the general agreement that he was not to blame: they would reserve their loathing for the demon preying upon their poor master.

Max had entered the Hôtel du Miremont neither flesh nor fowl, but now there was a name for his kind. Paradoxically, he began to be treated with frigid respect, for it was a natural supposition that he would carry tales. True, his fire often smoked and his shirts were regularly singed by the laundry, but such mishaps were followed by fulsome apologies, so that there was little he could do. And when he recalled Michel and the Oxen, he supposed he should be grateful for these minor discomforts.

But about the Buzzard he could—he must—do something.

In his first weeks he had contrived to shrug off the daily indignities heaped upon him but by now his hard-won control was pressed to its limits. Besides, as we know, it was not in his character to continue indefinitely without rebellion. A potent spur to his discontent was the life he lived at night and its contrast with his days in the library. It was not difficult to imagine how pleasant his existence would become if the only obstacle to his free contact with M de Miremont were removed.

Had he not been through the logic in his own head a thousand times? It was unshakeable: the Buzzard was aged and infirm and it would be a kindness to pension him off. Max was fairly confident that M de M, in his heart of hearts, believed this too. He appeared to feel the limitations set on their meeting even more keenly than Max. So why did he not act as logic dictated?

During Max's first week, as it had gradually sunk in that monsieur had surrendered him without terms to his secretary, he had sometimes wondered if the Buzzard had a secret hold over his master, knowledge of some past indiscretion that would explain why M de Miremont tolerated his lack of respect. Or perhaps it might be fear of the Buzzard's revenge that held him back; if the old fowl were sent packing, he might voice certain suspicions to M de Sauvigny and other members of the family. Yet it was evident that the Buzzard lived in blinkered innocence, for he would have been overjoyed to add depravity to his compendium of Max's faults.

No, the problem must once again be monsieur's indecision. The old boy would screw up the courage to follow his inclinations in the end, but he might act more speedily if he were nudged.

Max knew M de Miremont better by now than to approach him with a direct complaint about the Buzzard's behaviour: while in general they talked freely, the old boy still delicately avoided the discussion of personalities (with the exception, as it transpired, of the comte de Tarascon). Besides, monsieur already had evidence of his secretary's capacity for malice.

There had been that trivial business about the lack of a fire in Max's room: it had scarcely bothered Max, who had not imagined he was entitled to such a luxury, but it had apparently upset the old boy. However, much more distressing to monsieur was the Buzzard's meanness over the tailor's bill.

This had emerged on the second night of their reconciliation, when M de Miremont, to save Max from donning all his clothes for the brief journey up the service stairs to his room, had lent him one of his dressing gowns; although a handsome garment of quilted silk, it was inevitably too short at the hem and sleeves, prompting the old fellow to talk of commissioning Mathurin to make Max one of his own; and when Max had protested that he could not afford it, he had replied, looking somewhat surprised, that it would, of course, be a gift. During the ensuing argument—for Max was still resolved that both his pride and his independence should prevent him from accepting such presents—M de Miremont had exclaimed in frustration: "Oh, my dear impossible, infuriating boy, could you not regard it as a perquisite of your employment, like the other things?" At which he could not help noticing that Max was taken aback.

Once Max understood that the old boy had not broken his word about his wages and had never intended to saddle him with a debt, he no longer resented paying for the clothes, indeed was adamant that he should continue. But M de Miremont, although he endeavoured to conceal it, was clearly furious and so determined to make matters right that Max was obliged to concede the dressing gown.

Oh yes, the Buzzard had done his work for him there. He was free to choose some cooler, more impartial ground for airing his discontents. And he had one, laid out and ready.

"Oh, my dear, not now. Not here."

"But the whole thing is a travesty."

"Darling Max—"

"I know I am two months into the work, but I should be only too happy to make the necessary alterations—"

"Dear boy, shush! I am quite resigned to my bookshelves taking me on a voyage into the unknown."

They had been lying side by side watching the tendrils of their cigarette smoke drift towards the bed canopy. But at this, abruptly, Max sat up. "I see." From the moment he had mentioned the catalogue, his coolness had somehow deserted him. "So my work has in any case been pointless?"

Miremont reached out to stroke his back. "You know the point."

But Max's spine stiffened. "I thought I did."

Setting aside the cigarette, Miremont too sat up. "My dear, I'm not unaware…I agree things are difficult. But we simply cannot discuss this here. You must see how grossly unfair it is to the poor fellow."

"So when should we discuss it? Must I make an appointment—and pray he allows me to keep it?" Although Miremont was attempting to put his arm around his shoulders, Max shook him off. "Unfair? I'm a prisoner in your damned library, monsieur, and I'm not even permitted to read the books!"

There was a moment of silence. Then Max flung himself back onto the pillows, mortified by his loss of control, which could only encourage the old boy's evasion.

But Miremont, after considering him a little ruefully, heaved a long heavy sigh. "No, you are right, we can no longer avoid the subject." He reached for his dressing gown—perhaps he felt it would add some measure of propriety to the discussion. "I agree that I promised—I hoped—that you would be able to join me in my work and have time for your own study. And I still intend to keep these promises. But at the moment I cannot insist…poor Lesage will not…it can only make your situation more difficult. Darling boy, you have been admirable so far and I'm grateful for your patience. But we must give Monsieur Lesage more time."

"He has had two months."

"But you must see how it is. If I appear to be showing you favour, he believes it detracts from him. Try to put yourself in the poor fellow's position."

"Oh, I have, monsieur. Often." Since M de Miremont preferred to preserve his modesty while conducting the conversation, Max had swung himself off the bed and was pulling on his own robe. "And if I were him, at his age and with his infirmities, knowing that I had a generous master who would not leave me to starve, I should be grateful to take a dignified retirement and make way for someone younger."

Mathurin, as before, had rather exceeded his brief: although the fabric of the new dressing gown was an austere midnight blue, there was something in the cut, in the width of the sleeves and the flare of the skirt as it swept to the floor, that, as the boy settled cross-legged on the bed beside Miremont, made him resemble some sulky Eastern princeling, while the colour of the silk compelled Miremont to notice afresh the slate-blue of his eyes and their disconcerting intensity.

Miremont fought valiantly against this distraction. "Darling Max, how old are you?"

"Twenty-four."

"No, truly."

The boy looked for an instant as if he would brazen it out, but then he gave a resigned shrug. "I can't tell you truly, as I don't know my birthday. But I believe I have turned twenty."

"Well, when you are Camille Lesage's age you will think rather differently."

"But, monsieur, he doesn't give a damn about Ovid. And as for the other work he does for you, is it really so burdensome it is beyond mere mortals? This afternoon, when he professed to be very busy with your correspondence, I chanced to look over his shoulder and how was he engaged? Writing a billet-doux to one of his impoverished comtesses.

Added to which he can't see three centimetres in front of his nose, but when he makes a mistake it's naturally my fault. And then there's his manner—he's more of a marquis than you are, in fact I wonder if he doesn't believe—"

"Max, that is quite enough! I have made you certain promises. But I have never promised you that. Monsieur Lesage is my secretary and will remain so. I trust that is understood."

Startled by the unexpected force of old fellow's anger, Max lowered his eyes; he was once again furious with himself for letting his hatred of the Buzzard get the better of him. But to Miremont the boy appeared chastened, so that he immediately regretted the roughness of his tone.

"Dear boy, this may not be what either of us wishes. But you must try to understand. I have an obligation to poor Lesage."

"Because he is going blind?"

"In part, yes."

"It's a great misfortune, monsieur. But does it excuse him everything?"

"Max, I will not—" But Miremont once again, with a sigh, relented. "I concede the poor fellow can sometimes be...let us say, a trifle small-minded. But he is what we Miremonts have made him. My father—well, my father was in all respects such an admirable man that it is hard for me to find fault with him. Yet perhaps he should have thought...given greater consideration to the consequences...perhaps he too readily took for granted the way Lesage worshipped him. To serve him, Lesage gave up any chance of marriage, sacrificed his talents—he was, you must believe me, once very able—and surrendered all hope of establishing his independence. And I was just as thoughtless. When my father died and then my beloved brother, without Lesage's understanding of the family's affairs I should have been lost. It did not occur to me then that I was stealing another twenty years of the poor man's life, that, in return for his hard work and loyalty—and he is loyal, to the marquisate most certainly, if not especially to me—he would be left with—what? No friends, no family, no consuming interests, no place in the world outside these walls."

"Forgive me, monsieur, but was not that his choice?"

"But if my father—no, if I...But it is all too late now. My family is his religion and this house his church. How can I insist he retires? I have assured him repeatedly that he may end his days here if he wishes. Alas, he seems not to believe me."

"He doubts your word?"

"I do not think he hears me. Fear has made him deaf. As he feels his capabilities slipping away…Well, darling boy, you know how he is, refusing every offer of assistance, preferring to endure a cruel struggle rather than admit to anyone, least of all to himself…But it is not only that." Miremont laughed suddenly. "Ironically my father—he was a wise, kind man, but severely practical, not given to sentiment—my father would have sent Lesage back to Nogent when his cataracts were first diagnosed. And Lesage himself would not have quarrelled with the rightfulness of that. It would destroy him, of course, he dreads dying in provincial obscurity as he dreads nothing else. But it is what he expects. It is right, it is fitting. And I suppose he secretly fears that, whatever I promise, one day I am bound to come to my senses and act as befits my rank."

Miremont paused to look at the boy. "But I am not my father—I lack his resolve—so you see, my dear Max, we must try to make the best of things."

"You mean, continue as we are?"

"I promise I shall do everything in my power to improve your situation. And you—well, as I have said, you have managed commendably up till now. I beg you to make allowances for the poor fellow."

The boy appeared to engage in a struggle with himself; but, as Miremont observed with a heavy heart, it was never very likely that his better nature would conquer. "Allowances? I am to be insulted, lectured, treated like a slave and now, into the bargain, my heart must bleed for the old f—fellow?"

"My darling boy, it is in you to be more generous. Think of all the advantages you possess. You have your health, your youth—"

"That's an advantage, monsieur? In a world run by old men?"

Miremont endeavoured to ignore this. "You are young, handsome, intelligent, your future is before you. And you have one other significant, if very unfair, advantage." Tentatively he reached out to touch Max's cheek and was relieved when this time, although his gesture was not rewarded by any brightening of the boy's expression, it was at least not repulsed. "My darling Max, don't sulk. I know your worth—why else should I love you? And if Lesage wishes to find fault it is I who must judge the truth of the matter. So, in the end, what are his complaints if they fall on fallow ground and have no consequences? Mere pin-pricks. They may hurt your pride a little, but only if you allow it."

"I see." The boy smiled bitterly. "I am to put on my scapula again. I must submit."

Miremont's unruly forelock had fallen across his eyes. He thrust it back in a gesture of frustration. "Max, if you ever meet with real injustice in this house, you can be sure I shall defend you with everything in my power. But this—this is not the occasion for it. All I ask is your forbearance—if you can find no compassion for Monsieur Lesage then, please, I ask it for my sake."

But Max's only response was that ominous tilt to his chin. Miremont's anger turned to exhaustion: he had hoped, he supposed, foolishly and unfairly, that this personal appeal would draw from the boy the longed-for reassurance that he was loved; instead their quarrel seemed beyond resolution. He fell back against the pillows and closed his eyes.

"My dear boy, forgive me, I am apt to forget how very young you are. I should not have demanded of you something you cannot do. We will not talk of Monsieur Lesage again."

Yet, if Max's pride rebelled against submission to the Buzzard, it was goaded beyond endurance by this. "Monsieur mistakes me. Have I once said that I could not do it?"

Later, back in his room, Max berated himself. Right was on his side, he should never have given in. All the same, he had lost the argument the moment he had broken the old boy's rules. Moreover, just as before when he had quarrelled with monsieur, he could not escape the suspicion that despite the merit of his cause he had behaved less than well, which only intensified his anger.

But of course the matter need not end there. He could go back to monsieur and threaten to leave if he were not given the secretary's post. The Buzzard or him—the old boy must choose. Max would confront him with it tomorrow.

Yet, though he brooded on the idea for a couple of days, he did not carry it through. He was not entirely confident of success: in the last month he had come to understand M de M rather better and he could see the choice would cause the old boy much anguish; even if he won, it might be a pyrrhic victory, for it would very likely be at the expense of monsieur's good opinion—something, he discovered, he would rather not risk.

So where did that leave him? No further forward, in fact worse off than before. Now he not only lacked all hope of escaping the Buzzard's persecution, he was bound to tolerate it: a promise had been extorted from him that he would be expected to keep.

Despite his bold assertions, he was not sure he could manage it. Oh, he knew how to bite his tongue, stand straight, empty his face of emotion—had he not been tutored in these arts all his life by his subjection to one rule or another? And certainly he valued self-discipline—witness his annoyance when it deserted him. But he valued it on his own terms. Other people's rules only bound you in so far as you feared to break them—if you dared risk a beating or endless stations of the cross or your wages being docked, you could shrug off your fetters; and besides, what was obedience but mere observance, who could shackle your thoughts? In coercion, perversely, there were certain freedoms.

But what M de Miremont required was absolute. There were no sanctions but there was no escape either. Georges and Philippe might counter the Buzzard's insults with their mocking politeness, then give vent to a few choice curses in the safety of the servants' hall. But monsieur, if Max understood him aright when he talked of 'compassion' and 'allowances', did not mean the appearance of submission, but the thing itself. Max must not merely mask his hatred of the Buzzard, he must transform it, he must find it in him to feel genuine sympathy for his persecutor no matter how vilely he was treated.

It was absurd, impossible. Yet how typical of M de Miremont. It was all very well for the old boy to pardon the Buzzard's disloyalty, indeed it was downright saintly of him; however, it struck Max that monsieur's fastidious kindness was like his obsession with truth—admirable in theory, but in practice apt to inflict suffering on everyone around him. Monsieur's revered Papa, though he sounded an old brute, had taken the right approach to the Buzzard.

All the same, Max was bound to honour his word, for it soon emerged—and now he instantly forgave monsieur his troublesome virtues—that the old boy had been assiduous in keeping his part of their bargain.

The Buzzard did not let slip any chance to remind Max that his probationary three months were nearly up. There was a gleam of triumph in the old fowl's eyes when, as happened on a couple of occasions, he caught his underling dozing at his work-table (Max's nocturnal exertions were taking their usual toll). Then, one afternoon at the end of March, some days after Max's argument with the old boy, the Buzzard was called away from his letter-writing and did not reappear; two hours went by before Philippe informed Max that he too was required to attend upon monsieur.

Since M Fabien's term of trial had proved satisfactory, rewarding the faith M de Miremont and M Lesage had placed in his abilities— and thanks, of course, to M Lesage's rigorous tuition—it was time to consider how best his talents could be employed in the future. Accordingly, while M Lesage continued to deal with matters appertaining to M de Miremont's estates, investments and other business affairs, M Fabien would have his own separate responsibilities: since the cataloguing was well underway and making smooth progress, he was to have sole charge of this task and of the library itself; he would assist monsieur in his research; in recognition of his youth and his need to improve his Greek, he was to be granted two afternoons a week for his own study; and his wages were to be increased (this, Max understood, hastily computing the sum, was the old boy's method of recompensing him for the Buzzard's deductions).

The old fellow kept an admirably solemn face while announcing this, never forgetting to address Max with appropriate formality and making every effort, with glances and even the occasional smile in his secretary's direction, to convey that this arrangement was endorsed by the Buzzard. But Max need not look at Lesage, nor hear the squawk the old bird permitted himself when M de Miremont reached the part about his wages, to know that it was a charade, enacted to preserve the Buzzard's dignity; as Max had entered monsieur's apartments, even before he had encountered the two of them seated in silence on opposing sides of the study table, he had detected the rancid vapours of prolonged dissent.

Nevertheless, after Max had thanked them both, the old boy, fixing the Buzzard with a look his father would have applauded, remarked: "Good, then we are all content. Is that not so, Monsieur Lesage?"

To which the Buzzard, though screwing up his mouth as if he had mistaken tar for treacle, was obliged to reply: "As monsieur pleases."

CHAPTER THIRTY ONE

Under the new arrangements, it seemed that Max would have little difficulty keeping his promise. Whereas he had been cooped up all day with the old fowl, now he scarcely saw him: the Buzzard not only wrote his letters in his own rooms but avoided the library altogether, so that Max could come and go as he pleased; but in any case Max's duties for M de Miremont meant that he often spent the afternoons in the old fellow's study. His only prolonged encounters with Lesage were at mealtimes and, although he was obliged to endure the usual sneers—the sniffs when he dared express an opinion, the imputations of ingratitude when he declined monsieur's excellent vintages, the little clicks of the tongue like the tapping of a red pencil underlining his other supposed lapses of savoir faire—these could be shrugged off as a small price for the liberties otherwise accorded him.

M de M was scarcely a hard task-master and, besides, readily distracted. As for the library, while Max accepted the old boy's strictures about the catalogue, left at last to his own devices he was able to make changes—minor adjustments that would surely go unnoticed—which purged it of the oddities that most offended reason. And then there were the two glorious afternoons when he answered to no one: soon he would concentrate upon his secret researches, but first he decided to learn Italian. When he and Fabrice met at the Monkey the following Sunday, his jaunty air was no longer a pose.

Yet, sadly, this agreeable state of affairs was not to last. Indeed it had continued scarcely above ten days before Max, returning to his work-table after an hour or so upstairs, found his latest pages of calligraphy marked with schoolmasterly corrections. Two days later there was a note: why had he deviated from the agreed plan for the catalogue? After that, there was hardly a day that did not bring some billet-doux in the Buzzard's wavering hand: had Max sent to the printers for more bookplates, where was the latest consignment for the restorer, why had he failed to inform M Boussec that one of the doors to the anteroom creaked?

The cumulative effect of this barrage was maddening, the more so because it left Max at a loss. Since the Buzzard always cunningly delivered his missives when he knew his adversary was engaged with monsieur, he might simply pretend he had never received them, but he doubted this would meet the requirements of his promise. However, writing back was not the answer, as he discovered, having gone to the trouble of penning a courteous yet, he hoped, cogent justification of his catalogue revisions; notes simply generated more notes, as shots draw returning fire.

In the end he ignored some and acted on others: given his invidious situation with the servants, he was loath to tell them their duty by complaining about the door, but the Buzzard's reminder about the bookplates was timely and he gritted his teeth and thanked him for it. And yes, he supposed it was in accordance with his pledge, or at least a victory of some sort when, returning to his work-table to find the phantom pedagogue had subjected his fair copy of M de Miremont's first chapter to the same treatment as his calligraphy, he did not storm upstairs to the old fowl's rooms and seize him by the gizzard but, reminding himself that it had been sheer stupidity not to hide the manuscript, merely set about copying the spoiled pages afresh.

All the same, he wondered angrily about the value of his promise, when the Buzzard himself did not honour any agreements. And in fact Max's restraint seemed only to provoke the old lunatic, for he soon resorted to extreme measures—or at least did something he had hitherto found unthinkable: he asked M de Miremont if he could call upon Max's assistance.

Of course, if the old fowl were genuinely, as he declared himself, struggling with a sudden overabundance of work, or even if he had simply needed a keener pair of eyes to read the day's correspondence, it would not have required any pledge to persuade Max to help him: Max recalled what animosity had obscured, how bravely and adroitly Lesage coped with his affliction, and this, as much as compassion, would have made him happy to oblige. And, of course, it might be that the old fowl had experienced some illuminating vision that had brought him a change of heart, if not an alteration of character: at any rate that appeared to be what M de Miremont supposed, for he seemed delighted by this turn of events.

But Max was bound to feel the greatest misgivings, which were soon confirmed. Every time his help was required, things turned out disastrously. A pile of documents would be thrust at him and he would be asked to make digests or draft letters; but, as these papers were usually leases or tenancy agreements relating to monsieur's three estates, they were couched in impenetrable legal language that the

Buzzard explained only vaguely or, if pressed, elaborated upon with so many flourishes that Max was more confused than before. Once, M de Miremont came down to the library to find him puzzling over an opinion Maître Ladurie had given on a dispute over wood-cutting rights on the Vendée estate, where the land was apportioned between a bewildering number of tenants and even the château was rented out: despite the ban on discussing the Buzzard, which Max meticulously observed, the old boy insisted on knowing what was troubling him and within minutes had clarified the points at issue; but he could hardly run to monsieur every time he was in difficulty.

The result was that he frequently made mistakes. And even when he did not, his letter-writing style was likely to prove unsatisfactory: try as he might, his instinct for simplicity prevented him from ever reaching the florid heights required by the Buzzard. Letters had to be rewritten over and over, wasting hours—precious time that Max might otherwise count his own, since, by sinister coincidence, the Buzzard usually seemed in need of assistance on Max's study afternoons.

Max had to grant it—this time the old bird had been clever. Oh, it had been at a cost to his pride, but that was handsomely repaid, for he was now able to demonstrate conclusively how indispensable he was, while casting his adversary in the worst possible light. That M de Miremont did not seem greatly perturbed by these proofs of Max's incompetence, that he would brush them aside with "Well, my dear Lesage, we must give Monsieur Fabien the chance to learn," evidently caused the old fowl frustration but did not encourage him to desist, for, though he naturally knew nothing of Max's undertaking, he perceived that his prey could not escape his clutches without adding a lack of charity to his other deficiencies.

Max tried to persuade himself that it was only a game, but he could not help feeling angry and humiliated. For monsieur was wrong—it was not without consequence. No one likes being made to look stupid, and no one less than Max. Above all he hated appearing a fool in front of M de Miremont, for, although the latter showed no dwindling of affection—rather the reverse—he could not but feel lowered in monsieur's eyes, so that even the old boy's leniency towards his short-comings seemed a revolting form of pity. For the worst of it was that, while reason told him this was precisely what the Buzzard wanted, he could not help doubting himself—he who had believed he could so easily step into the secretary's post. He began to fear that, even in their private debates, M de Miremont secretly despised his opinions and only tolerated them out of indulgence.

Then came the business of the missing trust documents. Dr Gérard had been recruited to the board of the charitable institution for distressed young women founded by monsieur and his late sister to commemorate their mother, and Max was duly sent round to his consulting rooms with papers for him to sign. The Buzzard was not in his study on Max's return, so, only too happy to avoid him, Max left the papers on his blotter where he was bound to notice them—later he cursed himself for not giving the damned things into the old fowl's hands. For a day later the Buzzard announced that he had never received them. He made a great deal of fuss —Max must have lost them in the library or, worse still, dropped them in the street—and insisted on summoning him before M de Miremont.

Angrily repudiating his promise, Max opened his mouth to protest his innocence, but M de Miremont cut him off. "My dear Lesage, why do we not simply ask Ladurie to draw up the documents again? I can get the doctor to sign them when he comes on Thursday."

The Buzzard seemed to find this solution too easy by far and continued to harry monsieur with objections about the delay and expense, but these squawks were again dismissed with a tired smile. "The matter is not urgent. And an hour of some poor clerk's time will scarcely bankrupt us—in fact, it will be an infinitesimal price for peace and quiet."

Which should have made a merciful end to the business. Had not Max, the day after the duplicate document had been signed and safely returned to Maître Ladurie, come across the original, hidden in a pile of other papers Lesage had left on his table that morning.

A white-hot fury seized him. So the Buzzard would not let it lie. Having failed at the first attempt, he had contrived a second plan to incriminate him. It did not matter that the papers were now redundant, or that monsieur had not cared greatly about their loss. Nothing must stand in the way of the Buzzard's determination that he, Max, should be found wanting. Oh, he might destroy the damned things, but what would that serve, since the old fowl knew he had them? He would only seem to be admitting his guilt. Well, this time he would not stand for it. To hell with his promise, to hell with being offered up as a ritual sacrifice to monsieur's moral scruples! He would find the Buzzard and stuff these accursed papers up the old carrion bird's scrawny—

But at this point he seemed to hear his fulminations as if he had uttered them out loud and was immediately struck by their total absurdity. No one could shackle your thoughts? He had let himself get so enmeshed in the Buzzard's toils he was in danger of becoming quite as mad as his persecutor.

On cooler reflection, he understood precisely what had happened. It was, of course, as he had originally assumed: the Buzzard had lost the document himself—not deliberately abstracted it as part of some byzantine plot, but simply mislaid it; although the papers on his fastidiously tidy desk were carefully ranged in discrete piles so that he might know, without seeing, where everything was, he had absently picked up the trust document from his blotter and bestowed it upon the wrong pile, where it had become interleaved with the tenancy agreements, so that, even as he had combed through each pile in turn, peering anxiously through his magnifier, it had consistently eluded him.

Stupid old fool! Max could suddenly feel his panic. The waste of time and money, the loss of face before Maître Ladurie, the humiliating incompetence—these must have been accusations Lesage had levelled against himself, that had stoked his fear as he had hunted in every corner of his rooms, frantically, blindly, in vain. If only he had brought himself to ask for help. If only he could have grasped M de Miremont's lack of concern—but of course his entire relationship with the old fellow was bedevilled by his expectation that monsieur would behave, not as he actually did, but as the marquis de Miremont ought to. He, Lesage, had endangered the dignity of the house, his frailties would be exposed and punished. Unless, of course, he could save himself by laying the blame upon upstart M Fabien, who had no reputation to preserve except his renown for blundering.

And was he so wrong to try that, the mad old Buzzard? Perhaps Max would do the same if he were old, ailing and in fear of dismissal— he hoped not, yet, since he struggled to imagine himself in Lesage's predicament, he could not be absolutely certain.

Max considered the papers. They had caused a furore about nothing and were of no use to anyone now. The kindest thing would be to tear them up and keep silent about his discovery. But no, it was possible that the Buzzard was still fretting about their whereabouts, still living in dread that they would reappear to shame him. And besides, despite his sudden access of sympathy for the old fowl, Max was not so far along M de Miremont's path of virtue that he forgot all the other occasions Lesage had sought to do him down.

This was the hour of the morning when the Buzzard could be

found in monsieur's apartments. So much the better. Without giving himself time to change his mind, Max gathered together the papers and went upstairs.

"My...dear Monsieur Fabien?"

Monsieur's smile of delight at Max's unexpected appearance, that tiny but transparent hesitation as he reminded himself he must forego endearments—now Max was restored to sanity, he could see perfectly well that the old boy's affection continued unalloyed by either pity or contempt. The Buzzard, on the other hand, was scowling, and it was he who demanded:

"Young man, I presume you have a good excuse for this interruption?"

"I thought you would like to know that I have found the trust document."

As he unrolled the papers and placed them neatly on the table in front of monsieur, Max was aware that the old boy's smile vanished, no doubt in weary anticipation of the recriminations that must follow, and he could indeed be heard to murmur: "But, my dear, that is all water under..." But Max's attention was focussed on the Buzzard, who, he observed, wore a satisfying look of horror.

It was tempting to prolong this pleasure, but, as Max quickly recollected, revenge was not his purpose. On his way upstairs he had cautioned himself—what he was about to do could only be done with unaffected seriousness; he must, at least for the moment, mean it utterly. All the same, his pride suffered one last spasm of protest, so that if he had not noticed the Buzzard opening his mouth to forestall him with a denial, which would have quite ruined the effect, he might have been tempted to draw back. However, once he was underway, the whole thing was surprisingly easy.

"I found it in my drawer just now—I must have had it all along. I cannot imagine what I was thinking of and I can only apologise unreservedly and ask you, monsieur—and you too, Monsieur Lesage— to forgive me for the anxiety and inconvenience I have caused."

He saw they were both staring at him astonishment. The silence encouraged him to add: "I thought I should come and tell you immediately as, while I realise the document is no longer needed, I know Monsieur Lesage was concerned it might have fallen into the wrong hands."

The Buzzard's surprise was gradually being transmuted into incredulity, tinged with mistrust. M de Miremont, on the other hand, had recovered sufficiently to fix Max with his glance; they exchanged a rapid look of understanding before the old boy responded, carefully matching the gravity of Max's confession.

"Very proper, Monsieur Fabien. And in view of your...your remarkable frankness, which allows us at last to put the matter behind us, I think we must be disposed to be lenient—would you not agree, Lesage?"

Subdued by bewilderment and suspicion, the Buzzard could only assent through clenched teeth.

Max sailed downstairs to the library on a great wave of elation. When he thought about it, the sensation was not unlike the curious phenomenon he had experienced during his drain-digging days, when, after sweating in excruciating pain for hours, his every muscle screaming, he would suddenly, just as he thought he could stand no more, feel his limbs shrug off the fiery hoops that bound them, feel himself soaring like a phoenix, cleansed of his agony, god-like. The feeling did not last, of course, soon the pain set in again, worse than before. But for that short while he was omnipotent.

Max had not imagined—so far he had always considered that power lay in resistance, that to submit reduced you. Yet if you chose submission, not from cowardice, but as an act of free will—well, he had learnt there was power in that too. He could not suppose that this was what M de M had intended him to learn, for it was a far cry from compassion, but the old fellow, being disabled by his own noble motives from detecting the difference, seemed pleased with him nonetheless.

It could not be said that Max and Lesage began thereafter to like each other better; on the contrary, since the Buzzard now had cause to feel grateful to his adversary, his hatred of him was undoubtedly increased. However, the secretary had lost the main weapon in his arsenal: if his enemy could blithely confess to crimes he had not even committed, then, whatever blame was heaped on him, he would not be put to flight. Furthermore, Lesage's continuing suspicion that such a foolhardy act could only be explained by some complex and devious motive led him to reassess his underling and to treat him more warily, if not with courtesy then at least with restraint. For Max's part, he no longer cared whether the Buzzard was civil—now that he had found a way to rise above his intrigues, the old fowl could not touch him. So that all in all, while neither party had actually disarmed, there was the appearance of a truce.

Buoyed by his extraordinary discovery, which was bound to be invaluable in the future, Max forgave monsieur and could even grant there had been merit in his strictures. He would have been surprised to learn that the old fellow himself was not so sanguine.

Miremont could not bear to see the boy hurt: he found Lesage's behaviour detestable. Yet it was unworthy to blame his secretary when the fault was mainly his. In the tangled matter of the secretaryship, any clear-sighted man—his father, for example—might have cut the knot, might have judged that Lesage's conduct released Miremont from his promise. But Miremont's own sight was hopelessly fogged by his equivocal moral position. The guilty awareness of his suspect motives, the false pretences on which he now met Lesage, the shaming admission, which he had stifled for twenty-two years, that, despite what he owed him, he had never really liked the poor fellow—all dictated that his only proper path lay, not in brutal decisions, but in strict fairness to both parties. In the end, of course, he had been fair to neither.

Because he loved Max too immoderately to be impartial, he had compensated by being unreasonably hard on the boy; because he felt guilty about Lesage, he had been far too lenient with him. It had been pure wishful thinking to believe Lesage would accept any agreement into which he had been coerced; and then, to forbid the boy to complain—what sanctimony that was, as if Miremont's refusal to discuss Lesage in the bedroom somehow absolved him of his deceit.

Miremont shuddered to think what his hypocrisy had risked: for what had he done, with all his fine scruples, but put everything upon the boy; and, once Max bore it, the thorny encumbrance of Miremont's conscience, it seemed impossible to lift. Miremont shuddered again as he relived the past few dangerous days: had he truly forgotten Max's enthusiasm for the army? But instead, the boy had suddenly shrugged his shoulders and broken free. His absurd, generous quixotic gesture had miraculously freed them all. Even Lesage, though he was no more capable of stopping his rumblings than Mount Vesuvius, seemed temporarily quiescent. And on the boy's part, at least, there was genuine forbearance.

This did not prevent Miremont reproaching himself. Nonethless, it seemed he had been most undeservedly blessed. For he dared to think that Max's willingness in such trying circumstances gave evidence of his love.

CHAPTER THIRTY TWO

At the beginning of June, a month earlier than usual, Miremont decided to quit Paris for the summer. Although his excuse was Calvert, who was still making heavy weather of the model cottages, he was naturally impatient for Max to see Beauvallon; but, above all, it seemed to him that only in the country could he and Max live as he wished.

The château was small and his existence there simple. Most of the upper rooms remained permanently under dust covers; but in his own modest suite, communicating with his bedroom via a narrow dressing-room, was a room that could be prepared for Max without causing remark. Furthermore since, unlike the Hôtel de Miremont, the château had no service passage and servants' doors, these apartments could only be entered—as when Thomas came to wake him—from the landing: he and Max would no longer be forced to endure a nightly parting.

The informality and privacy of Beauvallon also suited Miremont's ideas. He felt none of Catherine's obligation to entertain the local notables. His parents had maintained tenuous connections with one or two neighbouring families, but the next generation had allowed this acquaintance to lapse. Apart from the interchanges required by the business of the estate—meetings with Calvert, conversations with his tenants, the annual celebration of the vintage with the commune's winemakers— Miremont's days were spent in unfettered solitude.

There were few servants, too. The only member of his Paris household to accompany him was Thomas: otherwise the château ran during Miremont's residence much as it did without him, under the stewardship of M and Mme Durand, with the assistance of a couple of maids who came in from the village. Or rather, if its daily routines flowed like some placid tributary, immune to tides or squalls, this was the achievement of Rosalie Durand, for while her husband Zacharie was in charge of the wine cellar and acted as butler on rare ceremonial occasions, his responsibilities were usually restricted to the supervision of the outdoor staff and the performance of odd jobs: it was she—housekeeper, cook, laundress, kitchen gardener—whose benevolent efficiency shone in every corner.

Miremont had the greatest affection for his Paris housekeeper, little neat Mme Mercier, sharp as a surgeon's scalpel (she too had twice the acumen of her titular master, poor ponderous Boussec); but he had a particular fondness for Rosalie, not only because she was Thomas' sister and a bond had been forged between them on the day of their rescue mission to the Old Manoir, but also because of her unvarying good nature and the extraordinary sweetness of her smile, which restored his faith that mankind, for all its excesses, was inherently virtuous. Despite Mme Mercier's evident devotion to him, Miremont was sensible that if he were once to step across the divide between master and servant she would be deeply shocked; but it was not unusual to find him in Rosalie's kitchen, sitting at her long scrubbed pine table, watching her big chapped constantly-working hands draw *poussins* or pummel dough while he sampled her pear tart and chatted to her as an old friend. In this easy atmosphere no one would expect him to maintain strict formalities with his young amanuensis.

As for Thomas himself, Rosalie would provide a soothing influence here too, together with the presence of his wider family—that was another advantage of Beauvallon. And a further source of not inconsiderable relief, Miremont acknowledged guiltily, would be the absence of Lesage.

Lesage loathed Beauvallon and did not conceal his resentment when his presence was required there. He had always found the lack of society hard to bear and latterly, Miremont suspected, his dislike had discovered a more practical objection; while he knew every unexpected step, every treacherous arrangement of furniture in the Hôtel de Miremont, he possessed no such mental map of the château. He had occasionally been invited by one of his noble ladies to spend the summer inhaling the fashionable ozone of Deauville; but if no promising invitation came his way he would rather endure the stinking heat of the city than expose his fastidious senses to agricultural effluvia.

This year, of course, things were different: when the secretary reflected that his rival would be left to his own devices with monsieur for four long months, he was torn. But once Miremont had assured him that the boy was accompanying him only to assist his work, that, as usual, he, Lesage, would continue to deal with all matters of business in Miremont's absence—and once he had seen the box of indigestible books the youth was packing to augment the resources of Beauvallon's library—the memory of stultifying afternoons and dim candle-lit evenings cut off from all the pleasures of civilisation was enough, if not to cure his anxiety, at least to contain it.

Miremont would at last have Max to himself. This longing for exclusivity was not, as he was shamefully aware, due entirely to the benign monomania of love. In Paris Max still took his days off and, after the first giddy week of their reconciliation, it was agreed that on those nights, so that he might catch up on his sleep, he would not visit Miremont. It was Miremont himself who had proposed this arrangement, out of a conscious wish to leave the boy some measure of freedom; yet this altruism made no allowances for the other less commendable trait in Miremont's character that his love had turned up like a malformed creature from beneath a primeval rock.

True, he need no longer fear Achille de Tarascon, but his jealousy merely sought other nourishment and was not appeased by the scraps it gleaned from Max's conversation, even though the boy's holiday pursuits seemed harmless enough—calls on a Russian family of his acquaintance, concerts sometimes on Thursday evenings and recently for the first time in his life a visit to the Théâtre Français, to see Bernhardt play Phèdre. These friendships already stirred Miremont's envy—how he would have loved to have been the one to introduce the boy to music and the theatre: but his jealousy refused to stop there, inventing other companions whose influence was the more malign for their being creatures of thin air. Although Miremont held to his resolution not to interrogate the boy and resisted waiting up for him when he returned late, he was unable to prevent himself from lying awake, straining to catch propitious sounds from the floor above. Ignoble though it might be, he could not regret that Beauvallon would deprive Max of his Thursdays and Sundays for a while.

And yet, at the same time and particularly as the date neared for their departure, he feared the boy might feel suffocated. They had already had a dispute which, although its occasion was once again the seemingly trivial matter of clothing, touched painfully, as Miremont by now recognised too well, on Max's notions of independence. It could not be helped: Mathurin's bill for the wardrobe the boy would require to feel comfortable in the country at high summer—the two coats, one of single-breasted cloth, the other a jacket of lightweight alpaca, the grey cloth trousers, the cream linen suit, the two waistcoats, the riding breeches and boots (Miremont was determined to see Max on horseback), the shirts with soft collars, the straw hat and another of shallow-crowned grey felt—was far beyond any ingenious plan of repayment Max might concoct, so that, if Miremont were not permitted to offer these things as a gift, he must put his foot down and declare (he who habitually rode around Beauvallon in an ancient sagging jacket and wearing gaiters instead of boots) that such attire was a matter of propriety, that it would reflect badly on him if his assistant secretary were unsuitably dressed.

As with the dressing gown, once Max understood that resistance was futile he seemed rather pleased with the additions to his wardrobe. But to Miremont, who hoped their time in the country would heal the divisions caused by Lesage, the boy's gratitude was almost as troubling as the disagreement itself: both pointed up the inequities in their relationship, which, if they were of no account to Miremont, could not seem negligible to Max. Nor was it just a matter of the boy's tender sense of self-respect; Miremont was forced to give fresh regard to the twenty-three years that separated them. Perhaps Max would pine for youthful company: although he had been brought up in the country and seemed to retain good memories of it despite his hatred of the enclosure, he now appeared entirely Parisian in his pleasures and recreations— perhaps at Beauvallon he would be as bored as Lesage.

Miremont's great-grandfather, Anselme, the eighth marquis, had been the first of the Varons to demonstrate the Anglophilia that was to be reinforced in succeeding generations by the family's years of English exile and through connections by marriage. Anselme had acquired the Beauvallon estate—six farms, vineyards, parkland and the ruined medieval manoir—as a retreat for his mistress, the actress and dancer Lita Lopez. Despite her raven curls and the gypsy glint in her eye, reportedly captured to the life in a portrait by Gainsborough (alas, destroyed when the château was sacked during the Terror), Mme Lopez had been born Clara O'Higgins and was of Anglo-Irish descent. To please her, Anselme de Miremont, instead of rebuilding the manoir, had demolished the substantial farmhouse attached to the home farm to construct a country house in the English style; and, not content with that, he had transformed thirty hectares of parkland into a landscaped garden after the manner of William Kent, complete with a lake, a grotto and an assortment of follies in various architectural styles, with the manoir's ruins supplying the requisite element of the picturesque. In Miremont's grandfather's time, the estate and with it the title, comte de Beauvallon, had passed to Miremont's great uncle Balthazar, who, dying without issue, had left it to Miremont's father, but not before he had painstakingly restored Anselme's *geste d'amour*.

As the château's venerable barouche turned in through the tall iron gates with Thomas and the luggage rumbling behind in the brake, Miremont, in his anxiety over this meeting between his two great loves, sought to see Beauvallon as Max must be seeing it. First, this somewhat austere approach, through open parkland, along an avenue of limes, with the house no more than a distant wraith; then, as it gradually took definition, the deceptive pomp of its colonnaded portico; then at last, as the trees gave way to a sweep of lawn and shingle, the first full view of its carriage front: not mansarded but with a shallow-pitched roof concealed by a balustrade, and wearing its magnificent entrance as an elegant woman wears an exceptional jewel, sparing other obtrusive adornment, relying for its effect on the purity of its proportions, it lay bathed in the sweet heavy stillness of the late afternoon, its sandstone glowing as though steeped in honey.

To the right was the wall of the kitchen garden and, beyond that, the Durands' cottage, the stables and a collection of other outbuildings a century older than the château; to the left, a path through the shrubbery led to a small orchard. This too pleased Miremont, this vision of his Palladian beauty slumbering beside the espaliered plum trees and the barns with their weathered pantiles, a goddess brought to earth amongst the homely and rustic. But her principal glory was yet to be revealed.

As Zacharie reined in the horses and the barouche halted before the steps, where Rosalie and the maids waited to greet their master, Miremont was already impatient to show Max the view from the garden front.

Of course, he need not have worried about the boy. Yes, Max was young—but his youth, as Miremont was brought guiltily to realise, had been caged for the past six months.

Even as they first stepped onto the stone balcony leading from the salon to the garden stairs and looked out, across the valley, to where the lawn rolled down to the broad, still expanse of the lake and to the wooded hills beyond, he seemed, from the slight but perceptible lifting of his shoulders, to be drinking the clear air as if it were an elixir.

Later, after an early dinner, they strolled down to the lakeside and settled on the steps of the Temple of Dionysus to watch as the setting sun cast bars of scarlet, turquoise and indigo above the château and the darkening hills, until one by one—the distant delicate arch of the Chinese bridge, the broken columns and shattered tree straight from a Piranesi etching that marked the entrance to the grotto, the domed Temple of Ancient Virtue crowning the nearest hill and, further eastwards, through a thick planting of firs, pines and larches, the medieval turrets of the Gothic Tower—all the joyous whimsies of Anselme's rustic fantasy were veiled in night and, as silhouettes merged, ink-dark, with their watery reflection, the lake seemed freed from its bounds, protean. Retiring to the musty interior of the Temple of Dionysus, they made love, unhurriedly and, so it seemed to Miremont, with a renewed sense of discovery.

As they steered a return path to the lawn with the aid of the lantern Miremont had brought to supplement the moonlight, Max stopped suddenly to glance back.

"Of course!" He laughed. "No wonder you like Claude."

Miremont was momentarily non-plussed.

"As the sun was going down—the light, the landscape, the water, the distant buildings—all it wanted was a little group of figures in antique robes."

This was so obvious and indeed so in keeping with Anselme's intention, which had been to create, depending on where you stood by the lake, a series of views, that Miremont was astonished that he had never consciously made the connection. But then to him the garden was—had always been—a repository of memories, a place of boyhood adventure, so that this first sight of it after absence, combined with its sounds and smells, the chatter of frogs, the chirr of a nightjar, the distant creak of the water-wheel feeding the lake from the river, the scents of grass and loam and pondweed, could not fail to evoke all the summers he had roamed wild there—the trees he had climbed, the dens he had built, his favourite hiding place, a giant fir whose hollow trunk could shelter two at a pinch, the reed bed beyond the bridge in which you could lie and watch dragon flies hatch, and all the other secret places he and Thomas had uncovered and which he now longed to show Max.

Thus it was with faint consternation that he said: "But you don't care for Claude."

"I've never stepped into the canvas before." The boy grinned. "How like you, Armand, to possess your own private Arcadia."

Again Miremont was uncertain how to construe this; yet, since Max had linked his arm with his and since it was the first time the boy had been persuaded to use his given name, he dared to let his happiness take flight.

Max's riding lessons, which began the next morning directly after breakfast, yielded a surprise—although perhaps Miremont should not have been so astonished. He had settled with himself that the boy's horsemanship had been confined to his bareback stunts on the monastery's spavined nag; but had not Max once told him he had ridden as a small child, that the scar on his temple was from being thrown by his pony? If Miremont had forgotten, it must have been from an urge to blot out the painful recollection of his own insensitivity that afternoon; but also—he must confess it—he had discounted this claim as being of a piece with the other inventions colouring Max's fantasy. Yet this was no invention; the boy was immediately at home in the saddle and fretting to be off the leading rein.

There were small faults Miremont felt obliged to correct—the position of the lad's knees and his feet in the stirrups, slapdash habits he had no doubt acquired from his bareback escapades—but to the skills he had learnt as a child Max added natural ability and the fearlessness of youth: by his second lesson, having exhausted the possibilities of poor old Hercules, the docile Holsteiner, broad and comfortable as a sofa, who usually pulled the brake, he had graduated to one of the carriage horses; by the third day Miremont judged that he could safely accompany him on his morning tour of the estate and within a week they had dispensed with the need for a groom.

Miremont was proud of him, although sometimes disquieted by that reckless streak of his: Max was never happier than when going at full gallop and, although Miremont had discouraged overuse of the whip, seemed determined to push his mount to the limits. The carriage horse, a six-year-old bay mare, was, despite her equable nature, a sprightly creature who by no means objected to being given her head. But the grooms had brought two horses down from the Paris stables for Miremont's own use, and he could see where Max's desires tended. Darius, a purebred Arab, chestnut with a white blaze, elegant, sure-footed and with a willing intelligence, was Miremont's particular favourite; but it was Pretender, the three-year-old Arab-English Thoroughbred cross, who inevitably attracted Max. Bred at Pompadour, nearly seventeen hands and jet black, from his disdainful Roman profile and elegant neck to his muscular shoulders and powerful hindquarters, Pretender was a magnificent animal; Max, Miremont was bound to admit, would sit superbly in his saddle; yet it was not this, he was willing to bet, that drew the boy, so much as a supercilious glint in Pretender's eye ominously akin to a challenge. Youth, strength and confidence could not replace experience and even experience was not proof against fate— Miremont needed no reminding of what had befallen his brother. He would go only so far as to surrender Darius to the boy, while he rode Pretender himself.

Yet if Max were inclined to be headstrong it was partly Miremont's own fault: the boy's competitive spirit transformed his once-solitary rides as mustard quickens a sauce. This was true, too, of the shooting. Although the Varons did not, by tradition, shoot game and Miremont could recall his revulsion during a stay in England at seeing the gorgeously plumaged corpses of over two hundred pheasants laid out by the beaters for the house party's admiration, in Italy as a young man he had learnt to aim at targets and he still liked to keep his eye in, choosing a deserted spot out beyond the Old Manoir as his shooting gallery. In this instance there could be no doubt—Max had never handled a gun before: however he proved a gratifyingly attentive student, every bit as enthusiastic as he was about riding. To begin with they shot at stationary targets with Miremont's revolvers: later, for variety and to appease the boy's lively curiosity about firearms, Miremont brought out Balthazar's silver-mounted flintlock duelling pistols. Max possessed a good eye and a steady hand: soon they were aiming at coins thrown in the air; by the end of their stay he would be a very passable shot and next summer Miremont must look to his laurels. Delighted, he made a mental note to talk to the fencing master on their return to Paris about instructing the boy in the art of foils.

When they were not on horseback or out at the Old Manoir, they swam in the lake, in the stretch near the Temple of Dionysus that was kept free of weed and water lilies for that purpose; they tramped the hills of Anselme's arcadia; they collected up flat stones wherever they saw them for fierce games of ducks and drakes. The boy even seemed interested in Miremont's visits to his tenants and in the model cottages, which, after a series of disasters, including a misreading of the plans in respect of the roof pitch and Calvert using timber for the rafters that was not only unseasoned but, worse still, too green, were being roofed for the third time; although, observing Max as he watched the men nailing pantiles to the battens, Miremont wondered if his true interest lay in a longing to be aloft with them, emulating their daring feats of balance.

Assuredly Miremont need not have worried. The sun had set a glow upon the boy's cheeks and, while he sat bareheaded after swimming, had streaked his hair with gold; he seemed freshly conscious of himself as a physical being, so that Miremont thought again of the leopard, liberated at last, stretching luxuriantly, testing the power of its limbs and rejoicing to feel its once-dulled blood course wildly through its veins. With this new freedom to take pleasure in his vigorous youth, the false gentility Max had learned as a servant dropped away; he showed his teeth when he smiled, threw his head back when he laughed, abandoned himself to all that was most spontaneous and, to Miremont's mind, most charming in his nature.

But it was not fresh air and exercise alone that had worked this transformation. Now they were no longer slaves to time and discretion, now they could satisfy desire when and wherever they wished, fall asleep in each other's arms and wake next to each other every morning, now that they need not guard their words nor store up thoughts to tip them out hastily like windfall apples that would roll away if they were not instantly snatched up, but might expand their intellectual debates or talk of nothing in particular or even award themselves the luxury of companionable silence, the affinity between them, which was Miremont's greatest joy but which he had feared might be diluted by propinquity, seemed only to grow the stronger.

This, Miremont found himself once again reflecting, was what he had so foolishly expected of his marriage: in the heat of the afternoon, as Max lay in a hammock in the orchard working his way through Balzac's *La Comédie humaine* while Miremont, as a gesture towards the ostensible purpose of their stay, sat in the library dozing over Ovid, he could not but marvel anew at this miraculous happiness, this strong wine that made the pleasure he had once derived from his solitary life seem as tepid as a watery tisane.

But of course there is no such thing as unqualified happiness; or rather to be aware of one's happiness is to break its spell. The closer Miremont felt he grew to Max, the more he was conscious that there was much about the boy he did not know.

For instance, it was a delight to him that their present sleeping quarters allowed him to observe the small practical details of his lover's existence, things hidden from him at the Hôtel de Miremont (where discretion had prevented him from ever setting foot in Max's room) and mundane in themselves, yet, like the flints and pot shards of some ancient tribe, fraught nevertheless with significance: the little stack of reading matter—a copy of Dante, an Italian dictionary and the literary review the boy had bought for the train—set carefully on the chair beside the bed; the cheap black-handled cut-throat, folded but lacking a case, lying on the wash-stand; the two solitary bone-backed brushes on the console beneath the looking glass and the modest, cloth-covered stud box; and, on the writing table, recalling an altogether gloomier occasion, the contents of the boy's pockets, a few coins, matches, the inevitable twist of tobacco and the watch Miremont had given him.

Miremont was gratified to see the watch, for he had wondered what had become of it; but he was principally struck by the emptiness of this room in contrast to his own, the spartan nature of these arrangements and their telling poverty, so that he longed, if only the boy's obstinacy would let him, to remedy these deficiencies. Yet what he also noticed was the uncanny tidiness, the clothes stowed neatly in the armoire, the few possessions disposed just so, exhibiting an orderliness surely unusual in a young man of barely twenty and certainly at odds with the wilder side of Max's character. Only later did he come to understand, with a chill, that this was not the discipline that Thomas worshipped, with its comforting ceremonies to tame and regulate the world; rather it was a recognition of contingency, of rootlessness, of the need to pack up and depart at a moment's notice. The cloister would have inculcated a disregard for possessions that the boy's time in service would not have discouraged, but this permanent readiness for flight spoke of something more: once Miremont had overcome his selfish fear, he was saddened to think that this was how the boy might see himself, belonging to nowhere and no one, forever on the alert like some creature in the savannah. He found his speculations reverting to the missing years of Max's childhood.

But here he must continue to rue his blunder of the previous summer, for where originally the boy had been so forthcoming he was now studiously vague. Naturally Miremont had asked about the riding, that first morning on their way back from the stables; this time Max professed not to recall where he had been taught or by whom. And the same blank denials, which discouraged further probing, greeted Miremont's concern about his nightmares.

It was during their third night together that Miremont had been woken from a deep and tranquil sleep by a harrowing cry, a sound so urgent in its distress yet so barely human that it was an instant before he realised it emanated, not from the darkness without, but from beside him. As Miremont reached out to the boy, Max gave a series of staccato groans, then, shouting something unintelligible, sat bolt upright; his eyes sprang open and he began to shiver.

Miremont held him, rocking him gently as if he were a child, until the shivering had stopped and he dared lean away momentarily to light a candle. But when he turned back Max had shed all trace of whatever the moonlight had veiled in those stark wide-open eyes; instead, he was grinning apologetically.

"Forgive me, I should have warned you. I'm told I make an abominable racket."

Miremont was disconcerted by the implications of this, until he reminded himself that servants shared quarters. But he was also taken aback by the boy's nonchalance. "But, my dear…You sounded…Are you saying this happens regularly?"

"Once in a while."

"Can you remember what you dream about?"

"Never. Not a thing." Max laughed. "So you see I don't deserve your concern. It's far worse for you than it is for me."

Yet as Miremont lay feigning sleep he could sense that the boy, despite his laughter, was also sleepless. And it proved sadly true that the nightmares were recurrent: on three further occasions Miremont woke to hear that unearthly howling; once he was even able to make out some words, rising with a terrible, frantic clarity from the gibberish. Like most words garbled in dreams, their emphasis was quite at odds with their banality, yet they were uttered with such heartrending desperation that Miremont at first scarcely took in their full significance.

"…*hundertelf, hundertzwölf, hundertdreizehn. Ach komm! Jetzt gleich! Hundertvierzehn…*"

Long after Max had fallen asleep again, Miremont lay awake and deeply troubled. Perhaps all the boy had tried to tell him was true, that he had indeed been born in Germany—where had he said, Waldavia?—that he really was the son of an aristocratic family brought low by some appalling disaster.

Miremont chose his moment carefully next day. And yes, for an instant Max did seem startled. Yet all he would say, before turning aside with a shrug, was: "As you know, Armand, I can't speak German. You must have misheard."

Miremont must learn to live with his bad conscience and stifle his curiosity. He could only hope that, whatever the misfortunes of his childhood, the boy would begin to see that he was no longer at the mercy of the fates. As for the particulars of his suffering, was he not entitled to his reticence? Yet this counsel of restraint was sometimes damnably hard to follow.

Nor was it easy to avoid dwelling upon the boy's other omission.

For all Miremont's fond hopes, Max had never returned his professions of love; perhaps he felt that the poem, sent so long ago now, had made further declarations redundant, or perhaps he was embarrassed to utter in his own words what he could confidently express through Catullus. With his deepening knowledge of Max's character, Miremont was forced to admit that neither excuse convinced.

In his bleaker moments, he found himself prey to the sort of corrosive self-pity that had attacked him last summer...But this, he saw, was madness. Did he forget where such thoughts had led him? Was he once again willing to condemn them both to months of needless anguish for the lack of three words, three trite little words, debased coinage compared with the riches Max had already bestowed?

CHAPTER THIRTY THREE

Here was Miremont's punishment for his doubts, that they had somehow conjured up Catherine! Not that he would have been displeased, in normal circumstances, to receive her; during Léonore's lifetime the Sauvignys had been in the habit of spending part of the summer at Beauvallon and he had several times invited Catherine to join them but she had always offered her excuses. Yet now she wrote that, as she was staying with the La Marnes and then travelling to the d'Issy-l'Évêques near Toulon before continuing south to La Boissière, she proposed to visit Beauvallon for a night or two en route. 'As you can see, dearest Armand, we are roaming the countryside like gypsies and must solicit your kindness for a roof over our heads.'

At this Miremont uttered such a snort that Max lowered his coffee cup enquiringly, obliging him, by way of explanation, to read the sentence aloud.

"Gypsies?"

"All very well for you to laugh, wretched boy. She's coming to make sure I haven't left you out in the rain or let you get woodworm."

"I doubt it's my welfare that concerns madame."

This was said lightly but with a wry smile that prompted Miremont to recall his first conversation with Catherine on the subject of the boy. His irritation increased. "And that's not even the worst of it. You note the word 'we'? She is travelling with that terrifying poetess and her niece. We shall have to be on our best behaviour."

"I shouldn't be so certain of that."

Miremont listened with some surprise to what Max imparted concerning Baroness Donyani and Mlle de la Falaise but his appetite for his breakfast brioche was not restored. There would be fuss, upheaval, poor Rosalie would need to get in help from the village, they would be obliged to make small talk and dress for dinner. His hospitable smile belied his heart as he stood on the steps a few days later watching the 'gypsies' and their caravan rumble into the forecourt, first Catherine and the other two ladies in the barouche with one of the duchesse's footmen up beside Durand, then a hired carriage from the station conveying the rest of their servants, then the brake, piled precariously with trunks, valises and hat boxes.

But perhaps Catherine repented her interference. It was true that she shot Miremont an appraising look as he handed her down from the barouche, but otherwise she seemed to have cast off her grand manner when she had tied on the simple straw bonnet trimmed with lilacs that crowned her country toilette, for she was as easy to please and as charming as he had known her. His other two guests were practically strangers to him (although he had encountered them at La Boissière he had scarcely exchanged a direct word with either and besides his mind had been occupied elsewhere) but they too realised none of his forebodings.

His principal recollection of the baroness, apart from her formidable size and presence—if not a Gorgon, she certainly resembled, in her antique robes and outlandish head-dresses, the high priestess of some ancient mystery requiring the type of emasculating sacrifice exacted by the cult of Cybele—was her habit of stirring up the dinner table with provoking topics, like someone prodding a wasps' nest with a poker. But this, Miremont came to realise, was because she shared his inability to concoct the frothy goblets of malice that passed for wit amongst the likes of Gilbert de Cressy and Princess Zelenska. In the small closed circle of Beauvallon she entirely forgot to press the Woman Question or dissect the latest financial scandal. Instead, she won Miremont's gratitude by enquiring about his work, while with Max she had a discussion about the Parnassians and the Symbolists that quite flowed over Miremont's head. Yet, while she was perceptive about literature, talked amusingly and had lived an interesting life— although married to a Magyar nobleman she had, she let slip, been born in Vienna, appeared to have made her home at one time or another in most middle European capitals, had met Nietzsche in Basle, Mickiewicz in Istanbul and Bakunin in Geneva, and, for all that, spoke with a faint Italian accent, so that her vast personage seemed a compendium of the conflicting cultural strains of an entire continent— she was modest about her own achievements and would only elaborate upon them if drawn, which prompted Miremont to recall that she did not stand on dignity, to remember the gusto with which she had joined in the Zelenski children's games.

Miremont could not but warm to her. He felt a pang of guilt that he had let her poetry wash over him at La Boissière as too overblown for his taste; he resolved to give it serious study when he returned to Paris.

Of Mlle de la Falaise, he had retained even fewer impressions. He had supposed she was very young and perhaps a little flighty. In truth, she would not see twenty-five again and this illusion of girlishness was fostered both by her penchant for figured organdie flounces reminiscent of first communions, and by her extreme liveliness, so that, although she could not precisely be described as pretty, having too large a nose and protuberant dark-rimmed eyes like a lemur, the animation of her features and her quick confident movements suggested a radiant health that might substitute for beauty. She was, Miremont realised, the epitome of those modern young women to be seen bicycling or playing tennis in the Bois de Boulogne, a strange and, to him, rather alarming species, so different from his own daughters. Nevertheless, she seemed touchingly devoted to her 'aunt'. Indeed he was envious of the openness with which they could display their friendship, the affectionate embraces their sex permitted them without prompting speculation.

This reminded him of what he had most dreaded. However, if the baroness and her niece recognised the handsome footman who had entertained the children at La Boissière, they did not betray it. Nor would Catherine, despite her misplaced sense of proprietorship, alert them—Miremont could rely absolutely on her friendship for that. But in any case—and this endeared them to Miremont above all else—they seemed refreshingly untroubled by snobbery and unconcerned to question their host's relationship with his young amanuensis; rather, taking their tone from Catherine, who treated the boy like some favourite nephew she was not above teasing unmercifully, they were inclined to make something of a pet of him as the youngest of the party. Thus, as they retired to the Grand Salon for coffee and brandy after a dinner that had surpassed Rosalie's usual exquisite standards, and during which there had been surprisingly little strain and a good deal of laughter, Miremont felt a sense of wellbeing he did not normally equate with social occasions.

That there were further admirable qualities to the New Woman he discovered the next morning. His guests had no wish to sit languishing in wicker chairs, waiting for someone to amuse them. Before he and Max had risen, the baroness and her niece, attended by the baroness's maid, had been out in their bathing dresses and hats for a dip in the lake. Mlle de la Falaise was a confident horsewoman, so they rode out as usual, with Catherine and the baroness following in the barouche. The baroness had one day measured her girth, she unselfconsciously admitted, and had ceased riding out of consideration for the horses: however, she proved impressive with a pistol when the little cavalcade diverted to the shooting gallery on its way up into the woods for a picnic luncheon in the Moorish kiosk.

Miremont began almost to regret that Beauvallon lacked a tennis court, as well as the equipment for archery, apparently another favourite sport of the two ladies; instead, Durand had been commissioned to hunt out the croquet hoops and mallets from Léonore's time and in the late afternoon, when the declining sun once again allowed outdoor pursuits, the party reassembled on the stretch of flat lawn behind the Temple of Dionysus.

From the shade of a holm oak, Miremont watched Mlle de la Falaise instructing Max in the rules of the game. It seemed to him that she was flirting with the boy—but then this was her way, Mlle de la Falaise flirted with everyone, with Catherine, even with Miremont himself, which for once, given his reassuring knowledge, did not alarm him. Yet, seeing how close the two of them stood, how their faces, as Max bent to absorb her talk of croquets and roquets, were separated only by the brims of their hats, it struck him that Max, although the source of that knowledge, was not discouraged by it from flirting too. And suddenly—perhaps it was the women's white dresses, or the scent of parched grass or the sound of laughter muffled by the afternoon heat—Miremont was back at La Boissière watching a tall young footman charming the children's nursemaid. And in that same moment—once again just as at La Boissière—he was aware, with horror, of being observed, of someone following his glance and divining his thoughts.

So acute was the sensation that when he glanced round he half-expected to see Tarascon's conspiratorial smirk. But it was the baroness who stood beside him, leaning on her mallet. She withdrew her gaze unhurriedly from Max, now bounding after the ball his over-enthusiastic practice stroke had sent far wide of the hoop, and from her niece, who was still laughing; her wise brown eyes favoured Miremont with a smile that rescued the precariously tilted dish of his happiness and set it gently on the level.

"They are beautiful, are they not, our young creatures? You and I, we are both blessed."

That night it was too hot for bedcovers; as Max slept, the moonlight etched in chiaroscuro the long sweep of his naked back, so that, still as he was, with the cast-off sheet caught in folds around his thighs, he recalled some recumbent Apollo from a Florentine frieze. Miremont, dazed by a fresh access of love, could not but reflect how far he had travelled, that he had felt no shame as he had smiled back at the baroness. This set him wondering what he would have made twelve months ago of this curious gathering beneath the roof of his beloved Beauvallon—the baroness and her niece celebrating their mysterious rites two bedrooms away, and further along the landing Catherine, in the arms of the taller of her two footmen, who, despite his bull neck and shifty eyes, was, according to Max, her present favourite. It amused Miremont to recall that he had once thought La Boissière louche. Yet Beauvallon, after all, had been built as a temple to illicit love, while Anselme, son of a less prudish age, had not confined himself to his dalliance with Mme Lopez, but had shown quite a taste for village girls and even, it was rumoured, for a succession of comely valets; the old libertine would have scoffed at his great-grandson's timid notions of debauchery.

"Hey-ho!" sighed Catherine, as they stood on the steps the next morning, watching her paramour and his fellow footman pile the party's boxes into the brake. "We vagabonds must be off to roam the highways and byways once again. And not a moment too soon. Another day of your rustic idyll, darling Armand, and I should be laid low with a sick headache."

However, from the sisterly kiss she reached up to plant on his cheek, Miremont gathered they had satisfied inspection.

Although the visit had been agreeable—surprisingly so—Miremont could not be said to miss his guests once they had gone. As July drifted into August and the nights became intolerably hot, he and the boy carried their mattresses out to the Temple of Dionysus and pitched camp there by the lake, plunging into the water on waking, then, still dripping and in their dressing gowns, sauntering back to the house for breakfast.

"Filth!"

That the voice was hoarse, scarcely above a whisper, did not diminish its ferocity: it little needed the thundering fist to give it emphasis nor the glass slammed down with such force that wine spattered the whitened boards of the kitchen table.

Durand's Adam's apple jigged assent. "What do I tell the gardeners, I'd like to know? How am I supposed to explain to Pichon why his boys must steer clear of that side of the lake in the mornings? If I have to pretend not to see what's as plain as the nose on my face, where's my authority?"

"Authority? You?"

Miremont would not have been surprised at Thomas nor perhaps even at Durand, who, he was aware, possessed those flexible principles which take a stand on any issue furnishing the opportunity for mischief: but he would have been astonished by Rosalie, sweetly smiling Rose, the woman he regarded as the personification of her sex's gentler qualities.

For she was not smiling now. Nor was she gentle as she whirled from the sink, still brandishing her filleting knife, to round upon her husband. "You'd like madame back, is that it? The lad's no trouble and he makes monsieur happy—"

"Oh well, that's all right then. So long as your beloved monsieur is—"

"Out!" The knife dripped blood and scales a whisker from Durand's nose.

"Go and pull me those scallions I asked for. And what happened to that mangle you were mending? And the blocked drain in the scullery? Go and make yourself useful for a change!"

"But, dearest—"

"Not another word. Out of my kitchen!"

Perhaps Thomas was amused by the sight of his crony gulping down the dregs in his glass and scurrying for the door, for his savage look seemed to relent somewhat. But even before Durand was gone, the accusatory knife was pointing at him.

"And as for you, my blockhead brother—leave aside the ingratitude, leave aside that Father and Mother would be wondering how to put bread on the table if Durand and me didn't have this place, and that it's a good place, where we can live as we please for most of the year—leaving aside all that, it's the hypocrisy of it that gets my goat. Didn't you and monsieur do the same when he was a boy? Sleeping out in the open, pretending to be wild men of the woods, lighting fires with sticks?"

Unlike Durand, Thomas had outfaced the reproaches of the filleting knife with a stony stare. But now, as his sister stared back, refusing to be deflected, he lowered his glance.

"Innocent!"

"And who's to say this isn't too? Don't talk to me about those priests of yours, if they don't see filth everywhere they're out of a job. If you spent less time whispering sweet nothings to Our Lady... But oh, what's the use?"

Rosalie's shoulders sagged, she flung the knife aside. Noting the splotches of blood and wine that besmirched her pristine table, she went wearily to fetch a cloth. "You've never used the brains you were born with, even before they were addled by that rock. Monsieur hung on your every word. You could have been steward by now instead of that thieving Calvert. Running off to be cannon fodder—what on earth possessed you I'll never understand."

CHAPTER THIRTY FOUR

Of course Max liked Beauvallon—even if Brother Bernard had not taught him to take pleasure in the countryside, how could he have disliked a life that might have been expressly arranged to delight him?

Although for the first few days he was uneasy. Every morning after breakfast he would offer to unpack the case of books in the library; but every morning, despite its contents having been chosen according to M de Miremont's precise instructions, the old fellow would demur: the weather was too glorious, perhaps later, after their ride, or tomorrow... "My dear boy, Ovid has waited for us for centuries, he can wait a little longer."

Having in one way or another been obliged to work all his life, Max could not shake off a certain guilt at not working. He felt that a compact had been broken: he was paid—continued to be paid—by monsieur to undertake certain duties; did not this idleness of his put an ambiguous slant on his situation? But his conscience was gradually soothed. After all, if this was what the old boy wished him to do, to assist him in his rural pursuits as he had in his studies, was not that work too, however enjoyable? And should he not bless his luck that he had escaped incarceration in the library?

To be in the saddle again, to fill his nostrils with the animal's scent, that sweet commingling of hay and dung, to feel the living breathing power of the beast, its muscles and sinews in communion with his own, to understand its foibles and command its will, to feel, as in his blood, that primal bond between man and horse—and not to be obliged to hold back, not to hear that distant but still-remembered voice ordering him to rein in, to keep always respectfully behind—shit, if he had ever been allowed on Bobik, he'd not have been thrown, he'd have put the little trickster through his paces all right!

He was eager for the afternoon's shooting practice too. Oh, not at first. He seethed with barely suppressed frustration for, while the old boy, despite claiming he needed to get his eye in, managed to pepper the centre of the target, all his own shots went wide and the more he willed himself to concentrate the greater his humiliation. But the old fellow was a patient tutor, correcting his stance and grip, showing him how to keep the sights aligned and to get his shot away fast without snatching at the trigger; until one afternoon he forgot to be angry with himself and found these things fell into place naturally, just as his body adapted itself to a trot or a canter. After that he loved it, the smell of powder, the feel of the gun in his hand, heavy yet well-balanced, a beautifully contrived object like monsieur's watch; he loved the satisfaction, the sense of power it gave him to use this beautiful thing as it deserved to be used, with calm precision.

Nor did it escape him that there was utility in these pleasures. The personages he must impress would expect him to ride and shoot—was this not presumed to be in his blood? And a further thought struck him. It might prove handy, in any case, to be a reasonable shot. While he disdained the fears instilled in his childhood—that went without saying—there was no harm, surely, in being prepared. He would buy his own revolver on their return to Paris.

As for Beauvallon itself, the old fellow's toy Arcadia amused him, while in many ways, not least that he was spared his furtive nocturnal excursions, he preferred the château to the Hôtel de Miremont. Compared with that Leviathan, it too was a toy, a doll's house, its decoration restrained, its graceful neo-classical furnishings all of a piece.

The library was modest; the pictures, once you set aside two Watteaus, a Fragonard and a Reynolds portrait of some Miremont relation by marriage, were mainly murky landscapes and stiff classical tableaux by deservedly unknown hands; and no amount of vigorous brushing and dusting by the two village girls who came in every morning could rejuvenate old Balthazar's damask hangings and Gobelin seat covers. All the same, there was something restful and even homely about this gentle decay: it reminded Max of monsieur's study. Nor did the lack of modern comforts trouble him as it had Lesage: he was perfectly content with candles, so long as it was Durand and not himself who must trim the chandeliers. Certainly it must be grim here in winter—if you ventured into any of the unused rooms on the upper floor you could detect, even though the sun was blazing outside, a distinct whiff of damp—but at the height of summer the faded salon with its dim, cool air and accommodating day-bed was a pleasant refuge.

Yet perhaps the most notable feature of Beauvallon was the transformation it had wrought in monsieur.

On their very first morning there had been the affair of the watch.

The increase in his wages had enabled Max to redeem it from pawn and now he carried it discreetly in his pocket. But it seemed monsieur had decided to fling discretion to the winds for, happening upon it in Max's bedroom, he had remarked with apparent surprise, as if having no recollection of his instructions: "You'd get much better use from it if you wore it, you know. That is, if you care to."

Once Max had recovered from his astonishment and when he discovered the other privileges that were to be bestowed upon him, he could not catch sight of the simple white-gold chain adorning his waistcoat without seeing it as the emblem of his freedom: here at Beauvallon he was at last permitted to exist in his own right. Naturally he was grateful. All the same this sudden nonchalance seemed most unlike the old boy.

Perhaps he had managed to cast off his hair shirt now he was away from his daughter's nagging and the scrutiny of his worldly-wise brother-in-law, not to say the squawking of the Buzzard. Yet if anxious ridges were no longer carved between his brows, if a new spring had entered his step, it was not simply because he had managed to stifle his conscience. Nor, however Max might flatter himself, was it solely due to his presence in the old boy's bed.

Initially Max had concluded that the estate, like the château and its garden, was another of monsieur's playthings. The old boy showed an improbable, almost childlike enthusiasm, not just for those precious cottages of his, but for threshing machine catalogues, grain yield figures, conversations about cattle breeds and the like. His relationship with his steward seemed perfectly to illustrate his naivety.

Admittedly, Calvert was not quite as Max had expected. A handsome, affable man of monsieur's age, hawk-featured, resplendently moustachioed, and affecting the manner and dress of a country squire, he did not seem at first sight an out-and-out rogue. Nevertheless he had a drinker's nose and Max distrusted his gold-toothed smile.

The steward had certainly done well enough out of monsieur. He and his wife, with their six children, occupied rent-free the rather grand stone house adjoining the home farm that monsieur's great grandfather had built to replace the original farmhouse. In addition, monsieur was supporting Calvert's eldest son in Paris as he studied at the École Normale. And, though Mme Calvert was never visible and the two youngest boys could often be found climbing the trees in the orchard or aiming their catapults at the hens in the yard, as muddy and ragged as any village urchin, Calvert himself appeared to live in some style and rode a fine bay that would not have disgraced monsieur's stable. Yet he was clearly abusing the old boy's generosity.

Take the cottages. A neat terrace of gabled dwellings, brick-built in two storeys after the English manner, each with its own yard and supplied with running water, they were intended to replace a straggle of ancient hovels on the road to the village. Drainage ditches had been dug and footings laid many months ago, yet here they were, still unfinished. Even Max, who knew nothing about building, could see some sort of fraud was involved. What else could explain this latest fiasco? Most likely Calvert had sold the high-quality wood cut from his master's coppices, then bought inferior timber and pocketed the difference. Max could see it, but could monsieur? True, the old fellow had summoned Calvert on their arrival and it was Max's impression that sharp words had been spoken. But all was amiable between the two of them now. And besides, so far as Max could gather, the old boy had been infuriated by the ridiculous delays rather than any suspicion of trickery.

Max did not forget the cunning ways of Brother Bernard: it was the instinct of every peasant to outwit his masters; how much greater the opportunity for someone in Calvert's position. Max felt outraged on monsieur's behalf. But when he ventured to hint at his concerns the old fellow's response was distressingly predictable.

"My dear Max, like the rest of us Médéric Calvert has his faults. But he has been managing Beauvallon on my behalf for fifteen years, as did his father before him, and his father's father in my great-uncle's time."

Max retreated with a sigh. It was Lesage all over again. Crazy old fellow with his sentimental loyalties, such a worshipper of truth, yet unable to recognise a swindle when it leapt up and bit him. But by now Max knew the old boy's intransigence where he felt an obligation: since Max's own interests were not engaged, he would do better to hold his tongue.

A day or two later, they were out for their morning ride when they encountered Calvert, also on horseback, on his way to call on one of the tenant farmers, who was complaining about a stolen cow. Since monsieur made a point of visiting all his tenants whenever he was at Beauvallon, they fell in with the steward and were soon walking their horses along an overgrown track. The farm, with less than two hectares of land, was not much more than a peasant small-holding and, in contrast to the two much larger farms they had so far visited, poorly kept. The tenant, a stolid man in his thirties who worked the land with his widowed mother, took them across a yard boggy with manure to a patch of scrubby pasture, where two white cows could be seen listlessly grazing; the third, as the widow herself explained volubly, had vanished just after morning milking as if spirited away by hobgoblins.

It seemed probable that, given the state of the hedges and the poverty of the grassland, the beast had simply made off in search of better fare. But Calvert's eyes narrowed: the old woman had barely got into her stride before he muttered something—Max thought he said: "To be sure, it's Thursday"—and, making his excuses, abandoned monsieur to the drawn-out end of the tale and to the litany of other complaints that followed. It was true that the old boy listened patiently and was even willing to be lured into the threadbare parlour to accept a measure of pear brandy; but surely here was yet another dereliction on the steward's part.

In any case, the matter of the missing cow appeared already to be resolved—as Max had surmised, the beast must have wandered—for, when they had finally escaped from the widow and were approaching the place where the track met the road, they encountered, coming in the opposite direction, a barefoot girl, a child of no more than ten, leading a dirty white cow on a makeshift halter. As they reined in to let her pass, the old boy, who appeared to know the entire population of Beauvallon by name, hailed her with a cheerful "Good day, Madeleine!" She was a pretty child despite her matted hair, and clearly not in awe of monsieur, for she looked him straight in the eye, almost defiantly Max thought, as she returned the greeting.

"No hobgoblins," Max observed. "Only a helpful imp."

The old boy laughed and was about to reply, when turning into the road, they came upon Calvert, keeping his horse at a leisurely amble in the girl's wake. To Max's amazement, in a reversal of proper form, monsieur tipped his hat to his steward. Calvert let out a chuckle that displayed all three of his effulgent teeth. Then, tipping in return, and maintaining the same unhurried pace, he rode off after the girl and the cow.

Although neither man had spoken, there was no mistaking the import of this exchange. Max suddenly understood the girl's defiant glance. "But how did he—? He's hardly been gone half an hour."

"He knew where to look. She's Plibou's eldest child."

Max vaguely recalled that Plibou was the village drunk and lived in one of the hovels that were to be demolished when the model cottages were habitable.

"They must have hoped to keep the beast under cover till the dead of night, when they could drive it to Soures. There's a market there every Friday."

"They?"

"Well, Plibou, naturally. But he sends Madeleine and his two eldest boys to do the pilfering. They're very adept, even though the youngest is only five. But the cow was perhaps over-ambitious."

"What will Calvert do? Fetch the constable?"

"Plibou would only plead innocence and blame the children. No, Madeleine will tell the Robinots some tale about rescuing the animal, which Madame Robinot will not believe—but at least they have recovered their property. The poor child can expect a beating when her father finds out, but that, alas, we are powerless to prevent."

Max too felt sorry for the girl: he had rather admired her defiance.

"However," continued M de Miremont, "Calvert will put the fear of God into Plibou and the hobgoblins will watch their step for a while. Very little in Beauvallon escapes Clavert. He's wise to the ways of all our elvish folk."

Max was tempted, despite his resolve, to reply that it took one to know one; but by now they had reached parkland and monsieur urged Pretender to a gallop. Nevertheless, the old fellow must have divined his thoughts, for later, over luncheon, when Durand and the maid had withdrawn, he reintroduced the topic.

"I observe, dear boy, that you still suspect poor Calvert of being Hobgoblin in Chief."

This uncharacteristic directness threw Max off balance. "Armand, it is hardly my place—"

"I'm an old fool, no doubt, but not that foolish."

"I certainly didn't mean—"

"Of course you didn't, my dear. I grant the poor fellow has his weaknesses—he's too fond of bezique, he keeps a mistress in Soures and, while he is no Plibou, he shares that wretch's devotion to the grape. But, to his credit, his accounts cannot be faulted. He is meticulous about collecting my rents—sometimes too meticulous and I have needed to plead leniency in deserving cases. He keeps a keen eye on contractors, he is ruthless at negotiating prices for our grain and wood, he manages the home farm on my behalf with commendable efficiency. Added to which, he is an agreeable fellow who, although Beauvallon is his daily responsibility and might more rightfully be judged his estate than mine, tolerates without resentment my interference for three months of the year. I only wish I could find someone as capable and trustworthy to sort out the endless problems at Miremont."

For all that this was a trenchant defence—it was notable that the old boy did not falter or search for words when the topic pertained to Beauvallon—Max could not resist enquiring: "Capable? Trustworthy? Even over the roof timbers?"

Monsieur smiled. "Perhaps there has been some chicanery. But there is another possibility."

"It's hard to see what."

"Sabotage."

Max had been in the act of lifting his fork to his mouth, but now he lowered it in astonishment. "Is not that worse?"

"Not if he believes it is in my best interests."

"To be rooked?"

"On the contrary, he hopes to save me money. Calvert rightly holds it his duty to extract the best possible income from the estate. But, you see, I also have duties. And sometimes I infuriate the poor fellow by going against reason. For instance, I cannot deny it would be rational to incorporate small-holdings like the Robinots' into one of the larger tenancies—the land would be better farmed and we could be sure of receiving our rent. But where would the Robinots go? Is it not preferable to help them make the best of their meagre hectares? And this is where I am truly infuriating. I oblige poor Calvert to conduct all manner of new fangled experiments on my own farmland. Sometimes they are dreadful failures but occasionally I am right. The new crop rotation scheme he has been trying out for me—"

"But the cottages?"

"Ah yes." Monsieur laid aside his knife and fork and took a sip of wine. "To poor Calvert they are my most lunatic whim yet. The style of building is not traditional to the village. He cannot see why labourers should need separate rooms upstairs for sleeping, or a tap in the scullery when they could go on taking buckets to the well. It offends him mightily, as you may understand, that Plibou will be one of the new tenants—yet we must consider poor Madame Plibou, to say nothing of the wretched children, who must somehow be prevented from going entirely to the bad. But his principal objection is this— given the rents we can realistically charge, we shall never recover the cost of these buildings, not in his lifetime or mine. Oh, he never argues with me, he is too clever for that. But since I first showed him the plans he has discovered practical problems and objections, until nigh on two years later we have arrived at our present situation. I think his hope was that the difficulties would make me lose heart. Now he fears that, if tenants finally move in and I am able, in spite of everything, to call the venture a success, I shall take it into my head to build more of these dwellings."

Max noted the glint in the old fellow's eye. "And shall you?"

"My dear boy, it will scarcely ruin me. And, if it were not my own inclination to provide the poor of the commune with somewhere decent to live, I should certainly be convinced by listening to Gérard, who has scientific evidence that soundly-constructed housing is fundamental to good health. Calvert will go on trying to save me from myself, but I can hardly dislike him for it."

Max remained sceptical: indeed, he was even somewhat shocked by the old boy's unsuspected capacity for pragmatism. If—when—he officially became monsieur's secretary, he would take a curry comb to the steward's 'faultless' accounts. Yet he could not help noticing that monsieur was more comfortable with Calvert than he was, even, with his friends from the Sorbonne. And, as they continued their daily rides, he was forced to admit that, at least where the estate was concerned, M de M was nobody's fool: he had a shrewd eye for detail and, although his courtesy never wavered and he listened more often than he talked, when he did speak it was with quiet authority. Lesage might complain he did not uphold the dignity of his rank: but at Beauvallon, while he did not invite deference and made not the slightest effort to impress, he was, it seemed to Max, to his fingertips M le marquis.

Max had once envied monsieur for instinctively knowing who he was. But now he understood this knowledge was not a weightless garment. In Paris, the old fellow's high principles were not ornaments but eccentricities. If he disdained to paint his escutcheon on his carriage and to put himself about in the smartest circles, what was the point of his ancient lineage and grand titles? What was left for him at the Hôtel de Miremont, except to become its curator, conserving past glories for an indifferent future? Small wonder he had gratefully discovered Ovid.

But, at Beauvallon, the old boy's notions of honour and obligation made perfect sense. Here his kindness was no longer troublesome, his sense of fairness no longer a curse. His generosity, as it gradually emerged, stretched far beyond the ill-starred cottages: as well as educating Calvert's son, he was sending two children from labourers' families to the Lycée at Dijon; he had paid for the village school to be rebuilt and for the casting of a new church bell; and he had a project afoot, in keeping with the lecherous doctor's precepts, to extend the drainage system serving the château, the home farm and the newly built dwellings until it reached the entire village.

Of course this was not monsieur's great-grandfather's time. As democracy required, the ruling power in the commune of Beauvallon was its mayor, who reported to the prefect at Auxerre. But there was no question where the actual power lay. Apart from a stretch to the west of the village, mainly given over to vineyards, monsieur owned all the land that brought most of the commune's four hundred-odd inhabitants their livelihood. The mayor, thrice-elected, was Hubert Saint-Séverin, the very same M Saint-Séverin with whom monsieur delighted to swap classical quotations when he visited the Maison des Vignerons, while all three members of the Municipal Council were monsieur's tenants. The old boy ruled this small corner of eastern France as a benevolent despot.

This could not but appeal to Max's private preoccupation with the exercise of power: he studied the old fellow with increasing respect. Yet he doubted monsieur viewed himself as a potentate. It might have been in the back of his mind that his philanthropy—the new school or the drainage scheme that the commune, with its modest state subsidy, could never otherwise afford—would win votes and ensure that his children inherited the estate intact. But if that were so, he never mentioned it. In fact, Max was intrigued to note, he did not even see himself as a philanthropist. Since he owned the land, he had an obligation to those who lived on it—it was as simple as that.

The inhabitants of Beauvallon seemed to have no particular quarrel with this state of affairs. Oh, there can have been few who felt Mme Rosalie's unqualified adoration: authority was authority, however benevolent. But, apart from the schoolmaster, whose wages were paid by the prefect, there seemed little Republican sentiment in the village. Certainly Plibou, a wild, emaciated figure with yellow eyeballs and a straggling beard, would shout abuse whenever he spotted the old boy, but otherwise, if there were hostility, it was reserved for Calvert: generally monsieur was held in grudging respect.

Poor old fellow, Max thought, seeing him for once full of purpose and comfortable with himself. If fate had allowed him to remain the second son, he might have been eternally content.

Max, too, was content as he lay reading Balzac in the orchard, lulled by the dense heat of mid-afternoon and its accompaniment of small sounds—bees, crickets, distant hens —muted to a gentle thrum by the heavy air.

Of course, he could not entirely relax. Lesage might be blissfully absent, but there was still Thomas, with whom he was thrust into closer quarters than ever before. However, the Cyclops' native territory provided him with distractions: as well as his ageing parents, who lived with the Durands, he seemed to have relations everywhere—the village constable was a Thomas, so were two of the grooms and the farrier—and then there were the temptations of the village *tabac*, run by yet another of his multitudinous cousins. Although baleful as ever, the Monoculus seemed generally content with giving his adversary a wide berth.

Still, that sister of his must be considered, too-good-to-be-true Mme Rosalie. Max remained circumspect about the Durands. But at least no dead birds erupted from his chimney and his shirts returned from the laundry unscathed.

Yes, he was made for this life: just as well that destiny, sooner or later, must requite her past cruelties by securing it for him as his right. He cursed his nightmares and would have much rather kept this weakness to himself, but perhaps in future he should bless them, for they had roused the old boy's interest again.

As Max lay in his hammock, immersed in *Splendeurs et misères des courtisanes* and the continuing adventures of the young and handsome Lucien de Rubempré as he scaled the slippery heights of society aided by his rich middle-aged lover Vautrin, he could not forgo certain comparisons. This time, he would not flounder in the shallows of detail when he made his appeal. But the moment for that was not now; he was learning too much and enjoying himself too well. Let the old boy puzzle over unanswered questions. Much better to keep him in suspense until they returned to Paris.

Of course it was mischievous to compare poor M de Miremont to Vautrin. Balzac's most compelling creation was, after all, a master criminal, devious, sinister and intent on domination. Whereas monsieur—Max laughed—while his respect for monsieur grew daily, he still considered the old fellow too virtuous for his own good. Unlike Vautrin's, his generosity set no terms. Yet Max would be a monster of ingratitude if he did not feel in his debt for these weeks at Beauvallon. And there was a way to repay him. There was something monsieur longed for, a small thing, easily granted.

The difficulty was that, when Max turned it over, it transpired not to be so small—indeed, as he considered its implications, it grew disturbingly.

Damn Catullus! Surely monsieur, of all people, recognised hyperbole. It had not occurred to Max—although he supposed it should have—that he would take poetic license literally. Poor M de M, he had borne his dashed expectations like a stoic. Yet Max could not fail to notice the wistful expression that sometimes appeared in the old fellow's eyes, a look that deepened into regret when he supposed he was unobserved. Max could not deny that, however he tried to shrug it off, this look left him unsettled. For he could easily end monsieur's pain: three short words would do it.

Three short lying words. Max had uttered them before when it had suited him—indeed had he not, in unhappier times, considered testing their effect upon monsieur? But he had not spoken them then and he would not speak them now. He could not, even when to say them would seem a kindness.

During their time together here, as his understanding of the old boy had grown, so had his affection. Yes, he was fond of the old fellow, very fond and, rather to his surprise, even after all these months, he could still be excited by their love-making. But what he had once asserted to Fabrice was surely as true now as it had ever been. He was not in love with him.

Painfully, he recalled the riot of emotion he had felt for Dom Sébastien, the worship, the idolatry, how the movement of his god's long limbs, the very turn of his head, would leave him weak, ready to pour out his heart, make a gift of himself, body and soul. No, he was not in love with monsieur. And he would not lie to him.

It could not be the old boy's fetish for the truth that restrained him: after all, when they returned to Paris he planned to present the poor old fellow with a whole screed of falsehoods. Nor was it that he quailed before Mme de Claireville's threats of retribution: besides, from her latest inspection—if her calling him 'my little bumpkin' and picking imaginary straw from his hair were to be gone by—she still judged him reassuringly stupid.

Well, she might believe what she liked. Stupidly or not, it would trouble him to mislead monsieur, at least in this. He had felt no such scruples in lying to her because she, old witch, had a heart as adamantine as the brilliants about her neck. But monsieur was another matter.

In any case, there were the consequences to consider. What longing deemed beyond price possession devalued. He could still taste the blood where Dom Sébastien had split his lower lip. Sébastien, whom he loved far more than God. Sébastien, whose smile was gentle, who had held him during his nightmares, whose touch brought him agonies of pleasure, who only the day before had covered that place on his lip with kisses, and who now stood before him, wild-eyed, sweating, raving that he had been visited by his name saint, pierced with arrows, who had told him he would burn eternally in Hell for what they had done together, for what he, Max, had tempted him to do.

Max remembered being puzzled as the blows struck him. How could the man he worshipped suddenly cease to love him? His own love had not ceased. He had tried to sneak into the infirmary, where Sébastien was locked away—they said he had attempted to punish himself as Hélouise's family had punished Abelard, though that doubtless came from Xavier, who liked to invent ghoulish tales—but in the morning Sébastien was driven off in a closed carriage, Dom Jérôme moved into the curtained alcove he had occupied as Magister of the postulants' dormitory, and Max never saw his beloved face again.

During the time afterwards of beatings, penances and interrogations, Max had sworn to the Reverend Father, sworn by Our Lady, that Dom Sébastien had never done anything bad to him. And that was true: he had done nothing that Max had not desired; indeed, compared with the Reverend Father's brutal detentions, their caresses had been of the most innocent kind. But if Sébastien were blameless, then it must be as they insisted: he, Max, was the guilty one. Had he not been told from infancy that he was seeded in sin, was he not reminded of it daily by the presence of the Other?

Max could little recall the dark months that followed. Yet something had flowered out of that mire of pain. He had ceased to be a child: God, Our Lady, Heaven, Hell, sin—that was when he began to see it was all mere cant. He could listen to Brother Bernard's wisdom and hold up his head in defiance.

For several years he had cherished a virulent anger towards Sébastien: what had his 'god' been, after all, but the ill-educated son of a Norman peasant who had let his wits—what wits he had—be overturned by ridiculous nonsense. Max could also see his own blind adoration for what it was: the mortifying infatuation of an eleven-year-old. But latterly when he thought of Sébastien he could understand what he had loved in him.

However that may be, he had learned his lesson: he would never again make a gift of himself, not to anyone.

The Temple of Dionysus sat where the lake bellied out around the island where the grotto lay hidden. Raised on a low artificial mound, the temple was cunningly situated so that its facade captured prospects of the lake and the lawns stretching up to the garden front, while its rear casements looked towards the Moorish kiosk and the wooded heights beyond, affording a view of the dawn breaking behind the Gothic tower's battlements.

Yet the temple was designed not just to feast the eye, but to deceive it. Despite its colonnade and its imposing pediment decorated with a relief of the god's majestic progress in his leopard-drawn chariot, it was built not of stone, but of stuccoed wood, while the relief was a painting in grisaille. In truth, it was a glorified summerhouse, rickety in construction and furnished only with a dusty opium couch and a couple of cane chairs.

At first Max, who had not forgotten his time sleeping in doorways, and to whom down pillows and chain springs, while no longer novelties, were not yet luxuries to be dispensed with lightly, was hard put to share the old boy's enthusiasm for the temple's rudimentary comforts. All the same, once they had pushed aside the chairs and covered the worn tiles with mattresses—Max was too tall for the couch—it was by no means a disagreeable place to spend a summer night. Beside the lake the air was cooler. From the colonnade, as you looked out upon the star-dusted night sky, distant sounds came to you with faultless clarity above the gentle threnody of the water wheel; horses shifting in their stalls, the hooting of owls, the crack of a shotgun as some villager kilometres away hunted rabbits. In the morning, a heady scent drifted in through the open casements from a shrubbery at the rear, where honeysuckle had been allowed to run wild over the bushes. It was possible in this solitary spot, as they made love on waking, then, flinging open the door to the sun, ran the few strides to the lake to meet the breathtaking shock of its waters, to imagine they were a world away from orderly life and its prejudices and prohibitions.

For Max, however, there was a disquieting element to their bucolic sleeping arrangements. As August advanced, spiders' webs began to appear in the shrubbery. M de M would pause to admire them on their way to breakfast; and, viewed impartially, the delicate filigree, pearled with dew, might be considered beautiful—if one ignored its artificer, set in the centre like a venomous jewel.

When Max had told Fabrice he was afraid of spiders, he had not spoken entirely in jest. In the cellar, during the long hours of total darkness while their captors slept, he and the Other had lived in terror of the invisible scurrying army that had invaded their bedding with its filthy, furtive, whispering touch. St Pons, and afterwards life in servants' quarters, had gradually inured Max to rats and mice. But, much to his shame—he would rather walk through fire than confess such a womanish fear—he had never succeeded in cultivating an equal indifference to spiders.

It was with a shudder, therefore, that he noticed one morning a web the size of a dinner plate, not out in the shrubbery, but within the summerhouse, suspended between the corner wall and the couch, a bare metre from his mattress. The web was empty and there was no sign of its occupant. But, just in case, when the old boy's back was turned and he would have no need to explain himself, he took up one of the candlesticks and with, a single determined stroke, demolished the structure and its pinions, so that not a strand was left.

The next morning as he and monsieur lay, still drowsy, letting shafts of sun from the open windows play upon their naked bodies, Max felt an ominous, abhorrent tickling on his upper arm. Instantly wide awake, his heart racing, he reared up, slapping at the place, unable to repress a cry of disgust as his fingers met something soft and living.

Monsieur also sat up. "My darling boy, whatever...?" Then his alarm vanished. "Oh, my dear, it's hardly a scorpion."

Max forced himself to follow the old boy's glance. At the bottom of the mattress, where he must have propelled it, the creature struggled to extricate itself from between two folds of the discarded sheet. It was about the size of his thumbnail, its swollen body almost too burdensome for its long slender legs, whose sinister points, as it finally levered itself out of the crevasse, gave it the mincing gait of an obese ballerina. Max could only look at it for a second before his gorge rose. He reached for the candlestick.

"Good heavens no!" M de M, to Max's astonishment, was on his knees, bending towards the repulsive thing. "She's harmless unless you're a fly. And she's quite a beauty."

Max watched, frozen, as the old boy, laying his index finger in the creature's path, let it perch there for an instant, before gently dislodging it into his left palm. Then, enclosing it with his right, he edged back towards Max. He parted his hands.

"*Araneus diadematus*. The common garden spider. But exquisite for all that. See how the white specks on her abdomen make the mark of the cross?"

Although his heart was once again galloping, Max knew he must look or reveal his cowardice. He glanced down but, despite his determination to focus, saw only a yellowish brown blur and repulsively waving legs. He attempted a laugh of bravado, but nothing came: "Ah—yes," was all he could manage.

The old boy abruptly closed his hands—because he was concerned the creature might escape, Max endeavoured to convince himself, not because he had detected Max's horror—then, rising from his knees while holding out his arms, as if he carried some precious piece of porcelain, he walked to the couch and climbed onto it in order to lean out of the window.

The laughter that had eluded Max suddenly convulsed him. Partly he laughed from sheer relief that the ordeal was over; but also he found the spectacle of M le marquis de Miremont, poised stark naked, tenderly decanting the wretched thing into the shrubbery, all at once irresistibly, unbearably funny. Daft old boy, kind to a fault, kind even to spiders. By the time monsieur had climbed down from the window Max's eyes were wet.

"Are you mocking me, miserable boy?" Monsieur's tone was light: yet he must have misunderstood the edge hysteria had given to Max's laughter, for he was clearly trying not to be offended.

Max felt ashamed of himself. "You're a crazy old fellow. But I love you for it."

His words brought them both up short.

The instant Max realised what he had said, he knew M de M would give it too much meaning. And yes, the old boy's expression confirmed it. However, he did not indulge in his usual outpourings. Instead, bending briefly to squeeze Max's shoulder and murmuring "Dearest boy" in a voice that was suddenly indistinct, he turned away and, snatching up his dressing gown, went out into the colonnade.

Max sat for a moment bewildered. He was glad. In fact, as if something tightly wound within him had all at once snapped, he felt overwhelming relief. He could not take back his words, nor did he wish to. While he might not have meant them in precisely the way they had been understood, they were not untrue. He did love the old fellow, loved him as he had loved Brother Bernard, as he loved Mitya Zhukovsky. He was glad he had been able to make him happy.

Max stretched luxuriantly, bathing his limbs in the sunlight: for once in his life, he was startled to discover, he too was happy.

That night, in the early hours, the weather broke and Beauvallon was hit by a tremendous thunderstorm. The flat roof of the temple proved unequal to the downpour and they were forced to decamp hastily to the château.

CHAPTER THRTY FIVE

The following morning, the sky was almost cloudless: apart from a new freshness in the air and the sudden verdant lustre of lawns and shrubs, the storm had left little trace.

In their present euphoria, Miremont and Max had viewed their precipitate evacuation of the temple as an amusing escapade, although they had rapidly been soaked to the skin and with the rain driving into their faces they could barely see their way—Max, who carried their only lantern, had narrowly prevented Miremont stumbling into the lake. When they had at last reached Miremont's bedroom, they had collapsed onto the bed, muddy and exhausted, but still laughing. They continued in high spirits when, having breakfasted somewhat later than usual, they left for their morning ride.

Three days ago, Miremont had surrendered to the inevitable and had let Max ride Pretender. He had done so not without misgivings nor without treating the boy to a lecture on the animal's uncertain temperament and the perils of recklessness. Max had taken this with a shrug but had nevertheless shown suitable caution so far and Miremont, who was pleased to have Darius returned to him, could not but admit, as he watched Max in the stable yard swinging gracefully into Pretender's saddle, that the two of them, tall, handsome and wilful, were well-matched.

Yet this morning's elation seemed to have woken a devil in the boy. Although the going was still slippery from the downpour, the moment they reached the parkland he urged Pretender to a gallop and, although Miremont had warned against it, began making too free with the whip, seeming determined to goad to the horse to his limits. Miremont's competitive spirit was not so fierce that he was prepared to belabour Darius, particularly in these conditions. As they fell behind he shouted to Max to ease up; but the only reply that drifted back to him was laughter.

Just beyond the Old Manoir was a gully that had once held a tributary to the river, long since dried to a mere trickle. Although the rain had augmented its flow, it was not a difficult jump, certainly no challenge for a horse of Pretender's power and reach, not if taken, according to the elementary principles of good horsemanship, straight on. But as Max and Pretender thundered towards it—what was he thinking of, was it simply carelessness or was it perversity, the pursuit of danger for danger's sake?—the boy made no attempt to change course but, as Miremont, from the rear, watched in dismay, set his mount to jump the gully diagonally.

Even then, Pretender might have been equal to it, had his front hooves not skidded in the mud on the far side, so that his back hooves caught the edge of the bank. His hind quarters began ominously to slew sideways while Max fought not to sail over his head.

As Miremont urged Darius to jump, he expected to see both horse and rider slide back into the gully. But Pretender, it seemed, was not willing to suffer such ignominy. By the time Miremont and Darius had landed safely on the far bank, with a great thrust of his powerful back legs he had regained his footing and was already several metres ahead of them, with Max still clinging on in the saddle.

What happened next Miremont would continue to see for days to come, over and over. Pretender reared up, immensely tall, on his hind legs, and with a contemptuous toss of his head, flung the boy from his back; then, with a leap and a vengeful backwards kick aimed at the prone body for good measure, he galloped off.

Max lay on his left side with his head turned away. Miremont, steadying Darius, who seemed disposed to follow Pretender, looked for him to move. But he did not.

Miremont froze. His heart seemed to stop beating and his mouth grew dry. It must have been only for a second or two that he sat in his saddle immobilised, begging, praying that Max would get up, but the moment seemed infinite. Then two parallel streams of thought began racing through his head: the first, coolly practical, reminded him that he would need Darius to ride for help, that he must tie him up somewhere before he went to the boy; the second, as he galloped towards a clump of hawthorn, kept asking why, why had he been such a fool, why had he ever believed Max would heed caution, why was it that one idiotic rash act could in an instant wipe out the whole of life's joy?

When he reached the hawthorn and looked back, the body on the ground was still motionless. Max had fallen off to the side and not, Miremont thought, on his head, but perhaps Pretender's kick had found its mark there, or perhaps he had injured his back or neck. The nearest doctor lived just outside Soures but one of the grooms could saddle up, it might not, could not be too late…

Dismounting and tethering Darius as best he could, Miremont began to run. He was still a few metres from the prone figure when his legs began to tremble as though they would give under him. For the boy was slowly sitting up. By the time Miremont reached him, he had regained his feet, albeit somewhat stiffly, and was brushing mud from the sleeve of his jacket.

Miremont was so weak with relief he could barely speak. "Oh, my darling, darling boy! I thought…"

"Just a bit winded, that's all." Max grinned. "Nothing broken." His grin widened. "But you're right, there's a devil in that horse."

Miremont had been rushing forward to embrace him. But he stopped stock still. His relief was obliterated by a sudden tearing anger, the anger that had seized him when Thomas had thrown away the pebble, the uncontrollable, unreasoning anger that until he fell in love with the boy he had not known he possessed.

"You stupid, stupid…! "

He raised his riding crop and struck Max across the face.

It took him a moment fully to realise what he had done. He had not even been aware that he still clutched his whip. Now, his rage vanishing as quickly as it had come, he looked down at the thing, bewildered. He had never before hit anyone in anger, never throughout the unendurable years of his marriage, never in his entire life. He dropped the whip as if it scorched him.

"Oh, dear God! Max! Oh, God in Heaven, forgive me!"

There was a thin red wheal on Max's right cheek and scarlet welled from his upper lip where the leather loop of the crop must have caught it. Otherwise his face was paper-white. His expression was indecipherable.

The sight of the blood filled Miremont with fresh horror. He fumbled in his sleeve for his handkerchief. "Here, my darling boy, please let me…"

But when Miremont took a step towards him, Max stepped back.

"Max, I'm so sorry. It was the shock. I didn't mean…I wouldn't for the world—"

"You won't whip a horse, monsieur. You won't even kill a filthy spider. But you'll take your riding crop to me."

It was not just the boy's icy tone that crushed Miremont, but his use of 'monsieur' and *vous*. Miremont watched, stricken, as Max wiped his mouth with the back of his hand, then ran his tongue over the cut as if he wished to taste it. He spat. Then he turned his back on

Miremont and walked to where his hat lay, some distance from where he had been thrown.

He was not entirely unscathed from the fall, Miremont noted with alarm, but was limping quite badly on his left leg. Nevertheless, punching the hat back into shape, he jammed it onto his head and began to walk away.

"Where are you going?" Miremont called out anxiously.

The boy did not turn round. "To find Pretender."

"He'll be halfway to Auxerre by now."

Max did not reply but continued walking, so that Miremont had no choice but to pursue him. "Max, stop! Come back with me on Darius, and we'll send the grooms to look for Pretender."

But Miremont knew, even as the words left him, that Max, whatever his injuries, would never accept the humiliation of riding into the stable yard clinging on behind him.

"Better still, take Darius."

At this Max at last turned round, but his face did not soften. "Thank you, monsieur, but I prefer to walk."

"But you're hurt. And you're going in the wrong direction."

Max shrugged.

Watching him hobble away, Miremont could not blame him for refusing to forgive him.

The grooms had gone out with an extra horse in case, as they searched for Pretender, they came upon Max as well. But the boy arrived back less than half an hour after Miremont returned from the stables: as he waited anxiously in the salon, he heard a commotion from beyond the portico doors and, when he went into the vestibule to look, there was Max climbing down from a cart driven by Robinot.

The boy must have cut back to the road, where he had chanced upon the farmer, but he disdained an explanation; although he could see Miremont standing in the vestibule, indeed must brush past him to gain the staircase, he went upstairs without a word.

Some time before luncheon, one of the grooms came to report that Pretender had also been recovered: he had scarcely gone beyond the park before he had allowed himself to be distracted by two mares in a nearby field.

While Miremont's immediate anxieties were stilled, his wretchedness in no way abated. The boy sent word by one of the maids that he would not be taking luncheon; and when Miremont, after his solitary meal, went upstairs to his bedroom, the door at the far end of the dressing room remained resolutely shut, with no sound from within.

It seemed to Miremont that he had forfeited any right to plead with the boy. Besides, it would be pointless. At the very least, Max's pride had been hurt: at worst— Miremont went down to the library, determined to think no further. Yet Ovid could not distract him and when the time came for the shooting gallery he had not the heart for it: throughout that dismal afternoon he could not escape its contrast with the day before and the joy that had burnished it. But now—Miremont struggled again to understand how this love of his, which rendered him so acutely alive, so aware of all that was beautiful in the world and so tenderly disposed towards it, could at the same time spawn his corrosive jealousy and now this vile anger: if these things lived within him—him, a man generally considered peaceable if dull, a dry stick lacking the sap of strong feeling—what else might he prove capable of, what other repugnant acts must he guard against committing?

No, he should not, must not beg Max for what he did not deserve.

All the same, when he went up before dinner to change his linen only to find the connecting door still closed, and when a message came that Max would not be dining, he immediately rued his preoccupation with his own misery. Although the boy had not been seriously injured, he would surely have felt the shock of the fall. And then—Miremont recoiled once more in shame—there was the damage to his face: mercifully, when Max had wiped away the blood, the cut on his lip had not seemed deep, but should it not be properly attended to? The boy may have set himself against all help but it was unthinkable to leave him where he was without at least enquiring if he were ill or in pain.

As expected, Miremont received no answer to his knock: he gently turned the door knob.

Max lay flat on his back on the bed. He had not pulled back the counterpane and still wore his riding breeches and boots. Otherwise, the room retained its usual spartan neatness and, apart from a few spent cigarettes, there was little evidence of how he had occupied himself during these long hours—the pile of books on the chair beside the bed seemed untouched. Perhaps he had passed the time staring up at the tester, blank-faced, as he was now.

Miremont could not but notice, too, the purple shadow below the boy's cheekbone and the dark thread of congealed blood bisecting the curve of his upper lip: recalling how he loved to kiss that wanton curve, he came for a moment close to weeping. He steeled himself to be matter-of-fact.

"My d—Max—forgive me for intruding. But you must...It would be a pity to miss dinner."

The boy adjusted his gaze to stare at Miremont coldly. "Did you not receive my apologies, monsieur? I can't come down."

"But you've had nothing since breakfast. Are you ill?"

"No."

" Does your...would eating be painful? "

"No!" Max seemed to wage a fierce struggle with himself, then, to his own exasperation, give in. "You don't understand. I *can't* come down."

"Well, I know the situation is awkward—"

"Oh shit!" The boy began to sit up, wincing, Miremont noted, and with some difficulty. "This is so idiotic, so damned feeble! I didn't want any sort of a fuss—I thought it would wear off. But, if you must know, I can't walk. My leg has seized up."

Miremont quelled the impulse to rush to him and take him in his arms: he retained his careful distance at the foot of the bed. "Shall I fetch the doctor?"

Max shook his head. "Thank you, monsieur, but it isn't broken, it brought me back here. But now—confound it!—it just won't work."

"Have you examined it?"

"How the hell can I?"

How stupid of Miremont not to comprehend the humiliating extent of the boy's predicament: he had not remained in his breeches and boots from choice. Miremont took a few steps forward. "Perhaps... if you would let me...?" Given the delicacy of situation, he hesitated. "But maybe it would be better if I rang for Thomas."

In other circumstances Miremont would have been amused by Max's appalled look. But at least he could take it that, however reluctantly, the boy would accept his help. For all that, Max might have done better with Thomas, since Miremont could not recall when he had last pulled off someone's riding boots—had they been his brother's or even his father's? Thomas, when not in one of his moods, removed Miremont's own boots with such proficiency that he was hardly aware of his doing it, but try as he might to replicate his valet's technique, even Max's right boot was a battle. And when it came to the left, although the poor boy did his best not to show it, Miremont could not avoid causing him pain. Then followed the business of divesting him of his muddy, grass-stained breeches.

The intrusiveness of this struggle sat oddly with the icy formalities of their estrangement. Yesterday, Miremont could not help reflecting, they would have made a joke of his clumsy ministrations. But although Max had asked after Pretender—while he had heard the horse had been found, he wished to be reassured he was unharmed—the few words they exchanged otherwise were those of polite strangers and confined to practicalities. As Miremont assisted Max to raise his pelvis and gently eased the breeches downwards, only the boy's quickly suppressed intake of breath broke the frigid silence.

A massive burgeoning bruise, or series of bruises, was revealed, crimson and magenta, scarlet where the skin was grazed, stretching from Max's left hip to below his knee. Apart from the bruising, there seemed nothing else amiss: the boy's toes moved freely, Miremont was relieved to see. Once the bruises had fully emerged the stiffness would vanish. There was a concoction traditionally used by his family for speeding this process, a receipt supposedly requiring all manner of medicinal herbs, although, from its vile smell, Miremont fancied it consisted mainly of comfrey: nevertheless, it was soothing and Rosalie always kept a bottle in readiness. Rather than press the bell, he went downstairs to instruct her in person.

As the little procession entered the bedroom—Miremont, Rosalie bearing a bowl containing the liniment and Pélagie, the housemaid, carrying hot water and towels—Miremont dreaded re-encountering the boy's stony face. It was true that Max allowed himself a small tight smile; but that was for the benefit of the servants. Likewise Miremont should not draw hope from his pleading glance when Rosalie offered to apply the potion: it was embarrassment that made Max prefer him for his nurse.

Once the women had left, Miremont helped his patient onto his right side and set to, bathing the bruises, then disinfecting the grazes with iodine before he painted on the concoction with lint. As he worked, the mingled smells of iodine and comfrey reminded him of the times Thomas had performed this ceremony after his own various childhood tumbles and, in spite of himself, he smiled when Max, who had scarcely uttered a gasp during the agonising removal of his boot, yelped like a schoolboy at the stinging iodine, just as he, Miremont, had always done. But apart from this, they continued in silence.

When Miremont had finished and was helping his patient to sit up, he quickly pulled the sheet up to his waist, for it seemed unsuitable, as things stood, that he should witness the boy's nakedness when it might be avoided. Yet it was impossible to forget his usual joyful familiarity with this naked flesh. His heart sank for he knew what he must do next.

"My dear fellow, I think I should have a look at your lip."

"No. There is no need. It is better left alone."

"Max, you must believe I would give anything—"

"Please, monsieur." The boy appeared to heave in breath. "I do not forgive you for what you did. But I must apologise to you."

Miremont stared at him.

It seemed the boy had made use of their silence, for what came next, delivered stiffly and in something of a rush, was evidently a prepared speech. "Naturally I was intending to leave at once. I should have asked Durand to drive me to the station if I hadn't suddenly felt unaccountably faint. I fell asleep and when I awoke—well, since then I have had plenty of time to think. I understand now why you were so angry. Pretender is a valuable horse and he could have broken a leg. Actually—" here his preparedness disintegrated suddenly into passion "—he's a superb horse. I know you think he is tricky, but he's also intelligent and strong and courageous. I should never have blamed him for what happened. I treated him badly—my stupid determination to show him who was master!—and I deserved to be thrown. So I can see, monsieur, why you were furious. To think I could have killed him—"

"Oh, damn the horse!"

Now it was Max's turn to look astonished.

"I don't mean," said Miremont, hastily regaining control of his voice, "that I shouldn't have been grieved to see Pretender shot. Or that I disagree with your verdict on your horsemanship this morning. But it is not—or rather it's only partly why I was angry." Sighing deeply, he set aside the bowl of liniment and sat down on the bed. "You must understand, love is profoundly selfish. When I saw you lying there, not moving, I saw my own grave open up before me."

"But I—I told you—I was only winded."

"How was I to know that? You seem to value your life so lightly—hurling yourself out of windows, taking jumps like some crazed bareback rider in a travelling circus. Do you imagine there is so much beauty in this world that it doesn't matter if you squander yours? That it will be of no account if you meet a futile end—that nothing will be lost? That one trifling instant of excitement justifies a needless, senseless, pointless…"

Miremont paused for fear the repugnant anger would reclaim him. "My darling Max, when you love and are loved, you are not free…" But here he paused again, now afraid that he presumed too much.

The boy was still staring at him, seeming both surprised and puzzled. "You mean—you struck me because you love me?"

"No! No, of course not. I was attempting to explain why I was angry. As for why I…for the other, I can neither explain or excuse it. I shall not even try. It was inexcusable. "

Miremont's cigarette case was in his jacket, hanging on a chair: he fetched it. At least Max did not shrink from touching his cupped hands as he proffered the match.

The boy blew out smoke thoughtfully. "It is a great insult."

Miremont winced. His shame had dwelt on the ignominy of striking any human being, let alone the man he loved; but of course Max would see the blow to his pride as his greater crime.

"Men have been called out for less."

Unsure where this tended, Miremont nodded. "Although not in these enlightened times."

"Of course," Max continued, "the difference in our ranks would be a difficulty."

"My dear boy, that is not the only—"

"But in any case it would be pointless."

Miremont, who had been reflecting that if he lost the boy he would be happy to let him put a bullet in him, were it not that Max would go to the guillotine, saw that he was all at once smiling. "Oh?"

"Knowing you, you'd fire into the air."

Miremont smiled too. "My dear, we should never even begin walking towards the barrier. My seconds would present you with an abject apology. And I do apologise, Max, from the bottom of my heart. Although, since my eloquent seconds are not to hand, I cannot see why you should accept it. I can only pray that you will."

And with that, since it had not escaped him that Max, when he had spoken last, had called him *tu*, and he feared to discover it had been a slip of the tongue, he rose and pressed the bell for Pélagie to bring the tray bearing the boy's dinner.

Miremont passed a drab and lonely evening: it mystified him to recall how he had once found his own company so enjoyable. When he went to bed he noticed a light beneath Max's door and it was still there when Thomas had finished undressing him—perhaps the boy's bruises made sleep difficult, particularly in this oppressive heat. Tentatively, as before, Miremont knocked and, when the only reply was silence, went in.

Max had fallen asleep with the lamp still burning. He lay, covered only by his shirt, on his right, uninjured side, with his right profile buried in the pillow so that the damage to his lip was barely visible. Yet Miremont could not avoid noticing it as he stood motionless beside the bed contemplating that well-loved face, made separate from him, unfathomable, by the infinite distance of sleep.

He bent and softly kissed the boy's cheek.

Having extinguished the lamp, he was nearly at the door when there was a creak of bedsprings. "Armand?"

Miremont could see by the moonlight that Max had turned onto his back and that his eyes were now wide open, so that he found himself wondering if the boy had truly been sleeping.

"Yes, Max?"

"I meant to ask you—about Pretender? Would you give me another chance with him?"

It was not a request that should have filled Miremont with any degree of enthusiasm, let alone with relief and joy. Yet he was so overwhelmed by both that he could not at first speak.

The next morning, although he was still inclined to limp, Max could bend his knee again and insisted they should ride as usual. Watching him make much of Pretender when he was brought out from his stable, Miremont was again prey to apprehension—it was possible that, of all the lessons learnt yesterday, Pretender's was the most deadly and Max would struggle to master him now. Yet to refuse the boy would be to strike a further blow at his pride. If nagging anxiety were to be the price of Miremont's own second chance, then he must pay it.

But that morning he could not criticise Max's handling of his mount or the way the horse responded and after a couple of days he was obliged to admit that as long as they could both curb their demons they worked well together. Life at Beauvallon resumed its usual course. Max's bruises faded and his lip healed. And if Miremont felt a lingering sorrow, as though some finely wrought thing, too fragile to sustain the weight of supreme happiness, had suffered an invisible but perilous crack, there was no outward sign to confirm it, either in Max's manner towards him or in their mutual enjoyment of their agreeable routines.

CHAPTER THIRTY SIX

It was now the middle of August. The labourers bringing in the harvest toiled in a haze of heat and dust, butter melted at the table and the water in the lake was no longer bracing but lukewarm and redolent of decaying vegetation.

As they sat at breakfast, Miremont went through the post as usual. Early in their stay there had been a steady stream of letters, mostly from Lesage on matters of business, but now the flow had dwindled; duty letters still came from Clotilde, who, with her husband and children, had gone to stay with her mother in Burgundy—these always left Miremont somewhat irritable—but, since Paris was on holiday, there had been little from Lesage in recent weeks and for the last week nothing. This morning, however, there was an envelope addressed in a hand which, although it seemed vaguely familiar, Max could not place: the old boy opened it with a smile but as he read it, then adjusted his pince-nez to read it again, the smile faded to dismay.

"Damn!" he said quietly. "Damn."

"More gypsies?"

Miremont stared at Max blankly for a moment. "No. Not that. But I fear, dear boy, that we must return to Paris, I cannot see any help for it."

"Paris? But I thought—"

"This is from Gérard. Lesage has taken a fall from the library steps and broken his wrist."

"Poor old chap." Although, of course, he was sorry for the Buzzard, Max found himself wondering suspiciously what he had been doing in the library. But he was also puzzled. "Surely—I mean, of course, it's wretched for him—but if Dr Gérard is already in attendance and has patched him up…?"

"Alas, there is more to it." Miremont sighed. "It is his right wrist and, according to Gérard, a bad break. When you take his eyesight into account he is left pretty-well helpless."

"But presumably the servants are doing all they can."

"Well, yes, Boussec is away of course, but Madame Mercier is there and Georges, so you would think…But it appears Lesage will not accept their help. For the last three days he has even been refusing to eat. He—if this were not from Gérard, I should scarcely credit it—he accuses them of trying to poison him."

"Good grief!"

"Added to which, it seems that room of his at the top of the house is infernally hot. For a man of Lesage's age, under-nourished and already not in the best of health, the situation is less than favourable."

"The doctor's like all doctors. He's bound to be alarmist."

"Not Gérard, dear boy. He wouldn't have written if he were not genuinely concerned. If he feels poor Lesage will continue to deteriorate unless he leaves Paris, I cannot but believe him."

"All the same, I don't understand why we must go back. I assume Dr Gérard wants to send him here, so why can't he simply put him on a train?"

"Gérard says…" Miremont despairingly cast off his pince-nez. "My dear boy, perhaps you had better read the letter."

Max could decipher the doctor's hand only with difficulty, so that when a sentence stopped him at the top of the second page he was obliged to read it twice to make sure he had construed it properly. "But that's—Armand, that's absurd!"

"I suppose, in his present agitated state, poor fellow, he feels he is only doing his duty."

"Refusing to leave your house unless you order him to do so? In person?"

"I allow it is—"

"And starving himself. That's blackmail. "

" I agree it seems somewhat unreasonable, dear boy, but we should not—"

"Unreasonable?" Max could not forebear laughing. "Does he forget which of you is the marquis?"

This provoked Miremont to frown. "We should not be quick to judge, Max. Poor Lesage has always…well, you know his fears as well as I do. I allow that by most standards his request is—inappropriate. But in these circumstances…If my presence can reassure him that he may return beneath my roof as soon as he is well again….You do see, my dear boy, I cannot in all conscience…."

Max was tempted to retort that if the Buzzard was so determined to die at the Leviathan, perhaps he should be permitted to get on with it. But he had already taken warning from M de M's frown. And besides, he felt sorry for monsieur, who had gathered up the doctor's missive and was glumly re-reading it.

"Armand, I understand the sense of obligation you feel. But what about the model cottages? Isn't it next Monday that the first tenants move in? You said you wanted to make sure all went well. And then there's the grape harvest—you told me you always stay on here for the celebrations."

"That is not until the end of September, five weeks away—I hope we shall have returned long before then. As for the cottages—" here Miremont smiled ruefully "—I must pray that Calvert concedes defeat." He put down the letter and ran his hands over his face. "I wish it were otherwise but it seems I have no choice."

"That's not entirely so."

Miremont shook his head. "What else can I do? Leave the poor fellow to suffer?"

"You could send me."

Miremont stared at the boy.

"I'm supposed to be his assistant."

"Well, yes, dear boy—but—"

"Should I not be the one to assist him?"

"No. No, my dear Max—" Miremont attempted to soften his refusal with a smile. "Aside from anything else, I cannot bear to part with you. And…well, I know you and Lesage are better friends than you used to be, but all the same…I fear if even Gérard cannot persuade him…"

"But I shan't need to."

Miremont raised his eyebrows.

"You shall do the persuading. I shall simply carry out your instructions." Max warmed to his theme. "If you write a letter guaranteeing you will honour your promise to him and urging him to take the doctor's advice, I shall deliver it into his hands. I shall read it to him and make sure he understands it. And, of course, I'll undertake the necessary arrangements for him to travel. I shall only be gone three or four days at the most. And you'll be here to see your tenants installed and toast the success of your venture at long last. "

The old fellow was frowning again. "My darling boy—"

"But don't you see, Armand? It's proper that I should go. I shall only be doing what you employ me to do. Whereas …" Max paused. He was tempted to try a dangerous gambit. He assayed a grin. "Well, what do you think Lesage himself would say if he were in my place?"

Miremont shot him a mordant glance. "He would presume. As you do, dear boy, much as I love you. What my father might have done is neither here nor there."

Yet Miremont's annoyance was increased by the knowledge that the boy was right. Compassion urged him to go to Paris; but compassion was not a quality his secretary esteemed. Lesage, despite the fear that inspired his demands, would be all too well aware that they were a violation of due form and, if Miremont acceded to them, his respect for his master would not increase: he might even become more intransigent.

But this was not what had first made him frown. It was the boy's enthusiasm that he found so troubling. The realisation that Max was keen to leave, accompanied by the inevitable phantasms Miremont's jealousy conjured up, would have been painful at any time. But now, so soon after the breach between them, whose wounds he sensed were not entirely healed, it seemed doubly hard to bear. He felt quite unreasonably furious with Lesage, for breaking into their peace, for being impossible, even for being, poor fellow, so inconsiderately ill; yet, at the same time, reproaching his anger, was the knowledge that, if it were Max lying sick in Paris, he would not hesitate to take the earliest train.

Meanwhile, Max was surveying him with raised brows. "Do you think I am not up to it? Do you not trust me?"

"Yes. Yes, of course, darling boy. Of course I trust you." Miremont was the more emphatic for this not being entirely true. But what was love without trust? And, if the boy truly wished to go to Paris without him, what would be served by preventing him? Would Max love him any better for keeping him here against his will?

Sighing, Miremont thrust his forelock from his eyes. "I am merely concerned...well, we both know Lesage. Even if I write as you suggest...he has been hard on the servants and he may be hard on you..."

"Which will surprise me?"

"I agree, dear boy, you have been admirable. But even so, now that he is ill..."

Max smiled. "I shall be the soul of patience, I promise you."

Miremont attempted to return the smile. It would only be a brief parting: he must tell his jealousy that, like the boy's free evenings, it was a necessary sacrifice. All the same, he could not restrain another sigh as he said: "Very well then."

Max's look of pleasure was painful to observe.

"But on condition you write to me daily. And that you return as soon as you can."

Max was already draining his coffee cup, rising from his chair. "I'll go and pack now. If Durand can have the barouche ready to go to Auxerre in half an hour, I should be in Paris by early evening, as long as I don't miss the connection at Laroche. Oh—" He paused with his hand on the back of the chair. "Am I to assume that I bring the invalid back here?"

Monsieur's bleak look answered his own feelings. "Lesage hates this place. If you are to succeed with him, we had better think of some alternative." Monsieur considered for a moment. "He has a younger sister still living in Nogent-sur-Oise, I believe. A sister's care and understanding is perhaps what he most needs at present. And Nogent has the benefit of country air, while being not too far distant from Paris. She married a local notary—what was his name?—Rochas, Royer? I'm afraid I don't know the precise address, but of course Lesage will be able to tell you."

While Max went to pack Miremont retired to the library to write the necessary letter. After offering his sympathies, enjoining Lesage to follow Gérard's advice and paying elaborate tribute to his secretary's long years of dutiful service, he wrote:

'My dear Lesage, while I fully realise that you have ever been actuated by the wish to serve rather than any thought of financial reward, I should not be fulfilling my own duty if I did not ensure that you were properly provided for during the—it is to be hoped—short period you are absent from the Hôtel de Miremont. Accordingly, as well as continuing to pay your usual stipend, I propose to add the same sum again to cover your board and lodging and any other expenses you may incur during the time you are not living under my roof. If, to my misfortune, you feel you are unable to return to your duties, I undertake that I, and my heirs after me, will continue to remit this sum to you annually for the rest of your life. However, it is my fondest hope that you will speedily return to good health and I must reiterate my promise to you, that your place as my secretary will remain vacant until such time as you are ready and willing to resume it, when I shall be delighted to welcome you back as an invaluable and indispensable member of my household.

'A signed copy of this letter will be lodged with Maître Ladurie as a binding document. M Fabien is aware of its contents and acts under my instructions, which are to assist you in every way he can. He will keep me informed daily of the steps he is taking on your behalf and I am sure I have no need to encourage you to place your trust in him, since he acts only in accordance with my own wishes for your comfort and well-being.'

Miremont concluded with the usual formalities. But even as he added his signature, his doubts multiplied. However Max might desire it, was it fair, after all, to send him to Paris alone? Lesage ought to be calmed by a binding written promise, but he was clearly at his most fractious; there would be the servants' ruffled feathers to be smoothed; and then there was Gérard, who had never relented in his antipathy towards the poor boy. True, Gérard was too good a doctor to let personal animosity stand in the way of his helping Max if the health of his patient were at risk, while the servants would follow Miremont's orders. All the same... If he rang for Thomas to pack him they could catch the later train together.

Miremont was moving to touch the bell when Max reappeared. He had changed into his grey worsted suit, carried the high-crowned felt hat he usually wore in Paris, and looked so distressingly cheerful that Miremont's determination faltered.

"My darling boy, I fear I am sending you into the big cats' cage."

Max laughed. "Armand, I have been shockingly lazy all these weeks. I'm only too glad to make myself useful at last."

Since Miremont could not begin to explain how acutely painful he found this last remark, he turned back to his writing table, giving the letter to Max to read and then to copy, while he wrote briefly to Gérard and to Mme Mercier.

CHAPTER THIRTY SEVEN

Night ablaze on the boulevards, the awnings of cafés beckoning, dim rooms fumed with wine and tobacco and the reek of sweat and pomade—Max could taste the city as the pistons of the train chorused his progress through the flat northern countryside ever closer to the Gare de Rungis. Paris. Freedom. For, of all that had been said since the incident of the riding crop, these words of the old boy's remained uppermost in his mind: "You are not free."

Even though he had known he was making a mistake, he had thrown his freedom away. He had trusted the old boy. And what had happened? Max should have done as honour required: he should have left as soon as he could walk. But somehow, because he had been unable to act at once, the situation had no longer seemed quite so simple.

To begin with, it was so damnably hard to remain properly angry with the old boy. Monsieur was not Sébastien, his moment of insanity had been as inexplicable to him as it was to Max: he had not tried to justify himself and he did not seek to conceal his mortification. Daft old fellow, on his knees like a penitent, dabbing away with his foul-smelling ointment. There was even something oddly comforting in the revelation that monsieur could suffer his lapses, that he was not entirely a model of virtue.

Oh, of course, if the old boy struck him again, if he ever again treated him as less than his equal...But here was Max once more, forgiving what should not be forgiven. It was a trap, this fondness, this sentimental attachment—whatever it was that he felt for the old fellow. Had he forgotten the code by which he had sworn to live on first arriving in Paris? Not for him loyalties, ties, obligations: he must recognise no duty beyond what he owed to himself. In the five years that had passed—yes, it must be granted—he had been guilty of slips and weaknesses. But these failures should not obscure the ruthless clarity of his vision.

He had somehow allowed monsieur to corrupt him. Why was it, for instance, that whenever he was angry with the old boy he would find himself wondering whether he, too, might not be altogether without fault? He was no longer the child who accepted blame as his lot. Oh, he had regained the upper hand for now, for the remarkable outcome of monsieur's insult was that, rather than lowering him, it had restored his power: it was as if his stupid declaration had been taken back. But how long would this state of affairs last?

Yet going would also betray his interests. He required monsieur for his grand plan: it would be the height of folly to throw everything away for the sake of a gesture. And besides...Although honour disdained such venal excuses, life at Beauvallon had rendered Max no keener to enlist; and when he took into account how much he was learning, could still learn...Also, he could not help recalling how he had missed the old boy's company in the past...He did not want...He would regret...Oh, damn the whole business to hell, here he was travelling full circle, back into the trap again!

Then Gérard's letter had arrived and he had seen a straight path at last. He did not wish to go and he would not go, yet he would keep his freedom. For he would stay on his own terms.

At first the Buzzard's predicament had seemed merely an excuse to escape, to seize a few days free from distracting influences to clear his mind. But, even while he was persuading monsieur, he had begun to see the scope of his opportunity. Now he smiled to himself as he sat watching the fields fly past, his copy of *Cousin Pons* lying unopened in his lap. The letter was there, above his head in the luggage rack, safely stowed away in his valise with the others.

Yes, he would make his own terms. It was not enough that he had learnt to rise above the Buzzard. When he and monsieur eventually returned to the Leviathan, he would not surrender the privileges he enjoyed at Beauvallon, revert to a life of pretexts and pretences, a half-life where he was constantly 'put in his place'. Monsieur did not require two secretaries.

On the whole the old boy's letter was highly satisfactory. In spite of himself, Max had blanched on reading the sentence that promised to keep the Buzzard's situation open in perpetuity—but then the Buzzard himself would never read nor hear it. The sentence above, on the other hand, guaranteeing the old fowl a substantial pension if he left the Leviathan—this, subject to a couple of minor amendments, could not be bettered.

It was a piece of good fortune that monsieur used the same writing paper whether he was at Beauvallon or the hôtel and sealed his envelopes with the same simple wafer bearing his crest. Lesage could hardly question why the letter he received was not in monsieur's hand, for he knew very well that the old boy frequently dictated his correspondence. As for monsieur's signature, Max had often practised it as an amusement for idle moments: he was confident he could produce a credible facsimile, good enough at any rate to deceive Lesage's eyesight.

There were the other two letters, of course, to Mme Mercier and the lecherous old doctor, but monsieur had considerately shown Max those too, so that he was relieved of any worry that their content might destroy his plan. The only difficulty remaining was the copy of the Buzzard's letter to be lodged with Ladurie. Of course Max could send them his version in its place, but he feared some eagle-eyed clerk might question the signature or monsieur might one day ask to see it. The alternative—simply to lose it—could cause similar problems: supposing the old fellow checked that it had arrived? No matter. A solution would surely present itself once Max had reached Paris.

Besides, monsieur might never enquire about the letter. Max recalled how tightly the old boy had embraced him, how sad he had looked as he had watched him climb into the barouche—sorrowful enough to afflict Max with a guilty twinge. But guilt be damned! Why, if the old boy had so little wished for their parting, had he given in and allowed Max to go alone? Why had he expended so many words reassuring the Buzzard that he should not starve if he chose retirement? Why, unless he knew what Max intended? The intrusion of Lesage upon their intimacy was an even greater source of frustration to the old boy than it was to him. Of course monsieur could not break his promise to the Buzzard, however much he desired to. But he could let Max do it for him.

To Max's satisfaction, the countryside was beginning to give way to the workshops and factories of the *banlieues*. He smiled to himself once more. There would be no recriminations once the Buzzard was packed off, safely and for good, to Nogent-sur-Oise.

He had not forgotten the monumental proportions of the Hôtel de Miremont but he was taken aback by how cavernous and dark it seemed after Beauvallon, how he missed the view out across the water of trees and hills and limitless sky. In monsieur's absence, too, the place had a contingent air: most of the shutters were closed against the August sun, the furniture in the *piano nobile* was shrouded in dust sheets, there were ladders here and there and the fountain in the courtyard had been turned off. His own room under the eaves, emptied of most of his belongings and half his books, seemed strangely desolate. It was also, despite the approach of dusk and even when he had flung open the window, abominably hot—he could understand why the Buzzard, two rooms away, was suffering. But an inspection of the old fowl must, thank heavens, wait until tomorrow, for he had ascertained from Georges that despite the earliness of the hour the invalid was asleep and better left undisturbed.

On monsieur's instructions, Durand had telegraphed from Auxerre to prepare both Gérard and the servants for Max's arrival. From Georges' sardonic welcome Max could see how the servants' hall had greeted the news. Mme Mercier, when he summoned her to the old boy's study, met him tight-lipped. She was somewhat mollified when he reassured her that he would not require dinner this evening and would be happy for the rest of his stay to take his meals in his room, saving the need to set and serve the table. But the old boy's letter turned her little hard black eyes into daggers again.

"Monsieur Fabien, we all know that Monsieur de Miremont has a heart of gold, but this suggestion that we should move Monsieur Lesage to madame's old apartments—"

"He wishes Monsieur Lesage to be somewhere cooler."

"The second floor of the east wing has been shut up for years. It will take the maids days of work to make the rooms habitable for an invalid. And these are *Madame la marquise's* apartments."

Max took from this that their occupation by a mere secretary would be an affront, not to her former mistress, to whom she was unlikely to feel great loyalty, but to all the other marquises de Miremont, past and future. He was fleetingly sorry for the Buzzard.

"Of course, you may assure monsieur that we will do it. We are doing all we can. Georges, who is without Philippe at the moment and has plenty enough to keep him busy, has offered to shave and dress Monsieur Lesage. Madame Dussardier has cooked his favourite dishes, we have cut up the food for him, I have even tried to feed him by hand. I have cared for him, I will have Monsieur de Miremont know, as a mother would care. And what is our reward? He has made these disgraceful allegations."

Once again a twinge of sympathy for Lesage afflicted Max as he contemplated the idea of stern, spinsterish Mme Mercier being motherly, but he attempted what he hoped was a consoling look. "Monsieur does not for one moment believe—"

"I should hope not, indeed."

"I assure you he understands—"

"Ha!" Mme Mercier shook the letter at him. "If he could see for himself what we have had to put up with!"

"Monsieur suggests the east wing only as a temporary arrangement. I hope— with your help, madame—to convey Monsieur Lesage to the country as soon as possible."

The housekeeper scrutinised him down the swoop of her narrow arched nose until he began to fear his collar was askew or his fly unbuttoned. Then she folded monsieur's letter neatly and stowed in her apron pocket. "If monsieur places his trust in you, then it is not for us to doubt him." She gave a thin, grim smile. "We look forward, Monsieur Fabien, to seeing you succeed where we have failed."

Max was all at once nostalgic for Mme Rosalie's indulgent smiles. Damn the Buzzard! The old fowl's antics had not improved his own invidious relations with the servants. And his brief spark of fellow-feeling was altogether extinguished when, on entering the library, he discovered that the Buzzard, before his accident, had managed to reverse most of his catalogue amendments.

At least a free night stretched before him, for the doctor had left a message to say that he would call in the morning.

He had splashed his face with cold water to purge himself of the smuts and grime of travel, put on fresh linen and exchanged the worsted suit for the cloth coat and trousers he had brought from the country. But even in this lighter attire he was sweating profusely by the time he had walked to the Boulevard du Montparnasse. Mercifully the concierge at the Rue Boissonade assured him that the Zhukovskys were at home.

As he climbed the stairs to the third floor, his anticipation heard the strains of a violin. But when the maid opened the door the sound that drifted into the hall from the parlour was of raised voices: apparently one of those impassioned and insoluble arguments about the future of Russia was in progress.

"Maxim Alexandrovitch!" Vera came into the hall to welcome him. "How wonderful! But—" her blue eyes darkened "—you wrote that you would not be back for another month. I do hope there is nothing wrong."

"Nothing whatsoever—"

"We were all so relieved that you had begun to like your new situation a little better. But it does seem rather unkind of your marquis to keep you working such long hours even when you are in the country."

From behind her came hearty laughter. "Oh, Verotchka, look at the fellow!" exclaimed Mitya, moving forward with his arms outstretched. "Does this look to you like a chap who has been cooped up for three months with—what was it, the odes of Horace?"

As they embraced, Max wondered irritably why he could never succeed in lying to Mitya. Certainly in his letters he had somewhat exaggerated the time he and M de M had spent in the library: knowing that Mitya must have a shrewd idea of the true nature their relationship, he did not want to convey the impression—well, he had not entirely banished the fear that, given the lack of proper work, his presence at Beauvallon risked appearing in an unflattering light. But Mitya, it seemed, damn him, had chosen to receive the wrong impression regardless.

Yet his friend must have caught his irritation, for he seemed instantly penitent. "My dear Maxim, we are merely envious, those of us who have been cooking in this stinking oven of a city with too little work and not enough fresh air."

"It is true, I did ride a little. Monsieur de Miremont is teaching me about the running of the estate."

"It is a delight to see you looking so well."

"And I am in Paris to conduct a rather delicate matter of business for him. I shall only be here for a few days."

"Well then—" Mitya put his arm around Max's shoulders "—let us make the most of it, my friend. We have missed you."

Vera nodded. "Mama is always asking if there has been another letter from you. We have all been very dull without you."

Max could not but be propitiated. He had missed them too: their apartment, with its comforting smell, a commingling of cooking and furniture polish, suggested homecoming in a way that the Leviathan's hallowed spaces never could. Regrettably, he would not see Mme Zhukovskaya, who, having suffered one of her bad days, was sleeping. But the parlour, boisterously untidy as usual, disarmed him with fond memories of convivial evenings.

The company had evidently just finished supper—Vera offered to see what was left in the kitchen but, since his visit must be brief if he were to call in at the Monkey, he crushed down his hunger and declined. To his surprise, there were only two guests. Arkady Lyudin Max knew. The other was a small square man with heavy-lidded eyes, narrow lips and a bulging forehead that gained additional prominence from his being, although probably much of an age with Mitya, almost completely bald: Mitya introduced him as Simeon Borisovitch Tretchikov, a viola player.

Whatever had been the argument over Mother Russia, it seemed to have taken a difficult turn, for while Tretchikov had carried his glass of wine to an armchair, where he sat smoking a *papirosa*, Lyudin remained at the table in the alcove, his chin mournfully in his hands. The cellist seemed rather drunk—although sadly not yet far gone enough for arias: his blurred gaze briefly acknowledged Max but fixed itself unsteadily upon Vera as she fussed over the newcomer, settling him on the sofa and fetching him a glass of tea.

Despite Vera's attentions, Max felt suddenly awkward, out of place in his single-breasted blue coat and tight grey trousers: Tretchikov in particular wore his tired frock coat like a badge of virtue. The conversation, instead of resuming where Max's arrival had interrupted it, languished in a brief uncomfortable silence. Then Tretchikov appeared on the point of uttering some pronouncement. But Vera, who had perched beside Max on the sofa, cut him off: "Maxim Alexandrovitch, you must tell us all about Beauvallon."

Glancing at Tretchikov, who seemed put out, Max hesitated. "I am not sure that everyone—"

"Oh, nonsense! These three have talked nothing but politics all evening. And you always describe the countryside so beautifully. Besides—" she shot him a teasing smile "—now we know your old marquis is not the terrible tyrant you paint him, you may tell us everything. Did you lie in the long grass listening to skylarks and eat grapes straight from the vine?"

Although Max endeavoured to make his account of the château and the estate as brief as possible, Vera was much taken with M de Miremont's Arcadia and he found himself describing the various follies and dwelling on the sunsets and the pleasures of bathing in the lake, until he was interrupted by a harsh laugh.

"You French astonish me," said Tretchikov. "While we cannot manage one revolution, M Fabien, you have had four. Yet your nobility is still living in splendour on its estates."

Mitya frowned. "Simeon Borisovitch, here the people at least have universal suffrage, things are not so—"

"Pshaw!" Tretchikov's heavy stare, ignoring his host, continued to fix itself on Max. "What price your so-called Republic if this marquis of yours still lives like some relic of the *ancien régime*, growing fat as a tick on the blood and sweat of the peasants?"

"Monsieur, I take great exception to that." Max flushed. He was aware that his anger would make an uncomfortable situation worse, particularly for Mitya, who, though he had tried to divert the attack, held views closer to Tretchikov's than his own; nor did he miss the impulsive touch of Vera's fingers upon his arm. But he could not let the old boy go undefended. "You insult Monsieur de Miremont without knowing him. If your objection is to hereditary privilege—"

"Naturally it is."

"Then I cannot agree with you that it is always a bad thing. Not if it is used wisely and well, from a sense of duty and obligation."

The violist's lip curled. "A duty to despise the masses and an obligation to grind them into the dirt? So much for liberty, equality, fraternity!" He had a high grating voice, shrill, almost girlish, which aggravated Max's anger.

"I know nothing of politics, monsieur, but I can't help noticing from all the scandals recently that our deputies and senators are just as likely to put their own interests before those of the people. At least the best of the nobility is not driven by personal ambition, but by an honourable tradition—"

"An honourable tradition of theft. Your Monsieur de Mortmont—"

"Simeon Borisovitch, Maxim!" pleaded Mitya. "You are neither of you going to—"

"Miremont," said Max. "Monsieur de Miremont. And far from stealing from the people of Beauvallon, he is their benefactor. He has built a new school, he is providing the poorest of the village with new dwellings built to the highest modern standards—at his own expense, for he will never recover a fraction of the cost in rent—"

"Aha! He does not forget to exact rent, this benevolent noble of yours?"

"Yes, of course, but that is—"

"So he is as they all are, a thief twice over." Tretchikov's overbearing forehead gleamed with triumph. "First his ancestors steal the land from the people, then he steals from them again by forcing them to pay for the use of it. Even his charity is financed by his ill-gotten gains. And you, sir, his lackey, with your rides, your dips in the lake, your fancy clothes—are you not ashamed that they have been paid for by blood money, by the toil and suffering of honest labouring men who have been denied their natural rights?"

Max was for a moment too stunned to reply and it was Vera who broke the silence: "Simeon Borisovitch, you are unkind."

Whereupon Lyudin, who had continued to stare absently at Vera as though he were deaf to the conversation, suddenly ceased to slouch on his elbows and sat bolt upright. "But you know, Fabien old chap, the fellow has a point. If your old marquis is the saint you say he is, wouldn't he be happy to give his estate back to the people?"

"Arkady Feodorovitch, you're drunk. Go back to sleep." Mitya rose and went to fetch the wine bottle. "Enough of revolution, I think. Let us return to the original reason for this meeting. If—and I say if—we decide to form a string quartet, there is the question of our repertoire. Maxim, you can advise us—should we play Haydn, Mozart and Beethoven, or should we, as Simeon Borisovitch believes, reject Europe and concentrate on works in the Russian tradition?"

But Max felt his anger would suffocate him if he remained for a moment longer in the same room as Tretchikov and Lyudin. Making a show of casually consulting his watch, he tendered his excuses.

Although Vera had risen to see him out, Mitya was there before her. In the hall, before they embraced in parting, he put his hand on Max's shoulder: "Please, my dear chap, if you can, come tomorrow to see Mama. And don't trouble yourself about Tretchikov—his playing is as melodious as his conversation."

All the same, Max's rage was unleashed the moment the door was closed. Lyudin's was the most inexplicable betrayal: although, when sober, the cellist spoke little, Max had never believed him ill-disposed towards him; and yes, on reflection Lyudin's mockery might also have been directed at Tretchikov, but it was a betrayal nonetheless. Yet Max's fury was not restricted to Tretchikov and Lyudin. He was angry with Mitya for being condescending while doubtless despising him, angry with Vera for leading him into Tretchikov's snare, angry with himself for looking foolish, angry, above all, with the old boy, who had placed him in this appalling position.

It was not as if he had avoided asking himself Tretchikov's question. During a period of vicissitude he too had wondered how the old boy and Mme de Claireville remained smugly ensconced in their palaces, but when he recalled his own aspirations he was obliged to brush the question aside. In any case, his time as a servant had left him cynical. However many revolutions you had, however passionately you spoke of equality, the world was inherently unfair. His reading confirmed it—Alexander, the Caesars, Frederick of Prussia, Napoleon—some men would always trample others to gain or retain power: he had no doubt Tretchikov would quickly stop brandishing his red flag if he ever tasted privilege. It had been so for as long as mankind had existed and it would always be so. The motto—and Max fully intended to heed it—was: 'be one of the powerful, not the trampled'. In the brutal impartiality of this eternal truth there was indeed something glorious; but not until he had risen to monsieur's defence had Max realised how the old fellow had confused his thinking, had seduced him into idealising it as the well-spring of altruism.

And that was not the only way in which monsieur had distorted his vision. A lackey! Yet, oh dear god, was it so wide of the mark? In fact, was not the truth worse? The idle months at Beauvallon, the riding, the shooting, the food Max ate, the clothes on his back—not only had he been paid in full for doing nothing, he had never once been required to put his hand in his pocket. How had he been so willingly blinded? How had he forgotten his pride? He had not so much lost his freedom as sold it.

In his anger the crowded streets he had longed for now irritated him beyond measure. As he strode up the Boulevard Saint-Michel, he cursed the idlers who blocked his progress, the oncomers who collided with him or jostled his shoulder. One particularly annoying individual, dressed to the nines despite the heat and sporting a topper whose brim curled like an aristocrat's sneer, not only halted to obstruct his path, but began a strange little dance, gesticulating with his cane.

"Angel!"

"My god! Fabrice."

"Hippolyte, petal, if you don't mind. Oh my, let me look at you!"

To avoid stemming the pedestrian tide, he had no choice but to submit as Fabrice—Max could never get used to thinking of him by anything but his *nomme de guerre*—drew him aside under an awning and, having embraced him, subjected him to minute inspection.

"Oh yes! Adore the low-cut waist and the single button. And the waistcoat— shawl collars are *le dernier cri*, although I'd have picked a brighter colour myself to set off the coat—rose, perhaps, or violet. And you simply must get some spats, dear heart, and a topper. But on the whole, joy! I deduce that little Mademoiselle Mouse continues to treat you well."

Max's rage had not been cooled by this inventory. "Monsieur de Miremont. And if you are implying—"

"I trust it's still true love. Your Tristan to her Isolde."

"I am not in love with him. And he does *not* keep me."

"Of course not, dear heart. On a librarian's wages you can easily afford the best tailor in Paris."

"Once and for all! I am not a librarian, I am his secretary. He requires me to make a favourable impression. There is no more to it than that. And if you or anyone else says differently, I shall be forced to…" But, as he spluttered impotently to a halt, he became aware of Fabrice's affronted look and was all at once ashamed. "Oh forgive me, my dear fellow. Monsieur has sent me back here on a rather trying errand and—and this heat is wearing. Truly, I am glad to see you."

"Likewise, angel."

To deepen Max's shame, he noticed, now anger no longer misted his vision, that Fabrice, despite his lavender gloves and impressive headgear, seemed sunken-cheeked and wilted. Some time ago Max had observed that he had taken to brushing his yellow curls forward *à l'empereur* to conceal a receding hairline. But habitude must have obscured what Max's months of absence suddenly made plain: Fabrice was beginning to show his age.

Max took his friend's arm. "In fact, it's the greatest good fortune, bumping into you like this. I was hoping to find you at the Monkey—"

"Oh, the Monkey." Fabrice grimaced, causing Max to recall that he had been walking in the opposite direction. "Everyone who's anyone is away."

"Then come and eat with me. I've had nothing since the station buffet at Laroche."

Fabrice pulled another face. "Regrettably, angel, I've just dined."

"Well, a drink at least?"

At this Fabrice brightened and, since they were already standing next to an empty café table with a waiter hovering officiously, they sat down.

"So how goes it with you?" Max enquired, having quickly scanned the menu and ordered a brandy for Fabrice and a plate of Jura ham, a *mazagran* and a bottle of Vitell for himself. "Why isn't your newspaper baron taking the sea air?"

"Oh she is, angel. At Cabourg. But she's one of those." From which Max inferred that, like M de Bellac, Fabrice's master was too mean to take his own servant away with him. Yet he observed that his friend was staring morosely into his brandy glass. And indeed a moment later, sighing, Fabrice said: "Actually, petal, I'm between situations at the moment."

"My dear fellow, I'm sorry to hear it."

"A trivial incident—a difference of opinion over a bottle of cologne.

Old Jouvert has promised to do his best for me. But it's August…"

Max was suitably sympathetic: although he could offer no helpful suggestions, he ordered Fabrice a second brandy and, when he saw how his friend eyed the ham, pressed the menu upon him until he was induced to try the *langoustines au gratin*. Once he had consumed this with alacrity, followed it with a slice of *tarte tatin* swimming in cream, and washed both down with a third brandy, Fabrice, brightening considerably, decided he would come to the Monkey after all—perhaps Old Jouvert at last had something for him.

Max too felt calmer as he sipped his coffee. But when he took out his notecase to pay the bill his anger was instantly rekindled: it was bad enough that he had forgotten his pride for the last three months, but most of this money was also the old boy's, thrust upon him as he was leaving to meet the expense of his journey. Well, he would draw upon the bank tomorrow and repay it. Meanwhile, he rapidly counted out a pile of notes and pushed it across the table towards the astonished Fabrice.

"Quickly, my friend. Or some street arab will grab it."

Fabrice demurred, but even as he did so he was cramming the money into his pocket. "Angel! Dear heart! How can I ever –? "

"Don't thank me," said Max grimly. "It is I who should thank you."

When Max returned to the Hôtel de Miremont the servants had long since retired and a single lamp had been left for him in the foyer to guide him upstairs. Although he had made a further reassertion of his independence in an alley near the Monkey, his temper was not greatly improved. He was certainly in no mood to show mercy to the Buzzard.

Despite the night air from the open window, the heat in his room was still oppressive. Tearing out the stud from his high stiff collar, tugging off his boots, which pinched abominably, then divesting himself of the rest of his clothes, he stood at the washstand and soaped himself all over, as if he hoped to scrub away the humiliations of the evening. Then, moving the lamp to the table, he sat down, naked, to the night's final task.

Before leaving for the Zhukovskys' he had taken the precaution of removing a supply of the old boy's stationery from his study. Now, breaking the seal on the envelope and unfolding the letter to Lesage, he began upon a rough draft of his amendments. 'My dear Lesage,' he wrote:

'…while I fully realise that you have ever been actuated by the wish to serve rather than any thought of financial reward, I should not be fulfilling my own duty if I did not ensure that you were properly provided for when the time comes—as I fear to my misfortune it has now—for you to enjoy a well-deserved retirement. Accordingly, I am proposing to pay you a pension of double your present stipend, to cover the additional expenses you will incur when you are no longer living under my roof, and I undertake that I, and my heirs after me, will continue to remit this sum to you annually for the rest of your life. It is my fondest hope that you will speedily return to good health so that you may reap the benefits of your new life of ease and tranquillity, a just reward for all your years as an invaluable and indispensable member of my household...'

On reading this over, he added 'full' before the word 'benefits' and substituted 'trusted' for 'indispensable.' Then, retaining the letter's original opening and closing paragraphs, he copied the whole onto a sheet of the old boy's writing paper. Having blotted and re-read it, he paused like an actor preparing himself for a taxing soliloquy before dipping his pen into the inkwell and executing monsieur's signature with a flourish. He was pleased with the result. Finding a fresh wafer, he folded the letter and sealed it into a new envelope. Then, having burned monsieur's original in the grate, together with the sheet on which he had practised the signature, he lit a cigarette and sat back in his chair contemplating his work with satisfaction.

The copy of the original letter would go to Ladurie without alteration, he had decided. It was safer that way. After showing the amended version to the Buzzard, he would get possession of it again and destroy it. If later on the old fowl cut up rough, the only available record would contradict him..

CHAPTER THIRTY EIGHT

Max had intended to give the Buzzard the letter before he saw Dr Gérard but, having retired to bed at dawn, he failed to wake when the maid knocked with his hot water. The aftermath of his anger seemed to have dulled his mind and left him feeling strangely uncomfortable in his own skin, as if he had matched Fabrice yesterday evening glass for glass. He nicked his chin as he shaved in haste, tripped over his boots and experienced unaccountable difficulty tying his cravat. When at last he was fully dressed in his sober secretary's suit and could pause to gulp coffee and collect himself, he contemplated the morning ahead without relish.

He might have taught himself to rise above the Buzzard, but all the same he did not look forward to their meeting. Nor was he keen to present himself to the doctor, who anyway disliked him and in these circumstances must be treated with the utmost caution. He needed a clear head and an air of assurance, not this vague but pervasive guilt that cast its clammy shadow even over last night's encounter at the Monkey—as if it had been any different from his usual adventures.

It did not help that on his breakfast tray, beside his napkin, lay a telegram from the old boy. It was brief and, in accordance with the rules they had agreed for their correspondence, carefully impersonal.

TRUST JOURNEY UNEVENTFUL STOP KEEP ME INFORMED OF YOUR PROGRESS STOP MIREMONT XLVIII

However, Max need not consult Catullus to recall that the numerals denoted the poem promising three hundred thousand kisses. He glared at the missive as if the heat of his glance might shrivel it to ashes. But it was no good—he would have to pen an answer at some juncture today or the old fellow would grow suspicious. And, as for the postscript, he would need to acknowledge that too if he did not want monsieur to arrive by the next train. Shit! Was he not to be free, even in Paris? And yet, at the same time, he saw the lake at Beauvallon in the crisp light of early morning, felt the dew beneath his feet and the old fellow's arm around his waist as they walked back to the house exhilarated from bathing, and he seemed to inhale from the paper the faint scent of honeysuckle, which filled him with an absurd and painful longing, as though for something already lost to him forever.

Shit, shit, shit! It was not as if he were doing monsieur a terrible wrong. If the old boy could be pragmatic about Calvert's misdeeds, he would surely understand that he, Max, was also acting in his best interests.

Dr Gérard had been shown into monsieur's study, where he sat on the edge of the worn leather couch with his large hairy hands planted awkwardly upon his thighs. His countenance, as always, reminded Max of a camembert cheese—round, pale, lumpy and furred with outcrops of mould in the form of colourless side-whiskers—and as usual he appeared painfully constricted by his ill-fitting morning coat. But the diffidence he affected in the presence of monsieur was notably absent as Max apologised for keeping him waiting. Nor was there in his eye the faintest gleam of lechery: instead Max received the unpleasant impression that the old quack had already seen through him.

He could only pray that the letter monsieur had addressed to Gérard, with its commendations of his trustworthiness and efficiency, might work its charm; but when the doctor had scanned it his look of prescient distaste returned.

He sighed. "I suppose I had hoped...but of course Monsieur de Miremont has other demands upon his time. Monsieur Lesage must make do with your good offices, it seems, Monsieur Fabien."

There was an edge to Gérard's voice that his irritating lisp did not disguise. Max found himself snapping back: "I am, after all, his assistant."

"Hmm. Precisely so. I take it you have seen him?"

"I arrived too late last night. And I thought I should wait until you had examined him this morning."

"Ah."

Although Max cautioned himself to control his temper, this impenetrable yet portentous response increased his irritation. "What do you mean by that, monsieur? Is your patient worse?"

"I mean by it, Monsieur Fabien, that he is no longer my patient."

Max stared. "So you have washed your hands of him?"

"I do not abandon patients, monsieur. Monsieur Lesage informed me yesterday afternoon that he would prefer Doctor Chevalier to attend him. I understand that he is the physician favoured by Madame la marquise."

Max hoped he betrayed no sign of his relief. All the same, he was stunned by the Buzzard's presumption. "But he can't—that's preposterous!"

"I trust you will obtain Monsieur de Miremont's consent to the new arrangement. Naturally I shall also write to him."

"But monsieur has great faith in you, he is bound to ask you to change your mind."

"As I have attempted to explain, it is not my decision." The doctor's clumsy hands twitched with exasperation, but he restrained them firmly in his lap. "I cannot continue to treat a patient who does not wish me to treat him. I should do him no good."

It struck Max that Gérard's grim demeanour was due as much to this slighting of his skills as to their mutual dislike. He smiled. "Monsieur Lesage can be somewhat—provoking."

But the doctor brushed aside this olive branch. "Monsieur Lesage is in his sixties. His long life may have confirmed him in certain fixed views. But that does not make him less deserving of our patience and understanding."

Max was obliged to consider himself rebuked. "Well—we shall not require Doctor Chevalier's services for long. I shall be conveying Monsieur Lesage to his sister's as soon as I can. I assume you approve this course of action. But perhaps, monsieur, now you have withdrawn from the case, you prefer not to give an opinion."

"Monsieur Fabien—" Gérard, Max was convinced, had been about to call him 'young man' but instead he drew in breath and held it for a moment. "Naturally I shall give you an opinion. Why else do you think I have called on you this morning?"

Max recollected that although he had mercifully escaped the old quack's surveillance, he still needed his help; and besides, it was foolish to antagonise him, since he would report back to monsieur. "Forgive me, Doctor Gérard. Monsieur de Miremont has given me a great responsibility and I am anxious to discharge it as best I can."

Gérard stared at him hard, but then appeared to relent. "Yes, Nogent is eminently sensible. The Yonne might be too arduous a journey for the poor fellow. But he must certainly be moved from this house. The atmosphere in his room is most unhealthy, for one thing—"

"Madame Mercier is making ready one of the rooms downstairs."

"That is good. But his hostility to the servants is of even more concern."

"These allegations of poison?"

"They have certainly not assisted the situation. I wondered at one stage whether to send him to Doctor Broissart's clinic at Passy. However, his condition is not sufficiently serious."

"Not serious? Your letter to Monsieur de Miremont suggested—"

"Oh, it will rapidly become serious if he continues to refuse nourishment. You will need to get him eating before you can think of moving him—thankfully he is not refusing water, but he is growing weaker by the day. Otherwise, however, he is more helpless than ill."

"I'm sure Monsieur de Miremont will be relieved to hear it."

"But in this, I'm afraid, our main difficulty lies." Gérard sighed. "I have seldom met a patient so determinedly—independent."

"Oh, he is certainly that." Sanctimonious old quack! Max still favoured his own description.

"I have splinted his wrist and prescribed laudanum for the pain, which is already diminishing. But it will be at least two months before he regains the use of his hand. However he resolutely refuses all assistance with shaving and dressing, with the result that, even if he were not starving himself, he would be confined to his bedroom like an invalid. Thus he deprives himself of the gentle exercise and mild mental stimulation that would be beneficial in his present circumstance. I have explained this to him, but to no avail."

"Independent, monsieur—as you say."

"And then there is his eyesight. His cataracts are now sufficiently well-advanced for surgery, after which, with the aid of special spectacles, his vision would be restored. I should like to have calmed his fears about this operation, which has an excellent success rate. But again, unfortunately, he will not hear me out. He still maintains that, apart from a little long-sightedness, there is nothing whatever wrong with his eyes."

Here the doctor's hands, like two sickly newborn pups, wriggled free and blindly essayed flight, so that he was temporarily occupied in recapturing them. Max might almost have been tempted to fellow-feeling, had he not he recalled how his previous peace-offering had been greeted.

"I'm sorry to hear that patience and understanding did not prevail."

The doctor continued to study his hands as if he suspected them of further mischief. "Let us not be trivial, Monsieur Fabien. There may be some physiological reason for his—resistance. We must ask ourselves why he fell from the library steps."

Max gave an astonished laugh. "Because he's blind as a worm."

"He retains some limited vision. And in my observation he manages remarkably well in familiar surroundings. I did speculate, when I first examined him—his left pupil was somewhat contracted and his pulse rather slow and full—I thought there might be some congestion of the brain. "

"A seizure?"

"An apoplectic stroke. But if so, it was not of any magnitude and has left him with no observable impediments. Although it might account for some of his—his more eccentric notions."

Max repressed a smile: it did not need apoplexy to render the Buzzard's notions eccentric. "So that is why he claims Madames Mercier and Dussardier are conspiring to murder him?"

"It is a possible explanation. There is another rather obvious possibility."

There seemed to Max nothing more obvious than that the Buzzard was mad and becoming madder.

Gérard raised his eyebrows. "You do not see it? Ah well. Madame Mercier did not see it either when I tried to explain it to her. Some people are equally adept with both left and right hands—you, Monsieur Fabien, are one of them—"

This startled Max, for he had scarcely spent enough time in the doctor's company for the old quack to notice a trait of which he himself was barely aware.

"Monsieur Lesage, however, has very little facility with his left. Combine this with his failing sight and, although in theory he can feed himself, in practice he has great difficulty conveying the food to his mouth."

"Yes, I see that, but—"

"What does a man of Monsieur Lesage's temperament do when—?"

"Ah!" Light dawned for Max. "When someone tries to spoon-feed him like a baby."

"Exactly."

"All the same, that seems a little extreme, even for the old— Monsieur Lesage. But if you are sure he doesn't truly believe the food is poisoned—"

"It is an assumption only."

"But if you are right, then he can be persuaded to eat again."

"Hmm. There is also a third possibility. Monsieur Lesage has asserted to me with distressing frequency that he wishes to die in this house."

"You mean he intends to starve himself to death?" It could not but cross Max's mind, however fleetingly, that this might be the best outcome for all concerned.

"I mean that, even if you can somehow assist him to eat, you may still struggle to get him to Nogent. He seems, for some reason, afraid to leave the Hôtel de Miremont."

Max cursed the old quack's sinister powers of divination, the more so because he could not help flushing. He rose. "I am grateful, monsieur, for your visit. And, of course, for your professional advice. But I fear I shall find it hard to follow. You advise me that Monsieur Lesage must be helped to eat, but you offer no suggestion as to how that might be done. You advise me that he urgently needs to leave for the country, yet you tell me he won't go. Altogether, I am at something of a loss."

The doctor had also risen and was cautiously manoeuvring his bulk between the couch and the table in the direction of the door. "I have given you my opinion, Monsieur Fabien. Advice you must get from Doctor Chevalier. However...you may tell him if you wish that I was entirely opposed to the patient leaving Paris. And for the rest— perhaps the way to help Monsieur Lesage is to be unhelpful. Something I venture, monsieur, you should not find too difficult."

Max did not immediately go to the Buzzard but paused for a while to calm himself. He should not have allowed the old quack to rile him: still less should he have retaliated. Yet even Mitya, if he despised him, had suppressed it. Max realised now what Gérard had recalled to him: the look Lebas' guests had given him all those years ago as he had waited to be summoned to the comte de Tarascon, the look that judged him both of no account and capable of any enormity.

Ah well. The doctor, bourgeois sycophant that he was, would doubtless avoid criticising him openly for fear of incurring monsieur's displeasure. Subduing his anger, Max went to his room to fetch the letter.

The rooms beneath the eves of the west wing, with their low ceilings and dormer windows, had once accommodated servants, until the smaller household suited to the old boy's modest requirements had meant they could all, including Thomas, find space in the servants' wing. Max and the Buzzard were now the floor's only occupants: Max had the room corresponding to monsieur's study on the floor below, while the Buzzard occupied the two rooms at the end of the corridor. The old fowl's study, above monsieur's bedroom, was spacious, but his bedroom had been partitioned to create a separate water closet next to the back stairs. Max had never before entered Lesage's inner sanctum and now, as he passed through the study, noting that the desk's carefully segregated piles of paper were in uncharacteristic disarray, he approached the connecting door with a flicker of trepidation.

Gérard had been right about the unhealthiness of the Buzzard's quarters. The study, with its windows firmly latched and the shutters half closed, had seemed to Max several degrees hotter than his own room. But the air in the bedroom took his breath away, as if someone had thrust a rank cloth in his face. Not only was the single window closed; to exclude the glare the Buzzard's weak eyes abhorred, the shutters were open no more than a chink, so that it took Max a second to adjust his own vision to a gloom made more oppressive by the quantities of furniture crammed into the narrow room. Two towering armoires, a tallboy, a chest and a washstand hemmed the bedstead, a simple wooden affair like his own, into the far corner, where, as his eye travelled through this mahogany twilight, he discerned a figure propped up amongst the pillows.

Whenever he thought of his adversary, Max recalled the minatory glint of the pebble glasses, the sharp chin coerced into permanent disdain by the absurdly high collar; he saw a man, no longer young, but driven by the vigour of his various obsessions, not tall, but punctiliously upright, as if pressed, brushed and starched to his very backbone. The old man in the bed, with his stained nightgown and six-day growth of beard, might have been some other person.

He appeared to be sleeping. His withered yellow face seemed pathetically exposed by the absence of his thick spectacles. His mouth, which memory saw pursed tight with disapproval, hung open so that his tongue lolled over his lower lip. Instead of the stiff wing collar, his shrivelled neck supported the sling that held his injured wrist across his chest—Max could see the tips of the fingers, pink and bunched as grapes, protruding from the bandage that secured the splint. And now he had become accustomed to the dismal light, he could see something else too, which transfixed him with horror: from beneath the old fowl's purplish eyelids, two tears oozed out and trickled slowly into his stubble.

Max was overwhelmed simultaneously by disgust and pity. On the one hand, he was choked by the miasma of the sickroom: he flexed his shoulders to reassure himself that his own healthy body could never succumb to this degrading senility. But on the other hand—poor old

Buzzard! How had he come to this in the space of three months? And now that the bedraggled old bird had moulted all his plumage, how could he, Max, possibly…? He felt the crackle of the envelope in his breast pocket like a reproach. Besides, it might not even be necessary. Perhaps Gérard was right about the apoplectic stroke. In which case—

But suddenly, as though alert to Max's thoughts, the purple eyelids snapped open and the milky pupils beneath were trained in his direction. "You!"

Max stepped back, startled. He was some distance from the bed and, if Gérard were correct, all the old fowl could see was a blur.

"Oh, I can smell the stench of the gutter when it invades my room. Besides, I knew he'd send you. He's too much of a coward to come himself." With difficulty, but with surprising strength, Lesage was using his left arm to lever himself higher against the pillows. His voice, too, was hardly the feeble quaver of an invalid.

Max's pity evaporated. "If, monsieur, you are referring to Monsieur de Miremont—"

"You can't wait, can you, *Monsieur* Fabien? You can't wait to steal my place. Not that you'll even need to steal it, he'll give it to you, weak fool that he is. Twenty-two years of my life I've devoted to saving him from his own mistakes. But oh no, youth must prevail and I'm for the dust heap."

"Monsieur Lesage, while I appreciate that you are unwell—"

"I am not unwell. I have a slight difficulty with my right wrist. Not that I haven't been fortunate to escape the infections that nincompoop of a doctor brings into this house from his charity patients. But that's Monsieur le marquis for you—he can't be satisfied with Doctor Chevalier, who attends all the best houses in the Faubourg. Oh no, he must try some new man with so-called modern theories, even if he wears a morning coat you couldn't give away to the boot boy. In madame's time—"

"Monsieur Lesage, Doctor Chevalier will be summoned as you have requested. Now, if you will permit me to speak for a moment—"

"In madame's time," continued the Buzzard, "we had a proper doctor. In Monsieur Guy de Miremont's time too. We had servants who knew their place. We received and were received in the highest circles, we kept lists—who could be invited to dinner, who might be asked to soirées, who to balls. We did not admit into this house every rag, tag and bobtail—bourgeois professors who are not only Jews, but most probably Socialists. Nor did we employ young persons of dubious origin and without proper references, merely because they could construe two sentences of Latin…"

Max opened his mouth to retort but decided to wait until these vile outpourings had ceased. The letter was all that was required to despatch his adversary. To hell with the old fowl's senile tears! He felt no remorse and would show no mercy. He took the envelope from his pocket in readiness for when the Buzzard next drew breath.

"I have a letter for you from Monsieur de Miremont."

"A letter, eh?" The Buzzard snorted. "I'm sure I cannot imagine what that contains."

"He makes you the most generous offer—"

"To whom?"

In spite of himself, Max was brought up short. "Forgive me?"

"Generous to whom? To you, no doubt, because it gives you what you've schemed for ever since you set foot under this roof. Oh, he's very generous, our Monsieur le marquis—to shiftless peasants, fallen women, cunning young flatterers who encourage the fantasy that he'll one day write that magnum opus of his—but to those who've attempted to remind him of his duty and give him sensible advice—"

"Monsieur Lesage—"

"Just you wait, young man. He'll make you promises. He'll swear on his honour to reward a lifetime of service. But find yourself laid up because of a trivial accident, even after twenty-two years without a day lost for illness—"

"Monsieur Lesage!"

"He can't stick to his word, he doesn't know his own mind, he has no judgement. I shouldn't care for myself, but what's to become of his poor grandson, Monsieur le vicomte, when the family fortune has been squandered and the dignity of the house lies in—?"

"Enough!" With all the force it had been accumulating for days, Max's anger exploded.

Lesage seemed startled, but not deterred. "Young man, you are impertinent!"

Max flung back one of the shutters so that harsh sunlight flooded the room. It was cruel but it served its purpose, for his adversary gave a whimper and cringed back into his pillows. Max advanced upon him. When he spoke, his voice was a low growl.

"I am well used to you insulting me, you old vulture, but I will not tolerate your insults to Monsieur de Miremont. My very first day here you spoke slighting of him and ever since then I have listened to you belittle him. If I were monsieur, I should not have put up with your insolence and your malice and your petty snobbery, not for one year, let alone twenty-two. But he, out of a sense of loyalty and obligation you are incapable of understanding, and out of compassion for your infirmity—"

Here the Buzzard gave a squawk, but Max overrode it.

"He has continued to treat you with a generosity you do not deserve. What is his crime? That he prefers kindness to tyranny? That he doesn't always dress for dinner, doesn't care for balls and soirées? If that's your famous 'dignity of the house' then to hell with it! When have you known him neglect any duty that matters? When has he ever broken his word to you? If you only paid attention to him for once instead of sneering, you would not dare to question his honour. And as for his judgement—having been forced to stand and listen to your filthy slanders, I might say only that he is too lenient with you, that if he understood what a vile old carrion bird you are, he would never... never guarantee to..."

Max faltered, realising that he still clutched the letter, the letter that gave the lie to everything he was saying.

CHAPTER THIRTY NINE

Later he would understand better why he did what he did next.

Later he would see that his deception, even if it were never found out, would have poisoned his relations with the old boy. For he could not fool himself: yes, monsieur might excuse Calvert's chicanery, but he would not readily forgive this breach of trust. Max could never again have felt entirely easy with the old fellow.

Later he would realise, too, that if he truly thought he had sold himself to M de M as he had to Lebas and Tarascon, then here was the means to redemption: to do the work for which he was paid in the way in which he had been instructed, however contrary to his own interests that might be.

But at the time, as, without a word of excuse, he rushed from Lesage's bedroom, through the old fowl's study and down the corridor to his own room, he had only one thought: while his code allowed him to lie and cheat on his own behalf, it did not entitle him to do so on monsieur's.

The copy of the old boy's original letter lay on his table, addressed and ready to be delivered to Ladurie. He ripped it from the envelope and, in fear of lingering for an instant lest he change his mind, ran back with it.

He expected his reappearance to be greeted with outrage. Yet, perplexingly, the old fowl did not appear much disturbed by his behaviour. Instead, he waved his left hand imperiously at the window.

"My girl, how many times must you be told? The shutters are to be—Oh, it's you. Come to pick my bones, have you? I might have known he'd send you."

Max, who was still sweating and had only just recovered his breath, was for a moment utterly disconcerted.

"Of course, Monsieur le marquis must do as he chooses. If he wishes to entrust the family's affairs to someone who cannot even catalogue a library—"

"Please! Monsieur Lesage." The fear that he was about to be caught up in an eternal circle was already making Max dizzy. "Forgive me, I brought the wrong letter before. Let me —"

"Letter? Which letter?"

"The letter from—Oh, for pity's sake, just let me read it to you."

And read it Max did, drawing up a chair to the bedside and continuing doggedly to the end despite a barrage of interruptions. Perhaps the Buzzard had been so intent on his protests that he had failed to listen, for he showed neither gratitude nor relief. Max began again. This time for the most part the old fowl was silent, until Max reached monsieur's promise to keep the secretary's position open indefinitely. Whereupon, suddenly leaning forward and stretching out his uninjured left claw, he tried to snatch the document.

"Give it me here. It is clearly a forgery."

The irony of this forced a startled laugh from Max.

"Forgery, young man, is no laughing matter. Let me see it. At once!"

This placed Max in a quandary. He would not put it past the Buzzard, in his present mood, to tear up the letter, yet something must be sent to Ladurie, and this not only bore the only genuine signature, but was now the only copy. Still, since it was after all addressed to Lesage, he could hardly withhold it.

Next to the bed was a small cabinet, the top of which, in a marked reversal of the Buzzard's usual finicky habits, was cluttered with objects. Amongst the medicine bottles, soiled handkerchiefs and novena cards, Max found the old fowl's spectacles, although there was no sign of the magnifying glass. He watched apprehensively as the Buzzard, his single functioning hand trembling with the effort, held the paper to within a centimetre of the thick lenses.

"You wrote this, this is your hand."

"Monsieur dictated it." Spying the magnifier all at once on the floor near the leg of his chair, Max bent to retrieve it. "Please, examine the signature."

Given that it was impossible for Lesage to hold up the paper and train the glass upon it at the same time, it would have been easier if he had permitted Max to hold the letter—easier too for Max to abstract it afterwards and restore it safely to his pocket. But alas, Gérard was right, the Buzzard spurned even this small act of assistance, preferring to use his raised knees as a lectern, despite the painful contortion this involved. He seemed to spend so long hunched there, spectacles pressed to the magnifier, nose all but resting on the paper, that it became more than Max could bear.

"So you see, monsieur. Monsieur de Miremont has kept his promise. You may take your slanders back."

At this, Lesage finally looked up. That he gave no sign of contrition was perhaps to be expected, yet he still refused to evince pleasure; rather, Max fancied he seemed almost disappointed. Casting aside the magnifying glass and spectacles and lowering his knees, he folded the letter as best he could and, to Max's dismay, proceeded to secrete it beneath his pillows.

"Let us suppose," he said, assuming a judicial air, "let us suppose for the sake of argument that this letter was indeed written by Monsieur le marquis—"

"Monsieur Lesage—"

"Where, may I ask, am I to be sent for this 'brief period of absence'? To Beauvallon? A rustic hell, devoid of all civilisation?" Suddenly his face crumpled. "Dear God, that I should end my days at Beauvallon!"

By now Max was both bewildered and exhausted by these rapid changes of mood. But, fearing the horrific tears, he endeavoured to sound consoling. "Monsieur Lesage, you are not about to end your days anywhere. Monsieur suggests you stay with your sister in Nogent, only until your wrist has healed. You need not even concern yourself with the arrangements. I shall write to your sister, with your consent, and arrange everything."

"Shall you, indeed, Monsieur Fabien?" Abandoning pathos, the Buzzard was all at once oddly smug. "I fear you may have some trouble. My sister is dead."

Max's heart sank. Yet he thought he detected something crafty in the old fowl's expression. "Forgive me, but Monsieur de Miremont seems firmly under the impression that she is still living."

"She is dead to me. We fell out years ago."

"So monsieur is mistaken in believing that you still correspond? And that she still lives in Nogent-sur-Oise?"

The Buzzard's narrow lips curled in a smile of triumph. "She may live in Peru for all I know."

Lesage was to be Max's penance and he could not but admit that he deserved it. Yet, even by the end of that first exhausting day, he had little idea how arduous, how time-consuming, how entirely maddening his journey of expiation was to prove. The delights of Paris? That evening he was too busy and too tired either to pay his promised visit to the Zhukovskys or go to the Monkey.

In the middle of the afternoon, desperate to escape from the sickroom, he retired to his own room and reviewed the tasks that now fell to him, so that he could draw up a plan of campaign. First he must organise his troops, shore up his defences and ensure his supply lines were in place—in other words, fetch Dr Chevalier, send the letter to Ladurie and write to M de M telling him all was proceeding smoothly. Then there were the three fortresses he must storm to be certain of conquest: the Buzzard must give up his fast, agree to be dressed and shaved, and must divulge his sister's whereabouts.

At least he had already made a start with martialling his forces. Having decided to risk calling in Chevalier straight away, even before he had obtained the old boy's official consent, he had been surprised by how promptly the doctor had arrived. Or rather, since Dr Chevalier was enjoying the sea breezes at Cabourg, the great man's locum, his nephew, Dr Vionnet, had arrived, immediately after luncheon. Small, neat, in his late twenties, with a self-important moustache and an unctuous manner, Vionnet became decidedly less unctuous when he discovered his patient was not M le marquis. However, he condescended to visit Lesage's lowly quarters, since it was M de Miremont's wish. The Buzzard was at first similarly disappointed, but brightened when he heard the locum was related to Chevalier, as one might console oneself with the cadet branch of a royal house. He did not seem put out that Vionnet's examination was cursory, to say the least—Max had tactfully withdrawn to the study when Vionnet had produced his stethoscope, but it seemed only a minute or two before the doctor came to join him.

Max had observed that, while Vionnet tut-tutted over Gérard's splinting, he evinced no enthusiasm for remedying its supposed defects. Nor, although he debated it, did he finally recommend letting blood, for that would have involved daily visits. Diagnosing the Buzzard's failure to eat as due to mild stomach catarrh, he prescribed mustard plasters, a camphor sleeping draught, a strychnine tonic to invigorate the nervous system, a glass of fortified wine daily to strengthen the constitution and continuation of the laudanum. If there were a dramatic change in the patient's condition, Max might, by all means, call him in again.

Serve the Buzzard right for being such an obnoxious snob! Yet Max could not help feeling angry on the old fowl's behalf, while Gérard went up in his estimation. But at least Vionnet's reluctance to earn his fee had prevented him from doing positive harm and he had been highly beneficial in one vital respect: on hearing from Max that Gérard forbade moving the patient, Vionnet had insisted to Lesage that he must seek healthier air forthwith.

By chance, Max had also happened upon a strategy for his first offensive: true, it had met with little success as yet, but it had promise.

He had only just abandoned asking the Buzzard about his sister when one of the maids, escorted by Mme Mercier herself, had brought in the old fowl's luncheon. Monsieur's letter had clearly not produced the hoped-for alteration in Lesage's resolve to starve, for he waved the tray away in a lordly fashion that caused Mme Mercier to bristle. Max had thought to use this interruption to make his escape, for his patience had been drained dry by the Buzzard's evasions. Yet it occurred to him that pride might be the new obstacle to the old fowl's accepting food: eating would be tantamount to retracting his accusations.

Max intercepted Mme Mercier at the door. "Please, madame, leave the tray, if you will."

The housekeeper shot him a sour look, but the tray was placed on its stand at the Buzzard's bedside. When they were alone, Max lifted the covers and the mingled fragrances of Mme Dussardier's artistry rose up, momentarily obliterating the odours of the sickroom. Max fancied he saw the Buzzard's nose twitch, but this might have been wishful thinking.

A herb bouillon, thoughtfully served in a cup. White fish—although it had been cut up it looked to Max like turbot—poached in a light broth, with leeks, thinly sliced, and creamed potato. A small dish of egg custard.

A sly confiding expression had crept over the Buzzard's face, a look Max would never have expected from the old fowl, saucy, familiar, as if, had he been capable of it, he would have nudged Max in the ribs. "It's poisoned, you know. They're trying to poison me."

Max sighed. He was scarcely in the mood to play games. Yet he wondered if the Buzzard's sudden changes of personality might be as much due to starvation as anything. He picked up the cup of bouillon and, noisily, so that the Buzzard could not mistake what he was doing, took a gulp from it.

The old fowl cackled. "They'd be even happier if they could poison you."

"No doubt." Max gave his attention to the fish, again making as much noise as possible, clattering his fork against the plate. Then it was the turn of the egg custard. He smacked his lips. "Delicious. You're more likely to be poisoned by your Doctor Vionnet. Won't you try a little?"

But the Buzzard was not to be beaten. "You shan't catch me that way, young man," he said with dignity. "You've taken the antidote."

Max's exasperation knew no bounds. Was the old carrion bird stark mad or was he merely play-acting? With a sudden tremendous groan, Max collapsed onto the end of the bed, one arm clasped tightly around his belly while the other hand clutched at his throat, from which there came agonised gargling.

"Monsieur Fabien!" The Buzzard was obliged to raise his voice above the din. "Have you no respect for a sick man? Stop this tomfoolery at once!"

"So we are agreed there is no poison?" Max decided he would put into practice Gérard's advice. "Well, that's a relief. I must confess I am famished."

Moving the chair and the tray away from the bedside, he took up the plate of fish. "This is very good, you know. Definitely turbot. Poached in white wine and parsley." He came and sat on the edge of the bed, so that the plate was a mere arm's length from the Buzzard's nose and was delighted to see his adversary struggling to hide a look that recalled Fabrice's perusal of last night's Jura ham. "Yes, Madame Dussardier has surpassed herself. The leeks too—so tender they melt on your tongue."

"Monsieur Fabien, what do you mean by sitting on my bed?"

"And creamed potatoes. I've always had a weakness for them."

"Young man, will you desist from—"

"Good Lord, I had no idea I was so hungry." This was, in fact, untrue, for the frustrations of the morning and the atmosphere in the room had quite removed Max's appetite. But, despite this and regardless of his adversary's protests, he continued to eat with apparent relish, even mopping up the juices with bread, until the plate was clean. By the time he had demolished the egg custard, the Buzzard was mute, his pained face turned into the pillow. Max left him the cup of bouillon, placing it next to the water carafe on the bedside cabinet.

Later, after Vionnet's visit, when Max sought out Mme Mercier to tell her she might cease her endeavours in the east wing since M Lesage was adamantly opposed to moving rooms, her grudging acknowledgement of these good tidings was tempered by a frown of suspicion.

"When Christine came to collect Monsieur Lesage's tray, the plates were clean."

With effort, for the contents of his own luncheon tray still sat heavily on his stomach, Max conjured up a grin. "Well, that's excellent news, is it not, madame?"

The housekeeper's eye did not soften. "It can't be at all good for someone who hasn't eaten for five days to gobble down all that food at once. If he did, that is."

"Did he drink the bouillon?"

"No, I think he left that. But—"

"Ah well." Shit! Still, it was early yet. Max recalled that the Buzzard had a very sweet tooth. "Perhaps this evening we could try him with Madame Dussardier's exquisite chocolate soufflé?"

"Chocolate soufflé, for an invalid? Doctor Gérard gave strict orders—"

"Oh, and a glass of monsieur's 1827 port."

"Monsieur Fabien!"

"New doctor, new orders, madame."

Max was pleased to see that, despite Mme Mercier's suspicions, the chocolate soufflé was on the Buzzard's dinner tray, as, having lain in wait for Christine, he followed it into the sickroom. The glass of port was there too, though heaven knew what objections Georges had raised to broaching one of the precious bottles. There was also a cup of chicken consommé and a *blanquette* of veal.

Having abstracted the port and placed it on the washstand, beyond the limits of the Buzzard's vision, Max proceeded as he had at luncheon, commenting on each dish in turn before setting the consommé on the bedside cabinet and devoting his attention to the entrée. This time, however, he not only sat on the bed but laid the tray across his knees so that none of its tempting aromas should escape his victim. The Buzzard, to his relief, made no mention of poison and indeed, after firing off a few salvos of protest, fell strangely silent: although his face was turned away, Max could observe that every muscle in it was taut.

"Damn, I forgot!" Max had finished the veal and was about to embark upon the chocolate soufflé when, all at once thrusting the tray unceremoniously into the Buzzard's lap, he rose and went to the washstand. "The port. Do you know, I think…" Carrying the glass over to the bed, he sniffed it elaborately. "Mmm, I might be wrong, but I think they've sent up—what was the vintage you and monsieur make such a song and dance about? 1867?"

The very mention of port had impelled the Buzzard to turn his head. Now his eyes popped. "1827."

Max sniffed again, then, as though offering the glass up to the light, held it for one enticing second within range of the Buzzard's nose. Many were the times he had watched the old fowl hold the glass thus before rolling the first sip of the liquid on his tongue, then expatiating upon its richness, its complexities, its exquisite finish. Many were the times too, that he, Max, had been castigated as uncouth and ungrateful for refusing to taste this nectar.

He snatched the glass away just as the Buzzard reached for it. "1827? Well, well. What a shame it must go to waste."

The old fowl let out an incredulous squawk.

"As you know, monsieur, I don't drink. Still, better not offend Georges. I'll tip it away."

"But it's mine! Doctor Chevalier prescribed it!"

"I'm not sure the doctor understood you hadn't eaten for so long."

"It's mine. I order you to give it to me."

"Truly, monsieur, I wish I could. But it will only make you sick. Let me pour you more water."

"Young man, I shall report you for gross insubordination. I shall write a full account of your disgraceful behaviour to Monsieur le marquis—"

"Careful!" Max steadied the tray with his free hand. "We don't want chocolate soufflé all over the sheets. Besides, I'm looking forward to it."

"He won't let you steal my place when he finds out how you abuse me. I told him, I said we should send you packing when your probation was over, but would he listen? But he'll listen now, you mark my words. Tormenting a sick man…"

Max let him run on. Keeping a weather eye on the tray as it bounced agitatedly in the old fowl's lap, he refilled the water glass, then retrieved the port from where he had put it out of harm's way and left the room. He did not hurry as he went down the corridor to the WC, where he flushed away M de Miremont's treasured vintage. Nor did he hurry back. In fact, he retired to his own room for a leisurely smoke.

Poor blinkered old Buzzard. Yes, a part of Max was enjoying this revenge. But, at the same time, he at last understood what Lesage's assaults upon his pride had always prevented him from grasping: he could comprehend perfectly why monsieur made such a fetish of trying to be fair to the old fowl. It might be merciful that the Buzzard could not see what the servants saw, yet, poor benighted carrion bird, it stripped him of all power. If Max were able to rise above Lesage, he realised with shame, it was not through any glorious victory of the will, but from the obvious and not very glorious fact that he always held the advantage: he had no need to forge letters, he could get away with anything he chose. And yet—to choose not to—was this, after all, where victory lay?

One minor triumph awaited Max's return to the sickroom. There could not be any doubt that, driven by rage or by the sheer agony of his hunger, the old bird had made an assault on the soufflé: there was plentiful evidence on the sheets and his nightshirt, but smears on his chin too, suggesting a small portion must have reached his mouth. Now he lay back on his pillows, exhausted from the effort: his squawks were feeble when Max seized the dish and consumed the rest. Once again, Max left the cup of soup beside the water carafe. Then he retired to his room to wait for Christine and the tray.

Christine was no more than seventeen, pretty and, despite Mme Mercier's undoubted warnings, more inclined to giggle and blush in Max's presence than to view him as Lucifer. They both agreed that the level of liquid in the soup cup had dropped, not dramatically, but sufficiently for encouragement.

Max had written to monsieur after Vionnet's visit, in time to catch the post. Now that his conscience was clear, the words came with surprising ease. There seemed little point in worrying the old fellow with such details as the Buzzard's peculiar state of mind or the business of his sister's address: once he had dealt with the change of doctors, he concentrated on reassuring M de M that his mission was straightforward and would take no more than three or four days. He was careful to obey the old boy's strictures, addressing him with due formality and, after concluding with elaborate and respectful salutations, signing himself Maxime Fabien; and when he came to the postscript—well, it was pointless hunting through Catullus for more moderate expressions of endearment, for moderation was scarcely the poet's stock-in-trade. So be it, XLVIII: poetic license. Curiously, once he had written it, he found he did not mind it.

The letter for Ladurie, on the other hand, was a more complicated affair. To begin with, Max must recover it from the Buzzard's pillows. Although Lesage still retained the use of his legs, rather than struggle to the WC in his present enfeebled state he preferred to use the close stool in his bedroom, so that no opportunity presented itself there. Of course, there was always the laudanum: Mme Mercier had apparently decided that, since Max thought fit to issue commands left and right, the care of the patient might now fall to him, and that included the administering of his medicines; it would be a simple matter to pour a double dose. However, Max did not relish the old fowl waking up while he scrabbled amongst his pillows.

In the end, taking the chocolate as his excuse, he prevailed upon Christine to change the sheets: a winning smile and the explanation that this was an important document he feared M Lesage might lose were all that was required to deliver the letter into his hands. Although it was somewhat creased it had thankfully escaped the soufflé; once Max had smoothed it out, refolded it and sealed it in a fresh envelope, Georges could take it round to Ladurie first thing tomorrow. But before that, of course, he must make a copy for Lesage.

Strange how honesty seemed to have blunted his forger's skills. The old boy's signature, which had flowed from his pen last night, now resolutely eluded him, and each failure meant he must copy the entire letter again. Only at the sixth attempt, close to despair, did he achieve anything halfway satisfactory. Still, it would pass so long as the Buzzard did not subject it to his magnifier. The thing was done. Max's treachery was expunged. He was surprised by the intensity of his relief.

CHAPTER FORTY

Now Max had sole charge of the Buzzard, it could not be said that conflict ceased. However, the first assault of Max's campaign brought encouraging developments.

The next morning, as he appeared with the Buzzard's breakfast tray, the old fowl announced that he was banned from the sickroom. "This young man," Lesage informed a perplexed Christine, "will do anything to step into my shoes. Now he's trying to starve me to death."

Complying obediently, Max returned on tiptoe to observe the invalid through the open door and noted that he ate most of his brioche. Relieved that he need no longer consume every meal twice over, Max went away light-hearted, but when he took up his observation post at luncheon it was a different story. While the brioche, broken and buttered in the kitchen, had presented no problem to Lesage's unsteady left hand, for it had only required him to use his fingers, luncheon's chicken fricassée, even with the spoon sensibly provided, was refined torture: most of the dish made its escape during the long tremulous journey from his plate to his mouth, and the same was true of the honey and almond blancmange. Poor old Buzzard. Spattered with food despite the napkin he had managed to thrust into the neck of his nightgown, he lay back on his pillows, breathless with frustration. Max contemplated this picture of despair thoughtfully. Then he went to consult Mme Mercier.

He did not expect to be congratulated on succeeding where the housekeeper and the cook had failed and in any case he gathered success did not count when achieved by underhand means. Indeed he wondered, were it not for the talisman of 'monsieur's orders', whether Mme Mercier would have responded to his summons. However, she agreed to a change in the Buzzard's diet, if with some objections and many sighs. Mme Dussardier might rightly pride herself on her sauces and light, soft food might be traditional fare for invalids, but the Buzzard had no difficulty chewing —he possessed a creditable number of teeth for a man of his age—while his digestion could be preserved by ensuring his portions were small until he had reaccustomed himself to eating. From now on, apart from soup, which he managed well from a cup, he would be served only food that could be speared with a fork or eaten with fingers.

But if Gérard had been right and thwarting the Buzzard had been the tactic to make him eat, Max struggled to see how it could help him find the Nogent address. Here thwarting was Lesage's weapon and he had mastery of it. Perhaps monsieur had been mistaken but Max doubted it; he was now certain the Buzzard was still in contact with his sister, the more so because of the old fowl's bizarre and contradictory denials. As to why he played this maddening game—for the sheer pleasure of outwitting his foe or because he refused to believe monsieur's letter—it was impossible to tell. After a second day of futile skirmishing, Max knew he must find another angle of attack.

Georges, who had clearly been conferring with Mmes Mercier and Dussardier, was not disposed to be helpful when Max enquired about Lesage's personal letters and whether he had a correspondent in the *département* of the Oise: Philippe usually dealt with the post and he was not due back until next week. There was nothing for it—Max would have to mount a search of the Buzzard's study.

He picked his moment, in the middle of the afternoon when the old fowl was sleeping, and, closing the bedroom door stealthily, prepared to set to work. But it was easy to forget that Lesage, whatever his other disabilities, still retained the use of his legs. Max had progressed no further than to take in the daunting quantity of papers, dossiers and notebooks the old fowl had accumulated over the years when the bedroom door burst open.

"Young man, you have no business—"

"Ah, Monsieur Lesage." Max snatched up a random bill from amongst the chaotic papers on the desk. "Just seeing if there was any work to be done."

"There is nothing, everything is up do date. Don't trouble yourself, you won't catch me out that way."

That left Max no recourse but night-time and the laudanum. Even with the Buzzard snoring soundly, the search was no easy task for, quite apart from the need for absolute silence, Max dared not light the gas, making do with a single lamp with the wick turned low.

He began by the door to the corridor, working methodically through every shelf, drawer and cupboard. Lesage, it seemed, had thrown away nothing during his forty years of service to the Miremonts: there were account ledgers meticulously chronicling decades of expenditure, including bills from Mathurin when monsieur was in knickerbockers; there were albums of invitations, preserved not because they were addressed to Lesage himself, but to commemorate the family's attendance at occasions of note—a reception to welcome Queen Victoria to Paris or a ball in honour of the Grand Duke of Tuscany; there were memorandum books, engagement books and, of course, the visiting books containing Lesage's precious lists. Letters abounded —in cabinets, in boxes, in document envelopes upon the shelves—more letters than Max could hope to scrutinise thoroughly in weeks, let alone in a few snatched hours; however, a cursory glance found none that could be deemed personal.

Indeed, it seemed that Lesage's personal life had gradually been subsumed by his devotion to the Miremonts. True, here and there Max came upon sentimental keepsakes that must date from the Buzzard's youth; a dance card, a lithograph of Rachel costumed for *Andromaque* and signed by the actress, a brown and disintegrating flower—a gardenia from a corsage perhaps—pressed between the pages of an almanac. A volume of poems by Alfred de Vigny was inscribed in fading ink to 'Camille' (Max still found it curious to think of the Buzzard possessing a given name like other mortals). But the sender of birthday felicitations in 1842 was not his sister, for she signed herself Violette, and monsieur, whatever his uncertainty about her married name, had seemed convinced the sister's given name was Edwige: while these traces of an unimaginable Lesage with romantic fire in his veins embarrassed Max, as though his prying had turned up a diagnosis of the pox, they were of no more practical use to him than the collection of religious medals he found in one of the desk drawers, together with two rosaries still in their presentation boxes, which, along with further bundles of prayer cards, were undoubtedly gifts from the more devout of the Buzzard's noble ladies.

Even the photographs that cluttered every surface unoccupied by papers seemed to deny any connection that was not with the Miremonts. (Max, who had never had the opportunity to study these closely before, was intrigued to see monsieur as a youthful bridegroom, pale and awkward as though daunted by the fragile blond beauty of his bride—later, if the camera did not lie, Mme la marquise had lost her finger-span waist, but not her power to intimidate.) There was a studio portrait of Lesage himself, taken at about the age monsieur was now, cutting an unexpectedly handsome figure in evening dress, yet already a stranger to the Camille who cherished fallen gardenias. But, apart from this, Max's search yielded only two photographs that might be of the Buzzard's relations, both taken years ago to judge from the ladies' crinolines.

While the first showed a respectable bourgeois couple, doubtless the old fowl's parents, the second was of a family group with three small children, the eldest clearly a daughter, the younger two still in petticoats. The paterfamilias, plump and balding with jaunty side-whiskers and an air of cheerful prosperity, was obviously not a Lesage, but there was no question about the wife; with her high crown, long face and sharp features and her reminiscent expression of extreme severity, this could not but be Edwige.

Yet what did this serve? Although Max carefully prised the frame apart in the hope of finding some inscription on the reverse of the photograph that would at least reveal Edwige's married name, there was nothing. His heart sank as, looking round the room, he realised his search had covered less than half of it. He had collected a pile of address books to examine in his own room; if they could not assist him, he would be forced to drug the Buzzard again tomorrow night.

Damn monsieur for being so vague about names. On the second night of his search, Max began with the bottom right-hand desk drawer, which had resisted him yesterday. Tonight he had brought along a length of wire fashioned into a lock-pick, yet it transpired the drawer was after all merely jammed. Rocking it by its handles as vigorously as he dared, he could at last open it far enough to ease his fingers inside; whatever was blocking it was wedged into the cavity between the runners and the side panel corresponding to the pedestal's ornamental pilaster. Max remembered the Mallarmé. Was this a favourite hiding place of the Buzzard's? Painfully edging his hand in further, he extracted a packet: a bundle of letters.

He untied the dusty red tape that secured the bundle with bated breath. But he had only to unfold the first yellowing sheet to see that this was another false trail; the letter, like the Alfred de Vigny, bore the signature 'Violette' and had been written over three decades ago from Algiers. Max read no further but, tying up the packet, thrust it hastily back into the gap and shut the drawer.

His search suddenly disgusted him. Besides it was futile—he might turn over every piece of paper in the study, but he could not search the bedroom, where the old fowl might easily conceal his sister's letters amongst his collars and shirts.

He was all too aware that by now he had used up the four days of his over-optimistic promise and that monsieur was already anxious as to the date of his return. Not wishing to confess his absurd but apparently insoluble dilemma, which would doubtless bring the old boy to Paris and prevent him from completing his penance, he wrote— what was after all true—that Lesage needed more time to accustom himself to eating and was at present too frail to travel. He did not add that he had yet to find a way of getting his charge shaved and dressed.

He had, it must be granted, made a minor advance on this front. On the night of the chocolate soufflé, after Christine had changed the Buzzard's sheets, Max had taken the liberty of opening the doors to the old fowl's armoire.

"Come out of there at once, young man!"

"Just finding you a clean nightshirt, monsieur."

"I do not need one."

Despite the Buzzard's protests, Max had ostentatiously shaken the folds from the garment and made quite a business of unfastening its buttons. "Here it is, on the bed."

"I don't want it, I tell you. You leave me alone!"

"With pleasure, monsieur," Max had replied, with a shrug. "I'm not your valet."

Yet, the following morning, the Buzzard's consumption of brioche had not been Max's only cause to rejoice: he was gratified to see that the old fowl was wearing the clean gown, albeit with the buttons still undone. He was rather admiring of the old carrion bird: with only one useful arm and with little sight to distinguish neck and armholes, heaven knew what effort it had cost him to struggle out of the dirty garment and into the fresh one; that same pride which spurned help must finally have rebelled against the indignity of his condition. But, if he could be driven to change his nightgown and to wash, it was another matter to expect him to shave himself or don his frock coat and stiff collar without help.

The solution came to Max by roundabout means when he was making a further attempt to discover Edwige's address. In despair, after he had yet again emphasised Dr Vionnet's advice, he asked: "If not to your sister's, monsieur, where should you like to go?"

The reply came back: "Deauville." Then, after a pause: "The Countess Kutchinsky often invites me to her villa to keep her dear mother, Madame de Thiviers, company—such a sweet-natured lady but sadly troubled by dropsy."

It seemed to Max that if the Buzzard wrote…No, the request should come from monsieur…

But the old fowl forestalled him. "Of course, one mustn't get into a rut. Besides, I couldn't have gone last year in case Monsieur le marquis

needed me at Beauvallon. And this year…Yes, Deauville can be dull if
one goes every summer."

Max understood at once, all too clearly. Even last year the Buzzard's
sight had told against him. Now that he could not be relied upon to
run errands or push a bath chair, he was no longer useful, indeed
might prove an annoying liability. The Buzzard's crestfallen look
confirmed it, so that Max wished he could take back his question.

But later, as he was pondering the problem of the old fowl's
toilette, he thought again of the noble ladies. They could not all be as
heartless as Mme Kutchinsky and her frightful mother. And, since they
were impoverished, they must mostly have remained in Paris. Of
course they were in ignorance of their friend's predicament, for he had
been unable to write; but, once they knew, surely some of them would
repay his devotion with a visit. Would the Buzzard be happy to receive
these delicate creatures at the Hôtel de Miremont in his nightgown
and with over a week's growth of beard?

Thanks to his clandestine activities, Max at least knew where these
addresses were to be found. He would write to the ladies himself
without telling Lesage, both to escape the inevitable protests and to
avoid raising false hopes. Two names on the list were pathetically
annotated 'deceased' and he could cross off the comtesse de Thiviers,
but that left four more, not including the two Miremont cousins
upstairs, who often received the Buzzard after mass on a Sunday and
had doubtless contributed to his drawer of devotional medals. Max
duly wrote to the baronne de Marsan, Mme de Bessé and Mmes
Sainte-Maure and Deneuville-Rivière, with suitable apologies for the
imposition, which he trusted they would forgive when they understood
the extent of their poor friend's suffering.

The princesse de Vaux and Mme d'Ancy-Miremont Max decided
to visit in person. Although he had seen neither of the sisters since his
return from Beauvallon, he was certain they had not gone away, for he
had glimpsed the lady companion scuttling across the courtyard and
he had heard footfalls on their staircase when he was passing through
the anteroom to the library.

As he entered through the side door and climbed towards their
apartment, it crossed his mind that the second cousins might also
relieve him of his other problem. Although it would mean the Buzzard
remained in Paris, he would escape from the hôtel's hostile atmosphere
and—who knew?—when he was staying with those who appreciated
him, he might be less cantankerous. Cheered by this notion, Max had

already knocked jauntily on the sisters' door before his ears caught the commotion that was distantly audible through its heavy panels. Deciding it had not been sensible to call unannounced, he was turning to go when the door was opened by a flustered maid.

It was not the smell that assailed him first, a stench of urine and faeces so powerful that unconsciously he took a step back. Nor was it the sight of the lady companion, her skirts gathered up and her bun uncoiling, emerging from a nearby room and running down the hall. It was the voice, high, eldritch, emanating from deep within the apartment like a damned soul screeching from some recess of hell: "Help me! In the name of the blessed Virgin, help me! Merciful God, help me! Help me!"

As she ran, the companion shouted over her shoulder at the maid: "Tell whoever it is the mistresses are not at home! They are not at home to anyone!" And the door was slammed shut on Max's mumbled apology.

This was a glimpse into a nightmare that made Lesage's tribulations seem paltry. Later Max wondered if he should have taken his dismissal so readily, without making some attempt to help. However, observing Dr Vionnet's carriage drawing up in the courtyard, he contented himself with sending over a note asking pardon for his intrusion and offering to be of service; he did not expect a reply and was relieved not to receive one.

There were still four noble ladies left and, after all, Max only needed one of them to further his scheme. But Mme Sainte-Maure, though replying promptly, regretted she was in deep mourning for a relation of her late husband's and could not pay visits. Mme de Bessé's servant left her card. Mme la baronne sent a basket of fruit. And from Mme Deneuville-Rivière there was silence—it was charitable to think that, like Mme de Thiviers, she had found some wealthy connection to stay with.

As his time at the Hôtel de Miremont extended into a second week, Max could barely recall the false confidence inspired by his early victories, let alone his state of mind as he had set out for Paris. He recollected that he had taken on Lesage as a penance but, although he remained glad that he had burnt his forgery and was abiding by the old boy's wishes, his reasons for inflicting this punishment upon himself seemed increasingly obscure. However, it was all one: there might be moments in every day where he longed to walk out into the street and hail a cab for the Gare de Rungis, but now the Buzzard was his responsibility he could not simply desert his post. He had undertaken to convey the old fowl to Nogent, or at least to some suitable place of convalescence, and he was damned if he would fail in the task.

It was, or so he had read, important in any war and particularly in a prolonged campaign, to gain an understanding of how the enemy's mind worked. But Max, it seemed, was no Wallenstein or Napoleon: his understanding of the Buzzard would always be limited. "Letter— what letter?" He had lost count of the times he had been drawn into this inexorable spiral of repetition, which peaked vertiginously with Lesage proclaiming: "I know you, you're trying to steal my place!" This daily torment made Max's previous scheming seem preposterously irrelevant. Of course, if the Buzzard were senile, then his ability to continue as the old boy's secretary must, in any case, be in doubt. But every time Max concluded he had lost his wits, the old fowl would confound him by some sign of acuity: he knew, for instance, that his study had been searched, although Max had taken particular care to return everything to its place. Besides, Max would catch him in a sly smile, just as when he insisted Edwige lived in Peru, so that it was possible these lapses of memory were a charade.

Sometimes Max wanted to take him by the shoulders and shake him. Sometimes he wanted to shout that he would not take his shitty job if he gave it to him, that the old fowl was welcome to his mountain of dusty paper, that wasting a lifetime keeping lists of precedence and writing out invitation cards was his, Max's, idea of hell. And it was true: now that he fully understood the power of his talisman, he could see it was his pride, merely, which had coveted the title of secretary. Let the old fowl fuddle his brain with leases and tenancy agreements, let him lie awake worrying about the dignity of the house. Max even forgave him his intransigence over the library catalogue. Sometimes, fleetingly, he even longed to tell him the truth.

Yet every attempt to divert the silly old fool from his *idée fixe* proved fruitless. As the days passed, Max wearied of the struggle and longed for a flag of truce. But the Buzzard, as he grew stronger, seemed to be regrouping his battalions. Yet to what end?

This was what defeated Max's understanding. He could see courage in the old fowl's obstinacy and even admire it. Yet what sane man acted so consistently and determinedly against his own interests?

One afternoon when Max was with Mme Zhukovskaya he found himself pouring out his frustration. She listened gravely and, when he had finished, leant forward on her cane so that she could touch his hand.

"Monsieur Fabien, forgive me, you have a good, kind heart, but there are some things you are not of an age yet to know. Contrary to what sentimental fiction tells us, illness does not make us saints. On my bad days, I am Baba Yaga—"

"Madame," protested Max, laughing, "I cannot imagine—"

"Oh, but I am—a crotchety old witch. It is so annoying, don't you see? To be unable to do simple ordinary things and, what is worse, to know you will never do them again. To turn from a parent into a child. Oh, Mitya and Verotchka are the best of parents, but like any child I don't want to listen to reason. I like to stamp my foot to show I'm still to be reckoned with."

She had spoken light-heartedly, concluding with a mischievous smile that defied him to feel a shred of pity for her. All the same, he could not but admire her fortitude: nor could he imagine that these lapses from her usual sweet nature, if she truly suffered them, would bear much resemblance to the ravings of the Buzzard.

"Besides," she continued, "it is frightening to become a child again. And your Monsieur Lesage, poor gentleman, is shut in the nursery in the dark."

The fleeting shadow of his own nightmares crossed Max's vision: he blinked it away. "I do see that he must fear what will happen when his sight fails completely. Perhaps that is why he can't let himself believe Monsieur de Miremont's promise."

"Certainly in a strange place he would be lost, poor man, truly a helpless child."

"But it would only be for a short time, until his wrist is healed. And if he were with his family...Or do you think it is Nogent that frightens him?"

She shifted uncomfortably against the cushions that supported her dowager's hump and he could see she was tiring, although when he rose to assist her she waved him away. "The difficulty with us invalids is that we have too much time to think. We invoke fears as mediums call up spirits."

When Max reflected on this conversation later, he concluded that the Buzzard's dread of leaving Paris could not be grounded in his failing vision alone—he would not have rejected Deauville if invited. Nogent appeared to be the problem. Perhaps monsieur was right and the atrocious old snob could not stomach returning to his lowly roots.

Or perhaps he truly had fallen out badly with his sister. Max began to cast about for other solutions.

Deauville might be made possible after all. The old fowl would need someone to accompany him: Max, who had never seen the sea, was for a moment tempted until he realised that monsieur, whose consent would be needed, would be appalled if he proposed a further prolonged absence and that, besides, his own sanity would be in danger. There was Fabrice, of course, still kicking his heels. But September was approaching, when there was every hope Old Jouvert would find him a situation. And in any case it would hardly be an act of friendship—did Max forget M de Bellac?

Max did not abandon all thought of Nogent, despite further discouragement. Philippe, on his return, although more obliging than Georges, could not be of much greater help: yes, M Lesage occasionally received personal letters from outside Paris, but no, he could not recall the sender's precise address or tell if the secretary ever replied to them, for M Lesage often took his letters to the post himself.

After this setback, Max was not disposed to place much faith, either, in a notion of Fabrice's.

"Dear heart, why don't you ask Old Jouvert?"

They were sitting in a café in the Rue des Écoles, where, as Max sipped a *mazagran*, Fabrice was engaged in the sacred ritual of filtering water through a sugar cube into his absinthe.

"How would Old Jouvert know?"

Fabrice did not answer until the last of the water had dripped through the slatted spoon. He lifted the cloudy mixture to his lips, drank, sighed. "Because she knows when the comte de Chambourd goes pee-pee."

"But this isn't Paris."

"Near enough for the hoi polloi to get ooh-la-la-ed and fall out of boats there every Sunday in summer."

Sometimes Max wondered whether Fabrice were not a bigger snob than the Buzzard. "That's Nogent-sur-Marne."

"Mind you, I've been capsized there myself —"

"This is Nogent-sur-Oise. In Picardy. Near Criel."

"Still not so far from Paris."

"And she's not a duchess, she's a provincial notary's widow."

"She's bound to have servants."

"A maid-of-all-work?"

Fabrice drained his glass. "If she has servants, angel, Old Jouvert will know of her."

Max thought he might have more chance of success if he took the train to Criel and investigated Nogent himself. However, when they arrived at the Monkey he ordered a bottle of wine and went over to Old Jouvert's table. The old soak, although he hummed and hawed as he always did when asked a favour, did not appear to think the quest beyond him—yet would he prejudice his reputation by suggesting otherwise?

There seemed nothing else for it: Max began to threaten the Buzzard with Beauvallon.

Max himself longed for Beauvallon. But most of all—although, as ever, he fought against admitting it—he longed for the old fellow. He could not accustom himself to the Hôtel de Miremont without him. In the old boy's absence the great marbled spaces rang hollow, the furniture and objets, like dislocated items in a curiosity shop, seemed bereft of everything that imbued them with meaning. Entering monsieur's study, he was startled not to find the old fellow deep in thought on the divan; in bed, between waking and sleeping, his arm reached for that familiar other presence. He felt, when he extinguished his lamp at night, as desolate as when he had first arrived at the Leviathan.

He could barely remember why he had been so angry with the old boy but, whatever it was, he forgave him for it; for if, as he vaguely recalled, it had been a matter pertaining to his own self-respect, was not he, Max, the only one who could remedy it? Dear crazy old fellow. Max thought of him riding out across the park or sitting on the steps of the Temple of Dionysus, watching the sun set on his Arcadia. Sometimes, when he was administering the Buzzard's medicines, he found himself smiling as he recalled monsieur dabbing away with his pad of lint, which in turn brought back the unholy struggle with the riding boots, so that he fought not to laugh out loud. He wished he were lying in the old boy's arms, describing every ridiculous detail of his battle with the Buzzard and finding the blessed relief of laughter.

But, as it was, he could not even write a proper letter: the rigid formalities imposed upon their correspondence precluded all but the practical or the trivial. There was the postscript, of course. Max no longer cavilled at including it: indeed it seemed altogether inadequate to express what was in his heart. But otherwise he was confined to giving evasive reports of his progress, while monsieur, when he was not enquiring about the date of his return, related day-to-day events at Beauvallon: the installation of the tenants in the model cottages had gone well, the grooms were exercising Pretender regularly, Saint-Séverin had gloomy predictions for the grape harvest, since some vineyards in the west of the commune had again been attacked by phyloxera.

Max could tell from the old fellow's stilted prose that he too was chafed by this epistolary corset: indeed, as their parting stretched beyond a week, monsieur's offer to come to Paris was repeated daily and ever more insistently. In moments of weariness, Max's longing to see him was such that he would have begged him to take the next train: yet—to give in now, to forget his amends, to fail in the work entrusted to him—was he once again to blame the old fellow if he despised himself?

One morning at the beginning of Max's second week, Dr Gérard called unannounced. Apparently, since he had been obliged to relinquish Lesage's case rather suddenly, he felt it incumbent on him—out of friendship only, it must be understood—to enquire how the patient was progressing. Max was not deceived by this lame excuse: there could be only one reason for the old quack's call.

Max's initial reaction was anger: was he not after all to be trusted? Had monsieur decided he was incompetent, out of his depth? Then it occurred to him that he might make use of this visit. Although his faith in Dr Vionnet was not such that he wished to summon him again, it concerned him that no one had checked the Buzzard's splint. If Gérard's ethics stretched to espionage, surely they would permit him to examine his own handiwork.

The Buzzard, as was usual now, was sitting in his study with his dressing gown around his shoulders. He greeted Gérard with: "Heaven forfend! The plague doctor!" But, this apart, he was remarkably compliant as the quack removed his sling and carefully unwound the top layer of bandages. Only when the doctor pronounced his verdict— that the fracture appeared to be healing well and the patient seemed much stronger—did he recover his customary form.

"Thanks to Dr Chevalier," he sniffed. "If it were left to you, monsieur, and this terrible young man, I should have been dead long since."

The terrible young man could think of nothing else but to pass this off with a grin. To his surprise, Gérard smiled too. Indeed, as they went downstairs to M de M's study, although the doctor could not be said to exude the warmth of friendship, he appeared to unbend a little.

While it went against the grain, Max thought it judicious to flatter him. "I have followed your advice, monsieur."

"So I see." Again the doctor favoured him with his annoyingly enigmatic smile. "You have done well to persuade him to take food."

Max preferred not to reveal his method of persuasion, but, since all would be reported back to the old fellow, he described his charge's new diet and his stratagem for getting him shaved and dressed (at this stage he could still speak of the latter with conviction for he had not yet given up on a reply from Mme Deneuville-Rivière). So far as Nogent was concerned, he stressed that the patience, forethought and cunning required to persuade M Lesage to leave Paris made it work that could not be hurried. Then, since Gérard had not manifested obvious disapproval and had even nodded once or twice, Max caught his eye and held it.

"Doctor, if you should happen to write to Monsieur de Miremont—" here he intensified his glance so that the old quack should not mistake his meaning "—please tell him that I miss—I miss Beauvallon very badly and shall not stay here an instant longer than is needed. But he has given me a duty to Monsieur Lesage and it is a point of honour for me to discharge it."

Later, when Max sat down to pen his own daily letter to monsieur, he reflected on Gérard's visit and decided he could no longer write like a dutiful servant. He confessed frankly to his difficulties with Lesage, then, having reiterated his determination not to give up, he repeated the message he had given to Gérard, only in more heartfelt terms and at much greater length. Reading the letter over, he wondered if he should tear it up. But since it contained nothing directly compromising and it had relieved his feelings somewhat, he gave it to Philippe nonetheless.

Evidently Gérard had submitted a favourable report, or perhaps his own letter had tipped the balance: monsieur, when he next wrote, no longer threatened to come to Paris and, far from reproving his indiscretion, responded with his own carefully coded declarations.

But while it was a consolation to communicate more freely with the old boy, nothing could compensate Max for the tedium of his present existence. Paris, city of light, city of freedom and delicious adventures? Incarcerated with the Buzzard on the third floor, pointedly ignored by all the servants saving Christine, who brought meals and made the beds, Max found his day had settled into a wearisome routine.

In the morning, he would give the Buzzard his medicines. Then, while his charge was breakfasting, since the old fowl could barely read letters even with his magnifier and, having rejected Max's offer to take dictation, was unable to write them, Max would seize the opportunity to rescue the post, forwarding to monsieur anything that warranted it and dealing with other urgent matters of business.

At about ten thirty the Buzzard would take determined possession of his study, fussing over the few unimportant papers Max had left him and making a great show of reorganising the piles of documents on his desk. Notionally this was a time at which Max would be free to go and sit in the picture gallery or construe Dante in the library. But, as the Buzzard's strength returned, it was wonderful how, while rejecting the help he needed, he did not scruple to send Max on unnecessary errands—to fetch ink and nibs he could not use or a newspaper he could not read. Strictly speaking, responding to these requests was at odds with Max's battle plan, yet it seemed petty to be unhelpful when it answered no clear objective. And, besides, the old carrion bird was relentless: if Max were not in his room to hear his imperious screeches, he would ring the bell in the passage for Christine to fetch him.

Before luncheon, Max would administer medicine again and after the meal, which they still ate separately in their own quarters, the Buzzard would take a nap, which gave Max the opportunity to write his letter to monsieur. Then Max would read to the old fowl.

This had been Mme Zhukovskaya's idea. "What the poor gentleman needs is distraction," she had said. "And you read to me so beautifully."

Max recalled that Gérard had recommended mild mental stimulation and undeniably the Buzzard had little except his megrims to occupy him. Perusing the old fowl's bookshelves, Max felt he could not stomach Alfred de Vigny but was intrigued by the entire shelf packed with Defaucompret's translations of Sir Walter Scott. He had not read any Scott but understood his novels had been admired by Pushkin and Balzac. He took down a volume at random.

Perhaps *Redgauntlet* was better in the original English, but Max had to confess that, although it contained some elements calculated to pique his interest—the mystery of the hero's true parentage, the plotting to restore a royal pretender—this tale of dour Edinburgh lawyers, rugged border folk and a mysterious beauty in a green mantle otherwise held little appeal. But the Buzzard, once he had stopped accusing Max of reading too fast or too slowly or mispronouncing the Scottish names, appeared enthralled: lying back in his chair, he let the high romanticism wash over him like some perfumed unguent until, with his eyes closed and his bony features relaxed, Max could have sworn he had been invested by the ghost of Camille. In due course he would begin to nod, then fall sound asleep, leaving Max in peace for the rest of the afternoon.

This, however, was only the briefest of respites, during which, usually too exhausted for Dante, he would visit the Delacroix murals in the church or sit by the fountain or wander the surrounding streets, grateful for fresh air. True freedom did not come until after dinner, when he had given the Buzzard his sleeping draught and checked that his splinted wrist was free of the sling and supported by a bolster. Then at last he was able to escape.

Most often he went to the Zhukovskys', where, as the Paris Opéra, like everyone else, was *en vacances*, Mitya was usually at home. Their breach was healed: in fact, Max could not but suspect it had existed merely in his own head. Lyudin, too, was his former shy but not unfriendly self. Vera, opining that her dear adopted brother was looking tired and required spoiling, plied him with strawberry conserve. They made him laugh and when they were playing he sank gratefully into the music, much as the Buzzard surrendered himself to Scott. On other evenings he met Fabrice and usually went with him to the Monkey: but not always. In his present state of mind his escapades there seemed as drearily predictable as the rest of his day.

It was not merely that he missed the old fellow. Cooped up in the Hôtel de Miremont, he felt hemmed in by sickness and senility. He could not forget the grim glimpse he had been given of the second cousins' apartment, where he had always imagined them at their embroidery in an atmosphere scented with mothballs and incense. During his afternoon wanderings, the shops selling ecclesiastical vestments, the dark figures of the seminarians flitting like bats across the square and the looming towers of the church itself oppressed him, not just with unpleasant memories but as if they were auguries of despair.

He was young. He had no business in this world of decay and death. Yet all promise of escape was rapidly receding. He had lost a week over the noble ladies. It was almost September and he could not think how to move forward.

But then, as the fortunes of war turn, he had two strokes of luck.

CHAPTER FORTY ONE

Max was crossing the forecourt on his way back from one of his dismal perambulations around the square when he heard his name called and saw the sisters' lady companion. His immediate instinct was to tip his hat and beat a hasty retreat, but she had halted and stood in his path.

"Monsieur Fabien—it is Monsieur Fabien, is it not? Monsieur Lesage's assistant?"

Max inclined his head in a brief bow.

"Forgive me for introducing myself, but I am Madame Radescu, companion to—"

"I know, madame." Realising that in his anxiety to flee he had cut her off rudely, he felt compelled to soften the interruption. "I trust your ladies are now in better health?"

"Much calmer, thank you, monsieur. The princess was so sorry not to be able to receive you last week, but Madame d'Ancy has suffered a paralytic seizure that has left her unable to move and, poor madame, she thought we had imprisoned her in her bed."

Although Max uttered sympathetic murmurs, this was sufficiently reminiscent of his difficulties with the Buzzard to make him all the more determined to escape. But Mme Radescu, it seemed, had something further to say and would detain him until she had said it.

"Yes indeed, monsieur, it was most distressing. But now we have the blessed Daughters of Charity to nurse her. And Doctor Vionnet and Abbé Pierrelle from the Institute visit every day. Poor Madame d'Ancy is more resigned, so the princess, thank Heaven, is also a little easier. She was touched by your kind message and she has written to Monsieur le marquis to commend you and to thank him for asking you to look out for us."

Surprise made Max speak without thinking. "Oh, but that was not why…"

Mme Radescu also registered surprised.

"I mean, if you are in difficulties again, of course I…" Looking at her properly for the first time, he took in a plain, flat, high-cheekboned face that might have been any age, curiously unlined, as if years of patient submission had abraded it like a stone. Yet this impassive look, he realised after an instant, was mainly produced by her strangest feature, a lack of eyebrows. By contrast her voice, with its faint foreign accent, was warm and expressive. She seemed, he thought, a good-natured soul.

"I came about Monsieur Lesage," he said.

"Monsieur Lesage? Is he not in the country with Monsieur le marquis? I have not seen him at mass for at least three weeks."

"Monsieur Lesage has had a fall and been quite unwell."

"Oh, the poor gentleman! The princess will be grieved to hear it. My ladies are very fond of Monsieur Lesage. They love to hear him talk of the old days, all the balls and the gowns and the dancing."

Since this enthusiasm for the Buzzard appeared unfeigned, Max was emboldened to explain the reason for the old fowl's present confinement and, when she still listened sympathetically, to outline the plan that had prompted his call.

She had smiled and seemed approving while he was speaking, but once he had finished she bit her lip. "I do not think the princess—apart from anything else, she would be most reluctant to leave her sister. Of course, I should be happy—" Here she blushed as if guilty of immodesty and continued quickly: "But that would not serve. On the other hand—" her eyes brightened again "—he could come to us. On Sunday as he usually does. The princess needs distraction and I am sure she would be delighted to see him."

The invitation to tea on Sunday, two days hence, arrived that afternoon. When Max read it out after dinner the Buzzard appeared overjoyed: indeed he looked—or so Max thought sadly—as if it had vindicated his existence.

"How unfortunate that you can't go."

The Buzzard rose so violently from his pillows that Max feared he might dislodge his splint. "Why ever not?"

Max folded the note and put it in his pocket. "Is that not obvious, monsieur? I shall decline on your behalf."

It was remarkable how the Buzzard's memory, while unable to retain monsieur's promise and his sister's address, did not lose hold of this invitation, not for an instant. Evidently he had fretted over it all night, for the first shots in the battle that raged the next day were fired well before breakfast. The barrage was intense: should Max attempt a strategic retreat the Buzzard's guns followed him down the passage, strafing him before he reached shelter.

Since victory could only be won by surrender it was important to judge the moment correctly—too soon and the old fowl might dig himself in again, too late and apoplexy seemed a real danger. At around noon, Max let himself be prevailed upon to take dictation as the Buzzard composed a florid note of acceptance, which Christine was directed to deliver forthwith.

The battle over how the old vulture was to be shaved and dressed was more prolonged and fighting, although fierce, was sporadic. All the same, Max grew weary of repeating: "Don't ask me, monsieur, I'm not your valet." At luncheon, concerned that the silly old fool would not eat, he let himself be cajoled into finding a barber for the following morning. This produced a lull in which he was able to retire to the library to write his usual letter to monsieur. But, when it was time for *Redgauntlet*, he found the Buzzard collapsed in a chair and clothes everywhere—shirts and cravats tossed aside like rags or spilling from open drawers, frock coats and trousers, some turned inside out, some flung on the floor as if in fury. This scene alarmed Max the more since the Buzzard, in the course of his futile endeavours, had cast off his sling: nor did he like to see the old fowl's trembling lip or the suspicious moisture welling in his eyes. He feared he had pushed his adversary too far, had not only captured the city but sacked it and put its inhabitants to the sword as well.

"Please—I have tried, but I can't. Monsieur Fabien, I beg you…"

There was a surprising absence of pleasure in seeing the old fowl humbled. With difficulty Max feigned a reluctant shrug. "Very well, monsieur. I'll dress you tomorrow."

The barber was due at ten-thirty the next morning but by eleven he had still not arrived and the Buzzard, as might be expected, was in a state of agitation. Max too displayed alarm, but in truth the fellow's dereliction was no surprise to him, since he had never been sent for: once the Buzzard's beard was gone, it would be inconvenient to summon a barber every morning.

At eleven thirty Max took pity on his charge. He sent Christine for a bowl and hot water and, having tested the old fowl's razor, went to his room to fetch his own, along with a pair of scissors.

The Buzzard's protests were predictable. "Not you! You'll cut my throat."

Max laughed—he was, for his own reasons, in an unusually light-hearted mood. "Please, monsieur, don't tempt me."

"Do not come near me! I need a barber! Whereas you—you have no more idea of how to shave a man than of—"

"Cataloguing a library?"

"Of civilised manners and respect for your elders. Fetch Georges. Or Philippe."

"Georges is away and Philippe won't come."

"Well, do something! Find me another barber."

Max shrugged. "Suit yourself, monsieur. After all, many men prefer a beard when they reach your age. And I'm sure the princess won't object to your looking like Robinson Crusoe."

Although he had never dealt with a full growth of beard, Max had shaved M de Cressy last summer to that fastidious gentleman's satisfaction: thus he was steady of hand and eye when, after swathing the Buzzard in towels, he began snipping away with the scissors. But he had reckoned without the old fowl, who commenced squawking before the blades had reached his chin.

"Ow! Ouch! Mind my nose! Young man, that was nearly my earlobe! Dear God, you've nicked me, I'm bleeding, I can feel it!"

Despite this, Max managed the trim without accident. However, once he had soaped the remaining stubble and had taken up his cut-throat, he put his face so close to the old fowl's that, even if the Buzzard could not read his eyes, he could feel his menacing breath.

"Move now, monsieur, or make a squeak, and you won't just bleed. You will be fillet steak."

This appeared to subdue the old fowl. But perhaps credit was not due solely to Max's thespian talent. As the Buzzard stroked his chin and pretended to study himself in the dressing glass Max held up for him, he all at once wore his sly look.

"It seems I misjudged you, Monsieur Fabien. They taught you barbering, did they, at the seminary?"

Damn the old fowl, here he was again, one minute doolally, knife-sharp the next. Max passed it off with a grin. "One never knew when one might be called upon to shave the Cardinal Archbishop."

Removing the Buzzard's beard had stripped him of ten years: after luncheon came the final stage of his transformation. Max had set aside his charge's best trousers and waistcoat, together with the only one of the old bird's frock coats with a sleeve wide enough to accommodate the splint, and all had been benzened, brushed and pressed in readiness. Still, Max hesitated as he eased the cuffs of the long underpants over the old fowl's gnarled yellow feet. Once more his spirit rebelled against this obscene intimacy with decay.

Yet he soon ceased to notice the Buzzard's withered shanks, slack belly and concave chest. For this was a work of restoration, concealing the tears in the canvas, renewing the cracked and muddy varnish, representing the subject in its true, clear colours. When he had finished he stood back with satisfaction. Gone was the old dotard with the sunken cheeks and lolling tongue. Here was the Buzzard in his full finicking officious glory, his crest clean and brushed, his grubby sling replaced by a silk foulard and all his accoutrements—spectacles, cravat pin, watch and chain— correctly in place. There was only one thing wanting.

In Max's room a glass of water held a single gardenia, purchased from the flower seller by the fountain in the square. Fetching the bloom, he secured it, like a signature to his handiwork, in the buttonhole of the old fowl's left lapel. He stood back once more. Fabrice would have been proud of him.

The Buzzard seemed not to recall Camille's fondness for gardenias: he protested the flower would give him asthma. But he, too, as he considered his blurred reflection in the cheval glass, seemed proud of his renovated self. Perhaps, after all, beyond the blur, he saw the society gallant who had posed for the camera long years ago. He could scarcely contain his impatience to present himself to the princess.

When the appointed hour arrived and Max had guided Lesage downstairs and handed him into the care of Mme Radescu, he watched him go with a proprietorial eye. But he, too, was impatient. During the Buzzard's brief absence he had a letter to write.

Max's second piece of luck had come as he was returning from his visit to the flower seller. As he was passing through the arch into the forecourt, the concierge had emerged from his booth to hand him a note delivered, apparently, by a ragged boy not a minute ago.

'With reference to your enquiry, we regret to state that we have had no success in Nogent-sur-Oise. However we are pleased to inform you that in Nogent-sur-Marne we have encountered a certain lady who may answer to the particulars. Mme Reynaud, née Lesage, is the widow of Maître Isidore Reynaud, has a son and two daughters and is known to have a brother employed as a functionary in one of the Faubourg's noble households…'

Shit! So Fabrice had been right. Damn monsieur for muddling his Nogents, damn the Buzzard for letting him chase a false trail. And thank god for Old Jouvert—he had splendidly upheld his reputation and Max would treat him to a bottle of the Monkey's finest cognac.

Max sat staring at the scruffy sheet of paper. Here it was, he realised: this was his release. Although at this moment he could scarcely believe it, in days he would be free. Meanwhile, as he adjusted his thoughts to this Nogent, he could grasp its advantages: since it was not much more than a hour's drive away, there would be no risk of exhausting the Buzzard and he could arrive in style in monsieur's brougham. Once he had been persuaded to go, that was. One final battle. But then it was over.

Max's impatience might be imagined during the two days he waited for Mme Reynaud's reply to his carefully composed letter. But when it arrived, its tone was not as he had anticipated.

'Thank you for your letter, which I note you have written on your master's behalf. I am naturally distressed to hear of my brother's infirmities. I have not, as M de Miremont well knows, seen my brother for nearly twelve years and my only contact with him has been by letter. Therefore I have been in no position to learn the true state of his health. I feel it would have been <u>considerate</u> of M le marquis—perhaps by writing to me in person, or is that vanity on the part of someone such as myself?—to give me warning that, having made use of my brother's services all these years, he now wishes him to leave his house, instead of <u>assuming</u> that I can take him in at a moment's notice. However, since my brother has nowhere else to go, it appears that neither he nor I are to be given any <u>choice</u> in the matter. I trust, monsieur, that you will have the goodness to let me know when I may expect him. You also mention that M de Miremont will provide for my brother's keep. Please assure M le marquis that this will <u>not</u> be necessary. We are not a family that has ever required the promptings of <u>charity</u> to do our duty.'

Max recoiled as if the paper had cut him. Clearly it had been a misjudgement to write to the lady himself. The old boy would have been glad to write if he had only thought to ask him, but he had been anxious to conclude the business without further delays. Now Mme Reynaud felt slighted. Yet could the tone of her letter be entirely in consequence of his mistake?

Max had not thought to keep a copy of his own letter, but he could recall stating clearly that the Buzzard's stay would be for a period of convalescence only: and while, yes, he had considered it better to mention the old fowl's stipend in case the widow were in straightened circumstances, he believed that, even despite his tactful circumlocutions, it would have been impossible for any reasonable person to conclude this money was a charitable gift.

Yet Edwige Reynaud had either misread his words or, more likely, deliberately twisted them to justify her anger. And there were other aspects of her reply he found less than reassuring. She lived a mere six kilometres from Paris, so why, if the Buzzard's welfare concerned her, had she been content with letters for twelve years? She had evidently boasted to her neighbours about his position at the Hôtel de Miremont yet had kept her distance as if she truly had emigrated to Peru. Nor did Max care for her assertion that monsieur was forcing the old fowl upon her with a *fait accompli*. And her use of the word 'duty' he found chilling.

He recalled the family tableau, the woman's forbidding look. It was there as much in her hand as in her words: the belligerently rounded letters, the peremptory vertical strokes and the underlinings, a couple of which scored the paper in their fury, told her character as eloquently as the laboured gravitas of Old Jouvert's script told his. Censorious, touchy, suspicious, obstinate, relentless, unforgiving. She might be the Buzzard's twin.

It seemed the old fowl had not been lying after all and there was no love lost between them: their very similarity must preclude accord. Could Max, in all conscience, deliver the poor old vulture, like an unwanted package, to a woman who had shown herself indifferent to his fate and whose only motive for taking him under her roof was a sour sense of duty? He had not told the Buzzard that he had discovered his sister's address and for some days now he had been preparing monsieur for the news that the old fowl must come to Beauvallon. He might tear up Mme Reynaud's missive without anyone being the wiser. Yet she was expecting a reply. Besides, he supposed he should learn the lesson of her letter; in this delicate situation, it was perhaps not altogether wise to act on the spur of the moment and take matters into his own hands. He would consult the old fellow. And, of course, however unproductive it might be, he must talk to Lesage himself.

The Buzzard had been in a curious mood for the last two days. He had returned from his half-hour with the princess in a state of elation, but, like the inspiriting rush of smelling salts, this had quickly evaporated and immediately after dinner he had retired to bed. Or rather he had asked—indeed ordered—Max to help him to bed. For it seemed he had found a way of justifying his defeats and even turning them into victories. Perhaps Max's shrug of "I'm not your valet" had put the idea into his head; or perhaps it arose from his finding his suspicions about his persecutor's origins so triumphantly confirmed: at any rate he had evidently decided there was no shame in accepting help if it came from a manservant. Max found himself addressed in a lordly manner as 'Fabien' and summoned on the slightest pretext. He could not object too strenuously: there was a pathos in the poor old fowl staking claim to a privilege that all his life he had watched his betters take for granted and, besides, Max had achieved his goal—his charge could be made ready to travel whenever required.

Yet there were also times when the old bird was curiously quiet and morose and even Scott failed to rouse him. When Max went in at the end of his nap to talk to him about Mme Reynaud's letter, he found him lying so perfectly still that for one horrifying moment, looking down at the waxen face with its milky empty eyes, he thought he was dead. Nor did the old fowl react to Max's news as might be expected. All he uttered was a resigned: "Oh." Then he closed his eyes.

Max hesitated, caught off balance. He waited for the Buzzard to say something more. When nothing further came, he drew up a chair to the side of the bed.

"Why did you and your sister quarrel?" he asked gently.

After a long pause, Lesage sighed. When he spoke it was in a quiet, tired voice quite foreign to his usual tones yet, for all that, lucid—more lucid, it seemed to Max, than he had ever sounded before. "We have never quarrelled. We merely expect different things from life."

"And is that why—?"

"You don't understand." Lesage opened his eyes suddenly and struggled to sit up. "Do you not see? I can't go back there like this!"

It was a cry of agony, although scarcely above a whisper, and Max realised it did not refer to the old fowl's failing sight or his broken wrist. He recalled how rapidly the old bird had been plunged into despondency after his half-hour with the princess. He recalled their conversation about Deauville and how the Buzzard had never otherwise mentioned the noble ladies, how it had been he, Max, who had naively hoped they would rally to their courtier. He recalled the expression on the poor fellow's face when presented with the baronne's basket of fruit.

Poor foolish, snobbish Buzzard, with his mementos of other people's triumphs. Even if he did not forgive it, Max better understood his bitterness towards monsieur, just as he could at last fully appreciate why monsieur's conscience was troubled. However, he knew the Buzzard too well to affront him with understanding or sympathy.

"Nonsense," he said briskly as he rose to adjust the old fowl's pillows. "In another month you'll be free of your sling and as good as new."

But the Buzzard still looked so anguished that, resuming his seat at the bedside, Max reverted to a gentler tone. "Monsieur, there is no need for you to go to Nogent if you would rather not. In fact, I'm inclined to agree with you. It is not a good idea."

"Then I can stay here?"

"Alas, no. You remember what Dr Vionnet said?"

"Dr Vionnet?"

"Dr Chevalier, then. He ordered you to the country to convalesce."

"But I wish to stay here."

"Doctor's orders, monsieur. I think it best if I take you back with me to Beauvallon."

"No!" At once the Buzzard reared up from his pillows and his mournful lucidity vanished. "Not Beauvallon. I'd rather go to Nogent."

"But I truly think you would be better—"

"I know what you're up to, young man. You're trying to kill me. Well, let me tell you, you've met your match. If I can't stay here, I shall go to Nogent. Nogent, do you hear? Nogent!"

It was unfortunate, if inevitable, that a stratagem which had previously served Max so well should come into play now, when he genuinely wished the old fowl to take his advice.

Max had telegraphed to Mme Reynaud that they would arrive on Friday. He had set the time at noon, so that the Buzzard would have little leisure to contemplate his departure once he was shaved and dressed, and he had even brought the laudanum in case the old fowl grew obstreperous on the journey. But Lesage appeared resigned to his fate. Max had sent another telegram to monsieur, asking for use of the carriage lest Théo refuse to drive them, and very splendid it looked too, drawn up in the forecourt, its gleaming coachwork and brasses amply compensating for its lack of escutcheons and with Théo, in full livery, on the box, reining in an elegant pair of bays: yet the Buzzard, as Max assisted him into it, seemed unmoved; allowing himself to be propped up on the cushions Max had provided and requesting a rug for his knees despite the heat, he closed his eyes and appeared to fall asleep.

Max himself was not nearly so sanguine. So deep were his misgivings that he had packed only a small valise for his charge. Indeed, he had determined that, given the slightest sign that the Buzzard would be ill-treated, he would take advantage of the short distance to convey him straight back to Paris.

After that—well, he could see why Lesage, who did not shoot, ride or swim, who could not see the sunsets or explore the delights of the old fellow's Arcadia and who, were he able to work, would be obliged to deal with Calvert, would find Beauvallon a very hell. Besides, it was nearly the end of the first week of September: it would be pointless cruelty to subject the old fowl to a long journey with a change of trains, merely to bring him back again three weeks later.

Altogether, it seemed that the reasoning which had dictated moving the invalid had been undone by the delays. Although it was still hot and the atmosphere in the Buzzard's quarters remained fetid, the temperature had dropped perceptibly in the last week and in any case the old bird, who seemed not to sweat like ordinary beings, had withstood August remarkably well.

Max recoiled from his inescapable conclusion. He would be separated from monsieur for a further three weeks and would renounce the pleasures of Beauvallon for the rest of the summer. Furthermore, without an objective to justify his new role as the Buzzard's valet, he would not be answerable if he took the old fowl's accusations to heart and slit his infuriating gizzard. And this left out of count monsieur's likely reaction: this year's poor grape harvest would increase the old boy's obligation to attend the festival, yet Max would be hard put, within the limitations of a letter, to dissuade him from returning.

But, after all, it was only for three weeks. And it was the best solution. Rather than leave the Buzzard with an unfeeling sister, Max would take him back to the Hôtel de Miremont, to complete his convalescence there as he wished.

CHAPTER FORTY TWO

Edwige Reynaud's house, according to the address Old Jouvert had provided, was nearly a kilometre outside Nogent. Max had in his mind's eye some unpretentious if respectable dwelling abutting the road, so that only when Théo made enquiries of a labourer scything the verge did they realise they had already passed their destination.

Guarded by wrought iron gates and approached up a wide drive bordered by lawns, it was the sort of substantial suburban villa a wealthy merchant might own. From its facade, stuccoed, pavilioned, pillared and dominated by a tall slate mansard, it must have been built about twenty years ago: it reminded Max of baron Reinhardt, which hardly disposed him more favourably towards Mme Reynaud.

A boy had run to open the gates and a middle-aged manservant in a tail coat now came forward to assist them from the carriage, but Max's eye was drawn to the two figures waiting at the top of the portico's brief flight of steps: two women, the younger in cream, the older in sober dark blue; at least, in marked contrast to the extravagances of the architecture, they appeared simply dressed, yet this restraint, when taken with iron grey hair scraped into a bun and a stance as stiff as a rule, served merely to emphasise the blue figure's severity.

However, Max was distracted from further consideration of Edwige by the difficulties of getting the Buzzard out of the carriage. Poor old fowl, he seemed utterly bewildered. Indeed, even if he could see he would have been disoriented, for this modern monstrosity must bear little resemblance to the family home he had left all those years since. Add the complications of easing him through the carriage door and down from the step without his falling or damaging his injured wrist, and it was small wonder that he began to whimper.

"I won't. This is Beauvallon, you've brought me to Beauvallon!"

But once Max and the manservant had at last lowered him to terra firma, he sniffed the air and seemed to discern some reassuringly familiar scent. Max handed him his cane and, with Max and the manservant on either side to guide him, he walked towards the steps.

At this juncture it might have been expected that Mme Reynaud would unbend, would rush down the steps to take her long-lost brother in her arms, or at least extend her hand to help him. But she did not move. She stood as if frozen in the portico and her younger companion, seeming to take her cue from Edwige, stood frozen too. On the companion's face was a look of dismay. On Mme Reynaud's there was the same stiff, cold look she had presented to the camera.

As the Buzzard reached the steps Max warned him in an undertone of their presence and number. He was halfway up when Mme Reynaud, though she still had not moved, suddenly found her voice.

"Camille!"

It was a strange cry, seeming to Max as much a reproach as a greeting, and it startled the Buzzard. Although he had only three more steps to climb, he stumbled, dropped his cane and would have fallen had Max not rushed to grab his arm. But he wrenched himself free and began to scream.

"Edwige, is that you? Help me, help me! This terrible young man is trying to steal my place. He has already tried to starve me and threatened to cut my throat. Please, Edwige! He wants my place and he'll stop at nothing. Save me, save me!"

At this, confusion reigned. Mme Reynaud, the lady in cream and the manservant all tried to haul the still-screaming Buzzard up the steps. Max, fearing for the old fowl's splint, moved to intervene, but Mme Reynaud waved him back imperiously.

"No, monsieur! I shall attend to you in a moment. Duval, show this gentleman to the Garden Salon."

A parlour maid in a starched apron had now joined the melée in the portico, allowing the manservant to disengage himself. Max followed him round the side of the house, past bay windows heavy with drapery, to the garden front, where they crossed a terrace to re-enter the villa through open French doors. The room in which Max found himself was light and by no means unwelcoming, despite its elaborate Second Empire stucco and ornate furniture: there was a grand piano with well-thumbed music sheets, a case of books which, unlike baron Reinhardt's, were clearly meant for reading; a set of delicate watercolours depicting Moorish scenes particularly drew Max's eye. All the same, he did not feel like kicking his heels there until Mme Reynaud thought fit to cast her basilisk stare upon him. At one end of the salon was a door through to a conservatory filled with fleshy hot-house plants. But it was fresh air he sought.

In the distance, where the lawn and its fringe of trees sloped away from the house, he could discern willows. The water, when he reached it, was no more than a stream, but fast running, doubtless a minor tributary of the Marne. He found a wooden bench shaded by willow fronds, sank down on it gratefully and reached for his cigarette case.

Curse the mad old Buzzard! But in truth Max was more exhausted than angry. If this was what the old vulture wanted, then so be it— Max absolved himself of all further responsibility. He would finish his cigarette, then summon the carriage and drive back to Paris.

Yet his escape was already cut off. He could hear his name being called and when he turned he saw the grim figure of Mme Reynaud striding vigorously across the lawn. With a sigh, he cast his cigarette into the water and rose.

"I trust Monsieur Lesage is calmer now?"

She shot him a glance that said it was no thanks to him. "Madame Colombier, my companion, is with him—she seems to know how to soothe him."

The lady in cream, Max reflected silently, must be possessed of supernatural powers.

"If you please, monsieur, be seated. We must talk and we may do it as well here as anywhere."

"Madame, I fear—"

But Max was quelled peremptorily. "If you will permit me, monsieur." As Edwige drew herself up, her resemblance to her brother was chilling. "I do not breathe the rarefied air of high society, so I speak as I find. My brother left here forty years ago a brilliant young man, handsome, educated and with a career as an advocate before him. Now you return him to us broken in mind and body. Your marquis no doubt thinks the world of himself, but he is heartless—no, monsieur you must let me have my say—he and his father, both, heartless, I tell you.

"To deny my brother visits home and days off, to require him to dance attendance every hour of the day—a scullery maid is treated better! He was going to be married, you know, but of course that meant he must give notice and your Miremonts could not let go of him. Mademoiselle Binet was my best friend, we all loved her dearly, but she could not wait forever, poor Violette, and went for a governess to a family in the colonial service. And so it has been all these years. He had only two days' leave for our mother's funeral and not a single day for our father's or my husband's, his nephew and nieces are strangers to him, he has great nephews and nieces he has never set eyes upon.

"If he had been permitted visitors—but heaven forbid our feet should dirty the portals of the Hôtel de Miremont! These past few years—this last year, since his handwriting has changed so much—I have been beside myself with worry. And when I received his last letter, saying he must work even harder to keep his place, otherwise Monsieur le marquis would give it to some young upstart...But what could I do? If I broke the rules, he told me, I should only make matters worse. And now you bring him here and deposit him on our doorstep like a bag of old clothes for the rag pickers. You, Monsieur Fabien, who do not look much older than my eldest grandson. But you are like my poor Camille—your master's creature. It is your high and mighty marquis whom God will judge..."

During this tirade, Mme Reynaud's countenance had undergone a surprising change, as if the sheer force of her anger and grief had breached her iron bolts, permitting escape to another softer, frailer and altogether more approachable being. But now, as she faltered, the iron shot back and she became a basilisk once more.

And yet...Observing this frozen mask at close quarters, Max could not but see his mistake. The photograph had misled him. This expression, captured when, unused to the camera, she had waited eternal moments for the shutter to click, was not the cold stare of a tyrant, but intended to hide distress: it had gripped her at the sight of her brother, returning after twelve years a doddering old man; and now she wore it because, manfully, she was struggling not to weep.

It was no longer hard to comprehend the tone of her letter. Cruel, lying old Buzzard. Max's first impulse, naturally, was to speak hotly in monsieur's defence. Yet pity for her left him in a quandary, for how could he do so without shattering her illusions about her beloved Camille?

He felt in his breast pocket for M de M's letter, which he had preserved carefully in a drawer in his own room. "Please, madame..."

She glanced up, sniffed, took the letter from him with a questioning look. He watched in silence as she read it. But it seemed he had reckoned without her habit of skimming impulsively over crucial detail. Her eyes blazed angrily again.

"He wants him back? Is he not content until he has the last drop of my brother's blood?"

"It is for Monsieur Lesage to choose. Read closely, madame and you will find he may return or not, as he wishes."

She commenced to read the letter again and this time when she had finished she looked puzzled. She read it a third time, glanced up, chewed her lip. "No, you are right, it is not as I—it is quite a kind letter…even a generous letter…" She studied Max for a moment with the same perplexity. Then she smiled faintly. "And you, Monsieur Fabien? It seems you are also not as I thought."

Max had the grace to feel a small pang of guilt. But at least he no longer had cause to reproach himself. "Monsieur de Miremont has never intended that I should replace your brother. He employs me as his librarian and to help with his scholarly research."

"And he will take Camille back. If Camille wishes it." She spoke slowly as if her mind still revolved upon the letter. "But why? He is blind. And his mind is…Will he ever be well enough?"

They were edging into difficult territory. "Monsieur de Miremont wishes to honour a promise."

She raised her eyebrows.

"It seems monsieur gave his word to Monsieur Lesage that he might end his days at the Hôtel de Miremont."

Her face stiffened. "I see."

"If that were Monsieur Lesage's desire."

"I see." She seemed to take a deep breath. "And tell me, is my brother in ignorance of this letter?"

There was now no escaping it. "I have read it to him innumerable times, madame. But of course…we must make allowances…his memory is not always –"

"So what did you do, monsieur?" Her voice once again quivered with rage. "Tie him up, drug him, put a pistol to his head? What did you have to do to persuade my brother to come here? To leave his precious Hôtel de Miremont and deign to honour us with his presence. We, his family, who are so far beneath him that we cannot number a single duke or marquis amongst our acquaintance."

"Madame, he wished to come." This was, after all, not entirely a lie. "He was most insistent."

"Monsieur Fabien, I can see you are attempting to spare me…And that is kind…But truly I…"

Here she gave up trying to freeze the contours of her face and began weeping in earnest. Her tears were not as horrifying as her brother's, since their cause was patent, but they were painful to observe nonetheless. Max offered her his handkerchief.

"Forgive me." She mopped her eyes. "I only cry when I am angry. But, of course, it is stupid. In my heart, I have always known." She rolled the handkerchief into a ball, which she kneaded in silence for a moment. "Our father was a wonderful man but, unlike my husband, he had little interest in the law and no head for business. There was no money for Camille to finish his studies, so he went as tutor to the Miremonts. It was only intended as a temporary measure, but it was like strong wine to him—he would come home boasting of how he had met countess so-and-so or princess such-and-such. We still had the king then and Papa used to say 'Fate willing, there'll be another republic one day and then you can be President of France. But you can't ever be one of them, my lad, however hard you try'."

Unrolling the handkerchief, she looked up with a watery smile. "Isn't it always easier to blame somebody else? I was angry at his treatment of Violette but in the end I put it down to him deciding they weren't suited. I knew he had adopted all these airs and graces but I thought he was bound to realise sooner or later where his heart belonged. And when he didn't come home when Papa passed on, or when I lost my darling Isidore, although he was not at the world's end but an hour's drive away—well, you don't want to think that your adored elder brother, whom you used to worship…"

Discarding the handkerchief, she picked up the letter again. "This was not written by a monster. I fear I have done Monsieur de Miremont a terrible wrong."

"He will forgive it, madame."

"Twelve years! For twelve years, we have been as good as dead to my brother!"

Little as the Buzzard deserved defending, Max could not but recall the old fowl's whispered anguish. "I think he has been ashamed to see you."

"Monsieur Fabien, you are kind, like your marquis—"

"No, truly, I believe he knows what he has lost."

"Maybe." She gave a little harsh laugh and her fingers plucked angrily at the handkerchief again.

Max considered her thoughtfully. With her red-rimmed eyes and crimsoned nose, she appeared to him now, as she fought valiantly to master her emotions, so much the reverse of formidable that what he said next came from concern for her welfare rather than the Buzzard's.

"Madame, I should perfectly understand and it would be no trouble to me if you would prefer me to take Monsieur Lesage back to Paris."

But she stared at him in surprise and horror. "Take him back? No, of course not, Monsieur Fabien. You will do no such thing."

"You are sure?"

"Of course I am sure. He is Camille, my brother, and he is ill." She smiled suddenly. "It is true I am a little angry with him, but it will pass. I shall sit here for a moment and it will soon be forgotten. In fact—" here she gave him another smile that was unexpectedly girlish "—you smoke, do you not? If I might be forward enough to ask you for a cigarette…?"

This was so far at odds with his preconceptions that he almost laughed. He wondered how the Buzzard would cope with finding his sister was a New Woman.

Once he had offered her his case and struck a match, he thought she might wish to be alone. But she shook her head and they sat in silence beneath the willow, smoking and watching the flow of the river and a pair of handsome mallards preening themselves on the bank.

Lesage's twin? Studying her covertly, Max discarded the lying photograph once and for all. She could be forceful, as she had proved, and she was undoubtedly used to command but he suspected she would be capable in happier circumstances of lively good humour. Looking back across the lawn at her villa, he forgave its pretensions: he too must beware the snobbery that brushed off from grand houses like the pollen from lilies.

Mme Reynaud had followed his glance. "My dear Isidore made some shrewd property investments in baron Haussmann's time. He bought this plot and built the house to celebrate our twentieth anniversary."

She handed Max her cigarette to extinguish. She smiled brightly as if, with it, she cast aside all thought of her brother's misdeeds. "Yes, life has been good to us. I had the best of husbands. My three children have also married well and I am blessed with eleven grandchildren. And now, late in life, I have the pleasure of sympathetic companionship."

They rose and began to walk back across the lawn.

"But of course," she continued, "you have yet to meet Madame Colombier—she plays the piano beautifully and she has inherited her mother's talent with watercolour."

Max recalled the Moorish scenes. "The watercolours in your garden room? They're rather fine. Are those hers?"

"You are a very observant young man. But no, those are dear Violette's."

"Then Madame Colombier——?"

"Yes, she is Violette's daughter. My dear friend married in Algiers and when she passed away eight years ago Cécilie came home to France. My beloved Isidore had been gone for two years by then, so she came to live here with me."

Max thought of the pressed gardenia and the packet of letters. "And does Monsieur Lesage know? Have you told him who she is?"

"Of course I wrote to him at the time, but he never remarked upon it. But do you know the most extraordinary thing?" He fancied her eyes glistened again. "She sounds very like Violette and when we were trying to get him into the house she spoke to him—and he stopped shouting, my poor Camille, and burst into tears." She paused, and Max realised her feverish glitter was hope. "So, monsieur, it must be as you say, mustn't it? He truly is sorry."

Despite being pressed by Mme Reynaud to stay for luncheon, Max was anxious to drive back to Paris—he had a package to collect before he left for Beauvallon. Once he had explained the Buzzard's dietary requirements and entrusted monsieur's letter to her safekeeping, he went to take leave of his charge.

In the small salon off the foyer, against a backdrop of ubiquitous red plush, a surprisingly peaceful scene presented itself. The Buzzard lay back on one of the overstuffed sofas, fast asleep, his head nodding gently, while in the embrasure of the window Mme Colombier sat watching him and stroking the large tabby cat curled up in her lap.

She was, Max, hazarded, in her early thirties, with black brows that met above her nose, dark eyes and red cheeks in a pale heart-shaped face. She had put her finger to her lips as they appeared in the doorway, but now, noting the traces of her friend's recent weeping, her single eyebrow rose in alarm.

"My dear, is all well?"

"Perfectly, dearest Sissy," whispered Mme Reynaud, and there passed between them an affectionate look that reminded Max of Baroness Donyani and Mlle de la Falaise. The irony amused him. What would the Buzzard make of that? But of course he would make nothing of it, for he would not notice. All the same, Max felt a pang of concern for them. Leaving without bidding the old fowl goodbye, for it seemed tempting providence to wake him, he hoped Mme Colombier's powers would prove equal to the challenge.

CHAPTER FORTY THREE

As Armand de Miremont stood on the steps of Beauvallon the following afternoon watching the barouche approach down the avenue, his joy eclipsed the torture of the past three weeks. The boy too, when he leapt from the carriage to meet Miremont's embrace, was grinning broadly. And after Rosalie had brought lemonade and finished fussing over the prodigal, and they could finally greet each other without restraint, the last whispering demons of Miremont's jealousy were vigorously put to flight.

Gérard, answering the question Miremont's letter had dared not ask, had written that he believed Max's wish to be with him at Beauvallon was heartfelt. And so it seemed. The boy had never been so openly affectionate. Miremont could no longer doubt he had been forgiven his shameful moment of anger.

Indeed, it was as if absence had wrought some subtle yet fundamental change in Max, as if he had returned, not from three weeks in Paris, but from a voyage to the South Seas. This was decidedly a homecoming, Miremont observed with delight: there were rituals to be performed, reunions to be celebrated—visits to the Temple of Dionysus and the shooting gallery, windfall apples for Pretender in his stable, a moment to catch the sunset before dinner.

As for Max's account of his ordeal with Lesage, it too had the lightly spiced flavour of a traveller's tale. Gérard had reported: 'It is remarkable what the natural callousness of youth can achieve where kindness and patience fail.' But to Miremont, remembering the fierce antipathy Max had once felt for Lesage, it seemed that Gérard was unjust, that beneath the boy's wry comedy ran a strain, if not exactly of liking, of compassion and understanding. How else could he explain Max's response when they discussed Lesage's retirement?

Gérard was of the opinion that the effects of Lesage's apoplexy would prevent the poor fellow ever resuming his duties. Miremont, of course, was profoundly sorry for Lesage, but he had been guiltily surprised by the depth of his relief. And Max could naturally be expected to feel as much and more. Thus Miremont was astonished when not only did he appear less than convinced by the doctor's diagnosis but seemed philosophical about Lesage's possible return.

"But after all you've said…and then there's the sister…Darling boy, you can't truly believe…?"

Max shrugged. "You never know with the Buzzard." Suddenly he broke into a smile that radiated pride and pleasure. "The main thing, Armand, is that you have kept your word."

After dinner, the mystery of the largish oblong package that Max had carried in from the barouche was finally revealed: he had brought Miremont back a trophy from his travels. When Miremont tore open the brown paper, he found a framed page from a sketch book, a study of hands worked in red and black chalks. Max had come upon it, he said, while leafing through a folio in the Passage Verdeau and, although it was amongst other chalk sketches attributed to Michel Dumas—a popular artist according to the dealer—it had seemed to stand out from the rest: there was something in its sinuous line and the effortless assurance of its shading that reminded him of the Watteau sketches in Miremont's study (later Korsakov was to confirm that the boy had a shrewd eye).

It was a beautiful thing, framed simply but to perfection, and Miremont was deeply touched. Yet he could not help being somewhat horrified by Max's extravagance. Even if it were to be believed that the dealer could not distinguish a Watteau from the work of a journeyman artist, a Dumas would probably command more than the 'mere trifle' Max claimed. And then there was the frame, from Vidler, Miremont's usual framer. The boy must have spent all his savings, even put himself in debt.

But Max had caught his slight frown.

"Yes," Miremont assured him hastily, "of course I am pleased with it. More than pleased. My dear Max, it is exquisite. But you should not…I cannot let you…"

"Give you presents? When you are forever giving them to me?"

Miremont would treasure the sketch, but naturally, sentimental fool that he was, he considered the boy's return the greater gift. That night, Max fell asleep the moment the lamp was extinguished and Miremont, drowsy himself with replete desire, drank in the smell of him, felt his heart beating against his own and was, as ever, consumed by his beauty. He was proud of him too: he had done well with Lesage and was growing into a fine young man.

Dreamily Miremont watched his happiness unfold. Tomorrow they would swim in the lake, ride, shoot, as if these pleasures had never been interrupted. When they returned to Paris, they would work together on his book. Then, in spring, he would see what real travel might inspire in the boy: Max had never seen Rome or Athens....

Ever since they had fled St Pons, the Other had been whispering temptation at Max's shoulder. Old Nick himself could not have been more persistent.

"You know you want it. You've always envied me. Well, come on, take it. It's the devil's work and I've dedicated my life to God. But you—what do you care for the devil, you're already damned to hell. I'm giving it to you, why don't you take it?"

As they had gone west into Brittany to shake off their pursuers (if indeed they were pursued), the Other had continued this refrain. During the weeks they lived in the woods to let their hair and stubble grow, and later while they were labouring in the fields, when he was not complaining about his blistered feet or his calluses, it was always the same.

"Don't you see? They will never stop looking for me, never, never. But if they think they've found me..."

"What if they also search for me?"

The Other, although never much given to laughter, had laughed at this.

"Besides," Max had objected, "we don't look alike."

"People think we do. When we were younger, they were always mistaking us. You're taller, I grant, but our eyes are the same colour, our hair is much the same."

"And what about God's will?"

"As if you care for that?"

"But you do."

"There is no sin in renouncing the world, the flesh and the devil. He will not judge me for obeying His command."

The Other, Max fancied, was less afraid of the flesh and the devil than of dying in a ditch. He recalled Brother Bernard's advice. After all, he had intended to flee on his own, had not asked for this burden. Twice he had packed up his bundle before sunrise and prepared to leave while his companion slept. But the Other had keen instincts for treachery.

"It suits your nature, not mine. And lying's like breathing to you. Why do you always do everything to spite me? Take it and we need never set eyes on each other again."

And so, after a while, Max had succumbed. For he could not but agree it would suit him and he deserved his revenge upon the world. Nor was there anything in his new code to forbid it—rather, it was the very exemplar of how he should live. Seize the day. They would both swear—he would swear on his life, the Other before God—that they would never, under any circumstances, speak of what they had done. Then there was only one detail to attend to and they could part for ever.

They had found the burnt-out farmhouse two hours before dusk and had gathered wood from the broken gate to make a fire. The Other sat on a fallen beam and ate his portion of the pie Max had stolen that morning, while Max set about his preparations. First his knife: at their last farm he had found a whetstone and ground the blade until its merest touch drew blood; he cleaned it with a rag from his bundle and set it carefully aside. Then he unpacked the piece of broken looking glass, parcelled in more strips of rag, and took from his pocket the twist of salt. The tin pot in which they usually boiled coffee was already filled with water from the well. He searched the debris that littered the flagstones for his final requirement; several slivers of timber, their tips burnt to charcoal.

The Other had finished eating and was watching him with indifference. Rather sullenly, he took off his cap and pushed aside his hair in answer to Max's request, but otherwise he showed no emotion as Max, sitting on the upturned bucket from the well, began to use himself as a living canvas. Glancing from the Other to his own reflection, he worked with the charcoal, checking in the glass, rubbing out, redrawing, until he was satisfied. It fretted his model to stay still for so long: the instant Max had finished he began scratching his lice.

Steam was rising from the pot on the fire. Max flung in the salt, then plunged the knife blade into the boiling water. He stood, waiting for it to cool a little.

"Make sure you cut exactly along the line. You need to cut deep, so there's a flap of skin."

The Other stopped scratching. His look of boredom vanished. "Me?"

"Who else? What did you think?"

"But I—I can't. It's disgusting."

"You're going back on our pact?"

"Of course not."

"Then you must."

"No!" The Other thrust his hands into his sleeves.

"Do it! Do it and free us both!"

But the Other shrank from the knife and began to snivel. Curse him, lily- livered in this as in all else. Yet perhaps it was a godsend. The Other could not summon a cool eye and a steady hand to slice an onion.

"Then at least hold the glass."

The Other's only response was to swing his legs over the charred beam so that his back was turned. For good measure, he covered his eyes.

The light was fading fast. Through the gaping roof, Max could see clouds gathering. Dusk would come earlier than he had predicted.

Searching for the lightest spot, he chose the blackened wall beneath the empty window. He pushed the bucket against it, propped up the glass, then, seizing the knife and some rags, got down on his knees. Thrusting back his hair, he positioned the point of the blade against his scalp just above the charcoal line and was relieved when even this gentle contact with his flesh drew forth a crimson bead. He must do it with one single rapid stroke that was finished before the pain came and the blood blinded him.

These days Max hardly noticed the scar. Automatically his eyes avoided it when he shaved, his hand swept his comb sideways to cover it. Only occasionally, when he caught unexpected sight of his reflection, was he forced to remember the taste of his own gore and the sound of the Other vomiting.

Nonetheless it was a mark of his destiny and in far-off days— those first callow years in which he had stumbled so often in pursuit of Fate's grand plan—he had been proud of it. Yet now it troubled him.

Damn the old fellow and his corrupting influence, stirring up confusion where none should exist. There had been nothing confusing in the Other's righteous virtue, it had been to Max as oil to water. But the old boy's goodness was an altogether more dangerous substance: it did not advertise its qualities or disclaim the imperfections with which they were admixed; yet nevertheless it drew you in, diluting your reason and dissolving your sense of purpose.

Of course, the old fellow was a throwback, not even to the *ancien régime*, but to some chivalrous and quite possibly mythical period long before. Whereas he, Max, was the coming man, cool, ruthless, unburdened by God or morality: the future. It was a weakness, his fondness for the old boy. It was a weakness to enjoy the pleasures of

Beauvallon. It was a weakness to believe that, now he could call himself secretary and had work that did not rely on monsieur's erratic pursuit of Ovid, he had recovered his independence. Attachments, sentiment, the craven desire for happiness—weaknesses, all, for the future man. If he felt a vague feeling of shame nowadays when he glimpsed the scar, it was only, the shade of his fifteen-year-old self whispered, because it reproached him. Had he any iron left in him, he would recall why he had cultivated monsieur and take action.

Yet he could not bring himself to do it. Indeed, he winced as he recalled his blundering attempts to interest M de M in his cause and was infinitely relieved that he had not succeeded. It was no longer the risk that held him back—he was certain now he could make the old fellow believe him. But knowing this rendered things no easier: it seemed all the more impossible to look the poor old boy in the eye and spin him the necessary tissue of lies. And even that was not the worst of it. There would, Max understood, be a greater betrayal.

Damn, damn the old fellow! Yet had Max forgotten the lesson of Lesage? If his resolve needed fortifying, should he not recall the Buzzard, who had set out to change his destiny but had eaten the stupefying lotus and wasted his life? Granted, the Buzzard had been chasing a chimera. 'You can be President of France, my lad, but you can't be one of them.' But Fate had altogether more glorious plans for Max. He could, he would, rise to the heights.

He no longer required a patron, for—thanks largely to the old fellow—he had acquired confidence enough to act alone. And act he must. So one day soon—not just now perhaps, but soon—why did it pain him so much to think of it?—he must leave. He must vanish from Armand de Miremont's life without trace. For this was the other lesson Lesage had taught him. He had taken a vow to uphold monsieur's honour. And he could not, as he now understood, involve the old fellow—by word or deed, by his very presence—in the spectacular fraud it was his destiny to commit.